D0899171

SAND MANSIONS

SAND MANSIONS
A Novel

Norman Gilliland

NEMO Productions

Madison, Wisconsin

This book is a work of fiction. Names, characters, places,
and incidents either are the product of the author's
imagination or are used fictitiously, and any resemblance
to actual persons, living or dead, events or locales
is purely coincidental. A railroad track, a church, or a hotel may
have moved from its strictly historical place because this is a novel.

Published by NEMO Productions
P.O. Box 260079
Madison, WI 53726-0079

ISBN 0-9715093-1-X
LCCN 2004102208

Printed by Banta Corporation
Harrisonburg, Virginia
Cover: *Cracker Horse & Rider*

Maps courtesy of the Rucker Agee Map Collection at the
Birmingham Public Library in Birmingham, Alabama
Photos courtesy the Matheson Museum, Gainesville, Florida

Attention Organizations and Educational Institutions:
Quantity discounts are available on bulk purchases of this book for
educational purposes and fund raising.
For information, please call NEMO Productions at (608) 833-0988.

For Terry Cassel

Once upon a time,
fellow traveler on the King Payne

Florida

1877

COUNTY MAP
OF
FLORIDA

SCALE OF MILES.

0 10 20 30 40 50 60 70 80

Longitude West   from Washington

SAND MANSIONS

Prologue

September 17, 1929

BREATHING WAS THE OLD MAN'S ONLY BUSINESS NOW. The rise and fall of his chest was fitful beneath the sheet but his heart was steady and kept chugging along like the locomotive that punched its way up West Main Street. The doctor's visit was merely a courtesy, his deft motions with the stethoscope little more than a way of keeping his hands busy while he passed the time with the woman and her son.

"It sure was kind of you to take him in, Flora, after all that bad blood. I've always heard it was your daddy who put that mark on his forehead."

The gabled room was hot and close. The woman watched lightning flicker through the open window beside the bed. Distant and silent, it illuminated the lace on the broad collar of her dress and cast the intricate silhouettes of tall loblolly pines. "Daddy forgave him a long time ago—in a rather startling way," she said. She patted the shoulder of the boy beside her. "In fact, he and Rex got to be friends this summer."

The doctor packed his stethoscope into an overstuffed valise. The rattle in the old man's lungs was clear enough without it. "A person his age ought not to be roughing it like a kid. How long do you suppose he'd been camping down there in the Porters Quarters?"

Rex volunteered the information in a voice that squeaked and broke. "All summer, maybe longer." He went on, testing his words "I was down there busting bottles one Sunday morning and suddenly there he was, right behind me, sitting on a pine stump. Like to scared me out of my skin."

Flora frowned. "It took us a while to get that story since he was supposed to be in Sunday school at the time."

"We got along real good." Rex's voice was behaving now and he was eager to take advantage of it. "He told me all kinds of stories from the old days. I was itching for him to tell me more about the Little Giant."

The doctor had picked up a photograph on the bureau. Two bearded grinning old men holding a mackerel that hung almost to the ground. He set it down and turned toward the boy. "The Little Giant? He told you about *him*?"

Rex was fired up now. "Got so I'd head down there whenever I could. Cost me a couple of whuppings but it was worth it."

Flora touched the wave in her new permanent. "Dr. Willis doesn't need to hear about all that."

The doctor glanced toward the window. "That Ford of yours fits into the old summer kitchen like a hand in a glove, doesn't it?"

Flora was glad for the change of subject. "Yes, but on days like this I wish I had the summer kitchen back."

"We get some rain, we'll all feel better. You've got the back yard so fixed up that I barely recognize it. When I was Rex's age I spent a lot of time tearing around back there, mostly throwing pinecones at your mama as I recall, and I'll tell you, she gave as good as she got, too. Pasted me real solid one time. Some of the boys and I had chased her out of the yard and after a while she came back and said real sweet, 'Billy, I've got something for you' and then she smacked one of those sharp green ones right there." He pulled back his collar. "After more than fifty years, I've still got the mark from it."

A swayback wooden horse lay beside the photograph. Flora set it on its feet. "Tell me more about my mother someday. There aren't many people left who remember her."

The doctor smiled. "Well, I can tell you this. She had her own way of seeing things and her own way of doing things. I don't doubt she'd have her own way of *remembering* things too, if she were here." He took a gold watch from his vest pocket and opened the cover. "I've let the time get away from me. I was due over at the Wards half an hour ago. Richard thinks he broke his wrist trying to crank up that new Packard he bought in Jacksonville. With a self-starter, I don't know how. You'd think a person who can make so much money would have more sense. Tell you what though. When I come back I'll tell you a story or two and you can tell me why your daddy came down here from Missouri in the first place. He always struck me as kind of a lone soul and he seemed to get quiet whenever that question came up."

The old man gasped and coughed and rose off the pillow. As Dr. Willis moved toward him he settled back down without waking up. Something was loose in his lungs.

"Could be pneumonia setting in," the doctor said. "They call it the old man's friend, you know. Well, I'll stop by around suppertime for the next day or so. In the meantime, if anything drastic occurs, call me."

Flora was still thinking about her father. "After more than fifty years, I guess it would be all right to tell you. He left Missouri for the same reason he eventually went back. Because he *had* to."

As they left the room the old man took in a noisy breath and pushed it out through dry lips.

Part I
Renegades
1876-1877

Chapter 1

LARRABEE LEANED LOW OVER THE SORREL MARE'S NECK, listening to her labored breathing, hoping that she would make it to the vast brown river that sparkled below. The horse was nearly spent. Spurring did little good. The man closing in on him was riding a fresher mount. They had exchanged shots half a mile back, but Larrabee's hand had been unsteady and, twisted around in the saddle while galloping on an uncertain road, he had fired far wide of the mark. The other's bullet had come much closer, close enough that Larrabee heard it hiss as it passed. That one shot had made him suddenly philosophical about life and death and convinced him that robbing banks was an undesirable way of passing from one to the other. But the die was cast. The man pressing him was intent on killing him.

He had little knowledge of this part of Missouri and less of jurisdiction, but he knew that this was the Mississippi he was breaking for and he believed that once he crossed it he'd be free of his pursuer.

Clods flying, the man was catching up. He fired twice. Larrabee felt the sorrel buckle beneath him, but she kept going.

Suddenly he was more angry than afraid. He turned and fired three more shots. The first exploded from the gun before he had finished raising the heavy .45. The second was a proper aim-and-squeeze, and the third went off before he saw through the smoke that the man had gone down. He stared stupidly for a moment at the empty saddle, then came to his senses and spurred the sorrel for all she was worth, down to the rushing Mississippi.

The road was muddy from a storm the night before, and as he picked his way down a treeless hill, he could see that the rain-gorged river was carrying snags capable of gutting any boat that blundered into them. The ferry was still on the Missouri side but the men on it quickly threw off their lines as Larrabee rode toward them. It was a miserable little affair, a teamboat, hardly more than an oversized raft enclosed in a rail. Crowding one end was a stack of crates stuffed with chickens. Occupying most of the deck were two teams of mules circling a capstan, and Larrabee was hard put to figure out how the contraption was supposed to get him to safety, but he wasn't about to let it get away. He pressed the sorrel forward, bracing himself all the while for another shot from behind.

One of the two ferrymen was driving the team. He was stout and ruddy faced and wore an infantry cap faded beyond affiliation, blue or gray. The other man was dark and bearded and worked in the shade of a black slouch hat. He hauled on the long tiller, moving the boat out into the water.

Larrabee gave a whoop, loped the sorrel onto the plank pier, and jumped the widening gap to the ferry. The sorrel cleared the rail and came down hard on the deck, breaking open a crate of Rhode Island Reds and throwing the ferry into chaos. Horse and mules collided with the capstan and each other and the twin stern wheels jerked to a stop, causing the ferry to surge crookedly. Half a dozen prize pullets squawked and flapped in outrage.

Larrabee vaulted out of the saddle, drew his gun, and took cover behind the winded sorrel as the ferry rocked against the current.

The gentlemen of the teamboat were unimpressed by the young desperado. Kicking a chicken aside, the teamster came toward Larrabee and told him to put the gun away or go to the bottom of the river with it.

Larrabee was looking back toward the landing, looking for the horseman to come over the hill, but no horseman came.

The helmsman craned his neck for a better view of the empty road and gave a long pull on the tiller. "Looks like you got him. You figger you killed him?"

Larrabee braced himself against the sweating sorrel in an effort to keep his knees from shaking.

"I don't know."

Several feathery passengers strutted among the mules, cackling their indignation.

The helmsman spat into the water and wiped his mouth on his sleeve. He adjusted his wide-brimmed hat. "Well, you don't get across this river without we take you and we can't hardly take you if you get us shot. So put it away like Pat told you." He shoved hard on the tiller and the ferry headed into the current for a moment and then started straight downstream. "Why was he after you?"

Larrabee continued to look back to the Missouri side. "I was trying to make a withdrawal at the bank."

The helmsman laughed, spat, and wiped his mouth again. "You and every other farmer's boy."

The team continued to turn the capstan even though the direction was still off. Low in the water a cottonwood tree came at them roots first.

The teamster turned his back on the nervous renegade. "You know, Bridger, it would serve him right if we was to take him right back to the Missouri side."

As the helmsman swung the ferry upstream, the cottonwood slid past them. "Well now Pat, back in Missouri this fine young feller just might get strung up—if he killed that man back there."

The teamster's belly strained his buttons, but his arms and legs were strong and he moved toward the uneasy bank robber, wanting a steep price for the passage, ten dollars, saying, "If you tapped a bank, you must be good for a thousand times as much."

Larrabee touched a fingertip to the ten-dollar gold piece in his vest pocket, a slim return for running scared and starved for most of a week, and he intended to hang onto it. Even after his enormous crime, he retained a boyish reluctance to tell a lie so he twisted the truth.

"There's not a dime on me, mister."

The teamster looked at him with disgust. "You had your way with a bank and came away without no money? You ain't good for much, are you now, bucko?"

"Never mind," the helmsman said. "Just put that gun away, boy, and set tight and we'll all get over to Illinois in one piece."

The teamster prodded his mules with a cottonwood stick and pointed at the sorrel. "You done run a good horse into the ground, boy. I'll tell you that. You'll be lucky if she sees another day."

Larrabee hadn't heard him. He was squinting into the golden disc of the western sun, waiting for his pursuer to ride over the hill and stop at the water's edge.

He never did.

Chapter 2

The sun flashing through the trees stirred the young renegade out of a shallow sleep just as a man hurled himself into the boxcar.

Larrabee had no idea how the new arrival had managed to catch the train because the right leg of his gray britches ended in a knot at the knee.

The man's Negro companion must have doubled back into the woods for some forgotten possession because he was losing his race with the train. He bounded after it, burdened with a haversack strapped to his back and a heavy-looking purple and green carpetbag that he swung in one hand. By the time he reached the boxcar he was sucking air and snatching for something to grab hold of. The man in the gray suit was in no position to help. He was flopped on his side, tangled up with a pair of crutches, holding his chest and gasping.

Larrabee's guts hurt and he wanted the boxcar to himself, but the running Negro had a kind face and a desperate look, and even though he didn't like the idea of touching him, Larrabee braced himself against the side of the door and reached out.

With a last burst of energy the Negro clasped Larrabee's hand, surged forward, chucked the carpetbag into the car, and jumped in after it.

He sprawled against the haversack, coughing and blinking. "Cap'm," he said, "I'm getting way too old to go chasing around like this. I am more than ready to go back home." He sat up, jerked the haversack from his shoulders and slid it away from the door of the car.

"Second the motion" the captain replied. He was putting himself in order, brushing hay from his sleeves, and smoothing his vest. He laid his crutches against the wall and combed his rust-colored beard with his fingers. "God," he said, " what I wouldn't give for a bit of the potion!"

"My heartfelt thanks," the Negro said. "May I present Cap'm Richard Fulton? And I'm Cameron Potts. We hail from Mossley Hall, down toward Raymond, Mississippi."

"Well, I'm Nathaniel Larrabee—from a farm in Liberty County, Missouri."

The captain's blue eyes lit up. "The gift of God!"

"What?"

"Nathaniel is Hebrew for *the gift of God*."

"Well, I don't feel like a gift."

"Where are you bound for, Nathaniel?"

"The Dakota Territory, the gold fields."

"Ah, quick money! But shouldn't you be going *north*?"

"I've had some reverses."

Captain Fulton laughed, making his sunburned face all the redder. "I should say you have! You look to have been set ablaze and then drowned."

"I was in a barn fire. I fell asleep smoking my pipe and woke up with my britches burning and my horse dead."

Cameron pulled a razor from the haversack and mixed some lather in a cup.

Larrabee took some comfort in the sight of the woods and cornfields scrolling away behind him. Each click of the tracks put him that much farther from the vengeance of law, and after three more days alone on the run, he was eager to talk.

"I walked to a landing and stowed aboard a northbound riverboat—the *Andy Johnson*—but as soon as I got on it, it turned right around and headed south."

"Well, sure," the captain said. "They often approach the landings against the current."

"It wasn't so glorious as it looked either. Full of hogs and pickpockets. At nightfall when we were coming up on Cape Girardeau, two toughs caught hold of me and pitched me off the sundeck. I came up clawing at what I thought was a log, but it was a dead man all stiffened up with his mouth open."

"They've had cholera on some of those boats," Cameron said. "They throw the bodies off before they come into port so as not to hurt business."

"I came to on a sandbar somewhere in Kentucky and grabbed the first train I got to. Got shut up all night in a boxcar. Couldn't see a thing. But I heard these two voices. One was high and drunk. The other one talked low and slow and was always trying to calm down the drunk and they argued all night long about whether or not to carve me up."

The captain shook his head. "What *has* become of the railroads?"

"The queer thing was that they never interrupted each other. I should've figured something from that. I wished I had my .45 but it was on the bottom of the Mississippi. Then when I was about to nod off, the train comes to a stop and I hear the conductor walking up and down outside saying, "Granada—Granada, Mississippi."

"A pretty little town," the captain said. "They've got a college there."

"Well, the door jerks open and before I know it somebody all but leapfrogs over me to get out of that boxcar and it's this little yellow-toothed tramp who dances a quickstep with the conductor then breaks loose and heads for the hills. Turned out that the whole time there wasn't but one man in that car with me. One lunatic talking in two voices."

"The Wild Man of Granada," Cameron said with awe. "He's famous in these parts. Some folks say he's death in human form."

"That was one hot little town," Larrabee said. "I walked around for a while with my stomach sticking to my backbone, then I ate a blackberry pie off a windowsill and it's been arguing with me ever since."

Cameron smiled through his lather. "There's nothing better than a fresh-baked blackberry pie,"

The train screeched and banged. Black clouds and cinders drifted into the boxcar.

Larrabee pitched toward the doorway and threw up.

Captain Fulton folded his arms and blew a stream of smoke. "See here, Nathaniel, you've done us a good turn. The least we can do is put you up at our place for a night. We don't have much to offer—just a home-cooked meal, a comfortable bed, and a roof over your head."

Cameron laughed. "And the guarantee that nobody's going to try to carve you up when you nod off. Of course, we'll understand if you've got other plans."

Before the sun had set again, Larrabee was gazing over fallow fields from the back steps of what had been an elegant home. "Where I come from we don't name farms, we name counties," he said, trying to stay clear of the captain's two playful hunting hounds. "But then this looks to be as *big* as a county."

One wing of Captain Fulton's plantation house had been blackened by fire and stood open to the wind. Its five big columns had been scorched six feet up. A sixth lay on the ground in hollow segments, giving the lie to the illusion of marble. The view from the portico was spectacular—massive moss-draped oaks, woods and fields that sloped toward the setting sun. Larrabee was dressed in the clothes of the captain's dead brother, tight britches and frock coat and a low-cut vest and cravat. He was twenty years out of style but he was clean and well fed. He felt restored and grateful.

Captain Fulton picked up a turtle shell and tossed it into an overgrown hedge. The hounds charged off to retrieve it.

"Now tell us, Nathaniel, why the allure of the gold fields? Isn't it harvest-time in Missouri?"

The heavy air and thick woods were another world and Larrabee wanted to tell his story so he was forthright.

"The bank took the farm. They said they were foreclosing but to us it was pure stealing. I was on my way back from a dance when the sheriff and his men came so I don't know for sure what happened, but the tracks in the yard and the blood on the steps were clear enough. My dad, with that hair-trigger temper of his, pulled the shotgun on 'em and they killed him several times over. They carried off my mother and my kid sister."

Cameron patted the returning hounds but declined to pick up the turtle shell. "Losing your home and your folks in one day like that. It's like the war."

"It was the beginning of a war for me," Larrabee said. "I was out for revenge. I met up with some other castoffs and we robbed that bank. I was going to use my share of the money to buy my way into the Dakota gold fields, then come back and buy the farm. But when things got hot on the road west, I broke away from the others and my share turned out to be what I grabbed off the floor on the way out of the bank." He took the gold piece from his pocket and held it toward the sun.

The captain sat down on the brick steps and struck a match. "My sympathies."

"I took the first open road I could get to, east I guess, and this one fella kept coming after me, just wouldn't let go. I lost him at the Mississippi. Shot him, I think. Killed him maybe"

"Well, no doubt many a renegade is prospering up in the gold fields."

"And I can too. All I need is a stake and I can get my share. When I do, I'll go back to Missouri."

"And buy the farm."

"That's right. And then I'll buy the *bank*."

The captain laughed and coughed through a cigarette. "Cameron and I are in much the same spot that you're in. We're trying to reclaim this farm. This disarray you see is a result of the late war and the taxes have gone sky high. But in its day Mossley Hall was a showplace, and with a little money we can turn it back into the thing it was."

"A little money would make a big difference to a good many folks," Larrabee said. "But nobody I know seems to be any good at making it."

The captain's eyes lit up. "Perhaps we can all realize our dreams if we throw in together for a few days. We can put this old place on its feet and you can buy your passage to the gold fields."

"As long as I don't have to rob any more banks."

"Just the opposite! You'd be restoring property to its rightful owner."

Larrabee thought he saw doubt in Cameron's face, but the captain went on.

"In New Orleans there is a Mr. Devane, a former Union colonel. In 1864, during the burning of this house, he personally removed an item of great value from it. After the war he become a shipping tycoon, but his scruples remain unchanged. In fact, he's been known to sell the same cargo to three different buyers."

"If he burned my house I'd nail him to the wall."

Captain Fulton shook his head. "Vengeance can eat you from the inside out. And anyway, I can't strike back at the whole Union Army. I just want my property back."

"And you want me to help you get this thing back."

"I do."

"Where is it?"

"In Devane's house."

"Won't he have something to say about that?"

The captain chuckled. "Once he finds out it's gone, he'll have *plenty* to say about it and I wish I could be there to hear it."

"At the house I mean." Larrabee had no time for humor.

"Devane won't be home. He'll be in the French Quarter with me, in a place called the Absinthe House, playing cards. By some stroke of luck he came out ahead in our last two encounters. Come Saturday night he won't be able to resist another crack at me."

"If you're so broke, what are you using for money?"

"Land. But this time we can turn things around. We can skin him twice in one night."

"Does he know who you are?"

"Not a clue. To him Mossley Hall was just another nameless place to plunder."

"Is his house guarded?"

"There's a butler, that's all."

"Just what is this thing you're after?"

The captain outlined it with his hands. "It's a bowl, a gold and silver bowl about so big. It's a precious heirloom. Been in my family for two hundred years. It was a gift from Charles the First of England. The Latin inscription on the bottom attests to that."

"I suppose you know right where it is."

"It's locked in Devane's study, upstairs. But every night at eight the butler opens the shutters. How are you at climbing, Nathaniel?"

"I've always had a knack for it."

"Good!"

"What about the family?"

"Mrs. Devane is an invalid. Her room is at the back of the house. Her only visitor after Saturday dinner is a man who delivers a bottle of sherry and a week's worth of *cascara sagrada*."

"Of what?"

The captain smiled. "It's for her bowels, my boy."

"Once I get this bowl, then what?"

"Bring it to the Absinthe House on Bourbon Street. Be discrete! Nod twice, I'll retire from the card game and we'll all beat it back to the hotel where we'll have a good howl."

"What if they come after it? How are you going to keep them from getting it back?"

Captain Fulton nodded to Cameron, who took a bundle of green chamois cloth from the carpetbag and handed it to him. The captain folded back the cloth, revealing the most beautiful pistol Larrabee had ever seen.

"It's a Leech and Rigdon .36 caliber," the captain stated with pride. "Made in Columbus, Mississippi. My men presented it to me when we were up there.

It's one of the last ones made before they had to move the factory. This'll keep the wolves at bay."

"Did you ever kill anybody in the war?" Larrabee asked suddenly.

"I don't know, but I damned near got myself killed by being in the wrong place at the wrong time. If we avoid that mistake in New Orleans we won't have to fire a single shot."

He handed the pistol to Cameron, who returned it to the carpetbag. "The long and the short of it is, Mr. Devane is a goose ready to be skewered and cooked."

"Once you get this bowl, what are you going to do with it?"

"I'm going to sell it, of course. There's a gentleman at the hotel who has a weakness for old gold. Part of the proceeds will go to Mossley Hall, part to you, and part for a potion to appease the ghost leg."

"The one that he lost in the battle at Raymond," Cameron explained.

"The one that *seceded*," the captain said with a pained smile.

Larrabee gazed out at the distant woods and tried to picture the gold fields of Dakota.

When the train dragged into New Orleans, the young desperado felt as if the city of massive facades and wrought iron had swallowed him. The best hotel in New Orleans was the vast, ornate St. Charles, whose manager had a soft spot for Confederate veterans. They put up in a first-floor room where they reviewed their plans for recovering the gold and silver bowl.

The captain had it right. Just past eight o'clock the shutters on the second floor of Devane's house opened up. As Cameron kept watch, Larrabee threw the knotted end of a rope over a balcony rail, tied a slipknot, and shinnied up to the large window. His borrowed boots creaked as he walked across the Morocco carpet in Devane's dim study. The gilt titles of books drew him to the mahogany shelf. He took out a tall volume and opened it. One page after another yielded engravings of a naked couple engaged in a variety of passionate embraces. At the sound of muffled voices he turned, and suddenly he saw the bowl in a niche above the door, glinting gold in the light from the street. He climbed onto a chair and laid his hands on the prize, tucked it into a linen bag, and slipped back into the night.

"I thought you had died," Cameron whispered in the darkness across the street.

At the Absinthe House Captain Fulton was upstairs enjoying a run of good luck, mostly at Devane's expense.

Larrabee stood beside him and nodded twice.

The captain tossed his cards down and reached for the carpetbag. "Well, gentlemen—"

The fleshy shipping magnate slammed his hands on the tabletop. "Sit down. Nobody leaves until I say so."

Behind him a tall pockmarked man started to reach for an inside pocket.

Suddenly the Leech and Rigdon .36 glinted up at the overfed merchant. Captain Fulton smiled merrily. Cameron began scraping bank notes into the carpetbag.

The captain handed the pistol to Larrabee and doffed his gray hat.

"Gentlemen, until next time. It's been a rare pleasure."

The three conspirators made their way quickly downstairs and into the dark, damp streets. The captain moved surprisingly fast for a man on crutches. Cameron carried the carpetbag stuffed with money. Larrabee hung onto the treasured Confederate revolver.

The captain laughed. "Finally the pay-off!"

A streetlight reflected in the bowl as Larrabee slipped the prize into the captain's carpetbag.

"We actually got the bowl and some cash at the same time," the captain was saying. "I can't wait to get home. Damn dogs'll be pissing with joy at the sight of us! Soon as I get some potion in me we'll get back to the hotel and divvy up the rest of the money. Nathaniel, gift of God, you can be at the gold fields within the week."

Cameron stopped for a moment, and then quickened his step.

The smile faded from the captain's face. "Damn that Devane. How many of them?"

They hurried past wrought iron balconies.

"Three."

Larrabee glanced back and saw the dark figures following them.

Captain Fulton quickened his swinging gait. "Gentlemen, we are a little short of firepower and a little far from the hotel. Damn! Why can you never get a hack in this town when you need one?" He turned a corner sharply. "Give me the weapon and let's see if we can draw them in here."

Larrabee handed over the pistol. He felt a knot in his stomach. He was about to get caught in the middle of a gunfight, unarmed.

Cameron forced a window and they tumbled into a derelict dance hall. The captain took the pistol from the carpetbag and moved forward. "You gentlemen take cover behind the bar and get their attention and I'll give them a little surprise up here." No sooner had he turned over a table and crouched behind it than the big window across from the bar splintered and a man stepped in. The captain's pistol flashed and thundered, dropping the intruder to the floor. The two behind him were more cautious. They knelt and fired from the broken window and then vaulted into the room shooting, scattering glass and wood. The captain fired again and one of Devane's men let out a sharp cry. Swearing, the two of them fired at the table.

Amid the blasts, Larrabee heard a clank like a hammer hitting an anvil.

The two men retreated back through the window.

In the smoke and darkness Larrabee broke from the bar and ran across broken glass to the overturned table where the captain lay on his back, open-eyed, his mouth agape, his hat pushed back. A red circle spread across his chest. On the floor beside him lay the gold and silver bowl, disfigured by a large hole in the bottom.

Cameron was at his side now, making a low sound deep in his throat.

"Stand away!" somebody shouted. The two men came back through the window, firing. Larrabee grabbed the pistol from the captain's hand and tried to shoot back but the trigger jammed. He threw the gun at the intruders, crouched and ran. Choking, he blundered his way into the street while Devane's men overpowered Cameron and gave him a pounding. He scrambled up iron grape leaves to a balcony, pulled at a dark green shutter, and stepped through a tall window. In soft light he caught sight of red-flocked wallpaper, a brass bed, and an armoire. On a bureau was an etching of Andrew Jackson like one in the parlor of the home he had left behind. He never saw the crystal decanter that sent him senseless to the floor.

Chapter 3

As the sun-struck river washed into the boundless Gulf of Mexico, Larrabee felt a growing sense of helplessness and despair. The water spread before him in a great green plain that turned blue far ahead of the schooner. The haze of morning had developed into low clouds that stretched over the sea and bubbled up into towering anvils. Larrabee was uneasy seeing nothing but the undulating water in all directions because he knew that out here he was on a string. The only plan he had now was to stay alive.

Captain Greenleaf of the *Belle Helene* laughed and pointed at a redheaded young man stumbling over a block-and-tackle: His accent was pinched, his voice nasal. "Penrod there was a newspaper reporter investigating corruption in the New Orleans city government and—guess what—he *found* some!" He turned the wheel a spoke closer to the wind and watched the newcomers dance to keep their balance. "I guess you other two are already acquainted since you were both at the Absinthe House last night. The Ethiopian is a creature to the late Captain Richard Fulton." He watched Larrabee struggle to his feet. "And sleeping beauty here is a planter's child of the Old South by the look of him. You, my lad, had the honor of being cold-cocked by one of the most popular whores in town—the only one in New Orleans who speaks French with an Arkansas accent."

The only other occupant of the *Belle Helene* was a grinning, spidery Creole named Philippe who worked the lines and scrambled over the deck as if born aboard the boat. Greenleaf made it clear that he and Philippe and any one of the three newcomers could sail the schooner, making the other two dead men if they caused trouble.

Through stolen bits of conversation with Jared Penrod, Larrabee learned that their cargo consisted of Army surplus muskets converted for the use of Cuban revolutionaries. He deduced that someone else was interested in the merchandise, too, because by dusk it was apparent that the *Belle Helene* was being chased by another vessel.

"You sold the guns twice, didn't you?" Larrabee said as Greenleaf glanced astern for the tenth time.

The skipper smiled. "The bottom line is that in order to survive you need to stay ahead of that vessel. So you'll all want to do your very best at running *this* one and jump to my tune, especially with this weather coming on. Am I understood?"

But they didn't have to deal with the pursuing vessel. Billowing storm clouds, pounding rain, and boiling seas made it disappear during the night while stretching the *Belle Helene* and her men to the breaking point. The schooner begun taking on water, and at sunrise on the third day Larrabee sat on the foredeck nursing hands raw from pumping the bilge and hauling ropes and canvas. He scanned the dark tossing swells of the western horizon without seeing a trace of the threatening sail.

"It's even more interesting over yonder," Cameron whispered from the bow. He nodded toward the low pink clouds before them. Larrabee looked to be sure that Greenleaf was still below, sleeping off the night's exertions. Philippe was at the wheel and seemed not to understand what Cameron was saying. Larrabee went forward and looked hard into the brightening east.

Gradually he made out a tree line and a few yellow lights steady in the dawn. "Where are we?"

Cameron folded his arms. "Florida."

"Florida?" Larrabee repeated the name as if it belonged to some fairytale kingdom. "I thought we'd be to Cuba by now."

"Don't wish that on me. Slavery is still legal in Cuba."

"If we ever get back to New Orleans, I'm going to pay Devane back right between the eyes."

"Don't do it on Cap'm Fulton's account. Didn't anybody love him more than I did. He gave me my freedom before Lincoln even thought of it. But if Devane's men hadn't killed him, the potion would have—and soon. We were running ourselves ragged buying and stealing that stuff."

"Did he need it that bad, that he had to quit the card game? That's what set Devane off."

"His head wasn't right when he needed the potion. The war cost him more than his leg."

"But what about his plan for Mossley Hall?"

"He wasn't going to put Mossley Hall back on its feet. That was just a fable we were telling ourselves to keep our spirits up. At least this way he died fighting, not seizing up in some boxcar. I'm glad for him. He died happy and he's finally free, free of that ghost leg!"

As the sun rose through scattering clouds, the *Belle Helene* began listing and they wallowed along close to the coast, within sight of a rough, scrubby little town. From the heaving deck Greenleaf looked at the harbor through a pair of binoculars. "Cedar Keys. It was bombarded during the war. Hasn't changed much since."

The pump had given out. Larrabee and Jared were scooping water out of the foul-smelling bilge and handing buckets up to Cameron. Larrabee spoke under his breath. "What if we just go ahead and swim for it?"

Jared looked toward the companionway to make sure nobody was coming. "The water's pretty rough but we'd probably make it when the tide starts coming in, except for Cameron. He can't swim."

"What? You sure?"

"I talked about jumping off this morning. He wished me well."

They hit on the idea of ambushing Greenleaf when he came out of his cabin, holding his pistol on Philippe, and forcing them to sail the *Belle Helene* right up to the town wharf, or to beach it if necessary.

They never got that far.

Greenleaf and Philippe had been arguing all day and the Creole started taking it out on Cameron. Cameron took his slaps with the rope patiently, which frustrated Philippe all the more. He started prodding Cameron with a cargo hook.

"If all he wants is a fight, I can give him one," Larrabee told Jared.

"We've got to take it till the time is right," Jared whispered. "Got to get Greenleaf first."

Cameron dodged Philippe's next pass with the hook and it caught Larrabee in the small of his back. In a fury, he swung hard and connected with Philippe's mouth.

Philippe came at him swinging the hook and the two of them fell fighting into the water in a blind, stinging confusion of froth and fists. Philippe was at home in the water, agile and confident, but he lost the hook and started ripping at Larrabee's face with his long nails, and Larrabee felt himself going down into the muddy bottom, but in a breathless spasm he ripped free of the slashing fingers and broke for the surface, shooting away from the boat with long, jagged strides. With great sweeps of his arms he pushed forward, kicking his cramped legs against their will. He heard a shot and pumped his way past the point where he though his arms had turned to lead, for what seemed like hours. Not for a long time did it dawn on him that Philippe had not followed.

The tide was out. He hauled himself across mudflats and into a patch of weeds and looked across the gray-green water. The *Belle Helene* was nowhere to be seen. A large white bird struck the surf and beat its way skyward on enormous wings. Larrabee watched the rolling waves for a long time as he dried off in the burning sunlight. He swore. Finally he got up and walked along a dirt road that brought him into Cedar Keys, a rusty, banged-up town of tin and pilings.

He tried to think of a way to go back out to the *Belle Helene* to help Jared and Cameron but he came up empty. Without any destination, he forced himself to go on. A mile or so farther down the road he came to a well-tended farm that reminded him of Mossley Hall. The frame house was set well back from the road amid tall moss-draped pine trees. Near it was a long, low tin-roofed building from which came the shrill, dire sounds of hog butchering. Between the hog shed and the road was a large pasture where a sorrel mare grazed, saddled, with her bridle trailing in the grass. Larrabee stared at her for a long time, weighing his crimes and the misery they had brought him, but the saddled horse seemed an invitation and now he had little left to lose.

Five minutes later he was loping down the road, the breeze of freedom on his face as he tried to calculate the distance to the Dakota Territory, although much of his progress seemed to be easterly, away from it. As the novelty of his speed wore off, he started to wonder if this endless gray track was punishment for his latest misdeed. Marshland and mosquitoes went on and on, and the steamy sunlight was relentless. An occasional sparkling in the tall grass suggested that he was in the middle of a vast swamp where he would be scorched and eaten alive by large dim forms that slithered there. The sorrel twitched constantly now in a miserable effort to shake off tormentors. Larrabee met a couple of wagons piled with lumber and the drivers looked at him as if he were deranged. His skin was beginning to burn but he unbuttoned his shirt the rest of the way because his clothes stuck and itched and pricked him. He began to wonder how he might have avoided this torturous ride through no man's land on a stolen horse.

The sun was still high when the ground became more solid and the road more firm. Broad fields bordered by thick scrub forests and studded with massive live oaks made him think again of Mississippi and Captain Fulton. He wondered what would have happened if he hadn't reached out to pull Cameron into the boxcar, and what would have happened if he hadn't lost his temper and struck back when Philippe hit him with the cargo hook.

The biting and stinging dwindled. A refreshing breeze came up. The slope leveled off and passing clouds provided relief from the heat. He stopped to water the sorrel in a roadside ditch and found five dollars in the saddlebags.

At last he came to a small, shady town that had a restaurant with the hopeful name Friends Café where he tied the sorrel to a porch post, adjusted his wretched clothes, and smoothed his hair. When his eyes adjusted to the darkness inside he found that he was the only patron, and yet he had trouble attracting the attention of the cook, a stout, flat-faced blond boy of twenty or so who sold him a plate of fried oysters and then went out back somewhere to resume cracking a whip. The oysters smelled like low tide at Cedar Keys and a fly struggled in the butter that came with the cornbread, but Larrabee was quick to stuff his napkin into his collar and dig in.

His enthusiasm was short-lived. Half an hour later, when the blond boy came back inside to collect, Larrabee was feeling queasy and in no mood to pay.

The blond boy came back with his whip and suddenly they were fighting like dogs, growling and snapping and tumbling across the plank floor. Larrabee swung a chair as the blond boy slapped at him with eight feet of stinging rawhide. They spilled into the dirt street. A crowd gathered. When Larrabee saw a hand go up for the sorrel's bridle, he dove at it, knocked it aside, threw himself into the saddle, and kicked the startled mare into a gallop.

He felt sicker than ever, but at least the country began to look friendlier. The late afternoon light softened on fenced fields of corn and beans, cotton and clover. Herds of well-fed beef cattle poked their way along grassy slopes. The air smelled of new-mown hay. This was the first territory east of the Mississippi that Larrabee had taken a liking to, but he was in no condition to enjoy it. He let the sorrel have her head while he tried to work through the ache in his gut. As evening approached it got worse.

He came to a fork and let the sorrel bear left, a more northerly route, which led him to another crossroads.

He asked a Negro gathering wood where he might find a doctor.

"Jus' up the road yonder in Gainesville," the wood-gatherer told him. "Up the hill and pas' the tradin' post, mind you. Not down there pas' the blacksmith or you'll end up in Hogtown!" He giggled. "In Gainesville mos' of the white folks goes to Doc Willis."

His stomach was starting to climb into his throat. Larrabee asked the wood-gatherer if he had something to drink.

The Negro favored him with a confidential smile, reached under the seat of his wagon, and offered him a nearly empty jar of whiskey. Without hesitation, Larrabee took two long swallows and thanked the man.

The hill was nothing by Missouri standards, but he could barely stay on the sorrel as she climbed it. He passed the trading post, a grim affair, half-clapboard and half log. The woods grew dark again, full of giant live oaks with gray moss hanging so low that sometimes it brushed his face. He rode in a tunnel of overarching branches with a scattering of blue and green light filtering in through shifting leaves. Although the air was moderate now he was sweating more than ever and his stomach hurt so much that he could hardly sit up. He stopped beside a massive oak scarred by lightning and passed his hand over the coarse bark thinking that he too might survive disaster. Then he fell off the horse.

After a while a middle-aged woman and her skinny brown daughter came along and helped him up. They were talking about a picnic that had been run into the ground by drunks and they thought that Larrabee might be one of the culprits. But they decided that as Christians they should set a good example, so they hauled him back onto his feet and propped him against the sorrel

The girl put her hands on her hips and shook her braids disapprovingly. "Mama, I do believe this man's *inebriated.*"

After a few tries, Larrabee re-established himself in the saddle and passed on down the dark tunnel of oak and moss. For the next two miles the sorrel was in control. Occasionally that meant a stop to savor some inviting shrub or weed, but eventually Larrabee began to see light and to hear horses passing and dogs barking. Soon it became apparent that this was not just another crossroads. The tunnel of trees opened onto a wide shaded street lined with well-kept frame houses and gardens. On one side he saw a stable with shingled walls and beside that a fine two-story house with twin brick chimneys. A huge white hotel, still under construction, opened its wide verandas to the street, dominating one intersection, and catty-corner from that, set in the middle of the muddy town square, behind a rail fence, was a tall white courthouse with jutting porticos. Beyond it was a massive brick building half a block long.

Larrabee had come to the end of his rope. He was sick, dirty, ragged, dog-tired and nearly incapable of thought. He hoped that his five dollars would make him acceptable somewhere. He had fallen a long way in the few days since he had left the lofty St. Charles Hotel.

Somebody was shouting at him but Larrabee wasn't sure what he was saying, something perhaps about riding the horse on the sidewalk. The hollow sound beneath the hooves continued for a while and then the sorrel stopped and Larrabee found himself beneath an awning, looking at a plain black-and-white sign that said "Alachua Hotel" that was nearly lost in the shadow of the palatial new place on the corner. Larrabee climbed down, tied the sorrel to a sweet gum tree, and went inside.

The trim young clerk looked put off at the sight and smell of him but could think of no reason to deny the rank visitor a room.

"Let me know if I can be of further service," he said from sheer habit.

Larrabee pulled himself away from the counter. "Get a doctor."

"Top of the stairs and to the right," the clerk went on. "Nice view of the square."

Larrabee stumbled into the room and collapsed on the bed, taking in the cool air that carried sharp noises through the window. Somewhere a gun went off. Men were running hard on a plank walkway. A chorus of cheers went up. Everyone in town seemed to be in the street. Out in the night, knuckles connected with flesh.

Chapter 4

The commotion down the street had blossomed into the semblance of a riot.

Lying across the bed face up, one arm flung over his eyes and the other trailing down toward the tobacco-stained carpet, Larrabee was unaware of the two heads poking into the room. The pair of visitors padded in and closed the door behind them. One of them was tall and angular, the other bald, his middle a muddle of dumplings and beer. They took up positions at the bedside. The bald one pulled up a cane chair and sat down, the tall one stood behind him like a shadow. The kerosene light on the wall flickered.

"A sad case," the tall man muttered. "Plans will have to be made."

"Pitiful," the bald man said. "It hurts to see a young feller so far gone."

The tall man hung over the bedside, clasping his bony hands. "What's wrong with him, doctor?"

At this point Larrabee brought his arm down and beheld the apparitions.

"It's all right, young feller," said the tall man. "Doc Choat is here now."

Larrabee thought that the hotel clerk, brusque as he was, must have summoned these angels of mercy.

The bald man leaned forward, nearly losing his chair. He collected himself and propped his feet on the bed. His boots were the widest Larrabee had ever seen. The toes were so square that they looked chopped off. The blunt-footed visitor asked Larrabee to stick out his tongue.

The patient couldn't bring himself to comply.

Choat looked mournful as he consulted his companion. "Paralysis has already set in. He's further gone than I feared."

Despite his infirmity, Larrabee's nose still worked and it was picking up the smell of turpentine.

"Young feller," Choat said, "you'll want to be wanting to put your affairs in order and that's why I brought Mr. Leary here."

The tall man removed his hat and forced a smile that showed large crooked teeth.

Choat said something about documents. Leary nodded and extracted some papers from his hat. He took the stub of a pencil from his breast pocket, put on a grave look, and began writing.

"Now then. I should ask do you have any kin in these parts?"

"I have a mother and a kid sister in Missouri," Larrabee said. He tried to remember his mother's face but the blunt-footed Choat and the long-faced Leary blotted out all other images.

"Ah, so no next of kin hereabouts?" Sympathy hung in the air like an odor. Choat sat up and put his hand on the edge of the covers. His broad foot clanged against something under the bed and he withdrew it.

Leary pressed his hands together. "Then perhaps you yourself would like to make arrangements for the disposal of the remains."

Larrabee blinked up at them, uncomprehending.

Leary put his hat over his heart and averted his gaze.

"The time comes for all of us," Choat intoned. "Some sooner than others. It's nature's way."

"Doctor, are you telling me I'm going to *die*?"

Choat cast his eyes downward before answering. "I have to ask you frankly, how do you feel? Let that be your guide."

His head ached, his stomach felt like he had swallowed spurs, he was parched and burned, bruised, cut, and pulled apart. He couldn't so much as raise his head from the pillow or lift the hand that dragged on the floor. Sharp voices down in the lobby were like needles in his ears.

Choat sat back. "Well, there you are. You are beyond anything medicine can do for you. I can perhaps achieve some comfort in this difficult time but we must prepare for the inevitable."

Leary smoothed the papers and laid them on the bed. "You will of course want a Christian disposition."

Larrabee wasn't grasping his meaning.

"I can attend to the details to your complete satisfaction," Leary assured him.

"But of course there will be *some* costs." Choat said.

Leary pressed his fingertips together. "May we ask whether your estate might be able to assume this burden?"

"He means what do you have to pay for it with."

"Property perhaps. Although one so young...."

"Any cash here in the room or on your person?"

"I do believe we saw a rather fine horse outside, with a saddle, a proper English saddle. Badly used, but under the circumstances that would just about cover the services, and a dollar or two for the visit. You understand of course." Leary's fingers curled over two dollar bills on the dresser.

"Now if you'll just sign here." Leary picked up Larrabee's hand and put the stub of a pencil in it. The smell of it reminded Larrabee of his frantic swim ashore at Cedar Keys, making him feel all the worse. He inscribed a large, shaky signature and then fell back limp on the bed.

His two visitors smiled. Back went the papers into the stovepipe hat. Up stood the sympathetic healer, and then suddenly both froze in mid-gesture— Mr. Leary with his hand still on his hat brim, Dr. Choat half-crouching, intent on some sound.

Someone was coming up the stairs and he was making a good deal of noise about it, raising his voice and thumping along with a walking stick. At his heels the hotel clerk made high-pitched excuses.

"I was on my way to get you, I swear it, Dr. Willis."

"Well, you were taking your sweet time about it, Bobby! That fight could've gone on all night once those fools got going. Now where is he?"

The stairs squeaked and the walking stick banged against the banister as the two came closer. "Dr. Willis, will you please keep your voice down, sir? We have other guests to—"

As the two of them came pounding down the hall, Choat and Leary rushed about the room looking for a back door that wasn't there. In came a rather short, substantial gray-haired man. The hotel clerk was right behind him, picking nervously at his waxed mustache.

Dr. Willis struck out at Larrabee's panicky visitors.

"Scoundrels! Frauds! Who let you in here?" He swung his walking stick and connected with Mr. Leary's posterior. Mr. Leary jumped up and emitted a squeal quite out of keeping with his former decorum. The undertaker hopped and jumped.

Dr. Willis was red-faced with rage. He went after Choat with his stick as if to impale him in a very tender place, prodding him into a clumsy little dance on tiptoes as he broke for the open window. The two were soon scrambling onto the broad awning that hung over sidewalk and, as the doctor swore and shook his stick at them, they somehow made their way down to the street.

"They got your horse," the hotel clerk reported from the window. "There they go."

Larrabee lay back and closed his eyes, relieved to be rid of it.

In the morning Dr. Willis sat on the same chair that the imposter Choat had occupied. He looked a little grayer and more creased now that the anger was out of him, but just seeing him made Larrabee feel better. He wore a black bow tie, a starched shirt, and a pressed linen suit. His salt-and-pepper beard was neatly trimmed. At once he set about appraising the patient with a variety of implements from an old leather valise. When he had finished he folded his hands over the ornate head of his walking stick, reminding Larrabee of a great eagle at rest.

"Baldy Choat and Sam Leary. They're headed for an evil end. They're just that much more trash chucked into the street."

"Well they won't set foot in here again," vowed the hotel clerk, whose name was Bobby La Rue. Having waved off several guests gathered outside the door, he himself was suddenly curious about the victim. "What looks to be the matter with him, doctor?"

"What doesn't look to be the matter with him?" The doctor rattled off a list. "Malnutrition, exposure, dehydration, abrasions, fungus, anxiety, insect bites, and a stolen horse." He stood up and set his valise on the chair. "I suppose those two cornpone confidence men got you to sign a bill of sale. They've done it before. How do you feel, son?"

"Like I'm going to die." Larrabee closed his eyes.

After a few more questions, Dr. Willis concluded that in addition to his other ills, the patient had contracted food poisoning in the town of Archer.

"Oh, Archer," Bobby La Rue said. "I've heard stories about the food down there."

Dr. Willis stood and picked up his valise. "By the way, Bobby, as long as you lingered to enjoy it, what was all that commotion in the street last night? It wasn't even Saturday."

Bobby took pleasure in reciting the details. "It started as a fistfight, of course. Then they went to shooting at pinecones. Then I think Penny Ward got them into redoing the battle on the square, maybe Olustee, too."

"Again? They'd do better to squeeze their juice running Leary and Choat out of town." He put on his hat and headed for the door.

"I hear Baldy has some honest work somewhere," Bobby said.

"Not exactly. He's cracking the whip over those poor misfits at John Howard's turpentine still. That's Baldy for you."

"Sam still burying folks?"

"Up at the work farm mostly." The doctor pointed at Larrabee. "As for you, you stick around for a few days. You're a one-man medical text. I'd hate to give you up too soon."

Larrabee was beginning to think that the events of the past week were some kind of fever dream, from the botched bank robbery to the counterfeit Doctor Choat.

Something under the bed caught the doctor's eye. He bent down to pick it up. "This yours?"

It was the ten-dollar gold piece.

Larrabee tried to sit up but settled for propping himself against the headboard. "It must've fallen out of my pocket last night."

"Be glad that Sam and Baldy didn't see it under there." Dr. Willis tossed the coin onto the bed. "Rest and decent food are what you need more than anything else in the world. You can get the rest right where you are for today and we'll see to the vittles directly."

"I need to be off." Larrabee was too weak to be convincing.

"Not today you don't. Now you just rest easy there for a minute while I talk to Bobby here."

The window faced east and the morning sun was hot, but Larrabee felt fifty shades better, although thin and weak. He managed to sit up on the bed and look out at the square white building across the street, the Courthouse. It looked worse in the light of day. It sat on brick pedestals that kept it off the ground, but something underneath had done a good deal of digging and the gray dirt was thrown out for the whole length of the wall. It needed paint. One of the windows was boarded. Larrabee found himself thinking of the *Andy Johnson*, the steamboat that had seemed so elegant from a distant ridge but proved to be full of filth and confusion. Then there was the *Belle Helene*. What had become of Cameron, gentle Cameron? Was he on his way to be sold as a slave in Cuba? Yesterday morning's events were hard to untangle. All he remembered clearly was swimming away, breaking free.

The streets were lined with lofty old oaks from last night's dream. Across the square, through a screen of gray moss, was a row of frame buildings, some turned sideways to the street, some end to. The square itself looked calm in the bright morning light, although apparently a night rain had made the streets like quicksand because wagons plodding their way through town spattered mud on everything they passed, including the occasional foul-mouthed pedestrian. Those afoot kept to the grass as best they could, but the green margin of the square had become a quagmire too, making for longer detours and shorter tempers. The only travelers unfazed by the sludge were small pigs that trotted briskly to and from the Courthouse. It seemed to Larrabee that this was a town where people bogged down and lost the will to move on.

He smiled at the thought of Captain Fulton thumping his way along those swampy thoroughfares, hopping and swearing and swinging his colorful carpetbag. He imagined the captain free of his addiction, free to play cards and drink whiskey and revisit his old war memories. If the captain had somehow lived, Cameron might laugh telling him about the beating he had taken in the dance hall in New Orleans. Larrabee would have stayed to fight beside him and this time Captain Fulton's battle would have been won. Except that it hadn't worked out that way and Larrabee had abandoned Cameron twice, first in the dance hall and then on the *Belle Helene*.

Dr. Willis was telling Bobby something about an account and Bobby was nodding his pomaded head in agreement. Despite the doctor's formal attire, the old cracked leather valise made him look relaxed and friendly.

He came back to the bed. "You know, they got your horse back this morning."

Larrabee had completely forgotten the stolen sorrel.

"Some farmer from Cedar Keys came up and swore it was his. Found it in the hands of Baldy Choat. Tracked him over to the turpentine still. Looks like you've got a scrap on your hands if you want it back."

"I'm in no shape for a scrap, doctor." For the first time in days, Larrabee smiled.

"Baldy's the one in a scrap," the doctor said. "The sheriff down in Levy

County wants him and so does our own man here in Alachua County. Baldy's saying he bought the horse from you but he can't produce the bill of sale he says he got from you. If he had one, he probably lost it on his way out the window."

Larrabee came away from the window and poured himself a cup of water at the washstand. "What do you suppose they'll do with him?"

"Last horse thief they caught got a thousand-dollar fine and thirty-nine lashes. There's plenty of folks around here would like to see Baldy get the same, plus some time in the stocks on the square. He's skinned enough of 'em one way or the other."

"And still stays broke somehow," Bobby said. "You suppose John Howard'll buy him out of jail? Or maybe the Little Giant himself?"

Larrabee peeled some skin off of his neck. "Who's the Little Giant?"

Dr. Willis set down his valise. "If you take my advice and stick around for the week you'll probably find out. And that's my fee. You stay right here in town for a week and eat three solid meals every day and stay out of the way of hard things and sharp things and hot things and scum like Choat and Leary. Then you come over and see me. And you're free. Do we have a deal?"

"I don't have anyplace to stay, doctor."

"I'm getting to that. Bobby here's going to get you some clothes that don't reek and you get yourself cleaned up and get over to a big white house two blocks over that way on Magnolia Street. You'll know it by the green shutters and the weathercock on the roof, and from the caterwauling coming from inside. Go over there and ask for Mrs. Newhouse. Tell her I sent you and they'll take you in for the week." He adjusted his hat and picked up his valise. "I'll see you in a week."

The doctor had left no room for argument. Walking stick and valise in hand, he was on his way out the door.

Bobby went with him. "I'll play my latest tune at Duke's just for you, Dr. Willis. It's about a grandfather clock."

Two hours later Larrabee threaded his way down the plank walk that spanned the mud on the west side of the square. He was elbow to elbow with armed men, black and white, whose eyes met his only briefly, men who swaggered like gamecocks, lean and ready to fight. Larrabee gave way to each of them, unwilling to let footing on a board become the flash point for another life-and-death struggle.

The Arlington Hotel was even bigger than he remembered from the night before. Its unfinished verandas looked cool in the watery sunlight. In front of the hotel, beside a carriage step that led to a brick walkway, lay a broken obelisk of a street sign that said *Liberty*. Apparently any other approach to the big hotel was perilous. All about him fair and proper buildings stood on brick pedestals as if raising their skirts above the mud. The heavy air smelled like rain and clouds that blocked the sun from time to time looked like dirty lint.

The smell of a sawmill reminded him of yesterday's street fight in Archer, and now that he was feeling stronger he considered going back to settle the account with the blond boy and his whip, but it seemed to him that Captain Fulton and Cameron would have put the quarrel behind them by now.

The next street went through a neighborhood of well-kept white houses and gardens. The trees lining the road here were unfamiliar to him. Most of them were not more than fifteen feet high. They had bright glossy dark green leaves and branches that hung low with round green fruit. Beyond them he found the house just as Dr. Willis had described it, large and white and square with deep porches on two sides. By the look of it, it had been a fine house not many years ago. But now the roof was overdue for re-shingling, a front window was cracked from top to bottom, and the gray front steps were half gone, replaced by a plank whose purpose seemed more to keep people off than to help them up. One of the two chimneys had lost several bricks and several pickets from the fence lay in the weeds where they had fallen. The weathercock leaned toward the bumpy brick walkway. The place was well used and ill repaired.

A scream from behind the house sent Larrabee running to the edge of a chicken yard where a girl of about twelve, a strawberry blonde in a blue-and-white gingham dress, was pursuing a very agitated hen. Several spectators were offering encouragement to the girl but the venture was not going well. The hen flapped and squawked and ran forward bobbing her head nervously while the girl stumbled after her with a raised hatchet that was a danger to both of them. Every time the girl closed in on her prey she shrieked and scared the hen off again. The girl's mother was starting to lose patience, causing the two men with her to redouble their encouragement while a younger girl, a cotton-top blonde, began rooting for the chicken.

"Caroline!" the woman shouted, "Stop this at once. You'll have all the neighbors thinking we run an asylum."

"Don't you?" asked the man beside her. His long white hair swept down from his broad-brimmed straw hat. He wore a black suit and clerical collar. He was puffing on a cherry wood pipe, making Larrabee yearn for a smoke.

"Run, Jenny, run!" cried the younger girl, who was about five.

"Martha, you be still!" scolded the mother, a tall, dark-haired woman who looked familiar.

Beside the preacher stood a stout and strong man wearing a collarless shirt and denim breeches. His thinning red hair swept straight back from his sun-burned forehead. His scruffy red beard looked accidental. He put his hands to his hips and shook his head. "We'll be half starved before this business is done. I should've gone huntin' today 'stead of roofin'. We could be feastin' on 'possum pie by now."

Caroline came to a halt and burst into tears. The hatchet shook in her fist.

Larrabee had been admiring an old Colt revolving-cylinder rifle propped against the wall of the house. He was an indifferent shot with a pistol but prided himself on his aim with a rifle. He hefted the weapon and lined the hen up in the sight. The shot was tempting and weeping girls had always made him uneasy. He pulled the trigger and the hen's head disappeared in noise and smoke. Larrabee blinked as Jenny the chicken took off again with a little red geyser shooting up from her neck.

The chicken yard erupted into shouts and screams, but Caroline stood clutching the hatchet as if on stage, staring at the strange antics of headless Jenny. The preacher sized up the marksman while bending over to pick up his pipe.

"Fancy shot," he said, "but next time warn us, will you?"

The red-bearded man got up from the dirt and snatched the rifle from Larrabee. "Won't be no next time. Give me that thing! You could've kilt somebody!"

Larrabee let him take it. "I was just trying to be helpful, mister, and anyway, with such a fine rifle, I was sure to hit the mark."

With a little flick of her wings, Jenny flopped over dead.

The man softened. "Well, now you're right about that."

Caroline dropped the hatchet and ran into the house. Her little sister was back on her feet now, staring at the twitching bird. She ran up to it and studied it, holding her hands behind her back as if the headless thing might peck. "You blew the head clean off!" she said with awe. "That *was* fancy shooting!"

Her mother walked through a cluster of noisy chickens that had reconvened after the shot. "Martha, I'm glad that you've gotten over your grief so quickly. Now will you please carry Jen—the bird into the summer kitchen so we can dress it?"

Martha backed away. "What if I just set the table, Mother?"

"I'm looking for Mrs. Newhouse," Larrabee said.

A strand of the woman's hair had come loose. She adjusted one of her pins. "I'm Mrs. Newhouse." She looked tired. She wiped her hands on an apron stained purple by berries.

The preacher motioned toward the house with his pipe. "The two that headed for the hills are Caroline and Martha. There's another one around here someplace. This here is Penny Ward and I'm Reverend Ezekiel Williams of the First Presbyterian Church."

Mrs. Newhouse seemed to be sizing Larrabee up. "Have we met?"

"I just got into town last night, ma'am. My name's Nathaniel Larrabee. Dr. Willis told me to stop by and see if you had a room to spare. Just for the week. Then I'll be moving on again."

Penny had cocked an ear to the way the newcomer talked. "You're from out west somewheres, ain't you?"

"That's right," Larrabee said. "Missouri."

"Whatever brings you away down here?"

"A wrong turn."

Penny laughed. "I guess *so!*"

"There's a problem with our only available room," Mrs. Newhouse said soberly. "The roof leaks." She was still trying to figure out where she had seen him.

"I've done some roofing, ma'am. I'd be glad to help with it."

"With two of us, it won't take but two or three days to git the whole thing done," Penny said, leaning the rifle back against the wall. "If nothin' don't happen."

"No guns," Mrs. Newhouse said. "If you have a gun it goes in the wood room as Penny's should have done and will do. No cursing and no chewing tobacco in the house. No smoking in the bedrooms."

"And no loud snorin'," Penny added. "We had a man git shot for that when John Wesley Hardin was in town. Shot through the wall."

"Absolutely no intoxicating spirits," Mrs. Newhouse continued. "Please be prompt for meals. The girls ring the breakfast bell at half past six. Luncheon is at noon and supper at five-thirty. Other than that we ask you simply to remember that ours is an orderly Christian home."

Martha burst from the house screaming with Caroline in pursuit.

Penny pointed a black-nailed finger skyward. "It's a heap *more* orderly up on the roof."

The cedar shingles were almost too hot to walk on. Larrabee kept in the shade of several big pine trees whenever he could, but Penny seemed to have leather skin and moved about on his hands and knees without any apparent discomfort. The town spread out beneath them in a neat grid of straight streets, frame houses, and church steeples half-lost in thick oak- and pinewoods. Every landmark inspired Penny to launch into some joke or story. The Courthouse set him to talking about the town's battles during the Confederate War, as he called it.

"It was August same as now only even hotter. The Yankees were comin' down from Jacksonville to cut off all that food we was sendin' up the railroad. They come down the tracks and took Baldwin and Starke and then camped over yonder at Boulware Springs and the next mornin' they come marching into town just like they owned the place. Set up all around the square with cavalry and artillery, thousands of 'em, almost all nigras." Apparently not bothered by being at the very edge of the roof, he shook his hammer toward the center of town. "We come up from the south with Captain Dickison—about a hundred and eighty of us on horseback—and come right up West Main Street. They had us ten or twenty to one but Captain Dickison done the smartest and bravest thing I ever saw. He split us three ways. He sent one bunch up each side of the street and me and th'other right up the middle." He chuckled and slammed in a nail with two hits. "Them Yankees thought they was surrounded and broke and ran—the whole pack of 'em—minus a few dozen—and they run all the way back up to Jacksonville! Lee pulled the same trick at Chancellorsville and

Forrest at Fort Pillow. Wouldn't you know it, I git all the way up here on the roof and then I have to take a leak."

Larrabee wiped the sweat from his eyes. He had been watching four barefoot boys chase a girl about ten years old. She seemed to be leading them on, taunting them as she paused to catch her breath, then sprinting on, her brown braids flying, her faded green dress aflutter. The boys pursued her into the back yard through scattering chickens, and after one more insult she ran an erratic zigzag through a neglected patch of grass and then turned and stopped, waiting for the boys to come on.

"Come on, Billy and you bullies! Come on and git me!"

They rushed on, but when they hit the tall grass they started hopping and crying out in surprise and pain.

Penny looked up from his shingle and burst out laughing. "Ambush, boys! She's got you right where she wants you!"

Larrabee wanted to know what all the hopping was about.

"Sandspurs! She run 'em right into a sandspur patch. She knew her way through it. Did you see her picking her steps as she went? She got 'em good'n stirred up and then run 'em right into it!"

She was flinty and brown-skinned and Larrabee had seen her somewhere but he couldn't figure out where.

"That's the middle girl," Penny said, wiping his eyes with the back of the hand that held the hammer. "That's Anna and don't you ever cross *her*!"

It was little Martha who walked around the house ringing the bell. Larrabee followed Penny onto the branch of an oak tree and from there down the shaky ladder. They took turns dousing their heads with cold water from the backyard pump. The afternoon was so hot that Mrs. Newhouse and the girls had set a table on the side porch where everybody could sit in the shade, including the flies and mud daubers. Everyone was taking places around the table while the women finished up in the summer kitchen. Larrabee started to sit at the head of the table but Penny waved him toward another chair.

A big bald man in shirtsleeves nodded toward the empty chair, smiling. "Looks like the seating assignments carry over from inside."

"Well, I expect he's just as hungry out here as he was in the house," Penny said.

The man in shirtsleeves leaned over his plate and explained. "That's *Mr.* Newhouse's place. He's always late for dinner. In fact, he's the late Mr. Newhouse. But she sets a place for him every day, in case he shows up I guess."

Penny laughed. "If he shows up I'll give him my place and skedaddle! Larrabee, this here's Duke Duforge. He's a Yankee but he ain't half rotten."

"Good to see you." Duke put out one of his bear paws and shook Larrabee's hand. "Mr. Newhouse has been gone for what, five years now, Penny?"

"It don't hardly seem that long but it was in '71, when the yellow jack come around."

"Sure. That's right. But it wasn't the yellow jack that got him, was it? It was the consumption. He came down here from Connecticut for the cure and got cured all right. Permanent."

"He come pretty high connected," Penny said. "He was in the cotton business with Mr. Dutton and come down here for some dealin' and that's how he got the idea to take the cure." He glanced around to be sure none of the ladies were within earshot. "You figger the missus and the preacher will ever, you know, tie the knot?"

The conversation broke off as two of the girls came onto the porch. Martha, whose skipping suggested that she had gotten over the death of Jenny the hen, and the lean, brown, freckly Anna. They sat with Larrabee between them.

Anna's brown eyes grew wide at the sight of him. "You was drunk last night!"

He had no idea what she was talking about. "What? I was not." The last thing he needed was to have his proper new landlady think he was a sot.

"You was too. Mama 'n' me hauled you up off the ground out by the lightnin' oak. You'd fell off your horse."

Mrs. Newhouse had come onto the porch. She was staring.

"You was too drunk to even stand up. You was downright *inebriated*."

Larrabee found the sinewy girl nettlesome. He sympathized with Billy and the other victims in the sandspur patch.

"By no stretch was I drunk. I was sick—sicker than a dog. You can ask Dr. Willis."

Anna stuck out her tongue to show her distaste. "Billy's old man."

Mrs. Newhouse tapped a silver serving spoon at the girl's place. "You will *not* speak that way of Dr. Willis or any of your elders, young lady! Is that clear?"

Anna's eyes narrowed. "Yes, ma'am."

"And you will apologize to Mr. Larrabee for what you said."

"Well, Mama, you thought he was drunk too. You said so, remember?"

Her mother's mouth came open. "I did n—that is, you just say you're sorry if you know what's good for you."

Anna closed her eyes for a moment. "Sorry."

Undaunted by the dispute, Penny plowed right on where he had left off. "Duke here runs the saloon."

"I'm just staying here at the house short-term." Duke spoke in a surprisingly soft, gentle voice. "We had a fire over at the saloon and we took some smoke damage. If Penny's fixed it right we'll be back in business by Friday. Just painting now."

"As soon as you open the door the place'll be chock full of card-players." Preacher Williams took his place at the table. He was in shirtsleeves now and he swabbed his brow with a linen handkerchief. He was a big man with a cowcatcher jaw and large ears. His bony knuckles cracked when he moved his long fingers. When he took his hat off, his waxy white hair showed thin at the top. His gray eyes seemed to take in and understand everything and he smiled often but never for long. When Caroline showed up with a platter of fried chicken he put his hands together and announced, "Praise the Lord! Guaranteed fresh too!"

Caroline was not smiling, but Anna leaned forward and cast a glance at Martha and before long the two of them were snorting and giggling.

"Anna wouldn't've been scared to pick Jenny up," Martha said. "Head or no head."

Mrs. Newhouse came onto the porch and put her hands on her hips. "Girls, didn't we agree that we were not going to talk about it?" She sat down quickly. "Preacher Williams, will you return thanks, please?"

The preacher rested his elbows on the table, put his large gnarled hands together, and bowed his head. He spoke in a loud clear drawl.

"Our heavenly Father, we thank Thee for this day and for this fellowship. Bless this food so that we may put it to Thy use in our daily lives as we strive to be better servants."

With bowed head, Larrabee had kept a watchful eye during the blessing and he saw Anna mouthing the words a syllable ahead of the preacher.

"In the name of Thy son, our Savior, Jesus Christ. Amen."

A chorus of *amens* echoed around the table.

Without so much as taking a breath, the preacher returned to earthly matters. "Now this combat we witnessed this afternoon, Anna, what was that all about?"

"Them boys was chasin' me." Anna flipped a braid over her shoulder.

"*Those* boys were chasing you," Caroline said. "If Miss Tebeau heard that she would shrivel up and die."

"Well, I don't go to no fancy Miss Tebeau School, Carrie, so—"

Preacher Williams put up his hand to stop the digression. "It's been my experience, Anna, that most every story has two sides to it and I was just wondering if you'd like to tell the other side, the side of those boys."

Anna thought for a moment. "We was down at the Sweetwater Branch catchin' tadpoles and lookin' for sharks' teeth and we got to throwin' stuff."

Caroline started to speak but the preacher put up his hand again. "And who threw *stuff* first?"

Anna's eyes narrowed and her lips puckered and her sun-bleached brows came together. "Well, it might've been me."

Mrs. Newhouse set a drumstick on Martha's plate and began cutting the meat from it. "What did you throw, Anna?" She spoke casually, as if to maintain control of her temper.

"Biggest, prickliest dang green pine cone—"

Mrs. Newhouse inhaled sharply. "*Anna!*"

"You ever saw. It must've came down during that storm we had Sunday night. Hurt me just to hold it in my hand. I caught that Billy Willis with it right in the neck and then you know what?"

Anna's glee was such that Martha started giggling again. Mrs. Newhouse tried to restore order but Anna wasn't to be stopped. "When it caught him right here in the collarbone the dumb cluck squished his shoulder up and mashed them prickles in good!"

Martha laughed so hard that chicken spilled from her mouth.

Caroline watched disapprovingly. "Mother, can't we send her to school? She's such an embarrassment."

Duke winked at Larrabee and turned toward Penny. "Sounds like the battle on the square all over again to me. Outnumbered four to one and still attacking those Yankees."

Penny rose to the bait without hesitation. "Four to one didn't have nothing to do with it," He had a watermelon pickle in his cheek but it didn't slow him down any. "We was *twenty-five* to one. Even if most of them was nigras. Hundred and eighty of us to five thousand of them. We split up three ways and come at 'em and they run so fast they left their shoes behind. You ask Baldy Choat if they didn't. He was there. And I'll tell you another thing—"

Duke spoke to Larrabee as if Penny were no more than music in the park on a summer day, a parade band, clanging and banging away in the background. "He gave you the whole story up on the roof, didn't he?"

Larrabee glanced at Penny, who was still going on, and nodded.

"Well, I've got news for you. You're going to hear it all over again this afternoon. If I was you I'd get that roof shingled fast as you can."

The flies discovered the luncheon and set everyone to swatting and flapping.

Preacher Williams brushed one from his plate. Unlike Martha and Anna, he didn't seem interested in killing them. "Were they this bad at the picnic last night, Mrs. Newhouse?"

"Worse," she said. "Toward sundown the mosquitoes came out. But the water in the spring was so clear and cold that it was worth the trouble. It was the young men that spoiled the evening with their drinking. Then one of them fell into the spring and you never heard so much carrying on in all your life. That's when we decided to pack up."

Duke patted his mustache with his napkin. "I can't promise you a dip in the spring, Larrabee, but if you're still in town Friday night, stop on by the place and I'll stand you to a drink. The place'll be all fixed up. You're invited too, Preacher. We'll have plenty of publicans and sinners for you to work on."

The preacher smiled. "I just might do that one of these nights. I imagine some of your folks need me worse than our churchgoing friends. It so often seems like I'm preaching to the converted."

Mrs. Newhouse's thoughts had remained on her wayward daughter. "I don't want you teasing those boys anymore, Anna. You might get the better of them today, but some night they'll come back and get even by soaping the windows or something even worse."

Just then the iceman drove up, his team fighting to keep the heavy wagon from bogging down in the mud. Mrs. Newhouse excused herself in order to meet him at the side gate.

Caroline stood in for her mother. "Mr. Larrabee, can I offer you some blackberry pie?"

Chapter 5

The rain held off for two days, allowing Larrabee and Penny to finish the roof with only one more retelling of the battle on the square. They decided to celebrate their work by walking over to Duke's newly restored saloon. Larrabee took a bath in the wood room off the kitchen and borrowed clothing from a former boarder who had died of an infected mule bite. One shirtsleeve had an ominous curved mark on it, but otherwise the garments were well mended and only a little too tight. Upstairs in his room overlooking the chicken yard, he took stock of himself in the mirror. He seemed to have shrunk and he had a bruise on one cheek, but otherwise he looked respectable. He picked his teeth with a straw pulled from his mattress and ambled down to the saloon with Penny.

"Y'hear that bugle call?" Penny asked. "They've been playin' that on the square twicet a day ever since the war ended, just so we know we're back in the Union." He rubbed his ruddy beginnings of a beard. "I don't mind being back in the Union, but I sure wish it paid better. I've pounded a passel of nails just to scrabble up a few dollars for the necessities. I'd sure like to find a shortcut. If there's a card game, maybe tonight will be my lucky night."

Duke's Saloon was a block south of the Alachua Hotel. It occupied the lower floor of a two-story frame building overshadowed by a more impressive structure identified above its cornices as "Roper's Hall." The saloon was as straightforward as its proprietor. On the sign overhead, a period after Duke's name left no doubt as to who was boss beyond the swinging doors. Inside, several brass sconces held kerosene lamps that lit the flocked wallpaper and glittered in the wall-length mirror behind the polished oak bar. A shambles of a piano stood against one wall. The scrubbed knotty pine floor and the high pressed tin ceiling reflected every syllable and footstep. Far overhead, large replicas of paintings leaned out from the walls in their gilt frames as if to eavesdrop on the conversations of the laughing, spitting, smoking men who lounged at felt-topped tables or propped their feet on the brass rail of the bar. A particularly prominent painting was labeled "Liberty at the Barricade" and more than once it had been remarked that Liberty was likely seeking independence from her clothing since one ample breast had already sprung free.

Beer was the beverage of the night and the games included dominoes and checkers and cards. At a table of poker players sat Curtis, who owned the icehouse and a sawmill, but still preferred to drive the delivery wagon himself each Wednesday. He was red-faced and genial with a succession of Tampa cigars poking out of his broad smile. "Only smoke 'em on Friday nights," he said. "It's the only time I get far enough from the missus."

Larrabee recognized another player from the stairs of the Alachua Hotel, a man who had made some remark about wishing that the Arlington would open soon so he could spend a night free of bedbugs. Their unlikely companions were two lean, tight-lipped men who seemed to speak to each other in a kind of code.

"Like in Valdosta," one said as he examined his cards.

"Better," the other replied without looking up.

Penny joined the game. Larrabee had only his hard-won ten-dollar gold piece and so he stood behind Penny and watched several hands. The outsiders were aggressive and didn't mind betting against each other but Penny won most of the hands, a dollar here, two dollars there, greenbacks and half-dollars and quarters. The bets got bigger and bigger. Before long, a gold half-eagle glinted in the pot.

Curtis folded and tossed his cards onto the table. "Coming home late's one thing. Coming home late and *broke* is another."

Penny looked at the two strangers. "Y'all're gittin' kind of pricey, ain't you?"

One of the outsiders glanced up at him. "You're good for it. The way your luck's been holding you'll take it anyway. So what you whining about?"

Penny was shaking his head. "I don't know. That's a pile of money."

"Five dollars to you," the outsider said. "Put it in and risk it or fold and lose for sure what you've got in there."

Penny looked over his shoulder for some kind of support but Larrabee looked away. He had no idea whether he would risk that kind of money.

Penny unpinned a five-dollar bill from his shirt pocket, held it over the pot for a moment, and then let it go.

"Okay," he said. "Let's see what y'all have."

One of the outsiders lowered his head and smiled and spread his cards. "Threes—three times over."

The cards fell out of Penny's hands. He pushed his chair back. "You boys sure know your game, don't you? You was milkin' me the whole time. Settin' me up and milkin' me." He pushed his chair back and knocked it over in his haste to exit through the swinging doors.

Larrabee wanted to go after him but decided that he had no right to. He felt as if he had abandoned Penny at the crucial moment.

A tall well-dressed man came over from the bar and set the chair back up. He appeared to be a year or two older than Larrabee. His thick, shiny black hair was neatly brushed. His mustache was trimmed short. His pale skin was smooth and clear. His dark blue eyes glittered with amusement. His self-assurance reminded Larrabee of a lion-tamer stepping into the ring.

Curtis took the cigar from his mouth. "Evenin', John. How are things up at the still?"

The newcomer adjusted his striped cravat and pulled his shirt cuffs back. "Evening, Curtis, gentlemen. It's been pretty quiet with Baldy Choat locked up. I haven't had a good laugh all day." He sat down and looked at the two outsiders. "You fellows going to provide one?"

"Folks, this is John Howard," Curtis said. "Owner of the San Felasco Turpentine Still. The rest of you I don't believe I caught your names." He turned to Larrabee. "You're staying over there at the Newhouses', ain't you? I saw you over there the other day."

"Name's Larrabee," Duke said from the bar. "He's a friend of Penny's."

Howard glanced from face to face. "Too bad Penny doesn't have enough sense to stay away from cards. Now I'm going to get all his money." He looked at the two outsiders. "So what *are* your names? I always like to know who I'm fleecing."

"Onslow," the one said, a little off balance. He was trying to tell if Howard was joking. "I'm George Onslow and he's Aldo Reynard."

"Where y'all from?" Curtis asked.

"Just passing through," Onslow said.

"Just looking for a game," Howard suggested.

"That's right." Onslow nodded. "Just looking for a game."

Howard smiled brightly. "Well, now you've found one. What do you say? Till there's just one man left standing?"

Reynard glanced around the room as if looking for a way out.

"All right," Onslow snapped. "Let's do it."

After just a few hands it was clear to Larrabee that John Howard was no ordinary card player. He kept his cards close to his embroidered vest. He never drew more than two cards and rarely had to show a losing hand because he usually folded or won. When he folded, he folded early. When he stayed in, he never hesitated to bet high. He played without any apparent emotion. Curtis changed his mind and decided to play a few hands but took such heavy losses that he quickly called it a night. Larrabee was reminded of a sharp cowboy cutting cattle. Once Curtis left, Howard went after Reynard. He worked him back and forth, losing low and winning high until Reynard's hands shook when he picked up his cards.

Communication between Onslow and Reynard began to break down. They started to argue. Larrabee counted $47 in the pot when Reynard put in his last greenback. Onslow had folded. Reynard's ace-high straight lost to Howard's flush. Onslow was looking very uneasy.

Larrabee wished Captain Fulton had been so successful.

But then Onslow began to win. Ten, twenty dollars at a time, each time Howard folded.

"You like to bluff, don't you?" he complained. "You like to toy with people."

Howard looked puzzled. "I'm just playing cards, George. And right now you're winning."

"That's right. I'm winning." But Onslow still sounded resentful.

"And we can speed it up." Howard remained cordial. "If you'd like to raise the ante."

"I like the ante where it is. Just deal the cards."

Duke had been watching from the bar and now he came over to get a closer look at the standoff between Onslow and Howard. Onslow had more chips and money but Howard had somehow gotten control of the game.

They shifted from draw poker to seven-card stud, two down, four up, one down. Slowly Howard's money drained away. Onslow had a pair of tens showing and Howard had only a two, a three, an eight, and a nine. Onslow started to draw him out. Curtis took out a gold watch and wound it. A quarter past twelve. Howard went along, a dollar, five dollars. Again the felt tabletop sparkled with gold.

Reynard stroked his long slick hair. "He's got a nine-high nothing to a pair of tens." He looked at Howard. "You know Onslow's got the third ten, don't you? And maybe a fourth. But you go ahead. Throw your money down."

Howard looked up from his cards. "My friend, when I buy a silver mine with your money, that's just what I'm going to call it. The Nine-High-Nothing Mine."

Howard and Onslow kept raising their bets until Larrabee reckoned the pot held more than a hundred and fifty dollars. Even as a would-be bank-robber he had never seen so much money in his life. It would take most men half a year to make as much.

Now it was Howard drawing out Onslow and everybody knew it, most of all Onslow. But the betting had become a matter of pride to him and he put his money down again and again, waiting for Howard to put a stop to the one-upmanship by calling.

Finally it was Onslow who slammed a banknote on the table.

"Call, damn your eyes! This time I'm calling your bluff."

He flipped over his cards and the third ten surfaced.

Without any to-do, Howard turned over his three cards. A ten, a jack, and a queen.

Curtis took out his cigar. "Can you believe that? A queen-high straight from a nine-high-nothing."

Reynard stared at Onslow but the attention was not returned.

Howard nodded toward Onslow's holdings. "You've got another thirty-six dollars there. How about a chance to double it in one hand?"

Not even Onslow knew that he had thirty-six dollars. Apparently Howard had been keeping track of every nickel. Onslow avoided looking at his money. "Thirty-six dollars in one hand? How?"

Howard was shuffling the cards with casual precision. His dealing had gotten faster and smoother as the night progressed.

"Simplest little game in the world. My card against yours. I turn mine up first. Then we bet on who has the higher card before we know what yours is." He waited for an answer to the challenge.

Onslow drummed his fingers at the edge of the table. He bit his lip. Everyone was watching his face. It was too late to back out without looking like a coward. It was an even chance, after all.

"All right. But I deal "

Howard pushed the deck toward him.

Onslow pushed it to Curtis. "Cut."

Curtis leaned forward, removed the top half of the deck and placed the bottom cards on it.

Keeping his hand on the table, Onslow slid the top card to Howard and drew the second for himself.

Howard flipped his card over. A four. Nothing but a four of diamonds.

He looked at the back of Onslow's card. "Well, what do you say? Thirty-six apiece?"

Onslow squirmed in his chair while he tried to calculate the odds of beating a four. The faces around the table gave no clue, not even Reynard's.

Onslow licked his lips. "All right." He pushed his money to the center of the table.

Reynard let out a breath.

"All right," Howard said. "Your turn."

Onslow looked him in the eye, trying to tell if he knew what was going to happen.

"Flip it over," Duke said.

Onslow turned the card. The three of spades.

He banged his fist on the table. "Damn it! Damn it to hell!"

Howard smiled slowly. He didn't bother to pull in Onslow's money. He owned everything on the table now, more than two hundred dollars.

The party broke up quickly. Onslow and Reynard fell over themselves on their way out the door. Curtis grabbed his hat and took off in hopes of slipping into bed without waking his wife. John Howard tied his money up in one of Duke's bar towels and walked off with it under his arm.

"Go home and try to cheer Penny up," Duke told Larrabee. "Maybe this'll teach him not to get in over his head. He's pretty good at dominoes. He ought to stick to that."

Larrabee watched him rub a wet circle from the tabletop. "You'll be staying here now that you have the place fixed up?"

Duke nodded. "You'd be surprised how often I've got to come downstairs to bludgeon some rowdy. Even after closing they try to get in here. I'll be over for lunch from time to time though. Emma Newhouse makes the best cornbread in town."

The night was warm and humid. The streets were dark except for scattered windows glowing amber. Larrabee crossed over to the square. He wanted to stretch his legs before turning in, and he followed his feet toward the white Courthouse that loomed as a great shadow under the cloudy sky. Someone had drawn a gallows and tombstones on the wall with charcoal, and even at this late hour hogs were stirring in the dirt underneath. He moved toward an oak-lined street that crossed a slow-moving creek, probably the Sweetwater Branch where Anna had begun her pinecone battle with Billy Willis. Ahead in the darkness he heard an owl, no, not an owl, a man in some kind of trouble. Pressing on, he saw three shadowy forms doing a kind of dance beside one of the great trees. Two of the figures were lunging at the third, backing him against the tree while they tried to outmaneuver him.

Larrabee didn't have to look long to determine that he was seeing Onslow and Reynard closing in on John Howard. As he came closer he saw that Reynard was thrusting at Howard with a knife while Onslow snatched at the bundle of money. Onslow had worked his way behind Howard while Reynard continued to pin him to the tree. Howard was shielding himself with his free hand, keeping up with Reynard's jabs, but Onslow was starting to get the better of him.

Larrabee thought of Captain Fulton dying in the dance hall and rushed forward.

Keeping to the shadows, he pried off a fence picket and ran forward baring the curved nails at its point. Reynard charged at Howard and Onslow grabbed at the towel full of money as Larrabee swung down with the picket. Onslow fell to one knee, regained his footing, and ran. Reynard turned on Larrabee with the knife but the picket caught him on the cheek and sent him reeling. Larrabee came at him again and knocked the knife from his hand. Reynard stumbled backwards, sat down hard, scrambled back to his feet, and took off after Onslow.

Howard straightened his cravat and tucked the bundle under his arm. Larrabee tossed down the picket and snatched up Reynard's knife. "A skinning knife. You're lucky he didn't get you."

"Lucky you came along too. Looks like my lucky night," Howard said. "You handle yourself pretty well in a street fight."

Larrabee threw the knife, burying the point in the trunk of a dark-leafed fruit tree. "You handle yourself pretty well in a card game. Do all the losers come after you like that?"

"No. But those two weren't your garden-variety losers. They were operators. I know their kind. If they can't win it, they'll wait till after the game and bushwhack it." John Howard smoothed his clothes and started down the dim street. "You're not a local, are you? You're from somewhere out west. What brings you to town?"

"Passing through on my way back west. I'll be moving on in a week."

"That so. Well, Mr.—"

"Larrabee. Nathaniel Larrabee."

"Yes. Well, Mr. Larrabee, about half the people in this town probably expected to move on in a week and yet here they are. It's one of those places that gets a hold on a person."

"You too?"

"Remains to be seen. But it beats the mill towns of New Hampshire."

"New Hampshire. That's a pull." Although he now knew the whereabouts of most of the southeastern states, thanks to Captain Fulton, Larrabee wasn't sure where New Hampshire was, but he thought its mere obscurity guaranteed that it was a long way off.

"That's the idea," Howard said with a smile. "A safe distance. I was a wanted man up there."

They had something in common. Larrabee was impressed by the man's openness. It took bravado to mention your crimes so casually.

"Something to do with card-playing?" he ventured.

Howard smiled and shook his head. "Debt. My father left debts when he died at Cold Harbor. It fell to me to pay them off by sewing on shoe soles fourteen hours a day. I decided I was fit for better things and struck out on my own."

"That ain't so much of a crime."

"Not to my way of thinking. Neither was being a digger."

"You mean a miner?"

Howard laughed. "No. Well—kind of. My friends and I trafficked in bodies."

"Bodies? You mean dead people?"

"I do. There was an excellent market for them in Boston. We'd move in after the hearse and the grief-stricken had departed and retrieve the deceased, then ferry them down to Boston where the doctors paid top dollar if the product was fresh. To our way of thinking we were performing a public service."

They were cutting across a vacant lot where the pulsating song of crickets was fast and loud. "What's the penalty for digging up bodies?"

"Oh, I don't know. That wasn't exactly the problem. The problem was that my friends got a little too zealous in their quest for freshness. One night we pulled up a German girl. Blond and blue-eyed. At least I assume she was blue-eyed. Still limp. And I could swear, still warm. It was just an impression at the time, mind you. After all, she had been in the grave for an hour or two. But then we started picking up very fresh corpses behind saloons and bawdy houses. On consignment. That the police frowned upon, and we were set to flight. Well, that's enough about me."

Larrabee tripped into something hard and low, something lost in the tall grass.

"And, speaking of the dead, it appears you just stepped on one. This is a little burying ground we're cutting through. Yellow fever victims from a few years ago. So quickly forgotten. It's a shame you're leaving town so soon. I'd offer you a way to make some traveling money."

They had come onto the street again, much to Larrabee's relief. "Truth to tell, I could use some traveling money. As long as I don't have to cross the law for it."

Howard chuckled. "Just the opposite. You'd be preventing other people from crossing the law, as you put it."

"What is it?"

"It's too late to get into that tonight. For now let's just say that it comes with a horse and a firearm. If you're interested, come to the Dennis Block at eight o'clock tomorrow morning."

"Where do I find this Dennis Block?"

"Just ask anyone and you'll find it. Well, I'm headed off that way. To our fine new jail. You really must see it sometime. From the outside of course."

By the time Larrabee got back to the Newhouse residence, the neighborhood was dark except for a light high in the back of the house. Going up the stairs to his room Larrabee saw that Preacher Williams' door was ajar. The man of God was bent over a writing desk, apparently deep in study, but at the sound of footsteps in the hall he looked up and pulled off his tiny reading glasses.

"Hello, Nathaniel." He waved a big bony hand toward a cane chair. "Come in and sit a while."

It was a fair-sized room made small by bookshelves that went from floor to ceiling. The window cast a trapezoid of light onto the garden and chicken yard below.

The preacher kept his voice down. "We haven't had much of a chance to visit."

Larrabee sat down and ran his eyes along the rows of leather bindings. The books were well used.

"I understand there was quite a card game at Duke's tonight," the preacher said.

"Penny lost. A couple of cardsharps cleaned him out. He was in over his head."

"Penny is a man of many attributes. But I don't believe he has the aptitude or the temperament of a poker player. He's too easily swept up by the enthusiasm of the moment. I'd take it as a kindness if you'd keep him from getting clipped like that again. Of course you may be long gone before he has the money to play again."

"That's right. I'm here for the week. I made a promise to Dr. Willis."

"I believe you'll keep it. This is a place that hangs onto people."

Larrabee began looking at the books again. Most of the titles were lettered in gilt. "You're the second person to say that tonight. Looks like *you're* pretty well settled here."

The preacher smiled. "My job requires a few props. But when the call comes, I'll follow. Just as I left the lumber camps of Wisconsin to come here."

"By your accent, I take you to be a southerner," Larrabee said.

The preacher's gentle nod was almost a bow. "South Carolina. After the war I became less rooted. The Wisconsin wilderness seemed like a good place to pursue my calling, but I was tested. I suppose you've heard of the great fire in Chicago?"

"Four or five years ago? Sure."

"Because the press was not there, few people know that, at the same time, a far worse fire broke out in Wisconsin. It killed entire families, entire settlements. I did not lose my faith in that fire, but I felt strongly that it needed a change of venue."

It was not difficult to picture the preacher in the lumber camps. He had a sinewy strength and a blunt way of speaking. He moistened his lips and continued. "This is a special house you have come to. It's not just anywhere that a five-year-old child will ask you if chickens have souls. Martha and I took that one on tonight. I believe I learned more than I taught."

"Well, Preacher, I don't know if they have souls, but that one today sure had flavor."

The preacher smiled again. He had even, ivory-colored teeth. "I sense that you are a young man with some wear on you, Nathaniel. May I ask do you have a family?"

"My father's dead. My mother and sister live in Missouri."

"Will you be seeing them soon?"

Larrabee hesitated. "I sure hope so."

"Have you written?"

"No. I'm not a writer and I'm not even sure where they are anymore."

"Do they know where you are?"

"*I'm* not even sure where I am. Do you always work this late?"

"On Fridays and Saturdays, yes. I work on my sermon. I seem to do my best work on Friday and Saturday nights. Inspiration and desperation make a great team."

"What's it on?"

"The Prodigal Son. As one wanderer to another, I'd be pleased to have you attend."

Chapter 6

Larrabee felt almost whole again and ready to face the dazzling new day. The horse was a big buckskin mare and his pistol was a Colt .44 army six-shooter that looked like it could blow the door off a barn. The sun was already burning through the live oaks and the 9:30 train to Cedar Keys had passed down West Main Street with enough racket to wake anyone still sleeping off Friday night revels. John Howard had gone into the Dennis Block with a tax assessor named Jacob Ford, leaving Larrabee and the buckskin to sweat and swat at flies.

Howard had explained that on the night of August twenty-first, Major Leonard G. Dennis—the famous "Little Giant"—had been giving a budget speech to the Hayes-Wheeler Club at a Negro school, the Union Academy, on the north side of town. From both sides of the crowded lecture hall, almost at the same time, two shots had been fired, both narrowly missing the major. During the pandemonium the major had rushed back to the podium, rung a large hand bell used by the academy's teachers, and restored order, after which he had launched into a powerful speech about social justice for the Negroes of the county.

"And who do you think would want to take a shot at the major?" Larrabee had asked at the end of Howard's story.

"Anyone in Alachua County who's not a Hayes backer," had been Howard's answer. "Tilden men, Conservatives, Regulators. Anyone after power or vengeance."

"Tilden men? Is this about the presidential election?" Larrabee knew a little about the close upcoming contest between Tilden the Democrat and Hayes the Republican. Some nervous Republicans had even wanted Grant to run for a third term, but apparently that had not set well with most in the party.

"This is about the *very* top," Howard had assured him.

"And who are the Conservatives you mentioned?"

"The men who ran the county before the war. Sons of the Old South. Their front man is General J. J. Finley. But he's of the Robert E. Lee school of honorable politics. You don't need to worry about him."

"And the Regulators?"

"The uncontrolled fringe. Men who ride at night, wear masks, and burn Negroes out of their homes."

Major Dennis was planning to swing through the county giving speeches on behalf of the Republican candidates, and his first stop was to be in the farming community of Arredonda, the stronghold of his sometime rival, the plantation-owner Josiah T. Walls.

Larrabee was beginning to lose track of the factions. "Is this Walls somebody who might be a threat to the Major?"

"Not by a long shot," Howard had said. "You don't have to worry about Walls for two reasons. Number one, he doesn't need power because he's already one of the richest men in the county. And number two, he's another noble warrior."

"Like Robert E. Lee."

"Not very. Walls is a Negro, a mulatto to be precise."

Larrabee was still sorting through it all when Howard and Jacob Ford emerged with a companion, a short, slight, fair-haired man with sparse mutton chop whiskers. He was not much more than thirty-five Larrabee reckoned, but he carried himself stiffly, like a man twenty years older. He wore a silk top hat and carried a walking stick that added to an air of self-importance. As he climbed into a rockaway he squinted up at Larrabee and asked, "Who's the new boy?"

"This is Larrabee, your bodyguard," Howard told him. "After Monday night it seemed to me we could use a bodyguard. Larrabee, this is Major Dennis."

Larrabee nodded politely. He wasn't sure what he thought of the major.

The carriage sank onto its springs as Jacob Ford climbed aboard and sat down beside Major Dennis.

The major studied the sky. "You really think we can make it all the way to Arredonda and back without a cloudburst? Seems like we're due for another dousing."

"We'll sure give it our best shot," Howard said. He hoisted himself into the driver's seat and shook the reins.

They followed the train tracks down West Main Street and Ford started a conversation with Major Dennis about the dark-leafed trees that seemed to be everywhere, lining the streets and yards and growing in vast groves right in town. "You could do a good deal worse than to put big money into oranges," he said. "There's gold on those trees."

Major Dennis was not impressed. "Better to buy and sell the property the trees are on. Save yourself all the trouble of taking care of those things. Deeds don't require upkeep."

It soon became clear that oranges were taking over Alachua County just as gold was taking over the Dakota Territory. Larrabee began to think that he wouldn't have to go west to find his fortune.

They passed through a forest of tall pines—loblollies Jacob Ford called them. "By the way," he said, "I hear that Sam and Baldy are out of the pokey. That was a pretty quick spring for horse theft."

"*Alleged* horse theft," John Howard told him. The horses' hooves were throwing mud and he guided the carriage onto the dry edge of the road.

Larrabee listened with great interest as he continued. "They swore they had bought the horse from some cow hunter. Said they paid $45 for the horse and $15 for the saddle. But they lost the bill of sale and the cow hunter disappeared."

"Where'd those two come up with $60? It's a cinch Baldy didn't make it working for you, John."

"Well, they're out anyway, Jacob, and the horse, only a little the worse for wear, is now safely back in Levy County. So everybody's happy."

A few miles to the southwest the woods gave over to hilly country, cattle land with sandy soil and thick grass. The fences and buildings were well cared-for. Here, too, was the occasional orange grove with its rows of dark-leafed trees marching up the slopes in neat array. Larrabee liked this open, hilly country because it reminded him of home and there were fewer hiding places for an ambush. A column of smoke rose above the trees, too straight and steady to be a locomotive and too narrow for a grass fire. He wanted to lope ahead and investigate but he stayed with the group.

Jacob Ford was first to speak. He half rose in the carriage as they passed a windbreak of scrub oaks and came to the smoking ruins of a house and barn.

"They've *burned* him out. They've burned him out and run off the lot of 'em."

"It's Caleb Green's place," Howard explained. "Many's the time we've stopped here for a drink of water or to wait out the rain."

"House and barn alike," Jacob Ford said in a daze. "House, barn, furniture, all up in smoke."

Howard brought the carriage to a halt and set the brake and everyone climbed out to have a closer look. Larrabee brought the buckskin mare into the yard, but she balked at the heat and smoke, so he took her across the road and tied her to a little scrub oak.

"Well, it wasn't lightning, that's for sure." Ford was coming back from what had been the barn, white ashes with a few uprights poking out of them. "Lightning don't take out a house and a barn neat like that."

"Not very likely." Major Dennis had left his walking stick behind and was walking through the yard with his hands clasped behind his back. Although he was slow moving, he had a martial bearing. He was sizing up the situation.

Beyond the smoldering barn an acre of ripe watermelons grew on their vines in orderly rows. Behind the remains of the house a vegetable garden showed a few full red tomatoes hanging from sticks and string. Part of the garden had been trampled and wagon ruts cut through the soft ground, took to the road and disappeared. The smoke changed direction, making the men cough and retrace their steps. Larrabee bent down and picked something out of a wagon track, a corncob doll like the ones his sister used to make. He set it back in the mud. Beside it was the print of a very wide square-toed boot. He was trying to remember where he had seen boots like that.

Howard had walked back to the carriage. "How do you figure it?"

"How do you figure it?" Ford was angry. "How do you *figure* it? Regulators is how you figure it!"

Something crackled in the woods. Larrabee put his hand to his gun butt. A cow broke through the brush and bellowed.

"They done a good job of running off the stock," Ford said. "There's probably animals wandering halfway across the county. Poor Caleb! What do you suppose has become of him?"

The major walked back to the carriage in silence.

Ford followed him. "What do you reckon we ought to do?"

The major got into the carriage. "We ought to go to Arredonda, that's what."

As Larrabee brought the mare into the road he was remembering where he had seen wide boots like the one that had made the print—on the feet of the very same Baldy Choat who worked for John Howard. He began to wonder how he was going to sort out friends from enemies.

They continued through woods and fields, crossed roads that disappeared over a ridge to the southwest, and came to a railroad track.

Ford looked down the tracks as they bumped over them. "How many trains come into Walls' place now?"

"Don't you know, Ford?" Major Dennis sounded annoyed. "You're the tax assessor, aren't you?"

Ford tried to recover from his effort at small talk. "I hear two a week. Likely be three when the oranges are ripe."

The road narrowed, so Larrabee rode behind the carriage until they came to a loose collection of warehouses, big weathered tobacco barns, and small clapboard houses with deep porches and slender brick chimneys. In the middle of a mowed field stood a blue-and-white striped pavilion tent and a platform draped with bunting.

Jacob Ford waved at a passer-by. "Looks like the Centennial all over again, don't it?" The field was full of people picnicking, playing horseshoes, chatting, laughing. About half of them were Negroes.

A handsome landau bobbed out of a side road and pulled onto the edge of the field a few yards from where most of the horses and wagons had been parked. A band began playing. Several men came up to the landau and a tall, elegantly dressed light-skinned Negro stepped down and began shaking hands. Howard guided the carriage onto the grass nearby and Major Dennis and Jacob

Ford got out and walked toward the gathering crowd.

"You're on," Howard told Larrabee. "You're looking at two of the most powerful men in the state. Get over there and stick to the major, but don't be obvious about it. Do whatever it takes to keep him in one piece, even if it means pushing him over or shooting women and children. There are men who would love to derail this assembly. It's your job to see to it that they don't."

The hours seemed endless to Larrabee as he scanned the crowd looking for the glint of a gun barrel or a sudden approach. There was a picnic, a series of tableaux put on by the Girls of the Greenbelt, a series of photographic sittings. Someone tried to make a plaster cast of the major's hands but somehow the plaster turned as sticky as pitch and the major spent close to a quarter of an hour at a pump trying to get his fingers clean while the artist fell all over himself apologizing.

By mid-afternoon local dignitaries began to take their seats on the speaker's platform. They were mostly farmers in their Sunday best—shirts that showed recent pressing, trousers too heavy for the day, hats that hadn't been broken in yet. Conspicuous in the center of the front row were Major Leonard G. Dennis and Mr. Josiah T. Walls. The crowd pressed toward the speakers and listened politely to a series of introductory speeches praising the productivity of the county and of Arredonda in particular, extolling the golden opportunities of the year ahead, and lauding the achievements of the Grant administration and the Republican Party.

Larrabee had taken up a position at the back of the platform, where he paced slowly from one side to the other, surveying the crowd. Many of the farmers carried rifles or pistols, so he looked for attitude—the way the men stood, the way they watched the speakers. If they stood with women or children, he focused somewhere else. Old men were safe. Boys under about fourteen were safe. That got him down to fifty or sixty men who might take a shot at the powerful Major Dennis.

Josiah Walls came to the podium and spoke in an eloquent tenor voice about opportunity. He was a believer, he said, in the opportunity offered by a prosperous county in a growing state in a secure nation that had as its steward a wise government elected by enlightened men. "This election is not for the Negro," he stated. "This election is for the people, white and Negro, who are heirs to the democratic process. I have withdrawn my candidacy from the race for the U.S. House of Representatives in order to unify this party. I support— and I urge you to support—Horatio Bisby as your congressional representative, Marcellus Stearns for your governor, and the honorable Rutherford B. Hayes for the President of the United States!"

The crowd responded with applause, whistling, and whooping, though it wasn't clear if the acclaim was for Walls' ideas or the dramatic loftiness with which he had expressed them.

Gripping the lectern, Walls waited for the noise to die down and then he introduced "a man with whom I have had my quarrels, but one with whom I have made my peace, for our ideals run parallel courses." With that he extended his hand and bowed to Major Dennis, who patted him on the shoulder as the assemblage cheered. Major Dennis came to the podium and raised his hand for silence. He leaned forward into the lectern, but apparently thinking that it made him appear too short, he stepped to one side and delivered a fifteen-minute oration that held the masses spellbound. He reviewed the slate of candidates and said, "I shall do all I can to cause their election, and if a faction calling themselves Republicans are determined to adhere to candidates preaching divisiveness, and by so doing turn the state over to the Democrats, they alone must bear the responsibility!"

The crowd burst into applause and the major started to leave the podium, but then he apparently changed his mind because he stood waiting for the outcry to subside. A murmur spread across the field. Had the major been taken ill? Was there trouble among the dignitaries on the platform? The major spoke in a loud, clear voice.

"Candidates and party platforms and planks are all well and good. But this election really comes down to one man. His name is Caleb Green. Some of you knew him. I say knew him because Caleb Green is no longer among us. He is gone. His house is gone. His barn is gone. His family is gone. Fired out! Was it lightning? No! Was it some accident? No! Caleb Green and his family were *driven* out. That's right, driven out! Driven out by other members of his race? No! By Republicans? No! What party may I ask you is the party of division?"

"The Democrats!" somebody shouted from the back of the crowd. "All those Democrats!"

"Not all Democrats," the major declared, waving his hand. "No, not all Democrats. But which is the party that sows the seeds of disunion in this state?"

"The Democrats!" called back a scattering of voices.

"And which party has held back the Negro in this state, denying him life and liberty?"

"The Democrats!"

"My fellow citizens, it's too late to save Caleb Green and his family. It's too late to save a thousand Caleb Greens. But it's not too late to save your neighbor and the man who bends his back in the sun as you do! Ten years have passed since the blood of martyrs restored the house divided. I ask you, is it not time to fulfill our promise to our honored dead by continuing the work for which they laid down their lives?"

Many of the women were weeping openly. Many of the men were visibly moved.

Major Dennis lowered his voice, but his words carried easily across the quiet field. "My friends, my countrymen, fulfill the promise by electing your Republican candidates."

"Yes!" came a voice from the crowd. "Yes, we will!" The field burst into a fury of shouts and applause. The band struck up a march. Walls and the major pumped hands. Walls grinned. Major Dennis blushed. The dignitaries clapped each other on the back and began climbing down from the platform. Pressing toward the major, Larrabee heard someone saying, "Well, that's why they call him the Little Giant. Not much to look at, but he sure can roar!"

Suddenly the crowd parted as a man pushed his way toward the platform. Pinned between two large, sweating dignitaries telling jokes, Larrabee could see only the newcomer's derby hat moving through the crowd and, not wanting to take chances, he rammed someone with his shoulder to give himself room to draw the .44. People were batting their hats and shoving at the man as he came on and Larrabee elbowed his way to the major's side, ready to push him out of the assassin's path.

Then he heard Howard saying, "Larrabee, there's some fellow here all excited because he knew you on the *Belle Helene*, whatever that is."

Larrabee tried to see through the crowd. "Cameron? Is that you, Cameron Potts?"

The man's hat came off, revealing a shock of red hair and the glowing face of Jared Penrod.

Chapter 7

The sound of the church bell carried through the woods and over the low hills that unfolded south of town. Jared rolled the cane pole in his hands until his cork and empty hook hung dripping over the water. An ibis beat its white wings from one end of the lake to the other and disappeared into the cypresses beyond.

"Well," Jared said, "there's another bait-stealer down there saying grace."

Larrabee's cork was still floating undisturbed. He figured something had cleaned his hook long ago but he was content. Slowly he let out more line and wound it back in just to give it some play.

Jared swung his line ashore and held it up while he dug a worm out of a peach can. "What did you say was in this lake?"

"Bluegills. This whole place through here, they call it Bivens Arm, is supposed to be full of bluegills. There's also rumors of bream and specks and shell-crackers."

"Unconfirmed rumors. This is our punishment for skipping church, you know. I hear Preacher Williams gives a sermon to stir the heart."

"If this is punishment, I'll take it." Larrabee settled back against a sweet gum tree. He had cleared away the prickly gumballs, but now one pinched his thigh and he chucked it into the water.

"What do you suppose happened to 'em all—Greenleaf and Philippe and poor Cameron?"

"Nothing good. You're lucky you got off of there, Jared."

"Cameron deserved better. Damn it. I shouldn't've taken off like that. "

Jared had told about his blind break from the *Belle Helene*, diving into the water while Cameron and Greenleaf wrestled for the Navy pistol.

"Things got out of hand," Larrabee said. "It all happened before we knew what hit us."

"What if they did get all the way to Cuba? Remember, slavery's still legal there."

"Maybe he got a lucky break."

"You really think so?"

"I will if you will."

Jared looked at a worm and put it back in the can. "I bet he would've liked it here. All that talk about justice for Negroes. That Walls is impressive."

"And you say he owns this newspaper you're working for."

"He sure does. Of course, your Major Dennis owns one too."

"That so?"

"Don't you know anything? Major Dennis owns the *Times* and Walls owns *The New Era*. If you'd read the papers you'd have some idea of what's going on around here."

"I got a pretty good idea down there at Arredonda yesterday. Dennis and Walls want to see to it that the Negroes have a say in running the county. Major Dennis was shot at last Monday night at a place called the Union Academy and nobody seems to know who did it. And somebody fired out a Negro farmer named Caleb Green and that's got the major good and stirred up and more determined than ever to win this election for the Republicans. I've been doing some thinking about that."

"About what?"

"About Caleb Green. I've seen farms where people were run off. Caleb Green's place didn't look the same."

Jared flicked off a mosquito. "What do you mean, didn't look the same?"

"Well, when somebody's been run off in earnest the ground's all cut up by horses and folks running around willy-nilly. That Green place had neat tracks. Like nobody was in any particular hurry. And there was a peculiar footprint of a wide boot with square toes, just like Baldy Choat's."

"What do you make of that?"

"I don't know. But it sure made for some powerful speeches yesterday. If speeches make votes, you'll likely see the major and Walls and all the Republicans elected, top to bottom."

"You figure to be here that long?"

"Maybe. I'm eating every day and I've got a little pocket money and nobody breathing down my neck. I might hang around for a little while."

"Weren't you talking about going west, to the gold fields? Or at least back to Missouri?"

"Jared, those gold fields might as well be in China. And as for Missouri, I can't go back. I may be wanted for killing a man out there."

"Oh, come on now. You didn't kill anybody."

"I fired the shots and I saw him go down. That sounds like two and two to me."

"What made you go and shoot at somebody?"

"He was shooting at me. They do that in Missouri. When you rob banks."

"Now I know you're telling tales. You didn't rob any bank."

"I sure did, even if I didn't get away with any money." He took the ten-dollar gold piece from his pocket. "Except this. Not much of a return for shooting a man."

"Why'd you do it?"

"I did it because our farm was one of those where everybody was run off. Only it wasn't raiders. It was all legal. Done before dawn by the Bank of Liberty County."

"Anybody else around here know that?"

Larrabee shook his head. "Only way they'll know is if you tell 'em."

"I won't. Even if I *am* a reporter. How long you been on the run?"

"Couple of weeks."

"Well, this is probably as good a place as any to lie low."

"I'd say so."

"Then if I was to hitch a ride on a northbound train you wouldn't want to come with me."

Larrabee smiled and shook his head. "I've had my fill of trains and river-boats and sailing ships for a while. You go on if you want to. I'm not going till I've got some money in my pocket. One way or the other."

"What if you *didn't* kill that man at the river?"

"I've been thinking about that. Either way I've put in a poor showing. I'm not going back to Missouri till I've made something of myself, till I've earned it." Suddenly Larrabee jerked forward. The tip of his pole was dipping toward the water

Jared stood up. "Looks like a big one! This could be our lucky day after all."

According to Jared the whole country was in a lather about the elections. He had it from newspapers as far away as Valdosta and Macon that the presidential contest would be very close indeed and that tensions were high between Republicans and Democrats right down to the local level. The more Major Dennis and Josiah Walls spoke of Negroes voting and owning land and sharing steamboats and trains with white men, the more strident the Democrats became about regaining control of the county, which had to begin with sending the occupying troops back north even though the troops no longer had much to do with the way the town was run. The bugler on the Courthouse Square became little more than an unfortunate symbol of the occupation, and as Election Day approached he was increasingly the target of unidentified assailants hurling corncobs dipped in mud or manure.

The Republicans continued to press for equal rights for the Negro and undertook a massive voter registration campaign. Larrabee and John Howard accompanied Major Dennis on day trips all across the county, some on excursion trains, some by carriage, one on horseback—and the major turned out to be a capable rider despite his brittle appearance. The retinue also included Thomas Vance and Richard Black, who were introduced as "clerk" and "inspector" respectively although it was never clear to Larrabee just what those titles meant.

"It's worked for the past ten years and it'll work this time," Vance told Black as they set out on one expedition. "If we can get every nigra in the county to vote Republican we can lick the Democrats and the old boys every time."

All the while, Larrabee was on the lookout for assassins. But since no one had ever seen the men who had fired on the major at the Union Academy, it was hard to know who to look for.

"They come and killed a nigra right on his farm six or seven years ago," Vance told Larrabee. "And they come after the major hisself during the election in '70."

"In that shooting at the Academy, what kind of gun was used?" Larrabee asked. "Did they get any slugs out of the wall?"

"Now that's a curious thing," Black shrugged. "Wasn't never any holes found in that wall. But everybody sure saw the flashes through the window and heard the reports and heard the bullets hit the plaster. You should've seen the way we dove out of there! Doors, windows it was all the same. Nigras and whites alike, flyin' right out and piled up together on the ground like cord wood!"

One night in September Larrabee had walked up from the Newhouse place and had a look at the Academy. It wasn't far. He could see the roof from the window of his room. It was a trim clapboard building with a steep roof and a bell tower. Larrabee opened the gate in the picket fence and followed the brick walkway to the long porch. Everyone had agreed that shots had been fired from the far left window of the porch and Larrabee leaned against the glass and looked toward the podium at the speaker's end of the room. The view was obstructed by the angle of the wall.

Whoever had shot at the major had been unable to see him.

When Larrabee got back to the house on Magnolia Street, Jared was on the sleeping porch whittling a horse out of soft pine. He had taken the room vacated when Duke moved back into the apartment over the saloon.

Larrabee described what he had found while Jared scooped out the horse's back.

"Interesting. What do you make of it?"

"I'm up here to ask you what *you* think of it," Larrabee said peevishly. Jared was always throwing his own questions back at him.

Jared was silent for a long time. The horse was becoming a little swaybacked and Larrabee wondered if Jared was carving a particular horse, faults and all. Although the forelegs were unfinished, the sculptor tapped the horse on the rump as if to stir it into life.

"It's sort of like the Caleb Green incident, ain't it?"

"How's that?"

"Well, like you said, after the shooting at the Academy the major got back up there and charged into a speech blaming the Democrats for running Caleb off. Suddenly county finances were not the issue of the night."

"Go on, Jared. What's the rest of it?"

"You know the rest of it because you were there. What happened after Caleb Green?"

"The major got up and gave a fire-and-brimstone speech about how the Republicans had to win the election or the whole county would go to hell."

"That's right. I'd say the major is quite fired up."

"You think he rigged the attempt on his own life and faked running off Caleb Green?"

"I don't know. We may never know."

Larrabee's thoughts went back to the man at the river and the uncertainty of what had happened to him. "It's like trying to work in smoke. What should we do?"

Suddenly Jared looked very wise. "We should do the best we can under the circumstances."

One of the voter registration tours had brought Larrabee back to Archer and the cafe where he had gotten into the fight over poison oysters. When Major Dennis suggested that they stop there for something to eat, Larrabee led the way in. The big flat-faced blond boy was there but, seeing the important men at Larrabee's heels, he settled for giving Larrabee a hard look from behind the counter and kept his distance.

"This is Walls country you're in now," Vance said to the entourage. "He taught school down here before he went into politics."

"I think it'd be perfectly all right if he goes back to teaching school," Black joked. The major's disapproving look cut his laugh short.

"They need Walls till after the election," Jared said when Larrabee told him of the incident. "Everything's at stake this time around. If any one of those elections goes to the Democrats the jig may well be up. They can't afford to antagonize Walls or any of his men. The Democrats are already putting pressure on the Negroes. Every Democrat with a black man working for him is telling that black man which way to vote. And there've been beatings. The Republicans may have the numbers but the Democrats want this election bad, and they're willing to do some scrapping to get it."

Larrabee was distracted because his mouth was sore. All around town the oranges were in full ripeness and Anna had showed him how to cut the top off and suck out the juice. She hadn't told him that after a while the peel would make his lips burn. There was nothing for it, Doctor Willis had told him, but to outlive it.

As the November elections approached, Larrabee became more and more convinced that his future and the future of the county lay in a Republican victory. The newspapers carried stories of Negroes being intimidated by Democrats, pressured either to vote for the Democratic candidates or to stay away from the polls entirely. Both sides used Caleb Green as a warning. The Republicans blamed the Democrats and said that the Civil War had been fought to prevent just that kind of persecution. The Democrats accused the Republicans of "waving the bloody shirt," blaming the war on the Democrats when it was really the fault of northern abolitionists and tariff-mongers. The Democrats claimed that theirs was the party to deal with extremists like the Regulators because the Democrats were the party of the people.

The election talk got so heated and so repetitious that Mrs. Newhouse forbade politics as a table topic. Preacher Williams began putting in vague references to "strife" when he said grace, but after a while even that stopped, and whenever talk of politics came up the offenders—usually Penny and Jared—would have to leave the room and continue their discussion on the porch. Jared wasn't going to say who he was voting for and that got Penny all red in the face because he thought it was as clear as rain that the Democrats had every right to win. With little provocation he would recite the wrongs that had led to the war, enumerate on his thick fingers the reasons why the Union had lost the war in Florida, and continue that line of argument right up to the present time, to the bugler who "crowed" from the Courthouse Square twice a day.

Mrs. Newhouse would look down to the opposite end of the long table to the empty place there as if wishing that her late husband would appear and set things right. But the election talk went on and on—in the woodshed, in the garden, on the porch, at the pump, and for all she knew, even up in the leafy embrace of old granddaddy oaks.

Billy Willis sported a Tilden ribbon on the lapel of his Sunday suit and had to give it over to Mrs. Doig, the Sunday school teacher, before he could take his place. That was enough to make Anna favor Hayes. She disliked the idea of endorsing a candidate just because a human worm favored his opponent, but she thought that Hayes must have some merits of his own if Larrabee was on his side. Larrabee was a very serious, hard-working man and must surely have made up his mind only after studying the two candidates at length.

Election Day was November seventh. Just after breakfast Larrabee was in the chicken yard chopping kindling for Mrs. Newhouse when Howard came by in a carriage and told him that the major wanted him to go to Archer.

Larrabee sank the hatchet into the chopping stump. "To Archer? On Election Day? What for?"

"To keep an eye on the polling place and bring the ballot box back. Get your horse and your artillery and meet me at the Dennis Block in a quarter hour."

They arrived at noon, dusty and windblown. The town under the trees was in a festive mood. On one side of the broad street groups of Negroes sat in rough wagons, talking and taking in the sunshine, for the morning had been chilly. On the other side of the street the white men of Archer chewed and spat and joked while their women held a quilting bee in one of the larger houses. Barefoot children squatted over games of marbles and mumblety-peg. Three or four older girls were making rag dolls at a table set up under the awning of a dry goods store.

The polling place was a long, low tobacco barn that had been cleared and cleaned for the occasion. Each end of the barn had an open window where voters came to have their names checked on the registration list. When a voter's name was found, his ballot was accepted and placed in a box by a Negro. A white man went back and forth between the windows certifying every twenty or thirty ballots and depositing them in the ballot box in the center of the room.

"Looks like the whole town showed up to vote," Howard said from the carriage. "That watcher's going to have his hands full."

The white man looked up at Howard then went back to checking ballots.

"He's a Democrat," Howard said in a stage whisper. "About to become extinct."

After an hour Larrabee went down the street to look for a drink of water. He caught sight of a pump in a small clearing and was heading for it when he heard the voice.

"You ran away fast, but I figgered you'd come back sooner or later. You ready to finish the fight?"

Larrabee's hand drifted to the .44.

The blond boy with the flat face flexed his coiled whip, "Go ahead and reach for it. Before you can touch it, I'll snap your fingers off."

Larrabee let his hand drop and backed away.

"I guess you're afraid to turn around, so go ahead and run backwards," the blond boy said. Two of his friends came into the clearing and moved toward Larrabee, one on each side, as the blond boy went on with his taunting.

"You going to go backwards like that for the rest of your life?"

Larrabee's hands tingled. The blond boy's chin jutted out, an easy target, but they were still ten yards apart and he didn't want to lose his livelihood to a street brawl. He was turning back toward the tobacco barn when he flinched at what sounded like a pistol shot and felt a sharp pain that spun him around by the shoulder. In an instant he realized that he was feeling the sting of the whip and tried not to let on that he had been hit. More voters were arriving at the tobacco barn and he walked toward the polling place with a slow, steady stride as the blond boy and his two friends trailed after him, calling him names and spitting at him. They followed him all the way up to the tobacco barn, where the watcher was just finishing his last tally and turning the ballot box over to the clerk, Thomas Vance.

The crowd was too big now for picking a fight so the blond boy and his friends slouched under the live oaks, slapping leaves off with the bullwhip while waiting for another opportunity.

"What's the vote?" somebody called out when Richard Black emerged from the barn. The poll inspector hesitated, obviously relishing the suspense and attention.

"What's the vote?" a few other voices demanded.

The poll inspector started to speak but nobody could hear him so, smiling awkwardly, he was hoisted onto a buckboard to announce the results.

He fished in his shirt pocket for a pair of reading glasses that he perched low on his nose as he scrutinized his papers. "The voting for this polling place shows 180 votes for the Republican ticket." He cleared his throat and a hush settled under the trees. "And for the Democrats, 136."

Half the crowd, Negroes mostly, burst into hoots and cheers. The other half, entirely white as far as Larrabee could see, turned from the polling place muttering and shaking their heads. The poll inspector was left to climb down from the buckboard on his own.

Thomas Vance came swaggering out of the tobacco barn with the ballot box under his arm.

"Come on down from there, Richard. We've got to get this back to town."

Larrabee climbed onto the buckskin mare and prodded her into a jog trot alongside the carriage. He heard someone whistle and felt a clod of dirt shoot past his ear, but he kept a steady pace and didn't look back until he and the major's men were out on the open road.

"You reckon anybody'll come after us?" Vance wondered.

"Not likely," Howard said. "If that box doesn't make it to Tallahassee it's no good to anybody. And it's got 136 Democrat votes in it."

He flipped the reins, snapping the team into a faster trot.

It was almost midnight by the time they got back to town. Lights flickered through dark trees and the cold wind carried the scent of pine smoke. They came up West Main Street past silent orange groves thick with ripe fruit and followed the railroad tracks until they came to the White Pine Livery Stable, where Larrabee turned the buckskin mare over to a sleepy stable hand and then climbed onto the seat beside Howard. He took the .44 out of the holster and laid it across his knee.

Howard nodded toward the gun. "Taking no chances in this last half mile? I'm surprised you didn't pull that out back in Archer." Off in the woods an owl hooted.

"Someone might've gotten killed," Larrabee said.

"Kind of quiet in town tonight." Vance looked around nervously.

Howard pushed his hat back. "That's because the saloons have been closed. It's Election Day after all."

"That's right, it still is," Richard Black pulled the ballot box close to his side. "It's been a long one. Seems like two days we've lived through since breakfast."

At a handsome two-story house Howard turned the team eastward onto a narrow oak-lined street that took them within a block of the trim, pillared Presbyterian Church and past a scattering of large unlit frame homes. After they had plodded on for another block or so, Howard pulled the team to a stop beside a low clapboard house shadowed by tall, brushy scrub oaks. Larrabee thought they were letting Vance or Black off but everyone got out. Clutching the ballot box, the clerk followed the poll inspector and Howard past the picket fence and up to the narrow front porch. It was a drab, pinched, suspicious-looking little place, Larrabee thought. He felt for his gun butt as he went up the front steps.

Before Howard had finished turning the bell, the door opened. Inside, holding a lantern turned low, was Major Dennis. His collar was open and he was wearing slippers, but otherwise he was fully dressed as if ready to do business. The lamp cast strange shapes in his mutton-chop whiskers.

"Everything go according to Hoyle?" He held the lamp a little higher as he studied the faces of the men at his door.

Howard nodded toward Vance and Black. "Got 'em here."

The door opened wider. "Come in." As the major went back into the house, Larrabee thought he heard him ask, "What was the count?"

Vance and Black went in. As Larrabee came up, Howard turned and blocked the door. "Job well done. Now take the rig back to White Pine and call it a night. I'll send for you tomorrow or the day after."

Fifteen minutes later, Larrabee was walking back up West Main. Instead of continuing north to his warm bed, though, he followed an impulse to walk back over to the major's house. In a gable overlooking the deserted street a light shone. He stood under an oak, watching shadows flicker across the window, increasingly intrigued by the indistinct voices from the house. On the third try, he had his foot on a broken sign that said *No* and his hands on the bottom branch of the oak. A moment later, he was wedged against the trunk of the tree with a full view of the men in the house.

They were sitting at a table. They were in their shirtsleeves. At first it looked like they were playing cards, but the ballot box was open at the major's elbow. Vance and Black were busily writing. Every now and then Black would stop and wring his hand. Howard was nowhere to be seen. The major picked up a stack of papers, paged through them, and began folding them. Stretching for a higher view, Larrabee discerned that the papers were ballots, just like the ones he had seen going into the boxes in Archer all afternoon. Was this some kind of validation process?

"How many more?" Vance asked.

"We've got a couple hundred. Give me some more yet," the major said. "I want Archer to speak with a clear voice."

Larrabee let those words sink in as Vance and Black continued scrawling.

Major Dennis was stuffing the ballot box.

Chapter 8

When the sun rose on November eighth nobody in the country knew which party had won the election for the United States presidency and, closer to home, nobody knew which party had captured the governorship of Florida. Both contests were too close to call, and cries of fraud echoed throughout the land. Jared folded *The New Era* and laid it in his lap.

Larrabee jabbed a pitchfork into a bale of hay. "But we do know that the Republicans carried Archer by three hundred and ninety-nine to one hundred and thirty-six. Two hundred and nineteen more than was announced when the ballots were counted in Archer."

"You have a good head for figures, Nathaniel. You should be doing something better than stable work."

"Maybe so, but I'm good at fixing wagons and carriages and I'm doing something better than working for Major Leonard G. Dennis. Why doesn't he just rob banks like the James Gang? That'd be more honest."

Jared folded his arms. "But not as safe. The James Gang got themselves all shot to pieces in Minnesota a few weeks ago. Instead of robbing a bank that had foreclosed on the farmers they picked on a bank that was *owned* by farmers. Then one of the gang stole a getaway horse that turned out to be blind. So I don't think we'll be hearing much from the James Gang anytime soon."

"And Major Dennis will just go on running the county with his crooked ballot boxes. There's no way they'll ever get him out of there as long as he controls the polls."

"Nothing around here lasts very long, Nathaniel. Haven't you noticed that the whole town is built up on footings? That way when things get too bad, the whole thing can just pick up and walk away. I hear John Howard's coming back tonight. It being Friday he'll probably show up at Duke's."

"If he doesn't get himself lynched somewhere or ambushed."

"I hear he's been up in Jacksonville. You still figure he was in on it?"

"The whole kettle of fish smells bad to me."

"Well, I admire your principles. To give up your horse and your dollar a day."

A roan gelding was tied to a hook on the wall and Larrabee pushed its rump aside with his shoulder. "The company's better. I kept the gun."

Just then a black boy about seven years old walked in from the yard carrying a shovel.

Larrabee propped the pitchfork against a stack of hay bales. "Jared, this here's Mr. Harmon Murray."

"Mr. Murray, is it? How are you, Mr. Murray?"

"I'm too good to work in this hole. That's how I am. Now quit messin' wif me."

"Feisty little scamp, ain't he?" Jared said. "A real barn cat. He sure has neat clothes though."

"His mother does that," Larrabee said. "She takes in laundry for some of the neatest. Bobby La Rue has Mrs. Murray do his things."

"Well, if I'm ever flush maybe I'll have her do my things too. You're holding that shovel like a weapon there, Mr. Murray."

"I'm fixing to mash me some more roaches, that's why. I hate roaches and I'm going to mash every one of 'em in this barn."

"Hard to get a day's work done that way," Jared said. "Hating things."

"Mind your own business." The boy shouldered the shovel and proceeded toward the main door. On his way out he spit on the wall.

Jared watched him go. "You've got yourself a real barn cat there, Nathaniel. Sure you wouldn't rather be riding for the major?"

"I can handle that one," Larrabee said. "I can handle Harmon Murray. At least I know where he's coming from."

At half past eight Larrabee went to Duke's looking for John Howard. He stopped to look over the frosted part of the side window and caught sight of the familiar dark hair and trim mustache. The night had a chill to it so Duke had the potbellied stove lit up, but most of the men were wearing their coats. Howard was deep into a five-handed game of stud poker, but unlike his stale-looking companions, he had the appearance of someone who had just stepped out of a ballroom. He had on a ruffled shirt with a wing collar, a velvet tie, a black serge coat and a lemon-colored silk vest. He was smoking a long slender cigar. His black hair was shiny with pomade and he wore a silver ring on his little finger. Apparently Jacksonville had been good to him.

Larrabee pushed his way through the doors and confronted him.

"Let's talk about the election."

The men looked up at him as if he had lost his mind. Duke was in front of the bar helping to pick up a man who had evidently fallen over. He eased the man back down on the floor and watched Larrabee with his steady blue eyes.

Howard looked perplexed. He took the cigar from his mouth and blew a jet of smoke across the table. "Election's over, Larrabee. It's up to the brokers to sort if all out. Anyway, some of these boys are Republicans and some are

Democrats." He smiled at the other players. "Better that we don't get into politics."

They all agreed with that. They'd heard enough about politics.

Larrabee had his hand on the table. The game wasn't going on until he got some answers.

"I want to talk about Archer," he said. "I want to talk about—"

John Howard stood up. "There's nothing to talk about. It's out of our hands." He looked over Larrabee's shoulder to Duke and raised his voice. "See if you can talk some sense into him."

Jared had come into the room.

Larrabee stayed where he was. "I want to hear it from you."

Howard moved past him. "Let's talk outside. Duke, keep an eye on these high rollers till I get back. If a one of them touches my stake, smack him with that belaying pin of yours."

"Hard to get through a game tonight," one of the players grumbled. "I think it's some kind of racket."

Larrabee and Jared followed Howard out to the walk. Amber light glinted through the clear upper panes of the front windows.

"Did you know?" Larrabee demanded. "Did you know that ballot box was going to be stuffed?"

Howard watched his cigar smoke curl up into the darkness. "My friend, like turning cards, I don't know anything until it's happened. If you know the box was stuffed, chances are you know I wasn't there when it happened. Am I surprised? Are you really surprised? You did your job and you were paid for it. Anything else is Major Dennis' lookout." He softened his stance. "And as long as we're speaking of money, I have come across a way that might bring in plenty of it if you and your friend are feeling adventuresome." Larrabee started to speak, but Howard put up his hand. "It's legal. It's a night's work. And the money is more than you've ever seen."

"How much?"

"It's nice to know that I have your attention. Enough to buy a house—or a farm."

"How much, John?"

"Ten thousand dollars. How does that sound? It's going to take some nerve to go after it. But you have to be in the deal before I tell you any more. And if you're in, you don't breathe a word to anyone until the job is done or you stand to lose everything. Cut your friend in on your share if you want. He just might earn it. But it'll be just the three of us. In or out? What do you say?"

The card players were calling for Howard to come back. Duke had propped the fallen man against the piano.

Larrabee watched the smoke drift past Howard's face. Inside Duke's saloon someone had started to play the piano, one note over and over, hollow and tinny.

"I say it's a pig in a poke. You keep it."

When they were well down the street, Jared looked back. Howard was still outside the saloon. His cigar glowed like a cat's eye.

During the next few days, Larrabee fell into a particularly sour mood at the stable. Harmon's killing had progressed from cockroaches to mice, and there was no lack of them in the barn since the cold weather drew them in. The boy found them under the hay bales and flattened them into the sand. He found them in the tack room and cut them in two with the lip of the shovel. He chased them out of the cracks in the walls, crushed them, and left the foul-smelling lumps as trophies.

Howard's moneymaking scheme nagged at Larrabee even though it was no more substantial than the smoke from his cigar. The fact was that Howard did have an ability to make fast money without getting dirty. And so far as Larrabee knew, Howard hadn't done anything illegal. Maybe it was true. Maybe the money was there for the taking for the man bold enough to take it.

One night he thought about the money all through dinner—during Preacher Williams' blessing, during the ritual passing of the dishes, during Penny's patter about shooting a large buck at the Sweetwater Branch when he was a boy.

"Polishing the silver tonight?" Jared's innocent question stopped all conversation.

Larrabee hadn't noticed. The usual heavy ornate tableware had been replaced with dull, mismatched tools.

Everyone looked to the end of the table where Mrs. Newhouse sat stiffly with her hands in her lap. For a moment Larrabee thought she would bolt from the room but she stayed in her place.

"Oh, *Mama!*" Anna fought back tears.

Caroline let out that a southbound tinker named Leo Bard had bought the family silver.

Mrs. Newhouse took a deep breath. "It's not important. Other things are more important. We will please not mention it again."

"I'm sorry. I—" Jared looked away.

Penny rushed to fill the silence. "Them pine woods th'other side of th'academy used to be full of whitetail. You could shoot 'em from the window when they put these houses up. We didn't none of us need money then. The land gave us everything."

Once dinner was over Jared wasted little time going outside. Larrabee followed him out to the empty chicken yard. The chickens were still settling in the hen house. The neat rows of the garden had withered into vague lines of decay. Stalks and leaves had been heaped up, waiting for the quickening of spring.

"I heard they were having trouble making ends meet," Jared said. "But I didn't know it was that bad. We've all been so caught up in our politics we didn't notice that they were going broke."

Somebody was playing the piano. It sounded better than Duke's instrument, sweet and tuneful despite the occasional errant note. One of the girls laughed and the playing stopped for a moment then resumed with a different song.

Larrabee looked back toward the house. The downstairs was well lit. Upstairs only the preacher's window showed light. Saturday night. He would be adding the finishing touches to tomorrow's sermon.

"What is it—the mortgage?"

"And keeping the place fixed up. And the taxes. They're due in January. That I do know."

Larrabee walked toward the summer kitchen. "Is the whole world going broke?"

The pianist went into a skipping melody that ended in the high notes. Larrabee was trying to figure out who was playing, Caroline or Anna.

"You want to go back to him, hat in hand?"

"To Howard?" Jared put his hands in his pockets. "I am kind of curious as to what he's up to. But it sounds like another dangerous shortcut. And you can't trust him."

"That's right."

"On the other hand, if it is ten thousand dollars, it can put us all back on our feet. We could *give* Mrs. Newhouse the tax money. You could buy back your farm and I could buy an interest in a newspaper. Editor-publisher. I kind of like the way it sounds. And what do we have to lose?"

"Let's just hope we don't find out."

It took Larrabee a while to find him. It was Sunday morning. He wasn't in his rooms over Jordan's Dry Goods Store on the square. Larrabee couldn't picture Howard settling down at a fishing hole. The picnic spots—Boulware Springs and Oliver Park and Magnesia Springs—seemed equally unlikely. Larrabee roamed the town on a bony roan gelding borrowed from the stable. He saw runaway pigs and stray chickens and two or three recovering drunks but no John Howard. Against the muddy clopping of the horse's hooves, the Presbyterian Church tolled its bell for the faithful. The Methodist choir was warming up with "Pleading Savior." As he passed, the raw air filled with the soulful tones of the African Baptists singing "We Are Climbing Jacob's Ladder." Larrabee could see his breath. On a hunch, he kicked the roan into a trot and rode north on the hard mud of West Main. He followed the train tracks past the edge of town to a flat place where the loblolly pines grew tall and straight. Then he turned west and rode half a mile, which brought him to a line of three clapboard cabins consisting of hardly more than a front porch, a chimney, and enough lumber to keep the weather out. He spoke to the roan, louder and more than was necessary to keep it moving. His reins and spurs rattled and clanked enough for a caravan.

A woman appeared on the porch of the first cabin. Her blond hair was pulled back, and although the morning was cloudy she seemed unaccustomed to the light. She shaded her eyes and hailed him in long syllables that reminded Larrabee of a taffy pull.

"You picked a funny time to come out here, sugar. Don't you know that it's Sunday?"

Larrabee brought the roan to a halt. He started to tip his hat off but thought better of it. "I'm out here looking for a fellow named John Howard. You wouldn't've seen him, would you?"

"Sugar, we don't use names out here very much. Did you say his first name was John?"

"Yes, ma'am." The roan lowered his nose to the ground. Larrabee rested his hands on the saddle horn.

She laughed. "Most of 'em are named John."

From the first cabin came the muffled sound of furniture moving. The blonde looked over her shoulder. Low down on her fair white neck was a raspberry mark.

The floor squeaked and the door opened on leather hinges. John Howard came out with his boots on, in black breeches and shirtsleeves. His hair was ruffled and his shirt was open at the collar but he still looked composed and fashionable. He came up behind the blonde and propped his hand on the porch post. "Watch out, Lucinda. This man could be dangerous. I've seen him fight two men at once with just a piece of fencing."

Lucinda looked at Larrabee with a sly smile, as if she might want to meet him alone sometime.

"Lucinda here was just giving me a manicure, Larrabee. There's nothing like a little attention to bring a man's finger to life. That what you're out here for?"

The second cabin door opened and a brown-haired woman came out. She was heavy and big-boned but she had a beautiful face and full lips. She reminded Larrabee of "Liberty at the Barricade."

He smiled. For once he felt as if he had the advantage over Howard. "I've come here looking for you, John. We've decided to take you up on your offer."

"Well, you must be in a hell of a pinch to come out here like this." Howard sounded casual, friendly. Was his cordiality for the benefit of the ladies or did this place relax him that much?

"You know how it is," Larrabee shrugged. "When you've got to have it, you've got to have it."

Lucinda laughed. "You know that, don't you, John? When you've gotta have it, you've gotta have it!"

Apparently Howard thought she had gone too far. He brushed past her so closely that she had to step back to keep from getting knocked into the rail.

"You go back to town, Larrabee. We can talk about it tomorrow. There's no hurry." He turned and went back into the cabin, leaving Lucinda and her friend to appraise the serious young man on the roan horse.

Chapter 9

John Howard made them wait a good long time. Jared was bringing in some money from Josiah Walls' newspaper but Larrabee was just barely scraping by at the stable. Caroline Newhouse was taking in mending although it was not steady work. Anna and Martha gathered eggs and churned butter for a handful of pennies a day. A few days before Thanksgiving another boarder came in, a plump, tired-looking New Jersey widow named Nelda Larson. She was hoping to set up a millinery shop in a city where the climate might agree with her lungs. She had some money saved up, so she was capable of paying the five dollars a week.

Penny Ward took his Colt rifle and spent half a day hunting turkeys in the woods west of town. He brought back an eight-pound tom and half a dozen squirrels that held up passably during the six-mile walk back to the house. The girls set to cleaning the animals while their mother made bread and orange relish and mashed potatoes with giblet gravy. Larrabee and Jared split enough pine and oak to keep the stove going day and night. Duke came over with bottles of sarsaparilla for the girls and a jug of Baptist punch for everyone else. Bobby La Rue dropped by from the Alachua Hotel. Preacher Williams put an apron over his old serge suit and helped roll crusts for the pecan pies. Mrs. Larson was drawn to the kitchen like a moth to flame and wound up using one of the preacher's crusts for a squirrel tart.

The dining went on all afternoon and into the evening, when Anna and Martha began to get restless, and the festivities spilled into the cluttered front room and the narrow parlor. The girls got Preacher Williams into a game of caroms that they played with nimble fingers and shifting rules. They had the board balanced on a footstool and swung it around to line up the best shots, making the board and caroms slide and roll so much that the preacher declared they would all be seasick.

When Larrabee went in to stoke the fire in the front room, Jared followed him, leaving Duke and Bobby at the table talking politics. Their voices spilled over from one room to the next.

"If we don't get a president picked by inauguration day, they'll have to give

Grant another term," Bobby was saying.

Duke scraped his chair back to get more comfortable after the big meal. "It's not the president that's going to make any difference, Bobby. By the time the Democrats and the Republicans get this all sorted out you won't be able to tell one party from the other. Tilden or Hayes—it'll all be the same. It's the governorship that's going to make the difference. You get a Democratic governor and you'll see some changes around here."

Bobby cleared his throat. "And how's that going to happen with the Republicans running the polls? It won't—that's how."

Penny and Mrs. Larson were laughing about something in the kitchen, something about a recipe for alligator pie.

"Now there's two I hadn't figured on hitting it off," Jared said. "Any bets on how long before he hits her with the war stories?"

Larrabee stared into the fire. "What do you suppose will become of this place?"

"It's a holiday, Nathaniel. You're not supposed to worry on holidays."

"First they foreclose. Then the sheriff comes and throws you out. It takes its course just as sure as the scarlet fever."

Penny and Mrs. Larson were still talking alligators. Somehow mushrooms had gotten into the conversation. "You're going to git killed by a mushroom before you'll git killed by any alligator," Penny was saying. "You eat one of them with the little ring under the parasol and you just might be talking in tongues when you go. Don't you pick no mushrooms 'less you're with somebody who knows pick from sick."

"Well, I'll just do that," Mrs. Larson said. She had a big low laugh that made Larrabee wonder if the Baptist punch hadn't fermented.

Martha was drawing a bead on "blackie," the one carom that was worth fifteen points. It was in the dead center of the board. Martha shut one eye and cocked her finger.

"I'm gonna get that booger."

Preacher Williams winced. "You must not use that word, child."

"She got it from them boys," Anna said casually.

Jared turned his back to the fire and looked up at the high ceiling. It bulged slightly but the dull white paint was intact. "At least the roof is holding up," he said. "You and Penny must've done a fair job."

Larrabee's eyes reflected the fire. "What do you suppose Howard's up to? Is he just putting one over on us?"

"No way of knowing with him. He still working for Major Dennis?"

"They're connected." Larrabee spread his hands over the fire. The pine was burning hot but it felt good. "And he's got his turpentine still."

"He runs that place on slave labor they say."

Larrabee looked up. "Slave labor?"

"Sure. Walls himself told me how it works. He brings in a man who has debts, pays him a starvation wage, and runs a company store the man has to buy from, and that just gets him in deeper. The debt doesn't get paid and that man's in Howard's harness for the long haul. It isn't slavery under the law, but you tell me what's the difference."

"Figure he owns Baldy Choat that way?"

"Well, Baldy owed somebody a thousand dollars for stealing your horse. And somebody got him out of a whipping. Who do you suppose it was?"

"You reckon Major Dennis owns Howard?"

"Don't know, but he's made him property appraiser for the county, I hear. And he gets a piece of him that way. Part of his salary every month, same as with everyone else at the Courthouse."

"Walls tell you that too?"

Jared nodded. "The major gets a cut of every salary of every man paid by the county. Must add up pretty good and he's got a finger in their collars at the same time. Signed letter of resignation from every man he brings in, in the desk drawer. Ready to pull out whenever he's a mind to. Did it with that fellow Jacob what's-his-name."

"Ford. Jacob Ford. I think he said something the major didn't like."

"Easy to do, I'll bet."

"Five minutes' wages of either one of those buzzards would pay this place off."

During the second week of December a cold snap froze what was left of the garden vegetables and scattered frost that lingered in low-lying fields and hollows. Anna danced in the yard and swore that she had caught a snowflake on her tongue. But by afternoon the sun was so warm that the morning frost seemed like a dream. Preacher Williams had rented a carriage and driven out to minister to a congregation at Fort Clark Church. On the way back the harness broke and the preacher worked up a sweat splicing it back together. By the time he saw the lights of town the evening star was bright in the west and the air had turned cold again. The preacher worked his way up the hills praying that the harness would hold, one hand pressed to the top button of his coat, the other clamped to the reins. The damp air penetrated his clothes and left him weak and shivering. When he pulled the carriage into the White Pine Stable, Larrabee insisted on driving him home. Mrs. Newhouse had Penny put him to bed while she heated bricks to put at his feet.

"I don't need all this fuss," the preacher protested.

"Maybe you don't," Penny said, "but you're gittin' it anyway. We lost six men to the cold one time. It was the winter of '64 and it wasn't near as cold as this." He helped the preacher out of his coat and vest and got a blaze going in the fireplace.

"I can't seem to get warm," the preacher said. His hands were freezing as he tried to undo his shirt buttons.

With his stubby, graceless fingers, Penny opened the preacher's shirt and got his breeches off.

A few minutes later Larrabee came upstairs carrying the hot bricks on a tray and looked at the man in the bed.

"He doesn't look so good, Penny."

The preacher lay shivering beneath two quilts. His long white hair fell away from his forehead. His skin looked thin and translucent. His lips were the blue-gray of river clay. The bones stood out in his big hands. He seemed to have aged ten years.

Penny put the back of his hand to the preacher's cheek. It struck Larrabee as a tender gesture from one so rough-cut. "We'd better send for Doc Willis before this gits out of hand."

The house was thrown into confusion. Mrs. Newhouse turned the dinner preparations over to Caroline and Anna who fell into an argument over who should peel the onions for the stew. Caroline said they should've been put in an hour ago and Anna insisted that they should be added late so as not to become too mushy.

Mrs. Newhouse hovered over the preacher, adjusting the warm bricks and fussing with the quilts and pillow while Larrabee and Penny watched the doctor listen to the patient's lungs.

"You look better when you've been eating," the doctor told Larrabee. "Have you decided after all that this town agrees with you?"

"I'll be around for a while. How's he doing?"

The preacher let out a long breath. "Good question. How am I doing, Warren?"

The doctor stood up. "Let's just say I hope those folks out at Fort Clark got the most out of your visit. It's likely to be a while before you can go back out there." In response to the preacher's concerned look he added, "You've taken a chill. Pretty astute, huh? The question is whether it's going to get into your lungs. If you mind your own business for a few days and keep warm and dry and full of Emma's chicken soup we might be able to fend it off."

Preacher Williams struggled off the pillow. "Warren, I have a sermon to deliver on Sunday. And between now and then I have two building committee meetings and a wedding."

"Let one of your brethren do the wedding. How about Sam Carrington? Even if he *is* a Methodist."

That sent the preacher into a fit of shallow coughing. "Sam Carrington doesn't even know the bride and groom. What kind of wedding would that be?"

"After the first day or so it will all be the same. One way of the other, Zeke, you're here for the duration."

The preacher glared at him with dull eyes. "I'll use the time to plan skinning you at chess. And don't you fiddle with that board either. I'm about to take your queen, you know."

On his way downstairs Larrabee ran into Jared, who had just come back from the newspaper. "You won't believe this," he said breathlessly. "Drew is asking the Supreme Court for a recount. Did you hear me, Nathaniel? The Democrats are contesting the governorship. Dennis may yet be out of business."

Larrabee glanced up the stairs to be sure nobody was within earshot. "We may yet be out of business here too. The preacher's taken sick. Looks like it's up to us to keep this place from going to the wolves."

Three days later, when Larrabee arrived at the White Pine Stable, Harmon Murray handed him a note. It was creased and dirty but the handwriting was clear and precise. It was from John Howard.

Harmon eyed the note as Larrabee began reading. "What's it say?"

"None of your business. When did he give this to you?"

"He come in here looking for you while I was pitching from the loft. I could've busted him with a bale if I'd wanted to. When I told him you wasn't here yet, he wrote it."

The note was on the back of a blank check. *Meet me in Arredonda tomorrow at three o'clock. Come armed on a steady horse. Bring J.P. Tell no one. This is your chance.*

J. P. That meant Jared Penrod. Larrabee was surprised that Howard even knew Jared's last name. And what did he mean by a "steady" horse? Presumably one that was unlikely to spook. He waited until Harmon had lost interest and then went to an obscure corner of the barn and reached under a moldy bale of hay. It was still there wrapped in a scrap of pillowcase, the .44.

At a quarter to three the next afternoon he and Jared rode cautiously into windswept Arredonda. They passed the parade ground where Major Dennis had given his grand speech and came to the tobacco barn, where they waited out of the weather. Larrabee was wearing a long duster with the collar turned up. He liked it because it afforded some warmth and hid the .44 on his belt. Jared wore his derby pressed down hard and an old gray overcoat that was a Confederate castoff by the looks of it, with the original brass buttons replaced by hand-cut wooden ones. The horses stamped and snorted restlessly while the riders paced, rubbing their hands as they waited for Howard.

He drove up in a buckboard just as Jared had pulled out his watch and said, "Three o'clock." Larrabee suspected that he had already been in Arredonda for a while.

Leading their horses, they walked out to meet him.

"What's up?" Larrabee said.

"We'll talk as we go," Howard told him. "We have a ways to go yet."

They continued in silence through the scattered crossroads, even though there was hardly a soul to be seen. The buckboard rattled and clattered on the rough road. Larrabee guessed that the back was loaded with tools, but it was covered with a piece of canvas. The clear, pale-blue sky was clouding over in the west where the red-gold sun was beginning to fade.

"You're figuring to dig something up in the dark," Larrabee said.

"Well, now you have put two and two together," Howard replied.

"Something to do with that piece of paper you mentioned at Duke's that time."

Jared looked at Larrabee, wondering where the conversation was going.

"That fellow you won it from—he wasn't a former Confederate officer by any chance."

"Let's ride, Larrabee. We have a ways to go yet. There'll be plenty of time to tell stories."

They rode through pinewoods and fallow vegetable fields and past small fruitful orange groves. As the sun flashed through the trees, they turned off the southwest road toward Archer and cut due north on a narrow track across flat, sandy land. They crossed a cow path and rode on for another mile or two into the pines and scrub oak before Howard spoke again.

"Somewhere up this road there's a sinkhole. And if this piece of paper is correct, there's enough money in it to put us all on easy street for the rest of our lives—if we invest shrewdly that is."

"Whose money is it?" Larrabee asked.

"It's nobody's money now," Howard said brightly. "As you surmised, it's war salvage. No less than the treasury of the Confederate States of America."

Jared laughed. "That again? I was hearing Confederate treasure stories before I left Indiana. No two of 'em lined up."

"No doubt, my friend. But did any of them come with a map?"

Larrabee stopped his horse and Jared came to a halt behind him. "The whole Confederate treasury?"

"That's right—twenty thousand dollars worth of English gold sovereigns. Give or take a few hundred. About sixty pounds of it I figure. That's thirty pounds for me and thirty for the two of you."

The palmettos and leafless laurel oaks picked and crowded Larrabee so he brought his horse back onto the sand track. "How come nobody else has come after it?"

Jared's horse shied at something and he tightened the reins. "The most sensible story I heard was that the officers with the train divvied up the money when they got to the end of the line."

Howard was unimpressed. "Did you talk to any of them?"

"To the officers? Not hardly. I imagine most of 'em have long since been living in Cuba."

"But your newspaper doesn't deal in imagining, does it? It deals in facts. And the facts are that there were nine well-armed officers riding with the train on its last day. Their names were Clark, Dickenson, Emory, three brothers named Van Benthuysen, Tilghman, Watson, and Scott. It so happened that a few weeks ago in Jacksonville Scott got into a card game in which he was dealt a

very good hand—a very good hand indeed—almost as good as mine. His good
luck caused him to bet more than he had. And so in a private conversation
he and I assigned a certain value to some information. Being an honorable
southern gentleman, Colonel Scott obligingly committed that information to
paper in the form of a map, and when he lost the hand he tendered the map
to me."

Jared continued to struggle with his horse. He pulled off the track so that
Howard could bring the buckboard alongside. "If this fellow, Scott, knew about
the treasure all along, why didn't he just get the treasure himself? He's had
eleven years to do it."

"Well, my friend, you'll have to ask him. Although last time I was in
Jacksonville I heard he had left town rather abruptly for parts unknown. Could
it have to do with the same good old southern honor that made him and the
others leave the money there in the first place?"

"All right," Larrabee said, "that still leaves at least eight other officers who
might've made off with it by now."

"So it does. There may be nothing but a sinkhole. But for a shot at twenty
thousand dollars wouldn't you say it's worth a look?"

With his free hand Jared was fumbling at the top button of his coat. "Whose
land is it on?"

"It's on Cottonwood Plantation, the old home of Senator Yulee. Who owns
it now isn't too important since our visit will be brief."

For a while the only sound was the thudding of hooves and the creaking of
wheels and harness.

The sunset was short, a deepening of blue to violet and then to black. Even
by starlight the white sand road was clear enough to follow without mishap.
Larrabee and Jared had fallen back, letting Howard take the lead with the
buckboard.

"This way they'll shoot *him* first," Larrabee whispered.

"He never quits, does he?" Jared whispered back. "Always working on
something. Trouble is, it seems to pay off."

"I'll tell you what. If we come back in one piece with just fifty dollars each
to show for it, I'll vouch for him to run for Congress."

"I'll settle for a good story. Money or no, one of the big papers'll probably
print it."

A few minutes later the track ended in a small grassy clearing. They were at
the edge of a large fenced pasture. Howard climbed down from the buckboard
and threw back the canvas. As Larrabee and Jared dismounted, he tied the
buckboard reins to a fence post. When the horses were tied, Howard looked
out across the field and in a low voice told them his plan.

"Take a shovel, gentlemen. We cross the pasture on foot, go past an old
foundation, then bear right down a path until we come to the old road. Then
we find the sinkhole, according to the map. We work without light and without

speaking if at all possible. Once we get the money we carry it back here, load it in the wagon and split it up in Arredonda. Then we go our separate ways back to town. I don't have to tell you that making a big show of being rich is poor policy. I think I can trust you, Larrabee, not to talk this up. I hope the same goes for your friend here."

Jared was starting to get into the spirit of the venture. "Once we pay off the taxes and mortgage, I'm taking off for San Francisco. I'll wait a month before I sell the story. What about you, Larrabee?"

"One thing at a time. Let's go."

Howard raised one of the middle strands of fence wire and slipped into the pasture.

By now the only light came from stars, but it was enough to clarify the broad grassy field. The three men crouched as they moved over the wet ground. To his right Larrabee saw a herd of cattle clustered around a spreading oak tree. They were large and pale in the starlight, and as he stole across the pasture he continued to stare at them, trying to make sense of their strange thick shapes. He had heard of expensive cattle imported from India into the hot, humid Florida cattle ranches, but such talk had been wild stories told by men at the end of long nights of drinking. He reasoned that if such farfetched tales could be true so might Howard's tale of the Confederate treasure train with its $20,000 in gold.

Their path across the pasture took them toward the Big Dipper, which hung like a great cup on a sparkling hook. They came toward the herd now and the animals began to move nervously. Larrabee moved toward the far fence. The other two shifted with him, taking the safer, more circuitous way to the opposite side, where leafless trees offered cover. They followed the faint cow-track at the edge of the field until the woods opened up for a sandy path. They were just raising the wire when a bull bellowed and trotted toward them.

Howard was bent over fumbling with the wire when Larrabee pushed past him and rolled onto the ground. Jared went over the top, caught his boot and landed on his head.

"I can't see!"

"Get down, man!" Larrabee got up and pulled him into the trees.

"I can't—"

"Your hat's over your eyes." With rough hands Larrabee jerked up Jared's derby.

The bull stopped twenty yards short of the fence, snorted, and trotted back toward the herd.

"Damn strange looking cows," Jared said.

Howard was already on the move again. "Come on. Down this lane. And keep quiet."

Larrabee took a last look at the retreating bull and followed.

At least they were in the trees again, hurrying breathlessly down the sand track without fear of being seen. An owl came wuthering out of a scrub oak and snatched up something that squeaked in its talons as it flapped back skyward.

"How much farther?" Larrabee was beginning to get uneasy.

As if answering, Howard quickened his step. The trees opened up again but this time there was no fence, and the clearing was overgrown with sprouting oaks and broken by the low ruin of a brick foundation. They worked their way past the obstacles and came to the overgrown road. They walked it until they came to the charred trunk of a live oak. Then Howard set off through the scrub.

"He's circling right back to that damned pasture," Larrabee whispered. In a minute they were there at the fence again, about a hundred yards beyond the herd. Far across the field an amber light glowed through the trees, but Larrabee's attention was quickly diverted by the great dark hole that opened up ahead of them. Within a circular fence the ground sloped steeply toward a ring of rough chunks of star-lit lime rock.

Jared watched as Larrabee followed Howard into the sinkhole. "You sure this is the place? It's nothing but a hole in the middle of a pasture."

Howard had already slipped through the fence. He slid to the bottom of the sinkhole and began looking at the rocks there. He took out his map and studied it in the darkness. Then he struck a match and held it a safe distance from the paper. Jared edged his way down for a better view, but by the time he got there Howard had shaken the light out. He waited a moment, apparently letting his eyes adjust to the darkness, and stepped across the bottom of the sinkhole to a long rock that seemed to point into the hole. He started lifting smaller rocks and setting them to one side.

Larrabee thought back to one of Penny's war stories about the Battle of the Crater during which Union troops had dug a tunnel and blown up the Confederate line and then rushed jubilantly down into the crater to collect souvenirs. The dazed Confederates had recovered and come back with guns blazing, shooting the Yankees like fish in a barrel. Off in the woods a dog barked and everybody froze. Larrabee heard what sounded like a door slamming. He edged toward the top of the sinkhole and scanned the pasture in the direction of the Big Dipper, off toward the pinpoint of amber light. He was becoming very edgy about being down in the hole, but being up on the surface was even more dangerous now.

Howard was back to the business of stacking rocks. He motioned for Jared and Larrabee to help. Within a minute or two they had exposed the ground below the long rock. It was black and damp and hard packed.

Howard stood up. "Get shoveling but keep it quiet."

Because they had to work quietly and in the dark, the digging went slowly. Howard got more and more wound up. "It's supposed to be at the point of this long rock," he said, stooping down and staring into the three-foot hole they had scooped out.

All Larrabee could see was dirt and more lime rock.

"It's been eleven years," Jared said. "It could've shifted or—"

"God damn that rebel conjurer." Howard stood up, took a scarf from his pocket, and wiped his hands. He started climbing toward the fence.

Larrabee thought he had heard voices in the woods. He scrambled to the edge of the hole and lay there, listening. Howard and Jared were on their way out of the pit when the shot cracked the stillness. It was a strange, old booming sound, not a rifle that could kill you with unseen accuracy but a breech-loading musket that could blow a big hole. Dogs were barking.

Larrabee threw himself down the slope.

Jared coughed, picking himself up from the limestone. "They won't shoot at us as long as we're in here with their precious cows."

Larrabee crept back up to the rim. "Somebody out there isn't that smart. Down here we're dead."

Howard was propped on his elbows, trying to see where the voices had come from. "Those fools think we're after their damned cows."

The cattle were on the move, bellowing and running the fence line.

A second shot rang over their heads, smaller but closer.

Larrabee looked over his shoulder. "They're coming at us from two sides now. Run toward the one with the breech-loader. He's got bad aim and one bullet at a time. He's not likely to get off many shots in the dark." He rolled out of the sinkhole and, keeping low, ran zigzag toward the way they had come in. Over his own breathing he could hear the other two following. Another shot cracked in the woods, nowhere near. A double pop came from the other side of the pasture, a repeating rifle, Larrabee figured. For once, he told himself, he had made the right decision. He vaulted the fence and hit the ground running, lost his hat and blundered into the sandy lane. He ran along the edge of the woods, so as not to make a target of himself, although the crashing of pinecones and brush was almost as much of a giveaway. Jared was running hell-bent down the lane with Howard not far behind him and now the voices were in the pasture, suddenly much closer.

The repeater fired again and a bullet hissed past Larrabee's elbow. He cut through the woods and came back out at the brick foundation. He jumped it once, twice, stumbled, and brought himself up on one knee just as Jared and Howard came running down the lane. Larrabee recovered his balance and ran toward the lower end of the pasture, and as he got to the fence he heard another shot from the repeating rifle. The cattle were coming their way now. Behind him he heard a cry stifled by oncoming hoofbeats. He turned and saw Howard coming up behind him.

"*Where's Jared?*" Larrabee was breathing so hard it was all he could do to get the words out. He ran back over the broken foundation. Jared was nowhere to be seen. He could hear men running down the lane, running toward him. He waited for a long time while the running came nearer and nearer. The cattle came to the fence, knocked over someone who tried to wave them off, and turned again, revealing a crumpled figure on the ground. Larrabee saw one arm go up. He ran forward, despite the oncoming riflemen, dropped hard and knelt by the twitching form. Jared was sputtering blood. Larrabee picked up his hand and felt it go limp.

He called out to Howard. "He's still alive! Help me get him in the wagon!"

Howard pushed past him and plunged into the pasture.

Larrabee grabbed at him, tore his pocket, and came up empty-handed. "For God's sake, man, help me with him!"

Far away, Howard was ripping the reins free of the fence post.

Jared's eyes rolled back, the silver white of a fish's belly. A bullet cut the grass beside him.

Larrabee jumped to his feet and ran, ran through the terrible pasture to the far fence, with the men gaining on him. He was clumsy now. He wrestled with the wires and nearly lost a boot getting through them. The horses pulled nervously at the reins. He freed them, clawed his way into the saddle, and galloped down the track. Catching sight of John Howard speeding away in the rattling buckboard, he wheeled his horse around and took off in the opposite direction.

He was coming up on Arredonda before he let his horse drop into a labored, heavy-legged trot. Trying to banish all thoughts of what was behind him, he concentrated on the road that unfolded beneath the rising moon. He no longer feared the cattlemen. Something far swifter was after him. The sinkhole seemed to be expanding mile by mile, rushing to swallow him. He half expected the ground to collapse under the horse's hooves, to crumble and drop him into oblivion. He dreaded returning to town but ran like a hunted fox. He rode the heaving horse straight to the house, left it in the yard, and ran upstairs to Jared's room. He stood trembling, listening like a thief to one of the girls talking in her sleep, to Penny's fitful snore. He snatched Jared's belongings—a gilt-edged book, a clay whistle, scraps of paper and bitten pencils—and bundled them in the few clothes that hung in the wardrobe. Then the impulse to run was upon him again and he dashed from the house, a frantic figure in the white moonlight, tearing through the deep shadows of trees and rooflines until he was waist-deep in the Sweetwater Branch. He fought his way across and collapsed beneath a great oak tree. He tore at the bare ground with numb fingers and buried the bundle there. As he smoothed the dirt, his hand grazed one small thing that had fallen free. The half-carved horse. He rubbed it for a moment as if to make a wish. Then he dropped face down in scattered leaves and wept until the cock crowed the dawn.

Chapter 10

Shortly after sunrise on Christmas morning Dr. Willis stopped by the house on Magnolia Street with a bushel basket of oranges that he hauled up the new steps and set by the front door. He stood on the porch for a minute admiring the garlands of green pine that wound around each of the four white columns, then tapped on the windowpane. He heard footsteps coming fast down the stairs, squealing in the front hall, and some kind of struggle at the door. Finally, Caroline and Martha yanked it open together and, seeing the doctor, did their best to look respectable. Caroline tossed her long strawberry blond hair behind her shoulders and hid the red hair ribbon that still trailed from her hand. Martha was still in her nightgown, a faded flannel hand-me-down threadbare at the elbows. She slid back behind her sister and raised her hands to her mouth to suppress her laughter.

The doctor waited for the commotion to die down. "Have young folks stopped getting up before the sun on Christmas morning?"

The girls' mother had caught up with them. She looked fresh-faced and happy despite the tax problem that had become common knowledge. She thanked him and saw to it that the girls followed suit. "Doctor, after all you've done for us, we should be bringing *you* oranges."

"Nonsense. We've got more than we can keep up with already. If we get any more, Billy's going to start throwing them at the girls."

"Well, won't you at least come in?" Mrs. Newhouse moved Martha out of the doorway to make way for him.

"No I won't. I have more deliveries, though the smell of your bacon is a temptation." He motioned toward the bushel basket. "You've got somebody around here who can tote that in I imagine." He tipped his hat and walked back out to his buggy.

Martha turned toward the stairs and yelled, "Pen-*ny!*" Before she could repeat it Caroline had clapped a hand over her mouth.

He came downstairs tugging at his suspenders. "It's about time you girls learn to kill your own roaches. I can't come a-runnin' every—"

Mrs. Newhouse removed Caroline's hand from Martha's mouth. "Penny, will you please take these oranges to the summer kitchen? But bring in half a dozen of them for sauce."

Penny hoisted the bushel basket onto his shoulder and carted it back through the house and across the backyard to the summer kitchen. Anna was at the woodpile trying to talk Larrabee into letting her split kindling.

"If I let you swing this ax, your mother would take it and chase after me," he was saying. "And the last thing I need is more trouble."

"Look, I'm just asking for one time. You can even pick the piece."

"You can pick your own piece when your mother says so. Just leave me out of it."

"Oh, come on! It's Christmas. It can be my present."

"I already have a present for you. That's what you were fishing for, isn't it?"

Frowning, she put her hands on her hips. "What the deuce are you talking about?"

"Don't you use language like that or your mama will wash your mouth out with soap. I'm talking about your present. But I guess you're too big to care about presents."

"Maybe. Well?"

He set a piece of pine on the chopping stump and with one stroke, halved it.

"Well what?"

"Well, what is it?"

He set one half back on the stump and gave her a puzzled look. "What is what?"

"My present! What did you get me?"

"Well, I didn't get you anything."

"But you just said—"

"No I didn't. You think about what I said."

Anna put her knuckles to her mouth and made a shrill sound. Then she turned and ran back toward the house. Halfway there she turned and said. "Well, I got you something but you're not getting it for five years. I'd rather die than give you anything!"

Her last word turned into another exasperated squeal.

Penny had come out of the summer kitchen cradling several oranges in his arms. "Merry Christmas to you, Larrabee! Did I hear a bobcat just now?"

Larrabee split the piece of pine again and pitched the sticks onto his kindling pile. "Merry Christmas, Penny. Just goes to show you. She's not to be trusted with an ax."

Mrs. Newhouse met Penny at the kitchen door. "What on earth has gotten into Anna? She's stomping holes in the floor."

"Just excited about Christmas I guess. By the way, I got somethin' special for the feed."

"Not snails again I hope."

"No, ma'am. That won't ever happen again."

"What is it then?" Caroline came in, light and graceful. The red ribbon brought out the traces of red in her hair.

"Well, they're right out here under the porch."

"Sugar cane?" Martha came up on tiptoes. "Did you bring us some sugar cane?"

Penny shook his head. "Nope, not this time." He led them down the front steps and pointed under the latticework of the porch.

Even Martha was reluctant to look very closely. She was wearing white stockings now. She and Caroline peeked from a distance.

"Here they are," Penny said proudly. He hauled out a washtub. In the bottom of it were two huge gopher turtles. At the first movement of the tub they pulled into their shells and stared out past their beak noses and multiple chins.

Caroline wrinkled her nose. "Penny, we're not going to eat those."

He misunderstood, thinking she didn't want to deprive him of a delicacy. "Oh, now don't give it a thought, Caroline! It's Christmas! These here are my gift to the cause. There'll be just enough for one good bite apiece."

The turtles looked completely uninterested in the life-and-death conversation. One of them tried to pull in his scaly forelegs but they were already in as far as they would go.

"Poor turtles!" Martha stooped down to pet one. It scraped its claws against the bottom of the tub and managed to turn its back on her.

"You ain't never had nothin' better'n a strip of turtle steak sozzled in butter'n onions! It makes my mouth juice up just thinkin' of it! I saved these here from a dog, one that Nathaniel didn't git to I guess."

Caroline glanced toward the sound of the wood chopping. "What do you mean, one that Nathaniel didn't get to?"

"Oh, well, he's been taking in bounties on the strays, y'know. For a little extra money."

"What? You mean killing dogs for money?"

"Just the strays of course. Four bits for every set of ears he brings in. Now, who's going to help me dress out these critters?"

Martha stormed into the house to report the looming crime.

Caroline did her best to be the dignified lady. "I wish you would just let them go as a Christmas present to me. I think they must be husband and wife."

Mrs. Larson came out to see what had caused all the commotion.

Caroline smiled as if everything had been settled. "Penny has just shown us some turtles and now he's letting them go."

"Oh, how lovely!" Mrs. Larson gathered her skirts and came down the steps to see.

"Of course, the last thing we'd think of doing is *eatin'* 'em," Penny said.

"Of course." Mrs. Larson's voice was low and melodious. She reached into the tub and picked up one of the turtles. "Did you know you can tell their age by the number of lines on the shell?"

Penny looked at her askance. "No, can't say as I did. You sure you ain't thinkin' of trees?"

"Certainly not! Of course, it's true with trees too, but we're talking turtles here. See here? This one's twelve years old."

"As old as me," Caroline said. "They should be free."

Mrs. Larson put the turtle back. "Thanks for showing them to us, Penny. Where are you going to release them?"

By the end of dinner Penny was grateful that he had not butchered the turtles because he had eaten so much turkey and venison that he could hardly move. He felt so fat that he slipped behind the wingback chair in the corner and loosened his suspenders. The house was bursting too. Duke Duforge came over early because the saloon had been closed for two days—the day before having been the Sabbath—and he had paced the empty rooms above the bar until he thought the time suitable for visiting. Bobby La Rue had come over from the Alachua Hotel with a plum pudding that had a brand new penny baked into it and smelled faintly of one of Duke's more expensive bottles. Preacher Williams, still weak and leaning on a cane, had forgone his usual black silk tie for green velvet neckwear that hung at his throat like a giant moth. Larrabee had gotten an old brown frock coat from somewhere and Caroline had reattached two buttons for him, one of which she had accidentally sewn right through to the hip, which at least kept Larrabee from his awkward habit of stuffing his hands in his pockets.

By sunset an array of china and polished silver spread from the dining room table to the sideboard and onto all level surfaces in the kitchen. There was a gravy boat, a large soup tureen, a punch bowl, two butter trays, a coffee pot, an assortment of serving forks and spoons, footed bowls, carving knives and butter spreaders, pickle forks and relish spoons, and two good-sized platters. Amid this bounty was a scattering of the ordinary, mismatched flatware that had replaced the heavy silver. For the lost silver there was no remedy. It was last seen leaving town in the custody of tinker Leo Bard, bound for parts south.

Mrs. Larson and Mrs. Newhouse cheerfully presided over this chaos of contentment with energy and good spirits. Penny came into the kitchen from time to time to pump water into a copper tub that he hauled onto the sizzling stove for washing dishes. Curtis the iceman came by with a basket of gingerbread men that he and his wife had baked. He pointed out that he himself had made the lighter, tastier ones. Everyone in the kitchen was too full to touch one, but Larrabee saved the moment by downing one and tucking another into his breast pocket.

After the women had tended to the details of kitchen management, the gift-giving began by the popcorn-laced Christmas tree. Martha and Penny had collaborated on a felt spoon case for Caroline. Caroline had made an apron for her mother and a sampler for Mrs. Larson. The girls had used some of their sewing and egg money to buy their mother a set of tortoise shell combs. Mrs. Newhouse had given each of the girls a mother-of-pearl shawl clasp. Preacher Williams had given books—a Bible for Caroline, *The Life and Memorable Actions of George Washington* by Parson Weems for Anna, and for Martha a thinned down version of *Little Women*. The preacher in return received a linen handkerchief, a pen and inkwell, and a blotter. Mrs. Larson sported a fan and gloves, Penny got a box of shells for his Colt rifle and a salmon-pink silk scarf that he said was sure to start fights. On behalf of the women and girls, Anna gave Larrabee a handsome nickel-plated harmonica in recognition of his ability to whistle like a whippoorwill.

When things had settled down, Preacher Williams stood by the fireplace and drummed his fingers on the oak mantle piece.

Penny put his hands in his pockets and wondered aloud what might be on the preacher's mind.

Mrs. Newhouse came in from the kitchen to see what was going on.

Caroline approached the fire. "Mama, there's an envelope up there."

Her mother was perplexed. She picked up the envelope. "It's addressed to me."

"Is that so?" The preacher moved away as everyone watched her open it.

She studied the piece of paper for a moment.

Penny and the preacher exchanged glances.

"It's a receipt from Ray Polk. The county clerk." She looked up in disbelief. "It's a receipt for the taxes."

"We paid 'em," Martha blurted. "We all paid 'em."

Mrs. Newhouse looked from face to face. "How?"

"We all done what we could is how." Penny started enumerating. "Martha and Anna collected double the eggs, Larrabee got the bounty on dogs. Mrs. Larson there made some real good-lookin' hats. And preacher and I finished off that little cottage over on Mechanic Street. His brains 'n' my brawn. Sold it to a druggist and his wife from up Baltimore way. 'Course the preacher, before he was even out of his sickbed, was the ringmaster of the whole scheme."

A slow smile spread over the preacher's face as Mrs. Newhouse clasped the paper to her bosom.

Penny cleared his throat. "Say, Nathaniel, why don't you strike up a Christmas tune on that mouth organ of yours?"

Larrabee didn't hear him. He was still marveling at what the preacher had accomplished.

The dishes were washed, the banquet put away. Penny had fallen asleep in the wing chair and Larrabee had carried Martha up to bed. The lamps burned low and the front room fire was down to glowing coals. Larrabee was on his way into the summer kitchen for one of Dr. Willis' oranges.

"Well?"

He turned and there was Anna, scarcely more than outlined in the dimness. Cracks in the smoldering cook stove threw bars of red light across the floor.

"Well what?" He closed the back door to keep out the cold.

"Well, what do you have for me? You said you didn't get me nothing. But what do you *have* for me?"

"Oh, you figured that out." He reached into his inside pocket. "I do seem to have something in here." He held it out to her.

She turned it over in her fingers. It was a horse, a fine, delicately carved horse.

"You made this?" She caressed the slender legs and flowing mane and swayed back with her fingertips.

He waited to answer, savoring her admiration. "Jared started it. I finished it."

She looked up at him with sadness in her eyes. "Why did Jared go away?"

He almost choked on the words. "I don't exactly know, Anna."

"You miss him?"

"Yes I do. More than I can tell you."

Her lips moved but he couldn't make out her words. He bent low to hear her better.

She rose up, kissed him on the throat, and ran silently upstairs.

Chapter 11

John Howard blew another smoke ring, watched it frame the Courthouse across the street, and thought again about what he was going to say to Major Dennis. The veranda of the Arlington faced south, and the noonday sun made it a comfortable place to wait for the major. It seemed to Howard that his future was as vague as the smoke. He was capable at cards and had made a nice nest egg whipping the local rubes and the occasional well-heeled traveler, but in his book poker was not a real man's game. It was nothing you could build on. It was a diversion and a fallback at best. Now it was time to put the money to work at something that would pay big steady dividends without the sort of risks he had taken last summer when those two cut-rate card-sharps had tried to rob him of his winnings. It was time for money that you didn't have to stuff in a bar towel and carry to the bank. It was time to deal with a better class of people. Even that alleged treasure at Cottonwood Plantation was a boyish dream compared to real money. And no one knew more about real money than the Little Giant—Major Leonard G. Dennis.

Politics had been good to both of them for the past two years. The Democrats had controlled most of the voters but the Republicans had run the polls and the county government. Major Dennis knew where the development of the county was likely to go. Even though the election was two months behind them, it seemed to Howard that he still had plenty of ideas to offer and a little to kick in for cash investments. But the major was not a man to read easily. He had no close friends so far as anyone could tell, and more than a few former friends. It was rumored that he had a wife somewhere but no one had seen her. He was secretive and manipulative and he usually had the upper hand. When Howard's predecessor, Jacob Ford, had let a careless remark slip in the major's presence, suddenly he was out as tax assessor. Howard had been careful not to cross the Major. But now the political structure was starting to collapse beneath them like a badly built speaker's platform at a party rally.

"The major has asked me, sir, to inform you that he will see you now."

The waiter seemed reluctant to interrupt Howard's thoughts. He stood at the edge of the veranda, bent forward slightly as if not daring to cross a line.

Howard took a long drag on his cigar and exhaled slowly, watching the smoke drift across his view of the square. He had been cooling his heels for the past quarter of an hour and he was not about to lose face by rushing off the minute the major snapped his fingers. So by the time Howard came into the spacious dining room of the Arlington, Major Dennis was pacing and smoking and brushing ash from his sleeve.

"Did you lose your way down from the veranda, John?"

The rebuke caught Howard off guard. He lied. "Someone from the turpentine still rode up with an urgent message. Or at least he thought it was urgent."

The major motioned with his cigar. "Well, sit down. I take it you have more than turpentine on your mind."

"A good deal more." Howard shook the folds from his napkin and laid it on his lap even though there was no need for it yet. "For one thing, turpentine doesn't return an investment that well."

"Even with the slave wages you pay out there?"

What did the major mean by that? "It's a dreary business altogether," Howard said. "It's time to move on."

"To politics?"

Howard tried to read the major's face. He looked in vain for a hint of a smile. "At least it looks like Hayes is in. That should be worth something."

"Not much."

"Well, he can put the right spin on the governorship."

The major leaned into the smoke. "Can he now? You're talking about a man who went up to his chin whiskers in political favors just to get into office. Now the favors will come due. He'll have to cut a deal."

"With the Democrats?"

The major shrugged. "With everybody. Tilden doesn't contest the findings of the Republican-dominated election commission and Hayes doesn't contest the results of the state elections. The result—Florida gets a Democrat governor."

"Then that's the end of the party in Alachua County."

"Well, not to put too fine a point on it, John, but it's the end of party *patronage* in the county. The next election's going to be one uphill free-for-all. In the meantime, you'll be free to pursue your business interests, which I'm sure are legion."

The waiter came and asked them if they were ready to order. He was starched and pressed and combed to excess and Howard took secret satisfaction in detecting a flaw that he seemed to have overlooked, a small burn mark on the side of his collar. The man seemed unduly deferential.

They ordered steamed oysters with fried potatoes. The waiter came back a minute later and set down two bread plates laden with orange slices.

"So what is this plan of yours?" the major asked.

Howard tossed his cigar butt into a polished cuspidor. "We make this part of the state a thoroughfare for traffic from west to east."

"How so?"

Howard was talking with his hands now. "Let's say you have a cargo that comes in at Cedar Keys. You bring it up the Withlacoochee as far as the river's navigable. From there you put it on a train and take it to the Arredonda spur, unload at Rocky Point Landing on Alachua Lake, take it through canals to Lake Santa Fe and east all the way to the St. Johns River. From there you can go to Jacksonville and Charleston and New York for that matter. You can buy up the right-of-way, buy up the steamboats, build whatever spurs you need, and run all that Florida produce right up the coast and you can haul in everything from herring to ice." He paused, not wanting to let his excitement show.

The major stared. "Instead of digging up half the state, wouldn't it be easier just to send everything by rail? Isn't it simpler and cheaper to put down rails than to dig canals? And don't trains usually go faster than steamboats?"

With a sinking feeling, Howard realized at once that the major was right. There was already a railroad from Cedar Keys to Fernandina, had been for almost twenty years, and it ran within a few miles of most of the lakes. He was relieved by the distraction of several men coming into the dining room. At the head of the group was a sour, heavy-set man of sixty or so.

Major Dennis turned and nodded but it wasn't clear that the other man had noticed him.

"General Finley looks preoccupied today. Congressman Finley I suppose I should say. It looks as if Washington hasn't entirely agreed with him."

Howard welcomed the opportunity to change the subject. "Apparently he still has the power of command. He has a dozen of his old soldiers hanging onto his coattails."

The major shook his head. "Not those locals. They were under Finegan. Penny Ward, your friend Baldy Choat, the lot of them, the veterans of Olustee. We were all up there."

"You were at Olustee?"

The major nodded. "In the 40th Massachusetts. It's nothing I brag about. The rebels whipped us in that one, you know. Walls was in it too."

It was strange to think that these men had once been shooting at each other. "You and Josiah Walls were together at Olustee?" Howard felt like a schoolboy at his grandfather's knee.

"That's right. We were both there shooting at those rebs. He was in the Third Colored Regiment. We were both under General Seymour. Not that we knew each other at the time. He was right here in town fighting Dickison's men."

Howard got the sense that there would always be that gap between him and the major. He watched General Finley ease himself into an oversized chair brought in by two of his followers.

"My advice to you," the major said, "is to set your sights on something less grand, less grandiose."

It was not a helpful conversation. The 11:29 pulled up West Main half an hour late and discharged several dozen sooty, dazed, half-starved passengers who poured into the dining room of the Arlington and wrecked the service. In the mayhem Howard was not about to ask the major what "less grandiose" schemes he might have in mind. Across the street a fistfight broke out between two farmboys, and for some reason the onlookers were partisan for the bigger of the two. Somebody said the smaller boy had fouled the town pump by priming it with trough water, and that was enough to infuriate the crowd. It got so bad that the sheriff came up on his big dapple-gray and fired two shots into the air.

Major Dennis had had enough. He tossed down his napkin. "I'm supposed to be photographed in a few minutes anyway."

"I'll gladly pay for the luncheon," Howard said, standing up and reaching inside his coat.

The major put a hand on his sleeve. "John, it's taken care of."

The major turned his back on him and went over to General Finley's table to pay his respects. "A pleasure to see you again, General. How are things in Washington?"

Startled, the general looked up from his big chair. With the back of his huge hand he wiped the sweat from his heavy brow. "How you doing? Good to see you."

It seemed to Howard that the general had probably used that same vague greeting twenty times since breakfast.

"I'm well, General."

"That's good. That's real good. Say hello to the wife and kids for me."

Major Dennis stopped smiling for a moment. "I have no children, General."

The general looked to the other members of his coterie for some kind of explanation but they had already stopped paying attention.

The room was noisy. Major Dennis leaned forward a little. "I'll hope to see you often when you're in town now that I'm one of the owners of this hotel. If I may be of service, just let me know. My office is down on the first floor."

"I'll do that." The general turned around as he spoke, so that he seemed to be talking to one of the other men at his table.

Howard left the Arlington deep in thought. This whole luncheon had been a waste of time, a mistake. In one minute the major had given more solid information to a distracted Confederate general than he had given Howard during the whole of the meal. And the information was that the major was already moving past his political setbacks and into something cleaner and more substantial—a share in the biggest and best and most expensive hotel in town. Howard smiled when he thought of the secrets he had kept from the major— the fake assassination attempt at the Union Academy and the successful if overdone banishment of Caleb Green. But the biggest trick of all—the stuffed ballot boxes—the major had trumped him there.

On January twenty-ninth the Republicans and the Democrats agreed in Congress to appoint a special commission to decide the presidential election. The commission would consist of five members from each house of Congress and five from the Supreme Court. Of the fifteen members, eight were Republicans, seven Democrats. A candidate needed 185 electoral votes to win the presidency. Tilden, the Democrat, had 184 solid. Hayes, the Republican, had 166. At dispute were 19 electoral votes from three states—South Carolina, Louisiana, and Florida, with one stray vote unaccounted for out in Oregon. For the next month every decision the commission made fell along party lines. On March second Congress accepted the commission's decision, which awarded all 19 votes to Hayes, who thus won by a single electoral vote.

Shortly after Hayes took office, Major Dennis' prediction came true. In Tallahassee the Board of State Canvassers determined that the Democratic gubernatorial candidate, George F. Drew, had won that election by 195 votes. The national government, in power by the grace of compromise, did not contest the results.

The conciliatory attitude extended to the Federal occupation troops. One warm January morning as Curtis the iceman began his rounds it seemed to him that some part of the day's routine was missing. He was on his fourth delivery before he realized that there had been no morning bugle. During the night the Federal troops had left the city.

Suddenly his turpentine still struck Howard as very unsavory, a barbarism of the past. He suspected that even General Finley, who had fought for slavery, would find the place repulsive. And Major Dennis—who had delivered such an impassioned speech on behalf of the Negro after the Caleb Green affair—would find it beneath a man aspiring to civic standing. For that matter, Howard's own father—never one to let principles get in his way—had put on the Union uniform in part for the cause of Emancipation. If the turpentine business had to be done, it was best left to men who lived in the woods, unwashed and unschooled crackers who came into town only on weekends to drink and fight. Howard decided that he wanted out.

During one of his infrequent visits to Duke's he picked up some interesting news. Back before the turn of the year, Preacher Williams had risen from his sickbed to lead a successful fundraising effort on behalf of the widow Newhouse and, more recently, had been condemning the turpentine stills as enclaves of slavery. Howard had no use for mawkish musings from the pulpit, but from the news he deduced that the preacher was a crusader, one who got things done. During an uncomfortable visit to the man of the cloth, Howard offered to lumber off the land and sell it cheap to the First Presbyterian Church, in the name of reform and civic progress.

A week after the reverend's surprising acceptance, John Howard became the new owner of a completely respectable business—the Kanapaha Moss Mill on South Factory Street, below the Doig Foundry, half a block west of Dugger and Dean's Planing Mill. He was strapped for cash, but the mill had been a bargain because the Dutton Bank had taken it into receivership. Howard welcomed the opportunity to put his mind to something other than politics and the inner workings of the Presbyterian Church. The mill consisted of a made-over barn that was hot and steamy and smelled like burned wood, plus a couple of outbuildings on a half-acre lot. Inside the barn two Negroes named Ludlow and Laird sweated over a large oak vat, one dumping fresh Spanish moss into boiling water, the other stirring it around and fishing it out with a pitchfork. Another two teams of men scoured the county for the moss, which after a good boiling, was turned into batting and stuffing for furniture assembled by yet another crew. The furniture turned up all over town. Even the Arlington had a few pieces that had been assembled at the Kanapaha Moss Mill.

For John Howard, the first item of business at the moss mill was the collection of past-due bills and he took it on with gusto. First on his list was Mary Leary, spinster sister of Sam the erstwhile undertaker. She operated the old trading post at the edge of the oak woods atop a slope two miles due west of town, where the road began its descent to Hogtown Creek before cutting through ten miles of woods to Fort Clark. How long the little store had been there was anyone's guess. It seemed neither to prosper nor to wither. It just *was*, and Mary Leary continued on in her faded way year after year. Like Sam, she was tall and thin, bloodless, humorless, and a little odd in the head.

Howard got right to the point.

"You owe the Kanapaha Moss Mill fifteen dollars for re-stuffing a couch—a fainting couch. I'm here to collect." He spread his hands on the dusty counter. He and Mary were the only people in the store.

"I ain't got no fifteen dollars." She spoke so slowly that Howard thought she might die between words.

He glanced around the store at the worn and faded merchandise. "When did you figure to have it?"

She put a white fist to her mouth, making it hard to understand what she was saying.

"Sam's workin' on a new kind of embalmin'. He's goin' to git the patent on it and then you'll git your money."

Howard removed his hands from the counter. "I suppose that old vulture's been practicing on those poor devils who drop dead on the work gangs."

Mary showed some sign of life. "He had one up at the still that he thought was fixin' to come out real good but then somethin' made the body turn green and spoil. Sam thought mebbe it was the sulfur in the water."

Howard lost his patience. "Look, it's going to be a hundred years before that brother of yours turns a dollar's profit. You're going to have to pay up some other way. Or I'll bring the sheriff out here."

Something caught in Mary's throat. She gasped and wheezed. Her eyes watered.

He looked around the store again, seeing nothing worth taking in payment of the debt.

"I cain't pay! I cain't pay!" Mary shrank back against the log wall, unable to catch her breath.

It occurred to Howard that for the moment his fifteen dollars had bought him complete control of this woman. He looked at her narrow gray face, her stringy hair and bony heaving shoulders. Then he turned on his heel and walked back into the daylight.

His other visits were more routine. He got ten dollars from the owner of the Alachua Hotel, thirteen from the photography studio on the square, eleven from the pharmacist, an engraved silver snuff box from the manager of the Land Office, and a hard-fought twenty-two dollars and fifty cents in municipal bonds from a planter's widow who had retired to a house in town. Although he never again resorted to threatening any of his debtors, he was ready to do so and he could feel the power of the law at his side. One by one, the payments went into the receipts column of his ledger, entered into the morocco leather-bound volume in his small, precise, rolling script.

Each morning Ludlow and Laird laid a fire under the big vat, got the water boiling, and stirred in the moss gathered the day before. Every afternoon Howard came in from his bill collecting to make sure that production kept its pace. He watched with fascination as the two rough, sweaty black men deftly stuffed moss and horsehair and cotton batting into chairs and sofas and ottomans, neatly tapping brass pins and piping into place on the frames that came by train from Jacksonville. The price of the upholstery was moderate, the price of the finished furniture, steep, but nonetheless cheaper than bringing finished items into town. He began to advertise via circular to the surrounding towns—Archer, Arredonda, Micanopy, Starke, Newnansville, Waldo. He kept a lookout for worn furniture in hotels and banks, called it to the attention of the proprietor or owner, and in general made a very good business for himself, something approaching a monopoly. He bought himself a new wardrobe, a Prince Albert coat, cravats, patent leather boots, a linen suit for summer, wool for winter, stickpins and studs and cufflinks, and an engraved silver watch from Switzerland. He moved out of his drab room in the Varnum Hotel and took up residence in a corner suite of the Arlington itself. Despite all of that success he was still uneasy, though, because he knew that sooner or later competition would move in, would find a cheaper way to transport, a cheaper way to manufacture, a cheaper way to market furniture. He started to cast about for something bigger, better, and more respectable.

One afternoon in April Howard was staring through the lace curtain of his sitting room. He had spent the morning comparing his revenues for the past three months and had just come up from his weekly Businessman's Association luncheon downstairs. Rubbing elbows with the county's most successful entrepreneurs always set him to scheming, and today as he gazed across the square to the Courthouse his schemes turned to real estate. He knew that land prices would be going up as the town continued to spread, but it was anyone's guess as to exactly which way that spread would go. The uncertainty made it impossible to know just what price to pay. There were no physical features that made one location particularly better than another. Clean water was plentiful enough if you drilled down a hundred feet or so. The railroad made one place about as good as another so far as access was concerned. But he knew enough of human nature to know that soon enough one part of town or another would become fashionable and expensive.

And then there was the orange question. You could grow oranges almost anywhere. Someone at the luncheon had even talked of cutting down the old live oaks on the square and planting orange trees. Might it be time to get on that bandwagon and not worry so much about the finer points of location just now?

As if in answer to his question, a golden orange sphere appeared above the treetops southeast of the Courthouse. He pulled the curtain back for a better look. As the object came slowly but steadily toward him, it took on the teardrop shape of a hot-air balloon floating lazily in the stillness of midday. Howard watched until it disappeared behind the truncated steeple of the Presbyterian Church. Then he went back to his desk and returned to the more immediate matter of cutting costs at the Kanapaha Moss Mill.

Penny Ward was on his way into town when he saw the balloon. He and Mrs. Larson and Anna and Martha were on their way back from a picnic at Oliver Park when it came over the tree line and dipped so low that it looked as if it was going to drop down into the orchard beside them. Its approach was gradual enough that the team had time to get used to it, but Anna's excited cries made them twitch their ears and quicken their trot.

Penny had been thinking about the picnic and the surprising conversation he'd had with Mrs. Larson. They had brushed away the acorns and spread one of Mrs. Newhouse's old patchwork quilts on the gentle slope of the lakeshore. They were watching Anna and Martha skip mud chips on the dark water.

"If they come back dirty I reckon Mrs. Newhouse will skin us." Penny said.

"Poor thing," Mrs. Larson said in that full deep voice of hers. "She frets so. I believe it's one reason she has come down with a cold. She needs someone to take care of her!"

Penny was surprised. "Well ain't Caroline there with her?"

Mrs. Larson smiled. "Yes, certainly, but I meant also that Emma needs someone to keep her from becoming overwrought."

"Oh. Well, I can put the *amen* to that! 'Course raisin' them girls alone for the past five years would be enough to make anyone a little jumpy." He thought for a moment, watching the breeze lift the Spanish moss that hung from majestic live oaks. "I reckon you're sayin' she needs a husband."

"I reckon I am."

"Yes, well. It'd be nice to fill that head place at the table again. It leaves kind of a hole in the middle of every meal."

Mrs. Larson nodded. She was sitting on a campstool that showed just the toes of her kidskin boots beneath the hem of her gray morning dress. Shading her round face was a handsome wide-brimmed straw hat with a mauve silk band ornamented with red poppies, blue grapes, and daisies. Just looking at it made Penny a trifle hungry.

He didn't think of himself as one to gossip, but the occasion seemed to call for it. "She and the Preacher've had a Christian fellowship ever since he moved in, but him bein' so busy with the church and all, he don't seem to have much time for...." He wasn't sure where to go from there and wished he hadn't started.

"Oh, a man will always be busy," Mrs. Larson said. "What's important is that a man and wife understand each other and make allowances for each other's interests and pursuits."

It took him a minute to conclude that she was aiming at something, but he wasn't sure what.

Down at the water's edge Anna and Martha had been talking to a girl about Anna's age, and now the three of them came running up, hats and ribbons fluttering, and asked breathlessly if they could go see the bear.

Penny made a face. "Y'all have looked at that bear enough to wear holes in him. You look at him every time you come down here."

"Oh, puh-*leeze*," Anna pleaded, wringing her hands and dropping to her knees for effect. "Amy ain't seen him."

Martha clasped her little hands and echoed her sister. "Oh, puh-*leeze*."

"A bear," Mrs. Larson said, "how exciting."

"Unless you're the bear," Penny drawled. "He's been in a pen over there by the hotel for about three or four years. He's probably so full of soda crackers that he's fit to bust."

"Puh-*leeze!*" the girls repeated, more or less in unison as Amy looked on hopefully.

"Oh, go on," Penny said, waving them off. "Just don't git too friendly with him."

"Have there been problems before?" Mrs. Larson asked half-seriously.

"None as I know of," Penny said, watching the girls run into the crowd of picnickers and boaters. "But then there's some folks could go in there and not be missed for a while."

"You're so *funny!*" Mrs. Larson adjusted herself on the campstool, which was uneven because of the slope.

Penny stood up. "Here, let me fix that. We can poke it right down into the ground where it won't never fall over."

"No, no, no. Thank you." She gave the impression that she had the stool well under control. "Now where were we? Oh, yes. I believe I was saying that the heart of a marriage is for the husband and wife to make allowances for each other, to take interest in each other's pursuits."

Penny thought they had gotten over that subject. He wasn't sure what pursuits a wife would have other than keeping everybody fed and clothed. And he wasn't sure what pursuits a man would have other than his business and hunting and the occasional horse race, unless there was a war on.

"The late Mr. Larson, wonderful as he was, had that one little failing," the woman on the stool was saying. "He never quite understood the importance of...." Her voice trailed. She was looking across the lake, but so far as Penny could tell, nothing in particular was going on there. A man and woman in a canoe were stuck on a pine log. They had managed to get caught in the branches and the man was standing up trying to push away with his paddle. The woman was holding onto the branch to steady the canoe so they weren't going very far.

Penny waited for Mrs. Larson to continue and when she did not, he prompted her. "Ma'am? The importance of...?"

She looked down at him and bent so close that the poppies and grapes and daisies on her hat cast a shadow on him.

"He never understood the importance of—*hats*."

Penny blinked. "Ma'am?"

"Hats." She nodded and then looked up at the great cottony clouds that drifted across the bright sky. "Yes, hats. Who can be without hats? Why, from the day we're born we wear them. Hats to keep off the sun and rain and flies, hats to keep us cool in summer and warm in winter, hats for women to wear in church to show their devotion, hats for men to take off in church to show theirs."

"I never did understand that one," Penny mumbled, pulling at his earlobe.

She hadn't heard. She had fallen into a reverie. Her smile was radiant as she looked heavenward. "That's what the late Mr. Larson didn't understand—the importance of hats. They say so much about us—who we are, where we come from, what our station in life is, whether we're sad or gay. Even the angels have their haloes. Everybody needs a hat."

Penny was sitting on his. It was an old faded green affair, a cloth cap with a canvas brim tainted by a drip line of white paint. He pulled it out and set it on his knee.

"So I take it Mr. Larson didn't understand the importance of...."

"It wasn't that so much. He wore a hat, of course. He had several hats. He even had a fez for his lodge meetings."

Penny had no idea what a fez was. He thought it might be some kind of sombrero.

"The thing was," Mrs. Larson continued with a sigh, "he had no appreciation for the importance of the hat in society. He didn't quite realize that everyone must have a hat, several hats in fact."

"Well, ma'am, that does sound like a deficiency, yes."

"He had no concept of how much money can be made with hats."

Penny's ears perked up. He had entertained girls all his life by wiggling his ears. Now he felt them slide right back as if it was show time again.

"You don't say. Just about how much money do you reckon there is to be made in them things?"

She stood up and made a sweeping gesture, knocking over the campstool. "Why, just look around, Penny! Everyone here has a hat on! And well they should because that sun is so strong! For a lady a hat saves her complexion. For a gentleman it lends stature and puts the bald man on an equal footing with the tonsorially endowed."

Had she slipped into a foreign tongue? Penny had heard of it happening at the African Baptist Church away out on the road to the Devil's Millhopper. It made his neck tingle to think of it occurring right here at Oliver Park among picnickers and boaters. He scrambled to his feet to be ready in case she fell over frothing at the mouth.

"Don't you see?" she asked fervently. "Don't you see that Mr. Larson had no vision? He toiled all day in his foundry until the Good Lord came and took him away, without ever realizing that the whole country was just crying out for hats."

"Yes, ma'am, yes, ma'am. I can surely see that he was lackin' in vision. What exactly happened to Mr. Larson if I may ask, ma'am?"

"Stomach upset." She passed hastily to the next subject. "Are you a man of vision, Penny?"

"Well, now, if I do say so I—" He straightened out his cap and put it on at a rakish angle. It was a size too large and fit low over his brows. His eyes burned through the shadow, zealous, if a little perplexed.

Mrs. Larson burst into laugher. She put one hand to her mouth and the other lightly on his shoulder, apparently to maintain her balance.

"Oh dear! Oh dear! I should be afraid to march into battle and see *you* at the barricade!"

Penny was reminded of Duke's painting "Liberty at the Barricade," with her bare breast leading the charge. His face went crimson.

Mrs. Larson tightened her grip on his shoulder. "Now, now! I fear I have made you self-conscious! Do forgive me! I can see you are a man who takes hats very seriously indeed!"

He straightened and swallowed. The hat slid down the side of his head like melting butter, to an attitude surpassing rakish. "Yes ma'am."

"Oh dear, oh dear." She started fumbling in her sleeve and produced a lace handkerchief with which she daubed the corners of her eyes. "Dear, dear!" At last she regained her composure and replaced the handkerchief. "Now. I do hope you will call me Nelda. We have known each other long enough that we need not stand on such formality, Penny."

"Yes, ma'am."

"Say it."

"Nelda."

"I do know that we shall be fast friends, you and I."

"Yes, ma'am. I reckon we already are, you and I—Nelda. Now where was we? Something about hats."

"Yes. And money. Would you like to know more?"

"Well, seeing as how the girls ain't back yet, it might be a way to while away the time."

So Anna saw the balloon before Penny did because his mind had been ten miles away watching the sunlight dance on the lake as Nelda told him in great detail about turning hats into money.

Chapter 12

Sheriff Tom Duforge was Duke's older brother. Like Duke he was big and congenial with a ready smile and a slow heavy footfall that let you know he was coming. Unlike Duke, Tom had a large deep voice that usually was blunted by head colds and allergies. When he lost the use of his nose, Sheriff Duforge tended to be edgy and irritable. He became short-tempered and physical. During one of his moods Baldy Choat had seen him take two fighting drunks by the hair and clap their foreheads together with the sound of breaking rocks. Then Tom had hoisted one over each shoulder, thrown them over the back of his big bay mare, and hauled them off to the lockup like sacks of coffee and flour.

Larrabee had heard this story and one or two others from Duke and knew enough to stay on the sheriff's good side. He made a point of making a polite amount of noise when he came to the jail to deliver the dog ears for which Sheriff Duforge paid him a bounty of fifty cents a pair. On this April afternoon he was coming in from a meager hunt. All he had was a single pair of ears belonging to a half-starved mutt whose ribs stuck out through a taut, mangy hide. He tied Ralph Pine's gray mare to the rail and banged his way up the steps swinging the pointed brown ears dangling from a loop of string.

Sheriff Duforge looked up from the lilies he was arranging in a jar. "Don't you put them things on my desk."

He sounded stuffy so Larrabee came no closer. "I wasn't going to do that, sheriff." He crammed the ears into his shirt pocket. "Anyway, you won't have to worry about it for a while. I think I've shot every stray dog in the county. And maybe a few that weren't so stray."

The sheriff laughed at his misfortune. "You've done run out, huh? Well, cheer up, Larrabee! You never know—they might put up a bounty on 'possums or coons—or gators maybe. You'll get that horse paid off yet. May not take more'n another six or seven years at the rate you're going."

"Well, if you don't mind, give me my four bits for this one here."

"Whatever did happen to that horse anyway?" The sheriff opened a lower desk drawer and took out a small gray cash box. "I've heard of folks buying horses and I've heard of folks stealing horses and I've heard of folks losing *cows*. But I don't think I ever heard of someone outright losing a horse."

Larrabee had told the story before, so he had it down. Without offering any details he could stick to the truth. He didn't like to lie.

"Jared Penrod and I took out two horses from White Pine. We were out toward Arredonda and someone started shooting at us. We split up and ran. Only Jared never came back. That was about it."

Sheriff Duforge stood up and handed him a half dollar. "Somebody just shooting at you? Just like that? Well, I'll tell you Larrabee, it's a dangerous county for man or dog. Just you—"

He broke off. Someone was coming up the steps two at a time. The door was open and a deputy by the name of Red Clay bounded into the room, sweaty and breathless and gesturing toward the Courthouse.

"Tom, there's one of them hot air balloons fixing to come down on the square!"

The sheriff put his hands on his hips. "A balloon?"

"Yeah, Tom! A balloon!"

"Well, what did you expect me to do about it?"

Clearly Deputy Clay was not prepared for the question. He wiggled and stammered under the sheriff's steady gaze. "Well, hadn't we ought to do *something?*"

Sheriff Duforge looked from Larrabee to Red. "It's up in the air you say?"

"Yeah! Yeah! Right up over the square!"

"Well, if it's *over* the square it's out of my jurisdiction, Red. Maybe we should call a preacher." Nobody laughed. He threw his hands out. "All right. All right. I'll go have a look. Just in case the thing comes down."

Red was out the door like a wild dog, and the sheriff motioned Larrabee outside and locked the door. His kept his big dapple-gray mare saddled in the jail yard. He slid on a bridle and took to the street in an easy lope that Larrabee's horse had to work to keep up with.

Hovering over the Courthouse was the huge red balloon. Across its vast dome large black cursive letters proclaimed: *Faulkner's Flights of Fancy*. The bulb was ornamented with great columns of gold braid, and beneath it hung the largest wicker basket Larrabee had ever seen. His horse balked and sidestepped, but he pressed her on with reassuring words and his heels, and she clattered back to the side of the sheriff's big dapple-gray.

The sheriff kept right on going as if he had five-story balloons come down on the square every day. A man in the basket was calling down to the crowd that had formed. He lowered an anchor, hand over hand, slowly, until they had made room for it, then he let it drop the last thirty feet and called for some of the men to pull while he lowered a second line. Gradually the balloon descended on the south side of the square, settling down among the live oaks like a great bird coming to roost.

Larrabee and Sheriff Duforge decided not to push their luck with the horses any further. They tied them on the opposite side of the Courthouse, where only the top of the frightening red dome was visible above the trees. Then the sheriff strode toward the giant, parting the crowd as he went.

The balloon was still about eight feet off the ground, and a man wearing goggles and a duster was climbing down from it via a rope ladder. About halfway down he turned, smiling and waving to the cheering crowd. He wore a ship captain's cap, leather gloves, and a scarf tucked into the duster. His broad smile seemed to say that he was very glad indeed to be out of the sky for a while.

A second head appeared in the basket. A woman. She somehow managed to follow the man down the rope ladder without tangling her skirts or showing an unseemly amount of lace. As she disappeared into the noisy crowd, a parasol opened up, and as he moved forward in the sheriff's wake, Larrabee determined that the woman from the sky was a very attractive brunette with a fair complexion and a dimpled smile. Deputy Clay had gotten there in time to push the crowd back to give the balloonists some room.

The man doffed his cap and bowed. "I am Captain Faulkner! And this is my pilot, Miss Diana Quarry!"

"Don't hardly seem right them being up there alone together if they ain't married," someone said.

Diana was curtseying, a pinch of her brocade-trimmed dress at her fingertips as she acknowledged the applause. Two faces looked on from the Courthouse windows, Ray Polk the county clerk and Judge Carlisle, who frowned at the proceedings as he did at any disturbance in his court. The judge moved away from the window and left Ray staring down in fascination.

"Miss Quarry and I have just completed an air journey of forty-five miles!" Faulkner declared.

The crowd clapped and whistled and cheered. Diana beamed at the attention. She had beautiful teeth. A black velvet ribbon held her curls in place under a gray felt bonnet trimmed with pink roses. She turned her parasol in a dainty gloved hand.

"Hot darn!" somebody said. It was Billy Willis. Larrabee wasn't sure if he was talking about the balloon or Diana.

"We have seen so much of your beautiful state," Faulkner said, "and now we would like to offer *you* the chance to see some of it—from our wonderful balloon!"

Almost to a man, the crowd let out an *ooh* of delight and anticipation. Everybody was going to get to go.

Mrs. Larson's laugh cut through the hubbub. "You're not going to get *me* to go up in that thing. I'd lose my hat!"

"I'd lose a durn sight more'n my hat!" Penny said. "I'd lose my grits 'n' gravy!"

Faulkner waited for the laughter to die down, put his hands up for silence, and then continued. "We can take each of you up for as long as there's daylight and the winds are light—"

A stillness of expectation set in.

"—for just one dollar." Some separation of opinion arose and Faulkner waited for the price debates to die out. Again he held up his gloved hands. "We will ascend to a height of two hundred feet, high above your fair Courthouse, then return you safely to *terra firma.*"

Someone had the notion that *terra firma* was in a northern state and another argument broke out.

Smiling, Faulkner held his hands aloft. "Who'll be first? Just one dollar— gold, silver, or paper!"

"Send the Little Giant up," one of his debtors suggested, "and then let go!"

Half a dozen people laughed.

"For that I'd pay *two dollars,*" someone else said.

"You reckon it's legal?" Deputy Clay asked the sheriff.

"I don't see why not," Tom Duforge said. "Ain't no different than a train except it goes up and down instead of back and forth."

Faulkner smiled patiently, waiting for people to get serious. "Who'll be first?" he repeated. "Just one dollar."

"I'll give you a dollar," Billy said. He came forward holding aloft a folded banknote.

"There's one," Faulkner exclaimed. "Who'll be next? We can send up four at a time."

A breeze lifted the Spanish moss and turned the leaves on the live oaks.

The sheriff folded his arms and surveyed the crowd. "Mister, I believe they need another demonstration."

Faulkner seemed a little disappointed. The lovely Diana stopped smiling for a moment.

"Very well, folks. Would another ascent convince you of the safety of Faulkner's Flights of Fancy? I shall ask for further assistance from the crowd. We can let out a hundred feet of line and bring the aircraft back down to your lovely Courthouse Square. What do you say?"

Again, Faulkner and the lovely Diana were smiling confidently.

There was no lack of volunteers. Sheriff Duforge and Deputy Clay had to help the helpers to keep things from getting out of hand. While Diana watched from the Courthouse steps, Faulkner climbed back into the wicker basket. Slowly, unsteadily, the huge balloon rose on its tethers, rose above the tallest of the old oaks on the Courthouse Square, rose above the Courthouse itself, past darting crows and circling buzzards, up, up toward the gathering clouds.

The breeze had persisted, taking away a straw hat or two, and Faulkner seemed to be less aware of the crowd now and more attentive to the drifting balloon.

"Seems to be pulling a mite to the south," Deputy Clay observed. His head was thrown back and his Adam's apple bobbed as he spoke.

"You could probably smell rain in the air if all these people wasn't here," Sheriff Duforge said in his low stuffy voice.

At Faulkner's direction the men were pulling in the lines now. The pulling was tough because the big red balloon, orange in the midday sun, was stubbornly pulling back, pulling toward the south, and a dozen men on each rope yanked and clawed and swore for every yard they brought in.

Somebody had thought to wrap the anchors and hard-won footage around the trees again so that the balloon wouldn't be getting away even if it shook off a few men. Then, above all the tugging and grunting, a voice cried out that something was wrong.

It was Diana, who had been watching from high on the Courthouse steps.

"It's caught fire!"

Suddenly fifty hands were pointing at the giant red mass that seemed to be breathing black smoke and licking its lips with a tongue of fire. The crowd scattered to make room for the descending air bag. The abandoned lines went slack because the balloon was coming down on its own now, puckering on one side where the tall script had been reduced mockingly to *Faulkner's Lights.*

"It's going to hit the Courthouse!" Deputy Clay shrieked. He ran over his hat on his way across the street.

Sheriff Duforge stood his ground, hands on his hips, as if about to command the balloon to retreat. "If it catches on those shingles, the whole Courthouse goes up!"

As if on cue, the wicker basket banged into the roof and caught on the eave, causing the deflating fabric to spill across the shingles in a wave of destruction. Faulkner seized one of the anchor ropes and slid into the crowd. Above the screams of women and children and horses the voice of Judge Carlisle cut through. He was standing in the back of a buckboard at the edge of the square.

"A hundred dollars to the man who gets up there and puts that fire out! A hundred dollars!"

The horses hitched to the buckboard had seen quite enough and spirited the startled judge toward a safer part of town.

Larrabee had been watching more in fascination than fear, but now he realized that the Courthouse was indeed in peril. He ran to his horse and grabbed the coil of rope tied to the saddle. He spread the lariat and swung the big loop up at the weathervane in the middle of the roof. The iron rooster spun around and tossed off the rope, but on the third throw the loop held and Larrabee walked his way up the clapboard walls until he was in the heat of the captive balloon. He ran to the spine of the hot roof and ripped off the shingles there. Some broke in his hands, some refused to yield, some came up with the slightest touch and sailed intact over the crowded square. He worked in haste, unaware of the smoking hulk that banged and flared in the rising wind. He ripped up every shingle he could lay his hands on, exposing the flat tough oak timber and tin flashing beneath. He slipped once, fell on his back and slid toward the edge as the crowd gasped, but on his way down he snatched the rope that dangled from the wind vane and hauled himself back up, more determined than ever to see the job to the end. He pulled and ripped and pitched until the Courthouse was nearly bald. Then he wrapped the rope around his blackened arms and lowered himself into the outstretched hands of his admirers.

"Mister, that was one hell of a show you just put on!" A large man in a silk top hat pushed his way through the throng. "Yes, sir, one hell of a show!"

"Judge says he's going to make it a hundred and fifty," the sheriff was saying. "Looks like you just paid off your horse with some to spare!"

"No, wait a minute!" the man in the top hat was saying. "Don't go! I need a man with your kind of gumption. I want to offer you a job."

Larrabee turned to get a good look at him. The man was middle-aged, well dressed.

"Young man, I've got just the job for you. You're the kind of man I've been looking for!"

"Well, what kind of job?" Larrabee smiled awkwardly. He was being crushed between two well- wishers.

"On the lake," the man said. "My name is Herbert Kline and I've got a steamboat down there that needs you to help run it."

"No thanks, mister. Boats and me don't get along."

"You'll like this one," Herbert Kline insisted. "You and your partner call the shots and you get a dollar a day."

As night fell, the crestfallen aerialist Faulkner and the lovely Diana Quarry dined at the Arlington as guests of one of the owners, Major Leonard G. Dennis. They dined on pheasant and oysters at the grand corner table that looked across the square to the still-smoldering Courthouse. The next morning, they carried a few salvaged belongings aboard the train for Jacksonville.

"I hope this train goes farther than that confounded balloon," Faulkner muttered through clenched teeth.

As Larrabee trotted his horse toward the lake, he decided that the balloon had gone very far indeed. It had carried him all the way out of debt and into a new life of steady income and respectability.

Part II
Partners
1877-1886

Chapter 13

THE BARN WAS DAZZLING. Lanterns hung from the rafters and sat on ledges sprinkled with sand. Bunting brightened the walls with crescents of color and the floors, swept to the pine planks, echoed with the rhythmic stepping and stamping of richly arrayed dancers. The place swarmed with young and old. Most of the families in town had come, and many from the farms scattered across the flat fields and tucked into the deep pinewoods of the county. The hotels and boarding houses and spare rooms of the town were full for the night. The streets overflowed with creaking wagons pulled by tired horses, with running dogs and trotting pigs and ambling men. During the day the blessings of the land had changed hands—corn and melons, squash and cucumbers, tomatoes, onions, turnips and beets and potted flowers, cattle and horses and all manner of leather and bone things made from them. Now it was time to celebrate the bounty.

Reluctantly Ralph Pine had agreed to the use of his barn. It was the biggest in town even if it was the dirtiest. An exchange was worked out whereby the neighboring field would accommodate the night's traffic so that the barn, cleaned and dressed almost beyond recognition, could welcome all who had come for the farmer's market. Ralph's rather flaccid sense of civic duty had been tweaked with the promise of a dime a head for every man, woman, and child who set foot in the barn for any purpose whatsoever, and by sunset the dancing had brought in such droves that Ralph was positively beaming.

The musicians were enjoying the occasion. Ray Polk played a worn guitar with a big, sweet sound. Curtis the iceman had made his own banjo out of oak and goatskin. Sheriff Duforge sawed away on a weathered, patched-up string bass. His brother Duke had closed the saloon for the night in order to do double duty as caller and harmonica player. Penny Ward spun out fast, smooth fiddle tunes, having inherited his gift and his instrument from two generations of fiddling Wards. From atop a platform of planking laid across four buckboards, they put out a big sound in the big crowded barn, a sound that carried well above all the merriment.

"We need a fourth couple over here," Duke the caller was saying as the musicians broke into a lively quadrille. "Someone over there's plumb worn out looks like. We need a fresh team to complete the square."

On a strange whim, Anna hooked Billy Willis by the elbow and swung him into the breach.

"I ain't dancing no dance," he said, breaking free and hurrying into the crowd.

She ran after him, mostly to avoid the embarrassment of being out there alone.

"The course o' true love," said the caller as the laughing crowd parted for the runaways.

Preacher Williams tipped his summer straw hat to Mrs. Newhouse, who was too surprised to make polite protests.

Once the dance got underway and the sides of the tight square pulled back, he smiled and said, "It seems like this would be the only chance we'd have to talk. We've both been so busy."

She smiled at the next couple as they went through the do-si-do. When they were face to face again she said, "Penny is playing uncommonly well tonight."

"I believe he has reason to."

"And what do you mean by that, Preacher?" Her tone suggested that she knew the answer.

Form a star, Duke chanted. *Form a star and circle all.*

The couples went, hand to waist, two by two, turning like the blades of a windmill.

"Preacher's light-footed tonight," observed Judge Carlisle's wife, Marianne. "He looks younger'n he did this time last year. I see he's put away his walking-stick."

"He's a hearty man," the Judge said, a little short of breath. "Used to work the lumber camps of Wisconsin. That's a toughness that stays with a man. It'd take more than getting caught in the rain to bring him down."

"Do you suppose he and Emma will ever tie the knot?"

The Judge rolled his eyes. "Oh, for mercy's sake, Marianne, how should I know? It's none of my business. Or yours."

The star, the circle, the do-si-do.

"When are you going to talk to Mr. Roper?" Dr. Willis' wife was asking him.

"Me, Julia? Why am I supposed to talk to Roper? I know next to nothing about the *situation* as you call it."

"Warren, it's got to be plain even to you that something very strange is happening at that school. For one thing poor Mr. McMarris looks like he's aged ten years in the past month."

"Why shouldn't he? He spent that month in a small room with the children of this community, including our own."

She frowned. "There's more to it than that and you know it. You're just sticking your head in the sand—as usual. Lilly Poinsett said she smelled liquor on his breath."

"Lilly Poinsett! How'd she get close enough to smell his breath? Will you tell me that, my dove?"

"Warren, if that man is drinking I won't have him teaching our child. I want you to talk to Mr. Roper."

"Has anybody considered talking to Mr. McMarris? Wouldn't that make some sense?"

"Go ahead. But just be aware that he claims the school is full of snakes. He swears he saw a coral snake in his desk drawer."

Hand in hand, form a circle again.

The fourth couple in the star lived on one of the large farms down by the lake. Colonel Lloyd Summerton was from a plantation near Charleston and his wife, Laetitia, came from the same city, which she found much deteriorated since the war. They had first seen Alachua County from the train during a trip to Tampa, and took an instant liking to its lush hills, its unravaged towns, and sun-flecked lakes. The colonel had bought the farm as a first anniversary present. Their son Jeremy—now being passed around by cooing women and girls—had been born in the handsome white house at the beginning of the year.

Although Colonel Summerton and his wife had never square danced in their lives, they found that Duke's calling made the steps easy to follow.

"I guess you know," the Colonel said, "that the man up there sawing on the fiddle is the very one that built that little lopsided house you like so much."

They touched their palms, left and right.

Laetitia was twenty years younger than her husband, but she wore her dark brown hair in old-fashioned ringlets that shook as she kept up with his nimble steps on the dance floor. "Is that so? I'll have to compliment him once I catch my breath. It's a dear little house—all the more so for its lopsidedness."

"He builds 'em solid. With the same amount of lumber he could've made it twice as big." The colonel's hair and beard were blond giving over to gray, making him look more distinguished than most men of forty-three. Occasionally a mischievous sparkle in his eyes gave him the appearance of a schoolboy. He gestured with their joined hands. "Look at that man there pushing his way in. Isn't he a long, tall drink of water?"

Laetitia studied the lanky, dark-haired man and said that she had seen him before somewhere.

"In the drugstore," her husband said. "He was buying some *oleum terebinthinae*. That's one thing you can get cheap around here since it comes from pine trees."

"What's it for?"

"Lung ailments mostly or soreness of the muscles. He looks like he's in a hurry."

Face your partners, left and right.

Julia Willis was looking for Billy. "For a minute there I thought that boy of ours was actually going to dance."

"*I didn't,*" the doctor said.

"That's because you have your eyes shut. He's not the little boy he used to be. He and Anna have been spending some time together."

"Yes, throwing things at each other."

"Oh, dream on! Our boy is growing up right under your nose and you're not noticing. Now when are you going to talk to Mr. Roper? Tell me a day and time."

"Well, he isn't here tonight or I'd dance a couple of tunes with him and we could get this whole thing straightened out right—"

He felt a hand on his sleeve. "Doc, a word with you?"

"You'll wreck our star, Sam. What is it?"

"It's Mary, sir. She's in a bad way."

The doctor dropped out of the star, leaving his wife to trail into the shadows. "Well, what seems to be wrong with her?" He was having trouble hearing because of the noise and Sam's tendency to swallow his words. They pushed through the onlookers and out the door to the yard, where cigarettes and cigars glowed in the darkness.

Sam turned and put his hands in the pockets of his old frock coat. "Doc, it's you're place to say. She's hurtin' inside. She wanted me to come for you."

After thirty years of practice Doctor Willis had seen just about everything—urgent calls to come see gluttons with bellyaches, drunks with the shakes, and casual calls to see people who were on the verge of bleeding to death or burning with fever. He took a cigar from his breast pocket and bit the end off it. "How long has your sister been sick?"

Sam stood there, swaying slightly, his dark height and black stovepipe hat giving him the look of some dread engine waiting for coal. "I can't exactly say, doc. It seemed to come on kind of gradual."

The doctor thumped him on the chest and ashes flew. "This had better not be another one of your tricks, Sam, because if it is my wrath will be of Biblical proportions. Do you take my meaning?"

All join hands and circle 'round.

Anna had followed Billy until they were well out of sight, deep into Ralph Pine's newly planted orange grove.

"I don't think anybody's caught on," Billy said softly. "So just you see to it that they don't."

"If anybody tells, it won't be me," she vowed.

"I'm not talking about telling," he said. "I'm talking about gettin' caught."

"Just give me the box," she demanded. "I ain't going to get caught."

"Do you swear?"

"Yes, I swear. Now let me see it."

He led her to the tall grass at the edge of the grove. Then he knelt down and picked up a Tampa Imperial cigar box. He handed it to her.

"Don't open it up."

"Why not?"

"Just don't. Not till you're fixing to use it."

"If you're pulling a trick on me, I'll get you."

"I ain't pulling no trick. Not on you anyway."

They both giggled.

"How long's old Lucifer going to be staying at your place?"

"For the month, same as at yours. Did your mama and daddy not suspect?"

"Not even once. Mama thinks he's taken to drink."

"Maybe he has."

"Well, then that'll be the end of him and we'll be free before you know it."

She tucked the box under her arm and started to go but he put his hand on her shoulder.

"What?"

"Let's seal it. For luck." He put his face close to hers.

She tossed her head so that her hair brushed his cheek. He pulled gently on a braid until he was looking into her startled brown eyes. Then he kissed her lightly on the lips and watched as she held the box close and ran toward the light.

Penny had taken a break from his fiddling. He scratched his back with the bow and headed for the door with his instrument held high to keep it from the crush of the crowd.

"Looking for somebody?"

He nearly dropped the fiddle, caught it and clasped it to him.

"Why there you are, Nelda." He said her name again because he liked the sound of it. "Nelda, what d'you think of the music so far?"

"You're playing very nicely, though sometimes it's hard to hear you over the hollering."

"Well, that's the way it's supposed to be! Sure sign of a good time!"

"When do you think you should make the announcement?"

"There doesn't seem to've been a good time just yet."

"What about when you go back up to play again?"

He pulled at his earlobe and looked at the people beginning to come back into the barn. "There's—there's likely to be so many folks comin' and goin' and settlin' down it might all git kind of lost in the wash."

She looked up at him with steady eyes. "Penny, you're not nervous are you?"

"Nelda, I ain't nothing *but* nervous. Fiddlin' in front of the whole town is one thing. This is somethin' else."

She began to feel uncertain herself. "Oh, dear. Maybe this isn't the thing to do after all."

He tried to swallow but his throat had gone dry. "You mean the whole thing?"

"It's too crowded to talk in here."

"I know I could use some air. I could use a drink even more. Two drinks. This ain't as easy as I figgered it would be. What if we just send everyone a letter?"

"Oh, what an awful idea!" She winced and then broke out laughing. "I suppose we could just put an advertisement in the newspapers!"

Penny hugged his fiddle to his chest. "Yes, you may have somethin' there. That would surely be preferable."

He was right about the opportunities to make the announcement. As he climbed back onto the platform and prepared to play again, the crowd was more unsettled than ever. Mrs. Newhouse, holding Martha close to her side, had sent Caroline out to look for Anna. Mrs. Willis had not come back since the last dance. Dr. Willis and Billy were gone. Bobby La Rue had broken away from the Alachua Hotel long enough to dance with a graceful blonde who had come in with her family from one of the farms out toward Magnesia Springs. But he had stayed away from the desk longer than was wise and had taken his leave with a rueful backward glance. Duke was there, of course, leaning down at the edge of the platform, laughing at someone's joke. But most of the people Penny wanted to tell weren't in the barn. He stalled around, plucking and tuning and re-tuning until the other musicians started to look impatient. Then with a toss of his head, he tore into the liveliest dance he knew—a driving, foot-stomper of a strathspey called "Brendan Mulvhill."

Caroline spotted Anna by her long, determined stride and swinging braids. "Where are you going? Mama is about to have a fit!"

Anna stopped in the middle of the street. She held the cigar box behind her. She thought she could still feel Billy's kiss on her lips and she was confused, but she knew that she had to keep the cigar box a secret no matter what.

"I was just going to take this fool box to Billy's house. He thought he could scare me with his beetles."

Caroline shrank back. "Beetles. *Ewww!* They're too much like roaches!"

"They're slower and not as sneaky. I'll be back." Anna started off again.

"No, you come now, beetles and all. But if you let them loose at the dance you'll be in for it."

"I can't come now! I've got to take this to—"

"*Now*, Anna!" Caroline gripped her skirt the way she did when she was about to burst into a rage, which was more and more often lately. Anna decided it would be better not to risk a scene with her. She would just have to hold that box like it was glued to her.

Penny had left the platform and was outside, fiddle in hand, rounding up everyone he knew.

"The show's about to begin. Come on in!"

Duke Duforge looked at his brother in bewilderment. "Now he's drumming up business?" He played a little run on his harmonica as if to call everybody back.

"Long as you were out you should've passed the hat," Curtis told Penny. He plunked his banjo and tightened a peg.

Penny climbed back onto the platform with a little help from Ray Polk.

"I'll tell you, boys. This is fixin' to be the roughest show this fiddler's ever played!" He straightened and came to the front of the platform, so close to the edge that the rounded toes of his boots stuck out.

Anna worked her way over to the wall, doing her best to keep the box out of sight.

"Anna, will you come over here?" her mother scolded. "What's come over you?"

"I was coming right back." Anna replied sullenly. "What's Penny doing? He's just standing there."

"Not for long," the preacher said with a mysterious smile.

Penny's eyes scanned the crowd. He licked his lips and rubbed his unshaven jaw. "Ladies and gents, uh...."

"Speak up!" Ralph Pine slouched against the wall, cleaning his ear with his little finger.

"Ladies and uh gentlemen, I uh...I've been asked to announce that two folks here tonight are fixin' to...join in the bands of...That is are goin' to git married! And they are me and...uh, Mrs. Nelda Larson!"

The last words came tumbling out so loud that everybody heard. For a long awkward moment everyone stood silently as Penny wavered on the edge of the platform, so delicately balanced that it seemed a mere swallow's feather drifting down from the rough-hewn rafters could have sent him tumbling into the front row of upturned faces. Then the air crackled with a sound unheard in town for thirteen years. It started as a low growl and rose rapidly in volume and pitch until the whole barn seemed to shake with it. None of the women and children had ever heard the sound but they knew what it was. To the northerners it was a myth come to life. To the men there who had worn Confederate gray it was a sound that brought back shining youth, hope and glory. But all of them, young and old, northerner and southerner alike, raised their voices in the wake of the Rebel yell.

Dr. Willis came out of Mary Leary's room and closed the door softly.

"Was I right to call you?" Sam Leary asked in his strange bass drawl.

"Yes, and it won't likely be the last time either."

He let Sam stand there wondering for a moment. After all the petty trouble the undertaker had caused over the years it seemed time to let him squirm for a minute or two. It was an odd place, this old trading post at the edge of town. Cramped and dark. Half lumber, half log, with furnishings thirty years out of date. Sam looked odd, too, in his antique frock coat. The customary stovepipe hat stood on a little lace-covered table, a relic from an earlier generation. Sam looked older and more serious without it.

"Sam, your sister's going to have a baby."

"Mary is with child? How can that be?"

"Well, you and I know exactly how. You didn't know she was pregnant?"

Sam stuffed his hands in his pockets. "Did *she* know she is?"

"Sam, she may be a spinster, but she is a female. She's known for a while I'd say. She's about six months along. Sam, do you have any idea who the father is?"

The tall, pale undertaker dug his hands deeper into his pockets. No answer came.

"She hasn't said anything to you at all?"

"Nothing, doc. What did she tell you?"

"It's between you two, Sam. You two talk it over."

On the drive home the doctor reviewed in his mind the condition of the woman he had examined. A routine enough pregnancy by the look of it. But he had a notion that word of it would spread far beyond the walls of the wayside trading post if Mary Leary persisted in her assertion that the father of her child was John Howard.

Chapter 14

They gathered at the Arlington on Friday nights for dinner and whist. Most of them had been members of the Hayes-Wheeler Club or the Tilden-Hendricks Club, and now that the Republicans had won the presidency and the Democrats had won the governorship, they found that they had common interests in developing the county. Their lynchpin was none other than Major Leonard G. Dennis, who had made a graceful transition from carpetbag political boss to gracious city father. The major had done a wonderful job of making money in one venture after another, and his business partners included men who had been shooting at him thirteen years earlier in a succession of battles and skirmishes from Baldwin to Cedar Keys.

John Howard had learned to move among them. He found whist an old man's game, slow and safe compared to poker, but he figured that in the long run the stakes would be higher. These were men who knew which way the county was headed, and allying his fortunes with theirs could only lead to prosperity. He was disappointed that his three years of service with Major Dennis had not been more productive. He didn't particularly care about winning the major's friendship. He had long since come to the conclusion that the major was a difficult man to know. It was the lack of information that bothered him. Howard had brought up the time-honored idea of linking the lakes and rivers to form a barge canal from the Gulf to the Atlantic and the major had dismissed it without revealing his own plans—to invest in the Arlington, in lumber, in a plantation, in who knew what else.

Howard had asked him directly about the advisability of investing in orange groves and the major had shrugged that off too, even though everyone else in the county was doing it, and very successfully.

"They're the same fools who had all their money in cotton until 1867," the major had said. "And when the rains came they had tens of thousands of acres of rot. Oranges will rot the same as cotton. Or they'll freeze. Read a little history, John. There was a killing freeze in this county in 1835. If you like the soil so much, put your money into farms but don't put it all on one crop any more than you'd bet your whole fortune on the turn of one card. From what I hear you're a more careful player than that."

In the meantime, fortunes were being made on oranges.

Now Howard was faced with a different problem, completely unexpected, and the very devil to deal with, and he thought it had something to do with the way he was getting treated at the whist club. He didn't know who to ask for advice, so after cards he drank an extra brandy and approached the major's table. The afternoon had been hot, but now the weather seemed to be breaking. The air had grown damp and chilly and the waiters were closing the French doors that opened onto the veranda. A fire in the corner of the room popped and spat sparks as its pine kindling caught. Howard carried his brandy in the palm of his hand. He didn't particularly care for brandy. He set it on the major's table and asked if he might sit down.

The major was smoking a cigar and gazing across the room. "I won't be here much longer, John. I have some important letters to write. But go ahead. Sit down."

Howard decided to be forthright. "I suppose you've been hearing the gossip."

"I hear gossip every day." The major sat back, tapped his ash in the direction of the fireplace, and looked him in the eyes. "But I suppose you mean the stories about you and Mary Leary."

"I'm afraid I do." It was a sorry topic but at least now it was in the open. "What should I do?"

The major sat and smoked for a long time. Howard wasn't sure whether he was thinking of the problem or of something else entirely until at last he said, "What do you *want* to do?"

"I want to get my name back, of course." It was the closest he had ever come to being short with the major.

"Your name. Your reputation," the major said. "Most of us in this room have the reputations of scoundrels. Why should you be any different?"

Now Howard was getting impatient. "Because I had nothing to do with that woman. For God's sake, have you seen her? She's as plain as a board! The idea of having—of having my name linked with hers is ludicrous."

Suddenly the major was ahead of him. "And you think this scandal is impeding your progress as a stalwart of the community. You want to associate with noble and prosperous men."

"Is that an unreasonable wish?"

The major leaned forward and put his elbows on the table. "Well, what can you do? You've got no way of proving anything—unless the child turns out to be a Chinaman or a nigger."

It was surprising to hear the major speak so disparagingly of a race he had championed with such fervor. It was as if some sourness had seeped into his soul.

"So what can you do?" he repeated. "I suppose you could sue her for slander."

"She has nothing—only that wretched old store. That's where this whole stink came from. Last spring I went to collect a few dollars that she owed the moss mill and she got her back up. I never got a cent out of her. I got nothing. The woman must be out of her mind."

The major stared at him. "I suppose you could have someone shoot her."

Howard looked through the smoke to see if he was serious. He thought not. "Tempting but impractical."

"Then maybe you have just one course left to you." The major threw his cigar into the fire. "You can outlive it."

"Outlive it?"

"That's right. It's what most of these men here do. As we've already established, all of them have their peccadilloes, but they see to it that their noble deeds far outweigh them. We all know that you don't eat pork without slaughtering hogs, John. But the people who sit down to dinner don't think about how you slit the hog's throat, do they? So why don't you pick out some grand cause and take it up and in time everybody will forget this little dalliance."

Howard had returned to his rooms deep in thought. He stared out the beveled corner window. Somewhere down the street came the sound of six quick shots. Another rough-and-tumble Friday night, he figured. In the street below he saw a young girl, running. His eyes followed her as she rushed north, past the large dark shape of the new brick Methodist Church, toward the edge of town. By the time she had disappeared behind the line of the roof he had conceived his grand cause. He unbuttoned his collar, tossed it on the bed, rolled up his sleeves, and went over to the basin to wash his hands.

Chapter 15

Penny wasn't sure what to think. Here he was working on the roof of a cabin inhabited by a pair of soiled doves. That was peculiar enough. On top of that he had been urged to do so by two very unlikely people—Preacher Williams and his own fiancée, Nelda Larson. It was the least—and maybe the most—they could do for the women who had taken in poor Anna on the most terrible night of her life, the night she had run away after admitting to everyone in Roper's Hall that she had slipped a king snake into the teacher's drawer because she didn't like school. When the seemingly delusional young man was about to be banished for drunkenness, she had rushed forward to confess her crime, only to learn that the serpent in the cigar box was not a king snake after all, but its far deadlier look-alike, the coral snake, which the sheriff dispatched with six quick pistol shots.

Preacher Williams had said something about how he would love to salvage the souls of the soiled doves dwelling on the outskirts of town, but thought that nothing short of kidnapping would pull that off. So he thought that in addition to expressing gratitude, this work on the roof might keep the lines of communication open so that those unfortunate women might know that the doors of the church were always open to them.

"Our Savior communed with the most miserable members of the community," Preacher Williams had said, "knowing full well that they were the ones most in need of salvation."

At the time of Anna's return she and a few others had also been in need of a little salvaging. Anna had apparently resolved to put the whole awful episode of the snake behind her. She was doing quite well in school, having patched her relationship with the maligned Mr. McMarris via a suppertime apology that seemed to embarrass him even more than it did her. In an effort to forget the whole horrible episode, she had concentrated on her studies like never before, and it showed. Nobody in the school knew geography better than she did. The class had put the incident behind them by planting an oak with a bottled note that said, "We shall love beauty forever."

Nelda's insistence surprised Penny even more than the preacher's had. She was always surprising him. She was already making—and selling—hats right out of the Newhouse front room, and for what he was worth, Penny was helping, carting things around mostly, when he wasn't working on somebody's house. The town was undergoing a building boom and Penny was starting to make pretty good money from it. Houses were going up along Liberty Street east of the Sweetwater Branch. South of the Doig Foundry on West Main there was a new planing mill. A finishing school had opened behind the Land Office. And west on Liberty Street, out past Roper's school, the woods were falling for fine houses with turrets and oval windows and wrap-around porches. The smell of sawdust was in the air.

Dr. Willis was putting up a new house in a bean field just a stone's throw east of the old one. Everybody said Julia Willis was the force behind it, but the new house would also have room for an office and an operating room downstairs, so Penny figured the idea could not have come entirely from her. Billy was helping to saw the big timbers, which Dr. Willis said would help to keep him out of trouble. It seemed that Billy's guilt in the McMarris affair was determined very quickly by the fact that the offending serpent had been housed in a Tampa Imperial cigar box—Dr. Willis being the only person in town known to smoke that particular brand. Other punishments Billy may have suffered were not being openly discussed, but for a few days he seemed to spend a good deal of time standing at the back of the schoolroom.

It was hard for Penny to tear himself away from the building boom—and gossip—in town. But Preacher Williams and Nelda were irresistible forces, and so he had promised to go up to the cabins for a day, which stretched into two when he discovered rot by the chimney and loose mortar in the first cabin.

"These here were slave cabins," he told a bear-sized woman called Sweet Betsy as she stood on the porch shaking out a bedspread.

"Still are," she said with a toss of her head. "How much did Lucy say she was going to pay you?"

"Well, it ain't an issue," he said, trying not to stare at Betsy's enormity.

"What if we pay you in kind?" Sweet Betsy said, leaning over the rail at him.

He put his hand to his chest. "No need, ma'am. It's all taken care of." He didn't know what he meant but he was eager to get back onto the roof where he belonged.

Sweet Betsy hadn't been listening though. She was looking down the road at three men who were approaching on horseback. They came on in a welter of flying mud.

Penny went toward his ladder. "Well, back to business."

"They ain't customers," Sweet Betsy said.

Realizing the double meaning of his words, Penny blushed. "Who are they?"

Betsy looked worried. "We're fixing to find out."

Penny didn't recognize any of them. They were young and they rode up looking at the cabins and the surrounding woods as if they wanted to be sure no one else was around. They reminded Penny of raiding parties he had seen during the war. They came into the yard at a lope, forcing him up against the porch. He wondered if the women in the cabins were watching.

The leader of the three had a flat face and blond hair that seemed to sprout from his slouch hat.

He winked at Penny. "Ain't nothing like gittin' a little in the morning, is there, my man?"

"I'm working on the roof," Penny said.

"Is that so? Well, you can knock off now 'cause in a minute there won't be no roof."

Penny looked at the three faces and found no humor there. "I don't know where you boys come from but you don't belong here. Now git along."

The leader came down from his horse and reached into his saddle for a long whip that he slowly uncoiled.

The other two men were smiling.

"I'm going to count to two," the flat-faced boy said. "You can turn and run for it or you can stand right there and take it. Either way these cabins is coming down."

"What are you talking about?" Sweet Betsy glanced over her shoulder, but no one came to back her up and she moved toward the door a little.

The leader looked up at her and snapped his whip in her general direction, forcing her back even farther.

"You git all those other doves out here and I'll show you. Are they all as hog-fat as you?"

Penny stood his ground. "You ain't takin' no cabin down. Now you just go along."

The other two men came down from their horses.

"Now, listen boys. I ain't after no fight. I've had enough of fightin'. I'm gittin' married in a few days and I ain't after no fight."

The blond boy flexed his whip. "Gittin' married! Who you gittin' married to, my man? This hog here?"

Sweet Betsy sucked in a breath.

"Well, you had your chance! I ain't even going to hit you with the business end of my whip. I'm going to put you down with—this end."

He coiled the long lash and shook the corded handle as he came forward.

Penny's hand was already up to protect his face. "I can't take the three of you. But I can take one of you and that'un I'll take bad. You want to be the one, pretty boy?"

He was doing what he had done with Captain Dickison, attacking a larger force. It was the only thing he knew. He charged the blond boy with so much fury that the whip never came into play. He gave him such a blow to the forehead that the startled boy fell over backwards. But the other two brought

Penny down and kicked him from one end to the other while the blond boy got to his feet and used what strength he had left to spit on him.

That's when they looked up at the porch and saw the blond woman with the face of a child. She was pointing a gun at them, a heavy old Perry breech-loading pistol, which shook even though she held it in both hands.

"You men git out of here before this thing goes off!"

"Well," said the one that had kicked Penny in the mouth, "they ain't all big and fat, are they?"

"Cain't shoot but one ball at a time," said the other slowly as he came closer.

She shook the gun at him. "My one takes off your two. What do you say to that, mister?"

They backed up and spread out a little. The blond boy spat again. Blood. Penny lay unconscious, face down in the dirt.

"You had your chance." The blond boy spat again and nodded to one of the men, who kicked Penny in the ear. Before Lucinda could cry out and before she knew what had happened, her hand was aflame with pain, the gun was gone, and she was falling off the porch. She hadn't even heard the crack of the whip. She knelt, clutching her swelling hand.

The blond boy was starting to feel better now. He held the whip out to his side, ready to strike again.

"Tell the rest of them women to come out. We're fixin' to have us a bonfire!"

Bob Harper was more than good-natured. He was calm in a storm, even-tempered in an argument, and apparently incapable of carrying a grudge. And he generally prevailed, perhaps because his lack of anger enabled him to think situations through clearly, to see what he could reasonably expect to get out of each encounter. He had been maneuvering the 38-foot sternwheeler *King Payne* on Alachua Lake for five years, and by all accounts had saved it from many a scrape by thinking out the best course of action. Other boats had stuck on mud flats, burned to the waterline or gone down in the fast, sudden cloudbursts that wandered across the lake, but Bob Harper had always steered his through, cargo intact, and he was a happy and prosperous young man for it.

When he wasn't on the water he spent most of his time working the sandy soil around a small brick house that overlooked the water about a half-mile up-slope from the landing on the northwest corner of the lake. The house was one of just a few brick structures in the county, and he had put it together himself from castoffs of the Methodist Church and the County Jail. It had more mortar than most brick buildings its size but it was a fine, trim piece of work with white frame windows you could raise and lower, a Franklin stove for warmth and cooking, a fine cross-draft in summer, and a reliable plank door hung with clean iron hinges. The roof was shingled with pine bark covered with dirt to reduce the risk of fire, and in the lush, warm weather it sprouted weeds and seedlings that required occasional clearing.

For much of the year the yard was thick with rows of corn, tomatoes that worked their way up stout stakes, cucumbers and string beans and squash. What wasn't tilled was given over to knee-high grass that took on the color of wheat in the dry months of fall. In the past five years several nearby white pines and water oaks had come down and gone into the ample stack of firewood at the back of the house. An overturned rowboat lay against the north side. In a small paddock enclosed by split rails a skinny bone-colored quarter horse mare grazed on what was left of the grass and poked her way through goldenrod and wild chicory.

Larrabee's half year on the *King Payne* had been the happiest months of his life. Under Bob's patient tutorship he had come to know the intricacies of the lake—the channels and the flats, the places where you could go through the lilies and the places to stay away from. He had learned quickly for someone who had little experience with boats and most of that unpleasant. His tiller hand developed its own memory so that he could steer gently to any pier on the lake regardless of the wind direction and the water level. He found shortcuts that brought the boat so close to the western shoreline that he could wave to the engineer on the train to Cedar Keys. By the end of his first summer the *King Payne* was carrying the largest share of the wealth of the farms and plantations on the lake.

"One more season like this and we'll own the boat." Bob glanced down toward the landing as he paid Larrabee his share for the week.

Larrabee laughed. "That's because away down here there ain't anything else to spend the money on." He still had most of the $150 reward the judge had given him.

Bob cut the end off a plug of tobacco and tucked it into his cheek. "That's the way it works down here. You're too busy making it to spend it." He worked on the tobacco for a moment and then spat toward a field of corn stubble. "It being Saturday night however, I thought it might be diverting to go into town and stay over till tomorrow morning."

Scarcely another word had passed between them during the hitching of the high-withered quarter horse, Maude by name, to the remains of a once-stately buggy, although during the drive Larrabee found himself talking more and more about his friends in town.

"I think you told me that, " Bob said more than once, for during their long hours on the boat Larrabee had spoken many times of the Newhouses and Preacher Williams and Penny Ward.

"I imagine the Newhouses won't mind putting us up for the night if we wash a little," Larrabee said, scraping the mud from his boot sole with a pine twig.

Maude pulled her way dutifully up the slope to town, unhurried by the horses and wagons that passed her on their way to Saturday night revels. The western sky had gone to indigo and violet by the time they approached the orange-bearing groves on the southern outskirts of town. After his months on the lake Larrabee felt as if he were coming home, although there had been conspicuous changes since his last visit. Open fields and oak woods had been given over to row after row of newly planted orange trees. Several fine houses had gone up—big white houses with broad porches and sharp gables that looked across the wide street to stately shade trees and picket fences.

They left the buggy at the White Pine Stable. Ralph Pine was as sour as ever, complaining of old wounds that came back in the colder weather.

"You ought to get yourself more help," Larrabee said. He was cheerful since he had paid his debt for the missing horse.

"Got help already," Ralph sneered. "Dobkin Murray's boy's back, for what he's worth. Runs away about oncet a week. At that rate it'll be a hundred years before Dobkin pays off his debt."

"What about your own boys?" Larrabee asked. He seemed to remember that Ralph had two sons.

"Run off with their cousin," Ralph spat. "Said they was going to make big money as wreckers in Key West. That'll be the day. They don't know nothin' about boats."

He slapped Maude on the behind as if he owned her. As horse and buggy disappeared into the recesses of the barn, Larrabee and Bob walked toward the Courthouse.

"There's a fire up there to the north," Bob said, pointing toward a gray wisp drifting into the darkening sky. "I didn't think there was much up that way."

"There isn't," Larrabee said. "The old Bailey plantation is north but farther west." He was reminded of riding up that way to roust John Howard and thought of the blond woman with a child's face, but he put the ill-fated treasure hunt out of his mind.

The streets were full of traffic and noise. Families staying the night after selling their produce at the farmer's market, travelers laying over on the Tampa & Jacksonville line or en route from Fernandina to Cedar Keys. Cow hunters from the western ranges and scrub, Negro farmers and laborers in for a drink. A light was still glowing in the Courthouse. Ray Polk, most likely, working on the tax rolls.

Northeast of the Courthouse, in front of the new pharmacy, a crowd had gathered to watch two men ply a basset hound with beer. They began singing "Dixie." Every time they got to the word "away" in the chorus the dog would throw back his head and howl along, much to everyone's delight.

"Dog's the only one in tune," Bob said.

The Arlington was aglow with amber light. Music spilled from the hotel's broad terraces. The silhouettes of men in fine suits and ladies in fancy hats and bustles showed through the French doors. Talking and laughter carried over the music of a string quartet and a cornet player playing "Linger in Blissful Repose."

Bob hummed along as they passed into the darkness. "Sure you wouldn't rather put up in there for the night?"

"At those prices?" Larrabee scoffed. "The view from down here is free. As for the music, I imagine Miss Caroline's piano playing is just about up to that standard by now. And on top of that you get all of Penny's war stories. Some of 'em may even be true, and the way he tells 'em is like being there."

When they turned the corner and came to the house, Larrabee stopped.

"Something wrong, chief?"

Larrabee was looking at the porch. A very fat woman was talking to Dr. Willis. Beside her was the blond woman with the child's face. He quickened his stride.

"We'll just have to see how he looks in a day or two," the doctor was saying. "Was he talking on the way in?"

The fat woman was shaking her head, trying not to cry. "No, sir, not a word. Not a sound."

"Did they hit him with a weapon? A gun butt or something hard like that?"

"I couldn't tell," the blond woman said. "But I don't think so. They kicked him mostly."

Dr. Willis took the blond woman's hand and pulled the sleeve back from the lurid welt on her wrist. "How'd you come by this?"

"From the whip." She answered as if it was of no importance.

Larrabee was on the steps before the doctor spoke to him.

"Hello, Nathaniel. What brings you up this way?"

"We thought we'd take the night off. This here's my partner, Bob Harper. Bob, this is Doctor Willis."

"This is Lucinda and this is Betsy," the doctor said without embarrassment. The women were oddly overdressed given their bedraggled appearance. Lucinda was wearing a hat with big black feathers that Larrabee thought must have come from a crow. Sweet Betsy's hair was half up, half down, but she was enclosed in an elegant peach-colored dress with black trim.

"Somebody sick?" Larrabee asked.

"Penny ran afoul of some troublemakers. None of it makes such sense."

"Well, is he all right?"

"I've seen him look better. He's unconscious. Broken arm looks like. He's lost a couple of teeth. Likely whistle when he talks from now on. For the rest we're going to have to wait." Dr. Willis took a cigar from his breast pocket, bit the end off, and lit it.

"How'd it happen?" Larrabee asked Lucinda. It was strange talking to her on the Newhouses' porch.

"These three men came to fire us out and Penny was working on the roof. They run right over him." She spoke calmly, as if things like this happened every day.

"Who were they?"

Sweet Betsy was shaking her head. "Nobody I'd ever seen before. There was this one fellow with kind of a flat face and blond hair. He was the one with the whip. He seemed to be running 'em until Penny knocked him down."

"Any idea where they went?"

She was still shaking her head. "They rode off the way they came. Toward town."

"They said something about going for a drink," Lucinda said.

"Doctor, do you have any idea what's going on?"

"There's been talk in the papers about cleaning up the community. To make it a better place to do business." Dr. Willis tapped the ashes from his cigar. "It's hard to see how this fits in though."

"Can we see Penny?"

"You can look at him. They've got him in the wood room there by the kitchen."

On their way into the kitchen, Larrabee and Bob ran into a nervous young man drinking from the dipper. "He isn't doing so good. This is all my fault."

Larrabee was getting impatient with all these strangers who seemed to have taken over the house. "Who in blazes are you?"

The young man set the dipper down and rubbed his hands. "I'm Ronald McMarris." He waited for some kind of reaction that didn't come. "The teacher?" Still no reaction.

He explained the incident with the snake and told of Anna's running away from home and her night with Lucinda and Sweet Betsy.

"Has this whole town been turned upside down since I left?" It seemed to Larrabee that the familiar smell of flour was at odds with the strange people and goings-on.

He heard voices inside the wood room, low and mournful. He went over and opened the door softly. Mrs. Larson and Mrs. Newhouse were sitting by the bed. A quilt was drawn up to the patient's chin. His face and thinning hair were red against the white pillow. It took Larrabee a second look to recognize the swollen features as Penny's.

He felt his throat tighten.

Mrs. Newhouse stood up and came to the door. "You heard about this?" she asked in a light whisper.

"Just now." His voice was louder than he intended it to be.

Mrs. Larson looked up and smiled through tears.

Mrs. Newhouse ushered him back into the kitchen and closed the door behind her. "Will you be staying here tonight?"

Larrabee glanced over at Ronald McMarris, who was standing by the drain board doing nothing in particular. "If you have room. Bob and I would like to stay the night. Especially if we might be of use."

"We'd be happy to have you. And that way the girls will get to see you. Won't they be surprised." Mrs. Newhouse's dolorous tone was at odds with what she was saying.

"Where do you want us?"

"Take Penny's room tonight if you don't mind sharing the bed. We have him down here because we didn't want to carry him up the stairs."

Bob was looking at joined cutout figures one of the girls had made from folded paper.

Larrabee nodded. "I imagine we'll be coming back pretty late but we'll try not to wake anybody up."

"Now what did you mean by that?" Bob asked when they were back out on the now-deserted porch. "Coming back pretty late."

"I mean I'm going to find those sons-of-bitches and kill 'em," Larrabee said. "You can come along if you want to." He took off across the yard.

"What makes you think they're in town?"

"Because they have money and it's Saturday night. If we don't find 'em here we'll go to Archer."

"Archer!"

"That's right. One of 'em's from Archer. He's the one I want."

Bob was having trouble keeping up with Larrabee's long-legged stride. "Don't you reckon you ought to let the sheriff take care of this?"

"There's no law against fights and I guess there's no law against firing out soiled doves. Anyway, this is something to be settled between him and me."

They stopped first at the Alachua and asked Bobby La Rue if he had seen the men from Archer. Bobby seemed to find the description unpleasant and was quick to say that he certainly would not admit anyone of that ilk. "But the streets are full of that kind," he reminded them. "Take yourself a torch and look around out there. You'll find worse."

There was a new bowling alley on the south side of the square and they looked through the large window. Some kind of commotion had broken out between one of the patrons and a pin boy. Larrabee studied the faces carefully and moved on.

They crossed over to Duke's, which was bright and noisy. Tied to a rail on the side street were three horses. One of them had a whip tied to the saddle. When they got to the entrance of the saloon Bob grabbed Larrabee's shoulder. "This is the place, isn't it? I can see him in there as well as you can. The one with the flat face. There's three of 'em, Nathaniel. Don't go in there and pick a fight."

Larrabee pulled away. "What would you do, Bob—buy 'em a drink?"

The noise came between them for a moment, somebody swearing at cards, a drinking contest. The flat-faced boy from Archer was brandishing a fifty-dollar bill.

Bob seemed to be thinking about something else. "As a matter of fact, that's just what I'd like to do—buy 'em a drink. You want those boys, chief? You can have 'em. But let me deliver 'em to you. Wait for me. Be patient. Can you do that? Can you be patient?"

"All right. I'll wait. For a while."

"Go back down to the stable and get a wagon."

"The buggy you mean."

"No, leave the buggy and bring a wagon. By and by we're going to need it."

Distant lights flickered at the edges of the lake. Bob cut himself a wedge of tobacco and slowed the *King Payne* to scarcely more than floating.

"Looks like this fresh night air is starting to revive our friends."

"It's not night anymore, Bob. It's morning."

"Hold that lantern a little lower. I want to get a good look at the water."

"You really know where we are?"

"Sure. Give or take a foot. Told you. I hardly drank a dram. Your friend Duke was in cahoots with me. But them three on the floor had the better part of a bottle apiece. Except your friend with the bruises on the face. He held back so Duke had to nudge him along with the bar bopper. You're letting that lantern creep up again, chief."

Larrabee tried to make out the shoreline. A few tall oaks poked above the dark horizon, but no proper landmark. The water was a circle of translucent brown light. The occasional spark flew from the narrow stack of the *King Payne* and disappeared into the blackness. Indistinct things moved in the water, jumped and dove without revealing their shape or size. The air from the lake was warm but it cooled rapidly as it rose. Larrabee watched the water fold back and smiled. It seemed to him that even Preacher Williams could not object to what they were about to do. After all, God would decide the fate of the three men from Archer.

"Okay, boys, up and at' em!" Bob stepped over the three bodies and brought the boat to a virtual standstill by disengaging the stern wheel. They swayed gently on the water.

Larrabee hung the lantern from a hook in the cockpit and picked up a bait bucket. He unloaded it on the three sleeping men. One of them sat up, sputtering and swearing and blinking. He looked up and saw Bob smiling, one hand on the tiller, the other holding a .36 caliber Navy pistol.

"This is your stop, boys."

The man looked around, uncomprehending.

Larrabee dipped the bait bucket into the lake again and dumped it on the other two. As they wiggled and thrashed they realized that they were tied together at the wrists and ankles.

"We got us some paper dolls here," Bob said. "Can y'all stand up?"

He gave the pistol a little shake and the three men wrestled their way to their feet.

"What in hell do you think you're doing, mister?" Water ran from the first man's whiskers and he sputtered as he spoke.

"Me? I ain't doing nothing. But y'all are fixing to walk home."

Larrabee said in a slow, even voice, "But first, tell us why you fired out those girls up there."

The men from Archer remained silent.

Bob watched Larrabee's hands curl into fists. He waved the pistol toward the water. "Better get going, boys! Be high tide in a couple of hours and we've got four feet of water out here already. Go on now."

"Are you crazy, mister? We'll drown!"

"Not if you go the right way. Well, there's a few drop-offs but y'all can walk it all the way if y'all're careful."

The blond man, still dazed, was in the middle and the other two were getting impatient with having to hold him up. "What about our horses?" asked the bearded man.

"We pointed 'em toward Archer and smacked 'em with this." Bob held up the whip and threw it far out over the lake. "Don't worry, they'll likely be waiting long before y'all get back."

The blond man started to throw up.

"Oh, get him off our boat!" Bob cried in disgust. "Come on, everybody off!"

"Mister, you—"

"Shut up! Shut up! Shut up!"

The third man jerked toward the side of the boat and the other two flopped along. They all managed a sitting position on the broad ledge and then they dropped into the water, one, two, three. They were not happy about it. Arguing and yanking at each other, they lurched off in the general direction Bob had indicated.

Larrabee took up the lantern again. "You guessed shallow a few inches, looks like. Ain't no more than their heads and shoulders sticking out of the water."

Bob wrapped the pistol in a cloth and put it back under a floorboard. "No, those fellers just weren't as big once we got 'em out here."

"And what was all that business about the high tide? There's no tide on this lake."

"Just a little humor, chief. To put 'em at ease." Bob engaged the wheel again and steered the *King Payne* toward the far side of the lake, toward the Sweetwater Branch. He looked over his shoulder at the three dark heads bobbing and splashing in the dim lake. "Damn near beats killin' 'em, don't it?"

Chapter 16

"I wasn't this nervous when we charged them federal positions." Penny Ward whistled when he said an *s* now, but he didn't look half bad for a man who had been whipped and kicked senseless not three months ago. His right arm was too stiff for fiddling and it hurt again when the weather was cold and damp, but today the air was warm and dry, so warm that Mrs. Newhouse had opened the parlor windows and the afternoon sun filled the narrow room with fresh air and promise.

"There isn't anything so much to be nervous about," his best man assured him. "All you've got to do is repeat a few words after the preacher. It's not like going up before the class and saying *The Wreck of the Hesperus*."

Penny worked his shoulders in the ill-fitting coat. Not enough room. Everything seemed to be closing in on him. "I know that, Ronald, and you know that, but that still ain't the way it is."

It occurred to the teacher that a little small talk might defuse his friend's nerves.

"Did I tell you that we're going to have a poetry recitation contest at the school?"

"If I'd ever had a proper uniform I could be wearin' it— 'stead of this circus suit."

So much for a diversion thought the teacher. "Nevertheless," he said, "the gray looks well on you. And you only have to wear it for half an hour."

"Oh, no. That's where you're wrong." Penny shook his head. "This shindig's going to go on all day and into the night and anyway, I don't think I can git this thing off now but with scissors. They're going to have to bury me in it. Look at this." He made a show of trying to peel it off.

"Don't!" Ronald clapped his hand onto Penny's arm and was relieved that the bridegroom did not cry out in pain.

"Don't worry," Penny said. "It ain't comin' off no ways." He leaned toward Ronald and whispered, "I just hope the breeches ain't this hard to git off."

There was a knock at the door. "Preacher says we're about ready down here," Anna told them.

"This has got to be the craziest thing I ever thought of," Penny lisped. "I can't believe I'm doin' this."

"Penny, people get married every day."

Anna banged on the door again. "Did you hear me in there? Preacher says to come down."

Penny glanced toward the window. It was only the second floor. He could climb through without anyone seeing him.

"Penny, be brave!" Ronald was brushing off his lapels.

Something clicked in Penny's consciousness. *Men, be brave. Make your state proud of you.*

"We-we're coming out." He felt as if he should have his hands up.

Anna was at the top of the stairs. She was wearing a white dress trimmed with lace. Her braids were tied with pink satin bows. Suddenly she looked pretty and grown-up.

Penny put his hands on his hips, carefully. "You look like a bride, Miss Anna. Just who is it's gittin' married around here?"

"Not me," Anna said. She turned and bounded down the stairs. Martha was in the front hall wearing a similar outfit.

"They're bridesmaids," Ronald McMarris said, although it was common knowledge.

The narrow parlor was soon overflowing with wedding guests. Bobby La Rue was in the front room playing the piano as Caroline turned the pages in the hymnal.

"I never saw you with a page-turner before, Bobby." Duke Duforge winked at Dr. Willis.

"This isn't your everyday saloon stuff," Bobby said without taking his eyes from the music. "I dug into the bottom of the piano bench for what you're hearing."

"Well, I don't know if your playing sounds any better this way," Duke said, "but it sure *looks* better."

Caroline hadn't heard him. She was intent on the music and on the evenness of her sleeves. This was the most grown-up dress she had ever worn, fine brown wool with black trim that her mother and Mrs. Larson had sewn. As for Mrs. Newhouse, Mrs. Larson had created for her the most elegant little bonnet imaginable. It was black velvet with a shirred brim, trimmed with pink rosebuds in a *chou* of black tulle, tied beneath the right ear with a bow of black silk.

"We should have her make hats for all of us once the honeymoon's over," Tom Duforge said in his big stuffy voice. "I fancy something in silk would get more respect for the badge."

The kitchen door and the front door banged continuously at the hands of running children.

Curtis the iceman came in from the porch. He was wearing an old-fashioned brown frock coat that smelled of mothballs. "Anybody know any of them kids or are they just strays?"

"If you paid any attention you'd know who every one of 'em is," his wife said. "That'un there is ours, by the way."

"Yonder comes the bridegroom!" Curtis announced, watching Penny come downstairs. "Don't he look all roped and trussed!"

"Buck up, Penny!" Duke called from the fireplace. "Last I heard this was a wedding, not a wake!"

Penny managed a nervous smile. He walked stiffly down the stairs, afraid that each step would be the one to rip his gray coat from top to bottom.

"Still sore from the branding?" Curtis asked as Penny moved into the crowd.

"Well, now, y'all know I have a load of bachelorhood on me. Going on forty years! This here is something that's hard to practice for."

"Where are y'all going for the honeymoon?" Curtis asked.

Penny turned toward him carefully, with his shoulders pressed in. "We're going down to Cedar Keys, Curtis. Going to do some fishing for a week."

Curtis' wife looked at him in horror. "Fishing! Do you mean to tell me your bride has agreed to let you go fishing? On her honeymoon?"

"Well, we're both going, Cora! Nelda says she'd like nothin' more than to feel the pull on her line."

"Well, I never!"

Sheriff Duforge nodded toward the parlor, where people were making way for Preacher Williams. "He's looking fit today."

"You reckon tomorrow's sermon'll be something cribbed from the wedding service?" Curtis asked.

Penny forgot himself and waved him off. "He don't have to do no cribbin'. He's got a sermon up each sleeve and two in his hat!" He pulled his arm in quickly.

"What *is* the matter with you, Penny? You look like a turtle!" Anna frowned up at him.

Penny laughed. "Like that Mr. and Mrs. Turtle you girls made me turn loose on Thanksgiving that time!"

The preacher bent over and said something to Bobby and the piano player shifted from the "Papageno Polka" to something more contemplative.

"Get me 'The Maiden's Blush' pronto," he whispered to Caroline. "It's in the stack there somewhere. I'll make something up till you find it."

She glanced over her shoulder. "They're at the top of the stairs." She stooped down and began a hasty search through the music on the floor.

Bobby missed a note but recovered his stately tempo. Caroline found "The Maiden's Blush" and set it on the piano. The second page slipped to the floor and she scooped it up and restored it.

"They're coming down the stairs."

"Already? They were supposed to stay up there for this piece."

"Well, they're coming."

Bobby went into a slow arpeggio that put "The Maiden's Blush" to an early end and went into the wedding march from *Lohengrin*. "It's on top," he told Caroline. "Now, please."

She picked it up and plastered it over "The Maiden's Blush."

He nodded quickly and changed keys to get into it.

Someone had rounded up the wild children, and two of the boys were snickering. Apparently they had their own words to the dignified march.

Nelda moved gracefully down the stairs with Mrs. Newhouse at her side. She wore a gray satin dress gathered at the waist and brought back to a modest bustle. She wore kid gloves and a gray felt hat edged with black velvet and a mauve taffeta ribbon and a gray tulle veil, elegant yet simple for a bride making her second trip to the altar. Mrs. Newhouse walked beside her, smiling faintly as she concentrated on making each step graceful.

"Darned if they don't both look like brides," Curtis said, elbowing Dr. Willis.

The doctor was about to reply when the front door banged open and in walked Larrabee, breathless and disheveled, mumbling something about being thrown by Maude. "After being in harness she don't so much take to the saddle," he explained to Sheriff Duforge. He quieted down as soon as he saw how far the proceedings had gone.

Nelda Larson had not missed a beat. She and Mrs. Newhouse came into the front room and seemed to float among the guests on their way into the parlor where Preacher Williams waited, Bible in hand, with Penny fidgeting at his side. Beside him Ronald McMarris absentmindedly smoothed the knot in his big four-in-hand tie.

Curtis felt compelled to comment again. "It sure was a kindness for old Penny to have McMarris as his best man after all that trouble. There's a parcel of old rebs who've been bubblin' to do the job."

The doctor edged away from the iceman's elbow. "Well, he's just got a way of bringing out the best in folks. When it's there to bring out."

A few feet short of the altar Bobby ran out of music, but he seemed unconcerned. He stood up and closed the piano and moved toward the parlor while Caroline took up a position with her sisters, both of whom were now holding bouquets of wildflowers in their gloved hands.

The preacher's voice crackled as if the crowded room were a great tabernacle.

"Dearly beloved, we are gathered in the sight of God and these witnesses to join this man and this woman in the bonds of holy matrimony."

Penny had heard the words many times before without paying much attention to them. He wasn't paying much attention to them now because he was so worried about his coat and his behavior in front of all these people, even though he had known most of them for most of his life. Somewhere out beyond the parlor window two dogs got into a fight, snarling and yelping while angry men tried to pull them apart, but Preacher Williams pushed bravely on, for he had competed with many a Sunday morning racket during his years in the pulpit.

"...speak now or forever hold your peace."

Penny was reminded of the time up near Olustee when several shirtless soldiers had placed wagers on a cockfight and then realized that some of them were Confederates and some yanks. They had all been too embarrassed to make an issue of it so they had fallen back to their respective positions without so much as an exchange of insults. You never did know what folks would do, he told himself.

Suddenly everyone was looking at him. Preacher Williams came a step closer and all but bellowed in his ear, "And do you, Penny, take Nelda to be your lawfully wedded wife? To have and to hold, to love and cherish, in sickness and health, for richer, for poorer, till death do you part?" He dropped his voice. "Say *I do.*"

With a gasp, Penny snapped to attention, accompanied by an audible ripping.

"I do, sir!"

One look from the preacher's penetrating gray eyes kept the crowd from laughing.

Nelda was giving Penny a strange, cautious look now, as if she expected him to explode.

"And do you, Nelda, take Penny to be your lawfully wedded husband? To have and to hold, to love and cherish, in sickness and health, for richer, for poorer, till death do you part? Say—"

"I do."

"Then by the authority invested in me by the State of Florida and the Presbyterian Church, I now pronounce you man and wife! You may kiss the bride."

Penny was unprepared for that part and he had never dealt with a veil before so he started to kiss her right through it, but she deftly lifted it in time for their lips to meet unimpeded.

The preacher spread his arms, everyone burst into applause, and Bobby dropped to the piano bench and pounded out Mendelssohn's wedding march with great flourishes and glissandos.

Penny and Nelda trooped quickly through the front door with the girls following them, Caroline, Anna, and Martha, then Mrs. Newhouse, daubing her eyes, then Ronald McMarris, feeling in his pocket and muttering something about rings.

"The rings, the rings. We forgot to put on the rings."

"Oh, they'll have all night to put those on." Duke laughed, patting Ronald on the back with his big hand.

The crowd spilled into the yard where there was a long table laden with cake and punch.

"You dang near wrecked the whole wedding," Anna told Larrabee. "You ought not to get any."

He put his hands on his hips. "Well, your highness, it just so happens that my horse threw me and it took me the better part of an hour to get her back."

Anna was proud of her grammar. She had worked very hard at it since patching things up with Mr. McMarris. "I will talk to you as I wish if you are uncouth." She looked around to the edge of the yard where the offending horse was tied to a laurel oak.

"Get up there, girl! She's fixing to throw the flowers!"

Mrs. Willis shooed Anna in the general direction of the porch.

Nelda's throw was so vigorous that the bouquet sailed right over the heads of the assembled ladies and hit Anna in the face. She bent down and picked it up and everyone laughed and hooted.

Curtis' boy snorted. "That means you're next gittin' married, you cootie!"

Caroline stamped her foot. "She wasn't even trying to get it."

Her mother was eager to end the argument. "Never mind. You're neither one of you in any hurry."

Duke clapped his hand on Ronald's shoulder and spoke in confidence. "Is everything ready for tonight? Penny's waited forty years for his shivaree and we don't want to disappoint him."

They spent the first night in Nelda's room because the train for Cedar Keys didn't leave until 2:13 the next afternoon. The curtains were drawn but the noise outside was phenomenal nonetheless. Duke and his confederates had found the basset hound and got him singing "Dixie." There were also pots and pans and what sounded like a cat being swung on a fishing pole.

Penny and Nelda sat on the bed with their shoes off, letting their feet dangle.

"Now I suppose you're thinking," she said, "that this sounds like one of your battles."

"No, ma'am. It sounds a good deal worse than any one of them battles."

"Penny, you're a wonderful man. I hope you won't regret marrying me."

He turned to look at her. She looked like she was about to cry. He touched her cheek with his fingertip.

"Regret marrying you. How could I ever do that?"

"Well, we did sort of rush into it."

"If you call a year rushing."

"You know what I mean. I kind of pushed you. In a way it seems like we hardly know each other."

A firecracker shot past the window, lighting up the lace.

"I figger we know all we need to know."

"Still, there was something I should have told you." She began crying now, big tears that dropped warm onto his hand.

He was puzzled. He patted her hand gently.

"It can't be as bad as all that."

She put her head on his shoulder. "Penny, I can't have children. I know I was a great disappointment to Mr. Larson in that way. But it—it just wasn't meant to be."

Penny swallowed. Sure enough. They had never talked about children.

"Well, now, wife, don't you give it another thought, y'hear? I imagine we'll do just fine."

He pressed her to him and watched the sky light up.

Chapter 17

"Well, the damned brat doesn't look like me, that's for sure. But what does that prove?" John Howard stared at the standstill traffic and wished he could pour himself a Spanish brandy. "All of this over fifteen dollars. I'd pay a hundred times as much to be rid of that woman."

Major Dennis was annoyed at having to raise his voice above the commotion. "Go ahead if you think it'll do the trick."

Howard regretted that they had decided to leave town via this route. He'd had no idea that the streets would be blocked by a mob. The 11:29 to Fernandina came through every day. Why was it suddenly so popular? This hardly seemed the place to discuss such a delicate matter but at least the racket would cover their conversation.

"I have no idea whether she can be swayed by money. But my fear is that she really is mad. I could give her a thousand dollars today, and tomorrow she'd thank me by accusing me of siring twins."

Major Dennis smiled and tipped his hat at a couple passing by in a stylish landau drawn by matching bay mares. "You let Mary Leary squawk to her heart's content. As long as you persist in your community improvement plans you'll have nothing to fear from her." His smile faded as the landau turned toward the Courthouse Square. "But woe betide you if some other woman starts crying paternity."

Howard snapped the reins at his plodding team, not because he expected them to speed up for more than a few steps but because it made him feel better. The major still seemed oblivious to his professions of innocence in the Mary Leary matter, and seemed in fact to assume his guilt.

"There will *be* no other woman," Howard declared.

"Good for you," said the major in a patronizing tone.

"The business with the soiled doves was a botch," Howard said. "Those dunces that Choat lined up couldn't even manage to do a clean job of burning the cabins down. I hear they only burned up the inside. Then they damn near killed Penny Ward. They could've wrecked the entire plan."

"John, the problem is eliminated. The women in question have left town.

Your letters in the paper have kept you on the high ground in the issue. Is it not working as I said it would?"

"I suppose so."

"And the moss mill is prospering?"

"God, yes! I can't believe it. You'd think we had a monopoly. We're filling orders all the way to Cedar Keys."

"Of course you are. Hardly a day passes without a house or a business going up around here."

"The Island House ordered four lobby chairs and a settee."

"The men in the group know you're good for the amount needed, John. We'll have quite the enterprise before you know it. And not like this orange business. This'll be year-round cash flow."

Howard tingled at the prospect. Finally the major was letting him into the inner circle. Individually they were well-to-do, collectively they were formidable— attorneys Sanchez and Hampton, Matheson and J.B. Brown of dry goods fame, McMillan the real estate agent, and Oliver, owner of the celebrated park on the lake. They were heady company, combining their resources to develop a series of fertile farms in the south part of the county, the bounty of which would be shipped by lake and by rail to the burgeoning markets of the north. The plan was big and it was stable, but it would require a fair amount of cash up front and some time to develop the land and transportation. Agriculture was still not Howard's first choice, but there was no denying its power and importance. After all, recessions could affect the furniture business, but even in hard times people would have to eat.

They looked at two farms on the south shore of Alachua Lake and two a mile or so farther south. The first had been well kept, but the owner had dropped dead behind the plow and his widow was eager to sell. McMillan and Brown met them there. They were sipping lemonade in the shade of a magnolia tree and watching the distant boats on the lake. The widow, whose name was Aurora Smith, was deeply tanned and wrinkled, suggesting that she had spent many years working the property, yet she seemed to have no qualms about selling it and moving on. McMillan and Brown greeted the new arrivals with raised glasses. They had removed their jackets and rolled up their shirtsleeves as if they were about to take up the plow themselves.

After the briefest of introductions, Aurora Smith excused herself and trudged back toward the white clapboard farmhouse for two more glasses.

When she was out of earshot the major got down to business. "Well, gentlemen, what do you think? Will it do?"

J.B. Brown drained his glass and set it on a stump. "At this date, anything on the lake will do. The first freezer car comes through in the first week of May. We can close within the week and get ready to ship across the lake. We'll have cash flow before the ink on the title's dry."

Major Dennis looked around the property. "What about the orange trees?

How much of it's planted in oranges?"

McMillan and Brown looked at each other. The major's lack of confidence in oranges was well known. "They're here all right," Brown admitted. "More'n we thought. But most of it's beans and cucumbers. So we can let the oranges go along for the ride."

"As long as the other three places aren't full of them too," the major said.

Nervously Brown rubbed the back of his neck. "You know, in a pinch you could do worse than oranges, Leonard."

"What else is here?" The major took a prospectus from his coat pocket, held it at arm's length and began reading it. "Cotton." He looked up. "Must've gotten through '67 somehow."

McMillan shrugged. "It's only twenty acres of cotton. It's far and away truck that makes this place."

"Leonard, we know all about your dislike of cotton and oranges," J.B. Brown said. "We wouldn't've gotten into a deal that hangs heavily on either."

"Still, some folks seem to be struggling along on 'em." McMillan observed sarcastically. "I hear Walls over there is planning to struggle along with more than ever this year."

J.B. Brown looked across the dark water of the lake to the roof of a large brick house flanked by orange groves. "I could settle for struggling like that."

"We, all of us, have our hobby-horses," the major said. "You look across the lake and see cotton and oranges. McMillan sees the beginnings of a good old ante-bellum plantation. Tell them what you see, John. Go ahead. Tell them."

It was true. Howard still clung to his idea of a lake-and-canal network that would run produce from the interior of the state all the way to the northern markets. He turned away from the lake and looked at them. "It's a simple enough idea. To own the means of delivering your goods."

"John foresees a canal all the way across the state from the Gulf to the Atlantic, linking lakes and rivers into a grand aquatic thoroughfare." The major spoke without any apparent irony.

"It's an old idea," Howard conceded. "But doesn't it make sense for us to own at least a couple of *those?*" He pointed to a small sternwheeler paddling up to Aurora Smith's dock.

McMillan lit a cigar and inhaled deeply. "He may be onto something, Leonard. It's cheaper than building a railroad spur and it goes to a good deal more places."

The major laughed. "All right, gentlemen! Why don't we just buy *that* one?" He started down the slope toward the pier.

McMillan gave Brown a quizzical look and they followed Major Dennis down to the pier. Reluctantly, Howard followed.

"Back her, back her." Larrabee watched the *King Payne* edge toward the pier.

"More?" Bob called from the tiller.

"No. You stopped her on a dime."

Ten feet of water separated the boat from the pier. Larrabee picked up a coiled line and twirled it over his head.

"This ought to be good," Bob said. "Are we betting on this one?"

Larrabee pitched the rope loop at a dark piling. The rope opened up and caught.

"What did we say—twenty dollars?" Larrabee started pulling the boat toward the pier.

"I don't believe we bet on that one after all." Bob brought the stern of the boat in and they tied up, fore and aft.

"Right on the money," McMillan said with admiration.

Howard had caught up with the rest of them. "Hello, Larrabee. I heard you were spending time down here on the lake."

"You down here looking for gold, John?"

Howard rocked on his heels. "After a fashion."

"We'd like to buy your boat," the major said.

"Don't own it," Bob replied. "At least not yet. We're about two years shy of that."

"Well, who does?"

"Man by the name of Herbert Kline. Of Pensacola."

Major Dennis tapped his foot impatiently. "Of Pensacola. What's his address?"

"Can't rightly say." Bob was bringing the *King Payne* down to idle with a dangerous-looking iron lever under the canopy. "I have it back at the house."

McMillan laughed nervously, looking to see if Brown, too, saw the humor in the situation. "Leonard, you're not really going to buy this boat."

Four farmhands were on their way down the hill, young black men with hard muscles that glistened in the blinding sunshine. Without speaking, they began loading crates of the widow's figs onto the deck.

Howard was becoming increasingly uneasy, uneasy about this argument over the boat and even more uneasy about Larrabee, who knew too much about his past. This was not the time, he thought, not the time to be face to face with this person who looked at him so accusingly. Larrabee and these new business partners were a bad mix. The sooner that boat was back out on the lake, the better.

"What do you say, John?" Major Dennis stepped back to let the farmhands pass. "Should we buy this boat or shouldn't we?"

Howard looked away from Larrabee and put on an amiable smile. "Gentlemen, we still have three more farms to see and plenty of time to decide if we want a fleet of boats, a plantation or—for that matter—an amusement park. I think we should see those other farms and let the grand plans ferment for a while."

"Well said!" J.B. Brown declared. "Next farm's just half a mile by road over that way. It comes with a splendid apiary. Now *there's* something that will produce all year 'round."

Larrabee climbed onto the pier, lean and nimble and sunburned, like something the lake itself had produced.

"Just one thing, John."

The buyers had started back up the hill. They turned to see what he had in mind.

"If you buy this place, don't get careless and let it burn down. Remember Caleb Green."

The hands continued to load but the businessmen stopped and turned, all except Howard, who continued on for a few steps in the vain hope that the others would keep going.

McMillan paused in mid-stride and turned, perplexed at this boat-handler that had spoken out of turn. "What are you talking about? What do we have to do with Caleb Green?"

"Tell 'em, John. Tell 'em what you know about Caleb Green."

Howard stood a few feet uphill from his companions. He smoothed the hip pockets of his coat, aware that everyone was looking at him, Major Dennis in particular.

"Caleb Green? How can we know what became of Caleb Green? Run off in the middle of the night by the Regulators most likely. It was an election year, as you'll recall? The Democrats and the Regulators were harrying the Negroes in every way to get control of the voting. Both the major here and Congressman Walls gave eloquent speeches about it. I remember Arredonda in particular."

J.B. Brown sniffed and started back up the hill. "Damn right."

"So what does that have to do with us?" McMillan pressed. "That was two years ago. Why are you raising it here and now?"

Bob Harper was listening with great interest, using his penknife to cut the end off a new tobacco plug. He tucked a chunk into his cheek and chewed slowly.

"Ignore him," Howard said. "He may be unbalanced. The sun out here will do that to you."

The buyers seemed convinced. They resumed their walk up the hill, Howard a little faster than the rest. Only Major Dennis bothered with a single backward glance at the wild young man on the pier.

Chapter 18

For several months no one saw Mary Leary or her infant daughter. It was as if the gloomy trading post had swallowed them. But the child's name—Joan—fluttered through town, mocking the upstanding citizen who denied being her father.

On the other hand, just about everyone in town saw the Ward baby. Penny basked in the afternoon sunshine that warmed the porch of the cottage he shared with Nelda. He rocked gently on the gray porch swing, handed out cigars, and with a pride bordering on smugness, told any passer-by about little J.J., whose initials came not in honor of General Finley, as everyone assumed, but from Jefferson Jenner, the maiden names of the boy's paternal grandmother and mother.

John Howard rebuked himself for letting his mind drift from his reputation to such an inconsequential thought in the presence of important personages—the quarrelsome members of the newly formed Alachua Steam Navigation and Canal Company. They were hoping to smooth things over during an Independence Day shooting excursion on the lakeshore. The biggest sore point among them was the departure of Major Dennis, who had dropped out of the group because he didn't trust oranges or cotton. Neither did he like the idea of investing in lake transportation. But it was an idea that simply would not go away. His words still rang in John Howard's ears as the *King Payne* chugged its way down the Sweetwater Branch toward open water.

"They're all fools, John. They're catching the gold fever—the orange fever—and they don't even know it."

"Everybody's got the fever," Howard had said. "They can't plant the trees fast enough. But if we don't go into oranges, don't you suppose we should at least make some money from the men who do?"

They were in the major's office, a lavish room of walnut paneling and brocade draperies that occupied the northeast corner of the Dennis Block. Most of the upstairs was leased to the city government. The downstairs was occupied by merchants—a druggist, a photographer, a dry goods store, a novelty emporium, a boot maker—all paying rent to Major Leonard G. Dennis. Clearly the major had something going for him, but his hardheaded dismissal of cotton and oranges and steamships suggested a character flaw to Howard. The major had a temper that could flare for no apparent reason and when his temper flared he was capable of ridiculing and belittling anyone who happened to be around, white or black, rich or poor, Democrat or Republican. He was not a man to be crossed, not even a man to be joked with, and Howard regretted at once having brought up the steamship idea again.

The major's eyes flickered as he looked up from his desk.

"Do you know what they called that lake when I first came here in the '60's? Payne's Prairie. Payne's *Prairie,* John. Now where are you and your friends going to be with all your steamboats if that lake turns back into a prairie, even if Lake Alto and Lake Santa Fe and Orange Lake and Newnan's and the others in your grand scheme don't go dry? Where are you going to be? And can you afford to be there? McMillan and Sanchez and Henry Dutton—they can afford to be left high and dry. But can you? Can you afford that kind of gamble? Because that's what it is. Some things around here may be surefire but that's not one of them, and anybody who's been around here even ten years knows that."

The words had been an unassailable fortress of logic in the major's well-furnished office, but out here on the substantial lake with its acres of neat groves sloping up from the shores, those words were like so many blocks of limestone to be blasted away for the sake of progress. As the *King Payne* beat its way to the mouth of the Sweetwater Branch, a nine-mile expanse of water opened up from east to west and more than three to the south. As they turned west and left the moss-draped water oaks behind them, the partners began to feel better about the wisdom of their proud venture, the Alachua Steam Navigation and Canal Company.

"It's the best compromise to get this company off the ground," J.B. Brown declared, waving his arm over the sun-struck waters. "Some oranges, some cotton, some boats."

"Mostly boats. To carry everyone else's cotton and oranges," McMillan said. He clapped Howard on the back and commended him for his thinking. "I know it's not an original idea, John, but you're the one who pushed it."

"How long do you think for the boats?" J.B. Brown asked. Seeing that Howard had his mind on something else, he repeated the question.

"For one this size, the man in Waldo said sometime in late fall." Howard was eager to lay the subject to rest. He went on as if listening to music that nobody else was hearing. "But of course the larger the vessel, the larger the cargo. He figures we can go sixty feet, maybe more. Make a fortune on it. We should have at least three or four by this time next year." He sank back into his distant thoughts.

"How much to clear the passage between here and Newnan's?" Brown asked.

"A fraction of what you'd get out of it. A fraction. Then it's just four miles to connect Orange Lake and then dredge Orange Creek to the Ocklawaha River and you've got an excursion route all the way from the Sweetwater Branch to the St. Johns steamers."

Brown gave up on Howard for the time being and spoke to Larrabee. "You, what do you think of that? A fleet of steamboats running from here to the St. Johns."

"I say I'd dig the channels first," Larrabee told him. "Some days it's all we can do to get across this lake when the water's low."

The water was not low that day, but the places they had chosen for their shooting were inaccessible even to the *King Payne,* so the gentlemen of the Alachua Steam Navigation and Canal Company had arranged to tow a canoe that they took through the shallower water. Their first foray took them up the shore toward Rocky Point, where the ground was solid but the birds scarce. J.B. Brown contented himself with shooting a gray squirrel as it ran up the trunk of a pine tree.

"I've heard folks say they make a pretty good stew." McMillan turned the animal over with the muzzle of his bird gun.

"Then leave it for them." J.B. Brown had heard a mourning dove and was scanning the trees for it.

"Pretty sad stuff if we can't do any better than a squirrel and a mourning dove." McMillan was pointing his bird gun toward the treetops, looking for something else.

"Not the best time of year for the good kills," Howard commented. "Go to the Sugarfoot Swamp in December. Bag yourself half a dozen of those great blue herons. You might even make a few dollars on the plumes."

The mourning dove had eluded J.B. Brown and he was ambling along with his gun lowered. "I hear that Mrs.—what's her name—Ward—is doing quite well with hats. I hear she's giving Mrs. Miller a run for the money."

McMillan laughed. "Maybe we should forget about steamboats and go into the hat business!"

"What do you suppose the major would say to that, John?" J.B. Brown had his gun muzzle back in the air. He fired and brought a mockingbird down from a high branch of a loblolly pine. "It's safe, it's steady, and it don't require much cash up front."

Howard answered with a shot of his own. A second mocking bird, startled into flight, came tumbling down. "You'd have to ask him, J.B. Nobody speaks for the major but the major himself."

Their next stop was farther down on the west shore, half a mile from Josiah Walls' plantation. The ground was softer than it looked, and J.B. sank in almost to his boot tops before he made his way to safety. The others worked the canoe in closer and tramped through the palmettos until they were in knee-high grass on the edge of a bluff. Everything had flown at the sound of their coming, so they crouched and waited for the birds to return.

J.B. was about to speak when Howard raised his gun toward a water oak. He held it there for a long time and when a top branch moved, he fired.

"A hawk, by God!" McMillan raised his gun. "A black hawk! Now we're getting somewhere!"

"There's quail over here too," J.B. said. "I just saw one move over there." He strode off, stopped and fired three times into the grass.

By the time Howard and McMillan caught up with him he was stooping beside a flat place in the grass.

"Whatever it was, you missed it," McMillan said. "Looks like you found yourself a deer bed though."

The toe of Howard's boot hit something and he stooped to pick it up, a flint spear point, fluted and chipped to a killing edge. He tossed it away and went looking for the quail. At the top of the bluff they saw three hens, which took off low to the ground. They dropped all three. "One apiece," J.B. said, rubbing his gun muzzle on the sleeve of his shooting jacket. "That's a sure sign that we're a committee."

"They're good eating," McMillan commented. "You'd pay a pretty penny to have one of 'em for dinner at the Arlington."

"By the time we got 'em back home you wouldn't want 'em," J.B. said.

At the top of the bluff they reloaded and walked on silently for a hundred yards, coming into a stand of live oak and hickory. Howard stopped again, making a low arc with his rifle barrel as a petite thick-bodied bird flew by awkwardly, legs dangling. His shot brought it down.

"I want to see this one," he said.

"You won't ever find it," J.B. told him. "Something that small in this undergrowth."

Without answering, Howard pressed on in long, straight strides, undeterred by the brush.

The shot had taken away most of the head. The bird was compact, hen-shaped, and mottled brown, with long legs and beak. "What do you suppose?" J.B. didn't seem bothered by being wrong about finding it.

Howard turned it over with his boot. "Nothing fancy. A rail. A young one by the looks of it. That accounts for the long beak."

J.B. and McMillan marched cheerfully back down the bluff. J.B. broke off whistling "The Girl I Left Behind Me" to say that once the company got going they could include shooting excursions on the schedule. "There's plenty of Yankees would pay a good price to come down here shooting. What are we paying? Thirty? I'll bet we could get sixty."

"They say there's still parakeets out here." McMillan was a little out of breath from the walk. "If we could play that up we could probably get sixty." He held his hand up as if framing a sign. "Get one while they last. We'll have old eagle eye John here go out with 'em. Knock a parakeet out of the sky on every trip."

"Those fellows on the boat seem to know this lake inside and out," J.B. said. "We ought to start by hiring 'em."

McMillan nodded. "Hiring 'em or putting 'em out of business."

By now they had come to the canoe, and they carefully worked their way through the palmettos and spongy ground. As if at a signal, the mosquitoes descended upon them, making their departure hasty and awkward. J.B. was pushing the canoe off before McMillan had quite gotten in and man and gun flailed wildly.

"Get us the hell out of here before we all get killed." McMillan gasped as he laid the weapon in the bottom of the canoe.

They were sunburned, mosquito-bitten, and muddy by the time they got back to the *King Payne*, where Larrabee and Bob sat under the canopy, engaged in pleasant conversation.

"There's something wrong here," McMillan drawled. "We're paying to get dragged through the water on a string and you're getting paid to sit there and reel us in."

"Just think if you'd paid us more," Bob told him with a smile. "There wouldn't hardly be nothing left of you. Ready for the next stop?"

"We paid for it." McMillan sneezed. "We may as well see if we can stand it."

With little enthusiasm they set out for the last landing, farther down the west shore, past Walls' plantation, where the ground was solid but favored by an enormous flock of crows that made a great racket and dispersed the minute the canoe touched. The gentlemen of the committee crossed the tracks of the Cedar Keys railroad and worked their way uphill to an abandoned cotton field. Howard shot a rose-breasted grosbeak through the wing and watched it flap and tumble and right itself. J.B. finished it off with a load of birdshot.

"Did you forget to shoot, John?"

"John's just thinking about his steamship line, aren't you, John?" McMillan gave him a reassuring pat on the shoulder.

They trekked uphill, farther into the cotton field, which yielded nothing but a rattlesnake trying to swallow a toad, legs first.

"Well, now there's a sight," J.B. said with awe. They weren't more than twenty feet from the spectacle. "Figure out how to stuff that and Barnum would give you good money for it."

McMillan came closer, fascinated. The cottonmouth's jaws were unhooked and spread wide as he tried to take in the toad. The snake was no threat to anyone else. McMillan continued to approach until he was standing right beside the wriggling snake and the kicking toad. He seemed to be trying to make up his mind about something. Then, gently, he set his gun down in the old cotton row, took out a pocketknife, and cut off the snake's head, toad and all.

"Christ, Jim, what are you going to do with that?"

"I don't know, J.B., but I took a fancy to it." He set about severing the rattle.

The toad jerked himself free from the gaping jaws and took a lopsided hop into the cotton waste.

McMillan bundled the rattle into a handkerchief. He stood up and put his hands on his hips. "Well, gents, I'm all for calling it a day. How about you?"

Below them the lake stretched its nine miles to the east, glinting in the slanting sunlight. The neat rows of dark green orange trees marched up from the shore to the north and west. Above them stood a series of grand homes, sand mansions built on the bounty of the sun-soaked soil—tall, substantial and secure. Howard's gaze followed the shoreline until it merged with clouds gathering on the purple horizon.

Then his eye came back to the hilltop houses and he realized that he hated them.

"It's been a good day," McMillan was saying. "We've thrashed out some fundamental ideas about the company and had ourselves a good lark to boot. When we have the meeting on Monday night we can speak with one voice. J.B., why don't you cover the canal proposal and, John, you can talk about this idea of the fleet of—what did we say—three or four boats by this time next year?"

"Look at that lake," J.B. said with a sweep of his arm. "Four boats would just be a start, don't you think, John? We can—"

Howard fired his gun into the darkening sky, startling the other two.

"Gentlemen," he said, "count me out."

That night, after most of the respectable citizenry had gone to bed and the Independence Day celebrations had degenerated into shooting and fistfights on the Courthouse Square, Howard returned to his old entertainment at Duke's Saloon. He was boiling with anger. He was angry at having to break with the Alachua Steam Navigation and Canal Company—which was certain to succeed speedily. He was angry at having stymied his rising passion by driving the soiled doves from their cabins. He was angry at Major Dennis for exerting such a hold on him—a hold that made him think deep down that oranges and canals and steamboats were tickets to ruin, even while men investing in them prospered, complacent in their palaces.

He was angry enough to throw it all off for a night, to return to what was safe and certain—and vicious.

"If it isn't Mr. John Howard," Duke said from behind the bar. The glass he was drying broke in his hand but he seemed unconcerned. "You still drink whiskey before the first hand or have you moved on to Spanish brandy now that you're sporting a walking stick?"

"Who's here to play cards?" Howard asked, ignoring him. Other than the usual scattering of domino- and checker-players there were two cow hunters at the bar who talked it over and took up Howard's challenge. He set his stick against the arm of his chair and took a whiskey, which he set on the table without taking a drink.

The cow hunters were half drunk when they started. They were spending Spanish doubloons and freshly minted silver dollars from a Tampa payroll, and they were spending freely.

"What're your cow ponies worth?" Duke asked them as Howard's winnings piled up on the table. "At the rate he's skinning you they'll be in the next pot."

One of the cow hunters muttered a curse and caught himself before he fell over backwards. When the diversion was over, the other was holding a .45 on Howard.

In an instant the table came up and the gun went off high, putting a slug through the celebrated breast of "Liberty at the Barricade." Howard's black walking stick came down on the cow hunter's gun hand with a loud slap and the .45 hit the floor. The second man snatched it up and Howard broke the stick over the side of his head. The first found himself lying on his back with the sharp stub of the stick hard on his throat.

"Get out," Howard whispered as he pressed the sharp stick harder.

The cow hunters scrambled to their feet, snatched up their hats, and bolted from the room. Howard tossed the jagged stick away and looked at the circle of men staring at him. He smoothed his shirt and sleeves.

"See to my winnings, will you, Duke? Happy Independence Day, gentlemen."

He picked up his hat and walked away from the scattering of cards, broken furniture, dollars and doubloons.

Chapter 19

It was Preacher Williams who talked the judges into letting Anna run in the foot race. The gentlemen of the Alachua Steam Navigation and Canal Company were not eager to admit a girl to the contest to promote their new company, but this particular girl was so adamant that they decided excluding her would give the whole affair a black eye.

"What can be the harm?" J.B. Brown had said as their Friday night meeting at the Varnum Hotel began to deteriorate into individual arguments. "The worst thing that'll happen is she'll lose! Then we'll be able to put the whole fuss behind us. Who knows? We may even get some extra publicity from it."

The treasurer, B.F. Jordan, was shaking his head. He slid the cuspidor closer with the toe of his patent leather boot. "If she gets hurt, you'll get *bad* publicity." He was trying to say that an injured girl would reflect badly on the safety of the company, but his fellow board member, Dr. Phillips, was talking at the same time.

"How's she going to get hurt? It's only a foot race for God's sake."

"Those boys are going to be more than just running to win," J.T. McMillan said. He turned to the doctor with an admonishing look. "Didn't you ever run for a prize, Ben? There's as much shoving as in one of those football games. How are we going to look if that girl comes out with her pretty nose bloodied?"

The doctor had to think about that.

"We could make a rule that—"

McMillan cut him off. "And make it look like we're regulating the race just for her? I say just let her run till she gives out. Chances are they won't bother with knocking her over if she's at the back of the pack."

It was a point well taken. If the girl never took the lead she'd be safely out of the way, and that would be that.

"I still don't like it," Ben Jordan said. "The whole idea of the contest was to put a good face on things—to put that ugly break with John Howard behind us and to launch a bright, shiny image in the county. Now instead we've got the makings of another set-to. But if the preacher wants to take the responsibility on his shoulders—more power to him."

Anna had done badly in school for the entire week. Whenever the boys got the chance they teased her about her intention to run in the race, all except Billy Willis, who hung back whenever the goading started.

The race was from the Courthouse, north and east to the summer home of J. T. McMillan, which required crossing the Sweetwater Branch. The nearest footbridge, an old log structure, was on a path in oak woods about three-quarters of a mile upstream. From there it was another mile through Bailey's fallow cotton fields, and most of a quarter mile up a grassy rise to McMillan's house, where the runners would be greeted by a hoard of picnickers and the board of directors of the Alachua Steam Navigation and Canal Company. And there, right there at the picnic, the prize would be awarded—a genuine cracker mare descended from the horses of Ponce de León.

It was a long way—two miles—and Anna's heart sank when she thought of what she had gotten herself into, fighting for the right to race even though she knew deep down that she could never outrun a boy for half that distance. What would she do when she finally came across the finish line dead last? She would never live it down. Should she pretend to come down with some terrible disease the night before the race? Or maybe two nights before, just to make it more believable? Maybe some small but genuine injury such as a bruised toe or some kind of cut. She couldn't picture living with that. She didn't know what to do.

She knew the first mile pretty well, the part up to the old footbridge. She had played in those woods many times when she felt like stretching her mother's permission. The trees were big and the path was perilous with roots. Wading the creek was not an option because it was deep and fast, even in the winter, and alligators sometimes attacked those daring enough to swim in it. And besides, even in dry clothes, the rest of the course would be tough going.

So far as she knew, the path on the far side of the Sweetwater was flatter at least, and went straight to Mr. McMillan's house. But she had seen boys race before, had seen how they jostled and pushed and tripped each other when they thought no one was looking. Plenty could happen to a boy in two miles, even more to a girl. After school on Friday, the day before the race, she broke away from the taunts, went home, did her egg-hunting and mending as fast as she could, and then asked to be excused to play at Iris' house.

Her mother looked up at her from the teacups she was bleaching.

"Anna, I want to talk to you about this race."

"Yes, Mama?"

Mrs. Newhouse took a breath, sizing up her daughter. Anna was tall for thirteen, as tall as some of the boys her age, and browned by the sun. She was tough and sinewy with strong hands and a willful look in her brown eyes, but her face had begun to take on a delicacy. She was still wild but not the least bit boyish. Her daughter was a strange creature now, on the verge of blossoming into a pretty and graceful being.

"I want you to know that this whole contest business is a mystery to me. I don't think I'll ever understand why you have thrown yourself into it."

"No, ma'am."

"It just doesn't make sense."

Anna started to speak but thought better of it. She rubbed her nose. She didn't know how her mother could stand the sharp smell of the bleach.

Her mother put her hands on the girl's shoulders and looked at her for a long time. "Just this, little Anna. As long as you're so stuck on doing it, run that race for all you're worth, but stay away from those boys. Don't let them hurt you. Because they will if you let them."

Anna nodded. "Yes, ma'am."

She never went to Iris' house. She made for the Sweetwater Branch as fast as she could without attracting attention, gathering her skirts as she took fast strides with her long legs. She wanted to walk the course again, at least the part up to the old footbridge, and she had very little time to do it. The path was every bit as bad as she remembered it—a thousand places to stub a toe. It had been a rainy winter and the creek was as fast as ever, full of snags and dark forms that drifted, caught, and lay vague and half-submerged, grim and menacing in the brown water.

The hulking oaks were everywhere, drying their lacy gray moss on a warm south wind. They lined up so close to the creek that some of them leaned over the water at dangerous-looking angles. Anna walked on, feeling sharp acorns and gnarled roots under her bare feet. She was still a good half-mile from the footbridge when she saw something that caught her imagination. She might not be able to outrun those boys and she couldn't outfight them. But she might be able to outsmart them. She might be able to win this race.

She'd had no idea there would be so many of them.

Apparently word of the big race had gone far out into the county because the Courthouse Square was full of boys. The usual market day crowd filled the damp streets and cramped stores and they seemed to have brought with them an army of boys, barefoot and boisterous, bragging and braying and bullying their way through the heart of town. Anna took some comfort in the numbers, thinking that she would be lost in the crowd, although she preferred not to think about the added humiliation she would suffer if she came in last in so large a field.

Sheriff Duforge sat astride his dapple-gray mare and explained the rules loud enough for everyone to hear.

"All the runners have to be between the ages of ten and fifteen! The course is from this rope here, along the Sweetwater Branch and across to the first step of J.T. McMillan's house a mile north and a mile east! First one across the ribbon takes the prize! The law will deal firmly with any killings or assaults! Wait for the gun—then run!"

With that he jabbed his .45 into the air a couple of times just for the fun of seeing a few false starts, and when everyone had settled back down, he fired a blast that sent the crows flapping from the Courthouse roof.

The runners were off with a shrill roar, pouring down Liberty Street, trampling shrubs and setting off every dog in that part of town. Picket fences came down, horses shied, worried mothers shielded children in their arms. Boys perching in orange trees cheered them on, some of them with moldy fruit that exploded on heads and backs.

The sheriff laughed from atop his mare. "This makes General Sherman's march look like a cakewalk! What have we turned loose on the world?"

At first it was too crowded for fighting. Anna was swept along with the roaring river of runners until they came to the Sweetwater Branch, where the racecourse turned abruptly left into the narrow path. There, beyond the following of adults, the fists came out and runners began to go down. Sheriff Duforge's son Barkley pushed over two smaller boys, one of whom grabbed at his feet as he fell, taking Barkley down with him. Another boy was throwing wet sand in the faces of everyone who came near him. Anna kept to one side of the path and kept pace with the mob to avoid attention, but after a hundred yards she felt a pair of hands hit her between the shoulder blades and she struck the ground hard.

She got up, ignoring the laughter of the boys who ran past her, and started walking, a brisk, swinging gait that enabled her to keep the runners in sight. When they had passed, even the smaller ones, she began running again, another three hundred yards, until she finally spotted the tree she had found the day before, a tall live oak pressed close to the edge of the rushing creek, from which a long severed vine dangled almost to the ground. She tested it, pulled with all her strength and found it secure high on a thick branch. She gripped it and pulled herself up, two, three feet into the air, and it held. Then she pushed away from the trunk and began swinging, swinging in a broad arc as if she were on the ride at Oliver Park. Back and forth she swung until she was way over the creek, hanging on for all she was worth. With one final kick of her legs, she sailed fast and sure beyond the dangerous water. She was late letting go and fell against the bank, but she scratched her way to the top, shook herself, and began running through the woods.

She couldn't remember her geometry exactly, but she knew that if she could hold a straight path she would be running the long edge of a triangle while all those boys would be taking the other two sides—if she could hold the straight line despite the absence of a path. Her dress was a curse here because every weed and bush caught at it, and the hem interfered with her long legs. But she was glad that she had decided to wear shoes. She ran her jagged way through the oaks and hickory trees, certain that she had lost her direction. When she came to a fallow cotton field she cut back to the north, thinking it would correct her angle, but the field and woods were strange to her and she had only the direction of the sun for her guide. Once she thought she heard the boys far behind her and to the left, across the field and through the woods, but the sounds died away quickly and she decided that it had only been squabbling crows.

She came to a set of grassy ruts running through high grass and she was tempted to follow them. But they seemed to be going northwest to southeast instead of the due east she needed, so she ran on, bearing slightly to the left to counteract her tendency to bear right. She came into a blackberry thicket and forced her way through it despite the constant ripping and snagging.

How far had she come? She had no idea. The house was about a mile from where she had crossed the creek and it seemed to her that she had gone twice that far. She was short of breath, torn, dirty, and perspiring. On she went, propelled by great awkward strides that brought her again into the woods— not the same woods, she fervently hoped—and broke through to a vast field of ripening strawberries. Now she could choose her direction again and make good time if only she knew which way to go. She stopped and bent over, catching her breath, and then she heard the sound again, louder this time and more distinct—shouts echoing through the woods far to the north.

She ran diagonally across the strawberry field, keeping the shouting to the left and behind her, hoping to intersect the running path ahead of the boys. At the far corner of the field she came to another rut of a road and this time she took it, following its leisurely curve through scrub oak and weeds until it crossed a cow path—*the* path, she wished aloud. She could hear the boys better than ever now, but she couldn't tell just where they were. She made her best guess, taking them to be directly behind her, and sprinted down the path on aching feet.

They were gaining on her, which made her nervous, but also convinced her that she was on the right path, so she ran even harder, throwing her arms in wide arcs and pulling the warm air deep into her hurting lungs. She wanted to stop now, just for a quick rest, but she knew she couldn't because she would never get her heavy legs back up to speed again. The path seemed endless and the noise behind her louder and louder. Then, suddenly, the tall grass gave way and she was in a mowed field that sloped up to a white two-story house. The field was crowded with people sitting on blankets. One man wearing a yellow hat took a drumstick out of his mouth and said, "Are you seeing what I'm seeing?"

People started laughing and hollering and Anna thought she must surely have made some terrible mistake, coming in long after the boys or at the wrong place, but then a middle-aged woman in a mauve dress approached her at a quick walk saying, "Run, honey, run! They're gaining on you!"

She was so tired and excited that for a moment she forgot exactly where the finish line was, but she was reminded by a chorus of well wishers who pointed her toward the gray front steps of the McMillan house. Ahead she could see a twisting of red, white, and blue crepe paper. A final desperate sprint carried her through it.

It seemed as if the entire town had come out to see the end of the race, everyone she had known in her life. Hands came out to congratulate her, to pat her on the back, and still the laughter continued. She was sitting on the steps, gasping, feeling the blood return to her legs, when the first of the boys broke into the field and looked up, confused.

"She beat you, boy! She beat every one of you!" J.B. Brown came up leading a tall, slender, white mare with a cinnamon mane and tail."I imagine you'd like to have your prize now," he told Anna. "She could come in handy getting home—unless you want to run back!"

Everybody thought that was very funny since the poor girl was red-faced, tattered, and dirty, and still catching her breath.

Anna stood up on shaky legs and stared at the horse, feeling strangely out of place. What had she accomplished after all? She had no use for a horse and she had never taken any pride in her running, so why had she gone through this ordeal? She couldn't quite remember.

"I can't believe you whupped all these boys in a foot race," J.T. McMillan was saying.

As they came up the hill, sweaty, bruised and bewildered, the boys had a hard time believing it too.

Chapter 20

The first touch had done it. The horse was named Tuscawilla after the daughter of Chief Micanopy. Like others of the cracker breed, she had a short, strong back and neck, but Penny pointed out that she was a little lofty because her withers were as high as Anna was tall. The noisy crowd at McMillan's house had made her ill at ease and, seeing the fear in her gray eyes, Anna had reached up to stroke her mane, which settled the horse a bit, giving Anna the idea that she had some special calming effect on her new possession.

Anna's mother had not expected the situation. It was still a mystery as to how the girl had come out ahead of all those boys. Anna had been quiet and vague on the subject since the rules of the race simply stated that the first runner to make it from the Courthouse to McMillan's via the Sweetwater Branch would be declared the winner.

Her mother had questioned the acceptance of the prize because they had no place to keep a horse. Then Penny had stepped in. "You can keep her on that parcel we bought," he had said as if refusal was out of the question. "The grass ain't the best but it's already fenced in."

"What parcel?" Emma Newhouse had asked.

Nelda pointed out the kitchen window. "He means that half acre of woods right there. We bought it last fall though I've never been sure why."

"To plant oranges I suppose," Preacher Williams had suggested.

"Nope, just to set there for a while. Like you're doin' with the old turpentine property. It's good to own a parcel of land even if you don't do nothin' with it for a while. Makes a body feel better just knowing it's there."

So now there was a horse on it—Tuscawilla, the beautiful and high-strung companion of Anna—browsing on grass and beggar weed and the occasional garden carrot or handful of oats pilfered from the feed store by the depot. Anna had been on a horse only a few times in her life and Tuscawilla apparently had carried a rider only a few times in hers, so they had some work to do. When Larrabee and Bob came up for one of their Saturday night visits, Anna took Larrabee by the sleeve and showed him the proud mare trotting the fence line.

"She looks a little twitchy to me," he said after watching her for a while.

"I heard you won her but nobody seems to know how you pulled it off."

Anna smiled. "I beat all them boys in a foot race—all *those* boys."

"That's what I heard. But why and how is what I'm trying to figure."

"Well, the why was to prove I could do it." The answer was an afterthought, but she gave it with a certainty that made it sound obvious.

"That figures," he said. "But how'd you outrun all of those boys—swing a vine across the creek?"

Her look said that he had caught her off guard.

He chuckled. "I've heard that speculated on, but of course nobody puts much credence in it because they know ain't any girl can swing that creek, especially since no boy seems to've thought of it."

"Well, you let 'em say what they like." She held his look for a moment with a strange little smile.

"All right. But how do you plan to turn this beast into a riding horse?"

"I thought you could tell me. You know horses, even if Maude did throw you that one time."

"Oh, I've been thrown plenty and sometimes I was asking for it. You got a saddle?"

"No."

"That'd make it a whole lot easier."

Tuscawilla held her head high, caught something on the wind and trotted farther down the fence line.

"You might've been better off winning the five dollars for second place," he said.

It was a sore topic and she turned her head, flipping her long brown braids from shoulder to shoulder.

"What's your mother have to say about you getting on that horse?"

"She was so surprised at first that she didn't know what to say. She would rather I'd won a milk cow. Now she says riding horses is unladylike."

He blushed, but the evening light was dim enough that she didn't see it.

"So will you help me or not?"

On Sunday morning he went down to the White Pine Stable and paid half a dollar to borrow a worn saddle and bridle that he carried back to the house and set on the fence. Anna watched as he threw the bridle over his shoulder, climbed the fence and followed the mare around for a few laps. Several times the horse let him get within an arm's length before she trotted out of range. Each time he walked patiently after her, studying her movements and gradually wearing her down.

"How long's this going to take?" asked a voice at the fence. It was Martha, elegant in a gray dress, white gloves and a straw hat with a red ribbon.

"What time's the dance?" Larrabee asked from the pen.

"It's church," she said solemnly. "I'm to recite the books of the Old Testament today. Mama says you're to come right now, Anna, or else."

"We're just starting to get somewhere," Anna complained. "How can I leave now?"

"Well, you have to. Caroline's in the pageant, too, remember."

"How can I forget? She's been blabbing about it for two weeks. You'd think she was Mrs. Doig or maybe the Queen of Siam."

"Mama says if you're going to have a—"

Anna rolled her eyes and peeled herself away from the fence. "If I'm going to have a horse then I have to be a slave for life." Exasperated, she made a sound in her throat that caused Tuscawilla to stop and look her way.

"Guess it's just you and me," Larrabee told the high-strung mare. "You stay right there and we'll get along fine."

Anna had so much running through her head that church was scarcely more than a nuisance to her. Mrs. Polk played the wheezing, droning melodeon for what seemed like ages. Even with the windows thrown wide open, the heat was stifling and made all the worse by the oppressive mix of perfume, pomade and perspiration.

Caroline's pageant seemed to go on and on. It had something to do with Deborah slaying some unsuspecting general. The boys had a hard time squelching their enthusiasm when she plunged the dagger into his throat. But even in her more attentive moments Anna had no idea why Deborah was killing the general or even if the assassination was a good thing or bad, although Caroline seemed quite convincing in the part and drew enthusiastic applause.

During Preacher Williams' sermon on the Beatitudes, her thoughts returned to her horse, and she twitched and wriggled in the hard pew, wondering what progress Larrabee was making with her.

At last Preacher Williams pronounced the final benediction: "May the Lord watch between me and thee while we are absent one from the other." Mrs. Polk burst into some chipper little hymn tune that seemed to be missing a few notes, and people rose and moved into the aisle. Although Preacher Williams had lived in their house for as long as she could remember, the three girls and their mother went through the formality of shaking his hand at the church door and saying a few words about the sermon and the day.

"And what a wonderful performance," he said, smiling as he shook Caroline's gloved hand. "We'll all be looking forward to the next one."

Anna missed the remark completely because, looking down the sunny street, she caught sight of Larrabee, tall in the saddle, trotting toward the church on Tuscawilla. She started to run toward him, but he put his hand up to stop her. He brought the horse down to a walk, climbed off and led her to the church steps.

"She's got as smooth a gait as you could want, but she's still more than a mite skittery, so you'd best not make any sudden motions around her."

"Can I ride her?" Anna raised a hand to pet the mare's neck.

"Anna, your gloves!" Her mother watched disapprovingly from the church steps.

The girl settled for a quick pat that the horse tolerated with only a slight pulling away.

Preacher Williams finished shaking hands and came down the steps. "She's a fine horse, isn't she? Just a little unsettled."

The mare jerked her head back as if in agreement.

"You'd think those folks at the steam navigation company could've smoothed her out a little before making a prize of her," Larrabee said. "This is a passel of horse for a girl to handle."

"I'm fourteen," Anna informed him. "Fourteen tomorrow. So I think I'm big enough to handle a few things." She became aware of the edge in her voice, smiled, and added, "especially this one, now that you've gotten the saddle on her."

At times it seemed that this horse had taken over her life. She had to be watched and worried over, soothed and saddled and walked every day, and she was often difficult to catch. And on top of that, Anna was now eight dollars in debt for tack and feed. Still, the more time she spent with Tuscawilla the more it seemed the horse responded to her and the better she could read the horse's motions. She knew when to pursue and when to let up, and she had never yet had to resort to a whip although plenty of people had advised her that a switching was the quickest way to discipline a horse.

School ended on April twenty-third, giving Anna more time to work with Tuscawilla, but the hours were not as vast as she had envisioned because she had more chores to do than ever, especially cooking, and she had to scour the town looking for jobs to pay off her debt for the saddle. She discovered a Negro doctor with an office behind the Varnum who paid a penny apiece for any kind of small bottles she could deliver to him, so she kept her eye out for those. She kept an eye on feisty little J.J. one time when Nelda and Penny had to go to Jacksonville on business. By the end of the month she had paid Sheriff Duforge a dollar and a quarter.

"I believe Barkley is actually glad that you won the race," the sheriff told her. "If he'd won, the Duforge family would all be in the poorhouse supporting that horse."

In the time left she did make progress in her riding. Larrabee came up on Maude once or twice a week and showed her how to guide Tuscawilla with her legs and to use the reins sparingly.

"Pull on her face and she'll just fight you all the more," he told her.

After a few weeks she was proud to say that she had fallen off a few times but she had never been bucked off. Tuscawilla had quieted down that much. Some things still made the horse balk suddenly or jump sideways, but Anna got better and better and spotting them ahead of time and working around them. Tree branches on the ground she apparently took for enormous multi-headed snakes, and puddles turned into fathomless wells of death, but Anna learned to avoid them all, and by summer she knew what to expect from Tuscawilla and the horse knew what to expect from her.

Although Caroline thought horses were big, dirty, unpleasant monsters, she began to envy Anna the freedom that Tuscawilla represented. Once her chores were done, Anna was free to roam town from where Liberty Street crossed the Sweetwater Branch all the way west to Hogtown Creek, which provided many a pleasant prospect of tall loblolly pines and spreading oaks and the sight of many a pleasant house and cottage going up. The north was forbidden because of its desolation and the bad incident associated with the forlorn half-burned cabins up that way. The south was similarly off-limits because the planing mill and foundry and moss mill harbored hard-looking men.

One afternoon in August when Caroline was feeling particularly oppressed by the demands of maintaining a restaurant and boarding house she resorted to asking Anna if she might borrow Tuscawilla for an hour.

"No," said Anna. "But you can ride with me if you want."

It was exactly what she wanted. She was nervous about riding that horse, or any horse, by herself. After reciting to her mother their litany of duties done, the girls received permission to ride until half an hour before suppertime.

"And stay on the road," Mrs. Newhouse reminded them before they had time to get out of the kitchen.

Caroline looked at the ceiling and said under her breath, "As if we haven't heard that a hundred times."

Anna bribed Tuscawilla with a handful of oats, part of a bushel bought dearly from Ralph Pine, and before long the two girls were off at a trot with the granddaddy oaks and pert young orange trees seeming to fly past.

"Slow her down," Caroline demanded. "This is very uncomfortable."

"You have to get used to it," Anna said over her shoulder. "You have to move with the horse."

"Well, not today. I'm being shaken to shreds back here."

Anna patted Tuscawilla on the neck, which always dropped her from a trot to a walk.

Still they were at the edge of town in no time, passing the Dutton Bank with its cool-looking shade trees and huge arched windows. Across the street and down a bit Dutton had just broken ground for what Penny said would be a fine two-story house for his daughter. Behind that was the moss-covered school, not looking so out-in-the-woods now. Here and there on the way west modest houses had gone up, bringing down the pines to make their yards. But Liberty Street quickly tapered into a meandering double track that seemed headed for the wilderness.

It was late afternoon and very warm, but gathering clouds kept the day from being downright hot. The sisters pressed on, with Caroline clinging to Anna's waist, as the sky grew darker.

"It's fixing to rain for sure," Anna said at last, and the horse's ears turned as if expressing concern.

"Not for a while yet." Caroline clung more tightly to Anna's waist. "It's been building up most of the day. I hope it comes down good and hard once we get back home. It'll keep things slow at the cafe."

She always called it a cafe, which sounded fancier than anything else you could call it. Penny referred to the Newhouse dining room as an eatery.

"Mama says we need the money," Anna said.

"Not that bad. Not tonight. I'm tired of carrying food to people I don't even know. I almost miss the days when it was just the boarders."

Anna didn't answer. She was preoccupied with the saddle. She bent low over the horse's neck and ran her hand over the cinch.

"I thought so, you old fraud."

Caroline wondered where Anna had gotten such a word.

"What's the matter?"

"She puffed out when I put the saddle on. Now the girth is loose. We'll have to get off and tighten it."

"Up there's a house," Caroline said. "We can stop there."

"Don't you know what that is?" Anna asked. "It's the trading post. Old Mary Leary and Sam live there. Barkley says she's a witch."

"Well, Barkley's a dunce," Caroline scoffed. "I never heard such nonsense."

"Well, she isn't completely latched either," Anna insisted. "I don't want to go there."

"Then fix it here, silly. If you like the looks of this tree any better."

It was the old lightning oak where Anna and her mother had first seen Larrabee lying by the side of the road. The tree towered and arched in every direction, calling attention to the black scar high in its twisted center trunk.

The woman seemed to emerge from the tree itself. Hollow-cheeked and raven-haired she was beside them before they knew it, her eyes dark and shining like the blackberries gathered in her apron.

Anna's hand froze on the girth. Caroline stared as if mesmerized.

"Ya'll young'uns ought not to be out with this here storm fixing to break." She spoke in a rasping monotone that reminded Anna of rotten fence rails breaking.

"We ain't—" In her anxiety Anna lapsed into her old way of speaking. "We ain't but fixing to turn 'round here, Mary Leary."

She thought that by saying the name of the thing she feared she would somehow gain control over it, or herself.

One by one the berries were dropping from the fold in Mary's apron. She reached up and laid a hand on the saddle horn. Tuscawilla twitched.

"It's a proper storm brewing, sure. Ye can smell it! Smell the brimstone in the air." She turned her head as if hearing distant thunder inaudible to human ears. "Sure, old Scratch'll be knocking over his ten-pins tonight!"

Caroline shrank back on the horse's rump as far from the woman as she could, marveling at the oddly young looks that went with the strained old voice.

"Storm on a full moon can work a powerful magic on a woman. Ye know that."

Anna nodded, having no idea what the woman meant.

"Yes, ma'am."

"Ye know that."

"Yes, ma'am," Caroline echoed. She pulled back farther at the sight of Mary's hand wriggling spider-like on the saddle horn.

Mary's hand came away and went to her flat belly. "It was during a storm on a full moon that I was got with child."

Caroline felt as if some part of the earth had cracked open, revealing a dark corner of hell.

"That John Howard," Mary said, "the devil's disciple, got me with child and now won't give me my due though he has King Solomon's mine as his own."

Caroline was listening to a small noise in the distance, like a cat howling in the night. As it grew louder it took on a human quality, like a child crying. The woman heard it too. She cocked her head toward the old trading post that stood low on the hillside, half-log, half-clapboard, darkening in the gray-green light.

"Mind ye the storm on the full moon," she warned. She released the saddle horn and grinned. Her teeth were small and yellow, like kernels of corn. "Mind ye," she said again.

But Anna had already turned the horse and kicked her into a lope that had Caroline hanging on for her life.

Chapter 21

Caroline looked in the mirror and felt the clasp at the back of her neck. "It's not right, I tell you. It's too loose or something."

Her sister waved her hand between Caroline and the mirror. "It's all right. Take my word for it. It's all right now and it was all right the first ten times you looked at it."

Now Caroline was peering around the interfering hand, frowning.

"Oh, for pity's sake, what is it, Caroline?"

"Do you think my mouth is crooked?"

"No, I think your *brain* is crooked. Of course your mouth is crooked! Why shouldn't it be? A crooked mouth shows personality, Caroline."

"I think one eye is higher than the other."

"Will you stop? You look fine. The play will be fine. We went over your lines ten thousand times. So many tines *I* even know 'em—backwards and forwards. 'I have lived my life for France—France for life my lived have I!' You can't go wrong unless a sinkhole opens up and swallows all of Roper's Hall."

"Oh, I wish it would! Roper's Hall is too big for the audience we're going to have. I just know it! We'll just have a few miserable people fidgeting in the front rows. I'll be embarrassed to death! How many people are out there now?"

Anna went to the corner of the stage and looked through a crack at the edge of the curtain. "It's starting to fill up."

"How many?" Caroline pressed. "How many would you say?"

"You're going to see for yourself in about five minutes. There's Mama and Martha. I don't see Preacher Williams but there's Penny and Nelda and J.J.—"

"Oh, I do hope J.J. behaves himself."

"Oh, I do hope so too," Anna echoed loftily.

The rest of the cast started to come into the wings. There was King Louis the Sixteenth in a red velvet coat trimmed with rabbit fur and topped with an iron crown cast at the Doig Foundry and painted gold. It was a heavy crown and the king tended to hang his head even in his proudest moments. There was a ragtag bunch of revolutionaries of both sexes and a frowning judge sweating under a long heavy wig made of carpet pad. On his way in, one of the revolutionaries bumped into the guillotine, nearly knocking it over, but Mr. McMarris saved the moment by catching the cardboard blade before it could come to any harm.

Even Anna had her doubts about the play, an awkwardly worded translation of the original *Marie-Antoinette* by Constantine Boelly. It had lines like "My heart hops up at the sight of you" and "May this bright blade bring your succor."

"What does he mean *bring your sucker?*" Caroline had asked, to which Mr. McMarris had replied that it might be a misprint or maybe some kind of French expression.

Caroline had begun to long for the simple little pageant they had put on last spring. In *The Pilgrims* she had starred as Pocahontas saving John Smith from getting his head whacked off by the Indians. It was simple and dramatic and the costume had felt a good deal better than this one. Now she was corseted in a stuffy, oversized getup, saddled with awkward lines that were hard to remember, and on top of that, this time she couldn't keep her man from being decapitated. In fact, she couldn't even save her own neck. What kind of play was that where the beautiful heroine gets her head cut off? But she had been overruled by the drama committee, particularly the boys, who had wanted something with shooting in it but were quite willing to settle for a couple of beheadings.

If only she had left well enough alone and retired from the stage after that simple, politely-received Pocahontas! Now she was in deep, about to make a fool of herself and bring her blossoming career crashing down in laughter and humiliation.

It was worse than that. Anna had not been forthright about the size of the crowd. On a good night Roper's Hall could bring in 250 people. A magician, a temperance lecture, the man who played musical saws, even the poetess whose verses were unintentionally so bad that crowds showed up to laugh at them behind her back. All had filled the place. When the curtains parted a good fifteen minutes late for *Marie-Antoinette,* Caroline was staggered to see just thirteen people in the audience, most of them sitting several rows back as if they wanted to be near the egress. Two of them were the squirmy, unpredictable little J.J. and the youngest of the smelly, ever-growing O'Dell clan.

"The O'Dells may not like bath water, but they do take to plays." Billy Willis, revolutionary, editorialized through his cotton beard.

Barkley was in the play thanks to his mother, who had drafted him despite his graphic protests. As a gesture of defiance, he had rubbed his beard in the dirt to make it look particularly realistic. "I heard tell of a girl who, no matter how many times she took a bath, smelled like a fish," he said backstage. "Just like a fish. She run off with a old man whose nose had been twisted off in a fight."

Caroline was still counting the audience. Thirteen people. Two of whom were likely to commit some gross breach of etiquette at any moment.

"Get ready," Mr. McMarris was saying. "It's show time." He went onstage and began addressing the audience.

It occurred to Caroline that there had been more people in the audience during some of the rehearsals. Where were they all? She tried to imagine the excuse each parent, each brother and sister had made not to attend *Marie-Antoinette*. Then she had a terrible moment of self-doubt. What if they were all staying away because she had the lead role?

She peeked at the faces of the people sitting on the hard cedar benches. Her mother, Nelda and Penny all seemed alert and attentive. Penny had taken off his coat and thrown it over the back of the bench. Certainly there was plenty of room for it. His suspenders were bright red. Nelda had no need to take off her hat. No one was behind her to have his view blocked. J.J. and the O'Dell child were playing some kind of hand game that was causing J.J. to wave his arms until Nelda held him closer to quiet him down. The O'Dell parents and next youngest child were staring, gawking actually. They couldn't keep their eyes off the guillotine.

Then there was Mrs. Willis and Barkley's mother, who applauded wildly after Mr. McMarris' opening address, even after he started floundering in the curtain on his way backstage.

The words of the young thespians rang terribly hollow in the empty hall. Preacher Williams had come in late with Martha and sat beside Mrs. Newhouse. Having missed the first few minutes of the play, he was probably trying hard to figure out what was going on. He leaned over and whispered something to her mother and nodded as she said something in his ear, apparently summarizing the plot.

Caroline went through her lines mechanically, taking and giving cues dutifully and prompting Billy once when he fluffed his short dual role as the king's minister. Her spirits sank lower and lower as the horrible night dragged on.

Then, in the third act, something happened.

It was the pivotal act of the overlong play, in which the doomed queen first realizes that she is likely to perish at the hands of the revolutionaries. Caroline's distracted thoughts had drifted back to the summer's encounter with Mary Leary, and slowly she began to take on some of Mary's wildness. Marie-Antoinette, for all of her forced and stilted lines, began to lose her mind as execution loomed inevitable. Caroline began speaking with a voice not her own. It was as if someone—could it be the real Marie-Antoinette—had begun to speak through her voice. The lines flowed and the cotton and pasteboard revolutionaries became real, the cardboard blade of the guillotine—a razor-sharp instrument of death.

The audience picked up on the change in the air and so did the other players. When the king went to his doom at the end of the third act, Marie-Antoinette became an increasingly tragic figure, unable to face the danger she was in, planning intrigues for her escape instead of reforming her attitudes toward the plight of her countrymen. Caroline was both haughty and distraught, increasingly confused and deluded so that even Barkley, who had agreed to be in the play just because he wanted to cut off some heads, stopped smiling beneath his beard and began to take pity on the condemned queen.

When it was over and she had laid her neck on the guillotine and the curtains swept shut just as the horrible blade came down, everyone just sat there, not sure what they had been seeing. They had come expecting some pleasant pageant, some charming amalgam of bungled lines and cutout characters and instead something remarkable had happened on the stage in Roper's Hall, something that had to sink in for a few ticks of the wall clock. Behind the curtain Caroline got up from the guillotine with the feeling that time had stopped. Everyone was so still. Mr. McMarris stood with his hand on the curtain as he gazed out into the hall. Barkley waited at the instrument of death, forever fifteen, holding the irritating cotton beard as he searched each face waiting for someone to move. Billy Willis held himself straight and tall as if expecting the pronouncement of a judge. Then the preacher stood and beat his big hands together. One by one the others joined him. Even little J.J. stood on the bench, clapping enthusiastically, grinning and looking up at his parents for approval.

The curtain parted and, timidly, the cast members took their bows. Caroline wasn't sure who everyone was clapping for—her or that mysterious voice that had begun to speak through her. But as the applause persisted, she put her doubts out of her mind, smiled, continued to curtsy, and warmed to the acclaim, happy that certain disaster had magically turned into a wonderful if mysterious triumph.

Within a few days it was being said at washtubs and in church, at the barbershop and over backyard fences and clotheslines that one performance of *Marie-Antoinette* had not been enough, that for legitimate reasons many people had been unable to see the play, which, after all, had not been ballyhooed, had in fact been put on practically in secret. Mr. McMarris saw an opportunity to garner some financial support for the little moss-covered school and suggested that for ten cents a head—a nickel for children under ten—the play might be re-staged at a more convenient time.

It had not occurred to him to consult the players, and now Caroline was beginning to feel more than a little like Marie-Antoinette being led again to the scaffold. What if she played the part again and failed? And, more frightening still, what if the voice came back stronger than ever? She was letting a genie out of a bottle and she had no idea how powerful it might become and what it might do.

Two weeks later it happened again, all of it. This time in front of two hundred and fifty people who nearly brought the clock off the wall with their applause. Caroline was the darling of the hour. Mr. McMarris was all smiles as he counted all the nickels and dimes, more than twenty dollars worth—enough to buy a copy of the very latest geography book for every other person in the class.

"You've done very, very well," Professor Roper told him with a big handshake.

The teacher shook his head. "Uncle Jim, I never taught 'em to do it like that in rehearsal. Something happened up there on that stage. All I did was talk 'em through the lines."

"Well, whatever it was, you ought to do it again. That was the finest entertainment ever put on by our own. We've had plenty of fine shows come through but nothing like this that was done by our own. If you want to put on another one in the spring I'll put up the money for the costumes and sets, Ronald. What do you say?"

Caroline began to get comfortable with her genie. She even found that reading dialogue aloud from various books brought out the voices. She found that she could be rich or poor, young or old, kind or cruel if the words on the page were right. She talked Anna into reading some pages of dialogue with her, but Anna was impatient with the process. Her reading was accurate enough but it was flat and forced and almost totally void of character. No one else in town was any better. Caroline came to the conclusion that she might as well be trading lines with the wooden Seminole in front of Miller's drugstore.

Their next play was to be *Joan the Saint* by another French playwright, Henri Vachon. Caroline saw all kinds of problems with the play but she kept them to herself because she was afraid that Mr. McMarris and the other students would think she was getting to be too big for her britches. In her imagination she could hear Anna saying just that: "Caroline, Princess Caroline, Marie-Antoinette Caroline, you are getting too big for your britches."

She thought this play was a little too much like Marie-Antoinette, with a woman who goes through mental anguish on her way to her execution. And Joan of Arc had to be burned at the stake. How were they supposed to make *that* work without sending Roper's Hall up in flames? And even if they could, wouldn't the burning scene overshadow the character? The guillotine had been bad enough, the way the O'Dells had spent the whole play with their eyes fastened on it. There was also the matter of having to dress like a man. She had enjoyed the gown of Marie-Antoinette even if it didn't fit quite right. The drab brown tunic of Joan might make her look like a sack of potatoes. And her hair! Her long strawberry blond hair would have to be tied back somehow. She wasn't going to have it cut off; that was for sure.

But all of those doubts shrank as she recited the lines over and over, savoring the role of a martyr betrayed by her people. She decided that Henri Vachon's voices were a masterstroke—having Joan respond to words that only she could hear. She experimented with her hair and decided that it actually looked pretty good pulled back in a big ponytail. She got a feedbag, which she gave a thorough scrubbing, and a pair of doeskin britches left behind by a one-night boarder, and she had herself a convincing costume for *Joan the Saint.* To her surprise, she liked it, liked the way it made her look like someone else entirely. She wore the costume when she practiced her lines before the oval mirror on her mother's dresser and found that Joan of Arc was beginning to speak through her.

This time Mr. McMarris decided to hold auditions. The decision was controversial since it implied that the school talent wasn't good enough to carry the show. Most of the applicants were terrible actors, rough country boys who could hardly read, let alone do characters. Iris Poinsett tried out for the supporting role of a peasant girl who becomes one of Joan's ardent followers. But she had a tendency to read every comma and semicolon as if she were still laboring through her McGuffy's, and Mr. McMarris dared to pass her over for one of the girls from Miss Tebeau's school.

The demand for tickets was such that Mr. McMarris planned performances on Friday and Saturday night. He was concerned that some of the slighted players would try to sabotage the show. He also worried about Roper's Hall being next to Duke's Saloon, but Sheriff Duforge had assured him that there would be no trouble even if he had to lock up every cow hunter and railroad bum in the county.

The Friday night performance was a standout. Even the parents of the slighted actors agreed that the auditions had brought in some fine talent. A boy who had just moved down from Charleston played with convincing seriousness the part of the haughty English commander. The peasant girl had trouble keeping her stockings up, but let them become sort of a running gag that added poignancy to her final scene with Joan. Caroline had taught herself to use her hands to great effect and, in the last scene, raised them in a delicate gesture of supplication as she walked to the stake. When it was over there was not a dry female eye in the hall and many of the men were seen to avert their faces lest they be caught in the throes of unmanly emotion.

By Saturday everybody in town was talking about *Joan the Saint,* including Duke's patrons as they nursed their beers and poked at their checkers and dominoes.

"God, what a village we have found ourselves in!" remarked one of two city-dwellers that had gotten off the train for the night.

"As I recall, it was your idea to mingle, Charlie," said his companion. "I was ready to try my luck in the sleeping-car."

"That's well enough for you, my young friend. But as for me, I've pressed myself into too many a so-called sleeping car. My bones are too far gone for such procrustean activities."

"This is a crowded little burg for being on the edge of nowhere. What do you suppose all these people are doing here?"

Charlie was feeling the effects of his second beer. Seeing a familiar face, he raised his hand in greeting. "I say there! Do I know you, sir?"

The well-groomed man with the pomaded hair and wing collar nodded courteously.

"You just saw him half an hour ago, Charlie. He's the hotel clerk. At the—what's the name of it?"

"The Alachua, sir. Bobby La Rue at your service."

Charlie glanced at his companion and burst into embarrassed laughter. "Of course! Of course!" He motioned for Bobby to join them at their table. "I am Charles McKenna and this is my associate, Arthur Mayse."

Bobby smiled politely. He never enjoyed talking to people whose tongues had been loosened by drink, and he had found that a man's necktie was a good indication of how he conducted himself. Charles McKenna's necktie was loose and his face was flushed.

"I remember your name, sir. From the register." He managed another smile.

McKenna laughed again, louder than before. "You're a sharp one, you are! I wonder if you can tell us though. Where are all those people going?"

Bobby glanced toward the big window at the people streaming toward Roper's Hall. "They're going to the play. Folks are coming from all over the county to see it."

McKenna looked at Arthur Mayse with bleary eyes. "Well, fancy that! The whole county!"

"Yes, sir," Bobby said seriously. "The whole county."

"As a matter of fact, Artie and I are in the theater business. We're on our way from New Orleans to Savannah and have passed through your lovely town of Cypress Keys and—"

"Cedar Keys—if I may," Bobby said.

"—And we are looking for a new Desdemona for our Othello, to replace one who absconded with—"

"Charlie, you don't need to bore Mr. La Rue with our problems."

"Perhaps your production has just the thespian we need, waiting to be discovered. What is the name of the drama in question, pray?"

Bobby waited to be sure he wouldn't be interrupted. "The play is *Joan the Saint*."

McKenna put his beer down. "For God's sake! You don't mean that old blotter by Vachon."

"I believe so." Bobby looked at Arthur Mayse in the hope of finding some common civility.

"It has potential," Arthur said, trying to smooth things over. "It's just that it's often done so badly."

Bobby straightened his back. "Well, they're doing a fine job of it next door. I saw it last night. Worth every penny."

"Is that so? Maybe we ought to go, Artie. You never know where you'll find a good show. Isn't that what you keep saying?"

Arthur lit a cigarette. "I suppose so." He made an effort to change the subject. "I'm surprised you were able to get away from the hotel on such a busy night."

"I get two Saturdays a year," Bobby said, trying to pretend that McKenna wasn't at the table.

"Look here," McKenna said with exaggerated geniality. "I think we should go to this play of yours."

"It's not mine," Bobby said. "And you'd be lucky to get tickets. Last I heard they were all sold out."

McKenna pushed himself away from the table and stood up unsteadily. "My dear sir, you are talking to a man of the theater! There are ways to get tickets—and there are *ways to get tickets.*"

He went out into the street and intercepted Ray Polk and his wife. He took out his billfold and offered them a dollar each for their tickets.

"Nothing doing," Ray said. "I hear this is the best show to come along since the war." He and the missus hurried toward the hall.

"You, my good man! Surely you can use a dollar for your ticket." He had stopped Bob Harper, who was in town just for the occasion.

"No dice, mister. I paid one-and-a-half for it."

McKenna motioned toward Larrabee, who was coming up behind him after stopping to take a sandspur off his ankle.

"Not hardly. I paid two to that old buzzard in the land office."

Now it became a matter of pride to Charlie McKenna. He approached Baldy Choat and offered him five dollars.

"Done!" Baldy flicked his ticket at him, snatched the bill, stuffed it deep into his hip pocket, and ran off as if he had stolen it.

"There!" McKenna grinned, holding the ticket aloft. "Now one for you, Arthur."

"I'd prefer just to go back to the hotel and call it a night, Charlie."

"No such thing, my boy! Nothing doing!" He found a cow hunter who was waiting for his friend to finish retching in the alley, bought his ticket for four dollars, and elbowed his way into the hall with young Arthur frowning in his wake.

The hall was packed and it was hot. Ladies fanned themselves with whatever bits of cloth or feather they could spare from their apparel, and the men's hats were in constant motion. McKenna caught sight of two seats near the back and pushed toward them, forcing the rather portly Mrs. Doig to relinquish some of her space.

"For God's sake," he said, "nine dollars for this."

Arthur decided to make the best of it. "It makes you suspect that this would be a good town for us to play in if they can draw a crowd like this for an amateur performance."

"If we ever have the misfortune to pass this way again. Next time we'll just go through Atlanta. By then the furor over the policeman's daughter will have died down."

Apparently the tickets had been oversold because people kept jamming into the hall until they were standing in the back and along both walls almost to the stage. Charlie began to sweat. Then, just as the lights were turned down, he slouched back against the bench and fell asleep, drooping dangerously in the direction of the disdainful Mrs. Doig.

Arthur considered going back to the hotel, but he was afraid he might be injured in the rush to fill his seat, so he folded his arms and glowered at the parting curtains.

Quickly he saw what people had been talking about. The production had a rustic charm about it. The props were simple but solid, the costumes were convincing, the voices loud though hideously Southern in most cases. There was something so straightforward and sincere about the whole thing that he thought it in some ways superior to their own *Othello*. There were none of the mannerisms of the New York stage, none of the exaggerated arm waving and rolled r's that he as a small-town boy from upstate New York still found annoying. Of course, it would never play anywhere else in the country. It was like a local wine, tied to the place and the moment.

Then a girl came onstage, the one playing Joan. Except that she was not exactly playing Joan so much as *being* Joan, acting the part from the inside out, so that he could actually hear Joan of Arc saying those farfetched lines. She was dressed in burlap or whatever it was in a way that was anything but flattering. Certainly none of the prima donnas he had worked with would stoop to putting on such rags. And yet she was all the more alluring for it. He admitted that to himself right away. He found her very alluring. She lit up the room like a glowing stove on a cold night.

He found himself talking to Charlie even though his companion showed no sign of waking.

"Wherever do you suppose they found her, Charlie? Do you see the way she folds and unfolds her hands like that, as if she's opening letters from a lover? The way she floats when she walks? And everyone in here knows it. Look at them. They're all under her spell."

Is it just because I was expecting so little, he wondered. But he ruled that out. Is it some magic brought about by the fatigue and stress of this interminable tour? He knew it was not. Suddenly everyone was clapping and whistling and stamping their feet and the girl was smiling shyly in the flickering footlights, curtsying and glancing around the hall as the storm of approval went on and on. It was over. The play had slipped through his fingers as he watched that girl work her magic. Not waiting for Charlie to come to his senses, he pushed his way into the aisle and moved toward the stage.

She was nowhere to be seen, the girl in the sackcloth tunic. He ascended the steps to the stage and worked his way through spear-bearing soldiers and sweating peasants. Backstage he found two brawny boys having a sword fight. He pushed past them and into the rear of the hall. He heard water splashing in one of the back rooms and he tapped the half-open door. When no one answered he let himself in, startling a girl whose face was still pink from washing. She had loosened her strawberry blond hair so that it lay in waves on her white shoulders. She was wearing the coarse brown tunic that he had found so mysteriously attractive.

"They said I could use this room," she said, a face towel still pressed to her cheek.

His hand was still on the doorknob. He stayed there, poised awkwardly between going and staying.

"I only came to tell you how wonderful you were." He found it surprisingly difficult to speak although he had spoken to more actresses than he could count.

She brought the towel down. "What?"

He took a step toward her and stopped abruptly. She looked so much younger close up. "I said I'm here to tell you how wonderful your performance was. Forgive me. I'm forgetting my manners. My name is Arthur Mayse." He held out his hand. When, reluctantly, she took it, he held hers softly, bent and kissed it.

She withdrew her hand quickly. "I'm sorry. I have to go." She hurried past him with a rustling of burlap.

He followed her into the busy back hall. "I'm sorry. Let me explain. I'm in the theater. I'm a producer with a touring company. We're in between performances. Most of the cast is somewhere in Georgia on their way to Savannah. My business manager and I are on our way there via Fernandina. We're leaving tomorrow at...." He was at a loss for a moment, trying to think of how to keep the conversation going but he couldn't remember what time the train left.

"Eleven twenty-nine," she said. She had turned and was looking up at him with crystal blue eyes, the clearest eyes he had ever seen. He couldn't imagine what she was doing in this dingy little scrap of a town. "I imagine you're leaving on the 11:29 if you're going to Fernandina tomorrow."

He smiled self-consciously. "Yes, yes. That's right. The 11:29." They were being separated as more people came into the hall. He squeezed his way back toward her. "May I ask you—I'm sorry. I didn't catch your name, Miss...."

"Newhouse." She looked at him warily, a little impatiently he thought.

"May I ask you, have you ever done Shakespeare?"

"Shakespeare?" She blinked as if he were asking something nonsensical.

"Yes. You know. *The Merchant of Venice, The Tempest.*"

"Well, no. That is, I've read some lines, some dialogue."

"Have you read *Othello?*"

"*Othello?*" She hadn't even heard of that one.

"For God's sake, Artie. What are you doing back here?" Charlie shuffled up, red-faced and sleepy, rubbing the back of his neck. "I believe I just slept through five good dollars. Hell of a crook in my neck for it too. I woke up with some dowager giving me the damnedest look."

Caroline felt uneasy. The young man kept his eyes on her. He was perspiring slightly in the hot, crowded hall, but his dark hair was neatly parted and brushed back. His sideburns were precisely trimmed and he was clean-shaven. His chin was strong with a hint of a cleft and he had earnest gray-green eyes a bit close-set. His serge suit was pressed and his collar crisply starched. His silk tie was held in place with a small diamond pin, and when he held his hand up to silence his friend Caroline noticed that his nails were clean and even.

"Would you entertain the notion of reading—"

Charlie was shaking his head. "Artie, come on! Have you lost your mind?"

"Of—of reading some lines from the third act of the play? The part where Desdemona—"

Caroline wasn't sure what was happening. She was to meet her mother and Preacher Williams at the front door and go right home so that she could get a full night's sleep and be fresh when she got up to help with breakfast before getting ready for church. And here was this earnest young man asking her to read something from Shakespeare.

"What for?" she asked without feeling.

"For our production," he said before Charlie could stop him. "We need a Desdemona for our fall tour and I believe you can be her! All you have to do to settle it is to read a few lines. From Act Three. Will you do it?"

"Artie—"

"What do you say? You're an actress aren't you?"

Caroline had never thought about it that way. "Well, I guess I am—but Barkley says everyone comes just to see me go up in flames."

"Then Barkley's an ass." Seeing that his bluntness had startled her, he went on hurriedly. "I'm sorry. I meant no offense." He was talking faster than he had ever talked in his life. It was as if his heart and all of his senses were suddenly going double-time.

"It's late," Caroline said with an apologetic smile. "My mother and—"

"There's always a mother," Charlie reminded Arthur.

"Of course," Arthur said, trying to think things through quickly. "Of course. What about in the morning, then? In the light of day, in front of every mother in town if you like. Will you read for me? Before the train leaves?"

Caroline didn't know what to say so she said, "Where?"

"Anyplace you like. The town commons if you want."

The town commons. What a strange turn of phrase. So northern. Her mind raced from one bad idea to the next and then settled on the least of the bad. "You may call at my home if you wish. At ten o'clock tomorrow morning. We can read on the porch. But only for a little while. I have to get ready for church."

"Church," Charlie said to himself. "Now that's a new one."

Arthur was more intent than ever. "And how do I find—"

"Just ask for the Newhouse place," she said. "Ask anybody."

"Newhouse," he repeated. Then, as if it were part of a new play, he said the name again two or three times as she hurried off through the crowd.

In the morning, when she heard the tapping on the front door window, she was confused all over again. She had wanted him to come, wanted to believe that last night's encounter had been more than a dream. But while she found the idea of being an actress—a real actress—thrilling, she wasn't sure what kind of life went with it. And this fervent young man, Arthur, worried her. He was so eager, so single-minded, that she thought he might be dangerous. On the one hand, she felt above all those humdrum chores now. After all, anybody could wash and mend and cook and clean but how many people could act? How many people could tap into the magic? But on the other hand, those drab tasks brought her a certain security and reassurance. The repetition of the pressing and mending and cooking and dusting—all they demanded of her was patience. Acting required more and more of her each time, making her wonder how far she could take it.

Of course, she had told her mother that he would be coming—or might be coming—but it was a difficult thing to explain because she didn't quite understand it herself.

"What is the point of this reading?" her mother had asked. "I don't understand."

"Just to see," Caroline had said, her voice trailing off. "And then he'll be gone on the 11:29."

"I never heard of such a thing," Mrs. Newhouse had said. "What do you think of this?" she had asked Preacher Williams, who was helping himself to an orange just then.

"I can't say as I understand it either," he had said. "But I can't see any harm in it."

It seemed that the whole neighborhood happened to be on hand when the mysterious Arthur arrived, book in hand, and tapped on the windowpane.

Preacher Williams answered the door and introduced himself without going into his vague relationship with the family. Arthur seemed not the least set back by the encounter, was pleasant and mannerly but clearly eager to get to the purpose of the visit. Caroline came out next, already dressed for church—a full hour ahead of the usual time—and her punctuality had been the subject of ridicule from her sisters.

When Arthur arrived, Anna was out at the fence saying some rather unfeminine things to her horse, which was following the wire at a brisk trot instead of coming when called.

"You're not going to ride her before church anyway," Martha was saying, "so what are you making all the fuss about?"

"I'm trying to train her to come when I call her," Anna replied. "Now mind your own business."

Mrs. Newhouse was now trying to keep up with breakfast for ten single-handedly and was dragged protesting to the porch by Martha who, at ten years old, was nearly her size.

Boarders were coming and going, Iris Poinsett came by, singing some terrible song called "If You've Only Got a Mustache." Caroline felt more self-conscious than when she had been onstage. Arthur seemed unconcerned, though, as if he was accustomed to people reading Shakespeare on their porches.

He waited until he and Caroline were more or less alone, then he handed her a small leather-bound book with gilt-edged pages. The binding said: *Othello, the Moor of Venice by William Shakespeare.* She opened it to the place he had marked with last night's ticket stub. He took off his brown Fedora and set it on the porch swing.

"There, where Desdemona begins in the second scene."

The lines were short; she was glad for that. But she wasn't sure what they meant. He responded with Othello's lines without looking at the book. He was looking at Caroline. The lines came easily for him, with meaning and that same directness that he seemed always to have, but there were terrible words in what he said—"hell" and "damn." She had no idea there were such things in Shakespeare and she worried that Preacher Williams or her mother would hear.

She stumbled over her words, timid and uncertain. "O, heaven forgive us!" she said at last, relieved that her part was over.

He was staring at the ceiling, as if studying the peeling paint there.

She closed the book and held it out to him. He seemed not to notice.

Anna called to her horse again in a harsh voice, breaking the spell.

"Your book?" She came toward him and held it out again. "I'm sorry. I might've been better if I had studied it first."

"Better?" He seemed to be emerging from a dream. He touched the book and came toward her so that they were both holding it. "Better? You were superb! You were vulnerable as Desdemona is vulnerable. You must be Desdemona. You must be *our* Desdemona! Will you come with us?"

She choked, put her hand to her throat. "Come with you?"

He took the book as if it were some sacred object and pressed it to him. "Yes! To Savannah! To Charleston! And then to Richmond and Washington and Baltimore!"

She thought that he must be out of his mind. She shrank back toward the door, relieved when Preacher Williams emerged, Bible in hand, on his way to church.

He glanced from face to face and asked if something was wrong.

"Far from it," Arthur answered. "I've just asked Caroline to join us on our tour." He turned to her and added, "We open in Savannah in September. That gives us six months. In the meantime, we'll be touring with some popular entertainments—vaudevilles and a one-act. Summer fare."

The preacher put a hand on Arthur's shoulder. "I'm sure that I speak for Caroline's mother when I say that it can't be, Arthur. Caroline's only seventeen."

Arthur absorbed the news gracefully. He lowered the book from his chest. "She's still the best Desdemona I've ever heard—the best there is!" He came forward and looked at her with his earnest gray-green eyes. "I'll be back. I vow it. Will you wait for me? And if I write, will you write?"

She glanced at Preacher Williams then back at Arthur's fervent face. She nodded.

"Then it will be," he promised. Snatching her hand, he bent and kissed it and hurried off to catch the train.

Chapter 22

John Howard dreamed occasionally of the Confederate gold. He knew that the real thing, the treasure that had been hauled to Cottonwood Plantation, was in the form of English sovereigns but he always dreamed of freshly minted American double eagles shining in yellow moonlight that broke through parting clouds. He was just reaching into the strongbox when the gold pieces changed to oranges that dissolved into juice and ran through his fingers. Then shots cut through the stillness and he heard men and dogs coming after him. The shots were a recent touch, having something to do with the President he thought. Garfield had been shot in July. Four days ago he had died.

It would make no difference in the running of the country, Major Dennis had told him, except perhaps that there would be a more fervent cry for civil service reform since the assassin was a disgruntled office-seeker. The major seemed to take no particular interest in the killing. It was rumored that his career in the state legislature was bottoming out as the state's Democrats became more and more powerful. Political favors in the county were no longer a part of the major's fortunes. He had turned his attention almost entirely to business—the lumber business.

"Think about the oranges that everyone has gone so mad for," he told Howard. "Subject to freeze and drought and rot. Then think about timber— subject to none of the above. Abundant and always in demand. Which would you rather have?"

Howard thought that he would rather have that $20,000 in Confederate gold, but he had long since convinced himself—during his waking hours—that it had evaporated with the ill-begotten government of planters and cotton merchants.

"You still have your moss mill I suppose?" the major asked.

"I do. We use some of that timber of yours to build our furniture. Furniture doesn't freeze either."

It was an unusually smart remark but Howard was still chafing about dropping out of the Alachua Steam Navigation and Canal Company on the major's advice. The company's boats were coursing the lakes and rivers day and night and were prospering mightily. And none of the board members were on speaking terms with him. He wished he had the money or the backing to put together his own fleet, but it was out of the question. His would-be partners had far too much of a head start.

The major was sitting at the mahogany desk in his plush paneled office. Most of the papers on the desk appeared to be deeds and stock certificates festooned with ribbons and seals. He lit a cigar and took in the pungent smoke.

"Got any money to invest?"

It was the most direct question he had ever asked, but Howard hid his surprise. "I have some. And more that I can scrape up for the right project."

The major was unimpressed by the investor's terminology. No doubt he thought the talk of projects faddish, and he disapproved of popular fancies.

"What I have isn't a project. It's the Arlington."

"The Arlington?" This time Howard was unable to hide his surprise.

"Yes. How would you like to be my partner in her? Fifty-fifty."

Howard didn't know what to say. It was an honor. It was also a large investment, a very large investment. He stalled for time.

"Your other partners want to sell?"

"My other partners have already sold—to me. At a large price, but a bargain price. I'm prepared to offer that half to you at the same price." He looked up from his cigar. "If you're good for it."

Now it was a matter of pride. The Arlington was the finest hotel in town, the finest between Jacksonville and Tampa. It catered to the best—two hundred rooms at a time—and every day the railroad brought in more and more guests, businessmen, speculators, politicians, recreators and rusticators. Even from the house he had bought down the street Howard could tell that the Arlington was prospering. The joke was that the Tampa & Jacksonville trains and the Cedar Keys-to-Fernandina trains might just as well forego the depot and deposit everybody directly at the front door of the Arlington.

As long as the major was being blunt, he would be too.

"How much," he asked, straightening his tie.

It was an enormous number, even greater than he expected, but he had every reason to believe that the major was telling him the truth about what he had paid and that it was a bargain.

"I'll need some time," Howard said.

"I can give you two weeks." The major seemed more interested in his cigar than in the partnership. "After that I'll be opening it up."

Just like that. No apologies, no regrets.

He had long since outgrown his corner room upstairs at the Arlington. He needed space—space for legal papers, space for meetings with customers, space for being a community leader. The last requirement and a wish to invest money rather than throw it away on rent had prompted him to buy a very respectable house next door to the expansive estate of Mr. Henry F. Dutton himself. It was more solid than elegant, with stout columns, a broad porch that included a round pavilion facing the Duttons, and a low-hanging roof that kept the house cool on all but the hottest summer afternoons.

He had a Negro named Henry Collins—a former house servant on the Haile Plantation—who kept the place in order, answered the door and went to the post office for the mail. Collins saw to it that the maid kept the rooms tidy and comfortable and he laid out Howard's clothing each morning, freshly washed and starched by Mrs. Murray, who came to the back door three days a week to exchange the old for the new. Howard thought that Collins and Mrs. Murray were a little too inclined to gossip, and he told himself that the minute Collins' work began to suffer for it he would put a stop to it.

In this house he had more room for pacing, and the major's offer provoked plenty of it. He walked from the red India carpet in the high-ceilinged front room across the foyer to the maroon Persian carpet in the narrow parlor, back and forth, letting his mind work on the problem before him. He was not altogether content with the moss mill. It was profitable but somehow beneath him, a stepping-stone to something better, and the Arlington was certainly something better. It would go a long way toward making him a community leader, privy to the best investment opportunities—excluding, of course, those damnable oranges and steamboats. He stopped in the doorway between the parlor and the front room, balking at the idea that he was hostage to the major's prejudices and convincing himself that it wasn't the major's prejudices but his ideas that governed his actions. At heart he believed that the major was right about the dangers of those investments. He went to the writing desk in the parlor and hastily scrawled out a note, but he smudged the last line, wadded up the card and threw it in the elephant foot wastebasket in the corner. He wrote another note more slowly, shook it through the blotting sand and sealed it in an envelope addressed to the major. Then he called for Collins and told him to deliver the note to the Dennis Block.

His walk to the Merchant's Bank took him past the very object of his quest. The major and his partners had added onto the original structure, filling it out to a fine square building terraced on all four sides of both stories. It was the second grandest building in town, after the Dennis Block itself, its only rivals being the big brick Methodist Church and the jail—which was also two stories and an extremely popular place to stay. He reassured himself that he was doing the right thing—major or no major.

He passed under the spreading live oaks in front of the bank, glanced into the big arched windows, and asked one of the dapper young tellers if Mr. Dutton was in. It had been a daring move, accepting the major's offer without the money to cover the amount, but he felt like taking the risk, just as he had once enjoyed taking risks at the poker table. Dutton was out, the teller said, in New York to be precise, not to return for a week. It was a setback Howard hadn't considered. He was ready for acceptance or refusal of the loan. He wasn't ready for a one-week delay before he even got the answer.

"Who else can clear a loan?" Howard asked confidentially. The teller's cage made it seem as if he were talking to a convicted felon.

"How big a loan?" the teller asked a little too loudly.

"A very big loan," Howard said softly.

"Mr. Dutton. He's your man," the teller said. "Be back Thursday."

It was a long week. For the first time in his life Howard felt poor and desperate. Even as a boot maker without a dime to his name he'd had little need for money, and in the early days of his first freedom from the stitching bench, smuggling the freshly dead to eager medical students, he had needed little to get by on. Moving from one inn and rooming house to the next to keep ahead of the police he had needed only a few dollars a week, and the sweet life of making his own choices had made the dim corners and rank recesses of Boston seem like palaces.

He met with the major as if he already had the money in hand when he knew that even selling the moss mill—assuming he could sell it tomorrow—wouldn't cover the amount he needed. He told himself more than once that if he failed, he would fail with the major only, but he never could convince himself. Even if the major kept the failure to himself—even odds at best—their association would end, and with it his access to the major's keen business insights.

He was glad when Sunday came. It meant one day in which there would be no meeting with the major. He thought about taking the train to Jacksonville— a diversion in which he had taken comfort since he had forced the departure of Lucinda and her sisters in the oldest trade. His adventures there had not always turned out well. It was in a Jacksonville bawdy house that he had picked up the infernal story of the Confederate treasure. And there an off-duty policeman with a possessive attitude toward redheads had shot at him. But these were minor displeasures compared to the disaster that now loomed over him.

Instead he did something extraordinary. He went to church. After all, a leading businessman should be seen in all the best places. He started for the Methodist Church but as he came across the big open lawn he heard a hymn, rather badly sung, which reminded him of his childhood in Manchester and the Sundays which he spent blacking boots at the armory across from the gray granite Episcopal Church.

He went across Liberty Street to the more modest frame Presbyterian Church. At least it was quiet in there. The service was just beginning. Apparently the Presbyterians got up later than the Methodists. He took a place in the back pew away from the rest of the congregation, watching as the service unfolded. It was hot in the church and people were cooling themselves with pasteboard fans that in Gothic lettering advertised the new Hutchinson Undertakers who had taken up residence south on Main Street. Howard knew most of the congregation although he had little to do with them. There was Ray Polk and his wife and fidgeting son; the brothers Duforge—Duke the bachelor saloonkeeper and Tom the sheriff with his wife and oversized son Barkley. The discharged tax assessor Jacob Ford was the deacon poking the long-handled offering basket down the pews, which struck Howard as rather amusing. He started to put in a five-dollar bill, having the vague notion that he was raising the stakes in a poker game, but tossed in a dollar instead. In one of the front pews was a woman with three daughters, the proprietress of the boarding house Larrabee had lived in, he thought, but the girls didn't look familiar. He thought one of them had been in a much-touted play last spring. He barely recognized a well-dressed man with a scruffy graying red beard and determined that it was Penny Ward looking very well heeled. He had heard that Penny and his new wife had been prospering mightily in a hat business of all things. Then there was the preacher himself—with his white mane, intense gray eyes and hooked nose—that reminded Howard of the American eagle. His smile was difficult to read, Howard thought, looking at times almost predatory, a bird of prey always on the lookout for souls to scoop up and take to the nest. Nonetheless Howard had been able to sell him a nearly played-out patch of pine scrub at a good price, and all the while the preacher seemed to think he was getting the better end of the deal.

A dreary, reedy tune on the melodeon signaled everyone to stand up and drone out some lifeless hymn that tempted him to slip out the back. Instead he stood with the flock and followed along in a dilapidated hymnal without singing. A strange phenomenon, he thought. People who were sensible six days of the week, on the seventh engaged in this awkward pastiche of bad music, banal entreaties to a Deity that must surely find them tedious, and the collection of pocket change. But then money was always there, wasn't it? Even in their loftiest moments people were never far from thoughts of smelly old cash.

The sermon had a curious effect. The preacher stood at the pulpit expounding on some little snippet of Biblical text and all the while those paddle-fans were going so that the words seemed to be going out to a field of prairie grass with cat-o-nine-tails nodding in the wind. The preacher opened his great book and read in a powerful if melodramatic voice:

Whosoever heareth these sayings of mine, and doeth them, I will liken him unto a wise man, which builds his house upon a rock. And the rain descended, and the floods came, and the winds blew, and beat upon that house, and it fell not; for it was founded upon a rock. And every one that heareth these sayings of mine, and doeth them not, shall be likened unto a foolish man, which built his house upon the sand: And the rain descended, and the floods came, and the winds blew, and beat upon that house; and it fell; and great was the fall of it.

The preacher went on to explain the relationship between faith and works, saying that neither could succeed without the other, like a rowboat with an oar on only one side. And on and on. Ray Polk's head began to bob and his wife brought him around with a twist of the ear.

All of it was entertaining in its way and it helped Howard to get his mind off his financial predicament. But he couldn't see how anyone could go through it Sunday after Sunday, and he thought that the preacher must be half-mad after devoting himself to it entirely for so long. He was glad when the preacher finally gave the benediction and the melodeon struck up a wheezing recessional that sent everyone churning into the aisle. The smiles Howard could definitely understand. What a relief to be free of the stuffy homilies of that long, long hour!

There were rewards. Mrs. Doig smiled at him, and it didn't hurt to be on the good side of one of the county's most successful businessmen. He had wished that Mrs. Dutton would be in church. That could be a real boon. But he had no idea if she was Presbyterian, Methodist or one of the stay-at-home heathens.

The preacher cleverly beat everyone to the door so that he could ambush them as they came out.

"Good to see you this Sunday," he said genially, pumping Howard's hand. "It's been a long time."

Howard wanted to say that it would be a good deal longer until the next time. Instead he asked the preacher how the property was working out.

"Oh, I've hardly had time to give it a thought," was the reply. "But I'm sure it will come to good one day. Town's growing so."

Everybody said that. *Town's growing so.* It got so that a person hardly noticed the phrase anymore. It was like commenting on the weather.

"Yes, I know," Howard said, not waiting to put on his hat.

Larrabee's former landlady was having some kind of dispute with the eldest of the three daughters. The girl was walking at a distance from the rest of the family and a little faster.

Coop them all up for another hour, Howard thought. Let the preacher pour some of his words over them. Soften them up proper for discipline.

By Thursday he was practically ready to run out and meet the train carrying Mr. Henry Dutton back from New York. He was nervous and irritable and short. Collins came into the study and asked him what to do about a letter that the postal clerk had given him by mistake.

"Don't do anything with it," was Howard's reply. "Let it rot, Collins. It's none of our business."

The letter had been lying around for a long time but Collins kept forgetting to mention it. He could not read well. He'd never had the luxury of learning at the plantation and he hadn't had time to make up for the shortcoming. Little need, though, he told himself from time to time, except that he was starting to get a little curious about this wayward letter. He held it to the light and studied it with his failing eyes. The old-fashioned wax seal on the back had made it stick to Howard's issue of *Harper's Weekly*. The letter was sent from Savannah, Georgia, and it was addressed to somebody named Caroline, but he couldn't make out the rest. He decided to give it to Mrs. Murray when she came on Friday. She'd know what to do with it. If only he could remember to mention it to her. Now what was it Mr. Howard had said he wanted for supper?

Chapter 23

The Poinsetts' dog let out a howl that set off everything canine in the neighborhood as a brightly painted wagon came dragging around the corner. The mules came to a dead stop in front of the fence and the driver seemed to think it was as good a time as any to get out and go to work. He was short and sinewy, brown from years in the sun, his beard white with a little pepper still in it. He went through the formality of tying the reins to a round black anchor that he tossed into the grass. His loose clothes flapped when he walked. They had been good clothes once, but the fit suggested that he was not their first owner. He came up with the sureness of one who had just bought the property.

"Afternoon, gents. My name's Leo Bard. Either of you the master of the house?"

Penny had been on his way back up the ladder to finish scraping old paint from the porch ceiling, but he stopped and put the chisel down on a windowsill. "You're about ten years late for the master of the house, Mr. Bard."

"That so." With his crooked fingers Bard put on a pair of pince-nez and took a small notebook out of his breast pocket. "I see that now, sure enough. Widow still live here, name of Newhouse?"

Bobby La Rue had stopped by on his way to work. He was reading the wagon. *Buy. Sell. Trade. Your Trash is My Treasure. Leo Bard, Prop.* "You came through here about two years ago, didn't you?"

Leo Bard nodded. The sun glinted off his glasses. "Sure did, and two years before that more or less. I come cycling through like a comet of commerce, every year or so. 'Specially during the cold weather." He pocketed the notebook. "Bought some silverware off of Mrs. Newhouse 'long about six years ago. You gents happen to know if she's got anything to sell this time around?"

"Not likely," Penny said. "Business has been pretty good. Fact I wouldn't be surprised if she'd want to buy that silver back."

"Not a chance," Leo Bard said, shaking his head sadly. "Long gone up in Ohio somewhere. But I do have a fine set I picked up in Virginia. Now I can't prove this, but I have reason to believe that it once belonged to the Lee family themselves. It's right there in the wagon—"

"That won't likely be necessary," Penny said. "She ain't exactly in a barterin' mood."

Leo stopped on the top step and stroked his beard. "Ah, the moods of the fair gender! I am not totally a stranger to them. Know anyone hereabouts that might do a little trading?"

Penny thought for a moment. "Well, I believe the Learys still do some barter out there at the old post, don't they?"

"Some of this and some of that, I believe," Bobby said. "If you're not averse to strangeness."

"Strangeness ain't no stranger to me," Leo said. "Whereabouts is this trading post?"

"Down here to Liberty Street, west to the fork, bear left half a mile past the lightning oak and it's dead ahead on the right."

"The lightning—" Leo Bard took on a distant look. "Would this be an old place half clapboard, half log, top of a long slope?"

"That's it," Bobby said.

"Thank you, gentlemen. Thank you very much. I'm beginning to recollect myself."

He returned to his wagon, hoisted up his anchor, and showered the mules with exotic oaths until they grudgingly jerked out into the street.

Penny looked out toward the woods to the north, past the fence where Tuscawilla scraped at the meager grass and pine needles. "Maybe should've gone after poor Caroline," he said to himself. "It's hard to know what to do."

Bobby was looking the other way, watching the colorful, top-heavy wagon clatter down Liberty Street.

"That Mr. Bard don't know much either. We just told him Mary Leary's place was west and he up and went in the opposite direction."

A little later, a plump, well-dressed Negro woman approached the Newhouses' back yard.

Larrabee had come up to mail the monthly payment on the *King Payne.* He and Penny had been making a contest of seeing who could split the smallest pieces. He propped the ax against the chopping block. "It's Mrs. Murray, the wife of Dobkin the wood man, mother of Harmon the wild boy. She looks worried."

Despite her worries, Mrs. Murray had a pretty smile. "How do, Mist' Larrabee, Mist' Penny. I got this here letter for Miss Caroline Newhouse. She be around here?"

"Well, she was a while ago," Penny said, "but you never know. She's been so restless lately."

He took the letter into the kitchen and hallooed. "Mail for Caroline!" The words were hardly out of his mouth when Caroline bounded downstairs and snatched the letter from his hands. Anna and Martha weren't far behind.

"Mind your manners!" Anna scolded.

Caroline told her to mind her own business and hastily apologized to Penny. She tore open the letter, scattering fragments of the wax seal on the freshly scrubbed pine floor.

"It's from Arthur!" She looked at the date. "This letter's ancient! He wrote me right after he was here and I never wrote back! How horrible he must think me!"

Mrs. Newhouse had been upstairs in the small, hot sewing room. She came into the kitchen to see what all the commotion was about.

"Caroline has received a letter from Ar-thur," Martha intoned.

"What took this letter so long to get here?" Caroline pressed it to her bosom. "Mama, he wanted me to come to Savannah *last August*—to read for their road show!"

Her mother looked uneasy. She adjusted one of the tortoise-shell combs that held her ample hair in place. "Whatever a road show is, I don't like the sound of it."

"Oh it's just where the company travels! They'll spend the whole summer traveling—to Charleston, Atlanta, Richmond, Washington, Baltimore—maybe even Jacksonville. Maybe even here! Oh, Mama, if he'll have me this year, I must do it!"

"Mama, I must do it!" mouthed Martha. Anna saw her but remained serious.

"Caroline, how can you *possibly?*" her mother said. "You're just a girl. You haven't even been farther away than Jacksonville since you were eight years old."

"Mama, I will be *eighteen* in October. What difference can a couple of months make?"

"Perhaps quite a large difference if you're not thinking clearly. Now let's hear no more about it. Anyway, that letter is months old. You can be sure he's forgotten all about you by now."

Caroline clutched the letter as if it were divine authorization. "I know he hasn't, Mother, and I *must* go."

"And I say you won't. You've waited this long, you can wait until October. Maybe by then you'll be wiser and know that things are not always what they seem."

Caroline gave her an angry look. "What do you mean by *that?*"

Her mother stiffened. "I mean what I say. This young man whom you hardly know is talking about you ranging around the countryside with a bunch of actors. It's not proper. You know nothing of the ways of the world. Who would look out for you, Caroline? Think of it—actors!"

"Mother, *I'm* an actor. I can't be happy doing anything else. Nothing will happen to me! You don't know Arthur. He's kind. He's not some kind of cad. He's a gentleman! He loves the theater. We all have to take some chances if we're to meet our destiny. Father went to war. I have to do this."

"Your father came back from the war with consumption. If you were to go running off to be an actress, what might you come back with?"

Anna and Martha couldn't believe what they were hearing. Caroline and their mother seemed oblivious to their presence. Anna began to feel as if she were swimming in water way over her head, and she wished this would somehow turn into an argument over mending or hogging the hot water on bath night. But she knew now that those days were gone forever. Caroline had changed and there was no going back. She knew that much, whatever the outcome of this kitchen quarrel.

Caroline wrote back that night, in feverish sentences scratched onto the page with a pen that bent under the pressure of her grip. The address was several months old, but with the fervor of Saint Joan, Caroline prayed that it would quickly find its way to the earnest young man with the intense gray-green eyes.

It did more than that.

A few weeks later she was sitting on the porch—the very place where her Desdemona had won over Arthur a year ago. She was knitting patches onto a frayed blanket. She had complained that it would be months again before the blanket was needed, but her mother had insisted. After all, there was the occasional boarder who had to have a blanket regardless of the weather. She envied Anna her long rides on Tuscawilla—a form of escape that she herself found increasingly less appropriate. She envied Martha the bliss of youth, but then Martha was tough and adaptable. She had even learned to cut the heads off chickens.

Caroline had the blanket spread on a high old rack that blocked her view of the front walk, so she heard the visitor before she saw him. The white picket gate swung on its rusty hinges and the footsteps came toward the porch. She stood up to tell the prospective boarder that there were no vacancies—and there he was.

She had said his name before her pride could hold her back.

"Arthur?"

In a moment they were embracing on the top step as the ball of yarn she had dropped slowly unwound itself along the porch and down the steps onto the walkway.

This time, Arthur did not take the 11:29 to Fernandina, not the next day nor the day after that. He stopped by the house each day and talked in the parlor with Caroline. On the second day, Anna saw Caroline emerge into the front room and thought she saw her tucking a small piece of paper into her dress pocket, but she remembered it only the morning they found the note on Caroline's pillow.

Martha was the one who found the note and told the others. She nearly tripped in her hurry down the stairs. Her excitement and undeveloped reading skills made a hash of what Caroline had intended to be a touching, romantic message.

"'Dear Mother,'' Martha began, too agitated to mock the opening, "'Arthur and I have decided to do the only right thing. We have elapsed.''

Her mother was just bringing in the morning's biscuits from the summer kitchen and she was in no mood for nonsense.

"Child, don't waste my time with your fairy tales. Now look out. These biscuits are hot."

Frowning, Anna snatched the note from Martha and reread the sentence in question.

"'We have-' Mama, what does e-loped mean?"

"Now don't *you* start. Go upstairs and tell Caroline to come down at once. I declare she gets lazier all the time."

"'We have e-loped and by the time you read this we will be on our way to becoming man and wife.'" Anna stopped to absorb what she had read.

"Man and wife?" Martha wasn't sure what those words meant either.

Their mother set the biscuit tray down on the drain board. Slowly she wiped her hands on her apron.

"Give it to me, please." She held her hand out.

Timidly Anna gave her the note.

The two girls watched in silence as their mother looked at it over and over. Anna was trying to remember if she had seen her mother's hands shake that way before. Her mother's face turned a shade of gray that reminded Martha of the woods path.

Mrs. Newhouse spoke slowly and distinctly. "Go to the church and ask Preacher Williams to come home as fast as he can." Each girl assumed the other was intended.

"Now!"

Both girls ran.

Before the morning was over, a checkered bunch rode in hasty pursuit of the young couple. The reward was a hundred dollars to the man who brought Caroline Newhouse back unharmed. No mention was made of Arthur Mayse.

Larrabee and Bob were just bringing the *King Payne* to the Sweetwater Branch landing when they got word of the elopement. Larrabee made a beeline for the White Pine Stable and asked for Ralph Pine's fastest horse.

"What makes you think you're going to catch up with a train on a horse?" Ralph asked with that sideways manner of his.

"Ten dollars says you know," Larrabee told him. "Ten dollars says that fellow Mayse came over here and picked up a rig last night. Am I right?"

"I don't know 'twas Mayse. I don't know what the feller looks like. But there was a feller come in before sunup wanting a rig. Damn near shot him through the door for a footpad till he started banging."

Larrabee had found a horse on his own. He threw a blanket on it and went for a saddle.

Ralph Pine lounged against the rough-hewn wall. "Now tell me how you know that feller come here."

Larrabee tightened the girth. "He wasn't going to wait for a train and he was smart enough to know that even if he did, we could telegraph down the line and catch 'em. So that means horses. Except that Caroline doesn't like being on horseback. So that leaves a rig, doesn't it?"

Baldy Choat saw Larrabee taking the road north and tagged along after him on a borrowed cow pony. "They're going to Georgia, ain't they? Won't no questions be asked up there. What say we th'ow in together and spilt the hundred?"

"Because I expect you'll try to steal this horse right out from under me," Larrabee said. He gave his horse a little kick that forced Baldy to keep up.

"Sam 'n' me was just diddlin' that time we got your horse. And anyway you stole it from that feller down in Levy County—and I was the one that paid for it—in jail."

"How'd you get out of your thirty-nine lashes, Baldy? And the thousand dollar fine?"

"You know damn well. I've got a friend I help out now and again."

"Was it you that fired the shots at Major Dennis in the Union Academy back in '76?"

"What do you think?"

"Then there was Caleb Green. Fired out right about the time you were sprung from the pokey."

"The plan was just to scare him off for a while but that fool with the whip went crazy with his fire. You can blab this all over town when you get back and I'll deny it, my word against yours."

"So you also brought those lowlifes up from Archer to fire out the soiled doves. Did you know Penny would be up there?"

"You go to hell. You think I'd hire somebody to whip my own cousin?"

Larrabee jerked his horse to a halt. "Penny's your cousin?"

"Did he never tell you? I'd've thought he'd be proud of it."

The riders came straggling back the next day, the lot of them, mosquito-bitten and rain-soaked. They had followed a track most of the way to Waldo and lost it where the road changed to mud.

"Wherever they're going, they're good 'n' wet," Baldy said. "Same as us, and all for a tumble in the hay. I hope they both drown."

The heat finally started to let up by the end of September, but the rain never let up, with one downpour after another filling the streets and yards, gardens and groves, so that just getting from house to house was a misadventure. Wagons bogged down, drivers cursed and horses thrashed. Curtis the iceman resorted to carrying half a load at a time and Dobkin Murray lost most of a face cord of fat pine in the quagmire that was Liberty Street. He tied his team to one of Henry Dutton's orange trees and slogged into the Porters Quarters looking for assistance, half-wishing that his runaway son Harmon were still around to help him dig it out.

Just as the world appeared to be coming apart at the seams, Preacher Williams and Emma Newhouse announced their intention to join in the bonds of holy matrimony.

Chapter 24

"John, I'd like you to meet my compatriot, Mr. Charles Webber." Major Dennis motioned across his vast desk at a smallish bespectacled man in a Prince Albert suit who sat with his brown derby perched on one knee.

Smiling pleasantly Webber rose to shake hands. "Just call me Carl. That's the way most folks know me."

Howard knew at once what the major meant by "compatriot." Webber's accent was just like the major's. Rounded r's and pinched a's.

"Carl's come all the way from Salem, Massachusetts to do a write-up of the county."

"Of the whole county?" Howard sat down in the other big leather armchair that faced the desk. He set his hat on the India carpet. "What kind of write-up, Carl?"

Webber pushed his spectacles up to the bridge of his nose. "Well, an article to be distributed in the northern cities. To bring in more settlement and investment."

"That should help to keep the Arlington full," Howard said, trying to read the major's impassive face. "Not that we've had much trouble with that."

"The Arlington? Of course not," Webber said brightly. "It's a beautiful place. A grand place! I'm staying there myself, courtesy of the major."

Webber radiated such sincere enthusiasm that Howard thought he might have a future in politics as a campaign manager.

"Carl's come at a good time," Major Dennis said. "In fact the timing couldn't be better."

"It is a fine time of year," Howard said blandly. He had a hunch that the major meant something else.

"Sure it is," the major said. "But we also have a special presentation in a few minutes."

"Very much looking forward to it." Webber smiled graciously. His ruddy complexion made him look all the more excited.

"Did you read the last issue of the *Times*, John?" The major gestured toward a copy on his desk.

Of course, Howard thought, the presentation. It was another of the major's pet projects. Howard knew very little about it, only what he had read in the papers, thanks to the major's secretiveness. Before he could answer, someone out in the street began banging on a drum. A brass band joined in, accompanied by cheering.

Major Dennis stood up and motioned toward the door. "Shall we, gentlemen?"

Carl Webber beamed at the sight of the musicians—the brightly uniformed members of the East Florida Seminary Band. They were performing "Nelly Bly" with such verve and punch that many of the children in the crowd started dancing. The cymbal-player was particularly inspired. An old man standing nearby tucked his ear trumpet under his arm and moved back a few steps.

"Isn't that something!" Carl Webber doffed his derby as they came out onto the steps at the entrance of the Dennis Block. "Isn't that something?"

The object of the excitement was a fire engine—a one-horse pumper wagon with about fifty feet of folded ladder and a much-admired coil of hose. In the sharp sunlight, the large polished brass bell and fittings almost hurt Howard's eyes. But he had seen a four-horse rig back in New Hampshire twenty years ago, and he figured that, despite his gushing, Webber must have seen something equally impressive in Boston if not in Salem. He was beginning to take a dislike to the irrepressible journalist.

The band from the East Florida Seminary played two or three more tunes with that obnoxious drum banging away and a cornet that seemed to cut right to the inner ear. The crowd loved it. Sheriff Duforge stood by smiling broadly beneath his big mustache, holding one hand on his hip and propping the other on the substantial brick wall of the Dennis Block. Howard supposed he thought the pumper wagon would somehow make his job easier.

Major Dennis gave a speech, something about "our great community realizing its destiny and coming of age." It was a short speech, right to the point, without any rhetorical flourishes or entertainment value. This fire engine was simply Major Dennis' gift to the community that had given him so much. Amen to that, Howard thought. The major must own half the town by now. It was particularly interesting that this was the major's personal gift. He said nothing about the long string of businesses he was involved in, nothing about the Arlington, as if he were now above business and politics. Howard wondered what he was up to.

Carl Webber stayed in town for weeks. He spent most of his time traveling to and from the farms and plantations of Alachua Lake, out to the timberlands in the north part of the county, talking to bankers and grove owners and riding the lakes, courtesy of the Alachua Steam Navigation and Canal Company. He spent three days at Walls' plantation. He seemed to like everybody, to take offense at nothing, and to be genuinely taken with the whole area.

His enthusiasm was infectious. Even Major Dennis was cheerful and outgoing when Webber was around. Now Webber was saying that a mere article could not contain all that had to be said about this glorious region. That would take an entire book and the book was to be called *Midland Florida—Eden of the South.*

Howard was not sorry when Webber finally left, and he figured the odds at about fifty-fifty that the much touted book-to-be would never see print. He suspected that Mr. Carl Webber was just as likely to find some other part of the country just as stimulating—and just as lucrative.

He also savored the irony of one of the fledgling fire department's first calls. The "Little Giants"—as they were known—had been summoned in the middle of the night to a fire at the East Florida Seminary. The place had promptly burned to the ground, band instruments and all.

During that summer of 1883 the gentlemen of the Alachua Steam Navigation and Canal Company became quite cordial to John Howard. Not because they needed his money. They were doing very well without it. When it came to moving produce and passengers they practically had the lakes to themselves. Summer had been good to them, with fruit of all kinds being plentiful, and by October the fall season was promising another bumper citrus crop. The live oaks on the Courthouse lawn came down to make way for orange trees. The lakes were ringed with gold, and the gentlemen of the company were gracious enough to offer Howard another chance at it.

He considered the offer very carefully. His partnership with Major Dennis had been profitable. Thanks in part to Carl Webber's book, the Arlington rarely had vacancies. The "glowing tome," as Henry Dutton referred to it, was in every hotel lobby, restaurant, barbershop, and train station in the county. The major saw to it that as quickly as copies of it walked off, they were replaced from crates in his outer office. At the same time, the major had added a horse-drawn trolley that ran from the depot to the Arlington. That way anyone who missed the book in the train station was sure to see it on the way to the hotel, and if they somehow missed it in the hotel they could pick up a copy on their way back to the depot.

Howard began to wonder whether Webber had been paid a flat rate or by copy sold. He suspected that the major had bankrolled the book and owned the rights to it.

Business was so good at the Arlington that after only seven years it already needed extensive repairs and refurbishing. The carpets were worn in the halls and on the stairs. Most of the rooms needed repainting, and the original building was beginning to separate from the new addition. A contractor from Jacksonville had come down and given a hideous estimate on the repairs, the cost of which Howard and the major would share equally. Howard figured the expense would hardly be enough to make the lumber baron blink, but for him it was a worrisome sum. He was having trouble keeping up with the major's pace of spending—no, *investing*—money.

So the offer to cast his fortune with the lake steamers was tempting. No hard feelings, B.F. Jordan had said with apparent sincerity.

He waited, watching the orange-laden boats collecting from the plantations along the lakeshores. Oranges in the fall and winter, then all the bounty of spring—cabbages, beans, cucumbers, tomatoes, corn, long cotton, oats, strawberries, plums, blackberries, nectarines, peaches, figs, grapes and pears. And every low-riding boat that he glimpsed from the road skirting the lake, every wagon that came groaning up the slope from the landings was a token of the opportunity slipping through his fingers. Still he waited, smoked and paced in his high-ceilinged study, snapped at Collins when the black man interrupted his thoughts, and watched as the carpenters and bricklayers and painters restored the sagging Arlington.

He had not become the civic father he had hoped to be. True, he had received congratulatory pats on the back for his work on the committee to improve the streets around the square. He had supervised the bidding for paving the streets around the Courthouse with crushed lime rock over clay. He had personally supervised the installation of sixteen kerosene streetlights on the corners within a block of the square. He had been one of the movers behind digging a new well for the square. That had been a strange experience because at about 280 feet the drill bit had brought up gold-bearing quartz. Henry Dutton, of all people, had also struck gold while having a well dug in his yard. The gold fever had died down quickly, though, when an assay determined that the vein wasn't rich enough to pay for digging it up.

So it was back to the little things. A brick walk around the square and board walks connecting the businesses facing the Courthouse. Howard was in on the improvements, but it was committee work and he found himself in the shadows of bigger men, men who had gotten there first, had invested more heavily, had taken the initiative.

Even the major was having limited success. The "Little Giants" were getting mixed results with the pumper wagon. The major had recovered very deftly from the first setback, the burning of the East Florida Seminary. He had generously invited the trustees to quarter the school in the Dennis Block until they could rebuild. And in May, when a grease fire in the kitchen sent the Varnum up in smoke the "Little Giants" had also come up short. They could send a stream of water ninety feet, and the Varnum was brick from the second story up, but after six hours the whole thing had come crashing down. The sick and exhausted firemen had performed heroically, concentrating their water on the adjoining buildings and saving them all. Meanwhile, of course, the Arlington's prime competitor had been reduced to ashes. The repairs on the Arlington were hurried all the more to accommodate the new business. With a twinkle in his eye, the major figured they could get two dollars a night for beds in some of the larger closets.

For all of his success, the major was still out of sorts half the time and

Howard could never tell what would set him off. One night he fired the dining room manager because of a soiled salad fork.

The house on Magnolia Street was prospering also. The revenue from boarders and restaurant patrons had kept it in good repair. When the letter came saying that Caroline was coming home for the first time since her elopement, her mother's confusion of emotions funneled themselves into a fury of house-cleaning. Wanting to defer the confrontation with her errant daughter, Mrs. Newhouse invited a houseful of friends to share the big day.

Penny Ward laughed and clapped Bobby La Rue on the back. A new gold filling flashed from one of his back teeth. "I'm glad to hear that you've finally gotten a job at the Arlington, but I hope the Little Giant hasn't drawn you into any of his drinkin' contests."

The dapper clerk smiled. "Oh, now that was all exaggerated, that incident with the guest. I doubt if the major drank more than a couple of glasses."

"How does he cotton to the prospect of having a demmycrat for president?" Bob Harper asked, twisting the end of his mustache to keep from smiling outright.

Bobby La Rue shook his head. "Don't rightly know. The major and I don't talk politics—any more than you and Larrabee talk table linens and bedclothes."

Larrabee went into the front room and stretched his legs toward the fire. "Seems like a week since Bob and I have talked linens."

"You still giving the canal company a run for their money?" Preacher Williams asked. "Every time I go down to the lake there's another boat on it."

"We just happen to be the best one," Bob said. "November's been good. It's right Christian of them to leave the best farms to us. Are all those boys Presbyterians or what?"

The preacher smiled. "If so, they aren't attending."

"Well, you must be getting the word to 'em all the same, Preacher, 'cause they're sure enough leaving us our niche. We've been going down to the Walls place a good deal lately."

"To Walls?" Penny sat forward. "I thought he was runnin' everthing down by rail."

Bob nodded. "Some by rail, some by us. He hailed us himself the other day, didn't he, chief? Right from his dock."

"That's right. We were so caught up talking about table linen that we almost missed the flag."

"That's how they hail us," Bob explained. "They tie a red flag to the end of the dock."

"He was in need of some medicine for his wife," Larrabee said. "We went clean on over to Vidal's and picked it up. Done it a few times. I expect he's grateful for that and goes out of his way to give us some business."

"He's got plenty of it to spread around," Penny said. "Has he bought up any more land over there?"

"You'd have to ask old Ray Polk," Larrabee told him. "He's still the clerk, isn't he?"

"Is. But you know Tom's stepping down as sheriff."

"No. When did he say that?"

"Last week. He's moving out on the Archer Road to set up in farming."

Bob had toasted his back at the fire. Now he moved around to warm the other side. "I can see how a man would want to quit while he was ahead. You never know when some crackpot's going to take a shot at you for no good reason. Be a hard man to replace."

The faint sound of a whistle brought the preacher to his feet.

"Early for the train, isn't it?" Bobby La Rue went into the front hall and looked through the trees toward Main Street.

The preacher pulled the watch from his vest pocket and opened the cover.

Everyone else looked at the clock on the mantle.

"Early by any account," Bob Harper said.

The preacher closed his watch and sat back down.

The ticking of the clock intensified the discomfort of the moment. Penny pulled at his earlobe. "What, uh, what news did she write in the letter?"

"She said that the man, Arthur, is performing and that she is not." The preacher said the word "performing" as if it might refer to something best left vague. He crossed his legs, knee over knee, and folded his arms.

Nelda came into the room with little J.J. tagging behind her. He was nearly six years old now. He had his father's ruddy complexion and his mother's robust good nature. He went up and tugged on Larrabee's sleeve.

"What did you bring for me, Uncle Nathaniel?"

His mother's scolding was lost amid the men's laughter.

Smiling, Larrabee dug into his hip pocket and pulled out a shark's tooth that covered most of his palm. "What do you think of that there, J.J.? That turned up right at the landing after last Friday's storm. How'd you like to meet up with the critter that dropped that?"

Wide-eyed, the boy snatched it up and closed his fist around it. "It don't hardly hurt now less'n you squeeze it real hard."

Just then a passing shadow caused Larrabee to look up, and his heart skipped a beat when he realized it was Anna. He hadn't been to the house since early summer and she seemed to have changed into a different person since then. Her long hair had turned a lighter brown and she wore it up now, though a wisp had come loose above her left ear. Her girlish freckles had disappeared, but she still had the russet complexion of someone who spent a good deal of time outdoors. Larrabee supposed that her long rides on Tuscawilla accounted for that. She was wearing a plain gray skirt and white shirtwaist. When she stepped over J.J.'s hobbyhorse and Larrabee caught sight of a high-button shoe he wondered if she ever ran barefoot in the yard anymore.

He stood up awkwardly, the timing being such that it was unclear whether he was acknowledging the presence of the ladies or merely stretching his legs.

"Look who's here," he said, trying to sound casual. "The fleet-footed girl."

She smiled and kept on going, giving him the notion that her smile was for everyone.

"Where you racin' off to now?" Penny asked.

"Oh, I thought I'd meet the train." She sounded nervous.

Larrabee put his hands in his pockets, still trying to look at ease. "Were you figuring to take that wild horse of yours down there?"

She laughed. "Knowing Carrie, I'd more likely need a pack mule!"

He moved toward the door with her. "What's the matter with that left hind of your mare's?" He followed her onto the porch.

She stopped and turned. "What about her left hind?"

"Seemed to me she was going light on it out there in the field."

"Are you sure? I didn't see anything yesterday."

"Could be there wasn't anything to see yesterday. Go ahead. Walk her down to the station and I'll show you."

For once Tuscawilla was easy to catch. Larrabee had brought a couple of apples in case he had trouble with Maude, and Tuscawilla readily accepted one in exchange for submitting to the halter.

"It's not so mannerly of you to leave the others this way," Anna said as she led the horse among the great shade oaks and fruit-laden orange trees.

"Not so mannerly of you either, Miss Anna. At least I didn't come through the room like it was a steeplechase."

"I can't stand the waiting. I wait better moving around than I do sitting in a chair."

"Well then I imagine you haven't changed so much after all."

Her thoughts were already back on her sister. "I'm so worried about Carrie and what's going to happen with this visit."

"Everything that's going to happen has already happened, don't you suppose?" He started to say something about how Caroline had made her bed and now would lie in it, but thought better of it.

"I'm afraid she and Mama will make a scene," Anna said, as if it were the most obvious thing in the world.

"Maybe you ought to just send us all packing and clear the floor and have at it."

"No, Mama wants to have you all there. She thinks it'll be better that way. I don't see anything wrong with that left hind leg."

"Truth to tell, neither do I now. Maybe she worked through it."

They had been walking along Liberty Street, past the Arlington's wrought iron hitching posts, when the Courthouse Square came into sight. Anna stopped suddenly.

"They're really doing it."

"Or *un*doing it," Larrabee said. "It don't look like much now, does it?"

The roof of the Courthouse was already gone. Larrabee stood stroking Tuscawilla's mane as he thought back to the day he saved the place from the burning hot air balloon. The shingles he had torn off that day were gone again, this time for good, and the open windows showed hollow in the late morning sunshine. The white picket fence still stood protectively, but the building it enclosed was hardly more than a shell.

"They say the new one will be like nothing you ever saw," Anna said. "I guess this town's just gotten too big for the old one."

Larrabee chuckled. "I believe the town got too big for the old one a long time ago. Penny told me old Tillman Ingram put it up in a few days just so the railroad would come through this way. They were off a mile or two at that. But I guess they got their money's worth out of it."

They fell silent at the sound of a distant whistle.

"That must be Caroline now," Larrabee said.

"You suppose Tuscawilla's well enough to continue on?"

Larrabee made a point of looking at the suspect leg. "I believe so. The problem seems to've cleared right up. Whatever it was."

"Is that so?" Anna turned her head too fast for him to see that she was smiling.

Caroline looked tired and a little heavier. Her strawberry blond hair had darkened and her skin was lighter, making her look less healthy. She wore a smart little hat secured to her chin with a black silk ribbon. She had on a plaid dress with a bustle, and broad belt that accentuated her bosom. She carried a parasol under one arm and, once she had climbed down from the railroad car, she reached up through the door where somebody handed down a sleeping baby wrapped in a pale blue blanket.

Anna looked at Larrabee with her hand to her mouth.

"Carrie! You never said anything about this!"

Her sister brought the baby to her bosom, looking down at him with dimpled radiance. "This is Edgar. He slept very well on the train, so well that I'm afraid he'll be up all night. He's so active. Just like his father."

"Carrie, what will Mama say?"

It was a while before Emma said anything at all about Edgar. Looking older than Caroline remembered her and a little stiff and brittle, she received her runaway daughter with reserve and dignity amid the friends and family gathered for the occasion of Caroline's homecoming. After the big mid-afternoon meal she took her turn cradling and rocking Edgar in her arms while Preacher Williams looked on with a faint, fixed smile. But when the friends withdrew after "picking the bones" for an early supper and the boarders had retired to their rooms, a silence settled over the house, a stillness that reminded Anna of a summer day heavy with clouds ready to break.

Now eighteen, she was ready to leave her childhood home, too, and she held nothing against Caroline for having done so, despite her doubts about the impetuous way she had gone. As she gazed out the window of the room she still shared with Martha, taking in the raw sawdust-scented air, Anna wondered if Caroline's elopement hadn't been driven by something more basic than love. For how could a girl fall in love with a man in just a few days?

She shook her head to banish thoughts of passion, even though more than once in the past two years she had let herself picture that first rain-soaked night that Caroline and Arthur had spent together during their escape to Georgia.

She heard a soft voice at the other end of the hall, outside her mother's bedroom, and then, softer, her mother's reply. Then the two voices became muffled as the door closed.

Caroline stood just inside the room, watching her mother brush her long hair. The preacher had kept his room. After all, it was his study. But Caroline imagined that he would want to come in before long. One of his black bow ties lay on the bureau.

Her mother looked younger in the low yellow light of the kerosene lamp beside the mirror. The gray in her dark hair was hidden in the shadow, and the lines at the corners of her eyes and mouth were washed away in the amber glow. But her features were somewhat distorted, so that for a moment, studying her mother's face in the mirror from behind, Caroline was reminded of Mad Mary, from whom she had taken the inspiration to play her first great role in the theater.

She watched her mother brushing until Mary's gap-toothed image went away.

"It's—I'm happy to see you again, Mama."

The brushing continued, slow and steady, toward the customary hundred strokes.

"Where's your baby, Caroline? I'd think you'd not want him away from your side. Such a beautiful little boy." Her mother sounded distant.

Caroline glanced toward the door. "He's sleeping, Mama. I think all that passing around must have worn him out. He fell asleep the minute Anna took him from Martha."

"What is your situation, Caroline? What are your plans?"

"Oh, well I won't be any bother. Edgar and I will be going back to Savannah in the morning. I just wanted to see everyone again and let you all know that I'm well and to tell you—"

The brushing continued in silence. Her mother had not yet turned to face Caroline.

"—and to tell you that I love you all and that—that I'm sorry."

Brush in hand, her mother turned to face her. "Sorry for what, Caroline?"

Caroline had maintained her strength and poise so far, had kept her voice steady as she had taught herself to do when she felt stage fright coming on. But now, under her mother's full gaze, she felt her knees shake and her voice falter.

"Mama, I'm sorry for leaving the way I did." She began to open and close her hands in a way that lacked theatrical polish. "I'm sorry I ran away but—my life with Arthur is good. We're happy and—Mama, I wish *you* every happiness. I'm so glad that the chair isn't empty anymore. Will you wish me happiness, Mama?"

Emma was fighting tears. She pressed her fingers to her lips, turned, and laid the hairbrush gently on the bureau, then carefully straightened the tortoise shell comb beside it. She coughed. "How can I not wish you happiness? You're my daughter, your father's daughter." She began to lose the evenness in her voice. "But you understand that it has been hard, so hard to have you go like that. I worried so. I didn't know what to tell people. I still don't know what to tell them. I just—"

Caroline closed the gap between them, put her arm around her mother's shoulder, and they both wept.

"I just keep busy," Emma said, "God knows *that's* been easy enough."

Chapter 25

John Howard continued to pace. He reached into his breast pocket for a cigar before he realized that he was already smoking one. In his mind he was debating between steamboats and timber. The gentlemen of the Alachua Steam Navigation and Canal Company had continued to be cordial. B.F. Jordan had even sent him a Christmas basket full of the biggest oranges he had ever seen with a great red ribbon tied in a bow. It reminded him of "the hat lady" who was rumored to be making so much money with her creations. Mrs. Nelda Larson Ward, wife of a one-time carpenter, now had a fine large shop on the west side of the Courthouse Square—the new Courthouse Square—now graced by an enormous red brick edifice with a clock tower.

Disgusted, Howard pitched his cigar into the cuspidor beside the desk. Half the time, smoking made his stomach hurt. Now he was having trouble keeping his mind on the question at hand: To put in with those annoyingly pleasant people with the steamboats or to accept Major Dennis' offer?

The "boatmen," as he now thought of them, were definitely continuing to prosper. They had their routes from Alachua Lake into Lake Santa Fe and were still talking about linking up through Orange Lake all the way to the St. Johns River. With the crops continuing to burst forth, the boatmen had kept buying up the plantations their boats serviced—usually at bargain prices because they waited until someone was in a hurry to sell. The advantages of the plan were so obvious. Yet the major persisted in his warnings about citrus and the proposed lake-river-and-canal route. And he was becoming increasingly militant about it. He had taken to foul language whenever the topic of oranges came up. For the first several years he had known him, Howard had never heard the major swear, but now, when certain subjects arose, he swore with verve and color.

And now the major was offering Howard a fuller partnership. He was inviting him to buy into his vast timber holdings in the north part of the county as "a logical extension of our arrangement with the Arlington." Howard had felt a flutter of honor at the pronouncement, but this was much deeper water when it came to finances. One false step and he could lose everything. But then how could you misstep with timber? As the major had said, it cost nothing to maintain. No one could steal it. The demand for it would grow as surely as the population of the county was growing. Even the fire hazard wasn't particularly great. And clearly the major's business instincts had panned out so far. After all, he was said to be one of the ten richest men in the north central part of the state.

Howard was almost relieved to hear the interruption, the tapping at the study door, although he sounded irritated when he spoke.

"What is it, Collins?"

The white-haired Negro carried a letter on a small tin plate. "It's from de major, Mist' Howard. His man ast could you reply right away?"

"Well, tell him I'm not about to cater to the convenience of his man." He let his voice drop so that the old man couldn't possibly hear him. He took the note and opened it without bothering to dismiss Collins. The major was asking to see him right away. It was a strangely courteous note. It piqued his curiosity.

Howard grunted. "Tell the major's man to tell the major that I'm on my way. Tell him that, Collins. Are my coat and hat ready? And my stick?"

"Yes, Mist' Howard. Dey shore is. Right in de front closet."

"If anyone calls, tell them I expect to be back within the hour. If I'm not, I'll probably go straight to the Arlington for dinner. Or maybe to Timbuktu."

He was back before Collins had finished blacking his boots. His business with the major took scarcely fifteen minutes, but for John Howard it was a long fifteen minutes, like an endless plunge toward oblivion. The major said that he was going to be away for a few days. He asked if Howard had made up his mind about buying into the timber partnership. "If so," said the major, "you have the opportunity to make a little money at once."

The major was squinting at him from across the desk. He seemed to squint more and more these days, indoors and out. Howard wondered if the habit was an indicator of his mental state, but he couldn't find any pattern to it.

Somewhere along the line, sometime during the pacing and smoking, Howard had already made up his mind about the partnership. No need to change horses in the middle of a race. This one was doing fine even if he was flying along at a dangerous clip.

Howard was nervous, but he decided that he might just as well put the best face on his anxiety, so he sat forward and nodded. "How could it be any other way, Major Dennis? I say we call it a partnership."

The major stood up and they shook hands across the desk. "I believe this calls for a smoke."

He opened a silver-plated humidor and offered Howard a foil-wrapped cigar. "We keep on sending cattle to the Cubans and they keep on sending us cigars in exchange. Damned if I don't think we're getting the better of the bargain."

"Absolutely." Howard lit up, wondering whether this would be the one to make his stomach start hurting again.

The major began speaking rapidly, as if he had a train to catch. "Now, here it is, John. As mentioned, I'm going to be in Tallahassee for a few days and I—we—need to cut a quick check to for that big purchase from the Santa Fe Timber Company. We'll have the exact purchase price tomorrow, but I'll be gone by then. So what you need to do is cover the amount until I get back on Monday and you'll get a hundred dollars on top of the repayment for your half."

Howard took in the spacious office with its Circassian walnut trim and handsome etchings of Paris street scenes. If the offer had come from a stranger he would take it for a swindle, but this office in this big brick building was built on the major's ability to borrow money and pay it back. More than a few bricks of Dutton's new bank had been put there by dealings with Major Dennis. Whatever amount they were talking about, it was obviously nothing to the major. Hundred dollars or no, it was clearly to Howard's advantage to cover the sum.

"Of course. I'd be delighted. What sort of price should I expect?"

The major was squinting again, perhaps because the cigar smoke was in his eyes. "Somewhere around fourteen thousand. If he goes higher than fourteen-two he's cheating you and the deal's off. But that's not likely to happen."

Howard coughed and muttered something about the grippe. He smiled. He was getting pretty good at smiling when he needed to.

"Of course. Delighted."

The major rose. "Very well. I'll see you on Monday then. I'm glad we're able to move quickly on this property. Biggest damn pines you ever saw."

And that was that. Howard was walking back home before he knew it.

He was on pins and needles for the next three days, dreading what would happen if the major were somehow delayed in coming back to town. A Tuesday or Wednesday return might work, but if the major so much as caught cold and was bedridden for a few days, it would come out that Howard had written a check for $14,120 when his account totaled scarcely half that. He fervently hoped that all the locomotives and train tracks held up between Tallahassee and the Arlington. He spent most of the three days smoking and pacing and snapping at the ever patient Collins.

Then the major was back. Howard could scarcely conceal his pleasure and relief. To the major it seemed to be just business as usual. When they met at the depot, he said a few words about the stubborn legislature, wrote Howard a check for his half plus the hundred dollars, and went on to the subject of the Arlington. The hotel was continuing to pull in good money, but was in constant need of painting and repair.

In one of his more serene moments Howard made up his mind that dealing with the major was just another form of gambling—bluffing in his case—since he didn't have nearly as much money as the major seemed to think he had. Most of his cash was tied up in the Arlington, the rest in a few high-priced timber holdings. During the first week of May he wrote another check while the major was in Jacksonville. It crossed Howard's mind that during his trips to Jacksonville the major might be availing himself of the hostesses of that conveniently distant city. After all, it was an arrangement that worked very well for Howard when he began to feel the itch. But he couldn't picture the major being similarly affected. The major seemed to have no more interest in women than he did in anything else that wasn't connected to business. He seemed to have no itch, just that squint, whatever exactly it meant.

Howard considered explaining to the major that the checks were getting too big for him to cover, but so far it was just a matter of buying time—a day or two—and then there was that hundred-dollar bonus when the major came back.

There was also the matter of the major's darkening temper. To back out of one of these checks would almost certainly lead to a fit that would end everything, perhaps publicly. There was no telling what the major would do. Better just to keep writing those checks and sweating out the days until he came back.

On a morning in early June Howard answered a summons from the major and came into the office to find him engaged in a conversation with a slender man of twenty or so, whom the major introduced as his nephew, Cary Dennis, of Salem, Massachusetts.

"Cary's down for a few days and so I shall be in and out of the office," the major said after some small talk about the heat. "John, I'd like for you to tend to the firm for the duration. I have no doubt it'll be in good hands."

Howard was thunderstruck, but he maintained his composure. The invitation was at once an honor and a breathtaking responsibility. Even the Arlington still held its mysteries for him. How could he possibly keep on top of the major's myriad business interests, even for a few days?

"Delighted," Howard said with a nod and a smile.

Cary threw his hands out. "Uncle Leonard, I hate to have you put yourself out on my account. I'd be happy enough to tag along in your footsteps as you go about your business."

"Not at all," the major said, putting a quick end to his nephew's polite argument. "John, there is the matter of a check that will come due on Friday—the twelfth. If you'll cover that, the usual arrangement will prevail."

Howard was surprised that the major was discussing their relationship so openly, but was relieved that for once he wasn't going out of town. This way he could be sure there would be no delay in the major's return.

He decided that the amount no longer mattered since the major always came in to cover the checks anyway. When Friday came, he wrote in a neat hand, without hesitation, a check for $16,223 for the purchase of timberland fronting the Santa Fe River. In this case he was relieved to find that the major intended to cover the entire sum and add the land to his personal holdings.

He blew the ink dry and, without so much as a blink, turned the check over to the seller's representative, a pale, angular person who reminded him of that horrible Sam Leary. He was glad to see him go and stood with his hands on his hips in the smoking room of the Arlington, watching the man head for the depot, satisfied that he was finally in control of this new, bigger business.

He took his evening meal at the Arlington, smoking and greeting guests as they passed by his table in front of the fireplace. It was the first pleasant meal he had enjoyed there in weeks because it had been that long since he had dined there without having to worry about the major blowing up at some poor waiter or cook. This new manager, Bobby La Rue, had been doing very well to keep everyone happy and seemed to enjoy the major's confidence, but there was no telling when it would all go awry. Howard made a point of complimenting Bobby to keep him at ease so that he'd be less likely to make a blunder in the major's presence, and the hotel was running smoothly although you could feel the tension in the air when the major was around.

Howard was so preoccupied with thoughts of the hotel and timber that he was halfway down the stairs before he realized that he still had his napkin tucked under his chin. He allowed himself a little laugh at his own expense and tossed the napkin on the reception desk on his way out. It was another warm night, close and steamy, smelling slightly of boiled vegetables, and he decided to pour himself a tall drink when he got home. As he walked the edge of the square the mammoth new Courthouse loomed above him like a mountain. Something brushed his cheek, a moth, and he quickened his step. As he opened the gate and approached the house he was surprised to see the parlor light on. He hurried up the brick walkway determined to have stern words with Collins.

He tossed his hat and stick on the front table, not bothering to take his coat off even though he was perspiring. He was headed for the kitchen when he saw the woman. She was standing at the parlor door, outlined in the light. He knew her at once by her slender figure and the plaiting of her hair.

"Hello, John. You're always in such a hurry."

He stopped, staring. "Good God, what are you doing here?"

She came forward, smiling. "Did you think I only exist in Jacksonville? I wanted to come down and see you. I hope you can put a poor girl up for the night."

He was brusque. "Yes, for two dollars. At a place called the Arlington. I'll have Collins go for a hack if you like."

"I had no idea your house was so beautiful, John. You've told me so little about yourself, about your other life, I mean." She ran her fingers over the marble mantle piece.

"With good reason. Where the devil is Collins?"

Again, that smile of hers, slight, from one side of her mouth. "I asked him to get me a headache powder at the drugstore, in case I get a headache."

She was not pretty, not exactly. Her skin was pale and her black hair a little thin. Her narrow green eyes had a way of looking at you too long before glancing away. She was almost too slender and her neck was very long. Her mouth was small and given to pouting and her chin came to a delicate point. She was not a siren and that was exactly what Howard had found so irresistible about her. At first glance she was commonplace, the girl you might see on the railroad platform or at the post office. Many were the times she had taken him into her bed for money and then disappeared in the dark as he lay spent, smelling her perfume in the pillows. He had never in his most passionate dreams expected to see her here in his house. She was right. He scarcely believed that she existed outside of Jacksonville. He wasn't even sure what her real name was.

He circled her slowly. "Maybe you *will* have a headache before the night is over. As long as you're a guest in my house I'm entitled to know what your name is"

Her look was innocent. "Jane. You know that."

"All right, Jane. Your last name?"

She was quite matter-of-fact. "Jennings. Ask anyone at the house."

"I'm afraid that's a luxury we don't have now, do we? And what exactly *does* bring you to my house, Jane Jennings?"

She wavered for a moment, her delicate jaw quivering, and then she said, "One of the girls was stabbed last night. You remember Lottie. She's the one you—"

"An occupational hazard, Jane. You mean to tell me you came all the way down here because of a brawl?"

"If you had been there you might have run too."

"Was she killed?"

"No, but there was blood all over."

Her face turned pale. She put a hand up as if to support herself and then fell forward. He caught her, held her in his arms, and brought her back to her feet.

"Poor dove. You'd think it was you that got cut."

She raised her head from his shoulder, laid the back of her hand across her brow, and started to sag again.

He half carried her into the parlor and stretched her out on the horsehair sofa. He had just brought the ottoman over to support her feet when he heard Collins coming in the back door.

Seeing the woman on the sofa, Collins stopped at the entrance to the parlor. "You want me to fetch de doctor, Mist' Howard?" His voice was high and forced.

"No, she doesn't need a doctor, Collins."

"I done brung dese powders she ast for."

"Well, leave them in the study. Bring a cup of water and then you're free to go."

Howard sat watching his visitor and listening to the hall clock, and when it chimed the quarter hour he spoke to her.

"Here's water if you want it." He held the blue enamel cup toward her.

Slowly she sat up. Her cheeks were flushed.

"You look hot. Here, have it."

Eyes closed, she sipped and handed it back.

"So. We're in a bit of a fix, aren't we, Jane?"

She let out a deep breath. "Yes, I suppose so."

He got up and turned down the lamp. The light went to deep amber.

She watched him with dark eyes.

"It's quite improper, you being here like this."

She responded with a faint smile. "Yes, isn't it. Quite improper. If you fear for your reputation, I'll go."

He laughed. "Go where?"

"Doesn't matter."

"Where's your baggage?"

"I didn't exactly take time to pack."

"A woman traveling alone without baggage? The hotels won't have you, and I'd be risking my reputation to put in a word for you at the Arlington. I suppose the Newhouses might take you. They're not too particular. But as long as you're here, maybe we should just make the most of it."

"You're so cordial, John." She was regaining her strength. She pressed her hands to her cheeks.

He sat back on the chair he had pulled up. "You are a curious person, you know. You're not at all like your business partners. You're a smart girl."

"Please, John, no business talk. I want to forget about business."

He laughed again. "You and me both! For the weekend anyway. So maybe you've come to the right place after all."

She rubbed her eye with her fingertip and gave him another of her slow, beguiling smiles.

Whether it was the heat or the light or the pounding that woke him first, Howard wasn't sure. He did know that he had slept hard. The half-empty bottle of Spanish brandy on the table by the bed reminded him of that. He sat up, naked under a single sheet. The woman was still there beside him, sleeping on her side with her back to him, wearing only a shimmy. They had been drinking the brandy straight from the bottle and he felt himself blush when he remembered what had happened after that.

The banging continued. It sounded like someone was trying to knock down the front door. He jumped out of bed, threw on his dressing gown and put his head out the window.

"Whoever you are, get away from my door before I have you arrested!"

A young man came out onto the brick walk and looked up at him. "Mr. Howard?"

"Yes! Who are you and why the devil are you banging on my door at this hour?"

"I'm Bill Willis, sir. My father told me to come find you. It has to do with Major Dennis."

Howard's head hurt. He lost his temper completely. "Then go get Major Dennis, you young fool!"

The young man came a few steps closer to the window. For a moment he looked up at Howard as if reluctant to speak, but then, seeing that he had no choice, he went ahead.

"The major is very ill, sir! My father wanted me to tell you."

Howard slammed the window down and turned back into the room. "Imbecile! Should be arrested!" He began walking in circles and ranting. Jane sat up. Her look told him that he wasn't making sense.

He fumbled his way into his clothes and hurried downstairs and rushed out the door without his hat and coat and stick. The slant of the sunlight and the farmers packing their wagons made him realize that it was not morning at all, but late afternoon, that he had slept most of the day, drugged by the passion of the night and Spanish brandy.

The major's private rooms were above his generous paneled office. Howard took the stairs two at a time and let himself into the apartment. The large sitting room was deserted. He followed the sound of subdued voices into the bedchamber, and there was the major, ashen and still, his head awkwardly high on the pillow, his hands limp and as white as the lace bedspread.

Howard thought he must have been shot, and he began thinking of names, the names of the major's enemies, but the list was far too long to be meaningful. People had been trying to kill the major for at least fifteen years.

Several men were standing at the bedside—Dr. Willis, young Bill, Cary the nephew, old Sam Carrington the Methodist minister. In the corner a Negro valet looked on, ill at ease.

"How'd it happen?" Howard asked, suddenly aware of being in his shirt-sleeves.

Cary kept his eyes on the quiet figure on the bed. He spoke in a monotone. "He woke up about three this morning and began dressing. I asked him what was the matter and he said something about not feeling so good, said he wanted to sit up. He sat down in that rocker there and propped his feet on the bed. I went back to sleep and when I woke up around eight o'clock he was still sitting in the rocker and I couldn't rouse him. I called the doctor here and we gave him salts and rubbed his hands with cold water but nothing brought him around. We put him here on the bed and he hasn't moved all afternoon. He's been lying there just like that."

Dr. Willis bent over and held a hand mirror beneath the major's nose. He waited for a long time before withdrawing it.

"He's breathing all right," Howard said impatiently. "What's this about him being so ill?"

The doctor looked at his watch then closed the cover and put it back in his vest pocket. "His pulse is getting weaker and his breathing's shallower. His pupils are dilated. They don't respond to light, not the way they should anyway." He put his hand on Cary's shoulder. "I'm sorry, boy."

Sam Carrington had been standing too long. He sat down in a ladder-back chair near the head of the bed and folded his long bony fingers. "In the midst of life. What do you suppose brought him down, Warren?"

Howard did not like minister's use of the past tense.

"It wasn't the drinking," Cary insisted tearfully. "I don't care what anybody says, Uncle Leonard was not what you would call a drinking man. He might have his nights like any man, but he was not a drinking man. He had nothing last night. I know that for a fact."

John Howard had stopped listening. He was thinking about the check he had signed. It had become routine for him to sign over his share of the Arlington as collateral even though it was worth far more than the amount of the check. A default would cost him the hotel. He would have a legally clouded title to timberland he hadn't even seen in exchange for a half share in one of the richest concerns in town. He looked at the man on the bed for some sign of life but saw none.

"This doesn't make sense," Cary was saying. "He got through the war, leading men in battle when he was scarcely my age. He had attempts on his life and now this—and we don't even know what it is."

"I hear his temperament had changed in the past few months," the doctor said. "There were stories that he was becoming quarrelsome, short-tempered. Any truth to those stories so far as you know?"

Cary seemed at a loss for words. "He was always so kind to me. I've been here almost two weeks now and he was always the kindest...."

Howard knew that plenty of people at the Arlington could verify the stories, but he saw no point in mentioning them. Did the damn squinting have something to do with it? The only thing that mattered was whether the major lived or died.

The doctor seemed not to need corroboration. He leaned forward again with his hand mirror, laid his finger below the upturned jaw, and held one wrist for what seemed a very long time. Then he took out his watch and said, "Five o'clock. Major Dennis died at five o'clock on June thirteenth. Probable cause of death, hardening of the brain." He motioned to the valet, who edged toward the bed, crossed the dead man's hands over the motionless chest, and tied a handkerchief under the sagging chin. The minister rose and put a half dollar over each closed eye. Cary Dennis sank down at the foot of the bed, weeping.

"Gentlemen," the minister said, "a moment of prayer, please."

Cary could not bring himself to stand, but the others bowed their heads awkwardly while the frail minister spoke in his reedy voice.

"Our heavenly Father, we commend to Thy care the soul of the Little Giant, Major Leonard G. Dennis. Some of his enemies would not hesitate to defame him even now that he is dead, but he was a man of many admirable qualities. He fought an open, fair fight, stood firmly by his friends, was brave, bold, and generous. As a youth he knew the depraving influences of war, its license and its violence, and its perils no doubt warped somewhat his impulsive, dashing nature. But he goes now to that place where there is no north or south, only the unending east of the Resurrection where he will await Thy judgment and mercy. We now commend his everlasting soul to Thy care. In the name of Thy son, Jesus Christ, we pray. Amen."

To which every man in the room echoed, "Amen."

John Howard walked back to his fine shaded house in a shambles, oblivious to the street clatter that promised another noisy Saturday night. He opened the gate, drifted down the brick walk, up the curved steps, and into the front hall, ghostlike. He felt a terrible emptiness. Shock. And grief for a man who seemed to have been known by no one. He was hardly aware of the slender, green-eyed woman who stared at him from the foot of the stairs.

"What is it, John? What's happened?"

Her words brought a sharp pain that cut through the numbness.

He scarcely brought his eyes up to meet hers.

"I'm ruined," he said. "Ruined."

Chapter 26

"You've sure gotten your money's worth out of that harmonica this summer. What's made you take it up all of a sudden?"

Larrabee left off playing "Camptown Races" and tapped the instrument on his arm. "I've had it for going on ten years. Anna gave it to me my first Christmas here. I just figured I ought to put it to use."

"Well, chief, I sure hope you gave her something better than what you got."

Larrabee thought back to that troubled time, the taxes due, Preacher Williams at death's door, and Jared Penrod lost under the hooves of panicked cattle. In a voice too soft to hear, he said, "I gave her a little swaybacked horse whittled out of soft pine."

"Better keep practicing," Bob said. "If business gets any thinner you might be playing that thing for a living. You and Bobby La Rue could play duets for dimes down at Duke's."

"Bobby La Rue hardly goes down to Duke's anymore. He's all tied up at the Arlington."

Bob gave the tiller of the *King Payne* a shake to clear some duckweed from the rudder. They were finishing up for the day after making another special delivery to Walls' plantation, some new kind of medicine from the drugstore. The evening was hot and still, and the spreading wake of the boat was visible half a mile back. The low gray clouds had held their rain all day, and now in the west a copper sun was breaking through.

"I hear old John Howard still owns a share of the Arlington. I thought he lost it when the Little Giant died."

"I don't follow John's business as close as some do, but I've seen him over there on the veranda a time or two, so you can figure he still has a share in it."

Larrabee went back to his playing, one note at a time instead of a whole mouthful.

"I saw him up there on the square the other day at the battle of the ice blocks. That's a sorry-looking place now that the Dennis Block's burned down. Being brick you'd have thought it would've held up better than that. The Courthouse did."

"Did you bet on those ice blocks, Bob?"

"I did not! For one thing, I was not about to stand around watching a couple blocks of ice melt. That's not my idea of sport."

"They had shotgun guards on that ice. Somebody thought it was *more* than sport."

"Ice is ice, chief. I don't care if you cut it out of a pond in Maine or conjure it up artificial. You don't prove nothing by watching a couple of ice blocks melt."

"I still don't see how you can make ice, Robert. Can you tell me how they do that?"

"No. You ask Mr. Mack and then see if you can explain it to me."

It was so warm that Larrabee figured he'd sleep on the boat that night as long as the mosquitoes didn't get to him. He found it very hard to imagine how anyone could make ice in such weather.

"I bet old Curtis'll be right interested in it. They say—who is that fella?"

"Mr. Mack? Mr. A.J. McArthur. Hails from up in Wisconsin."

"They say he's fixing to put up an ice factory down there near Doig's foundry."

"I tell you, chief, I'd buy a piece right now. Put it in the house and cozy up to it all night."

"I thought you'd rather be cozying up to the widow Summerton. How long's the colonel been dead now?"

"I couldn't tell you exactly. And where'd you go getting ideas like that?"

Larrabee did a run on the harmonica, making each note in the scale separate and distinct. "Just seemed like more than business passing between you. She's a fine-cut widow, Bob. Not all of 'em come with ringlets like that, kind of old-fashioned. I believe I've seen her smile right pretty at you a time or two. It was only polite for you to smile back. She's become quite the steady customer too. When the Steam Navigation Company's taken over this whole lake, I imagine we'll still have her and Walls to carry for."

Bob took a plug of tobacco from his shirt pocket and started whittling off a piece. "All right then. I'll keep on smiling at Mrs. Summerton and you can smile at Josiah T. Walls." He cut his piece and tucked it in his cheek. "Unless of course you'd rather save your smiling for somebody else who don't even live on the lake."

"Lake seem low to you?" Larrabee was eyeing the southern shore where the water oaks and stout cabbage palms bowed toward the dark water.

"I've seen it lower. Days it seemed like we were plowing instead of boating. That's to our advantage as long as we've got enough water for the *King Payne*. Let all the rest of 'em run up in the mud and we'll wave as we go by."

It proved a good season for all of the lake boats. In September the cargo was watermelons and tomatoes and a host of other vegetables; in October— the second crop of sorghum and the first oranges; in November, December and

January—more oranges. In February it was sugar cane and honey.

On a chilly Sunday afternoon in February Larrabee and Bob hitched Maude to the wagon and drove into town with a load of cane to have rendered into sugar at a small mill about a mile west of town. While they were waiting for their sugar, they drove into town to see the Wards and the Newhouses and to see if they couldn't trade a little sugar for some coffee.

"I believe Nelda has taken up tea-drinking," Larrabee remarked as they nudged Maude up West Main Street. "And didn't I hear Mrs. Summerton allow as to how she has a fondness for tea?"

"Maybe you did." Bob watched a boy with a chameleon chase a girl in Sunday white.

"I hear Nelda gets her tea all the way from New York City and that the New Yorkers get it all the way from China."

"That so?"

"Have to be pretty fine tea, wouldn't it? To come all the way from China like that."

"I wouldn't know. I ain't so much of a tea drinker."

"Well, maybe you ought to be, Bob. I'll bet a person could meet some mighty keen folks drinking tea from China."

"Then you just try it and report back to me. What is that racket coming from the Wards' house?"

Bob started to tie the wagon to the picket fence in front of the Ward cottage, but saw that Penny had left a black-and-yellow anchor near the gate and so he tied up to that.

They pushed through the gate and followed the commotion around to the back of the house where about two dozen men and boys were squaring off in a field for some kind of contest. Penny was standing at the edge of the fray smiling and talking to Preacher Williams.

"What you got here?" Bob asked. "Re-doing the Battle of Olustee?"

"Hello there, boys!" Penny clapped Bob on the shoulder. "What we have here is likely more dangerous. It's a game of football."

"Football!" Bob dug into his hip pocket for his tobacco plug and penknife. "Don't believe I've ever seen it. How's it work?"

"You'll have to ask J.J. about that. This here's his seventh birthday party— a little late. He got in his mind that he wanted to celebrate with a game of football, which takes a herd of about fifty men, don't it, Preacher?"

The preacher nodded. "Twenty-five on a side." He was still in his black church suit. He was puffing on his pipe in an effort to keep it from going out.

"We had to argue about that for a while," Penny said. "Bill Willis says it's fifteen by the latest rules."

The shoving and taunts passing between the two mobs perplexed Larrabee. "How do you play? Looks to me like it's all arguing."

"Well, you've got a goal on each end of the field there, in between where them chairs is set. You git the ball through there one way or the other—on the other feller's side of the field—and you git one point."

"And how do you decide who gets the ball?"

"My friend, that's what you're about to see."

Barkley Duforge stood in between the two teams and tossed a coin, and before anybody knew what had happened somebody had grabbed the ball and was running for the end of the field. A bull-necked man of about twenty—Larrabee thought it was one of the O'Dells—came running at the ball carrier with his head lowered. They collided like two locomotives and the ball popped up into someone else's hands. That man took off in the other direction pursued by a rabble of men and boys who threw themselves on his back and neck and brought him down kicking.

"Preacher's here to keep the swearin' down," Penny said.

Nelda came out the back door accompanied by Emma and Martha and Anna. Emma looked worried and seemed to think the game should be stopped, but Anna went to the edge of the field and watched, fascinated. Martha came up beside her trying to figure out what all the excitement was about.

J.J. was having the time of his life, running after everyone who got the ball, but staying well back when the pile-ups started.

"Now I know why they start with twenty-five to a side," Bob said. "They need plenty of replacements. Who wins—the side with the most men left alive?"

"The side with the most points," Penny said wisely.

Barkley had the ball now and his opponents were coming at him with outstretched arms. He ducked and sprinted through the defenders. One remained between him and the goal. He feinted right, lunged left, and bolted through the chairs to the loud acclaim of his teammates and Anna and Martha.

Larrabee took off his vest and started rolling up his sleeves.

Bob gave him a strange look. "Now what's come over you?"

"Looks like those fellas over there need a hand. They're one short. Can't be so much different from running cattle."

"Then maybe you ought to play on horseback."

Larrabee ran onto the field and spiked the ball out of Barkley's hands. A free-for-all ensued with everybody wrestling and bucking and snorting. Somehow J.J. wound up with the ball and he broke for the opposite side of the field but tripped, leaving Larrabee to scoop it up and pass through the undefended goal for him.

Apparently nonpartisan, the onlookers cheered. Anna broke into a little hop and let out a whoop.

"See," Larrabee called to Bob, "there ain't much to it!"

At the kickoff Bill Willis knocked the ball out of the air and tried to run it down the side, but Barkley and his men mowed down his defenders, and the doctor's son found himself cornered. Amid much loud advice from the sidelines he simply threw the ball over their heads.

"That's against the rules," Preacher Williams said.

"What rules?" Bob wondered.

Larrabee, still picking himself up from the stampede, pulled in the ball and ran with it.

It went on that way until each team—noticeably reduced by scratches, bruises and exhaustion—had four points.

"Shall we call an end to the carnage?" the preacher asked Penny. "Next team to score wins!" he announced.

Again the ball went into the air. Larrabee, who was slippery with sweat, wiped the matted hair from his eyes and punched the ball toward his team's goal. The field was wide open and everybody ran after the leather sphere. Bill got to it first and was overwhelmed in an instant. Anticipating the threat, one of the defenders had rushed to the goal and was joined by a second. Larrabee threw himself on the ball, staggered to his feet and charged, cheered on by his entire team and everyone on the sidelines. He reached the first defender and broke to the right, then knocked into Barkley, leg to leg, with a loud cracking sound.

He hobbled the last few feet to the goal, knocked over one of the chairs, and went sprawling on the grass. Where the ball had gone he had no idea. He was doubled up, rolling on the ground, gripping his right leg.

As if they were still playing, everyone came running up and crowded around him.

"I heard that snap clean across the field," someone was saying. "You busted that leg for sure."

"Well, let's leave that for a doctor to say," someone else said.

"You poor thing! What are you going to do now?" Anna cut through the crowd and knelt beside him.

Chapter 27

"If you keep thrashing around like that it never will mend," Anna said. "But it's your limb."

"My limb," Larrabee grunted. "The way I drag it around it *feels* more like a limb than a leg."

He was sitting on the porch swing with his crutches propped against the rail. He was restless and uncomfortable.

Anna was sitting on a rocking chair. She smiled and leaned toward him. "A limb," she said in a husky, confidential voice. "That's what Mama calls it—a limb. She thinks it's improper to have *legs*."

"Is that so. And what do you think?"

"About legs? I'm all for them."

He watched a gray squirrel scurrying up a pine tree, envying its nimbleness. "It's warm out here. You'd think it was already spring."

Another squirrel was chasing the first round and round the trunk. They wound up in the branches and then the first squirrel jumped onto a branch of an adjacent tree. Anna smiled. "That's because you've been working so hard at just getting around. Now that you're sitting, you ought to settle down and stop fidgeting."

"I'm not fidgeting. I'm trying to get comfortable. I'm banking on that woman being wrong. Two months is a long time."

"Nathaniel Larrabee, she is not *that* woman. She's Dr. Sarah Robb."

"It just seems peculiar. A woman doctor."

"Oh, don't be so provincial."

"Whatever *that* is, I still wish Dr. Willis wasn't in Charleston."

"Don't you suppose one doctor's about as good as the next when it comes to fixing a broken leg? Even a woman doctor."

"What's this the preacher's going to announce at supper tonight?"

"I don't know. I think Mama's the only other one who does. I guess you'll be around for supper?"

"Very amusing." Larrabee folded his arms and glowered at the pine trees across the street.

Anna sighed. "Poor Bob. What's he going to do?"

"Poor Bob! Don't go feeling sorry for Bob! He's got two solid legs under him, a boat, and all the business he can handle. And to add insult to injury, he's got your hard-shinned friend Barkley Duforge working in my stead—for the duration. So let's not hear any more about poor Bob."

Anna picked up her feet and let the rocking chair carry her back and forth gently. "The duration's going to be longer than two months if you insist on fixing things around here day and night. Dr. Robb told you to rest that leg or risk having it re-set."

"There's one woman doctor in this whole town and I had to get her instead of her husband. Look, I've got to do *something* to earn my keep."

"You could whittle me another horse like the one you gave me for Christmas that time."

"That was Jared Penrod who whittled that horse mostly. I ain't half the whittler he was."

Anna stopped rocking. "You never did tell me just what happened to him."

"It was a long time ago." Larrabee got up, supporting himself on the rail. "What's all that yelling over there?"

Anna had heard it too. She was accustomed to the shrill voices of children at play, but this was a man and there was no playfulness in his voice.

"It's coming from over toward the Arlington," Larrabee said. "Sounds like Baldy Choat." He rose up higher. Somewhere in the distance a bell sounded. "He's yelling about fire!"

After that, everything seemed to happen at once.

Two horses came galloping down the street, then a third, wild and headlong. The loud voices of men mixed with shrill whinnying and the erratic stamping of hooves. Smoke rose black and thick through the trees. The bell continued to clang, its tinny sound nearly lost in the increasing uproar of men and animals. A woman screamed. A hot wind swept across the porch where Larrabee and Anna now stood staring toward the noise and heat. Emma and Martha came out. The preacher's wife still had a scrub brush in her hand.

"What do you suppose it is?" Emma asked. "Not the new Courthouse."

Larrabee leaned on his crutches as if to propel himself toward the fire. "No, see it's coming from over there—and the horses came from the stable. It's the Arlington. The Arlington's on fire!"

He began working his way down the steps.

"Nathaniel, you can't go over there!" The preacher had come out in his shirtsleeves.

"I can pass a bucket as well as the next man. I think it's going to take more than the Little Giants to stop this one."

"Well, wait for me! We can't have you falling over on the way there!"

"Anna, where do you think you're going?" Her mother came down the steps after her.

"I can help fill the buckets, Mama!"

"You just stop right there! I won't let you!"

"Mama, I'm nineteen years old. I want to help."

Her mother stopped at the foot of the steps as if the yard were water. "Those men aren't going to want you there, Anna."

Her daughter was already out of earshot.

The preacher turned as he hurried down the steps and called back to Martha. "You stay and take care of your mother now. You wet down as much of the house as you can get to in case the fire comes this way. We'll be back soon's we can."

The Little Giants were already there, pumping an arc of water fifty feet into the air, dousing the broad veranda without any noticeable effect. The water brigade had formed across the street at the Courthouse pump. A dozen heavy wooden buckets passed from hand to hand, discharged their meager contents onto the burning face of the building, and looped back to the pump. Anna and the preacher served as bucket runners, Larrabee spelled the man at the pump, who moved up near the head of the line just as the windows in the dining room doors began shattering.

"Son of a bitch is going up fast," said the man who grabbed the bucket at the pump.

"It's been so dry," said the man next to him.

"Little Giants ain't too good on the bigger places, er they?" said a third.

"It's going so fast it's hard to tell whereabouts it started at."

"It was in the stable. You should've seen them horses come running out of there!"

"It was Baldy Choat got 'em out. He come roaring like thunder 'n purty and near cleared the whole place out afore she went up."

"Baldy Choat! Last time I saw him he was clapped into the stocks on the Courthouse Square."

"Well, today he shore was in the right place at the right time."

The Little Giants and the bucket brigade moved back as parts of the hotel began falling from the upper stories. A railing peeled away and crashed into the street. Moldings and siding and ornaments dropped away. Shards of hot glass flew like shrapnel.

"This one's done for!" shouted somebody near the pump. "Start putting your water on these other buildings before they go up!"

The Little Giants kept it up for a while longer, bravely pressing close to the roaring fire until the heat was too much to bear. Then they too withdrew and began wetting down the trees and stores across West Main, the drugstore, the photographer's studio, the tobacco shop. By the time the lofty Arlington had been reduced to two tall brick chimneys and a large jagged stack of black flickering rubble, it was clear that the other buildings had been spared. Men sat on the Courthouse lawn, shirtless, black-faced and sweating. Larrabee and the preacher were drinking from a bucket as if it were a big cup. Anna dipped her hand into another and drank until she could drink no more.

"Craziest damned thing," somebody said. "No sooner do you build a decent Courthouse than the rest of the square burns down around it."

Everybody around him chuckled at that.

"John Howard still owns a share of it, don't he?"

"*Did* own," someone amended. "Haven't seen him today."

"I heard he was up in Jacksonville. Took himself a wife, y'know."

"Well, he's done lost the honeymoon suite."

Everybody laughed at that too. Bad as the ruin was, they were all relieved that nothing else had caught fire. The hotel had been something they could point to with pride, but few of them had any real stake in it except for a forlorn figure that Larrabee recognized as Bobby La Rue. He sat on the Courthouse steps, his knees drawn under his chin, blinking at the charred sticks across the street.

Larrabee gathered his crutches and swung his way over to him.

Bobby looked up and moved over to make a place for him on the steps. "Hello, Larrabee. I heard you busted your leg."

"Playing some crazy game." Larrabee took up a place beside him. The former occupants of the hotel were wandering around the square. A few of them were carrying baggage. Mostly they were just drifting back and forth, dazed. Men who looked like railroad bums, women in dirty dresses and drooping hats, children with red faces and runny noses.

"It's a sorry pass," Larrabee said. "What do you reckon you'll do, Bobby?"

Bobby stretched his legs a little and brushed some sand from a step with his foot. "I'm about running out of hotels. First the Varnum, now this. There's still the American and the old Alachua, but they can't hold a candle to what the Arlington was."

"Well, I don't know if Duke's aware of it, but his place could sure use some livening up. He's been real short of music lately, could definitely use some more piano-playing."

Bobby stood up and patted him on the shoulder. "All my music was in there. But thanks for the thought, Larrabee. I'll see you around. Take care of that leg now." He straightened what was left of his coat and walked into the crowd.

Chapter 28

Not since the preacher's wedding had the church been so full. Rumor had it that Preacher Williams had more in mind than just introducing his new assistant to the congregation. By now most of them had met "the new man," a trim, brushed twenty-six-year-old by the name of Roland Bonds. He had a pleasant smile, a firm handshake, a fondness for mashed potatoes with chicken gravy, and a tendency to quote Scripture even when it didn't quite match the point he was trying to make. The question circulating among backyard fences and laundry lines was how the church was going to pay for the two of them, a point on which the elders were annoyingly mum.

Lily Poinsett, who broke out in a rash when she kept a secret for more than a day, was driven to distraction when her own husband, Virgil, apparently suffered no discomfort while withholding the privileged information from her.

She decided to proceed without solid information and told everyone that Preacher Williams was about to leave town and turn the church over to young Mr. Bonds.

No one was more surprised than she was on that warm, stuffy February morning when it turned out to be perfectly true.

Preacher Williams did a fine job of weaving the announcement into his sermon. He took as his text the story of Christ's forty days in the wilderness and indicated in his firm, crackling drawl that Christ's sojourn had been an inspiration to him of late. Then he took a turn and got onto the subject of spreading the Gospel beyond the borders of Christendom.

"And so," he concluded, gripping the pulpit with his big, gnarled hands, "and so, in consultation with my dear wife, I have decided to quit this place where I have found so much fulfillment for these fifteen years and to spread the good news of the Savior's coming in a distant land." The members of the congregation looked at each other, conjecturing what land this might be. "I am sad and I am happy to announce that on the eighteenth of April my wife and my daughters and I will be leaving this Eden of the South for four years to take up missionary work near Canton, China."

China! He had to quiet them down with raised hands.

Anna and Martha, sitting in the front pew as usual, couldn't help turning to see who was saying what. They had received the news only the day before, and neither of them had had time to let it sink in. Anna believed that she was now living in a very strange dream. She was sure that she would wake up and find that she had fallen asleep again while looking at the atlas. China! It was nothing but a strange green bulge on the map. She knew not the first thing about China and she knew no one who did. She did know that she had no wish to go there. She knew that as the eighteenth of April approached—which just happened to be her twentieth birthday—she would find it harder and harder not to cry and she wasn't entirely sure why.

Martha had been strangely excited about going to China, and Anna had done nothing to dampen her enthusiasm although she was sure that Martha had no concept of how far away China was and how long they would be there and what a weird place it must be. Martha seemed to think that going to China was something like going to Oliver Park for a picnic—not something that would take them away from home for a large part of their lives. During those four years they wouldn't see Penny and Nelda or the Willises or the Poinsetts or Mr. McMarris, who still came down from Tennessee in the winter, or Duke Duforge, or the surprisingly polite and good-looking Barkley, or—or any of them.

And if it turned out that they *never* came back, what then?

Three days later, after supper, she felt the tears coming and she ran out to the summer kitchen to cry. In her haste she nearly knocked Larrabee over as he hobbled in from shutting up the hen house for the night.

"Whoa there, Miss Anna! You'll break my other, uh, limb!"

Without saying a word, she swept past him. He went after her, moving swiftly if unevenly on the crutches. He caught up with her at the door to the summer kitchen. She stood with one hand on the doorjamb as if gathering her strength.

"It's too pretty a night for the blues," he said as if speaking to someone else. He was looking up at Venus glowing steady and bright in the purple twilight beyond the paddock. "Every so often a night like this just makes you stop and enjoy it no matter what comes before or after."

She turned toward him. "That's easy for you to say. Nothing ever bothers you."

He swung around and looked at her. "Plenty of times I wished that was so. I suppose you're not so keen on going to China."

"Why shouldn't I be? I'll be with my family. Preacher will be doing important work. I'll get to see wonderful palaces and mountains that cut the sky."

"Mountains that cut the sky, huh? They have those over there?"

"That's what Preacher says. He got it in a letter from the head of the mission."

"Then it must be so. How's Martha feel about it?"

"She's just as keen on it as I am."

"Or as you make out to be."

"What do you know about it?"

"I'm sorry, Anna. I didn't mean anything. I was just hoping to cheer you up."

"If you want to cheer me up, why don't you buy my horse?"

"Buy Tuscawilla? I wish I could. But most everything I have is tied up in the *King Payne*."

She seemed to think that he had missed the point. "You don't have to pay me right away. You can send me a dollar or two a month for as long as it takes. Four years for all I care. How's that? Or would the postage be too much? After all, it's China."

He didn't know how to handle her anger. He tried for the fastest way to please her. "All right if that'll help. I can give you about three dollars—"

"Don't give me *anything!* Just take the horse! She'd be a sight safer to ride than Maude. Soon as your leg gets better, just take her!"

She turned and ran into the night and this time he didn't dare pursue her.

The stove in the office was working too well. Dr. Willis opened the window a crack to let in some of the sweet damp air. When the window started to slide back down he propped it up with a piece of kindling. The preacher used the opportunity to study a bottle of Jack Daniels on the roll-top desk.

"For medicinal purposes," the doctor said.

"I had no doubt about it," Preacher Williams told him. "The bottle's dusty."

"Well, Zeke, I have the pleasure of informing you that you're healthy. Though your chess game was a little off tonight. You might consider taking a shot of that stuff every now and then to loosen the strings. Do you suppose they even have whiskey where you're going? I mean China, not heaven."

The preacher smiled. "I hear it's a big place. China, that is. There's likely a bottle or two around for those who feel the need."

Dr. Willis sat down in his swivel chair and pressed his fingertips together. "Then I have just one more question, Zeke."

"Yes?" The preacher sounded wary.

"That road that goes from Tallahassee to link up with the military road to St. Augustine. The one they cut through the year you and I were born. What do they call that?"

The preacher thought for a moment, wondering if the doctor's memory was starting to fail him. "It's the old Bellamy Road. Everybody knows that."

The doctor gave him a knowing look.

"Oh, I see. Thank you very much, Warren. I needed that."

"You're not the proverbial spring chicken, Zeke. You're sixty-two. Isn't it kind of late in life to be picking up and traipsing off ten thousand miles away or whatever it is? Aren't there enough pagans right here in Alachua County to last you a lifetime?"

"Maybe being old has something to do with it, Warren. I've spent too many years to count, preaching. Preaching politely to folks who nod politely, knowing their Scripture well enough but don't have the fire of it burning in them. That's all I want, Warren—a chance to see souls coming fresh to the Gospel. You remember that teacher who came down here for a few seasons? Roper's nephew?"

"Ronald McMarris."

"That's right. Well, I used to envy him holding forth in that little moss-covered wreck of a school because he was right there on the front line between ignorance and knowledge and he was turning over young minds every day."

"Once they stopped putting snakes in his desk."

"Or, how about this? What if you were spending all your time trimming hangnails when down the road—in Newnansville or Starke—there was a whole town full of people dying from the yellow jack or scurvy?"

"If it was scurvy I could do something for 'em."

"Warren, you take my meaning I think."

"I take your meaning. How are the women in your life taking this? They happy about it?"

"Happy enough I think. Happy enough." The preacher paused. "I'm a little worried about Anna."

"She's almost twenty. It's a hard time to know a person's mind. Tell you a story about one of my Scottish Presbyterian forebears, a young woman by the name of Catherine McClusky whose folks were setting sail from Londonderry to Philadelphia in 1726. Catherine had taken a shine to a Catholic boy, and when the ship pulled out of the harbor she jumped ship. I mean, literally jumped into the water and swam to the boy. The family never saw her again."

The preacher got up and lifted the bottle. "You got a glass or shall we just pop the cork and pass this back and forth?"

Iris Poinsett pretended not to be listening. Her mother and Nelda Ward were talking about China with Emma, Emma Newhouse, as they occasionally called her from habit.

"Tell me about the mission," Mrs. Poinsett was saying. "Will Preacher Williams have to learn Chinese?"

The questions went on and on, and to her dismay Emma didn't know most of the answers. She couldn't even remember the name of the city they were going to, and she didn't know if it was in the cold, dry north or the lush, tropical south. She was able to tell them that the term of her husband's residence was four years, although the distance made her think of it as permanent. After all, so much could happen in four years if you were halfway around the world.

"And what will you be doing with the house?" Mrs. Poinsett was asking. "Now that you have the restaurant so successful and all."

That was one of the happier tidings Emma could report. They had worked out a lease with Bobby La Rue. With the Arlington burned to the ground he had no prospects except for the undersized Alachua Hotel and the rundown American. Those were no sure thing, and the chance to run his own place was one that Bobby jumped at. As for the rooms, he could live in one himself and rent out the other four or five out as he saw fit. The money would be a long time getting to China so Preacher Williams had told him to deposit it in his account at the Dutton Bank.

"We'll expect to have quite a fortune waiting for us when we get back," the preacher had said.

"Of course, you'll want to give ten percent of it to the church," Bobby had replied with a twinkle in his eye.

"What about the girls?" Iris asked. "Are they getting more excited as the time draws nigh?"

Emma didn't know how to answer that one. Martha seemed eager to discover that strange new land far beyond the loblolly pines and beggar weed. But Emma wasn't sure that she fully comprehended the distance and the time involved. Martha was almost fifteen years old now. She would grow to full womanhood in China. She would receive her first gentlemen caller in China, a merchant or missionary's son perhaps. It was so hard to picture how it would all turn out.

As for Anna, she had put the best face on her feelings, but her acceptance of the move seemed to be more for Martha's sake than a true willingness to go. In unguarded moments she had shown tension. Someone whistling, the clomping of boots on the front porch, the sound of a rider approaching at dusk—those things had jerked her from deep thoughts and it took a while for her usual bright mood to return.

All of those shadows would disperse, Emma told herself, once they had said their good-byes and climbed onto the mail coach to Newnansville. And once they were on the westbound train there would be wonders to behold, too many exciting new things to see for anyone to dwell on what they might be leaving behind in Florida.

The eighteenth of April came sooner than anyone expected. The packing had gone on for what seemed like weeks, even though they were leaving all of the furniture, many of the preacher's books, and all of the household goods. Clothing and a few reminders of home were all they carried, but it was enough to fill four fair-sized steamer trunks and half a dozen hatboxes.

"Let us know if they like them hats in China," Penny said as they waited for the mail coach. "We might strike up a business relationship."

Nelda laughed. "Don't you pay him any mind. I'll have him all straightened out by the time you get back."

Dr. Willis looked at his watch and then tucked it back into his vest pocket. "Late as usual. You'd think they were coming from Key West instead of Micanopy."

"We'd probably have time for one more move in the chess game," the preacher said. "Seems to me you dug yourself a bit of a hole, Warren, by throwing away your rook."

"I didn't throw it away. I sacrificed it for position, as you would find out if you weren't rushing off to some godforsaken corner of the map. The game of chess is about location. That's what's important—location. Maybe you'll figure that out some day. Location."

"I was serious about continuing the game by mail, Warren."

"Do you know how many years it would take to play chess between here and China? We'd still be at it into the next century."

"Seems to me worse things could happen. Tell you what. I'll send you my move and you send one back if you aren't stumped completely."

"That'll be the day when you stump me, you old geezer. When I knock over your king you'll be able to hear me crow all the way to China!"

"This has got to be about the biggest turnout the mail coach ever had," Bobby La Rue said. "You have most of the town here. Most of the folks that count anyway."

He and Anna got into a polite conversation about how the restaurant would work out. When Larrabee came up and tried to give her ten dollars as a down payment on Tuscawilla she pretended not to hear him.

"I suppose you'll want to spend it before you get to China," he said to nobody in particular. "I don't imagine they'll take it over there. But I expect there'll be an opportunity to unload it between here and San Francisco."

She was going on about linen napkins and tablecloths. "I always thought we should have them," she was telling Bobby. Then she startled him by giving him a big hug and telling him how much she was going to miss him.

"You sure have a way with the ladies," Bob Harper told the innkeeper. He put up a hand to settle the crow on his shoulder. Children eager to pet the bird were making it beat its wings nervously.

"Is that crow for rent?" Larrabee asked. "I need to get someone's attention."

"No, Old Flap stays with me. We're like toast and jam, ain't we, Flap?"

Larrabee nodded toward a dust whirl far up on Main Street. "Yonder comes the mail coach. I imagine that'll be that."

Bob straightened up and Old Flap moved high on his shoulder beyond the reach of little hands. "The place won't hardly be the same without you folks. We won't know what to do with ourselves next time we come into town."

Preacher Williams watched the mail coach come rattling up the street. "Well, Bob, you come on up to the house from time to time and make sure that Mr. La Rue keeps it proper. You might even stop by the church now and then to see how Preacher Bonds is doing. How long before you're back on two feet again, Nathaniel? Didn't you see Mrs. Doctor or Mr. Doctor Robb this morning?"

"I saw the Missus. Doctor Willis said she'd been the alpha of it so she may as well be the omega. Whatever exactly he meant by that."

Bob laughed so loud that Old Flap took to the air for a moment. "You and the ladies, Larrabee! You run afoul of 'em everywhere you turn. What'd she say?"

"About three or four more weeks if I stay away from ball games. Otherwise she'd have to bust it all over again to set it straight."

"Well, you get any better on them crutches and you'll be a sure thing in the three-legged race."

The crowd fell back out of the street to make way for the mail coach, which was coming on with an excess of yipping and whiplash. The driver was a fat man with short red hair. Beside him was a bony boy who clung to the seat and the rail as if he expected to be pitched over the horses' heads at any moment.

"Well, this is it!" Everybody seemed to be saying the same thing. "It sure looks like this is it!"

Puffing and grunting, the drivers got the steamer trunks loaded, two in the back and two on top. Martha was smiling and blushing at all the good wishes. Emma was nodding and embracing her old neighbors, one and two at a time while the sweating coach driver and his boy stood by patiently.

"Ain't seen such a commotion down here on the square since that balloon set fire to the Courthouse," Penny said.

"Or that hanging in '75," Duke Duforge said cheerfully. His bald head and bright blue eyes towered over everyone, except for his red-nosed brother Tom, who had come in from his new farm to see everyone off.

"Looks like that country air don't agree with you any more than here in the big city," Dr. Willis told Tom. "You still sneezing the walls down at this time of year?"

"No, I'm just fine, doc. And there's a bridge in New York I want to sell you cheap."

Larrabee stood by the coach door and helped Martha in, then Emma. When Anna came forward she smiled politely and said, "No thanks, I can get it. Take care of yourself now. It's been a pleasure knowing you."

He reached out to touch her, to touch her shoulder, her elbow, her hand, but the preacher came in between them, and, surprisingly fast, the fat driver was back in the seat with his boy beside him. Hands went out from the crowd as the mail coach pulled into West Main Street. Handkerchiefs waved from the coach windows. Martha's face appeared for a moment and was lost in the dust. Larrabee saw Anna glance toward the throng and then look away.

Bob put his hands on his hips as the coach disappeared past the black ruins of the Arlington. "Well, my friend, I guess that's that."

When he turned around for a reply, Larrabee was gone.

Chapter 29

Ed Wheeler wiped his mouth on his sleeve and took another sip from his flask. "The thing of it is, Corky, this here's mostly water, just plain water from Boulware Springs. Sweetest water in the county, with just enough yahoo to give it some bite and keep the yellow jack away. And you know I ain't been sick a day in my life! It's on account of the fresh air and a little of this here mix. That's all there is to it."

Corky clung to the handgrip behind him. "I b'lieve I could use a little of that to numb the bruises, Ed! This here road's the worst I've ever seed it. I'm sure my hind end is black and blue and I s'pose them folks down b'low must be rattling their teeth out. Them girls wasn't bad looking when they got in, but they'll be bruised goods getting out. Cain't they do nothing 'bout this road?"

A front wheel struck a pothole and Corky nearly left the coach, but Ed sat comfortable and secure, held down by his sheer weight.

He shook his head. "You should've been here ten years ago! When it rained you didn't have nothing but a river and when it didn't the whole road liked to blow away! There wasn't hardly no potholes because there wasn't hardly no road! I recollect I was carrying a load of produce one time, including eggs if you can believe that. That's right, about a couple gross of eggs right up top there, clean into Newnansville from some farm or other up this way. Well, I was coming along at a fair clip 'cause I was a foolish young buck like you, cocky because I knowed every hole in the road that was there the day before. That was the thing of it. The day *before*. Well, I was along in here somewheres and before I knew what was up, the road clean dropped out from under me! The whole rig must've fell down about half a foot in a wash and rammed into the team, which took off like a firecracker with everthing clattering and banging till I thought the whole coach would come apart before it stopped! And you know what finally stopped it? Right up about there a pine limb 'most clean across the road. I'm damned if the team didn't haul off and jump it! But the coach didn't! Them wheels hit the wood and I took to the sky like a goddam cannonball! When I sat up in the road I saw that by some miracle the coach was still up, with produce all over the road! But, get this. You know them eggs?"

Corky eyed him suspiciously "Don't tell me they—"

Ed grinned. "Splattered all over God's green land, every one of 'em. One miracle a day is all you git on this route."

Corky twisted and laid his hand on the top rail to steady himself. Something far behind them on the dusty road caught his attention.

"Ed, was there ever...."

"Say up, boy! Was there ever what?"

"Was there ever holdups on this road?"

"Holdups? Sure there was holdups! Did you think your rifle was for decoration? Now, mind you, I personally was never held up and neither was nobody else for about eight years now. But there was blood and murder on this road in them years after the war."

"Well, we don't have nothing worth taking, do we?"

"Not as I know of, but who's to say what's in them steamer trunks? What are you going on about?"

"There's a feller coming after us. Fast. On a cracker horse."

Ed turned his bulk and glanced, but couldn't make anything out through the dust. "Corky, last I heard, highwaymen come at you from the sides, sometimes after a ruse or blocking the road. It would be a different highwayman who would come flying up at you from behind."

"Then it just might work, mightn't it?"

That stopped Ed for a minute. He had been in Finegan's army at Olustee and he knew something about surprise. He took a swig from his flask and laid on the whip to see if the pursuer would keep pace.

"He's gaining, Ed."

"Well, I figgered he would if he stayed on his horse. Can you make him out yet?"

"Not hardly. Except he's riding funny."

"Riding funny! What's that supposed to mean? Riding funny."

"He's got one leg out to the side straight as a board. It's a wonder he's staying on."

Ed found that strangely troublesome. A drunk wouldn't ride with a straight leg like that. But a deranged man might. A few years back he'd heard about one of Finegan's wounded who had a steel plate in his head and shot at anybody wearing a blue coat until finally he was done in by rust. This wild man on the cracker horse was starting to make him nervous, and when it came to the safety of his passengers—and himself for that matter—it was better to get the jump on the other fellow.

"Git the rifle out. Be ready."

Corky muttered a dirty word and fumbled for the firearm. It was in a canvas case lashed to the top rail. In his haste to load the coach he had set one of the steamer trunks on top of it and now he was paying for his carelessness.

The rider was coming up fast. Corky tore at the lashings and yanked at the rifle, hoping that it wouldn't shoot him in the shoulder, all the while uttering odd little swear words that nobody else would've understood. Finally he had the long gray barrel. He laid the rifle across the top rail with one hand while using the other to keep from falling off the bouncing coach. The rifle went off and Corky yelled a word that everybody understood. The younger of the girls poked her head out the window to ask what was going on.

Ed told her in no uncertain terms to stick her head back inside the coach and leave it there until he told her to do otherwise.

"What the hell are you doing, Corky? You'll git us all killed!" He allowed himself another quick look through the dust. Their pursuer was low in the saddle. It sounded like he was hollering something, possibly to get his horse to go faster.

"I was trying to grab hold and it went off," Corky explained.

"Well, if he shoots back, I know who'll get the better of it. Just do me a favor, Corky, and don't drop that rifle. Them Sharps don't come cheap."

"I'm glad you're so concerned about my welfare, Ed. Here he comes!"

Now Ed was glad to have the bulky steamer trunks up top. The rider would have to come abreast of them before he'd even see the driver.

Corky was getting bolder now, or more desperate. He braced himself with his left hand and got up on his knees, pointing the Sharps with his right hand. Then the coach slammed into a giant pothole. The rifle fired and kicked Corky over backwards, down onto the rumps of the closer pair of horses.

Ed assumed Corky had been shot, and in any event he wanted to keep him from getting trampled on his way down through the harness, so he gathered the reins and pulled hard. To his surprise, the horses actually came to a halt. The coach swung to one side, threatening to turn over, but Ed threw his considerable weight to the high side of the seat and everything came crashing to a standstill.

Before the smoke and dust had cleared, the rider was beside him. Ed dropped the reins and poked his hands into the sky.

"Don't shoot, mister! Whatever you want, just take it!"

Then, to his embarrassment, he saw that the presumed highwayman wasn't even carrying a gun.

Corky sat up between the horses and stared as the newcomer goaded his horse to the coach window, reached down and raised the canvas shade.

"Anna?"

She glowered up at him. "What are you doing here? You almost scared us to death!"

He seemed a little surprised at that. He sat up in the saddle and dropped the window shade. Anna caught it and held it up.

The rider seemed to have lost the power to speak.

Corky was coming to his senses. He untangled himself from the harness and stood in the road on wobbly knees.

"There's your highwayman," Ed told him. "He don't even have no gun unless he swallered it."

The cracker mare began to get impatient. She tried to back away from the coach, but the rider pushed her forward with his good leg.

Ed listened as confusion arose among the passengers. "Don't be too hard on him," the young woman's mother was saying. "He's come a long way for something, Anna."

Anna laid a gloved hand on the window ledge and scrutinized the wild man on the horse. "Yes, you *have* come a long way. What for?"

Her younger sister had now taken on the awkward business of holding up the window shade. The preacher raised the shade and secured it with the cord. "There now," he said.

"Well?" Anna asked. "I already told you, you can pay me later for the horse."

The man on the mare bowed and swept his hand in a gallant gesture that reminded Ed of a Confederate cavalry officer.

The words came out slowly at first, then gushed forth like a river breaking a dam.

"Anna, I...I cordially invite you...to marry me."

"*What? What did you say?*"

He glanced over his shoulder as if hoping to find a translator. He looked from Ed to Corky thinking they might relay what he had said.

"I'm asking you to marry me." This time he spoke as if saying the most obvious, ordinary thing. "Marry me."

After a terrible silence Anna said, "Why?"

"*Why?*" Now he was getting annoyed. "Why? Because we're meant for each other, that's why. Can you say we aren't?"

He crossed his hands on the saddle horn and waited for her reply.

She looked at Corky standing dazed and smudged and rubbing his backside. The ceiling of the coach creaked as Ed shifted his bulk in the seat. Larrabee sat patiently, waiting for her reply. She closed her eyes and quickly shook her head. Then she came to her senses and some of the anger returned to her voice. "And what do you propose to do about it now? We have a train to catch."

He shrugged. "We can get married at the next town—at Newnansville. What do you say to that, Anna—dear Anna?"

She looked from Corky, who stood there blinking the dust from his eyes, to Ed, who was standing in the road now, daubing the sweat from his forehead with the back of his arm. The earnest young rider patted Tuscawilla on the neck.

She leaned out the window and said something he couldn't make out.

"What?" He brought the horse a step closer and bent down.

"Yes!" She leaned farther out the window in case he hadn't heard her the second time. She was irritated at having to repeat herself. "I'm saying yes!"

Ed saw fit to butt in at this point. He came to the coach window and asked the preacher. "May I inquire as to where exactly y'all are headed?"

"China," was the immediate reply.

Ed gave him a strange look. "That in Florida or Georgia?"

"Neither," Martha declared. "It's just plain China."

Ed put up his hands. "Well, wherever it is, if we can all git ourselves glued back together and beat it for Newnansville y'all can do whatever you're doing, and whoever's going on to Lake City to catch the train just might git there in time if nothing don't happen."

The man on the horse swooped down and kissed Anna. Then he took off down the road with a yell that startled the team back into action before Ed and Corky were quite ready. The whole improbable parade clattered up to the post office at a breakneck speed that made dogs bark and sleepy old men sit up and wonder.

"Why are we stopping at the post office?" Martha asked.

"Because this is a mail coach," Corky said with authority.

A whiskery, slightly overweight man wearing sleeve garters came out to see what all the clatter was about.

Ed greeted him and explained that this was a wedding party. "If nobody's changed their mind. We've even brought us a preacher, Bill. Where do you reckon we ought to set up?"

"Do it here if you've a mind to," the man said.

Anna got out of the coach and shook the dust from her clothes. "I'm not getting married in any post office. The least you can do is take me to a church, Nathaniel Larrabee."

"Ma'am, it being Sunday, they're all pretty much spoken for," the man said. "Fact is, the post office ain't usually open on the Sabbath but I happened to be here 'cause I was expecting Ed with some circulars that need to go out tomorrow." He sniffed. "Well, post office is there if you want it or you can go on down to the stage depot."

"We'll need some documents," the preacher said. "A marriage certificate and a title transfer."

"A title transfer? What do you need that for?" asked the postmaster.

"No time to explain right now. Can you break a lock somewhere and bring the papers up to the stage depot? I'd surely appreciate it."

At least the stage depot had room for everybody, and it was more cheerful than the drab, severe post office. The wedding party went in and Ed explained to the sleepy ticket agent while a few disheveled travelers looked on.

"Soon as Bill Geiger gits back with the papers, we'll do this and be on our way," he promised.

"This is not the dress I would've picked for my wedding," Anna said. It was plain and gray muslin that she had chosen for its durability.

"You're going to need a best man," the preacher told Larrabee. "Who do you have in mind?"

He chose Ed, who was still red-faced and sweaty from the ordeal on the road. Ed wiped his face on his sleeve again and slicked back what hair he had. Bill Geiger hurried in breathless and gave the preacher the documents he had asked for. The preacher went over to the counter and borrowed the agent's pen long enough to fill out the papers while Anna talked to Martha about being the maid of honor.

The preacher shook the papers through a sand-blotter. "Now we'll need two witnesses plus the signatures of the bride and groom and my own. This other one here is your wedding present or Anna's dowry if you wish. I'm signing it right now so your witness can sign too. It isn't much, Nathaniel. It's just that patch of pinewoods I bought from John Howard for the church. I took it off the church's hands when my brother Arthur died and left me a little money. There's not even any trees on it anymore except for some scrub oak, but it might farm off some day or make somebody a place for rusticating if the town doesn't spread right across it. So here it is, for what it's worth." He signed the title transfer and gave it to Ed and the ticket agent for their names.

He laid the document on the counter. "Now, we're going to have to do this ceremony in jig time if we're going to catch that train." He positioned everybody and said, "We're just going to talk our way through this."

By now the stage office was beginning to fill up with passersby who had heard about the impromptu wedding that was to take place. Most of them were well dressed since they were on their way to or from church. Ed continued to look nervously at the ticking clock behind the counter, calculating his fastest time to Lake City and coming up just a few minutes shy of catching the train for Tallahassee and points west. After all, they would certainly have to take time pulling Anna's steamer trunk off the coach or—worse still—separating her things from someone else's.

It seemed to go very slowly. This was a preacher who didn't cut any corners. There was a prayer, the familiar quotations from St. Paul, the bride's mother stepping stiffly forward to give her away. The groom had to do without a ring. The bride received one from her mother. All of the women started crying, including the ones who had come in from the street. The groom was dusty and leaning on a borrowed walking stick, but he looked tall and lean and handsome and he and the bride seemed to be looking at each other more and more as the ceremony went on.

"What God has joined together let no man put asunder! I now pronounce you man and wife!"

Just then the bells of not one, but two churches began ringing.

As the bride and groom kissed, Ed decided that maybe the wild man on the horse had been right. Maybe the two of them *were* meant for each other.

Part III
The Sour-Apple Tree
1886-1888

Chapter 30

John Howard watched Dr. Phillips' hand move across the map and decided that things had turned out very well indeed. Thanks to a timely investment in fire insurance and the discreet work of Baldy Choat, he had managed, literally, to snatch most of his fortune from the fire that had destroyed the Arlington Hotel. He had sold off the Santa Fe River timberland that had nearly ruined him, and was now quite free from the entangling debts of the deceased Major Dennis.

And yet the major's way of thinking was still very much with him. Since the major's death he had found himself strangely incapable of investing in anything the major had disapproved of—oranges, lake steamers, or cotton. He had done passably well with artificial ice and had sunk some money into the development of refrigerated railroad cars. If he couldn't bring himself to buy orange groves, he could at least profit from the transportation of the crops—which were continuing to thrive mightily despite the major's many grave warnings.

But now here was something that was certain to pay off. It was not dependent upon the caprices of the weather or the steady hands of lake pilots, and on top of that, the major himself had invested in it. His name was engraved in cursive on a drawer of the lock box that was to go in the proposed hotel.

The Hygienic Hotel—as it was to be called—was to be the centerpiece of New Gainesville. But the hotel was really the least of the project. The land and the parceling out of the land were the heart of it.

Dr. Phillips' silver cufflink caught Howard's eye as his hand moved to the circle in the center of the map. The hotel itself was to be grander than even the major might have imagined. It was to have a four-story rotunda. It would spread through the pines in four three-story wings. It would boast of piazzas and balconies that would put the memory of the Arlington to shame. The site, the doctor was explaining, was just eighteen inches short of being the highest point between Fernandina and Cedar Keys.

A quarter mile east of the hotel, toward Newnan's Lake, was a 560-acre parcel to be carved up into 112 five-acre plots to be sold at a hefty $1000 to $1500 each. That was the clever thing, Howard thought—to create a demand for housing. Lure people in—well-to-do people—with the promise of a healthy climate and handsome vistas and then sell them otherwise undistinguished land for $200 to $300 an acre. And these personages in the Alachua Improvement Company had the cash to make the plan work—$180,000 in working capital, and going up.

He supposed he should pay attention to the artistic aspects of the project. He lit a cigar and watched through the smoke as Dr. Phillips traced the blocks of cottages forming a circle around the hotel. Outside the cottage blocks there was to be a vast circular drive called "the Arena," which would be a hundred feet wide. Howard couldn't for the life of him figure out what good a hundred-foot-wide road would be, except maybe as a racetrack. But anyway, outside this Arena would be two blocks of business buildings. Radiating from there, four big parks named after various trees for no particular reason. And going out from the center of that, a target-like configuration of several avenues eighty feet wide, extending to the outer edge of the circles. The whole contrivance would be connected to town with various streets running west. A central avenue, also a hundred feet wide, would run west to town and east to Newnan's Lake.

Howard thought the project lacked only a Tower of Babel. But seeing Dr. Phillips' enthusiasm and the excitement of the others in the room, he figured this sort of grandiose undertaking was just the thing to draw many a well-heeled northerner into the county. After all, these were grandiose times. The men packed into the meeting room had money and push. They would make this idea *happen* and once it happened they would make it pay.

Which was a good thing because the land itself—about a square mile of it from what Howard could tell—was of no particular value. It was high, rolling pineland not worth anything near $200 an acre. The investors were relying heavily on the healthy climate to attract the first flock of nesters who would then fly back north and spread the word among their friends. Renters would become buyers. After a few years Howard and the others could sell out and move on to the next venture. The doctors in the meantime would develop a steady business from the less healthy arrivals since the cost of treatment would be folded into the rent.

It was just the sort of scheme Howard needed. It had the sheen of public welfare. It involved respectable people with considerable wherewithal. It was short-term and set up for a clean exit. It had an aura of modernity about it.

He walked home whistling a tune he'd heard on his way past Duke's Saloon, something about a silver horn. Old Collins was just leaving and he went out of his way to bid him good night. The detour brought him in the back door, which he found strangely appealing after all the high talk.

Jane was in the kitchen polishing a copper vase, a gift from their neighbors, the Duttons.

"Here now," he said, "what is this domestic turn you've taken lately? You could've left that for Collins."

She didn't look up. "I wanted to do it myself. I just felt like it. That's all."

"And the cooking yesterday."

"The same. After all, I have to do *something*."

He put his arms around her waist as she continued to shine the copper. "Are we not happy in our new home? Are we left too much alone?"

She set the vase down on the drain board. "And what do *we* mean by that?"

"Only that your life in the big city must've been more exciting, more full of people coming and going."

"That's a cheap crack, John."

He backed off. "Sorry. I didn't mean it that way. After all, you're Mrs. John Howard!"

Her lip curled and she gave him a sidelong look. "That's right. I am as far as anyone around here is concerned. And believe you me, I think it's as funny as you do. It seems to me, though, that it's opened some doors for you. Hasn't it, John? To have folks around here think you're a married man."

"You're nobody's fool, Janey. That's what I like about you. Always have. I swear you should go on the stage, too. You're the perfect little counterfeit. You'll be very interested in the meeting I just attended."

"With the Improvement Company."

"You remembered. I'm impressed."

"I remember plenty more than that. The ice company is short $137 this month by the way. If I were you I'd check last month's books again. You may flush out an embezzler."

"Good God. You think just like a man."

"Not quite. I *can* think like a man, John. It's not so hard. I can talk like a man, too, when I want to. Wouldn't that surprise your friends at the Improvement Company? What did they say at the meeting?"

"They're building an entire town from the ground up, that's what they said."

"They've been planning that for three years. You said so yourself."

"Yes, but tonight Dr. Phillips showed the latest plan. And of course it's the first time I've actually seen it since I'm new to the company. I've got to say it's even bigger than I thought. They will do very nicely. There's nothing to stop them."

She touched his cheek with her fingertip. "And nothing to stop you then. How long for the payoff?"

He laughed. "You *do* talk like a man! Next time I come home you'll be smoking cigars!"

She shook her head. "I hate the taste of them. How long, John?"

"About two years. After all, they've got to build the place first. I suppose we can sell some lots beforehand, but the gold rush won't come until that hotel and all those cottages are up."

"That didn't stop the Wards."

"The Wards? What do you mean?"

"According to Mrs. Polk they sold off a good chunk of property at the edge of town and it's got nothing but trees on it."

"Well, since Ray Polk hasn't been the county clerk for a couple of years now, Mrs. Polk may well be talking off the top of her head. But if they did make some money, it's by virtue of Mrs. Ward's business acumen. There's a woman who can make a fortune out of *hats* for God's sake."

"Aren't you lucky then. You have a businesswoman of your own."

Chapter 31

Anna pressed her hands to the small of her back and listened to the rain beating down on the roof. It was hard to believe that she still had three months to go! She had taken on the shape of a pear! Her face looked swollen and it was all she could do to stand up straight. She was not one to wish the time away, but occasionally she found herself counting the days to January. At least the early days of throwing up and the sweltering heat were gone. May and June had been brutal. Hens in the coop had stifled and died overnight. The still air was so humid that clothes never dried. Boys heated pennies on railroad tracks and used them to burn holes in magnolia leaves.

Larrabee reported that even the lake provided no comfort. She was certain that he said it to assure her that he too was unhappy about his being gone all day. It was something they hadn't worked out in their rush to say, "I do." How were they going to keep body and soul—and the house—together unless he went back to work on the lake? So in June, by the time his leg had mended, he went back to Bob Harper and the *King Payne*. The money was good but Anna hated the separation.

She welcomed this hard rain because it kept him off the lake for a few hours. The beans and tomatoes and squash and the thousand other crops could wait another day.

Somebody in the kitchen dropped a stockpot and the racket woke Larrabee up.

"We banging a gong before breakfast now?" He sat up rubbing his head as if he had been hit.

She turned and smiled. "No, just a pot by the sound of it. Empty I would guess or we'd be hearing a good deal more noise down there."

"Well, Bobby and his gang of thugs should be more careful. What time is it?"

"Sometime before sunrise."

"So I see. What are you doing up anyway?"

She came away from the window. "I was just thinking."

"In the morning?"

"I'm so fat!"

"You're supposed to be fat. You're going to have twins."

"Ugh! What gave you that idea?"

He made a vague motion with his hands, as if sizing up a watermelon. "You're cargo hold is so.... You know...."

"Do you hate me because I'm fat?"

He laughed. "No! You look good like that—kind of prosperous. You were too scrawny before. All edges."

"You're just making that up so I'll feel better. Before I was fat you came riding after me at a full gallop, risking your life to ask for my hand."

"Well, but you were risking your life too, rushing off in a coach driven by those two birdbrains. It's a wonder any of us lived through it."

She put her hand to her mouth and sank down on a chair, crying.

"Hey now, what's that for?" He untangled himself from the covers and came over to her in his nightshirt.

"I don't know."

"I swear, Anna, you get more complicated and mysterious every day."

She looked up at him with red eyes. "Thank you."

He put his hand on her shoulder. "What's the little spud going to think with it raining inside and out like that?"

She bent over and daubed her eyes with the hem of her nightgown. "I don't know."

He patted her on the belly. "We'll have to take over the entire upstairs if this keeps happening."

"And how are we going to keep it from happening?"

He chuckled and put his arm around her shoulder. "I hope we're not."

"You just want to be sure you get a boy."

"Where did you come up with that notion?"

Anna swallowed and gave her eyes a final brush with her sleeve. "Iris Poinsett. She says all men want sons."

"Well, I wasn't aware that Iris knows all men. I don't remember her knowing me."

"Nathaniel, that's shameful!"

He kissed her on the cheek, taking away the last tear. "All men are shameful, Miss Anna. It's in our nature. We're all part human, part roving dogs. It's up to the women to bring out the human part."

She stood up. "I'll hope you'll do some of that on your own."

"A day like this gives me a strange notion, my girl."

"To re-shingle the roof?"

He shook his head. "No, it's held these ten years. Penny and I did a fine job. I'm thinking of that little patch of land the preacher gave us. Your dowry."

She tied her hair back with a piece of black silk ribbon, a remnant from one of Nelda's hats. "My dowry. I wish he'd never said that."

"Never mind. I was just thinking about that patch and wondering if we might build on it."

She turned, surprised. "You mean a farm?"

"It would answer the need. Wouldn't have to go to the lake every day."

"But *this* is our home. And anyway, how is it as farmland? Wouldn't we be better off here?"

"I was hoping you'd say that. Just thinking out loud."

"Maybe you could farm closer to town?"

He looked out the window at the pinewoods and the horse paddock where Tuscawilla walked the fence line in the rain. "That'll all be going to houses. That's the way Penny and Nelda sold it. I hear that all the land east of town is owned by that improvement company. South of the road is mostly groves. I suppose I could become an orange farmer, could sell my interest in the boat and buy a grove."

"Is that what you want to do?"

He shrugged. "No."

"I didn't think so. I can't picture you doctoring orange trees."

"Foreign to a boy from Missouri."

She dipped her hands into the water basin and began washing her face. "You've never told me much about your family. Our baby's going to want to know about his—or her—grandparents."

"There's not so much to tell about 'em."

"Your father was killed when they took the farm?"

"That's right."

"Were you there when it happened?"

"No, I'd been out all night and by the time I got home it was all over. I sometimes wonder what would've happened if I'd been there. Nothing good I imagine."

She took his hand in both of hers. "Then I'm glad you weren't there. But why did you leave your mother and sister?"

"It was hard times. We got separated." He touched her cheek. "There's more. I should've told you before we got married but there wasn't time."

She finished drying her face and regarded him with her dark brown eyes. "Would it have made a difference do you think?"

"Anna, a man was shooting at me. I shot back."

She sat down on the bed.

"Did you kill him?"

"I don't know. It was ten years ago. We were on horseback. He was shooting at me and I was shooting at him. One minute he was there, the next he was gone. I didn't see him get hit and I didn't see him go down. And I didn't have the luxury of going back to look for him. So for ten years I've had that hanging over me."

She sat for a moment, absorbing what he had told her. The rain was terrible now, driven by a northwest wind that shook the pines. Tuscawilla was nowhere to be seen.

She lowered her eyes. "Why was he shooting at you?"

"I fell in with a couple of boys who fancied themselves highwaymen. Castoffs like me. We were going to strike back at the banks. Maybe even give some of the money to farmers who were going to get thrown out. That's what I *thought*. We robbed the bank that foreclosed on us. I stood inside the door and served as lookout. It was a botch all the way. We weren't half out of that bank before men came after us shooting. We split up and ran like rabbits. On my way out, I grabbed a ten-dollar gold piece off the floor and that was all I ever got. I never even looked back till I was clean across the state, almost to the Mississippi. When the man started shooting close, I shot back."

"So that's it."

"They had already run my mother and sister off the farm, so I didn't know where to write and I couldn't go back without risking a noose. I meant to go west. Gold-hunting or some wild scheme to get rich quick. I took some wrong turns."

She sighed. "I'd say you did. Who else have you told about this?"

He put his hands on his knees. "Only Jared Penrod."

"Did that have to do with his leaving so quickly?"

He wasn't sure how much he should tell her. It was so hard to read her moods lately. But after all these years, he wanted to tell someone.

"Jared died in a stampede on the Cottonwood Plantation. Looking for Confederate gold. John Howard and I were with him."

She closed her eyes and took a deep breath.

He was afraid she was going to faint. He put his arm around her.

"I'm sorry," he said. "Where do you suppose we ought to go from here?"

She stood up and kissed him on the forehead. "We go right where we were going. There's nothing you can do to change what might have happened ten years ago. There's plenty you can do to change what happens here and now. You go where you can do the most good. Don't you think?"

Chapter 32

"Has it occurred to anyone," John Howard said, "that the new town ought to be supplied with gaslight if it's going to be so modern?"

"The city's got to build the gasworks first," Henry Dutton said, "and they'll be doing just that within the year. There will be plenty of time to lay in the lines before the hotel and the cottages go up. We'll let the city try it out first to make sure nothing blows up!"

Everybody on the porch laughed, but after all, they were in a jovial mood. The Duttons were throwing a New Year's Eve party for what seemed like the entire town. Howard was surprised at the variety of people drinking punch under the light of the Japanese lanterns that threw orange circles across the vast lawn. Rich and not so rich alike and their children too, the latter being herded into the summer kitchen for a taffy pull supervised by Dutton's Negro cook and maid who kept the sticky proceedings on track with iron discipline.

Howard couldn't help wondering what Major Dennis would've thought of the gas works idea and decided that he probably would've been at least a year ahead on it and would probably have owned at least half the company.

As Dutton and his companions faded into the darkness between lanterns Howard caught sight of an unlikely couple conversing on the porch. It was Jane, punch cup in hand, looking up at a tall, sinewy man with an intent expression. Larrabee. What in blazes was he doing at Dutton's party and how had he and Jane fallen in together? She looked quite intent on whatever it was he was saying.

Larrabee was wearing a brown double-breasted coat and vest. The vest revealed no watch chain or fob. His black silk tie was loose and he wore brown boots that implied a readiness to spring onto the nearest horse and gallop into the night. He was hatless and his ruffled hair gave him the look of a man who had just been in a fight. It had been some time since Howard had seen Larrabee close up and he tried to remember if he had always had that wild look.

Jane set her punch cup on the porch rail. "I thought you had gone home," she said with an insincere cheerfulness. "It hardly seems fitting for you to leave your bride that way."

"Well, I had not gone home," Howard said, trying to match her false cheer. "I was only circulating with our host."

"Say hello to Mr. Larrabee here."

"Hello, Nathaniel. How are you?"

"You've met then?"

"Yes. We go back quite a ways, don't we Nathaniel?"

"We've had some mutual acquaintances. Seems like most of 'em aren't around anymore."

Howard smiled. "Hard times. Dangerous times."

"I guess you know Penny Ward." Larrabee's look was hard to read.

"The husband of the hat lady," Howard said.

"That's right. He was out hunting a few weeks back and he ran into one of your old cronies—the hero of the Arlington—Baldy Choat."

Howard stiffened. "He's done some work for me over the years but I hardly know him."

"Folks have been kind of wondering where he went after saving all those people out of the burning hotel. You'd think a fellow would want to stick around and bask in the glory a little, wouldn't you? And yet Baldy was holed up in a cabin down by Hogtown Creek and didn't want to talk about the Arlington. But then a few years went by before he wanted to talk about Caleb Green."

"Don't be tedious, Larrabee. Choat is nothing to me."

Jane was eager to defuse what was becoming a frightening exchange of words. She broke in with desperate enthusiasm. "Mr. Larrabee's wife is going to have a baby. Very soon, didn't you say?"

"A week or two, ma'am."

"I hope she's not unwell."

"She's well and in good spirits but thought it best to remain in confinement from now on."

"And it's her first, didn't you say?"

"Yes, ma'am."

Jane felt in control again and began to enjoy herself. "Now, none of this 'ma'am' business! You are to call me Jane. And I hope that you and your wife will call on us when she's up and about again. We live just next door, you know. We'd be happy to entertain you, wouldn't we, John?"

"Unutterably."

An explosion shook the air and a shower of color lit up the sky.

"There go the gasworks!"

Everyone laughed at Henry Dutton's joke. He came up the porch steps, leaned on the rail and addressed the crowd.

"Folks, Mrs. Dutton and I are proud as can be to have you here and to have you for our friends and neighbors. We've arranged a little holiday entertainment to help bring in 1887 for you and we hope you like it. You'll probably like it most if you stand away from the back corner of the yard there where my man is sending them up. You'll want your inventory of fingers and toes to carry over from the old year to the new."

More laughter. Howard looked back to see if Larrabee had gotten the joke, but he was nowhere in sight. Jane had moved to the rail and was leaning out, smiling at the general merriment.

After the fireworks people began to haul off their sticky, argumentative children and to drift off into the night. Howard and Jane had just taken leave of their host and hostess when a gaunt figure appeared at the front gate. At first Howard took it for some passing shadow, but the gate opened and in she came, right up the brick walk with the departing guests making way for her.

Henry Dutton folded his arms and looked down at her. "Mary, it's not proper to be out so late. And you alone so far from home. How will you get back?"

It was then that the people on the porch saw the person with her, a young girl, by her face not more than nine, but uncommonly tall, with hair past her waist.

Mary Leary raised a thin finger. "I'm not alone but with my daughter and the daughter of yonder John Howard, though he never yet has seen fit to acknowledge her. And yet he should, for my Joan is a fine girl with many unusual abilities."

Among the departing guests an indistinct hissing of syllables suggested the word "witch."

Howard wished fervently that he had brought his walking stick, for he would brandish it like a wand to strike her dead. But since he had come from next door he had dispensed with it, so he contented himself with advancing to the edge of the steps and pointing back at her.

"Woman, you are mad! Continue to spread these falsehoods about me and I'll put a stop to them, one way or the other. My wife and I are going home. Now clear the walk."

With Jane on his arm he advanced down the steps, Jane holding back just a little, so that their progress was uneven. When he was within a few paces of Mary and her longhaired daughter, he sprang forward and startled them into full retreat. Mary and Joan ran through the gate with their dark skirts and tattered shawls fluttering like giant bat wings.

As if to make the ungainly pair disappear, Henry Dutton raised his hands, smiled, and bid his guests good night and Happy New Year.

While Jane undressed in the bedroom, Howard quietly turned the key in the front door and blew out the sentinel light in the study. Then he ascended the stairs with a flickering lamp. When he came into the bedroom and pulled off his tie he was surprised to hear Jane laughing.

"Apparently you had a good time at the Duttons," he said. "Maybe better than anyone else. How much of that punch did you have?"

Her dark brown hair hung over the shoulders of her flannel nightgown. She had not yet brushed out the twists from its pinning.

"It's the New Year, John! You shouldn't be so grim. I just couldn't help laughing at the thought of you and that old witch, as they say, in *congress*." She broke out laughing again.

Howard set the lamp on the bureau. "Well, you can forget that thought because nothing of the sort ever happened. She's a madwoman, a lunatic, and everybody knows it. I've never even been alone with her except when I went to collect fifteen dollars due on her account with the Kanapaha Moss Mill. I had just bought the damned place and I was young and overzealous in collecting the bills."

She laughed again, harder than ever. "Overzealous? I would say you were!"

"Get a hold of yourself, woman! I'm telling you, I had nothing to do with her."

Jane began to take his anger seriously. "Well, somebody obviously had something to do with her. Why does she insist it was you?"

"How should I know? Probably because I have money."

"Has she asked you for money?"

"Of course not! I mean, no—not yet."

"Not yet? John, her daughter must be about ten years old. If she was going to ask you for money I would think she would've done so by now."

"She's mad I tell you! There's no telling what she'll do."

Jane had finally recovered from her laughing. "From what I could tell the girl doesn't look much like you. Can't say as she looks like anybody in particular."

"That's the most sensible thing you've said all evening."

Jane threw back the covers and climbed into bed, showing her white legs up to the knee. It was that casual attitude toward her sexuality that Howard had always found irresistible.

"Actually, I said a great many sensible things this evening. It's just that you weren't around to hear them. I spent a while talking to that tall cowboy. What's his name?"

"If you mean Larrabee—"

"Yes, that was it—Larrabee."

It seemed indecent for her to be mentioning his name when she was sitting in bed with her nightgown barely covering her.

"Larrabee's no cowboy, my dear. If you'd gotten any closer you'd probably have discovered that he reeks of lake muck. He's spent most of the last ten years shuttling beans and tomatoes around on a little steamboat. Before that I believe he was shooting dogs at fifty cents a head."

"You don't mean it. Really?"

Now he was glad to see her smile.

"Ask anyone. Ask Larrabee if you ever again get close enough."

She seemed to be losing interest in the subject. "Maybe I will. What was all that about mutual acquaintances not being around anymore?"

"Just small talk, my dear."

"What's the matter? Why are you holding your stomach like that?"

"Indigestion I suppose. I could use a cigar to settle it."

"Oh, not now. Get your clothes off and come to bed before you catch cold. We'll see how you feel in the morning."

Chapter 33

"I really should get up! I feel like a piece of furniture."

Nelda laughed softly. "Anna dear, once that baby comes you'll be up plenty! Enjoy your bed rest while you can get it. That's my advice."

"J.J.'s fixing to turn eight years old. I can hardly believe it. As I recall he didn't give you much trouble as a baby."

"Oh, there were moments! We were just getting the hat business going and I had to drop what I was doing every time I turned around. Penny said it wasn't natural for a mother to run a business. But he never really meant it. At least we got to sleep through the night pretty early on. J.J. was always a good sleeper. Takes after his dad that way."

Anna hadn't heard everything Nelda had said. She pulled herself up on the pillows and put her hand to her swollen belly. "I think that was a contraction."

"Now that's *exciting*." Nelda spoke with such control that she might have been talking about a hand of whist. "You sure it wasn't just the baby kicking?"

"Oh, yes. I've been in this condition long enough to know the difference."

Nelda looked for a clock and, not seeing one, pulled out a pretty little gold watch on a chain. "Half past seven. Let's see when the next one comes. Do you want me to get Nathaniel?"

"Oh, I think he must already have left for the lake. Will you go and see if Tuscawilla's gone?"

Nelda went to the window and pulled back the curtain. They were in the big corner room that had been Anna's mother's, the one Emma had later shared with the preacher, and its view of the paddock was partially obstructed by loblolly pines. Nelda couldn't see the horse, but she hurried downstairs to see if Larrabee might still be in the shed getting the saddle and bridle.

The three boarders were already in the dining room having breakfast while Bobby La Rue and his cook finished up the morning meal and got ready for the luncheon crowd. The cook was Mrs. Murray, wife of Dobkin Murray the wood hauler and mother of the troublesome Harmon, now seventeen years old and a source of constant worry. Mrs. Murray was just getting the cornbread pans from the corner cupboard when Nelda came breezing through the kitchen on her way to find Larrabee. The two nearly collided as Mrs. Murray was saying something to Bobby about her errant boy. It was the fastest anyone had seen Nelda move, and Bobby and Mrs. Murray thought that surely some wild animal had broken into the house.

"Miz Ward, is something the matter?" By the time Mrs. Murray got the words out, Nelda was already hurrying toward the shed, scattering the chickens as she went.

Much to her relief, Larrabee was inside, cleaning Tuscawilla's bit and oiling the bridle. Neither was in particular need of the attention but Larrabee had dragged out his morning leave-taking in anticipation of the baby's birth. His tardiness had thrown the *King Payne* behind schedule more than once. But Bob Harper, as fidgety as he got waiting for Larrabee to show up, never held the delays against him.

"I'm getting as eager for this baby as you are," he had said to Larrabee a few days ago. "I think even Mr. Josiah T. Walls himself will be happy to see this baby born just so the county gets back its rhythm."

When Nelda came into the shed Larrabee knew something was up. He hung the bridle on its nail. "Is it happening?"

"She's had a contraction," Nelda reported calmly.

Larrabee knew about the birth of horses and cattle but he had tried not to think about how it worked with women.

"Does that mean soon?"

Nelda shrugged. "Could be soon, could be tomorrow. Could be next week. We won't know until she's had a few more contractions."

They avoided the kitchen this time, went around to the front porch and straight up the stairs to the corner bedroom where Anna sat breathing heavily.

"What's wrong?" Larrabee asked.

She looked up and smiled. "Nothing—yet. It just feels better to breathe."

"Good idea. How do you feel? You want me to get Doctor Willis?"

"No, no. Not yet. I haven't even had the second contraction yet. In fact I'm beginning to wonder if I ever had the first. Why are you here so late?"

"I was cleaning the bridle. Last thing I want is to get halfway and break a rein."

"I thought you cleaned it yesterday morning."

"Look, are you warm enough? That fire hasn't caught yet."

In the fireplace off the foot of the bed a small oak log smoked atop stirred embers.

"It feels plenty hot to me," Anna said. "Does it feel cold to you?"

"No, it feels warm to me too but I've been outside. Can't be much above freezing out there. It's a wonder Tuscawilla hasn't grown her coat out."

Nelda kept a steady eye on her neighbor. "You sure it wasn't just hunger, Anna? You didn't eat much for breakfast."

"Whatever it was, it wasn't hunger. I ate plenty! I've been eating like a mule for months now. Maybe I'm not even pregnant at all. Maybe I've just been eating my way up to this size! Would you love me if I was to stay this fat?"

Larrabee asked Nelda if his wife was delirious.

Anna's face twisted. "That was another one. Walk—don't run—walk over to Dr. Willis' and ask him what he thinks we should do."

Larrabee left the room and took his time getting down the stairs and across the porch. Then he ran to Dr. Willis' house.

After he had knocked on the back door for a while, Mrs. Willis came and apologized. "I was turning butter. Couldn't hear a thing. How's Anna?"

"Looks like it could be time," he said.

"Uh-oh, and I'm afraid Warren isn't here. He left early this morning. Drove up to see Billy. He's camping with the Guards up near Starke. How close together are the contractions?"

Larrabee was embarrassed to say that he wasn't sure.

Mrs. Willis wrote a note for her husband, snatched up a sweater she was crocheting, and went back over to the house with Larrabee. "As long as I get back in time to get my bread out of the oven. Maybe we'll manage to keep things under control till Warren gets back. And if not, it wouldn't be the first time a baby was born without a doctor. Our own child is proof of that."

When they got back to the room Larrabee was disappointed to find that nothing had changed. Nelda was still sitting by the bed, although now she appeared to be knitting something.

Mrs. Willis greeted her and Anna as if this were just another market day encounter.

"I brought mine too," she said. "What are you making, Nelda?"

Larrabee found this small talk annoying, but when the "female" talk began, he found it too much to the point and said that he was going downstairs to have a smoke.

"If you plan to smoke until this baby is born," Julia Willis said, "you may end up as cured as a ham."

As the door closed behind him he heard Anna asking Mrs. Willis a question about bearing down.

He took up a position in the wicker chair in the foyer and lit his pipe. He figured that Bob would wait until about nine o'clock and cast off without him as long as the lake wasn't acting up. Through the front door window the sky looked gray but not threatening and the trees were still, so there was no wind to speak of. He figured Bob enjoyed the occasional opportunity to show what he could do with the *King Payne* single-handed. He supposed Bob might also welcome a chance to see the widow Laetitia Summerton without company.

"One of these days maybe she'll invite you in for tea," Larrabee had said just last week. "We've hauled that New York tea over there from time to time.

She must have plenty by now. All she needs is a handsome young buck to drink it with."

"The widow Laetitia is beyond my reach," Bob had said. "She's got a plantation and I've got half a boat. And speaking of that, why don't you put your mind to running your half of it before we run aground?"

She still wore black. It was a good color for her, Larrabee thought. She stood at the top of the slope on the veranda of her handsome house while the hands loaded the crates and sacks onto the *King Payne*. She was elegant and inaccessible, but Larrabee figured that one day she would change from black to gray with black trim, and then to a more social hue as the time for mourning passed. He couldn't remember when the colonel had died, but it seemed to him that the customary year of grieving must be long over and that perhaps tomorrow, when he told Bob of his new baby, Bob might be prodded into reporting some progress with the widow Laetitia.

His daydream seemed to have been going on for half the morning and still nothing had happened upstairs. He lit his pipe again and smoked and watched the boarders come and go. He had a conversation with Curtis about artificial ice.

"It don't make so much difference as I thought it would," Curtis said. "And the price being a little cheaper, I'm doing a few more deliveries than I was."

"You'll get rich yet," Larrabee told him.

Curtis chuckled. "No, I'm one of those folks that money just rolls off of like water off a duck. Anyway, my cut's about the same. Now, Mr. John Howard is likely doing handsomely. I hear he's working on developing some kind of train car that'll stay cold all the way to New York. How do you reckon that'll work?"

"I don't know, Curtis. But if he can make ice down here in the summertime I imagine it's no great shakes keeping a railroad car cold. You working for him?"

"That's right. Can't say as he's such a likable fellow. He's a mite frosty. But he pays the right amount at the right time and if we run into a deadbeat, he's the one who goes after the money. I like that about it."

"I'll bet you he gets that money, too. He seems to have his ways."

Curtis laughed. "I hear that's what old Mary Leary was saying at Dutton's the other night. I hear she come right up to the steps with the little girl in tow and pointed the finger at John again."

"She sure did. I was there."

"What you doing setting here anyway? I thought you'd be down to the lake by now."

Larrabee tapped his pipe on the arm of the chair. "Anna's upstairs getting ready to have that baby and I'm down here keeping out of the way. You been by the Doctors Robb today?"

"They ain't here. Canceled ice for last week and this. I hear they was visiting in Tennessee."

"How about McKinstry?"

"Far as I know he's around somewheres, but he wasn't at the house this morning. Least ways his rig's gone."

"We're coming up right short of medicine men today."

"Good deal of fuss to move a ten-pound load a foot or two. Who's with her?"

"Nelda Ward and Julia Willis."

"I expect they'll figure it out. Somebody figured it out for every one of us that's walking around this town. I'll leave you a little extra ice if you think it might come in handy."

Larrabee had no idea whether it would or not. He thanked Curtis and told him to go ahead and leave some extra, without specifying an amount.

An hour passed. He took the ten-dollar gold piece from his vest pocket and flipped it, watching it catch the light that poured in from the porch. Boarders and visitors came and went. Some of them spoke to him, others seemed not to notice him. He got nervous. He got restless. He got inattentive and burned a hole in the arm of the chair with his pipe. Finally he went upstairs and asked through the door if there had been some progress.

"It's likely to be a while," was the reply from Mrs. Willis. "Just relax."

He wanted to go for a walk to stretch his legs, but didn't dare. So he returned to the scorched wicker chair and lit up again.

The dining room began to fill with lunch customers. Each time a door opened he thought it must surely be Dr. Willis. Penny and J.J. came by to find out why Nelda had never come back to the house.

"Today's the day then," Penny said.

"Well, I hope it's today," Larrabee told him. "One day of this is enough."

"Anything we can bring you from the store? We're stoppin' by Matheson's to get us some fish hooks."

"Fish hooks! Don't you ever work these days?"

"Not so much the way I used to, a-slammin' boards together. We're doin' just fine with hats and property. It don't hardly seem like workin' no more and the money's better. It's peculiar, I swear."

"I see the houses are starting to go up out here."

"Yes, all back behind the Dutton Bank, clean to that field of beggar's weed! Houses and a store or two. I ain't buildin' 'em but we're helpin' to bankroll 'em. There's some fellers in town that have money in it. Ray Polk and Irv Poinsett and a few others. Myself, I kind of miss the hammer and nails. So back to Matheson's. Can we bring you anything?"

"Not unless they have a baby we can buy down there. Be a sight easier than this."

About once an hour Bobby La Rue came in from the kitchen.

"Any news?"

"Not yet."

"I declare, it's worse than waiting for well-water to boil."

"That it is, Bobby. That it is."

Early in the afternoon Larrabee extended his range to include pacing back and forth on the front porch. He used up all of his tobacco and wished that he'd thought to ask Penny to bring him more. He was on his way up the stairs again when he heard a horse out at the front gate. The familiar voice rebuking the animal made him hurry out to the gate.

"Doctor, am I ever glad to see you! I was afraid you were gone for good!"

They moved up the walkway at a brisk pace. "That's probably because Mrs. Willis heard me wrong this morning. Somehow she got it in her head that I was going up to see Billy. How long's your wife been in labor?"

By now Larrabee had had plenty of time to think about it. "Going on twelve hours."

"And how far apart are the contractions now? Any idea?"

"I don't know. But Nelda and your wife ought to know. They've been up with her all day."

When they got upstairs Dr. Willis tapped on the door and, without waiting for a reply, went into the room with Larrabee at his heels. Anna was lying down again, pale and perspiring, her dark brown hair pressed to her temples and forehead.

"And how's the mother-to-be?" the doctor asked.

"Ready to *be* a mother," Anna replied hoarsely.

"Well, let's see what we can do about that." The doctor asked to be alone with Anna, and Larrabee took it as a bad sign that Mrs. Willis brought her crochet work out of the room with her.

"What do you figure?" he asked as they went downstairs. "Is this going to happen today?"

"I don't know, Nathaniel. The problem is, her water hasn't broken yet."

That was more than he was ready to hear. He tripped on the last step.

They had been sitting by the fire in the front room for a few minutes when Dr. Willis' voice came booming from the top of the stairs.

"Mrs. Willis!"

She rushed into the foyer. "Yes, Warren?"

"Come on up here. And bring your knitting with you."

She gave Nelda and Larrabee a strange look. "It's crochet, Warren."

"You take my meaning, woman! Now bring it up, will you?"

She tucked her work under her arm, gathered her skirts and hurried upstairs.

Larrabee drummed his fingers on the round table and gazed into the fire. Nelda put her hand on his shoulder. "I believe we'll be hearing something very soon now."

Bobby La Rue came out of the kitchen drying his hands. "Are we about to hear little footsteps upstairs?"

Nelda made a face. "It's a little too soon for *that*." She smiled at Larrabee. "We'll settle for a good healthy yowl."

Just then, from upstairs, they heard precisely that. Larrabee ran upstairs with Nelda only a step behind. Bobby stopped at the newel post where Mrs. Murray joined him.

"I believe that was it!" Bobby said with a grin. "I believe that was it!"

"O' course that was it!" Mrs. Murray laughed. "That was sure enough a baby!"

"You give us a couple of minutes," Mrs. Willis told Larrabee before he could get the door open. She raised her voice. "Nelda? Will you come here please?"

The next few minutes seemed as long as all the time Larrabee had waited since Nelda had come for him in the shed. The women scurried up and down the stairs with sheets and towels and laundry baskets and a pitcher of water while Larrabee stood fidgeting outside the bedroom door. Finally Dr. Willis told him to come on in.

Anna half-sat, half lay in bed, bolstered by the big feather pillows. The linen was fresh and still bore the creases from the closet. Anna had brushed her hair and her color had come back so well that her cheeks had taken on the flush of a winter sunrise. In the crook of her arm, wrapped in a green blanket and wearing a yellow bonnet, was the baby, red and blinking in the late afternoon light that slanted in through the tall windows.

"It's a girl," Anna said, smiling up at Larrabee. "Isn't she pretty?"

Larrabee came closer. "Well, it's hard to say the way she's trussed up. She looks more like a flower than a baby."

Mrs. Willis laughed and clapped her hands. "A flower! Land sakes!"

Dr. Willis shut his valise. "Fauna or flora, this is what you've been waiting for."

Anna stroked the baby's cheek with the back of her hand. "Flora. That would be a pretty name for a little girl."

"Ain't it kind of soon to be naming her?" Larrabee asked. "Shouldn't we wait a week or so?"

"I think it's already too late," Nelda said. "I think she's already become Flora."

Larrabee stooped down beside her and held out his finger. Flora was decidedly uninterested. She shook her little red fists and turned toward her mother.

"She's fairly quiet after that squawk she let out a while ago," he said.

"That squawk was because I rapped her on the feet with a knitting—a *crochet* hook," Dr. Willis said. "Sometimes it takes a little shock to get 'em to breathe."

Larrabee was preoccupied with the pinched face in the yellow bonnet. "We never had to do that with the horses and cattle."

"No, I suppose not. You can hold her if you want to. That is, if the mother approves."

"It's likely to happen sometime," Anna said. "May as well try it now."

Dr. Willis picked up his valise and pushed a chair toward the bed. "Better try it sitting down the first time or two. It's easier on everybody's nerves."

Larrabee sat on the chair, reached down, and scooped the bundle into his hands. "She doesn't look half bad. But I'm not so sure she's thinking the same about me. She's got her peepers shut tight."

The doctor went to the window near the head of the bed and pulled down the shade. As the room darkened Flora blinked up at her father.

"She's got blue eyes," Larrabee said. "She's not smiling though."

"It takes them weeks to learn to smile," Nelda said.

Larrabee looked at her skeptically.

"It does. You've got to teach them that the same as walking and talking."

"Well I never. We'll hope to teach her to smile plenty."

Dr. Willis moved toward the door. "I'd say it's about time to leave this family to themselves for a while, and I for one would like to get home and have some of Mrs. Willis' bread."

His wife jumped to her feet. "Oh no."

"What is it?" Nelda asked.

"My bread. I completely forgot to take it out of the oven."

"Well, don't have a conniption," her husband told her. "I took it out before I came over here. And it didn't come out half bad if I do say so myself."

Chapter 34

They laid their saddles on the porch swing, took off their boots and ponchos, and came into the house passably dry. While Bob took the time to shake some of the rain from his clothes, Larrabee headed straight for the kitchen, where Anna met him with a reluctant hug that left a wet imprint on her apron.

"I was worried about you. How was it on the lake?"

"Bad enough," he told her.

"Tell her the whole story, chief." Bob took a plug of tobacco from his shirt pocket but thought better of it and put it back.

"We had us a little invite," Larrabee said. "Where's Flora?"

"Upstairs sleeping. I put her down about an hour ago. What kind of invite?"

"Seems like she sleeps all the time."

"You wouldn't think so if you were here all the time. What kind of invite?"

"From Mr. Josiah T. Walls himself," Bob beamed. "That's what kind."

"From Walls? How'd that come about?"

Larrabee went on into the kitchen and began snooping in the pots on the stove. "He had the red flag out this afternoon so we went over figuring he needed something from Vidal's."

"His poor wife. Sick all the time." A sound in the yard drew Anna's attention away until she was satisfied she hadn't heard the baby crying.

"So no sooner do we pull up at the dock than lightning strikes not a two-count away. We're laying low on the boat when this darkie comes skittering down the hill, full of the fear of God, apparently thinking the next bolt's for him. As the rain starts to come down he asks us if we want to sit out the storm up at the house. Well, Barkley was with us and he said he didn't care to be in the house of no nigger so he stayed on the boat getting soaked to the bone and swearing at the lightning whilst Bob and I drank tea up in the parlor."

Bob laughed. "Now, don't that knock your hat in a creek! One minute we're out cleaving the scum with the sky fixing to crack open and the next we're high and dry and taking tea with old Josiah T. Walls himself. Larrabee and I and Old Flap! Old Flap took to that tea after a while, didn't he, chief?"

"After it cooled off."

Anna wasn't interested in the crow. "Did you see his wife? What does she look like? Does she dress nicely?"

"His wife? No. Why should we see his wife?"

"Well, she lives there, doesn't she?"

"Anna, this is about Josiah. He's about the friendliest cuss you'd expect to meet."

"Didn't you tell me you'd met him before?"

"Oh, that was ten years ago or more when he was giving a speech down at Arredonda. I didn't meet him, just saw him. Where'd the fish come from?"

"Penny and J.J. brought it over. They were down at Bivens Arm again. Caught more than they could eat."

"Especially seeing as how J.J. doesn't care so much for bluegills." They sat down in the dining room. Larrabee flipped the cloth from the bread and helped himself to a slice. "You make this loaf or did Julia Willis?"

"I did. I seem to have better luck with it than she does. The blackberries for the pie came from her though. I thought Bob might like some even if you don't care for it."

Bob nodded with enthusiasm. "How can you not like it?"

"I did—until I stole one out of a window and didn't have any better sense than to eat the whole thing right on the spot. Took me half a minute to eat it and half the afternoon to be rid of it."

Anna gave him a disapproving look.

Bob bit into a slice from a deep red tomato. "These are good, Anna."

"I can hardly keep up with them. I pick a colander full just about every day."

Larrabee glanced toward the stairs. "Well, before too long you can train Flora to help out."

"It's going to be most of a year before she'll be able to walk. So I don't think she'll be picking tomatoes anytime soon."

Bob watched the chickens through the back window. They were pecking at something in the yard, worms forced up by the rain most likely. "Nathaniel was real eager to get back to y'all. He kept wanting to go the whole time we were there, didn't you, chief?"

"Now, how's a person supposed to answer that, Bob? Didn't we both want to be on our way soon as the weather cleared?"

"All right. All right. Walls asked him why he was so fidgety and Nathaniel wouldn't come right out with it so I told him about little Flora and all and he allowed as how he has a daughter too and knew just how Nathaniel felt about getting back. He was very jocular for such a rich feller, didn't you think, chief?"

"All in all, I suppose so. He was smiling and laughing all the time."

"That's what I said. Jocular."

"He's got orange groves far as you can see up that slope."

"What's the house like? Did he show it to you?"

"Why would he do that? No, we just stayed there in the parlor drinking tea."

"Well, what was it like?"

"It was like hot brown water. It—"

"Not the tea. You know very well what I mean. The parlor."

"Oh, that. I don't know. It was about the size of our front room and looks down toward the lake. That's about it, wouldn't you say, Bob?"

"He made close to three thousand on his tomatoes last year. Six thousand crates. We've heard that once or twice around the lake. I'll bet ain't a one of them tomatoes are as good as this here though. Maybe we ought to give him a run for his money."

"You'll never get off that lake," Anna said. "You'll always be going down there in the morning and coming back here wet or sore or dog tired at night."

"It's a living."

"That's right and I'm thankful."

"Me too. It's a far cry from doing without."

"I just wish we could all be under one roof again. Every day I'm sorry that Mama and Martha and Preacher Williams went to China."

"It's not forever. Just four years."

"Three to go! And just one letter in more than a year. Six months old."

"It's a long pull to China. Clean to the other side of the world."

"You don't need to tell me. Who was good at maps in school? And who was bad?"

He listened patiently. "I should never have told you about losing track of Louisiana that time." He explained to Bob. "I got here in the first place thinking I was going north on a southbound riverboat."

Bob shrugged. "Long as you know which end of the lake is which—and which way is home."

Anna was listening again for the baby.

The sound came back, a cat in the Poinsetts' yard. "Kind of quiet in here now that Bobby La Rue's pulled out," Larrabee said.

"How's he making it in the new place?" Bob asked.

"Fair enough from what I hear. He still has time to go down to Duke's on a Saturday night and howl by the piano."

"Oh, he's a good singer, don't you think? Nothing tops the way he does 'Hard Times Come Again No More.' You figuring to take on a boarder from time to time?"

"No, except for the likes of you, overnight when it rains. I'm no nursemaid and Anna's got her hands full. You never know—we might need all those rooms for family." He winked at Anna.

Three days later they found out they would need one of the rooms for family—for Carrie, her actor husband, and their four-year-old son Edgar.

Anna ran to Larrabee to tell him the news. "It's like a wish come true! Here, read the letter!"

He hugged her and kissed her and took the letter, noting that in her excitement she had wadded it so much that reading it was next to impossible. "It looks like Flora got a hold of it," he said.

"They'll be here in three days! What are we going to do?"

"What do you mean what're we going to do? We're going to sit around the table and chew the fat and tell stretchers and an outright lie or two to puff ourselves up and then prick ourselves back down to size so we're all friends again. That's what we'll do."

"What are you talking about? We've got to clean this place from top to bottom. We've got to get some really good clothes for Flora. We've got to—"

He laughed and stooped down to pick up a rattle. "Before you know it you'll be wanting to borrow the Walls place to put on a show!"

"I'm serious. We don't have any time to waste!"

"Be easier just to entertain 'em on the boat."

"Will you quit? How can I keep track of Flora and get this place in shape in just three days?"

"Put her on your back like a papoose."

He was joking, but the next morning that's exactly what she did. She sewed up the hem of a baby gown that Flora had outgrown and tied it to her waist and shoulders. It worked for about an hour and then, despite her best efforts, it sprang a leak that forced Anna to change the baby's clothes and her own. She settled for moving Flora's crib with her from room to room—through all the upstairs bedrooms, through the upstairs hall, through the front room and the parlor, the dining room, the kitchen, the wood room—even the summer kitchen. Then it was time to do the cooking. So by the time Carrie, Arthur, and little Edgar were due to arrive, she was exhausted and feverish.

She insisted on going to meet them nonetheless. She and Larrabee drove down to the depot in the old buggy the preacher had left behind and found it completely inadequate to the task. They had to hire a buckboard to haul everything.

"I had forgotten you tend to travel fully," Anna said.

Caroline was too overwhelmed to pay attention. She was gawking at the town, a place she hardly recognized. "All this in three years," she said, looking from one grand building to the next.

"It's a wonder what a couple of fires can do," Larrabee said.

"You won't even find some of the places we used to know," Anna told her. "The roof of the old school collapsed in a rainstorm and our pine fort disappeared when they put a house up."

"You'll find the Courthouse a little different from what you remember," Larrabee said.

Young Edgar was jerking at his collar and complaining about the heat while Caroline tried to keep him tidy.

"If he's hot, we've got the place for him," Larrabee told Arthur. "There's a spring up north of town that'll cool him off plenty. We can go up there Sunday if you want."

By the time two days had passed, all of them were ready to cool off. The heat was relentless. Children walking on sand byways burned their feet. Dogs died under porches. Preacher Bonds gave his sermon outside in his shirtsleeves, under the shade of the pines. Tuscawilla was slow and crabby as she pulled the two families the several broiling miles to the spring.

"I haven't been here since I was girl," Anna sighed as they came at last into the comfort of thick woods. "I always thought of this place as one of our family secrets. Until that time all the drunks showed up."

Edgar had been chafing against the heat all the way and had fallen into something like a stupor. He lay against his mother, gently puffing his red cheeks like a fish out of water. Larrabee found a grassy spot where Tuscawilla could graze and tied the buggy to a sapling at the edge of it. Arthur followed Anna and Caroline with the picnic basket and they spread out in a clearing that sloped down to the gurgling spring.

"It's going to be cold," Larrabee reminded Edgar as the boy walked out of the woods in his swimming clothes.

The boy was quick to contradict him. "No it won't. *Nothing* here is cold."

He jumped into the little pool that welled up from the spring.

"Whooh-whooh-*whooh!*" He threw himself out of the water, gasping.

Anna smiled as she rocked Flora in her arms. "Maybe we should've started him out at the Sweetwater Branch."

They broke out the chicken and lemonade and the two sisters began to talk about old times. "It was chicken that introduced us," Caroline told Larrabee. "Remember?"

He squirmed. "I'd just as soon forget. It wasn't the best way to say how-de-do."

Arthur looked skeptical as he listened to Caroline's explanation.

"I think the idea of blowing the head off a chicken is foreign to him," Anna said.

"Well, I think it a trifle strange myself—now," Larrabee told her. "I did some things back then that seemed reasonable enough at the time but seem downright crazy today."

"That's because you're a family man now," Caroline told him. "That makes all the difference in the world, settling down, doesn't it, Arthur?"

Arthur didn't seem interested in pursuing the subject. Apparently it reminded him of something unpleasant.

"We sure were wild enough when we were younger," Caroline suggested.

"The preacher offered a hundred-dollar reward for bringing you back," Larrabee told Caroline. "That was enough to put about fifty men on the road, none of 'em having any idea where they were going."

"I think he regretted that," Anna said. "He wanted to do something for the family, but he just didn't know how to handle it. He just thought he had to do something fast."

"To preserve my honor," Caroline said with irony.

"Maybe we didn't do things the finest way," Arthur said, "but they've turned out for the best. Wouldn't you agree?"

Before Anna could answer, Edgar fell down in the pool and Arthur jumped up and ran down the slippery path to make sure he was safe.

At Anna's prodding, Larrabee took a slower but more certain route to see if he might be helpful. "Now he's cooled off for the rest of the day," he said as the boy slid from his father's hands and jumped back into the water, wetting the actor to the skin.

"Uh, you beggar!" Wincing, Arthur hauled Edgar back out of the water and set him down.

Larrabee glanced up at the mothers. "Boys and water," he said. "Once they find each other there's no pulling 'em apart."

Arthur was not taking his wetting well. He gave Edgar a pop on the behind. Edgar tried to jump into the water again, but his father caught him by the arm and set him on the path back up the slope. The boy seemed unaffected by the spanking and ran back to his mother with his wet clothes flapping.

"This is what happens when we spare the rod," Arthur said. "The boy's unmanageable."

"Oh, he's just high-spirited," Caroline replied. "Not so different from his father—or the way his father used to be."

"I'm going somewhere to dry off," Arthur announced. He continued down the path that followed the spring.

At a look from Anna, Larrabee went with him.

"If I remember right there's a place up on the other side," Larrabee said. "Open, with some good places to hang clothes."

They crossed the flowage at a narrow point and climbed up the opposite bank, where the sunlight broke through the canopy of moss-covered pines. The day was so humid that Larrabee doubted Arthur's clothes would dry anytime soon, but he figured that the actor mostly just wanted a walk to cool his temper. Fifty yards past the spring they came to a glen where deer had flattened the tall grass.

"I suppose I shouldn't have lost my temper," Arthur said. "It's just that he always catches me off guard when he does those things. It's probably all the traveling that's made him that way. Always trying to get attention."

"You're still on the move then," Larrabee said.

"Not as much as we were. The touring was getting to be too much with a baby and all."

"I know what you mean. Myself I'd just as soon not track down to that lake every day. There's pretty good money in it, but it doesn't seem altogether healthy. I've hardly seen Flora."

Arthur took off his coat and vest and hung them on a sapling. "I suppose we're similar in that way, aren't we? Each of us did some desperate thing to have his wife and then spent too much time traveling to see enough of her."

"Only you were traveling with Caroline, weren't you?"

"Not always. We—that is, I was put in a position which forced me to— Look here, Larrabee, the fact is I had a falling-out with the road manager and we've been on our own a bit."

Larrabee studied Arthur's face. The once-dashing actor looked nervous and out-of-sorts "Sounds like you've had a tough row to hoe. What do you figure to do?"

"The truth of the matter is, the company was in trouble anyway. The road manager absconded with half of last summer's receipts—and the leading lady."

"What about Caroline? I suppose motherhood slowed down her acting."

Arthur went to the sapling and pulled a flask from his inside coat pocket. He unscrewed the cap, pulled the cork and took a quick drink.

"Don't worry. I'm not a drunk. But I do need a drink from time to time, though Carrie disapproves." The silver flask flashed in the sunlight as he held it out to Larrabee. "It's not half bad on a hot day."

"Just don't buy any of this stuff off the locals." Larrabee took a swallow and handed it back.

Arthur took another swig and tucked the flask back into his coat pocket. "You see, the thing about Carrie is that, well, after we were married she seemed to lose her gift." He looked up at the tall pines as if addressing a soliloquy to the squirrels. "It's a sore point between us. Oh, she was acceptable. A provincial actress. But nothing like what I saw that night on your rough little stage in that nameless play. That night she had an edge, but it just seemed to get more and more blunt with each passing day. After Edgar was born, that was the end of it. She had nothing left. She turned away from it and never once looked back. Even though there was an opportunity or two." He took out the flask again and had one more quick drink. "So there you have it."

Larrabee looked toward the spring. No one had come after them. "I wish there was something here for you, but I don't imagine this little scrap of a town has much to offer you after Washington and Savannah and Richmond."

"No, no," Arthur said. "We wouldn't expect that. Carrie just wanted to get her spirits up by seeing the family again."

"Sorry you missed Mrs. Newhouse and Martha and the preacher."

"That's what happens when you're gone for three, four years. Things change. We're going to try our luck in New Orleans."

"New Orleans. Be careful in that town."

"You've been there?"

"Long time ago. They've got a hotel so big you could lose a coach-and-four in it. The St. Charles."

"I've heard of it! You've been to the St. Charles?"

"Oh, yes. And they've got hospitals bigger than the Courthouse. They need 'em too. It's a dangerous town."

"Nonetheless," Arthur said, "it's a town—a city—rich in theaters. We hope to start there and create a circuit up to St. Louis and over to Chicago, perhaps as producers. It's the only thing we know."

Just then they heard Caroline calling from the spring.

Larrabee stooped and picked two plants that looked like large, broad-leafed clover. He put one in his mouth and chewed it. He offered the other to Arthur.

"These are kind of sour but they're not half bad and they take away the smell of whiskey just like that."

Arthur nodded, smiled sheepishly, and started chewing.

The rain returned and stayed for the summer. When she wasn't running from the cover of one house to another, Anna worked hard at keeping her own in order.

"Oh! No! No! No!" She lifted her skirts, showing an improper amount of petticoat as she climbed the makeshift fence in the front room and pried the carpet from Flora's mouth.

"It may not be too bad as carpets go," Larrabee said.

Anna scooped the girl into her arms and followed Larrabee into the kitchen for his customary cooling-off ritual. "I envied you today," she said. "Being on the water the whole time. I would've dipped my hands and feet into it whenever I could."

Larrabee put his head under the kitchen pump and let the cold water run through his hair. When he had toweled off he said, "Don't envy me too much, my girl. This is the first chance I've had to dip all day. And it was plenty hot out there on that lake. How's Flora taking it?"

"She gets red as a berry but she keeps right on going. She took seven steps today. Here, look at this."

She set the toddler down at the doorway to the front room and took up a position at the opposite end of the kitchen. "Come on, sugarcane. Come on, Flora."

Larrabee smoothed his hair with his fingers and joined Anna. "Come on, Flora. We've got a nice juicy piece of carpet for you. Come on, girl. Come on."

Anna looked up at him, frowning. "You sound like you're calling a dog."

"Always thought we should have one. There's nothing like a good dog for keeping a place secure and homey."

"I wouldn't have one. Not with the baby."

"Well, we'll have to work on her, won't we, Flora?"

The little girl was smiling, taking wobbly steps.

"Look at that, Nathaniel. And not even ten months old."

"She walks better than some of those boys around Duke's place, and she's a darn sight prettier."

"Look, there's another one. It's twenty steps from the front room to the back door. Let's see if she can do ten."

Flora sat down abruptly on her padded behind, looking frightened and bewildered.

"Some days are like that," Larrabee said.

"Oh, dear. I suppose she must be tired. It's too close to bed time."

"It's another night for the sleeping porch. That's for sure. We'll have moths batting into us the whole time."

"Speaking of running into things, guess who I ran into at the post office this afternoon."

"Well, I suppose it was Mr. Andrew Carnegie."

"Not today. No, it was John Howard's wife. Jane."

"She's a queer duck, ain't she?"

"Oh, I don't know. She just doesn't seem to have any friends."

"Look at the company she keeps."

Anna went over and put Flora back on her feet. "Come on, sugar. How about just six steps—for Papa?" She pulled back a few feet and knelt on the floor. "Come on. Just six little steps. Anyway, you can't judge a woman by her husband."

"I'm not sure how to take *that*."

"Never mind. The point is I invited her over. And I think she just might come."

"Let her come. As long as she doesn't bring the other half with her."

"Oh, I doubt if she will. But would that be the end of the world if she did? John Howard isn't poison, is he?"

"Well, he's not exactly a tonic and he's got a way of bringing out the worst in people. Sooner or later you'll see him come up with something rotten. One thing I can say for him though—you may not like what he does, but you pretty much know what to expect. Sort of like snakes and skunks."

"That new town they're going to put up sounds like it's going to be a marvel. It might even do your business some good."

"That's John. He thinks big. Building a whole town. Now who'd've thought of that? I suppose next he'll be wanting to set up his own state, which is just fine as long as he stays out of mine. You can thank your lucky stars he hasn't bought in with the canal company or he'd be trying to sweep Bob and me and the *King Payne* right off the water."

"Look. Two...three...."

"We stopped by and had us a visit with Miss Laetitia Summerton this afternoon. Or I should say Bob did. You know I believe she's sweet on our man. I've been telling him that's why she's stuck with us instead of going with the canal company."

"Four! And I suppose that's why Walls has stuck with you too."

"Nope. That's the shallow water. We're the only ones who can get in there. And maybe a sense of loyalty for us ferrying his wife's medicines all these years. It's a strange business."

"Mrs. Summerton's been a widow now for several years."

"That's right. It would be respectable. She doesn't dress in mourning anymore. This being the United States of America there ain't no reason he can't court her—even if she does own five hundred acres and all he has is a boat—or half a boat. She has a smart, sensible farm. She's a smart woman. Grows about twenty different crops. Always has something going and never too much to lose if something goes wrong. It's no wonder he's smitten."

"And I suppose she's not bad to look at."

"Not so bad. Old-fashioned ringlets such as they must've worn in Charleston before the war, though she can't be much more than thirty. She's come down to the dock to talk a time or two. She's a cut above most of those folks down there."

"And what do you think of Jane Howard?"

"What do I think of her? I never gave much thought to her at all. I met her over at Dutton's that night. Then old Mary Leary came up and put the finger on John. If you ask me, that's the couple that deserves each other."

Flora had given considerable thought to the business of walking. Smiling uncertainly, she ventured out for another step.

"There! That's five! Come on! Show Papa you can do six."

Larrabee decided that if Anna wanted to invite Jane Howard over, nothing need come of it. It was better not to resist, not to stir up old animosities, better just to let her go ahead and he would put the past behind him. He figured that Anna and Jane wouldn't have much in common anyway.

"Six! That's six!"

Flora was more wobbly than ever, but she was beaming. Larrabee looked at her thin, fair, light brown hair—almost enough now for little braids—and it seemed to him that she was no longer just a baby with no life separate from her mother, but a fast-growing person in her own right. He stooped down and held out his arms.

"Here, darlin.' Come over here to your papa and make it an even ten."

Anna protested. "Ten, Nathaniel? She'll hurt herself."

"Sev-en," he counted. "Don't fall over now. Mama been putting whiskey in the milk again?"

"Nathaniel!"

Flora caught some of their energy and took a big eighth step.

"This is too much, Nathaniel. I'm going to pick her up."

He put his hand out to stop her. "She's steady. Look at that. She's got good legs on her."

"My mother would die to hear you talking that way."

"Here she comes!" Flora was within one step of Larrabee's outstretched arms. She smiled as if teasing him and gave a coquettish turn of her head.

He tapped her on the shoulder and when she turned back she lost her balance. He caught her, swept her into his arms, and stood up so fast that Flora was startled.

"Ten! That's what goes in the record books."

Anna scolded him. "Look, now you've scared her."

He made a face at the little girl and then cracked a big smile that made her laugh. She grabbed his lower lip and pulled.

Anna pulled away Flora's hand and kissed it. "Nelda says that before we know it she'll be walking a mile."

Larrabee chuckled and gave the girl a squeeze. "I believe we'll have all we can do to keep up with her. I believe she's a girl who's going to go places."

Chapter 35

"I think it's the most beautiful house in town." Jane Howard moved her parasol to one side for a better look.

It was a tall, graceful, two-story structure. The finely cut balcony railing and cornice-work resembled lace. The high windows were open to the warm September air. Jane fancied that the single-story wing to the right was an elegant study.

"Beautiful or not, he's got plenty of *my* money in it," John Howard said. He tapped the picket fence with his walking stick. "If I'd known there was so much profit in it I would've become a dentist. I would've saved myself a peck of trouble too."

"Think of it as an investment," she told him. "You can figure that all the money you've spent on your dentist is going into the Hygienic Hotel. That way you're getting some of it back."

"That's a twisted path to comfort, Jane."

"Sometimes the path *is* twisted, wouldn't you say?" She turned her parasol again to provide a view down the street. "Well, look who's coming."

Howard pulled at his collar, as he tended to do when he was impatient. "Who? I don't see anybody."

"You don't see a woman with a baby buggy? Maybe you need to invest in an eye doctor too."

"Oh, her. Who is she?"

"It's Anna Larrabee. I met her in the post office a few weeks ago. I talked to her husband at the Duttons' New Year's Eve party. You disapproved, remember?"

"No, I do not. You can talk to anyone you want to."

"Now, now. She'll hear you. Better mind your manners, John."

A long row of fair-sized oaks separated the neighborhood's picket fences from the broad sandy streets. Howard counted the trees Anna passed as she approached, but Jane spoiled the tally by going forward to greet her.

"How are you doing, Anna? My, I believe that baby's grown an inch since I saw you at the post office."

Howard held back, leaning on his stick and pretending to watch two boys chasing a pig across the street.

"John, oh John! Come say hello to Anna! Don't be such an old galosh."

He came up slowly, tapping his stick as he went.

"Come on now, John." Jane hooked her arm through his elbow and patted his hand. "You must know Mrs. Larrabee, John."

He touched the brim of his white felt summer hat. "Of course. From a distance."

Anna couldn't help smiling at his stiffness. "Sure. I've seen you here and there ever since I was a girl. My husband's told me so much about you."

Howard raised a brow skeptically although there was nothing ironic in her tone. "How is your husband, Mrs. Larrabee? I see him so seldom anymore."

"He's working very hard like he always does. Riding down to the lake every day—except Sunday of course. I wish he could stay right here in town and work. I'd get to see more of him."

"Of course. Maybe it'll work out that way somehow."

"That's the prettiest hat you're wearing, Anna! Is that an ostrich feather?"

Anna blushed and touched it. "Yes, I'm sure it is." It was a modest hat. A small affair of light brown velvet and ivory lace. She had admired it at Nelda's house and Nelda had given it to her on the spot.

"Well, it's very elegant indeed and just the thing with fall coming on. Wouldn't you say, John?"

"Absolutely. Well, well."

"I think that means that he wants to be on," Jane explained. "You know how men are. Always business." She patted his hand again and they moved on as the two women renewed their intention to call on each other.

"You could've been more sociable," Jane told him when they turned the corner. "And why do you trail your walking stick along the fences? You'll ruin it."

He chose not to answer her statement and went instead to her question.

"I drag it because it suits me. I find it as relaxing as the walk itself. In fact, sometimes more so. Maybe you should get a stick too, Jane."

"I'm perfectly well relaxed," she said. "More all the time. After two years I'm actually starting to like this town."

That night he took a walk by himself, with his stick in one hand and a Cuban cigar in the other. Something Anna Larrabee had said had set him to thinking. Smiling to himself and smoking as he went, he played out the scenario in his mind. The ice company was not going as well as expected. There was simply too much competition. Some of the air compression equipment was patented but there were plenty of ways to get around the patents, especially when the demand for artificial ice was so high. His own man, Curtis, had gone over to an upstart firm down near the Doig foundry. And that wasn't his only competitor. He was making some money, but just barely enough to keep the house going, and his client list wasn't getting any longer. He needed some other way to get cash flow.

Fall was coming on and the orange trade looked likely to be as profitable as ever. The trees on the Courthouse Square were still too young to produce, but practically every other free foot of soil was about to pay off. The ripening fruit was thick in the trees and the demand in the growing northern markets was stronger than ever.

That meant that there would be more money than ever in transporting those oranges. He decided to make an offer to the gentlemen of the Alachua Steam Navigation and Canal Company, and what Mrs. Larrabee had said made him confident that they would listen. The next morning he walked to B.F. Jordan's store on the east side of the square. Finding Jordan out, he left his card and went to the icehouse to see how production and delivery might be made more efficient—for the next owner. It was another hot day. As he stood in the pleasantly cool storage room he wondered if there weren't some way that buildings could be made cool year round by fanning air over blocks of artificial ice, or for that matter, compressing the air and somehow blowing it directly into the room to be cooled. He thought that a fortune must be waiting for the man who could make that work economically, but he couldn't begin to see where all the necessary electricity would come from.

That pipedream ended abruptly when one of the ice handlers, tongs still in hand, told him that he had a caller in the front office.

The caller turned out to be none other than B.F. Jordan himself. They shook hands as if they had been doing business together all along.

Howard was heartened by Jordan's quick and personal response. He invited him to take a chair by the open window. Then he closed the door to the small, high-ceilinged corner office and made a point of bringing his own chair away from the battered roll-top desk.

"Thanks for coming, Ben. As you can imagine, I have a proposition for you."

Jordan put his hands together as if in prayer. "Of course, as the secretary of the company—I assume this is about the company—"

Howard assured him that it was.

"As the secretary of the company I'll be glad to forward your proposal to the board."

"Of course. If you like what I have to say—and I think you will—I'll be happy to restate it for the board."

Three nights later he was in the big boardroom over Jordan's store doing just that, and he had an attentive audience in the gentlemen of the Steam Navigation and Canal Company. He had brought a map of Alachua Lake with him. He tacked it to the wall. "It's already October, gentlemen, and the orange trade will soon be upon us. What share of it will you have?"

"On that lake—about seventy percent," boasted J.T. McMillan, the treasurer.

Howard came forward, his hands on his hips. "Why not a hundred?"

The gentlemen of the board looked at each other as if the answer was obvious. "Because we can't get to it all," McMillan said.

Ben Jordan started to say something, but Howard raised his hand to stop him. "Let's take this one step at a time. Why can't you get to it?"

"Because the water's too shallow and unpredictable," McMillan replied.

Howard waited for the words to sink in. "But *somebody's* getting that other thirty percent."

Dr. Phillips had been with the company all along, but had recently moved into town from Waldo. He was tired and impatient. "It's the *King Payne*. They've got Bob Harper. He and Larrabee can read the channels on that lake like the lines in their hands. We made Harper an offer—about the same time we made you one, John. But he didn't come over either. Said he likes working for himself and paying his boat off. So he gets everything from Rocky Point all the way over to the Summerton farm. Including what Walls doesn't send by train. Thirty percent."

Howard looked around the room. "And there's nobody else who can reach those places?"

McMillan shrugged. "Harper's been on that lake for fifteen years—longer than anybody else. Larrabee almost as long. Plus they've got the knack. How you going to beat them?"

"That's what I'm getting to, gentlemen. And I'll pay for it."

"I'm listening." Dr. Phillips' statement echoed among the others in the room.

"What're you going to do—kidnap Bob Harper?" McMillan laughed and so did some of the others. Sitting off to one side, Ben Jordan folded his arms and remained serious.

"Gentlemen, the obvious answer—if I may say so—is to do what your company says you do—use a canal. You start by digging it."

"A canal?" Dr. Phillips wasn't sure he had heard right. "To seventy different farms and plantations? It'd be cheaper to dig through to the St. Johns River."

"All you need is one canal," Howard said, relishing his position as educator. "Along the southwest shore of the lake—here—from one dock to the next if you want to think of it that way. It's a mud bottom. Easy to dredge."

"And easy to fill up too," McMillan said. "That lake bottom shifts about every week from what our men say."

"So you dredge it out every week," Howard said. "It'll be even cheaper to maintain than it'll be to cut in the first place. You can keep your dredge out there all year, working back and forth."

Ben Jordan tapped his finger. "Anyway, you won't have to worry about it, Jim. He's going to pay for it himself. If he buys into the company, that can be his pet project."

"Won't be any good till next year," McMillan said.

"That's right," Howard told him. "You won't turn a dime till '88, end of the summer probably. But in plenty of time for next year's oranges."

"And what do you want from the company in the meantime, John, while you're building this canal of yours?"

"Well, Bill, just the same share every one else in this room gets. An equal share of the net."

"Before you've put in any money? There won't be much of a net."

"Sure there will, Bill. You've seen those trees out there. They're hanging with oranges. You've got a good six months of big money to look forward to."

Jim McMillan rubbed his goatee pensively. "And when do you propose to start building your canal?"

"*Our* canal." Howard made an expansive gesture to include everyone in the room. "As soon as I can find the low bidder on the job. Won't take long once we get the boat in the water."

"Well, just see to it that they keep it deep enough for our boats. The *Harris* and the *Chacala* float high enough, but the *Santa Fe* needs some water under her."

"We'll put eight feet of water from one end to the other, Jim. At sixty-six feet the *Santa Fe* doesn't draw that much. You can get yourselves a bigger boat if you want to."

They went on past ten o'clock, smoking and talking over the details of the canal project. Finally they stood up, stretching and shaking hands and patting each other on the back. Jim McMillan summed up the evening.

"John, as I recall you bowed out of the company by firing a pistol in the air down there on the southwest shore of the lake. I'm glad that your return has been quieter and more harmonious."

For the next three months Howard walked and smoked and evaded their questions about how the bids on the dredging were going. He needed the cash flow from their investments before he could afford to lease a dredge, let alone buy one. He did manage to sell the ice company, though the terms were marginal at best and he had to carry a second mortgage on the place, but if the new owner—a consumptive New Yorker down for the climate—were to default, the business would revert to Howard. It compromised his ability to pay for the dredging, but he leveraged a deal with Dutton's bank whereby he was able to get a one-year lease on a dredge in Fernandina—one that would be dismantled and loaded on the railroad for delivery during the second week of January.

Chapter 36

Dobkin Murray huddled in his overcoat, wishing that he were already home. His shoulders ached from the sawing and he had pinched a finger between two knotty pine logs when he was loading the wagon. For a while the exertion and his throbbing finger had taken his mind off the cold, but after a couple of miles on the wind-whipped road he was shivering. He shivered as he reached under the seat for the warming comfort of a sip of whiskey. He pulled his collar around his chin and pushed his limp felt hat down over his forehead. Then he gave Ralph Pine's team another crack with the whip and settled back into his coat for what little warmth was there.

He was so intent on the cold and pushing the team up the hill that at first he didn't see the girl standing at the edge of the woods. She had a shawl over her head and shoulders and clutched its stringy ends together in one skinny hand. With the other she waved a linen handkerchief. She was a white girl and he didn't know what to do. Perhaps because he was so bundled up, she had not been able to tell that he was a Negro? He had no wish to stop in the cold with night coming on, and the strange, rhythmic way this girl was waving was unsettling. Dobkin Murray had plenty of reasons to keep on going, but the sermon last Sunday had been about the Good Samaritan and so, against his better judgment, Dobkin pulled the team to a stop and asked the girl what she wanted.

His misgivings flared up again when, instead of speaking, she waved a crooked finger toward the weather-beaten old trading post across the road. He thought at first that she was asking to buy some of his firewood, although that seemed unlikely with so much of it lying around in the woods that surrounded the place.

"This here wood's too green," he told her, forcing a smile. "Maybe next year." It was the truth, he told himself. The armload of dry pieces he had hidden away on the bottom of the pile was not worth mentioning. He was looking forward to throwing them on his own fire tonight.

The girl persisted. When she turned and gestured again toward the trading post, he noticed that she had the longest hair he had ever seen on anyone.

Straight and light brown, it covered the entire length of the shawl and then some. Those crooked white fingers of hers looked like roots, and in the dimming light her face seemed to fall away from high, prominent cheekbones. Her small dark eyes never let go of him.

He could think of no reason why anybody would want to attack a poor Negro with a wagonload of green wood, and he was eager to break from the girl's gaze, so he quietly said, "Yes, ma'am" and nudged the team toward the lonesome pile of clapboard and logs.

The girl kept up noiselessly and without any apparent quickening of her pace, as if she were gliding. Dobkin felt the skin tingle at the back of his neck. He shivered from cold and at the thought of something unholy that seemed to inhabit this desolate place. He considered turning the team and whipping it toward town but instead he drove the last few yards to the trading post.

As if by magic the wagon came to a halt. He said an unseemly word and climbed down from the seat. He knew little about the people who lived here. Like everyone else, he had heard the stories of Mad Mary, had seen her shuffling along the streets as if sleepwalking, had heard people laugh at her claim that John Howard was the father of her strange child. He knew that her weed of a brother, Sam, was an undertaker given to professional misadventures, a shadowy figure that turned the occasional dollar at the edge of the law and was somehow connected to the devious, Negro-hating Baldy Choat. He knew that before the war Baldy had been a mean young man to work for at a slave-rich place called Haile Plantation, knew that the Choats and Learys had come here from God-knows-where and set up this trading post before the Seminole wars, when his own kinfolk were still being bought and sold in the bottomlands of eastern Virginia.

As the girl motioned toward the plank door he took some consolation in the new brass hinges on which it hung. Here at last was something of the everyday world and he pressed them into his mind to take with him, whatever might come.

As the girl swung the door open he told himself that there was only one reason he was going inside—the potbellied stove that squatted in the center of the square room. Except for a few crosscut saws outlined against the stripes of log and mortar, the merchandise was dark and formless. The smell of overripe apples mixed with the scent of kerosene, wood smoke, and machine oil. He stood by the glowing stove, warming his hands and pressing so close that he felt a pleasant burning from the nickel slides of his suspenders.

But the girl had her own agenda. With a skinny hand she motioned him toward the back of the room, away from the warmth and light.

"Child," he said in a voice that barely rose above the crackle inside the stove, "child, the sun's going down and I's got to be going. Do you hear me, child? I's got to be going now."

Tilting her head, she looked toward the back wall, toward another door. He was in deep now, and a contrary feeling came over him. He was curious to see what was behind that door, horrible as it might be. He kept telling himself that he had nothing to fear because he had nothing anyone could want. Even the team wasn't his. It belonged to Ralph Pine and it had kept him in debt for as long as he could remember.

He followed the girl into this second room, smaller and warmer than the first, with an unhealthy smell of unwashed flesh and drying vomit. A single kerosene lamp turned low lit the room and the remains of a fire gave off an orange glimmer. Half buried in a sagging brass bed was a pale gaunt woman. Dobkin thought at first that she was dead, but as he and the girl came closer, the woman's eyes fluttered open. At the sight of Dobkin she gasped and flopped on her side so that her back was to him. "You done brung a nigra into my bedchamber, you foolish girl? Did I teach you nothing? Come 'round here."

The girl did as she was told, keeping out of her mother's reach. She stuck two fingers in her mouth and waited for her mother to speak again.

Dobkin pulled back toward the door, hat in hand. "I'll be on my way now. I reckon I'll be on my way."

Suddenly Mary rolled onto her back, staring at the ceiling with bulging eyes. "Fairies! Them fairies took off the rings!"

He found himself stuck to the threshold, straining to hear what she was saying.

"Them fairies took off the rings and I did eat! Come down, ye peerie fairies. Come down, ye pretty ones."

Dobkin had heard that years ago up in Newnansville Mad Mary had fallen down in church, spoken in tongues, and had never come back normal, and now it seemed to him that she was doing it again, for the strange words were beginning to creep in. But she continued to stare at the ceiling, at the rough, shadowy pine rafters, as if something were moving among them, unseen to anyone else. The girl was not looking up at all, was gazing at her mother's face as if waiting for the storm to pass. But Mary arched her back and reached a bony hand upward and shrieked something about rings again, then fell back against the pillow so violently that he thought she must be dead. She lay panting like a fox hunted through the night and Dobkin thought now that the devil must surely have entered into her. He expected her to rise from the bed spewing venom, but she did worse. She lay quietly for a moment, turned toward him and spoke with a tenderness that was the most terrible of all.

She reached out to him. "I'm here. Hold me back from the spirit world. Hold me!"

Dobkin put a steadying hand to the doorjamb and dropped his hat. Mary continued to look at him beseechingly. He was torn between pity and fear. Her hand was so thin and white. It trembled, waiting for his. The girl came around to his side of the bed and looked up at him with large brown eyes that reflected the flickering of the fire. Slowly he lowered his hand and took up the cold fingers of Mary Leary. He knelt by the bed, folding her hand in his, patting and stroking it.

"There, there now. It'll be all right. There now."

She seemed more at peace, spoke softly of a hot day, a fever, and the sound of big guns. He thought she must be remembering something from the war, but she started mentioning tar and he couldn't for the life of him figure out what tar had to do with it. The smell of tar, she said, wrinkling her nose as if there were tar right there in the room. During his long life he had come to believe that dreams had significance. They always did in the Bible, after all. And his own dreams seemed to ring true sometimes, although occasionally, when he was only half asleep he caught them in lies, jumbling unimportant things together just because he had thought about them during the course of the day. So now he was trying to decide what poor Mary Leary's dreams were meaning as she grasped his hand all the tighter.

His head was spinning so much that he didn't hear the voices until they were inside the store. He knew them at once for what they were—the low whine of Sam Leary and the drawn-out rasp of Baldy Choat. All at once he became aware of the danger he was in. He tried to pull his hand away from Mary's, but her fingers closed around his all the tighter so that he had to wrench himself free. He knew there was no way past the two men, but at the very least he wanted to be out of the bedroom when they found him. Even that he was denied, though, for by the time he had broken away from Mary's grip, Sam and Baldy had crossed the store and opened the door to Mary's room.

Baldy was carrying a birding gun, small caliber but grim and deadly at close range, and before Dobkin knew it, the muzzle was at his throat. He swallowed, closed his eyes, and prepared to meet his maker, but the blast did not come, just the jabbing of the cold muzzle at his throat. Of course, he told himself. They would want him outside. They'd shoot him there. Probably skin him too.

"The girl called me in." Dobkin said in a pinched voice that he didn't recognize as his own. The words came out wrong, like he was placing blame, but he didn't know how to fix them.

To his surprise he heard Sam's low voice say, "Joan, is that so?"

"It stinks in here," Baldy said. "What's going on? Tell me." He jabbed the bird gun so that Dobkin's chin jutted up painfully.

"She's sick," Dobkin rasped. "I think maybe she done et something poison. Now she's gone into visions. I was just fixin' to fetch the doctor but—but she wanted me near."

Baldy's thrust with the bird gun told him that he had said something wrong.

"That true, Joan?" Sam asked over Dobkin's shoulder.

Dobkin now felt sure that they would kill him just for the sport of it. After all, the girl was obviously mute. How would she tell the truth even if she wanted to?

"Speak up now! Is that true? Did you and your mama ask this nigra to come into this room?"

Baldy seemed angry with the girl now, but he was expressing it by jabbing the bird gun into Dobkin's throat. Dobkin dared to swallow again, but it hurt. He wished he could see what the girl was doing, could see what her mother was doing. His life lay in the hands of a madwoman and a mute.

"Joan! Is it *true?*"

Dobkin felt something snap in his neck.

The girl had been sitting at the foot of the bed. She got up and took her fingers out of her mouth. "It's *true!*" Her voice was thin and shrill, but the words were sweet to the wood hauler. Dobkin felt his knees buckle. He had taken too many shocks to stand up to.

Baldy pushed Dobkin with the rifle bore. "Go on. Git out of here."

"I can get the doctor if you wants," Dobkin offered. He felt sorry for the woman.

Baldy ignored him. He spoke to Sam instead.

"What do you think? Them goddamned mushrooms again?"

Sam covered his nose with a long hand. "Smells like it."

Dobkin made his way to the door, glad now to feel the bite of the cold air and happy to see his old unreliable horses and wagon. After two tries at climbing onto the seat, he turned the team toward town, he felt relieved and free. His son might be in jail up in Georgia and his wife might give him hell for coming home late with a far-fetched story about big guns and tar, but he thanked the Lord that he lived in a world of fresh air and daylight, straight talking and sanity.

Chapter 37

Bob Harper cut himself a generous plug and tucked it into his cheek.

"There may not be much left of this old tub by the time we're through, Larrabee, but by thunder it'll be ours. Eleven years we've been sending drafts off to Mr. Herbert Kline and his son, and in one more year we're through." He spat into the lake, laid the tiller in the crook of his arm, and took in the chilly air. "Damn, don't them oranges look good today!"

"They look best to them that owns 'em," Larrabee said. "Same as this boat will look like the *Andy Johnson* to you once you've paid it off."

"*We,* Larrabee. You'll own a half. Don't let's forget that."

"I'm not forgetting, Robert. It's just that I never figured myself to be a boat owner. I always had it in mind to take up farming. That is, once I wised up about the gold fields."

They were well out onto the lake now and Bob let the boat steer itself for a moment so he could spit. "There's a secret to gold, you know."

"A secret."

"That's right. As to why it's so valuable."

"And what secret's that?"

"Why, if just everybody could find it, it wouldn't be worth nothing. So don't it figure that most folks who go out panning or digging or whatever ain't likely to find nothing?"

"I don't call that much of a secret."

"And I'll tell you who makes most of the money off of gold."

"I just bet you will, Bob."

"It's the camp followers. The soiled doves and the card sharps and the hardware dealers—"

"And the second-story men."

Bob nodded. "And them. There was more money made off of folks looking for gold than there ever was off of the gold itself."

"And do you reckon that's so with oranges?"

"I do not. I'd heap rather have me a farm full of oranges than be out here patching my boiler every other day. What do you suppose the Yankees will be paying for produce come summer?"

"'Bout the same as last I imagine."

"With all that harsh weather they've been having? With twenty-foot snowdrifts in New York City?"

"Who says there were twenty-foot snowdrifts in New York City?"

"The newspapers. They're saying there was never a blizzard like it."

"Well, you can have snow without it ruining anything. Just because you have snow doesn't mean it's so cold."

"Larrabee, there was ice floating in the St. Johns River the other day or Ray Polk's a liar."

"Maybe there was, but everything looks healthy to me, Bob. Does it not to you? Don't those oranges over there look as hale as ever? And over there? Maybe Ray Polk saw ice and maybe it snowed twenty feet in New York, but that doesn't mean the crops are to be ruined. You southern boys don't understand snow. That's the problem here."

They were silent for a while as their tempers cooled in the sharp February wind. Bob cut himself a sliver from his plug and took up the subject of Bobby La Rue, asking whether he still ran the restaurant on the south side of the square.

"I haven't had the heart to ask him," Larrabee said. "Last I heard he was just hanging on. Seemed like there were enough folks going in there, but somehow he just can't keep the money up."

Bob was looking at something on the far side of the lake, toward the Walls plantation. He nudged the tiller to work around a half-submerged log. "There's people like that. Can't hang onto a dollar. And then there's the other kind—can't let go of one."

Larrabee had seen the thing too. It had to be a boat but the shape was very strange. "And then there's the kind that money just sticks to no matter what. Bobby's giving Anna piano lessons. Did I tell you that?"

"No. What's he teaching her? Saloon tunes so she can play at Duke's?"

"Not that I know of. She didn't say. Could be saloon tunes I suppose. If she was to play at Duke's I could be home and away at the same time."

"You and your Anna. Maybe I'll just tell her you said that."

"Go right ahead. Just don't tell her that her new hat's too small. I already made that mistake."

"Larrabee, even though I'm a bachelor l know better than that. Did you have to spend a night in the summer kitchen?"

"No, I spent an hour smoking in the wicker chair. Then she came downstairs and forgave me. Sometimes I think the subject matter's got little to do with the argument."

"It seems to me that women are kind of like fertilizer. Most of the time you can handle 'em safe enough, but every now and then—without warning—they'll blow up in your face."

"I wouldn't tell her that either if I was you. Or any other woman. And I predict a long life alone for you, Robert."

"Me too. But only because I can't afford a lady good enough for me."

"You mean, *the* lady good enough for you. You still figure half of a sporting craft like the *King Payne* won't impress Miss Laetitia?"

"I do not. Nor three quarters, nor one-and-a-half for that matter. She was raised high in Charleston and widowed high on that smart farm down yonder, and I ain't no Confederate colonel."

"Maybe. But you've got one thing over that colonel—you're still up and about. Don't you suppose a living mud pilot's got high card over a deceased colonel when the night's cold and lonely?"

Bob whistled and shook his head and thought sweet thoughts. "Miss Laetitia. She's got a son, you know. Must be about nine or ten. 'Bout the same age as J.J. She keeps him close to the apron strings, but he peeps out now and again. I've a notion he cottons to boats."

"Well, now, that's a start." Larrabee squinted toward the Walls plantation as the *King Payne* churned its black smoky way in *that* direction. "What do you suppose that thing is?"

"I'll tell you what it is," Bob said. "It's two things. It's a dredge—and it's stuck."

Larrabee went up to the bow and studied the strange lines some more. The basic shape wasn't so different from any of the other boats on the lake—low-slung with a cabin that poked up as if stuck on as an afterthought. But then there were those two black arms that jutted over the water.

"What's it doing away over here?" Larrabee asked. "Canal's on the other end of the lake."

"That's a good question. You can be sure he ain't over here to dig a canal."

"You figure it's a channel?"

"I do. I wondered how long it would take those fellers to come up with the idea. They couldn't buy us out, so there're figuring to run us out of business."

"Can they do that?"

"Don't see why not. Doesn't anybody own the lake. I'm just not so sure how practical it is. They're going to have to keep dredging it all the time."

"Be a shame if that dredge was to sink some night."

Bob laughed. "Wouldn't it though! But if they can't keep off the bottom better than that, we won't have to worry about competition from them."

"That so?"

"No."

"What do you suppose we ought to do?"

"Don't know. Guess we'll start by running over there and seeing what's what."

The dredge wasn't going anywhere and didn't seem to be trying to. Bob put the *King Payne* on a perpendicular course as if he were expecting the newcomers to fire a cannon at him. There were five men idling on the dredge. Two of them were eating lunch in the stern, one was sunning himself on top of the cabin, and the other two were forward, talking by the giant iron arms.

Larrabee addressed them from the bow of the *King Payne*.

"Ho, boys. Pretty day to be out."

"Canal company took their sweet time sending y'all over here," said one of the men by the arms.

"Longer'n you think," Bob said from the tiller. He swung the *King Payne* around broadside and kept it about ten feet away. "We ain't the canal company and I don't see anybody out here who is."

Off to the west a small sloop cut the blue horizon with its triangular sails. It was bearing away. A faint puff of smoke rose from the vicinity of the Sweetwater Branch. It was impossible to tell whether the boat was entering or leaving the lake.

The man lying on the cabin sat up and eyed Bob and Larrabee suspiciously. "Who are you then if you ain't with the canal company?"

Bob ignored the question. "Ya'll are stuck pretty good, ain't you?"

The man up front put his hands on his hips. "We could use a tow if you've got a line, mister."

Larrabee went back to the tiller to see what Bob wanted to do.

"Let's rig something up," Bob said.

Larrabee wasn't sure what he was hearing. "You mean haul 'em off, just like that?"

"That's right."

"Sure as we do there'll be boats running right through here every day of the week and Sunday too, and you and I'll be out of a job."

"Could be. But let's get to it. Better rig something. About twenty feet to make sure they don't ram into us."

"Seems to me we at least ought to make 'em pay," Larrabee said. "Otherwise we're just shooting ourselves in the foot."

Bob put a hand on his shoulder. "Never mind, Nathaniel. Go ahead and splice those docking lines together. Let's get 'em off of here so we can get on with our business."

The docking lines were twelve-foot lengths of hemp rope the diameter of a quarter dollar. Larrabee tied them together with a sheet bend, tied it off on a bow cleat, and heaved the free end over to the men in the bow of the dredge. They started to carry it back to the stern but Bob called over to them to tie it up front.

"What for?" Larrabee asked.

"So they'll think I know what I'm doing," Bob said.

They called over when they had the bow tied off and Bob signaled Larrabee to ease the throttle into reverse. The line stretched its full length and went taut across the bow of the *King Payne*. The dredge sat tight. The line pulled and groaned and the cleat squeaked as the water boiled up around the churning stern wheel. Bob worked the tiller slowly to the left and the stern swung around until the two boats were perpendicular.

"More," Bob told Larrabee. "Go to half."

Larrabee opened the throttle farther, sweating from the heat of the boiler. "That line ain't going to hold," he said. Vainly he looked for some movement of the dredge.

"Go to three quarters," Bob told him.

Larrabee couldn't hear him above the noise of the engine and the surging water, so Bob raised and lowered his fist three times. Larrabee looked back at him as if he were crazy.

Bob signaled again.

The *King Payne* made a noise that neither of them had ever heard—a screeching that came up from the engine and cut through everything else. Larrabee wanted to back away to save himself when the boiler exploded, which he thought it surely would, but he stood his ground, with his hand on the throttle, waiting, daring Bob to signal him again.

The men on the dredge seemed unconcerned. They had collected in the stern of the clumsy boat and paid no particular attention to the straining, top-heavy bow that had jammed into the mud. Apparently they assumed that the operation would succeed.

In the end it did. The nose of the dredge turned toward the straining sternwheeler and broke free with a sideways motion that threatened to pull the whole thing over. A bubble of black smoke shot from the shiny stack and the two boats surged into free water. Larrabee steadied himself and brought the throttle down. Bob straightened the tiller and the motion settled into a smooth gliding through the water.

Bob wiped his forehead. "What did you think of that?"

Larrabee watched the dredge pull toward them. "I think we damned near lost the boat. That's what I think."

Bob dug out his tobacco plug and sliced off an end. "You know, I imagine we damned near did. Wonder what she'd do if we brought her up full."

"Blow us up," was Larrabee's reply.

"Well, now, there ain't no reason to get sore. Everything turned out for the best."

The dredge came up and a man with a handlebar mustache heaved the line back over to Larrabee. "Many thanks, boys."

"Not at all." Bob gave them a friendly wave. "Nothing to it."

Larrabee coiled the line and watched them go. "Was it your boyhood pastime to feed snakes?"

Bob laughed and worked the *King Payne* out into deeper water. "No, I was more likely to bust 'em with rocks—friend and foe alike."

"They're just going to go and dig their channel, and in a week or so the canal company's going to be going through here like it was a thoroughfare. They've got that sixty-six-footer all ready to go I hear."

"And they'll go with it no matter what we do."

"You think they would've pulled *us* off?"

"We'll never know."

"Well, I know."

"They're just pawns of the canal company, Nathaniel. They don't mean any harm."

"And I suppose a snake doesn't mean any either. Just doing his job. Who do you figure put 'em up to this?"

"Don't know. But if you're really curious you can always go to the Courthouse and find out who the shareholders are these days. There'll be a record of it."

"Maybe I'll just do that. Somebody set 'em off."

For the next two months the dredge spent most of its time poking along the southwestern quarter of the lake as if it had lost a gold piece in the water. It managed to avoid running aground again, but at the same time accomplished nothing that resembled the dreaded channel. The *King Payne* continued to pay scheduled visits to the farms and plantations as the citrus season gave way to vegetables.

"If we're living on borrowed time," Bob said. "We're living pretty high. I just hope we've borrowed long-term."

"Don't count on that," Larrabee told him. "We're borrowing from John Howard and that means trouble. Sooner more than later."

That was the name he had seen in the Courthouse records. Added to the familiar names associated with the canal company was that one new one, John Howard.

Bob smiled as he watched the meanderings of the new boat. "The whole pack of 'em's going to go broke sooner or later if they keep paying that dredge to go wading like that. I'm glad I don't own stock in that company. You don't think it's personal between you and Howard, do you? It can't mean that much to him to bring you down."

"I figure if he can bring me down and make money at the same time he'll do it."

They were well out toward the Walls plantation and gathering speed in the deep water. "Well, call off your dogs," Bob said. "You're supposed to be celebrating today. Your anniversary and Anna's birthday all rolled into one. I'm surprised you didn't stay home."

"Who can afford to do that? Forty-six more weeks and we're paid off. It's going to feel mighty good having that money go into the bank instead of an envelope sent to Herbert Kline."

Bob didn't answer.

Larrabee looked back and saw him studying the water.

Bob swung the tiller sharply. But before he could complete the arc, the *King Payne* hit hard with a sickening metallic scream that reminded Larrabee of a hound having its belly laid open by a coon.

The boat came to a halt with the water welling around it.

"There's nothing out here to run into," Larrabee said.

Bob looked at the thrashing stern wheel. "There is now."

Larrabee brought the throttle down until the boat had slowed almost to a standstill. Both of them looked back at what they had crossed. The wake of the *King Payne* swirled around an angular form that lay just below the surface.

Bob brought the boat back a little closer and stared. "Now that's damned ugly. Someone's lost a skiff right in the middle of the lane."

"Who do you suppose?" Larrabee asked.

Bob continued to stare at the metal shafts that rose up from the bottom of the lake. "Could be your friend John if that's what you're thinking. But it'd take some doing to find out, and right now we've got bigger fish to fry. We've got to have a good look at this boat."

"It'll cost us the day to go back to the landing," Larrabee said. "Not that we have any choice."

Bob swung the tiller and pointed the *King Payne* back toward Rocky Point.

"We got off cheap," he said at dinner that night. "I thought sure we had busted the piston rods and bent the cylinder, but a shave and a haircut'll take care of it." He shifted in his chair and patted the birthday girl on the wrist. "Now enough of that foul old lake. How've you been, Miss Anna?"

Before she could answer, Flora toddled up to her side with a complaint about some kind of itch.

"Miss Anna's been busy," Larrabee said. "That's how she's been. She thought it would get easier once Flora learned to walk, but she totes her around more than ever to keep her out of mischief."

"She did some of her own walking today," Anna told them. "We went all the way over to the new opera house. And isn't that a sight to behold!"

"Town's gittin' too fancy to live in," Penny said. He had been out to the kitchen to dish the ice cream, which was too hard for the women to scoop. "That artificial ice must be colder'n the real stuff. I ain't never seen ice cream harden up like this."

"It's because you took it out before it was all turned," Nelda said. "We had a discussion about that at the time."

"I did it, Ma!" J.J. spoke up to put a stop to what sounded like a dispute in the making. "Pa let me do the whole thing. Only we wasn't going to tell you. We wanted to make it a surprise. But I was getting powerful tired of turning the crank and so I took it out before it was ready."

"Never you mind," Penny said. He set a dish in front of the boy and gave him a reassuring squeeze on the shoulder. "It's goin' to taste just as good. I could about git drunk smellin' that vanilla."

"Two years married!" Nelda said. "How does it feel?"

Larrabee and Anna started to answer at the same time.

"Best wife I ever had," Larrabee quipped.

"I'm glad to hear *that*," Anna said. "It's hard to believe it's already been two years, except when I think how long ago Mama and Martha and Preacher Williams left for China. Two years ago!"

"Another two and they're due back, ain't they?" Penny wagged an admonishing finger at J.J., who had gotten most of his bowl of ice cream on his spoon and was getting ready to stuff it into his mouth.

"Seems like a while since you've gotten a letter," Nelda said, trying to ignore her men.

"It has been. And that was from Martha, which made it a little hard to know what was going on because she goes on and on about people as if we know who they are even though we've never heard of them."

"Preacher must have his hands full," Penny said, smiling. "'Course it may be that not all the letters are gittin' to you. Like it was durin' the war. I don't suppose half the mail got from here to Baldwin. It's hard to keep up correspondence that-a-way even if you work at it."

"Not that you ever wrote a letter in your life," Nelda said.

"I don't know about that. It's just that a feller keeps busy with his work and don't often have time to take up the pen."

"That old property of yours is about all built up now, ain't it?" Bob said.

"Fast as we can sell it they build on it," Penny said. "If I was still doin' carpentry I'd be employed for life. The woods is fillin' up with houses."

"I suppose you'll be building one of those palaces before long," Bob said.

Penny shook his head. "Too much trouble to move all that stuff we have, and anyway I like a place that's got some wear on it. It's taken us the better part of ten years to git the right wear on that place we have."

"We'll swap you for this one," Larrabee said. "It's got all the wear you need and then some."

Penny looked around at the corners of the ceiling and the tall, wide windows with their heavy oak sills painted gray green. "This is a fine old house with some fine livin' on it, and that roof's about as good as the day we put them shingles on. When was that? Ten years ago."

"More like twelve," Anna said. "I remember it like yesterday. Maybe even better than Nathaniel."

"You were out there in the yard," Larrabee said, "with the boys chasing you through the sandspurs. It was hotter than the kitchen stove up on that roof. I remember that. And noisy down below! I've never seen such a bunch of wild women as lived in this house."

"It's going to get wild again if Flora here gets any faster," Anna said. "She's into something every time I turn around."

Penny winked at Larrabee. "What she needs is a dozen little brothers and sisters to keep her company, fill the place up."

"We're going to have to fill it back up with boarders the way the lake's treating us." Larrabee glanced at Bob to see if the subject was too sore to mention, but saw that Bob had been preoccupied with his own thoughts.

Penny leaned forward with one elbow on the table. "Don't tell me them canal company boys're actually dredgin' their channel."

"Not that we can tell," Larrabee said. Seeing that Penny's words had gotten Bob's attention, he went on. "But we ran into something out there today. A wreck in the middle of the route we take to Walls' place."

"You figger somebody put it there on purpose?"

"We don't know," Bob said. "If we find another one you can be pretty sure something's doing."

Penny sat back. "Well, now. I never figgered those boys to act like that. I've known some of 'em half my life."

"How long've you known John Howard?" Larrabee asked.

"John Howard." Penny turned the name over like something he had found under a rock. "He just keeps croppin' up, don't he?"

"Well, it may be nothing," Bob reminded them. "It wouldn't be the first wreck in that lake. And there's nothing we can do about it tonight. Can't go out and guard the lake! We'll just have to be more careful from now on, that's all. Miss Anna, what's this ruffian going to give you for a birthday present?"

Four days later, on Sunday morning, Larrabee woke up to the sound of church bells. He had been up late the night before. Flora had been suffering from an earache and had finally fallen asleep crying somewhere around two o'clock. He had just begun to drift off too when he became aware of Anna's warm hands under his nightshirt. They had made love with a passion that seemed to come only from the depths of the night. In the morning the April sunshine poured so brightly through the loblolly pines that even the room on the northwest corner of the house was brilliant with light.

Anna was gone. Hearing voices outside, Larrabee went to the window and pulled back the frayed lace curtain. Anna was in the garden, hunched down talking to Flora. He dressed and went downstairs, taking a biscuit from the dining room table on his way outside. The day was already warm. The chickens flapped out of his way as he crossed the yard to the garden gate.

Anna looked up at him and smiled from under the brim of her big straw hat. "We could, you know."

"We could what?" Flora came up and hugged his leg and he patted her on the top of her plaid sunbonnet.

"What you said. Fill the place back up with boarders."

"My land, Anna! You're just like those letters of Martha's. Going on when nobody but you knows what you've been thinking about. That was a couple of days ago I said that."

She went back to her gardening, weeding and harvesting at the same time. "We *could* do it. It's just that I'd have to roll up my sleeves and learn plenty of good recipes."

He dropped down beside her. "And you figure me for some kind of a cook or bed maker in this scheme of yours?"

She touched him lightly on the knee with one of her dirty hands. "Oh, now, nobody said that."

"Then what?"

"I don't know. But it'd sure be nice to have you around. 'Stead of seeing you go off first thing every morning."

"Except for Sundays."

"The Sundays go pretty fast once church is over."

"I don't see you rushing off to it this morning."

She made a face. A mosquito had brushed the tip of her nose. "It just wasn't a morning for it. I don't know."

"The Reverend Bonds will be thinking you're backsliding."

"Let him. We'll invite him over for dinner and that'll set everything right. The truth of it is, his sermons don't go to the heart quite the way Preacher's did."

Flora had stooped down and was getting ready to put a centipede in her mouth. Larrabee intercepted it and flicked it toward the outhouse.

"This girl's going to take some watching, all right. Just like her mama."

Anna eased out a small thistle and placed it in a basket of weeds. "So what do you think?"

"About what?"

"About what! About what we've been talking about! Do you think we can run the place for room and board again?"

"Well, let's not write off the lake just yet. Bob's still the best man out there and I'm second if I do say so. Those men of Howard's seem to know even less than most of 'em. He must've picked 'em up cheap somewhere. They've got no channel and they haven't gotten the first boat to a pier yet."

She shifted her weight from one knee to the other. "But don't you think they will sooner or later? That's what they're out there for. We've got to face up to that."

Chapter 38

They saw the second wreck just in time. The wind was driving clouds up from the southwest and Larrabee spotted the fine whiskers of water streaming from the corners of what turned out to be a discarded harvester baring its iron teeth just inches beneath the surface.

"Now we know," Bob said quietly from his place at the tiller. "At least now we know."

Larrabee looked across the lake to the lush slope of Josiah Walls' house and groves. "Do you suppose there might be a law against this kind of thing?"

"Might be." Bob nodded. "'Course you'd have to catch 'em doing it before you could sic the law on 'em. And that gets back to watching about a quarter of the lake. And sooner or later, if they keep this up, they're going to start running into their own wrecks."

Larrabee was watching something emerge from the shoreline on the western side of the lake. "There's our friends now. That's one of the canal company boats trying out the new channel by the looks of it."

Bob studied it for a while. "Nudge us up a little and let's have a closer look."

They entered the channel that was threatening their livelihood and moved toward shore with the stern wheel churning. The wind was down and the water was flat and silvery under a slate sky. It was hard to see what the canal company boat was up to until they were within a half-mile of it.

"How do you suppose they got out here so early?" Larrabee wondered.

"I've been thinking about that. Don't you suppose they killed two birds with one stone and just tied up out here somewhere? That way they could keep an eye on their channel and get the jump on us at the same time—whenever they decided to start doing business."

"If they've started doing business they're already six places up on us. They're heading for Walls."

"Can't see as they have anything aboard. Maybe they're just making passes as yet. Let's just tag along a while and see how they do."

The canal company boat, the *Santa Fe*, was making good speed compared to the clumsy dredge that had cleared the way for her. Perhaps because she had seen the *King Payne* closing on her stern, she plowed the tepid water of the lake as if the Walls pier was her one and only object.

"She's got us," Larrabee said from the bow. "Do you suppose they've already talked to Walls?"

"The way they're beating for it, I don't think so," Bob said. "If they'd already cut a deal why would they be in such a hurry to beat us? I do believe this is a little demonstration run to show what a bigger boat can do."

As they came closer it became clear that the *Santa Fe* would have an audience. Several of Walls' Negro hands were standing on the pier watching the two boats approach. Gradually the men took on individual shapes and voices, but it was impossible to tell what they thought of this apparent duel of the steamboats. Bob had Larrabee keep up speed and the *Santa Fe* continued to press on, even when she was within a hundred yards of the pier.

"What's the big rush?" Larrabee asked.

"That's what I want them to wonder," Bob said from the tiller. "Give us a little more."

Too late, the men of the *Santa Fe* saw the error of their ways. In their haste to beat the *King Payne* to Walls' pier they had failed to gauge their momentum. At the same time they were in no position to steam past the pier and make another pass because the *King Payne* would surely get there first. They reversed engines, but too late. The men on the pier were shouting and waving them off, and when it became clear that the *Santa Fe* was out of control, some ran for shore and others dove off the far side of the pier. The helmsman of the errant vessel had the presence of mind to throw the tiller over hard at the last moment, but the brunt of the twenty-ton behemoth swung heavily into the eight-inch pine planks that until now had constituted one of the finest piers in the county.

Even Bob and Larrabee turned away at the sight. With a horrible squealing and scraping and a deafening crash the last third of the pier collapsed into the lake, leaving only one very crooked piling to mark where it had been. Larrabee slowed the *King Payne* to a funereal swish-swish. Bob stood with one hand on the tiller and the other over his mouth. Somehow the *Santa Fe* righted herself and drifted away from the remains of the pier. Running down the hill was Josiah T. Walls himself. He was hatless and in his shirtsleeves and he had a napkin flapping at his throat. By the time he got to the pier, the *Santa Fe* had already hobbled back into deeper water. Bob swung the *King Payne* in as close as he dared, keeping a respectful distance from the confusion of splashing Negroes and settling timbers.

"A little more practice!" he shouted across the wreckage.

Walls responded by tearing the napkin from his throat and flinging it into the water.

"Do you know what a Pyrrhic victory is?" Bob asked Larrabee after they were well on their way to the next stop, a vegetable farm and nursery under the management of an old couple from Pennsylvania. He had to repeat the question because Larrabee was lost in thought.

"No, I don't," Larrabee replied. "But I have a hunch you're planning to tell me."

"Well, a Pyrrhic victory is one that the victor can't afford. And that's what we just had back there. The canal company doesn't get Walls until he rebuilds that pier—and neither do we. 'Course he may not bother to rebuild the pier. He may just let everything go by train from now on. And he can always send a man on horseback for his wife's medicine. So that was a Pyrrhic victory. And the war's not over yet either."

He was right. By the beginning of July another canal company boat was poking around the west shore of the lake. The *Santa Fe* had been patched up and sent to work the eastern side and all the way up the canal to Lake Santa Fe. Whoever was running this new boat knew his business. The *King Payne* had to scramble to keep customers. The farms and plantations along the lake had signed no contracts. They simply paid whoever got there first to collect their produce. Only the last farm to the south—the pretty, fertile holding of Laetitia Summerton, remained true to the *King Payne*, and both Larrabee and Bob found themselves wishing that her place was five times as big.

"The joke would be funny if it wasn't on us," Bob said. "The closer we get to paying off this boat, the less we get to do with it. This lake's not big enough anymore."

They were on the way back to Rocky Point. The sun was setting and the gnats were starting to come out. A dragonfly buzzed past Larrabee's face. "Bob, if you want to go ahead and go in with them, you ought to. Anna's been wanting me to stick closer to home anyway. I couldn't work for Howard but you could."

Bob spat in the water. "Never mind that. You go on and do what you want regardless but I ain't going in with no canal company! I can hire out as a ferryboat or an excursion boat or a fisherman if I have to. Once we're paid off, it's just a matter of upkeep, and as long as I stay clear of Howard's wrecks out there I can keep this boat patched together. In the meantime, we'll just keep pushing right along and get the most out of it. The canal company may decide that it's too expensive to keep their channel dredged—and to pay for fixing the piers they run over."

Larrabee took some comfort in Bob's determination. Bob had come to the conclusion that Howard was behind the wrecks, which meant that destroying Walls' pier might have cost Howard money out of his own pocket. That made the Pyrrhic victory a little more favorable for the *King Payne*. Larrabee refrained from saying that the best solution would be to line up the men of the canal company and shoot them.

By August of '88 they were making half of what they had a year before, and

Howard's wrecks—as they now called them—were in a complicated configuration so confusing that one of the canal company's own boats ripped her belly on one of them. Under pressure from the board of directors, the helmsman had quit and turned up drunk at Duke's on a Saturday night when Bob was staying over with Larrabee and Anna. Barkley Duforge had been at Duke's sneaking a quick drink before returning to the farm with his father, the retired sheriff. When Barkley figured out who the man was he whispered to Duke to see to it that he didn't get away, and hotfooted it up to tell his friends. They came down and kept the man plied with Jack Daniels long enough to learn quite a bit about the workings of the canal company.

Thrums—that was what they called Howard's wrecks. Each of the canal company's captains had a map of them, but this man had been given a map that was three weeks out of date, and he had hit upon the newest thrum just two days after it had gone in. Bob listened with narrowing eyes as the man said that the plan was to remove the thrums as soon as the canal company had the lake to itself. Bob and Larrabee had been so intent on the man's information that they had failed to take full notice of his condition, and in mid-sentence he fell off his chair and collapsed into a very limber, uncommunicative heap.

"Now what?" Larrabee said.

"Now we've got a goose that lays golden eggs," Bob said. "But he's no good to us like this. We need him sober."

They took turns carrying him down noisy boardwalks and past barking dogs to Larrabee's house, where they loaded him face down onto a reluctant Tuscawilla, tied his hands to his feet under her belly, and carted him over to the jail. They accused him of enough misdeeds to keep him there for at least a week.

"Sounds like he's a one-man crime spree," Sheriff Fennell drawled. "You all boys sure he did all that?"

"Would we make up all that stuff?" Bob asked innocently.

The sheriff ran his fingers through his big mustache. "Don't know, and right now I don't care. Deputy's overdue and I'm going home to supper. We'll talk to him in the morning—if he lives through the night. He looks like something from the bottom of the bait bucket."

As soon as the sun was up, Larrabee and Bob walked down to the jail to see what their man would say sober. He was in a cell with two other drunks, one of whom lay sleeping on the brick floor. The deputy had been dozing in the desk chair. He stood by impatiently as Bob tried to get the hung-over man to repeat some of what he had said the night before.

"I say plenty when I'm drunk," the man said with his head in his hands. "I couldn't tell you what it was if I wanted to."

"It was about the thrums out there in the lake," Bob said. He stood with his hands on the bars as if he were the one in jail.

"I got no reason to tell you about thrums or anything else," the man said.

"Now stop talking. You're making my head hurt."

"What about the canal company?" Larrabee said. "They cut you off. Isn't that reason enough to speak up?"

The man buried his head in his arms.

"Let him out and we'll get him to talk," Larrabee said.

Bob shook his head. "Won't do any good unless he's willing to talk in court. He's not much use to us."

The deputy started a conversation with the drunk on the floor and Larrabee used the opportunity to ask Bob what they could do.

"I don't know," Bob said. "Maybe we ought to start by finding out who he is. That may give us some idea of how to get to him."

Larrabee looked at the pale, unshaven wreck of a man. "Which approach do you favor this time? Honey or vinegar?"

"It's a little more dangerous treating him good," Bob said. "We'd have to get him out of jail."

"Well, we can't hardly get to him if he's *in* jail. So there we are. What do you propose, Bob? Take him home and fix him breakfast?"

That's just what they did. They talked the deputy into letting the man out and half carried him up to the house, where they got him up the steps and onto the porch. Hearing a strange voice—or strange moans—Anna came down from the sewing room with Flora to see what was the matter.

"Who is he?" she asked. "He smells awful."

"You noticed that too." Bob patted the man on the cheek and asked him his name.

"Allen," the man said.

"That your first name or your last name?" Bob asked.

The man nodded.

"Well, which is it? First or last?"

"Allen. Henry," the man said with great effort.

"Well, Mr. Henry, how do you do? I'm Bob Harper and this here is Nathaniel Larrabee and that there's his wife Anna and their little girl Flora."

"No, no, no," the man muttered. "My name is *Henry Allen*."

"Oh, well, Henry, we're sorry to hear about you losing your job."

Henry Allen mumbled something unsuitable for the presence of ladies.

"This man's a wreck," Larrabee said.

Anna giggled. "Just like you when Mama and I first saw *you*."

"Not hardly. I was not drunk," Larrabee insisted. "I was sick."

"I ain't drunk either," Henry Allen croaked. "I'm *real* sick." He proved it by lurching forward and throwing up in the azaleas.

Anna seized Flora's hand and withdrew into the house.

"Reckon we ought to get a doctor?" Larrabee asked.

"Naw, I've seen worse. Hell, I've *had* worse. What he needs is a good soaking."

They held him over the rail to make sure he was empty and then hauled Henry Allen into the wood room off the kitchen. The room still had a cot in it and half a cord of wood, as well as the oversized claw-footed bathtub that Larrabee had given to Anna on their anniversary.

"You're not putting that man in my bathtub," she said.

Larrabee left Bob to struggle with him for a moment. "If this bathtub does the trick I'll buy you a new one. If you want to be useful you can help us get his clothes off."

"Nothing doing!" She made a hasty retreat into the kitchen.

Bob and Larrabee scooped up their drooping ward and loaded him into the tub, clothes and all. The first water Larrabee brought from the backyard pump was warm, and Henry Allen seemed to fall asleep as they emptied the first few buckets over his shoulders. The first cold one made him jump like a mackerel.

"Whoa!" Bob pushed him back down then gave him a friendly pat on the head. "We'll have you feeling better in no time, Henry."

After a terrible commotion of swearing and splashing, Henry was deemed fully alert and ready to accept the hospitality of the Larrabee household. He was dried off and dressed and plopped down on a chair at the head of the dining room table. Anna pointed out that this once-sacred place of her late father and Preacher Williams was not getting its due respect.

"You're the one who was talking about running a rooming house," Larrabee reminded her.

"Now that we have him, why is he here and what are we going to do with him?" she asked.

Larrabee drew her into the kitchen for the explanation.

"Maybe we *should* run a boarding house," she said, frowning. "I hate to think that the man in there is the key to our livelihood."

"Well, he is," Larrabee told her. "So let's make him as happy as we can."

Henry Allen drank coffee and ate warmed-over oatmeal and bacon and grits without saying more than a few words between smacking mouthfuls. When Sheriff Fennell stopped by, bristling at their removal of the prisoner, Larrabee and Bob did their best to assure him that last night had all been a misunderstanding. But the new sheriff was not one to be toyed with. He shook an admonishing finger at them and said he never wanted to see Allen Henry again.

"*Henry Allen*," sputtered the prisoner from the dining room.

The sheriff strode down the walkway. On his way out, he tried to slam the dragging gate.

"It's hotter'n blazes today," Bob said. "I could use a turn in that tub myself."

Mr. Allen continued to enjoy the hospitality of the house. Although his knees were a little weak when he made his way from the dining room to the big wing chair by the front fireplace and back, his head seemed to clear and his disposition settled into a pleasant blandness.

"I have nothing to say about that," he sniffed when Bob raised the subject of thrums. "Say, you wouldn't have a newspaper would you? It don't hardly seem like a proper morning without a newspaper."

Anna found what was left of the latest *Weekly Sun & Bee*. The rest of it she had used to start the kindling in her stove.

Henry Allen crossed his legs and sighed comfortably as he settled into the chair with last week's news and musings. Church bells tolled the morning services, boys chased by the windows on their way to swimming and fishing holes, dogs barked at a treed 'possum, and Mr. Allen drifted in and out of a comfortable sleep while Bob and Larrabee fidgeted and paced.

"Maybe honey wasn't the best way after all," Larrabee said.

"He ain't exactly the sort you can warm up to," Bob admitted. "But I've got an idea."

They roused Mr. Allen by shaking his knee gently and removing the newspaper from his face.

"Damned if it don't look like we'll have a Democrat for president," wheezed the sleeper.

"Well, friend Henry," Bob said, "Demmycrat or no, it looks like you're out of a job."

Henry Allen blinked and stuck his finger up his nose. "I do seem to recall that."

"But we've seen you out on that lake and we think you're just the man for us. You see, we've got a boat out there too and we've got just the place for you."

Larrabee looked at him as if to say, "You bet we do, but the lake isn't deep enough."

Henry Allen looked at them as if they were out of their minds. "Thanks but no thanks, boys. I've had it up to here with that scum hole. I'm going back to Fernandina where there's real water, blue water." He tried to get up but he seemed stuck to the leather embrace of the chair. "That damned lake is a killer. And if I was to go back on it my life wouldn't be worth a nickel."

This time he did manage to get up. "Gentlemen, it's been lovely and now I must be going." He wove his way past the round table in front of the fireplace and got as far as the wicker chair in the front hall before stopping to rest.

Bob sat down on the broad arm of the chair. "Now, tell us about why your life wouldn't be worth a nickel."

"You know damn well," Henry Allen said. His face looked pale and doughy in the harsh morning light that poured in from the porch. "All I want to do is get to Fernandina and ship out."

"That may not be the best place to go," Larrabee said. "I hear there's a longshoremen's strike up there. There's talk about sending troops up to keep the peace."

"Well, I won't be there long." Henry Allen sneezed and swore. "Just long enough to ship out."

Bob and Larrabee consulted on the porch. "This could be the chance to take care of two things at once," Bob said.

Larrabee snorted and put his hands on his hips. "I don't see how."

"Here's how. If Henry wants to go up to Fernandina, we'll let him. In fact, you'll go with him to see to it he gets there safely."

"Ain't that a little *too much* honey, Bob? You sure you don't want me to give him fifty dollars spending money too?"

"Now come on. Hear me out. You get him up there and get a sworn statement from him, written, signed, and witnessed—two copies. One you file at the courthouse in Jacksonville, the other you bring back here. Once you've done that, we're through with Mr. Henry Allen. While you're at it, look for some new pistons and rods. We can't keep patching these forever. Do those two things and we can beat the canal company at their own game. You can go up on the Thursday night train and come back Sunday."

Larrabee didn't much like the idea but admitted that he could see its potential.

"While you're up there, Barkley and I can give those boys a run for their money."

"I'll tell you what else I'll do when I come back," Larrabee said. "I'll root out Baldy Choat and wring his neck till he tells everything he knows about the burning of the Arlington. We'll expose our boy once and for all."

Henry Allen was trying to get up again. "That is the last goddamned drink I take in my life."

All it took to convince him to stick around was the offer of train fare. "You sit right there," Bob said, "and Thursday night you'll be on that train for Fernandina."

"You expect me to sit around here until Thursday?" Henry Allen said. "I don't have that kind of time. I have business!"

Anna liked the idea even less than Henry Allen did. She didn't want Larrabee to leave town. After all, they'd never been separated for more than a day in the entire two years they had been married. She had heard about the longshoremen's strike and it was the last place she wanted her husband to be. On top of that, she was the one who was supposed to put up with Henry Allen for the next four days while Bob and Larrabee were working on the lake.

"What am I supposed to do with that reptile between now and Thursday?" she asked.

"Just keep him entertained," Larrabee told her. "You can think of something."

For the first three days she had nothing to worry about because Mr. Henry Allen spent most of his time falling asleep in the big leather wing chair by the fireplace. She kept him supplied with newspapers—anything she could get her hands on—and he fell asleep reading them. On Wednesday morning, during a light rain, he fell asleep before he even had his shoes on. He fell asleep after breakfast when the rain had let up. He fell asleep after lunch as the rain returned. She had no doubt that he had been asleep when he had hit one of those thrums. She figured that if his life were ever in danger he could survive quite nicely just by playing 'possum.

She had been eager to get back to her gardening, but the ground was too wet to work so she left the house long enough to walk with Flora to the post office. While she was there she ran into Jane Howard, who was reserved and seemed as lonesome as ever. Just for the sake of making small talk, Anna mentioned that she was going to be doing some pickling and Jane let on that she knew nothing about the process.

"It's about as much fun as it can be," Anna joked. "And you're welcome to come over and learn all about it anytime. On Thursday I'm going to do up some watermelon pickles."

To her surprise, Jane accepted the invitation.

Chapter 39

"It's Mr. Larrabee's way to cut things close," Anna said again. "I'm sure he'll be here in time for the train. He's never missed a train yet." That last was complete nonsense, she knew, because he had only been on a train two or three times since she had known him, and those had been short last-minute hops taken when the weather was too bad for driving a team.

"A drink would sure steady my nerves," Henry Allen said irritably. "I've waited long enough."

At half past seven Anna heard the familiar pounding of Tuscawilla's hooves coming faster than usual. She went to the porch in time to see her husband jump off the horse.

"Do you know what time it is?" Her voice had a scolding edge.

"I saw the Courthouse clock," he told her. "There's one big commotion down there for some reason."

"That train leaves in one half hour," she reminded him. "How are you possibly going to get there in time?"

He pulled off Tuscawilla's saddle and hung it over the porch rail and smiled at his wife's concern. "I could get to the square one-legged in half an hour!"

"But you have to get cleaned up and packed first."

He pulled off Tuscawilla's bridle and turned the horse into the paddock. When he got back to the porch he gave Anna a quick kiss. "I can get to that train and still have time for another smooch. How's that girl of ours today?"

"She was helping Jane How—She was helping Jane and me do the pickling. You'll never believe what Jane told me. She and John aren't even legally married."

"When it comes to that cutthroat, I'd believe almost anything. Is Mr. Allen all set to go?"

"Gossip's wasted on you. He's more than ready!"

The errant skipper felt much revived by his convalescence of hearty meals and long naps. Even on the pinching cot in the wood room he had slept until midmorning.

"Your dinner's going to be all dried out," Anna said, following Larrabee to the dining room table. "It's been warming in the oven for over an hour."

"We came real close to hitting another one of your thrums today," Larrabee told Henry Allen. "We could've used that map of yours even if it is outdated."

He tore into the pork chops, mashed potatoes and gravy and string beans as if they were all one conglomeration. He washed it down with a glass of water, ate a piece of apple pie over the kitchen sink, took off his shirt, and dumped the basin of drinking water over his head and shoulders.

"You'll want a towel," Anna suggested as he stood there in his blindness.

She was always a little envious of the way he could make himself look presentable in a quarter of the time it took her. He changed clothes, slicked his hair back, threw half a dozen things into a worn valise left behind by a boarder, and was ready to go.

She hadn't seen him pack the revolver.

"Let's hit it," he said. He set the valise down long enough to scoop up Flora.

"Nathaniel! You'll drop her if you carry all of that."

"Will not. Come on. No time to argue. Train's going to leave, remember?"

The streets and sidewalks were much improved from when he had first come to town, and Anna got all the way to the square without getting the hem of her dress muddy. The train was nowhere to be seen. The tracks were lined with people, whites and Negroes, marching and shouting.

"Why are all these people here?" Anna asked, but she was drowned out by a salvo of cheers and applause and male voices bursting into "John Brown's Body," except that the words seemed to be different.

"It's the Guards," Larrabee said. "Looks like they're going to be getting on the train. What do you suppose they're doing here?"

"They're going to Fernandina!" said someone behind them. It was Dr. Willis. "The governor called 'em up to keep the city from being burned and looted by the longshoremen. The Ocala Rifles are going up too."

Larrabee looked around to make sure Henry Allen was still there. "You picked a fine time to go to Fernandina, Henry."

Anna took Flora from him. "Oh, Nathaniel, I don't like this."

He put his arm around her. "We're safer than ever now, my girl, with these bully cadets to protect us. And don't they have fine voices!"

The crowd picked up the words of the song and it spread down the street as the guards marched toward the depot.

We'll hang Yellow Jack from a sour-apple tree!

"What kind of nonsense is that?" Dr. Willis said. "One of our own doctors—who shall remain anonymous—just came back from there and assured us there's no fever in Fernandina."

"Is Billy still in the Guards?" Larrabee asked. He thought the doctor looked unusually tired and tense.

"He is. And I hope he'll have sense to stay clear of trouble."

We'll hang Yellow Jack from a sour-apple tree!

"Nathaniel—"

"Anna, we're not going anywhere near that strike. We're going to the courthouse up there and then Henry's going to get on his boat and I'm going to pick up a couple of pistons and rods and come right back. Whatever the longshoremen do, they're likely to avoid where I'm going."

We'll hang Yellow Jack to a sour-apple tree as we go marching on!

"But about the fever—"

He pulled her close. Flora tugged at his ear. "I'll be moving too fast for the yellow jack to catch me. If there's even any up there, which everybody says there isn't."

"Then why is everybody singing about it?"

"Just to burn some time. The train's late. I could've had second helpings. Of everything."

The song about Yellow Jack died out and the Guards launched into a powerful rendition of "Onward Christian Soldiers," which suddenly turned the mood somber.

Still the train did not come. The Guards took up "Dixie" and continued to keep things going with one song after another, including "Crossing the Grand Sierras" and "The Camptown Races" and "The Blue-Tail Fly." The crowd swelled around the depot, joining in the songs. Someone in the Guards with an unusually fine and forceful voice began "Hard Times Come Again No More" and five hundred onlookers joined in. His voice was so powerful and so beautiful that when he started "Gentle Annie" everybody just stood and listened. They were just starting to applaud when the train came into view and gave a shrill whistle that the crowd greeted with wild cheering.

"Clear the tracks!" was the call from the depot. "Make way!"

Anna tugged at Larrabee's sleeve. "Nathaniel, you don't have to go."

"Now, come on, my girl. We've been through it twenty times. I'll see you Sunday. And don't fix dinner. We'll go over to the American and see how old Bobby's doing with the cooking."

Henry Allen pushed through the crowd, eager to get aboard. Larrabee climbed onto the first step of the car, bent down and kissed Flora. "You take good care of your mama, will you now?"

"I will," said a little voice nearly lost in the rush as the Guards started getting into the car ahead.

Anna took her husband by the lapel and gave him a long kiss that would've caused a scandal if there hadn't been so much pandemonium. The train started to move. He climbed onto the step and his hat came off. As he grabbed it back the surging crowd pushed him into the car.

He elbowed his way to a window, where he got one last look at her pressing Flora close and waving.

Chapter 40

He was two days overdue and she had busied herself with one task after another, not to take her mind off him, which was impossible, but to keep from worrying herself sick. She sewed a winter dress for Flora even though the hot, damp September days made merely touching the wool uncomfortable. She weeded the garden clean, although the emerging green tufts refused to come out of the warm, wet ground intact. She whitewashed the hen house and buried two heat-struck pullets beneath the pine needles in the little scrap of no man's land that still remained between the garden and the new houses that had gone up in the woods. Most of all she listened for the train whistle, hour after hour, even though the rumors of yellow fever in Tampa and Fernandina had reduced the rail traffic to one train a day. Each day she carried Flora to the depot and each day the train was late and each day she waited until the last passenger had gotten off before she turned and walked back home in the hot sun.

At times she longed for her childhood days of swimming in the Sweetwater Branch or wiggling her toes in the deliciously cold water of Hidden Spring. She thought of hinting to Penny and Nelda that they should go for an outing in the shade of Boulware Springs, but then she remembered that they had already left to spend a few days at their new cottage on Newnan's Lake.

Late in the afternoon of September eleventh she met the train as usual and found that the twenty-five guards who had gone to Fernandina five days earlier had come back. They were not singing and they were not greeted by the jubilant masses that had seen them off. They were a tired, silent lot and they dragged off the train as if they were returning from some terrible battle. Billy Willis was among them and she asked him if he had seen her husband, but he had nothing to tell her. She followed the men back to their barracks above the dry goods store that had replaced the ill-fated Arlington. She had never let social convention stand between her and what she sorely wanted, and she went to the men as they lay exhausted on their cots and asked each of them if he had seen her husband.

What she heard—or overhead—was a story of rough going in Fernandina. The striking longshoremen had proven a force to be reckoned with, but the

Guards, along with the Ocala Rifles, had been able to wrest an uneasy truce between the strikers and the waterfront businesses. Several of the guards had been assigned, in fact, to protect the house of the leader of the longshoremen, a large black man who rode a spirited white horse. During a downpour they had taken shelter on the man's porch even though his wife was said to be suffering from typhoid fever. Now, as they sat on their cots in the armory, they argued about what had actually happened in Fernandina, whether they had accomplished anything, and what had become of the woman. Had she lived or died?

The captain of the Guards, a big man named Webster, came upstairs and, seeing Anna listening in the shadows of the rafters, told her to have some consideration for his exhausted boys. In a large, kindly voice that provided no room for argument, he asked her to leave. So she went back to her pickling and sewing and cooking with little Flora cooing and wiggling at her side. She considered taking the train to Fernandina to look for her husband, but she knew that it would be a nearly hopeless act since none of the guards had seen him once he had gotten off the train in that troubled city. Time and again she convinced herself that the best thing she could do was to wait, even though it was the most difficult.

She waited another day, working in the hot garden until dusk, when the mosquitoes drove her back into the house. She waited another day and still another and then she had a new concern. When Larrabee was five days overdue, she felt a headache coming on. She had brought her sewing downstairs to be out of the hot little room, and figured that she had moved too late. The pain between her temples spread to her back, and once she had finally put Flora down for a nap, Anna went to bed too, hoping that a little sleep would make her feel better, as it often did. But when she woke up to Flora's crying she felt stiff and heavy and feverish. Her head throbbed as she got up and drank most of the warm water from the bedroom pitcher, then pushed herself to attend to Flora, who had wet her clothes during her nap.

She had to lie down again, but someone was knocking and hallooing at the porch door and she made her way downstairs, leaning heavily on the rail as Flora came down behind her with big, nimble steps. Whoever had been at the door was gone before she got there, so Anna went out onto the porch and sat down in the bentwood rocker in a cool patch of shade. Flora climbed onto her lap and together they rocked for an hour or two as the sodden air dropped cones and branches from the tall straight pines in the yard.

Iris Poinsett found her late in the afternoon with Flora playing by her side. She helped Anna inside, washed her face with cool water and put her to bed.

The next day, September fourteenth, Anna woke up feeling considerably better. Dr. Willis was in the corner of the room talking to Iris.

"The fever's broken," he was saying, and his words were so soft and comforting that Anna immediately drifted back into a light, refreshing sleep.

She returned to the simpler chores, wanting to strike a balance between too much idleness— which she thought would give her the attitude of sick person— and too much exertion, which she thought would surely bring back the aches and fever she had shaken. She knew she had to do something, though—not to keep Larrabee out of her mind, but to keep from caving in to despair. On Saturday the fifteenth Iris came over early and stayed with her for most of the day, playing with Flora and helping with the cooking and cleaning.

"There's hardly anyone to cook for," Anna sighed as she and Iris harvested tomatoes from the garden. She wanted to cry but felt that she couldn't give in to tears, not yet.

Another night's sleep made her feel better, and though she was still weak, she was already up and dressed on Sunday morning when Iris came over with a basket of phlox, bachelor-buttons, and sumac. Iris made sassafras tea, the very smell of which restored Anna's sense of well-being.

"It seems like we hardly ever get a chance to visit, everyone's so busy," Iris said. "Your mama and mine were real good friends, and you and I had many a fine evening playing in our fort with all those boys. They tore that down, you know."

Anna was still taking in the steam of the tea.

"They flattened it out and let the grass grow right up to the trees and some little feller comes along all summer and mows the grass and swears like the dickens when the Spanish moss gets wrapped up in the blades. I tell you, Anna, if you and I were to talk like that your mama or mine would've washed our mouths out."

Those days seemed so far away now that Anna felt more than ever like crying.

"You all right, honey?"

She nodded. "The steam feels so good."

"Now don't go getting sick on me again, y'hear?"

Anna put her fist to her cheek to stop the tears. "It's just that he was supposed to be back a *week* ago and I haven't heard a word."

Iris laid a comforting hand on Anna's shoulder. "Well, you know that Fernandina's a complete mess, Anna. I'm sure he's holed up safe enough. Didn't he say he was going to the courthouse or something? I mean, how much safer could you be? And you know they aren't letting but one train a day into the county and they'll throw you off it at the county line if you don't have a letter from your doctor saying you're healthy and all."

Anna hadn't heard that. It must have developed during her illness. She asked what became of the people thrown off the trains.

"I don't know for sure, but I hear they put 'em in quarantine camps. Daddy says the governor authorized it on account of the fever in Tampa."

"You don't think they have it in Fernandina?"

"They sent Dr. Phillips up there and he came back and said they didn't."

Anna put a handkerchief to her eye. "Well, that's good."

"It's a mess, I tell you."

"Iris, you don't suppose Nathaniel was on one of those trains."

"Oh, honey, now I doubt it."

"He might be in one of those camps right now. He might've left Fernandina late and gotten into one of those camps just a day or two ago. Iris, what if he's in one of those camps and I don't even know it?"

"Honey, if he's there, he'll come in. If I know that man of yours, nothing'll stop him from coming in." She listened for a moment, thinking she had heard Flora waking up from her nap, but it was only a cat out in the yard somewhere. "Listen, Anna, there's going to be a union service at the church tonight. Why don't you let Mama watch over Flora and you and me'll go—if you don't mind throwing in with us heathen Methodists for a night. I swear I can't believe old Reverend Carrington's still going at it. He must be sixty-five. What do you say? I believe it would be just the ticket."

Everyone agreed that the Methodists had the finest church in town. It was a large trim brick building that stood next to where the East Florida Seminary had burned down five years ago, and—splendid as the new Seminary building was—the new Methodist church dwarfed it. Anna had never been very taken with the lackluster sermons of Roland Bonds and had seen Samuel Carrington speak only at the wedding of her mother and Preacher Williams, so she welcomed the opportunity to participate in something that was both spiritual and diverting. At the same time she had the comfort of Iris' rather verbose but uplifting company.

It was another hot, humid night and the tall church windows were all thrown open from bottom to top, though the outside air was hardly more refreshing than what was inside. Anna found the service dry and businesslike compared to the friendlier Presbyterian gatherings, but she was so taken with the fresh prettiness of the place that she was content just to sit and admire the white woodwork of the pews and gallery while the words rolled over her.

The better part of two hours had passed, if the wicks in the wall lamps were any indication, when old Samuel Carrington, leaning heavily on his cane, came forward to give the final benediction. He was distracted by a slight commotion behind him, a confusion of rising voices that caused him to turn and look back almost to the point of falling over. Roman Siegel, the watchmaker, came forward, sweating and breathless and stood beside the perplexed Reverend Carrington.

He twisted his hands, cleared his throat and waited impatiently for the murmuring to die down.

"My—ladies and gentlemen. I regret to make this announcement."

Everyone leaned forward in the pews to hear what he had to say.

"Ladies and gentlemen, as you all know, last Tuesday the Guards came back from their heroic mission in Fernandina. Since that time several members of the corps have been confined to their beds with what was reasonably thought to have been exhaustion. Tonight, with their condition unimproved, two doctors were called in by their captain, and those physicians have just now confirmed that six of the guards have come down with the yellow fever."

Samuel Carrington moved surprisingly fast to follow the dread tidings with the benediction, but not fast enough. No one waited to hear it. Those in the handsome gallery ran down the stairs and broke for the open door. Those unable to get to the door jumped through the open windows without hesitation, as if they had been planning for this event all their lives. Anna's only thought was to get back to the Poinsetts' house, collect Flora, go home, and close the windows and shutters and doors. But even that was more than the panic-stricken crowd seemed able to allow. She and Iris were forced to take shelter between pews until the church was entirely empty except for poor old bruised Reverend Carrington, who raised himself up on his cane, collar askew, and beheld the desolation in open-mouthed bewilderment.

Anna and Iris helped him to a bench and, with apologies, hurried on.

By the time she had reached the house, Anna knew what she had to do.

Half an hour later, as Tuscawilla plodded into the night, the sounds of the frantic town gradually faded away. The sounds of people running and packing, the desperate bargaining for horses and wagons, the crying of babies. Anna became aware that she had left with nothing but her horse, her daughter. and the clothes on her back. But even as she moved into the darkness and quiet she became convinced that she had done the right thing. Her horse was nineteen years old but still a prize for anyone bent on leaving town. With the fever in town she no longer wanted her husband to come to her. She would go to him, wherever he was. She would go first to Newnan's Lake to see Penny and Nelda, and in the morning set out for the quarantine camp where the rails entered the eastern edge of the county.

Tuscawilla had been reluctant and confused at first. She was unaccustomed to being out at night after her portion of hay and oats. She took tentative steps until Anna tore off a small pine branch and slapped her on the rump. Tuscawilla jumped forward and then settled into a leaden walk once they were past the town lights.

Anna had taken precious time to lash Flora to her back as a papoose, but at least the little girl had nodded off quickly once the darkness had set in and Tuscawilla had dropped into a steady rhythm. This place east of town was still open woods, though Anna realized that she was riding through what was to have been a grand planned city with a giant hotel at its heart. Even though she had little interest in such schemes, she knew that the yellow jack had killed that community in its cradle, for who would come to restore his health in a place where an epidemic had broken out? Here and there, winking through the woods, were the lights of isolated farmhouses that would keep their solitude after all, for a long, long time.

After she had been on the road for about an hour, a light rain began to fall. She worried that Flora would wake up crying, but the rain was only a passing cloud and she moved on, listening all the while for the sound of men and horses behind her. She slowly went numb in mind and body, not quite believing that she was in such a predicament. She no longer felt the rhythmic plodding of the horse's hooves. She thought back to the foot race almost ten years ago when she had outdistanced all those noisy boys and had been received by a rush of congratulatory hands at the finish line. How proud and happy she had been when she first climbed atop Tuscawilla! Now the horse was old and she was feeling pretty old herself. Her back ached and she felt a terrible desperation and emptiness come over her when she thought that she might never see her husband again.

She had never been to the Wards' new lake cottage, but she knew it from their description. It came after a sharp bend in the road that Penny had complained about because the extra loop seemed unnecessary. With returning strength she guided Tuscawilla down the narrow wagon road that sloped through the sandy hummock. The cottage, with its two chimneys and unusually steep roof—a reminder of Nelda's northern origins—stood in darkness, outlined against the faint light that came from the broad lake.

Before Anna had finished tying the reins to the porch rail a faint glow appeared in a window and in it the distorted features of a face lit from beneath. She was relieved to recognize Penny, who continued to squint at her for a moment before his face broke into a broad smile. Apparently unembarrassed, he came out onto the porch in his nightshirt and sleeping cap, said how happy he was to see her, and hoped that everything was all right.

"There's fever in town," she told him. "The yellow fever. It looks like the Guards brought it back from Fernandina."

"The fever!" He dropped his voice back to a whisper. "You're lucky you got out. I saw what the fever did to that town the last time, in '71. Are you all right, Anna? Have you heard from that man of yours?"

She shook her head and put the back of her hand to her mouth to keep the tears from coming. "I'm fine. Flora and I just need some rest. It's beautiful out here. You'd never guess."

"Let me just get my shoes on and I'll turn your horse out." He started for the door.

She began to tell him that she could do it herself, but she felt her numbness giving way to the ache, and she contented herself with sitting down on the porch and untying Flora from her back.

She woke up to another gray, humid day, feeling rested but weak. She had been roused by the smell of coffee and found Penny and Nelda, still in their nightclothes, tiptoeing through the preparations for breakfast.

"Told you we should've waited," Penny told his wife. "Here we've gone and woken up our girl."

"Did we dear? Oh, I'm so sorry." Nelda came over and sat beside Anna on the horsehair sofa and put an arm around her. "You don't know how happy I am to see you. I'm so glad you got out. What awful news! And Nathaniel still hasn't come back?"

Anna smiled wearily. "I'm on my way to the quarantine camp. My best hope is that he's there."

Penny rubbed his stubbly jaw, not wanting to bring up bad news. "Trouble is, there's more'n one camp. You could go out east to the county line. That's one place they've been takin' 'em off the train. There's another one down by Oliver Park. If he got stopped on his way back from Fernandina he's likely at one or the other. That's a big if though."

As if she were responding to the dilemma, Flora woke up, but at least she wasn't crying. She burped.

"There's some other problems there too," Penny said. "You go in one of them camps lookin' for Nathaniel and they won't let you back out till the governor says so. And then there's the little matter of the fever itself. You'd be askin' for it."

Anna could hold the tears back no longer. They streamed down her cheeks and dropped off her chin. "I didn't want Flora to see me doing this," she said through her fingers.

Nelda gave Penny a reproachful look even though what he had said was perfectly true and necessary. She pulled Anna to her side, hugged her and patted her until Anna seemed to feel a little better.

"There's a way," she said. "I'll go with you."

"Now, hold on—" Penny put up a hand to stop her.

Nelda stood up and smoothed her dressing gown. "I'll be in no danger. I had the yellow fever during a visit to Charleston when I was twelve years old. Nobody gets it twice."

"Well, there's something," Penny said. "But how about Anna here?"

"She can wait outside the camps while I look for Nathaniel." She stroked Anna's hair. "If I have to, I'll bully my way in and then bully my way right back out. We'll make a little tour of it."

"I don't like it," Penny said, shaking his head. "Two women out on their own like that."

"Sometimes circumstances force us to do what we wouldn't ordinarily do," Nelda told him. "Right now the only thing is to find Nathaniel."

"But you don't even know—" Penny realized that his doubts would only make Anna feel worse. He knew that Nelda had made up her mind and that nothing he could say would change it, so he raised a more conciliatory concern. "How about little Flora here?"

Nelda smiled and touched his cheek. "The two of you will get along famously. As soon as J.J. wakes up the three of you can play cards." She explained to Anna that Penny had taken a shine to card playing again, but not to betting. "You can show them some of your tricks."

And so by midmorning they were off. Nelda didn't want to bother with the complexities of the wagon so she rode Penny's short, stout-legged little draft horse while Anna set out again on Tuscawilla, who was content to go since she had some notion that she was heading back to the comfort and security of her paddock.

Penny kept his advice positive and tried to sound as if this were just another outing to Oliver Park or Boulware Springs.

"Don't let that horse git the idea that he's the boss! He's a whole different animal when he's under the saddle. And don't let him git too close to Tuscawilla. When he starts puttin' his ears back, he's gittin' ready to bite. He ain't no gentleman, Nelda."

His wife rolled her eyes and adjusted her hat. "You'd think I'd never been around a horse in my life. Are you ready, Anna?"

It was another hot day and Anna was glad to be wearing one of Nelda's wide-brimmed gardening hats. They followed the gradual southward curve of the lake for a while, then cut farther south to the railroad tracks, which they followed in a line that swung wide of the shore of Alachua Lake. When Anna saw the sun glinting off the distant water she longed to see the familiar slant and angles of the *King Payne*. There was not a boat to be seen, though, and she wondered what Bob and Barkley would have left to do while the yellow jack brought everything to a standstill.

The camp was a miserable affair, thrown together back in April when word first came out of Tampa that the fever had hit there. Word had it that the camp had been little more than a wayside, a turning-around point for train travelers without the proper health reports. But the rumors from Fernandina had made it into something more serious—a place where people were detained at gunpoint until they could be turned back to the county they came from. As Anna and Nelda clattered down the empty tracks, a tall man with a shotgun confronted them.

"Y'all don't come no further." He poked the shotgun in their general direction. "Go on back now, hear?"

Nelda's horse took a few extra steps and she worked the reins to create the impression that she was in control. "We're here on business," she said. "We're looking for a man."

This time the sentry set his feet apart and pointed the shotgun at her. "Now I said stop, didn't I? You can go on in if you want to, but you don't come out. That what you want?"

She put her hands on her hips and glared down at the man. "We're looking for Nathaniel Larrabee. Do you know him?"

"Never heard of him. Like I said, you can go in if you want to, but you don't come out till the governor says so."

Nelda didn't know what to do. She had assumed that someone could tell them if Larrabee was there. She wasn't expecting to deal with strangers.

Something startled the man and Nelda turned to see Anna doubled over, sliding slowly down Tuscawilla's shoulder. Nelda wheeled her horse, but by the time she got there Anna had dropped to the tracks. Clumsily, she pulled her foot from the stirrup and leaned against the sweating horse.

"Child!" Nelda climbed down and put her arm around Anna's waist to keep her from falling. Anna's cheek brushed her lips. "Burning up," Nelda said to herself. She pushed Tuscawilla off the tracks and sat Anna down. She pretended to adjust her hat while she figured out what to do next.

"Sir, I'm afraid my friend has been in the sun too long. I believe we'll have to take you up on your offer of hospitality. She's—she's with child, you see, and it was foolish for us to be out on such a hot day. I thought the air might do her good."

"Whereabouts y'all from?" the man wanted to know.

"Oh, just over by Newnan's Lake. I'm sure we'll be heading back in no time."

Chapter 41

The tent was a cast-off from the Guards, from happier days when their chief concern was their appearance. At a dozen places in the ceiling Nelda could see pinpricks of gray light and the corners were mottled with mildew. She longed for some bleach to clean away the stains and purify the musty air that baked slowly as the afternoon grew hotter.

"I hope he's here," she said to herself. "Dear God, I hope he's here."

When she had Anna settled on a cot she went out looking for Larrabee. What she saw instead was a jagged row of mostly empty tents on uneven ground recently cleared of brush. She came to the conclusion that the empty tents had not yet been inhabited, which she considered preferable to the thought that they had recently lost their inhabitants to the fever. Anna had spoken of having been sick for a few days and then recovering, something Nelda took comfort in because she assumed that Anna had suffered from some sort of grippe before the epidemic had broken out and was now suffering a relapse of that relatively mild illness. Now that the door had swung shut on them, though, they would have to wait out the epidemic here in this place and keep as much to themselves as they could so as not to be exposed to people who might actually have the fever. Nelda tied the horses close to the tent and set about making Anna as comfortable as possible.

First there was the matter of the floor—or the lack of one. The tent had been thrust up in a field of blackberry bushes and beggar weed, and although the brush had been stomped down and chopped to a few inches, it was impossible for Nelda to pass from the cots to the door without tearing her hem. So she took off her wedding ring and set about digging at the roots with her bare hands until she had a tolerable path and clearing. It was hot under the heavy canvas, but when she raised the door flap, she was beset by mosquitoes and thought that Anna must be suffering terribly since she was too weak to raise a hand against them. She experimented with raising the tent slightly where it touched the ground and found the result a bearable compromise between heat and mosquito bites.

Her next concern was water. Anna's fever seemed to be getting worse, so

Nelda hurried through the beggar weed to find a pump. She headed for a brick foundation and a scattering of weathered boards on the top of the rise and found the pump. She had nothing to carry the water in, though, so she contented herself with holding the hem of her dress under the spurting water and cooling Anna's forehead that way. She daubed Anna's glowing cheeks until the water itself felt hot, then she returned to the pump.

When Anna seemed to have dozed off, Nelda sat on the other cot and thought for a moment. Then she straightened her hat and went out again to see if there was any sign of Larrabee.

The camp was about half full. Most of its inhabitants were young men, but she also saw families with small children, older couples and, away off toward the pinewoods, a contingent of Negroes who sat fanning themselves in the shade of their tents. She wondered how each of them had come to the camp, wondered if any of them were sick or if they were just biding their time until the governor finally told them that they could go home again.

As she looked from face to face she was surprised to find that she knew none of them and supposed that they were travelers caught when the roads were sealed off and the trains emptied. She had imagined that these people would be her friends and neighbors and customers who could tell her at once if Larrabee had been there, but she found that she had to describe him to weary, worried people who showed no sign of recognition.

She fought back a growing hopelessness and went looking for something to carry water in. The best she could do was a castoff peach can and a dirty whiskey bottle. Waiting her turn at the pump now, she cleaned both and filled them, and finding herself suddenly very thirsty, drank from the musky can and refilled it before returning to the tent.

They had brought a little lunch and now she remembered it, went to the grazing horses and got it from the saddlebag. It was only strips of dried beef, hardtack and blackberry preserves. Soldier's rations Penny had called it, but said that it would last a lifetime, even in the hot September sun. And what would Penny be thinking now, she asked herself as the day wore on and she and Anna failed to return to the cottage by the lake. Would he find a way to come after them?

Anna was still asleep. Nelda set her lunch aside and went out again, wanting to know the best or worst by the time she woke up. Walking down the hill toward Oliver Park, she finally caught sight of someone familiar. He was standing beside a large tent, leaning on a fine walking stick as he listened to a tall, thin pale man in a top hat and old-fashioned black frock coat. The man she recognized was also tall but younger and better dressed than the other, though his shoulders were slightly hunched and he seemed to rely heavily on the walking stick, as if he were lame or very tired. At one point he turned to leave the other man but then stopped as if suddenly the other had something important to say.

Nelda hesitated for a moment, smelling the hot straw of her hat, then made up her mind and broke into the conversation.

"I am sorry to interrupt, but I believe you know a Mr. Larrabee."

Both of the men seemed caught off guard by the question.

"What of it?" asked the well-dressed man.

Nelda stood her ground. She looked up at him with steady eyes. "Have you seen Mr. Larrabee in this camp?"

"I have not. Do I know you?" he asked as an afterthought.

"I am Nelda Ward."

"Oh, Good God. I am one of your admirers. I'm John Howard."

They shook hands. His was warm and firm and slow to release hers.

"And you say that Mr. Larrabee has not been here? Is there anyone else who might have seen him?"

"I see everyone who comes in," Howard told her. "You see, I'm the commandant of this charming facility." He gave the other man a hard look that sent him on his way.

"That's very civic-minded of you," Nelda said. "And very brave if you haven't had the fever."

"Maybe. But it so happens that I suddenly find myself with a good deal of time on my hands and no immediate prospects."

"What about the canal company?"

"Trade is stopped. There *is* no canal company for the time being."

"I'm sorry. Everybody seems to be suffering."

"How true. And will continue to. Those who live. But then they'll always want hats, won't they?"

"Always."

"And groceries, of course, and dry goods. I hear that some of the businessmen are going back into town today, working their stores, fever notwithstanding, for a few hours."

"And have you no business then, Mr. Howard?"

"My dear lady, I own a prime portion of the business district, the only drawback being that the town it's a part of exists only on paper." He dropped his voice as if talking to himself. "And now will continue to exist only on paper. There is no urgency in that business district."

Nelda weighed her next words carefully. "If you are the commandant of this place and an admirer of mine perhaps you will see fit to grant me a small favor."

He bowed slightly. "At your service."

"There's a woman here. Suffering from a fever having nothing to do with the crisis. I would like to take her back to Newnan's Lake with me."

Howard seemed to be making connections in his mind. Perhaps he had seen Anna and Nelda ride into the camp.

"That I cannot do," he said.

"She is separated from her husband and child, sir."

"Many of these poor devils are, madam. All of them have stories. All of them have fallen off the edge of the earth in someone's reckoning. If she's clear of the fever, let her count her blessings. Her family will be all the happier to see her once the governor lifts the ban."

"And what about your own wife, Mr. Howard? Does she know of your whereabouts?"

"My own wife knows only that I'm *here*. As to whether I'm dead or alive, it's hearsay only."

"You are a hard man, Mr. Howard."

"They are hard times, madam. I wish you the best of luck."

Nelda returned to the tent, sitting and thinking, waiting for the heat to dissipate, waiting for Anna to wake up. As she sat on her cot, taking the occasional sip from the water can and picking the sticky green arcs of beggar's lice from her skirts, she realized that Mr. John Howard didn't care whether he lived or died.

The heat refused to let go. From early morning and into the long afternoon hours the two women sweltered in the heavy tent. At times it seemed to Nelda that the monotonous drone of cicadas was actually the sound of the ground frying. The sand that she scuffed up on her way to the pump was hot. The pump handle was hot. Even the can in her hand grew hot in the relentless sun. In the evening a light, refreshing rain came and after it an onslaught of mosquitoes that had no respect for poor Anna as she shivered and twitched on the damp cot.

On the morning of September nineteenth Anna sat up and Nelda thought she must be feeling much better, but the fever hadn't yet broken and Anna seemed disoriented.

"Poor dear," Nelda said, stroking her neighbor's flushed cheek and brushing back a strand of fine brown hair. "You haven't eaten in a day. You must be wanting something to keep your strength up."

She broke off a piece of hardtack and moistened it and held it under Anna's nose. She was heartened when Anna put it in her mouth and chewed. She nursed her through a palm-sized piece that way and got her to drink cool water from the whiskey bottle.

"You should lie down now," she said.

Anna looked at the half-open tent flap and tried to get up. "Nathaniel. Where's Nathaniel? Has he been here?"

Nelda put her arm around her shoulder and sat her back down. "Not yet, dear Anna. And maybe that's all for the best. He's still out there somewhere, healthy and coming home."

"Where's Flora?"

"She's at the lake with Penny and J.J. Remember?"

Slowly Anna nodded. She put her hand on the edge of the cot and lay back down. "I was having such strange dreams."

"What was it, Anna?"

"A garden. And a mansion. So many rooms. And the sand drifting through the fence and Nathaniel was trying to keep the sand out, trying to build a wall to keep the sand out. And Flora and I...."

"It's the heat, child. It's enough to give us all bad dreams. Try to think of something soothing, something to cool you."

Anna looked at the pricks of light in the sloped ceiling and smiled. "A swim in the creek, feels...."

Anna drifted back to sleep, leaving Nelda to wonder what the strange dream meant.

Sometime in the middle of the morning, when Nelda was checking on the horses, she thought she heard a train approaching from the east and she hurried to the camp gate to get a look at the tracks. If there had been a train though, there was none now and the rails merged into the scorching sun without a trace of a locomotive. The guard was there, half-asleep in a cane chair, the bright-barreled shotgun resting on his knees.

About noon Anna woke again and asked for Larrabee. She asked what the date was and Nelda lied for the sake of keeping her spirits up and told her that he was only a day late. Nelda bathed Anna's face in cool water, made her drink and got her to eat a small piece of dried beef, though she was afraid all the while that she would choke on it. Anna's fever was stubborn, but Nelda nurtured a secret hope that once Anna had recovered from it, they could convince John Howard to let them leave the camp.

Half an hour later, the worst happened. Anna jerked to a sitting position and threw up blood. "It's nothing," Nelda told her. She tore off pieces of her petticoat to bathe her neighbor's forehead and cheeks, cleaned her dress, and then coaxed her back to sleep. She took the bloody rags out and hid them in the weeds, knowing now that in the tent she had seen the face of Yellow Jack.

In her own bout with yellow fever she had never gotten that far. She stayed as close to the tent as she could now, swabbing Anna's face and fanning her until her arms ached, thinking that her neighbor could not go on this way much longer.

Another night passed, hot and damp and restless with mosquitoes and muffled coughs from the distant tents. In the morning of their third day in camp Nelda heard rumors at the pump. An old man brought in a week ago had come down with the fever, no doubt about it. He was hot as an oven and throwing up.

"They ought to put him out of his misery," someone said. "Sooner they bury him the better."

"Old Sam's already got some holes dug and Baldy's made coffins. How do you like that?"

In the evening a hard rain came—hard enough to keep the mosquitoes away—and Nelda opened the tent flap wide to let in the cooling air. This was the best thing that had happened to them in days and Nelda took comfort in it. She slept soundly, even as the water seeped under the walls of the tent.

The next morning, the twenty-first, was hotter than ever and the air heavy with humidity. Her clothes stuck to her skin and she longed for a cool bath and something clean and dry to put on. Anna had eaten nothing for more than a day, and in the harsh light that slanted in through the tent flap, her complexion was the color of moldy straw.

"What day is it?" Anna asked when Nelda put a hand to her feverish forehead.

In truth, Nelda wasn't sure, had lost touch with the days of the week, had let the numbers slip too, so it was easy for her to lie and say it was only the eleventh.

"Two days late," Anna said in a thin voice. She tried to get up. "Flora's crying. I'd better see to her."

"No, she's not crying, dear. It's the wind. Flora's playing with J.J." Nelda fervently wished it were so.

Half an hour later a commotion arose at one of the other tents. Nelda looked out and saw two masked men going inside it. She thought it strange that men would dress like highwaymen going into a tent in a quarantine camp.

Anna woke up again but without raising her head from the cot, and said something about bright sand by a river.

Nelda came closer and picked up the girl's hand. It was hot. Nelda felt a mosquito blunder into her ear. She slapped and it fell away.

She kissed the back of Anna's hand. The girl seemed to be staring at something outside and Nelda slipped free and went to see what it was. Seeing nothing but a few people gathered around the tent visited by the masked men, she turned and looked back at Anna. She stood there for a long while, slowly losing her sense of touch, of place and time. She put her fingers to her lips. Then she went back into the tent and closed her neighbor's lifeless eyes.

Chapter 42

He had walked from the county line, stopping to rest during the heat of the day and pressing on by night when he was stronger. It had damn near cost him his life, but in his pocket he had what he had gone to Fernandina to get. Three badly written sentences and a signature in the hand of one Henry Allen, witnessed by the clerk of Nassau County, stating that one John Howard representing the Alachua Steam Navigation and Canal Company had contracted him to sink wrecks in Alachua Lake for the purpose of harassing the boat of a rival transit company. He figured it wouldn't go far in court, but would probably be enough to put Howard out of business anyway since a man's reputation was still his most valuable asset among the people of the county.

After the little signing party and Allen's hasty departure from the courthouse, things began to blur. Larrabee had planned to come back on the train with the Guards, but there were delays and arguments and the not-so-distant sounds of glass breaking as the longshoremen carried their grievances into the heart of town. Larrabee tried to remember what came after that, but could come up with no more than scraps of conversations and the recollection of waking up in a large, bare room that reminded him of a giant hospital he had seen in New Orleans. A woman wearing some peculiar kind of cap had come to see him every day, had held his hand and said soothing things, placed light fingers on his forehead, taken his pulse and told him that he had a strong constitution and was lucky to be alive, luckier than most. He seemed to recall an enduring headache, the feeling that his back would snap every time he moved, and nausea that made the smell of food sickening.

For some uncounted number of days, he lay on his back and looked at the high pressed tin ceiling, the tall, arched windows, and the sympathetic nurse. Then he was walking toward the train station, valise in hand, light-headed and hungry.

The train had turned back at Waldo, and now he was walking again, stronger but still good for no more than a mile or two at a stretch. He walked the edge of the muddy road from midmorning until the red sun was well below the crowns of the tall pine trees, walked and rested, eyeing the threatening clouds as he shifted the valise from one hand to the other. He had thought of leaving it in Fernandina, but knew that Anna would be angry with him for losing even a hand-me-down possession. And then there was the .44, which the orderlies at the hospital had apparently overlooked. Better to have it out of sight.

He had heard about the fever coming to town. They were talking about it in the streets of Jacksonville and on the train. He figured Anna would have withdrawn into the house with Flora. After all, there was water and plenty to eat and at the same time no reason for anyone to come in on them. She may have gone to stay with Nelda and Penny if they weren't out at their lake cottage, but he thought it more likely that she would stay home to see to her garden. And what would she say to him when he straggled up the walk, scrawny and tawny and two weeks late?

He stopped to rest at the three forlorn cabins that had refused to yield more than their roofs to fire and time. He sat on the stoop of the place that had been Lucinda's, remembering the morning he had ridden there looking for John Howard, thinking back on that terrible night when Jerry Penrod had lost his life in a treasure hunt gone wrong. And then Penny had been beaten within an inch of his life here. He got up and pushed on.

The road was straight and he could see well in advance that it was blocked, but he knew half a dozen shortcuts through the woods and he took the one that brought him in behind the garden. His heart froze when he saw it. Weeds had sprung up everywhere. Peas had split their pods and spilled into the mud. Tomatoes lay broken and scattered. Rain had beaten down the squash and cucumbers. Chickens wandered in the yard. The rest were nowhere to be seen. He looked toward the paddock. Tuscawilla was gone.

He walked up the back steps without hope, went into the kitchen and from room to room calling Anna, faster and louder. The house was hot and mildewy. On the dining room table a bouquet of wildflowers had wilted, staining the cloth. Beside it he found an old business card. On the back of it, scarcely legible, in what he barely recognized as Anna's handwriting, was the single phrase *at the cottage*. Below it was a star and a beautiful cursive A.

Something like a thunderclap startled him, an explosion coming from the direction of the Courthouse. He walked through the front room and the entry-way to the porch. He heard a distant shout and a second explosion that rocked the windows. He had already made his mind up to go east, to the cottage, and the Courthouse was on his way. He hurried down the walk, closed the front gate behind him, and cut across the street toward the square. A dog approached him, head down, tail wagging tentatively. It was a hound mix of some kind and its ribs showed through its short tan coat. It trotted after him as he crossed the muddy street and came to the center of town. At the corner of the square, across from the dry goods store and armory that had replaced the Arlington, two men in blue-gray uniforms were loading a cannon pointed down West Main Street. As he came closer Larrabee smelled burning tar and wondered if some kind of insurrection had broken out.

He skirted the square to the south and found it deserted except for the two cadets reloading their cannon. The stores were empty, the houses shuttered, the streets littered with clothing and furniture. A cow grazed on the Courthouse lawn, her bag heavy with milk. Larrabee worked his way back up the eastern side of the square, listening for the next volley from the cannon but it didn't come. He crossed Liberty Street at Vidal's drugstore and went to Dr. Willis' house.

Billy answered the door. He was taller than Larrabee remembered. He was barefoot but neat. His thick brown hair was parted down the middle and pomaded. He had grown a mustache.

"Jesus," he said softly, "you look like the very devil. Where've you been, Larrabee? Come on in. Looks like you've picked up an orphan."

Larrabee glanced back and saw that the hound had followed him all this way. It sat on its haunches and looked up hoping for a handout.

"That's the story around here," Billy said. "Wish I could do something for him, but there's too many of 'em. You feed one and they just keep coming back and pretty soon you're feeding 'em all." He ushered Larrabee into the parlor and lit the lamp. When he got a good look at his visitor he shuddered. "How did you get here?"

"By train to Waldo. I walked the rest of the way."

"It's a wonder they let you on the train."

"I wasn't this yellow when I got on."

"Have you come to see Father?"

"I've come to see if anyone knows where Anna is." Larrabee sat back on a horsehair chair, out of the light, as if to minimize his thinness and sallow complexion.

"It's been such a mess around here," Billy said. "So much coming and going—mostly going. I doubt if anyone can help you. Two of the guards died, you know."

"Where is everybody?"

"God only knows. Scattered. Scared. You should've seen 'em take off the night the fever was announced. You never heard so much running around and screaming in your life. I suppose the war must've been like that. Soon as I came home from Fernandina Father locked me up here in the house and told the captain I was down with the ague. It was the first time that I ever knew him to tell a lie. I figure there are probably hundreds of liars out there now. Lying to get out of town and lying to get back in. They're in camps, you know. Wherever the train tracks come into the county. There's a big one down at Oliver Park run by John Howard. They say he's wearing a gun. Of course those that can do it are hunkering down at the lakes—Santa Fe, Newnan's. That's the place to be—away from all this." His face lit up. "You know, I do recall that when we came back from Fernandina Anna was asking about you. That was a long time ago though. A couple of weeks."

There was a stirring now in the back of the house and Dr. Willis appeared at the parlor door. He looked old and tired. His shirt hung open at his throat. His vest was unbuttoned. The light showed creases in his face.

"I thought I heard voices. You look like a ghost, Larrabee. How are Anna and the little girl?"

"I was hoping you could tell me, doctor. Town seems to be turned upside down."

"It is. How'd you get in?"

"The long way. You don't know where Anna and Flora might be?"

Dr. Willis gave Billy a questioning look. "Haven't seen 'em. Why don't you come into my office for a moment?"

Larrabee got up and followed him to the back of the dim house. When they got to the office, Dr. Willis lit the lamp on the roll-top desk and turned it up. He motioned for Larrabee to sit down in the swivel chair and then he took up a position on an ottoman against the wall. Beside it stood the small round table with the chess set on it. Dr. Willis' game with the preacher was still in progress. It was covered with dust.

"When did you come down with the fever, boy?"

"Couple of days after I got to Fernandina. I don't remember exactly."

"Well, you can count your blessings. You won't ever have to worry about getting it again."

"Is it bad around town?"

"Two of the guards. I hear some have died in the camps, but I don't know who or how many. There's plenty of talk but not much fact. It's going to be rough. The horse there?"

Larrabee deduced that he meant Tuscawilla. He shook his head. "Anna left a note saying she was going to Penny and Nelda's cottage."

"If she's out there, you're ahead of the game." His words were cut short by a rumble from the cannon.

"What're they doing?" Larrabee half rose in his chair.

"What they can, which is nothing," the doctor said. "Somebody gave 'em the idea that vibrations keep away the contagion. So they're shooting cannons. When I was a kid folks used to do that to bring drowning victims to the surface. It worked about as well. You've probably smelled that tar too. Same thing. Smoke and mirrors to make 'em think they're doing something. You know, you don't look half-bad for a man who's been through the fever. I suggest you get some sleep though. Not that I expect you'll do so."

Larrabee spent most of a restless night in the house. Before sunrise he was on the road. In the darkness he easily slipped past the sentries at the barricade east on Liberty Street, but the going was slow because the road was so muddy. It was well past sunup by the time he came to the boat landing at the edge of the dark lake. It took him several tries to find the cottage he was looking for. People were suspicious and standoffish, but at last someone knew about the cottage with two chimneys and Larrabee worked his way through the meandering hummock road to it.

When she saw him, Nelda burst into tears, and in a sickening moment he knew the worst. They stood embracing at the threshold. She held him tight saying over and over, "I'm sorry, I'm so sorry. There must've been something I could have done."

"What about Flora?" he said at last, in a way that was more like a long breath than words.

She pointed toward the lake. At the end of the pier Penny was hunched over a fishing pole. Beside him J.J. stood fumbling with a tangle while a small girl tried to help.

He took Nelda's hand and pressed it in his. "Where is she? Where's Anna?"

"We were at the camp." Nelda gulped, almost broke down again, but held back her tears. "It's where the Florida Southern goes past Oliver Park. On a ridge to the north. Toward the cemetery. I'm sorry. I left your horse. I was afraid to come back with both. I'll go there with you."

He shook his head. "You've been through enough and this is a walk I have to take by myself. Will you watch my little girl another day?"

She bit her lip, was reluctant to let go of his hand. "It seems like a dream," she said. "If you squeeze my hand hard enough maybe we'll both wake up."

He squeezed her hand and started back down the road.

He wrestled with his sorrow the entire way. He kept asking himself *what if?* What if I had never gone to Fernandina? What if Bob and I had been content to outmaneuver the clumsy boats of the Canal Company? Things would've come out a world different and Anna would be alive. *Anna would be alive.* If there had been no confrontation on the lake, Anna would be alive. If John Howard had not sent out his dredge and sunk his wrecks, Anna would be alive.

He wanted pure sorrow devoted to the person he had loved more than any other, who had loved him more than any other, but as he walked, his sorrow was more and more entwined with a growing rage that rose up and choked it, like a vine strangling an oak.

Soon he veered away from Newnan's Lake and picked up the Florida Southern tracks that took him west and south to the sun-struck edge of Alachua Lake. He walked on, remembering many a happy day on the *King Payne* when the thought of riding home warmed a winter afternoon or made light of the summer rain. One by one he put those thoughts aside, passed the deserted entrance to Oliver Park, ascended a rise, and saw the scattering of tan tents on the hillside. In the near lower corner of the camp, toward the train tracks, he saw two mounds of earth and three open graves. Camp discipline had deteriorated from its early days. The place was unguarded. Empty tents had been allowed to collapse under rain and wind.

It was such a strange place, so unlike anything he had seen, that at first he was simply numb. It made no sense that Anna was in any way connected to this squatter's den. Then he saw Tuscawilla.

He went through the motions of patting her and saddling her and straightening her bridle as he had done a thousand times for Anna, but the sight of those graves kept pulling him back to this strange, desolate place. He led the horse a few steps, also a matter of habit, and then he saw the tall man in the black frock coat. The tall man had seen him too and had ducked behind a tent. Larrabee quickened his pace, leading Tuscawilla down the hill. When he was within a few yards of where the man had disappeared, he released her. He found the man crouching behind the hollow trunk of a long-dead oak tree.

"Where is she, Sam? Where's Anna?"

Sam Leary unfolded part way but remained pressed against the remains of the tree. "Well, now you know, Larrabee, I didn't do the actual digging. That was done by some boys that Mr. Howard hired, but—"

Larrabee seized him by the throat. "Where is he? Where's Howard?"

Sam made a gurgling sound. His collar came loose and he managed to squeeze free. "Well, I don't know. He was running the camp. He was running this here camp and now he's gone. Me, I'm just laying out the graves for drainage and such and them boys was supposed to do the digging—only they run off—but—" He held a protective hand in front of his face.

"Which grave is hers, you old fool? Which grave is Anna's?"

"Bu-bu—" Sam had fallen back into some long-forgotten childhood speech impediment. He averted his eyes as if the distant scrub oaks had something to tell him, held a trembling hand in front of his face.

"Which grave, Sam? Which grave?"

"I don't know!"

In his blind rage, Larrabee thought he must have hit the man, for Sam fell to the ground and rolled until the dead leaves and bark stuck to his sunken cheeks and thinning white hair. Suddenly he seemed half a century older, a brittle shell of the resilient trickster.

Larrabee thought he must have asked again of Howard's whereabouts because Sam was saying, "in town, he went to town." He jumped onto the startled horse, only vaguely aware that Sam was calling after him.

"He's carrying a gun, he is! He's carrying a gun!"

It was a hot, hard mile up the tracks to the road and the nineteen-year-old horse wasn't up to it, but Larrabee ran her over the ties and then north toward town and she was wet and winded by the time the barricade came into sight. Even then he kicked her on so that the mud flew from her hooves as they came within hailing distance of the sentry. The barricade consisted of a hay wagon behind bobbed wire strung across the broad street from oak to oak, from Doig's foundry on the east side, to Ralph Pine's orange grove on the west. At the sound of hoofbeats, the sentry came out from behind the wagon and stood with his shotgun resting in the crook of his arm.

"Hold, mister!"

Larrabee circled Tuscawilla back—three, four steps, charged, and jumped the wire, knocking the man over in mid-threat. He kicked the horse into a frantic run that had him out of range before the sentry could raise his shotgun. He ran her past the huge new opera house, past Duke's and the Alachua Hotel, past the vast dark Courthouse and the armory, and home, where he threw himself off the horse and bounded up the porch steps. The valise was still on the floor by the dining room table. He tore it open and dug through the clothes for the thing he wanted. He yanked open the cylinder and, satisfied that the gun was loaded, ran back outside, jumped onto the horse, and galloped down the street to Howard's house. He tied the horse at the gate and, holding the gun behind his back, walked slowly up to the house. Jane Jennings had seen him riding up and came out onto the porch. She had been fixing her hair and still had a pin in her hand.

Larrabee stopped six feet from the foot of the steps and looked up at her.

"Ma'am, where is he?"

She poked the palm of her hand with the point of the pin. "John? He's not here. He's—" She was nervous. She didn't know what to expect from this grim, yellow, mud-spattered man who was somehow still handsome. "He's out walking." She glanced in the general direction of the square. "He's out walking," she repeated. "Shall I tell him you called?"

Larrabee backed toward the gate and rode away. The town was still small enough. He'd find the man.

Somewhere a bell started ringing. It sounded like the Presbyterian Church. Slow and even, as if marking the hour. Larrabee let Tuscawilla drop down to a trot. He rode east down Liberty Street past the drugstore and the photographer's studio and then he turned north into a neighborhood of fine new houses and well-kept picket fences. The bell continued to ring. He dropped the spent horse to a walk. Coming down the street, a few houses away, John Howard dragged his fifty-dollar walking stick along the fences as if he were a boy with a hickory staff. Larrabee sat and watched him for a while, then dismounted and walked over to the fence. He set the gun on top of a post and waited for Howard to see him.

They were not more than fifty feet apart when it happened. Howard looked up and saw the horse first, then stopped and caught sight of Larrabee standing with one hand on the fence.

"Sam tells me you have a gun," Larrabee said.

Howard leaned on his stick, started to come forward but thought better of it. "Well, Sam's a damn fool."

"Anna died yesterday. It should've been you."

"They're dying all around us. We did everything we could."

"You have a gun. Mine's over here. I'm faster, but I'll have to reach across to get to it. That should make us just about even."

"Don't be foolish, Larrabee! This isn't some range war. These are modern times. A civilized country! People don't settle anything with guns. I threw mine away."

Larrabee's right hand remained a good six feet from the fence post, but poised.

Howard felt the need for a cigar. He reached for his inside pocket.

Larrabee snatched up the .44 and fired. Through the smoke he saw Howard's head jerk to one side. The walking stick flipped up and the gambler went over backwards, hitting the fence on his way into the sand.

All that Larrabee remembered afterward was the church bell tolling through the hot, still, deserted morning. Where the gun went, how the horse got into the paddock, he would never know. Or how he got the scratches on his hands and forehead. He had some vague recollection of rushing headlong through the woods beyond the Union Academy, but he could not be certain even of that. He lost the sound of the bell as the realization grew that history had repeated itself. He had killed a man in Missouri and spent his life a fugitive separated from his family. Now he had killed again and was a fugitive once more and had to pull up his roots or face the hangman's noose. After all, despite his true character, John Howard was a prominent citizen, a hero of the terrible epidemic, shot down in the street by a man who had failed in all endeavors. With a single furious stroke Larrabee had blasted away everything that had taken him twelve years to build, and as he lay on the kitchen floor, gasping like a landed fish, he knew that all he had left was the chance of one last visit with his daughter.

As his head cleared, he wanted at least to explain himself to someone who could tell the story right. He walked through the quiet streets to Dr. Willis' house and turned the bell.

Mrs. Willis answered the door. She looked worried at the sight of him, but before words could pass between them the doctor himself appeared in his Sunday best.

"You look like hell," he said. "Didn't I tell you to rest?" He motioned Larrabee inside.

As they shut the door, Larrabee glanced back, thinking that the sheriff would be coming into the yard at any moment.

"Let's go back into the office," the doctor said in a way that was more like an order than an invitation. "It's kind of a mess, but then so are you."

They remained standing.

"I came to tell you my side before I leave," Larrabee said. He looked from the dusty chess set to the doctor.

Dr. Willis closed the door.

"Anna's dead. The fever."

"I'm sorry. When did it happen?"

"I don't know. Yesterday I think."

"There was no finer woman than your Anna."

Larrabee was not saying what he wanted to say. He couldn't get past Anna. All of his thinking was drawn into her death.

"Have you seen Flora?" the doctor was asking.

"She's with the Wards at Newnan's Lake."

"Why don't you go out and stay with them? It's easy enough getting out of this town."

Larrabee was staring at the floor. He didn't want to say what came next. His eyes followed a thin trail of red coins. Fresh blood.

The doctor put a hand on his shoulder. "I want you to leave town. Call it doctor's orders."

"Will you say good-bye for me? To the ones who were our friends?"

The doctor looked as if he thought the question strange. He offered Larrabee his hand. "Count on it."

Larrabee was sure that the sheriff and his men must be on the front porch by now. He started for the office door but the doctor stopped him.

"Better go out by the front. There's blood all over the steps. John Howard was in here not half an hour ago. Some sniper creased his skull with a bullet. He bled like a stuck pig, but head wounds often do. Even the superficial ones."

Larrabee stared at the blood, letting the words sink in.

The doctor had just handed him a great gift, the gift of freedom itself, for all at once he *was* a free man again. He shook the doctor's hand on his way out the front door and vowed to himself that never again would he let his anger deprive him of his liberty.

He wasn't yet ready to acknowledge that the gift of freedom had come from John Howard.

In the steeple of the Presbyterian Church, Roland Bonds gave another tug on the bell rope. There had been no services in the week since the epidemic had begun. After all, the congregation was scattered to the four winds. But Preacher Bonds wanted to salute the dead, and so this Sunday at the gathering hour, he rang the bell. When he had sat praying in the sanctuary for a while a new thought struck him. He climbed back up the stairs and began to ring the bell again as a message that even in the darkest hour the church would be there, waiting to serve the living.

Part IV
Fortunes and Sacred Honor
1889-1899

Chapter 43

THE ENTIRE STORE OCCUPIED a part of the Dennis Block scarcely larger than the late major's sumptuous office. John Howard couldn't help making the comparison because this was the original site of the vast brick monument to the major's moneymaking. Howard had been to the old man's grave not long ago while taking a shortcut through Evergreen Cemetery and was reminded by the bold sculpting of the major's life span that the major had lived to be just forty-five years old. At thirty-five John Howard was quickly catching up. At the age of thirty-five the major already had most of the town, most of the county, in his pocket. He had made questionable decisions, had missed out on the ever-fatter profits from the orange trade, and had lost most of his political clout, may even have died down a few dollars. But he had always lived well and had never found it necessary to retreat from the position of a wealthy, influential, widely respected man.

He had never fallen so low as to be a mere shopkeeper just to keep a roof over his head. But then the major hadn't invested heavily in a town doomed by a yellow fever epidemic. As he surveyed the dreary, work-a-day stock on his shelves, Howard took some comfort from the failures of others. The canal company had taken huge losses. Virtually the entire fall citrus income had been wiped out by the fever that had brought lake traffic to a standstill. The steamers were doing double-time to transport the citrus before it rotted. But the railroad was eating up more of their business than ever, and the trouble-some little firm of Larrabee & Harper had resumed their run on the southwest quarter of the lake. They had hung on because the canal company—Howard in particular—had run out of money for dredging a channel and could scarcely afford to pay for another pier like the one their clumsy skipper had rammed at Walls' plantation.

So there he was, strapped for cash and stuck with a large parcel east of town that was worth half as much as he had paid for it because the entire nation had heard that sixteen people had died of yellow fever in the supposedly healthy climate of Alachua County.

One of the unlucky sixteen had been a certain Mr. Cipher Choat, better known as Baldy, who apparently had taken with him to the grave his complicity in various illegalities, including the fire that had freed Howard from the ruinous Arlington Hotel.

Howard couldn't afford to pay a helper to run his store. He was forced into the awful embarrassment of manning the counter himself. For a moment he had been tempted to enlist Jane's aid in the cause but couldn't stand the thought of her laughing at him. He thought she might leave him anyway now that most of the money was gone, but she had stayed. In fact, since the epidemic, she seemed more settled than ever. Although she had not come down with the fever herself, suddenly she seemed older and more tired, more apt to sit at home and gaze out the window. She wasn't so fast with a sly comeback in response to his little jokes at her expense. But then, he had been telling fewer jokes lately.

Although he had become less self-conscious about the scar on his temple, the red line where the bullet had grazed him, he dreaded seeing any of his former business associates in the store, to have them see him brought so low—reduced to little more than a clerk. At the same time, though, he desperately needed business, needed cash. He responded to each footstep at the door with mixed emotions. He was relieved to find that most of his customers were women who seemed not to recognize him as a former partner in the ambitious plan east of town. They were more interested in gardening tools than gossip now that the azaleas were beginning to bloom. He had bought most of the stock from a failed hardware store in Starke, had rented a wagon and driven up there himself on a warm, sunny January morning. There were some things he didn't want—cases of neat's-foot oil and bag balm—but he offered the bankrupt owner a chillingly low price for all of it.

"Surely your peace of mind is worth something," he had said. "Come on, my good man, you can have it all off your hands with the stroke of a pen."

And so he had obtained a pretty fair basic inventory at a cutthroat price. He called the store the Sunrise Emporium because a person standing on the Courthouse lawn could see the sun rise over its cupola and he thought the name sounded promising. He had rounded out his opening-day merchandise with a collection of china bought from a very persistent traveling salesman named Leo Bard, a short and fibrous little prune too long in the sun. He had a salt-and-pepper spade of a beard, spotted hands, and sharp little brown eyes that wouldn't let go of you. He reminded Howard of a gamecock, all advance and no retreat. He even had a way of squinting up his eyes that made Howard think of a rooster, and he had strange crooked fingers that came at you like a pitchfork.

"If I had your tenacity I'd be on easy street," Howard said when he realized what had happened.

"You ain't seen the silverware yet," Leo Bard told him. "Some of the best you'll find between here and the Ohio."

"And I don't want to see it either," Howard insisted. "Unless you want to take payment in trowels, shovels and hatchets."

Leo Bard sniffed. "This stuff is 1837 pattern made about 1860 by the looks of it. Probably spent the war buried in somebody's well. That's how precious it is. To tell you the truth I've gotten used to having it. I'd be loath to part with it."

"Good," Howard said.

"I'll show it to you next time I come through," Bard said nonetheless. "Next winter likely." With that he clapped his oversized straw hat on his head and wished Howard luck with his new venture.

"This here is usually a good town for selling," he added as he climbed into his top-heavy wagon.

"So good that there's plenty of competition," Howard said, rubbing one of the china plates in a last-minute search for hidden cracks.

On his first day of business Nelda Ward came into the store. She was thinner than when he had seen her at the quarantine camp, but she still had her self-assured walk. She wore one of her trademark hats, a finely woven straw accented with a white satin ribbon and two small white silk roses. She came right up to the counter as if she owned the place, and she seemed not the least surprised to see him reduced to a clerical position. When he saw her coming he wanted to take off his sleeve guards and hide them, but she was there before he knew it.

"An honor," he said with a polite nod.

"You flatter me." She was dismissive and distant, as if she wanted to recover some of the dignity she had lost at the camp.

"What might I show you, madam?" He was even more formal than usual. He, too, wanted to put the camp in the past. He wondered what she thought of him, if she blamed him in some way for the death of her friend.

She was looking for a birthday present for her son, who would be ten next week. She wondered if the emporium had any fishing tackle.

He had cane poles and a new kind of wound cotton line that could pull ten pounds.

She asked if he had one of those rods that had an attached reel.

Regrettably, he did not, but he would certainly look into getting some. He thought that they would surely be popular once the sportsmen started coming back into the county.

On her way out the door she turned and told him that it was a brave thing he had done, taking charge of the camp. "The town should be grateful to you," she said. Apparently she held no grudge although her friend had died in one of those awful tents. The burial had been a miserable, hasty business. Baldy Choat and an old man had died in the camp that same day and the graves had been filled so quickly that no one seemed to know which was which.

"The only gratitude I ask is that the town buy some hardware," Howard replied.

"I believe they will in time," she told him. Half an hour later a suntanned boy about ten years old came in and bought $10.50 worth of shingles and nails.

"It's for a doghouse," he explained. "My pa got me a hunting dog for my birthday and we're going to build a house for it."

"A palace I should think." Heartened, Howard tried to picture a ten-dollar doghouse.

An hour after that, one of the new grove owners bought some bee-keeping equipment that Howard had thought would never sell. When he finally closed shop at five-thirty he didn't have to count the receipts. He had kept track in his mind and knew that he had $62.80 to show for his day's work, an amount he would've squandered on a night of entertainment in Jacksonville during his high-living days. An inconsequential sum. He had won more in a single pot at seven-card stud. And yet, as he smoothed the bills with his fingers, he was strangely content.

As he approached home he put his hand to his inside pocket—the gesture that had nearly gotten him killed back in September—and treated himself to a smoke. More than two cigars in succession usually made his stomach hurt, so he restricted himself to one, which he smoked with great pleasure while standing on the front porch. He had saved the house and he had his wretched little store, and if tomorrow proved as good as today he would muddle through until the next thing came along. He was not riding high, but he had survived, he would muddle through, and then come roaring back.

Chapter 44

The afternoon was so warm that the children needed a cold drink. After all, they had been tearing around the yard ever since lunch. Penny had arranged for Duke Duforge to bring over bottles of sarsaparilla from the saloon and they had been sitting in a barrel of Curtis' artificial ice ever since church had let out. Penny and the men had been sitting on the back veranda smoking and talking politics while the boys of the younger generation played football.

Nelda questioned the wisdom of letting J.J. and his friends roughhouse in their Sunday best.

Penny waved his cigar. "Well, did their mothers expect a bunch of ten-year-old boys to set down to a game of bridge? Soon's they opened that football there wasn't anything in the world going to keep 'em from it."

Nelda went over and uncorked a sarsaparilla for herself. "You can do all the washing and mending then. All of us women will be happy to cheer you on."

The football players were in a world all their own, pushing and grunting and grabbing at the ball in a disorderly clump.

"No kickin'!" Penny hollered.

"Better tell 'em not to bite too," Bob Harper said. "But I wouldn't get too close. What's your leg say about the weather, chief?"

Larrabee didn't hear him. He was seeing a game of three years ago, when he was running for the goal line with Anna cheering him on from the terrace. Three years that might as well be three hundred because Anna would never return.

"I say, how's the leg today, Nathaniel?" Bob explained to Penny that Larrabee claimed he could predict cold weather by the tingling in his once-broken leg.

"What? My leg says it's too cold for me to play football, that it'll always be too cold for me to play football. It's a young man's game."

"Well, you're plenty young from where I set," Penny said. "I turned fifty last June, you know."

"A mere pup!" Bob said. "I'm surprised you're not going out to Oklahoma with the rest of them young fellows."

"What young fellows?" Larrabee asked.

"The ones going to Oklahoma," Bob said.

"All right, Bob. But what for?"

"Don't you ever read a newspaper? They're giving away land out there. Sooner you get there, the better you get. Going to make a big race of it."

"So that's what he's up to."

"Who?"

"Caroline's man, Arthur. Caroline wrote that he was going up to Oklahoma in April. Hanged if I could figure out why a city man like Arthur would be going into the Indian Territory."

Penny had been watching the football players to make sure they obeyed. Apparently satisfied, he sat back down on his rocking chair and joined the conversation. "They talked the Creeks and Seminoles into takin' an allotment per head. Figgered that since the tribes were gittin' smaller, they could give each Indian a bigger parcel and still have plenty left over for settlement. I hear there's some good land in there. Grass and water."

For the rest of the day Larrabee contemplated the patchwork his life had become and thought of Oklahoma. The epidemic had set him and Bob back four months in the final payoff on the *King Payne*. The citrus season had finally picked up again in January, about halfway through, but much of the fruit had rotted for want of transportation—a boat or train—to take it out of the county. The canal company presumably was feeling the pinch too because they had made no further inroads into the southwestern quarter of the lake, but it would be early summer before the money started coming in again full force. That had made it necessary for Larrabee to put in longer hours than ever, and so he saw little of Flora, who split her time between the Wards and Preacher Bonds and his bride.

Flora was fully two years old now and walking—as Penny put it—fit to lead a parade. She asked often about her mother despite the preacher's explanation that her mother was in heaven with the angels. The girl seemed to have some notion that her mother was upstairs somewhere in the dim and quiet house, and she asked for her more and more and was harder and harder to calm when Larrabee was off to the lake for long days.

Larrabee was more deeply troubled by something else. He was starting to have dreams again about the wild man of Granada, of being locked in a dark boxcar with two voices, one friendly, one hostile, and not knowing which would prevail as he dozed during the long night. Then somehow that dream drifted into one in which the two voices in the boxcar began talking about Yellow Jack. And then someone else was in the car with him—someone with the small voice of an angel whom the voices addressed as Flora.

The end of February was unusually warm. In the afternoon wool became oppressively hot and itchy, and the little things people said suggested that the fear was already returning, the fear that Yellow Jack would pay a return visit.

During the long hours on the lake Larrabee hit upon a very simple plan. He had heard that Preacher Bonds and his wife would be taking the train to New Orleans for a Bible convention, and one mild Sunday afternoon in March he asked them if they would take Flora with them. He had already written to Caroline and Arthur asking them to take the girl with them to Oklahoma. They had replied with a hesitant yes since Flora was the closest Caroline could ever come to having Anna back. Larrabee gave the reluctant preacher $89 for the train fare and sent Caroline $10 for Flora's first month of expenses. The land rush was scheduled for noon on April twenty-second. Arthur was to go up alone and then send for Caroline, Edgar, and Flora once he had staked his claim. When Larrabee had saved up some money, when the *King Payne* was paid off and the business was stabilized, he would go up and help Arthur work the land.

He tried not to think about the improbability of Arthur's being able to farm. Arthur was from a small town in New York and apparently had never turned a clod or scoured a plow in his life, but everybody believed that somehow he'd make a go of it, and so Larrabee was able to put that doubt out of his mind.

Only after the arrangements were made did he make his plan known. On a Saturday night in the middle of March he came home from the lake, put Tuscawilla in the paddock, and walked over to the Wards' house. J.J. had worn out his dog, Mallet, trying to teach him to jump through a barrel hoop, and Flora had sat drawing stars on the terrace with a piece of chalk while Ray Polk and his three-year-old grandson told Penny about their adventures as the Devil's Millhopper.

Larrabee had cut through alleys and backyard hedges. As he broke through a gap in the privet, Mallet burst into a fit of barking.

"Ain't you goin' to go after him?" Penny said with disdain. He sat forward in his rocker for a better look at the dog.

"What'd you pay for that dog?" Ray Polk asked. "Does he always just set there and bark his head off like that?"

"Papa!" Flora had stood up, chalk in hand, to see who the intruder was. She started to run toward Larrabee but Penny caught her by the hand.

"You stay here now, Flora. You never know. Old Mallet might start thinkin' he's a dog, unlikely as that seems."

"Papa!" The girl was delighted. She had been asking about her father ever since lunchtime.

Penny scooped her up, sat her on his arm and carried her out to meet her Larrabee. "You've got one single-minded girl here. If you didn't come home I think she was goin' to come git you."

"How've you been, darlin'?" Larrabee took the girl in his arms and gave her a squeeze.

"Papa home!" she said with a gummy grin.

Mallet had finally given up his act. He was wagging his tail and sniffing

Larrabee's boots with fascination.

"What do you suppose he paid for that dog?" Ray Polk asked. "He won't tell me."

"I was figuring I might ask to borrow him," Larrabee said. "We could use a dog down by the landing. Somebody's been poking around down there at night."

The air was still cold around him and he smelled like pitch from breaking a pine branch on his way through the next yard over.

Penny grew serious. "Up to something you figger or just fidgetin'?"

"Well, I don't know, but they've been on the boat. We're going to have to start sleeping down there, looks like."

"You don't think that Howard's boys are up to trouble again, do you?"

"I guess it doesn't matter too much who it is. We probably should've had us a dog a long time ago. The boat's so far from the house."

Penny nudged Mallet with his foot. "You won't want this one. While you were down shooin' off the intruder he'd likely stay behind and raid your cupboards. He eats like a damn hog. I have yet to figger out what he's good for."

"He was jumping through the hoop real good toward the end there," J.J. said cheerfully. "I think he's starting to get the hang of it."

"A hound dog that jumps hoops," Penny scoffed. "Maybe we should train the cat to go a-huntin.' You're lookin' kinda glum there, Nathaniel. You really think you've got trouble on your hands?"

Later that night, after Flora had fallen asleep on the guestroom couch, Larrabee told Penny and Nelda about his plan. He did his best to put it in a good light, talked about what solid folks Caroline and Arthur were, how little Edgar would make a fine playmate for Flora, how fertile the land was in the Indian Territory of Oklahoma.

Penny lit his pipe and rocked by the fire for a moment. "And when do you figger to go out there?"

Larrabee sat down in a ladder-back chair. He was smoking the pipe Anna had given him for his birthday a year ago. "Probably not more than a few months. Once we get the *King Payne* paid off and start making some real money. Soon as we get settled down there on the lake I'll be going out."

Penny and Nelda exchanged glances that said something wasn't right.

"You know Flora hasn't been any trouble at all for us," Nelda said. "In fact J.J. has benefited from having her around. It's taken some of the rough edge off him." She laughed. "In fact it was *her* idea to teach Mallet to jump hoops."

Penny took his pipe from his mouth. "Well, now. See here, Nathaniel, why do you want to go traipsin' all the way up to Oklahoma? Everything you could ever need is right here. I hear the wind blows right mean out there all the time, with nothing to stop it."

Larrabee got up and emptied his pipe into the fire. "Penny, the wind out there doesn't have the yellow fever in it, and—truth to tell—I guess I'm still a westerner at heart. So as soon as I have the wherewithal I'll go up and get her. I just can't live with the thought of the yellow jack taking her."

None of them mentioned what was most on their minds—Anna. It was clear that what Flora needed most was a mother, but no one could expect Larrabee to marry only half a year after Anna's death. He didn't wear a mourning band on his sleeve, but everyone knew that his mourning had scarcely begun. Neither Penny nor Nelda saw fit to argue the point any further. Sending Flora away seemed a terrible and unnecessary thing on the one hand. But on the other, maybe it was best to let things settle for a while. Maybe once Larrabee felt that he could pull his life back together he would rethink things and bring her back to Florida.

No one could take issue with her traveling companions. While Preacher Bonds had yet to develop the oratorical power of his predecessor, he was likeable and tried hard to do what was best for the members of his congregation. He mentioned the Old Testament far less frequently than Preacher Williams had done, stressed forgiveness over retribution and punishment, self-sacrifice over righteousness. Which was why some people thought he was a weak, bland man, but the sympathy he aroused stirred their Christianity and led them to think kindly of him all the same. They questioned why he had found it necessary to cast all the way to Mobile for his bride, but seemed a trifle disappointed to find the reason so simple and pure. Victoria and Roland had been childhood sweethearts. She had followed him through confirmation classes. They had missed each other when he had left for Florida. They had exchanged letters. He had asked for her parents' permission to marry her. They had readily consented. The marriage had taken place on a sunny June morning in Mobile's largest Presbyterian Church. The couple had returned to Florida. The life of Roland and Victoria Bonds was an open book. She was pleasant-looking but not uncommonly attractive, spoke well without being openly opinionated. She was kind without being a pushover. Always neat, even in the warmest weather. When she shook hands her hand never lingered too long nor withdrew too abruptly. She had a ready smile and a light laugh. Larrabee could not imagine her ministering to the sinners in the absinthe-spattered alleys of the French Quarter. But at the same time, he couldn't imagine anyone more trustworthy when it came to the safekeeping of Flora.

Nonetheless, he was unprepared for the sendoff. He had imagined that he would hand Flora over to Victoria Bonds, kiss his daughter on the cheek, and fade gradually into the crowd at the train station so that the parting would not be too difficult for daughter or father. He had imagined a fair March afternoon turning chilly so that Flora would welcome being bundled up between the preacher and his wife on a warm train. He had imagined a pale crescent moon in a pale blue sky and the smell of wood smoke and sawdust in the air. He had imagined riding quickly back to the lake in order to get there before dark and having his thoughts preoccupied by threatening sounds from the boat landing.

None of it worked that way. The train was late and the afternoon muggy, so that the platform was full of hot, irritable people. Roland and Victoria Bonds stood patiently, waiting for their baggage to be tagged and loaded, none of which happened until the preacher practically grabbed a porter by the blue lapels and raised his voice in protest. Instead of being comforted, Flora was impatient and confused. She wanted nothing to do with the preacher and his wife. When they put her down, she clung to Larrabee's leg. He had left her so many times when she was asleep—for an hour, a day or two—that she was reluctant to let him out of her sight. For a time he kept her amused by making a gift of the little carved horse, but the longer they waited, the hotter it got and the more unruly the would-be passengers became. Flora was no exception. She tore off her sunbonnet and threw it onto the tracks. One of her shoes came off. While she wiggled her little foot, defying Victoria's efforts to put it back on, the other came off. Flora's face was flushed. She had a runny nose. She had to go to the bathroom. Larrabee was certain that the Bonds would turn her back over to him unless the train came by at once and snatched them all up.

When the familiar whistle finally sounded far down West Main Street, everyone was too wrung out to be happy. Flora was fit to be tied, but it was impossible to tell whether her agitation and tears were from the parting or simple heat rash. When the moment of separation arrived, Larrabee was almost too distracted to notice. Roland Bonds offered his warm, limp hand while Victoria wrestled with Flora. Somehow they got up the steps and more or less poked Flora through the door, and the long black train swallowed her. The conductors waved back the crowd and with a burst of steam, life jerked forward, courtesy of the Savannah, Florida and Western Rail Road.

Chapter 45

The long summer evenings were Dobkin Murray's favorite time of the year. The air was unfailingly mild and he could always get home from his rounds before dark. On Saturdays he was particularly careful to be in before sundown because gunfire made him nervous and Saturday night invariably included shootings and fistfights and vandalism. It was bad enough to be threatened by a member of his own race in his own part of town. The thought of being caught near the square while the saloons were overflowing with hot-blooded white boys made his hair stand on end. If a Negro—even a good Negro—got cornered in some drunken fray, the best he could expect was a twenty-dollar funeral with some heartfelt gospel singing. No one was going to come to his rescue. No one would be so foolish.

He had gotten past Mad Mary's house with an hour of daylight left and two half dollars jingling in his pocket. Come Monday morning he would stop during his rounds long enough to buy a pencil and pen set as a birthday gift for the missus. The fellow at the Sunrise Emporium had one he was willing to sell out the back door for six bits. He seemed to make a few extra dollars that way, selling to the colored when no one was looking. Dobkin figured the open-mindedness came from working with the late Major Dennis, who had been a steadfast friend of the Negro.

As he nudged his tired team past the cane mill he reflected that the major would be sad to see the state things had come to, what with the passage of the new poll tax. That had put just about every Negro voter out of business. Not that Dobkin was much of a voting man, but he had savored the idea of the right to vote, even if he was usually too busy or too tired to exercise it.

On second thought, he brought the team up to the cane mill and asked if he might buy a quart of syrup. In town he would have had to pay a young white boy to do the buying for him, but out here beyond the edge of town customs were lax enough to permit the transaction so long as he minded his place. He was careful to remove his hat before asking.

"Cost you a dime," the white proprietor said, to be sure that Dobkin had the money.

"Yes, sir. Yes, sir." Smiling to himself, Dobkin dug one of the half dollars out of his hip pocket. "Sure smells like fine syrup y'all are makin' today."

"You stay there. We'll git you some from the shed."

Dobkin watched a man feed cane stalks into a grinder powered by a mule that bobbed along in a circle. Nearby, under a tin awning, the cane juice was boiling in an iron tub.

The man came back and handed him a quart jar about three quarters full of dark, rich syrup. For a moment Dobkin considered mentioning the skimpy measurement but thought better of it. He smiled and nodded and handed over his half dollar.

"You enjoy that syrup now, y'hear?" As he made change, the proprietor was looking down the road, perhaps to see if any other customers would be coming at such a late hour.

Dobkin set the jar between his knees and headed the team toward town. His last stop for the day was at the Main Street Cafe, where the owner was friendly but a little fussy about his wood. Dobkin smiled at the thought of the man with the fancy name wanting fancy firewood. Mr. Bobby La Rue, burning only the finest oak and pine in the stove of his cafe! The oak and pine smelled the same and burned the same as what went up the narrow chimneys in the Porters Quarters, but for Mr. La Rue the wood was somehow a little bit better.

The fireflies were already out by the time Dobkin had stacked Mr. La Rue's wood. The kitchen had smelled of warm apple pies and fried chicken, making Dobkin was all the more eager to get home. But first there was the matter of dropping the team off at Ralph Pine's. The team got older and more tired every year but Mr. Pine charged him a few dollars more each year for its use. It didn't make any sense to Dobkin but he wasn't about to argue. Mr. Pine was vinegary enough with white folks. Somebody said he had killed a Negro one time before the war although nobody seemed to know just who or under what circumstances.

He brought the wagon up to the side gate and climbed down carefully with his jar of syrup. At first he wasn't sure that old Mr. Pine had heard him. He waited, wondering if he should call out, but after a few minutes, amid the sound of crickets and horses snorting and kicking in their stalls, he heard him coming.

"You're cutting it close, ain't you, Dobkin?" Mr. Pine always had that way of walking at you sideways with his bad arm hanging straight.

"Yes, sir, I reckon I is, but the night was so nice I stayed out a little late and stopped to buy this here syrup for the missus."

"You're a fool buying syrup when you can't even pay for your team."

"Yes, sir. I reckon I is. I'll be back in earlier come Monday. Monday won't be as nice as today, Mist' Pine! Couldn't hardly be!" He chuckled at his prophecy.

"You ain't been running these horses, have you? They look sweaty."

"No sir. I reckon they's just heated up a little on account of it being so fair out." He had to smile at that too. The very thought of those horses running was ludicrous.

He tucked the jar in the crook of his arm and made his way across Main Street over past Duke's Saloon, which, fortunately, had not begun to get noisy yet. He had been stopped over that way a time or two, poked at and shoved around a little by white men with whiskey on their breaths. Farther on, toward the Porters Quarters, a deranged Negro had shouted something ugly at him. Those were the risks of walking through town after dark, and he put some spring into his step, thinking about how good that syrup was going to taste in the morning and how sweet it would be to sleep past sunup in the morning, Sunday morning.

He was into the shadows, the old familiar black man's shadows beyond the saloon, when he felt the hand on his shoulder. It was a firm, powerful hand, not one to be resisted by a middle-aged man with a bad back and mashed fingers.

"I begs your pardon." Dobkin stopped, not knowing what else to do.

"Don't you beg *nothing!*"

Dobkin slipped from under the hand and peered into the darkness.

"Harmon?"

"Hello, Daddy. Did you think I was going to kill you?"

Dobkin dropped the jar. He stooped to pick it up, relieved to find that it hadn't broken. He brushed the sand off it.

"Son, I thought you was in the penitentiary."

Harmon Murray stepped from the shadow of a magnolia tree. "You thought right. They done sent me up for stealing Pinkoson's horse. Only I didn't steal no horse."

"They said you had it when they found you. How did you come by it if you didn't steal it?"

"I borrowed it, Daddy! I was on my way to bring it back when they found me. I was just out romancing my woman friend, that's all."

"From what I hear, you've got a heap of women friends, Harmon. Them women's going to be the death of you. Ain't but one is all I can handle." Dobkin chuckled. He was relieved. He figured his own son wasn't going to harm him.

"Didn't you hear that we done busted out of that penitentiary?" Harmon seemed angry and disappointed at his father's ignorance. "We was working on a turpentine farm and at quitting time I snuck my ax helve into my shirt and after supper everybody caused a ruckus while I busted a board loose. Then after dark we slipped out of there just like that." He spat through his front teeth. "Nine of us! What you think of that?"

"Have you seen your mother?"

"You reckon she'd want to see *me?*"

"Your mother's always your mother, boy."

"I killed me a man, Daddy. Didn't y'all know?"

"I sure hope it wasn't no white man."

"What if it was?"

"If it was they'll never stop hunting you and when they catch you they'll hurt you and string you up."

"They ain't caught me yet."

"You oughtn't to be around here, Harmon. If they find you, they'll kill you sure."

"Hell, Daddy, them white men don't know *nothing!* I've been here under their noses two, three days and me being wanted all the time. If they ast you, tell 'em I'm in Tampa. And you know what—it's the truth and they still won't find me."

Chapter 46

Bob Harper pulled at the oars and watched the V spread out behind the boat. The shots had come from somewhere between Walls' plantation and Arredonda. He was glad to be well out onto the lake.

"Sounds way too big for bird-hunters," Larrabee said. "But there's nothing else to shoot up there. Except two-legged critters."

"Don't you pay any attention," Bob told the two men in the stern of the dinghy. "These are civilized parts."

"*Too* civilized," replied the one with the red mustache and the deerstalker's cap. "That's why we came down to fish. We heard the hunting down here is about finished."

"Depends on what you're hunting," Bob said with a smile. "The wolves and the bears are gone but there's still deer and gators."

"I have no intention whatsoever to hunt gators," said the second man. He wore a fashionable sack suit buttoned just below the collar, a black silk tie, and an odd hat of black felt that looked like a derby with the brim turned up. He passed his hand over his shadow of a mustache—to see if it was still there, Larrabee thought.

"What does a man do with a gator once he's got it?" wondered the first man.

"Why, just about anything," Bob said with enthusiasm. "There's shoes and belts and billfolds out of the hide, baby rattles from the teeth, and from the meat—steaks."

"What would gator meat taste like?" asked the other in a way that suggested no one had been so bold as to try it yet.

"Good," Bob said. "Like turtle, only it's easier to get at."

"Well, I never," said the man in the deerstalker's cap.

"Y'all come a long way just to do a little fishing," Bob said. "Don't they have fish where y'all come from?"

"In *Manhattan*?" The man with the shadow mustache seemed to think Bob had lost his mind. "Now there's one we can take back with us, Jack. Fishing in Manhattan."

Jack smiled without ridicule. "Y'know it doesn't take all that long to get down here. We left on the Jacksonville express on Saturday night and got to Indian River by Tuesday. I have to say, I like it a little better up here though. The wind's not such a bother."

Everyone waited a while to see if the shooting would resume. The only sound was the swishing of the water over the oars and the rattle of fishing tackle.

"Where y'all staying?" Bob asked.

"What is the name of that place, Jack? It's a little boarding house."

"The Cozy Corner," Jack said. "Best grits you ever had."

The other New Yorker stuck out his tongue. "Damned if I can figure out what they're for."

Bob cut a sliver from his plug and tucked it in his cheek. "You've got to get the southern air in your lungs and drink the southern water and eat our southern beef before you can know what grits are about. You stay down here long enough and you'll figure 'em out. Ain't that so, chief?"

"I believe I'll take your word for that," Jack said. "I'll be confining my visits to the winter. It's healthier."

"We read about your fever last fall," his friend remarked. "Had to think twice about coming up this way."

"It's the ones who go in where the others are scared that get the spoils," Bob said. "And anyway, that wasn't last fall. It was the year before. It was in '88."

"I beg your pardon," the New Yorker said, realizing that he had touched a nerve.

They were about a half-mile off Walls' new pier when Bob pulled in the oars and suggested they put their lines in the water. The wind was on the rise from the north and so they drifted as they fished, which catered to Bob's inclination to be moving constantly. The sky had begun to slate over with cold-looking clouds. The crows and ducks seemed to fly with increasing urgency, but the boat was stable and the fishing good and so the men from New York and their native guides paid no heed.

Jack Tebo and his fellow New Yorker—Truman Wister by name—had nothing but praise for the charms of the county. They had run afoul of a cold north wind down on the Indian River and had ventured ashore to shoot ducks and snipe and found the so-called prairies to be man-catching bogs of waist-high water rippling with big snakes.

"You can forget all about it when we get back to the landing," Bob told them. "We'll fry up a mess of these bass and have a smoke up at the house. It's the kind of day a feller could get used to."

They followed the bass along the southwest curve of the lake, making stops to throw out their lines along the way, until they were not more than a few hundred yards off the pier of the Summerton farm. Here the fish congregated in a hole at dawn and dusk. They were early for dusk but Bob thought it worth a try.

"Had good luck fishing out here for fifteen years," he said, throwing his wrist and casting his line far out over the gray-green water. "Just using cane poles. We didn't have these fancy reels to tangle up."

Truman Wister had managed to snarl his line and picked at the tangle of loose ends. "I imagine the old-timers must've tipped you off about this hole."

Bob laughed. "Lake's only been here seventeen years!"

"How's that?" Jack Tebo felt the tip of his rod go down, but the tug was steady so he figured he'd caught a weed.

"Lake's a sinkhole," Bob explained. "Same as the Devil's Millhopper if y'all have been up there. Limestone gets saturated with underground water and when the water goes down, the limestone collapses and you've got a big hole. Sometimes they fill up with water; sometimes they just sit there. Millhopper's one of the biggest. This one's the granddaddy of 'em all."

"Then how'd it turn into a lake and why aren't they all lakes?" Jack was like a kid, full of curiosity and eager questions.

"Sink clogged up is all." Bob pointed off to the southwest. "Down there not so far from Oliver Park is the sink that fills or empties the whole lake. Ain't much to look at but it feeds this whole lake, nine miles by four."

Jack looked at Truman in disbelief. "Can you imagine nine by four miles of ground collapsing under Manhattan?"

Truman had finally gotten his reel unsnarled. "It may happen if they keep building those subway tunnels."

"That there real ice or artificial?" Jack watched Bob put another bass into the fish box.

"They make it up south of town. We don't hardly bother with your Yankee ice anymore." Bob smiled to show that he wasn't seriously trying to stir up regional animosities.

"I'm surprised these folks around the lake don't just send everything out by rail," Truman said. "Those refrigerator cars get it from here to New York in two days or less."

"They do send it by rail," Bob said. "We just take it the first leg. Up to the Transit Railroad at Bivens Arm. That's mostly what we do, six days a week."

"What you boys need is more folks like us to come down. Then you wouldn't have to haul anything but a few passengers and a box of fish. A good deal less trouble."

"I could get used to that," Bob said. "Trouble is we might run out of fish after a while if everybody in New York came down here with rods and reels."

They drifted around the hole until the sky began to take on an unwelcome darkness, not the towering thunderheads of spring and summer, but a thick, gray opacity that smelled of cold rain.

"What do you suppose?" Bob said. "Do we have enough?"

Larrabee was looking to the north at distant palm trees waving the pale undersides of their fronds at the sky.

The weather was upon them faster than they could have guessed. It was as if the rain had closed in from three sides, leaving only the south temporarily calm. Larrabee took over the oars and began pulling for shore with long, powerful strokes.

"If we go over there we won't likely get back by morning," Bob said.

"Unless we leave the boat," Larrabee said. "We can always come back for it tomorrow. That wouldn't be the end of the world." He gave Bob a knowing look.

"Where are we headed?" Jack asked. He was still winding in his line.

"We'll put in over there at Summerton's," Bob explained. "Long enough to sit out the weather. If it gets dark, we'll get you a ride back to town soon's it lets up,"

The rain caught up to them just as they connected with the pier. Bob threw a hasty clove hitch over a piling and helped the gentlemen from New York out of the boat while Larrabee put away the oars. Up the slope, on the porch of the broad white farmhouse, a dog started barking.

The men ran for a wagon shed and took cover between a hay wagon and a moldy old landau. Three black field hands had gotten there first. Having acknowledged each other with quick glances and nods, the two groups stood apart, watching the sky darkening and listening to the rain beat down on the shingles.

"In New York this'd be snow," Jack said. Nobody replied. They were trying to figure out how long they'd be stuck there. Truman Wister consulted his silver pocket watch. Bob looked at a figure running down the slope under cover of an oilskin slicker. It proved to be a boy about twelve or thirteen years old, slender, with a thin face and dark hair made almost black by the rain. He didn't bother to come into the wagon shed, just stood at the entrance and raised his voice above the rain that dripped down from his hat.

"My mother asks if y'all would care to dry yourselves in the parlor?"

"We'd be proud to, Jeremy." Bob didn't wait for a vote. He took off toward the house.

Larrabee followed and the gentlemen from New York tagged after him.

Larrabee had never been in the house, but he had a feeling that Bob had because he didn't bother to watch Jeremy for guidance. He seemed to know which door to take before Jeremy got there, knew where to hang his hat and which way to go without tracking on the carpets.

"Pretty place," Truman said. It smelled of pitch and rosewater and faintly of freshly ironed linen.

The long, narrow parlor overlooked the lake. Two corner windows showed that whoever built this house had ideas and money to spare. The worn carpet was of a rich Persian design. The tables and chairs had the simple, stately curves of the Queen Anne era, but the couch and ottomans were the plush and brocade of the post-war years, suggesting to Larrabee that the colonel had bought the furniture not long before his death. When Laetitia entered the room he calculated that she could not have been more than eighteen when she married the retired Confederate officer, for she was still in her thirties, yet she reminded him of the city women of his childhood. She wore full skirts that rustled when she walked, a shawl over bare shoulders, and those ringlets that had been the fashion twenty-five years ago. He had caught glimpses of her many times during his thirteen years on the lake, but this was the first time he had been close enough to speak to her.

The men rose and the New Yorkers introduced themselves with bows and courtly phrases worthy of Southerners.

"I fear you will be inconvenienced by our inhospitable weather," Laetitia said, gathering her shawl in her small white hands. "I hope you will accept the hospitality of our farm as compensation."

The men allowed that they would be happy to wait out the rain in the comfort of her house.

The wind picked up and the rain tatted against the parlor windowpanes as the men engaged in small talk with the mistress of the farm. She sent Jeremy to have two of the hands bring the fish box up from the boat, and the men came back cold and wet and delivered the cargo to the kitchen. Within half an hour the aroma of fresh bass and mashed potatoes drifted into the parlor, making the men smile and turn their backs on the lake.

"She is a Southern belle of the first order," Jack Tebo whispered after Laetitia had left the parlor to see about bed linens for the guestrooms.

Truman Wister started to pull a pipe from the hip pocket of his tweed jacket but had second thoughts.

"We'll hitch a ride back to the landing in the morning," Bob said, "and come back with the *King Payne* to pick up the dinghy."

"I don't know about you," Truman said, "but I'm not in any particular hurry. It can rain all day tomorrow for all I care."

"It'll blow over tonight," Bob assured him.

"What happened to her husband?" Jack asked, looking through the open door to see if she was returning.

Bob waited a long time to reply. "A chest wound from the war took a bad turn a few years ago."

"And she's been living down here all this time without a man? What a waste!"

Something in the way Bob looked at him put an end to the subject. They talked of fishing and shooting, of ducks and snipe on Hogtown Prairie and of hunting dogs.

The dining room table would have accommodated three times their number, and Larrabee thought it must have seen some of the county's most prosperous ladies and gentlemen in its day. The room was well kept, but the only indication of grandeur was the cut glass chandelier, apparently disused because of the effort required to keep all its candles lit. Laetitia sat at the head of the table with Jeremy to her right. She began dinner with a short, simple grace that she said while clasping Jeremy's hand. The talk was of rain and crops and the details of the day. The only time she mentioned her late husband was in the context of his clothes fitting Jeremy, who liked to wear his father's hunting jacket. When the topic changed to travel, Laetitia and the New Yorkers did most of the talking. Laetitia had been in England and France when she was a child. Both Truman and Jack had been to England, France, and Germany within the past three years.

"So little change compared to here," Truman said. "The great cathedrals and castles. Always abiding."

"There is one thing that abides here," Laetitia began, and when she had everyone's full attention she said, "Change."

Truman laughed. "Ain't it the truth!"

"Amen," Bob said.

"I say!" Jack raised his glass, which was filled with a cloudy red wine. "I propose a toast to change—that which is for progress!"

Reluctantly Larrabee raised his glass and joined the clinking of rims.

The two fishermen were quartered in a corner bedroom, Larrabee and Bob in the one adjoining. When they had stripped down to their britches and long underwear, Larrabee sat on the edge of the cotton-stuffed mattress, turned the light down, and sat watching the line of flame at the edge of the wick as Bob flopped onto the sagging bed.

"We've had a passel of rain lately, haven't we?"

Bob rolled onto his back and spread his hands under his head. "That's right."

"Kind of a stretch getting to that pier today though."

"I noticed." Bob's voice had a touch of irritation in it.

Slowly, Larrabee turned the wick down into the slot to see how far it would go before it snuffed out. "All that rain and yet the lake's down."

"That's right." Bob said.

Larrabee turned and looked at him in the amber light. "We're losing the lake, aren't we? How long have you known?"

Bob rose up on one elbow. "I wasn't sure till today. Craziest damn thing."

"Is it the Sink?"

"Most likely. The Sink giveth, the Sink taketh away."

"How long d'you suppose?"

"Before the last drop goes down? I don't plan to be around to see it."

Larrabee got impatient. "A month? A year before we're out of business?"

Bob fell back onto the pillow. "Who knows? She's only borderline navigable now in places. We'll lose our part of it first. From Walls on down."

"To here."

"You bet. *Now* is when we could use a canal. Except it wouldn't be good but for a few weeks." He chuckled. "How about that? We done paid off the boat and now we won't have a lake to put it on."

The bed lashings creaked as he rolled back over onto his side. Larrabee turned out the lamp. He fell asleep to the sound of the rain tapping on the window glass. Only once did he wake up in the darkness, when he heard Bob slip on his clothes and leave the room. A little later he heard two voices conversing in low tones, a man and a woman. But he had been dreaming of Anna sweeping sand from the kitchen steps, and he returned to that dream with no further thoughts about the couple talking in the night.

Chapter 47

The pianist was no Bobby La Rue, but that didn't matter because Duke's Saloon was so noisy that you could hardly hear the music anyway. Duke had a theory that even music you could barely hear had an effect on people. If it was jovial music they tended to be jovial and joviality was good for business. On this hot June night business was very good. Cow hunters had come in from the scrub and open range. Farmhands and clerks had developed a thirst for whiskey and beer that they had indulged until they could hardly tell the difference between the two. There were half a dozen saloons around town now, but Duke's was the best known and nobody had ever been killed there. Duke's belaying pin and sledgehammer fists stopped things from getting that far. He had a smile for the friendly, an arm for the drunk, and a roundhouse punch for troublemakers.

Larrabee and Bob had come in for a bittersweet celebration. They now owned the *King Payne* free and clear—or as Bob put it—high and dry.

"That lake is really starting to stink," he said.

"Drink this," Larrabee said, pouring him a second glass of Colonel Jim's Kentucky Bourbon.

"You know I hate this stuff," Bob said. "I got the devil's own hangover off it one time."

"Well, now it's the closest you'll come to floating." Larrabee poured one for himself. "Here's to the best chicken coop on the lake."

"The best damn chicken coop. Long may she set!"

"Long may she lay! Who was King Payne anyway?"

Bob put a hand on Larrabee's arm. "You mean to tell me you were on that boat all these years and you never even knew about King Payne?"

Larrabee shrugged.

"He was a Seminole chief. One of the biggest. Used to graze his cattle down there on the prairie—before it turned into a lake. That's what they used to call it twenty years ago—Payne's Prairie." He swirled the bourbon in his glass and took another drink. "It's a good name. Worth dusting off. You really didn't know all this time?"

"Back off, Bob. No."

"Well, you have got some lackadaisical way of drifting along! Some lackadaisical way."

Larrabee was glad for all the noise in the place. He didn't mind getting drunk as long as he didn't call attention to himself.

"What do you suppose we ought to do?" he asked at last. "To make our fortunes."

"Chief, our boat is rotting at a dry dock. That fortune's going to be precious hard to come by."

"Well, I have a parcel of land." Larrabee said absentmindedly.

"You don't."

"I do. Out west of town. Preacher gave it to Anna and me as a wedding present. He bought it from the church. We called it the Preacher's Patch."

"What kind of land is it?"

"God awful I suspect. Had a turpentine farm on it. Owned by John Howard. He lumbered it off before he sold it to the preacher. I've never been up there. Never had any reason to go."

Bob drained his glass and made a face.

"I'll sell you a half interest for $50." Larrabee broke into a smile. "Tonight."

Bob reached into his coat pocket and started counting bills. "Twenty-four dollars." He dug a little deeper and slapped a dime on the table. "And ten cents."

"Close enough!" Larrabee raked in the money. "You are now property-rich. Congratulations!"

They shook hands, knocking over the empty whiskey bottle.

Larrabee was glad they had brought Tuscawilla to the saloon. His original idea had been to try to sell her while she still had some cash value, but tonight her value was in getting the partners home. They stumbled along, one on each side of her, grabbing at her mane and saddle horn for balance as she worked her slow way down the crowded gas-lit street. By the time Larrabee had pulled off her saddle and bridle Bob was already asleep in the porch swing. Larrabee roused him and half-hauled him through the door and they made their way into the dark front room. Bob mumbled something about Laetitia and dropped onto the floor beneath the round table. Larrabee collapsed into the vast leather wingback chair.

Sometime in the middle of the night Larrabee woke up with a throbbing headache. He found his way into the kitchen and scooped a cup of water from the basin. He splashed his face and pressed his hands to his temples. He had forgotten how bad a hangover could be, had forgotten that he usually got his before morning. He knew that he could shake it by sunup if he could get back to sleep, but after what seemed half the night he was more awake than ever, so he decided to try to walk it off in the cool night air.

Someone was yelling down near the square so he wandered toward the quieter neighborhood to the east, past the stores and stables and into the narrower residential streets. The occasional dog barked from beyond a well-kept fence. Chickens and horses stirred behind fastened doors, but no one was on the street and Larrabee walked without worry until he approached the dark hulk of the Presbyterian Church. From a few houses down he heard the faint sound of the melodeon, the reedy, asthmatic parlor organ that Mrs. Polk had wrestled for a thousand Sundays.

Beyond the ten holes of his harmonica he knew next to nothing about music, but he knew at once that the organist was not Mrs. Polk. Instead of the predictable procession of bold chords he heard a continuous play of high notes against low in light, rapid patterns, almost like singing. It was so foreign that he didn't know what to make of it or even whether he liked it or not. He stood across the street, leaning against an old live oak and listened, thinking the church seemed to have developed a voice of its own.

The music stopped and he hurried across the street, tried the rattling front door and found it locked. He walked around to the side of the building, looking for a light and found none. The music began again, softer now and higher. He could hear the working of the pedals and the wheezing of the bellows, but the player pattered on without the least hesitation, certain of every note. A back window was open half a foot. Larrabee edged it up higher, jumped for a handhold, and hauled himself in.

As he eased along the side aisle the floor creaked softly beneath his feet, but the music continued. He could see the back of the organist in a trapezoid of faint moonlight and he stopped to watch the man's pale fingers crabbing their way over the keys. Suddenly the organist stopped and looked over his shoulder.

Both men gasped.

Larrabee was certain that he was seeing the ghost of Jared Penrod, thirteen years dead.

The man at the organ stood up and raised his hands over his head.

Larrabee looked at him and saw that this man was shorter and a little heavier than the boy who had died under the hooves of stampeding cattle during an ill-starred treasure hunt.

"Jesus, Joseph, and Mary," the man hissed. "Are you with the church?" He eased his hands back down.

Larrabee put his hands on his hips. "Nope. You?"

The man steadied himself against the melodeon. "Uh, not this one, no. I was just bending my fingers on the keys, don't you know?"

"You're not from around here."

"Not hardly," the red-haired man said. "I'm from Galway. That's in Ireland, my good fellow. Have you come to arrest me then?"

"No, I was just passing by."

"Oh, so an aficionado of Bach."

Larrabee thought the man was ridiculing him. "Well, mister, you just go on. But don't cross the sheriff. That's my advice. He has a mean temper." Larrabee's head was starting to hurt again. He was ready for more air.

"Tell me more about this sheriff of yours." The man followed Larrabee toward the open window.

"He's got a bad temper, especially lately. Don't let him catch you in here, no matter what you're doing, unless it's a Sunday morning."

The organist followed him through the window. Apparently it was the way he had come in. "What does this sheriff look like? Not by any chance a big galoot with mustaches out to here and a spotted horse?"

"That's him. Rides an appaloosa. I hear he's real proud of that appaloosa. Had it brought in from the Indian Territory."

"So. I think I know why he's cross. But never mind that. I don't suppose you'd know where a person might spend what's left of the night? Damned if that hotel didn't lock me out!"

Larrabee looked him over in the long shadow of a loblolly pine. Anyone who could play the melodeon that way couldn't be too dangerous, he thought, and talking to this strange person seemed to lighten the hangover.

"You can flop till morning at my place if you want to, but if you steal anything I'll have your head on a stick."

"How can I pass up such a cordial invitation? I'm much obliged, my good sir. Much obliged. And here's a hand on it. They call me Michael Kelly."

Several hours later, Larrabee woke up feeling much better. He sat for a while, listening to the squirrels chasing up the pines in the yard before he remembered the red-haired organist. He got up and found the Irishman sitting on the porch rail, trying to darn a hole in his sock.

The sunlight hurt Larrabee's eyes.

Kelly laughed at the sight of him. "And a good morning to you! Chipper as a lark I see!"

"Well you can be chipper for both of us." Kelly—that was the man's name. It came back to him now. "You wouldn't be so cheerful if you'd drunk as much as I did."

Kelly motioned with his needle. "Oh, but I've done a whole lifetime o' drinking already! So I'll not pass judgment on them that's still catching up." He put his shoe on and laced it. "A thousand thanks for the hospitality! And now I must be on my way."

Larrabee leaned against a column. "The sheriff after you?"

Kelly laughed and set down the darning egg. "Just the opposite! I'm going to church!"

"Let me guess which one."

"The very same! I'll ask if they have need of an organist." He tucked the sock in his back pocket.

"They do, but they've already got one for free."

"Now that's what gives the profession a bad name. Giving it away. Well, thanks again." With that the Irishman was off, whistling a tune as he passed through the gate.

Larrabee and Bob rode out to the Preacher's Patch on their tired old horses. Maude was blind in one eye and Tuscawilla's joints snapped as she walked. The morning was hot, and during their ride west they stopped at the cane mill for a drink at the pump. They found the men there armed and nervous.

"Looks like we're a little underdressed," Bob said as they dismounted. "What's the news?"

"Murray and his gang was through here," said the man at the grinder. He had an old cavalry pistol strapped to his hip. He wouldn't be able to fire fast but he could make a big hole.

"Murray who?" It seemed to Larrabee that even the horses were uneasy.

"*Harmon* Murray." The man spat. "He and some gallows bait. They've been robbing their way up and down the county."

"Got us yesterday," said the man boiling the syrup. He wiped his brow with the crook of his arm. "We didn't have no money so they took our watches and a horse. I wouldn't be on the road without a gun if I was you."

Bob and Larrabee pumped themselves a drink and continued west past isolated farmhouses, then cut north into tall, palmetto-choked pinewoods that went on unbroken for miles. Finally Larrabee stopped at a wasteland of fallen trunks and sprouting scrub.

"How much farther?" Bob asked.

Larrabee climbed down and looped the reins over the saddle horn.

"I hope you're not going to tell me—" Bob looked away and then back to see if there weren't some mistake. "We rode all the way out here for *this*?"

Larrabee flipped a possum skull with the tip of his boot. "It needs a little work."

Maude snorted and flicked her tail as if in disapproval. Bob dismounted and tied her to a sapling. "It's nothing but stumps! How drunk *was* I last night? Will you tell me that? How drunk was I? How much did I pay you anyway?"

"I don't know. Twenty, twenty-four dollars I think."

"Twenty-four dollars! You cheated me!"

"I sure did. I'm broke. I ain't above cheating a drunk."

Bob shook his head. "How low we have fallen. A fool and a cheat."

"Oh, simmer down. I'll give you your money back." Larrabee reached into his pocket. It was empty.

"What's the matter?"

"It's not there. The damn money's gone."

"Lay off. I'm not *that* big a sucker."

"That little weasel." Larrabee looked in the general direction of town.

Bob sat down on a pine stump and propped his elbows on his knees. "Who?"

"That Irishman. That damned Irishman. I told him I'd skin him if he took anything. Now I'm going to do it."

"Well, look at the bright side. At least we don't have anything else to lose."

It was a dreary place. Larrabee couldn't believe that the preacher had ever seriously planned to build on it. He began thinking out loud.

"We could put a cabin up. Have the stumps pulled by fall and put in some Irish potatoes and peas and beets in January. Nothing fancy. A start."

"Irish potatoes? I hate farming. It's hot and dirty and my head hurts."

"If he's still in town I'll get the money out of him if I have to carve it from his hide."

"Damn!" Bob jumped up, slapping at his rear end. "Damnation! Ants! Goddamn!"

They were quiet all the way back to town. Bob shifted uncomfortably in the saddle. Larrabee snatched at horseflies that settled between Tuscawilla's ears. Grimly they rode the sand track back to "the retired boatman's home" as Bob called it.

Larrabee left Bob to soak in the bathtub in the wood room and went looking for the Irish thief. The first place he looked paid off. The clerk at the Alachua Hotel remembered an unshaven red-haired man coming in about noon and noted that his bed had not been slept in. Larrabee went upstairs, sat down in the hall, and waited.

Eventually the thief came up the stairs whistling a skipping little tune. Before he could speak, Larrabee had him by the throat.

"No, no. No need for pleasantries." With his free hand Larrabee started pawing through the Irishman's pockets. "I'll just help myself—like you did."

"It was just a loan don't you know." Kelly coughed. His face was turning purple.

"What's this? Only twelve. What'd you do with the rest—put it in the collection plate?"

"I'd've paid it back, sure!"

"Sure! Well, I'm here to help." Larrabee knocked Kelly's head against the wall for emphasis.

"Here now. I'll get you the rest. On my honor."

"Don't make me laugh. Which room is yours?"

"Right here."

"Open it up."

Kelly straightened his collar and took a key from his coat pocket. He unlocked the door and Larrabee pushed him into the room.

"Sit there. On the bed."

The springs squeaked as the Irishman did as he was told. He seemed perfectly relaxed now, as if people roughed him up every day.

Larrabee started pulling drawers open without finding much—a change of clothes, a scarf pin. A Bible. He held it up questioningly.

"I never travel without it," Kelly said righteously.

"Try reading it sometime. What is it—the sixth commandment?"

"No, that'd be killing. It's the eighth you'd be wanting."

"What do you know—a preacher."

"No, but I did study for the priesthood. At the College of the Jesuits, Isle of Jersey."

"Travel light, don't you?"

"My own little vow of poverty!"

"Come on. Let's go."

"Where to?"

"Fennell. He'll make you work it off."

"Ah, but—"

The door burst open and two black men strode in. Each wore a pistol tucked into his belt. One was wearing fancy boots with pointed toes. He was tall and heavy, his face shining with sweat. The other was half a foot shorter than Larrabee, lean and muscular, with eyes that took in the room at a glance.

He wiped his boots on the rug. "Hello, Larrabee."

A drawer crashed to floor. "Hello, Harmon. I heard you were around. What are you doing here?"

Harmon Murray laughed. "You heard I been around! I like that. There's some folks know I've been around all right. Ain't that right, Mike?"

The Irishman sat cross-legged on the bed. "I'm here to tell you. We've put on many a mile together."

Murray looked over his shoulder. The hallway was empty. "What you doing with Mike, Larrabee? You trying to shake down our man?"

"For twelve dollars, of my own."

"You take some of Larrabee's hard-earned money, Mike?"

"Well, now, Harmon, I didn't know he was a friend of yours."

"What'd he do—hold you up, Larrabee?"

"He grabbed it out of my pocket while I was asleep. After I made the mistake of putting him up last night."

Murray laughed again. "You done trusted the wrong Irish son-of-a-bitch, Larrabee!" He pulled the gun from his belt. "What if I settle it by shooting one of you?" He pointed the pistol first at the Irishman, then at Larrabee.

"You may be reckless, Harmon, but you don't want to die. You shoot either one of us and before suppertime Fennell's going to be parading you through town in a box."

"What do we do with this one?" the other black man said fiercely. "He knows we're here."

"So what?" Harmon said. "He ain't going to tell nobody till we're gone."

"Where you live, mister?" the big man asked. "You got a house?"

"He has a house up that way," said the Irishman with a gesture toward the window. "A nice big house with just one other fellow in it. If he's still alive."

"Shut up, Mike." Harmon stuffed the pistol back into his belt. "What for you want to know about this man's house, Tony?"

"What for? We's risking our necks every time we comes into town if we meets in a hotel. We need a place that's private like."

"Yeah? Well, I think you're one crazy nigger if you 'specs to hole up in this man's house. He's a *white* man for God's sake! Well, ain't he? Ain't he white!"

Tony looked embarrassed. He glanced around the walls even though there was nothing to see but the roses on the wallpaper. "Sure he's white."

Murray had picked up the scarf pin. He pointed it at Tony and twisted it as he ridiculed him further. "So was you just spectin' to mosey in and out of this here white man's front door with all his white neighbors saying how-de-do, Mr. Black-ass Tony Champion? Is that what you 'spected?"

Tony folded his arms and glowered. "All right. Let it go, Harmon."

"You just let me do the thinking for this gang now. I got you out of the prison farm. You leave it to me to *keep* you out. You understan'?"

Tony Champion pulled a second drawer from the bureau and slammed it against the wall.

"Yeah, I understan'."

Harmon glared at him for a moment and then ordered everybody out of the room. Champion pounded into the hall and down the back stairway in his pointed boots with Kelly in his wake and Harmon following. Larrabee took his time going out through the lobby.

As he passed the counter he was surprised not to see the clerk lying dead on the floor.

Chapter 48

Larrabee was on his way to the barbershop when a postal clerk bounded toward him waving a letter.

"We've had this for a good two weeks thinking you'd come to get it, Mr. Larrabee. Seeing you just now brought it back to mind."

He hoped it was from Caroline with news of Flora. It had been the better part of a year since he had received any word from Oklahoma. But he didn't recognize the handwriting. It was a careful, flowing scrawl, not as elegant as Caroline's but more feminine.

He thanked the clerk—Iris Poinsett's younger brother—and sat down on the steps to read the letter. It was postmarked St. Julien, California. Larrabee thought that the clerk had made a mistake, but it turned out that the letter was from Martha. More than two years had passed since he had written to the missionaries of Anna's death, more than four had gone by since Martha, her mother and the preacher had pulled out of the station in Newnansville. He remembered *that* date well—April 18, 1886—the day he had raced after the coach to propose to Anna. He skimmed the rest of the letter. Martha didn't mention her mother and the preacher, simply said that she was coming home— coming home to see all the people she remembered as if from yesterday—Penny and Nelda, the Willises, the Poinsetts. She was coming home to see him and Flora.

He folded the letter and put it in his pocket, at a complete loss to know what to tell her.

Three days later he appeared at the depot with the notion that he would recognize Martha as soon as he saw her. He did not. Like Caroline, she had put on a few pounds, but unlike Caroline, she had grown prettier. Her hair was a rich brown, thicker than Anna's had been, and she wore it fashionably, rolled back like a crown and pinned beneath a handsome gray velvet hat adorned with pink and white rosebuds and a white satin ribbon. Her dress was a plain gray with black trim that accentuated her well-turned figure. Larrabee found himself blushing at the sight of her.

He helped her down from the car, released her gloved hand, and then they embraced. There was so much to tell, too much, and he knew that he would have to begin with Anna's death. He had rented a buckboard from Ralph Pine, and he tipped a porter a dime to pull Martha's trunk first and another dime to help him load it onto the wagon. He was glad that he could keep the talk to pleasantries and the procedures of leaving the station. It bought him time to think of what he was going to say as he headed the team toward the Wards' house.

She was so busy looking at the new opera house, fine new cottages, and a plush hotel, that she didn't question the route. When they reached the Matheson Store he stopped the buckboard and spoke of Anna's death. Leaving out any reference to John Howard, he told of his chaotic departure for Fernandina, of the epidemic, and what Nelda had told him of Anna's last days at the quarantine camp.

She lowered her head. Her long lashes fluttered. She brought a handkerchief out of her sleeve and touched it to the corners of her eyes. "That makes me feel suddenly empty."

He felt awkward trying to comfort the pretty young woman. He wanted to change the subject to something happier.

"When will your mother and the preacher be getting back?"

She watched a blue jay fly from the top of a live oak. "Nathaniel, I've made a mess of what I wanted to say and how I wanted to say it. I thought that coming here would be better than writing. I'm sorry. On our way back from China the ship foundered and they drowned."

He stared, not knowing what to say.

She went on slowly, as if writing down the words. "We were coming back together, the three of us, last spring. There was a storm. The ship hit a coral reef in the Sandwich Islands. Some of us were saved and some of us—" She put her face in her hands and wept.

He put his arm around her shoulder. It was improper, out in the open, in the bright sunshine like this, but in a few minutes he had come to feel a free affection for this girl—suddenly a woman—whom he had not seen for four years.

In his mind he saw the broad sinews of the Mississippi. Fourteen years ago its abrupt switchbacks and whimsical loops had confused him with its indifference to the destination of a boy rushing headlong from trouble. Now he realized that the meandering river had been nothing but a map of a life yet unlived, powerful, unstoppable, and driven by some inner force with a mysterious itinerary all its own.

Curtis came rumbling up the street with his wagonload of artificial ice, pursued by a vociferous dog. Larrabee gave Martha's hand a final squeeze and snapped the reins.

The reunion with Penny and Nelda was bittersweet. Once the four of them had buried their dead, they moved on to the concerns of the living. Martha had taken up the first position she could find once she got back to the United States. She was teaching Indians at an old mission school south of San Francisco. The salary was modest to say the least, and she had found herself increasingly restless as she held off writing to Larrabee of the fatal shipwreck in the Sandwich Islands. Finally she had obtained a leave of absence to return to her family in Florida with the news.

"Now that I'm here," she said. "It comes home to me that I *have* no family."

"*We* will be your family," Nelda insisted. "And then the two of you have to find Caroline and Arthur and Flora. Families are not meant to be torn asunder that way." She held J.J. to her side, but he wriggled free, retreated to the corner, and fidgeted with an arrowhead his father had turned up where a house was being built.

"Been plenty of changes since y'all left," Penny said. He got up and closed the window onto the terrace.

"One thing that hasn't changed is my beloved husband's intolerance for northern air," Nelda commented. "One day I'll take him up to my old stomping-ground in New Jersey so he can see what real Yankee weather is like."

"No need at all," Penny said. "Along about October I git the idea. Or I can just go set in Curtis' ice house." He smiled at Martha. "They make the ice right here in town now, you know. And most of the buildins are puttin' in gaslights. You'll see them things all around the square tonight."

Larrabee had been quiet all the while, trying to see in Martha the little girl he had once known. When he had last seen her—at the end of the fateful ride to Newnansville—she had been fifteen, and even that had seemed like a jump. He still thought of her as a toe-headed five-year-old, and here she was a woman of the world.

"I hope you can stay a good long time," Nelda was saying. "We can use a fresh young face around here."

Martha twisted her gloves in her lap. She sat lightly on the horsehair sofa, with poise her mother would have been happy to see.

"I don't know what I'm going to do. The session at St. Julien won't begin again until January. But I—"

"Then you have to stay with us," Nelda insisted. "We'll surely find enough to keep you occupied! This town is growing so fast. There's an entertainment of some kind just about every week."

Martha smoothed her gloves and clasped her hands on her knees. "What I'd like most of all is to go out on the lake again. After the cruel Pacific I'd love to see some friendly, familiar water."

Larrabee and Penny glanced at each other.

"Canal company's still running boats on Lake Santa Fe," Larrabee said. "From Melrose to Waldo."

Penny explained. "The big lake's gone down to a big swamp. The water don't come within five hundred yards of where it was." He tugged at his earlobe.

"I—uh, don't think of it as losing a lake. I think of it as gittin' back a prairie! During the war that was some of the best grazin' land in the state. They used to fatten the cattle up out there before sendin' 'em north on the train. They say the Spanish and the Seminoles both had cattle out there. The old-timers used to say that King Payne hisself and old Micanopy ran herds out there. In another year or two a feller will be able to do pretty well for hisself on that prairie."

Larrabee frowned. "You find anyone who wants to swap some of it for a piece of prime woodland, tell me."

"Beats me why the preacher ever bought that parcel," Penny said. "'Taint nothing but stumps and clay. He went to all that trouble to buy it just to git that turpentine still off of there, and then he was left with one shabby patch of ground. I never could figger out what he had in mind for it."

"Now we'll never know," Larrabee said.

A few nights later, Bob fell asleep the minute he sat down by the fire. The fat pine hissed and popped not a yard from his feet, but he slumbered on, his tobacco pouch open in his lap and his boots drying on the brick apron.

"Now there's a picture of a clear conscience," the Irishman said. He was playing solitaire at the round table. Larrabee noticed that he cheated.

"You ever spend a day digging pine stumps, Mike? They've got a taproot that goes halfway to China. Try pulling one up sometime and you'll probably sleep too—no matter what's on your conscience."

"Here now! I tried to give you your twelve dollars back, didn't I?"

"You tried to give me *somebody's* twelve dollars. One thing I'll say for you, Mike, you're resourceful. You ever considered going straight?"

The Irishman flipped over a red jack, tucked it back into the deck, and drew a card that suited him better. "Have *you*, Larrabee? We're all crooked in one way or another."

"But not all of us are running with Harmon Murray. He's headed for a noose."

Kelly was dismissive. "Oh, now, he hasn't done so much harm! Hoisted a few watches is all. The rest of it's just bluster."

Larrabee put his hand on the cards. "He's dangerous, Mike. I knew him when he was a kid and he was dangerous then. He liked to kill mice with a shovel. He's had all those years to work up to something bigger. You don't want to be with him when it happens. And you don't want to be with him when Fennell catches him."

Clearing the Preacher's Patch was worse than either Bob or Larrabee had imagined. They broke ax handles hacking at roots that seemed to have turned to iron. They sweated and swore as the thick stumps resisted the straining horses. Harnesses snapped, gloves wore out, hands blistered, and spring planting seemed more and more like a pipe dream. Horses and men dragged back into town, exhausted at the end of the day, seven days a week.

They tolerated the Irishman because he was cheerful and he liked to cook. He would disappear for two or three days at a time and then turn up as if he had never been gone. Not far behind followed rumors and reports of robberies and beatings. Gradually a picture emerged of a nine-member gang comprised of six Negroes and three whites led by Harmon Murray. Some of their names were known: Tony Champion, Alexander Henderson, and Michael Kelly.

At the end of January they broke into the Sunrise Emporium and stole three Winchester rifles, ammunition, and hunting knives. On their way out they smashed a row of mantle clocks and knocked off the stovepipe.

The next night the Irishman was sitting at the round table, doing a clumsy job of darning another sock and drinking whiskey from a tarnished silver flask. The cards lay scattered before him.

"Do not shake thy gory locks at me," he said to Larrabee. "I thought it was foolishness and told 'em so."

Bob had fallen asleep again.

"You're scared, aren't you?" Larrabee brushed an ember from the floor with the toe of his boot. "You'd better hope that when you're caught it's Fennell that does the catching. That way at least you'll end up at some nice safe prison farm."

Kelly spoke deliberately as if to overcome the slurring that came from drinking heavily. "There is no such thing, my lad. And no way out of my little circle of friends, short of a very, very fast horse."

Larrabee pulled up a chair and sat down. "Mike, how did a slippery little piano-player like you get mixed up with that bunch in the first place?"

"Oh, just on a little lark, don't you know? Damn, I'll get the hang of stitchery yet."

"A lark? Didn't you say you were a priest?"

"Ah, but I didn't take the orders. Can't condone a cloistered virtue, I told myself. That's Milton. Have you ever read—but I suppose not. Anyway, I went to sea. Sailed the world! Saw the many ways men live and worship their creator. There are so many different ways as it turns out. The irony, dear Larrabee, is that while seeing all those other faiths I seem to have lost my own. Isn't that peculiar?"

"I couldn't say, Mike. I guess I haven't traveled that much."

"Count your blessings. I was totally adrift—spiritually, I mean, as well as nautically. After seeing all those remote places—China and India and Australia—I found my way back to New York. I tried to think of the wildest thing I could do next. I was trying to break away from that set path of the priesthood, don't you see—and so I joined the army."

"Then I'd say you broke away all right."

"That I did! And damned if they didn't send us out to Arizona to fight the Apaches! Can you believe that? Me a failed priest, better at Latin and Greek and the ways of the sea than shooting at the screaming Apache!"

"You're lucky you didn't get skinned."

"Oh, I don't know about that. I made my own luck. After a year of eatin' dust I deserted and found my way to the wilds of the Wisconsin woods. Then—can you believe this—one of my old army chums recognized me one night in a lumber camp near Oconto so I lit out for Canada."

"What did you do for money all that time?"

"Lived off the charity of the land you might say. Would you judge me harshly for that?"

Larrabee sat back. "There's bigger thieves in wing collars and calfskin shoes right here in town."

"After freezing in Canada I thought I might actually settle down and live a righteous life. I took a position as an organist! Got myself a job at the prettiest little church you ever saw in the bosom of the Kentucky mountains."

"And started writing letters home."

"So cynical! *Tsk-tsk*, Larrabee! In fact, I had better in mind. I went back to New York, thinking in the back o' my head that I'd at last be going back to Ireland. Instead I fell into sending others on their way. It was so easy after the first time."

Larrabee thought back to waking up scared and sick on the deck of the *Belle Helene*. He wondered how an Irish priest would have gone about shanghaiing men from the streets of New York.

"That sort of informality was frowned upon by the magistrates," the Irishman continued. "They had some pointed questions when they apprehended me, but I slipped the loop with the cleverest ruse—I disguised myself as a *priest!*"

Kelly's coughing laugh woke Bob. He sat up in the chair and blinked at the windows. "It ain't morning yet I hope."

"Not by a long shot," Larrabee assured him. "We're just sitting up telling yarns by the fire."

"That's what it is, o' course," said the Irishman with a smile. "Doing the mending and spinning yarns."

On the first Sunday in February a cold rain fell. Out in the paddock Tuscawilla and Maude stood with their heads down and their bony haunches to the wind. Larrabee could see his breath when he went to the woodshed for more kindling. The Irishman was already out there, rummaging for pieces that would split easily.

"Like to make me homesick, a day like this," he said.

"You ought to go back," Larrabee told him. "Any way you can. I've got a little money. Enough to get you to Savannah. It's a start."

"Oh, *that* money!" laughed the Irishman. "I found that days ago!"

"I'm not pulling your leg, Mike. I want you to have it."

The Irishman grew serious. He tossed down a piece of kindling and put a hand on Larrabee's shoulder. "I bless you for your kindness, my friend, but it would be too easy. And anyhow, there's no harm done yet, and I plan to be on my way before there is. If you're worried that Fennell will find me at your house—"

"I don't care about Fennell. I'm telling you, Harmon Murray is a dangerous man. Dangerous for you, dangerous for everybody."

"That's right! My lad, do you remember where the Savior went after the crucifixion?"

"What's that got to do with it?"

"My lad, he went to hell. Don't you know your Apostle's Creed? He went to hell so he could know earth and heaven the better. So I must run with Harmon Murray to know the saints. The cloistered virtue—remember?"

"The money's in the newel post, Mike. People around here are scared, and when people are scared they're like cattle. It won't take much to set off a stampede. Don't be in the way when it happens."

Four nights later Kelly was drinking more heavily than ever. He lit his pipe from a lamp and went upstairs to bed. That was the last thing anyone remembered before the fire. Bob, as usual, had fallen asleep in the front room. In his stocking feet he ran four blocks to the fire station while Larrabee hauled the Irishman downstairs and did his best to smother the flames with a quilt. By the time the Little Giants arrived with Major Dennis' pumper wagon, the back bedroom that had once been the preacher's was spitting glass and dropping plaster. Larrabee backed down the stairs without any hope of salvaging beds, bureaus, or trunks, and fell over the Irishman, who was lying on the floor by the wicker chair. He grabbed him by the shoulders and pulled him across the porch and down the steps without taking time to be delicate.

Kelly started coughing, came to his senses, and blinked at the fire. People were coming through the pines, from the new houses. The Poinsetts rushed over from next door, Mrs. Poinsett in an old-fashioned bonnet and frayed sleeping-robe. Iris gaped up at the boiling smoke.

"Roof needed work anyway," somebody quipped.

Aware of the crowd forming, Larrabee pulled the Irishman to his feet and hauled him to the gate.

"You goddamned fool! And I was worried about you and your friends. Get out of here before I come to my senses and wring your neck!" He shoved him by the collar. The Irishman bounced off Dr Willis and stumbled into the street.

The Little Giants managed to save the house, but the preacher's room and the room Larrabee had shared with Anna were charred and open to the sun and rain. Bob and Larrabee spent the day boarding them up.

At midnight on Sunday, February fifteenth, a policeman walking his beat heard the sound of breaking glass coming from the rear of the Sunrise Emporium. Impulsively, he ran toward the noise. Someone fired a shot at him. He heard the bullet whistle past his ear and retreated hastily to safety behind a rain barrel.

Hearing the commotion from across the street, Dr. Philips came onto his terrace. Someone fired three shots at him. One shattered the window behind his shoulder and the other two just missed him as he dove for the herringbone brickwork of the terrace.

By daybreak Sheriff Fennell was riding his appaloosa at the head of a formidable and determined posse. They combed the entire town, white and black sections alike, for anyone who knew anything of Harmon Murray and his gang.

When Fennell started to threaten Dobkin, Mrs. Murray broke down sobbing so piteously that one of the posse saw fit to remind the sheriff that Mrs. Murray came from one of the finest Negro families in the county and was probably as horrified by Harmon's doings as anyone.

"I figger you'd tell us if you knew where he was, wouldn't you?" the man said.

"If we knowed where he was we'd be the first to tell you," Dobkin said bravely. "Just 'cause he's our boy don't mean we like his robbin' folks any more than you does."

Eventually the trail led them to Alexander Henderson. Fennell knew that he had broken out of the prison farm with Harmon and the others in 1889, and he knew that Jerome Ludlow had spotted Henderson down near the Kanapaha Moss Mill. Ludlow knew of a woman Henderson liked to see when he was in town. The woman hadn't seen Henderson, but she knew of another who had and was happy to tell them where to find her.

Fennell and his men had no interest in the other woman, but they were very interested in her companion, who was still pulling his suspenders up when they broke in on him.

Alexander Henderson poked his hands at the sagging ceiling and promised them the moon if only they wouldn't shoot him.

Sheriff Fennell put his .45 in the holster. "We have no intention of shooting you, Alexander, as long as you tell us what we want to know."

"I don't know where he is," Henderson protested. Even though his nose was running, he kept his hands up high.

"You can have plenty of time to think about it, Alexander. We have a nice big room for you over at our hotel. Or we can let you go. What do you think of that? We get what we want and you get what you want. What do you say, Alexander? Ain't no good going to come of letting Harmon run around like that. Sooner or later he's likely to get into some real trouble. We put him behind bars and he won't likely be out for six to ten years. You can do a heap of traveling in that time, can't you?" He was not six inches from Henderson's ear.

"He'll kill me sure if he finds out I tol' on him."

"Not if he's locked up. What do you say? Lock him up—or lock you up?"

Henderson looked nervously from face to face in the room of angry white men with loaded weapons. He lowered his eyes, stared at his bare feet and began speaking in a fast, quiet monotone.

"He's at a place near the F.C. & P. Depot across from Porter's warehouse. There's a girl do mos' anything a man want. It's a green house with a magnolia tree in the front yard. They was going to meet up there. He and Tony and the Irishman."

Sheriff Fennell took his gun out and placed it against Henderson's temple.

"Truth?"

"I swear."

"Then go and sin no more, Alexander." The white men hurried out of the room, upsetting furniture and nearly knocking the front door off its hinges.

They were just saddling up when Tom and Barkley Duforge joined them.

Sheriff Fennell reined in his appaloosa. "Hello, Tom! I was hoping you'd come join us this morning! Looks like we're about to get our man."

"If you do, take him seriously," the former sheriff said. "Last night the gang killed a man—a farmer named McPherson—down at Millard Station. Seems he had testified against some of 'em for robbing him. McPherson's wife and daughter were about out of their minds according to the neighbors. Said the gang burned the barn and then came back for McPherson and said they were going to do what they wanted with the women. Then they took off again."

The sheriff took it in, then put his heels to the appaloosa's sides, and the posse thundered through the narrow, oak-lined streets to the depot. The green house with the magnolia tree appeared to be vacant. One of the men went forward and peeked through the windows. He came back and reported that he had seen only a wrinkled old black woman sewing a sheet.

"Well, they say sometimes the old ones is the best ones," quipped a rider named Tim Darling. They took up a position behind the warehouse across the street. After a long discussion in hushed tones, the posse came to the conclusion that the gang was running late because of the attack on the McPhersons.

"If he's headin' for that house to get hisself straight, sooner or later, he'll be here," Darling said. "Sooner or later he'll come riding down that road."

The afternoon was raw and wet and the men of the posse were rubbing their hands for warmth when they heard the hoofbeats. Darling reported from the roof of the warehouse that he had seen three riders—two Negroes and a white.

"That's the winning combination," Fennell said. He raised his .45. The posse fanned out behind trees and fences, waiting.

Before they were quite into position, one of the horses hidden behind the warehouse whinnied, a shot rang out, and the three desperadoes jumped from their mounts and burst into the green house with wood and glass splintering all around them.

"We need some men over there on the double to keep 'em from coming out the back," the sheriff said. He jumped on his appaloosa and broke for the road. The three outlaws were regaining their wits. A bullet slammed into the appaloosa's neck and Fennell and his horse crashed into the mud. The sheriff kicked himself free from the thrashing appaloosa and ran back toward the warehouse, shooting all the way as the posse laid down covering fire that took out both front windows and a flowerpot.

Tom Duforge turned to Tim Darling as he was reloading. "I'll bet your sewing girl in there has about filled her drawers by now."

"I think we nicked Champion," Tim said. He dropped a bullet in the mud but didn't stoop to look for it. "We had 'em where we wanted 'em for a minute there."

"We ain't doing so bad now," Tom replied. He was pumping bullets into his rifle.

"You've got one of them damned Henrys," Tim said.

"Load it on Sunday and fire all week." Tom smiled. "That's what they say."

The smoke was so thick that nobody could see much, but the lawmen continued to pump away at the house until Sheriff Fennell led a small charge across the street, past his dead horse, toward the back porch. There was very little to stop them. They ran from tree to tree, arriving breathless in the back yard, where they took cover behind an outbuilding and the remains of a split-rail fence.

"Just keep up your fire," the sheriff said. "We've got 'em outnumbered."

"We'll shoot the goddamned place off its foundation if we have to," said a man with a powder burn under his eye.

When their fire had gone unanswered for close to five minutes, Barkley Duforge ran crouching to the back door and kicked it in. He fired three shots into the house and then went in as the men in the yard ran forward. Inside he found a black man sitting on the floor with his hands up and a red-haired man crouched against the wall with his head wrapped in his arms.

"That's him!" barked the man with the powder-burned face. "You got Harmon Murray!"

Sheriff Fennell came in waving his .45. "The hell you did. The son-of-a-bitch got out the back before we even crossed the road. That's Champion. Looks like we creased him all right. Stand up, boy."

Tony Champion stood up just as Tom Duforge broke down the front door.

The seamstress was making a commotion about being stuck under the bed. The sheriff kept his back to the wall. "Your son's a hero, Tom. He was the first one in here."

Tom's smile was brief. "Glad I didn't see it. Where's Harmon?"

Fennell motioned with his gun. "Out the back. But we'll get him. In the meantime, we got these two." He pointed his gun at the kneeling Irishman then poked the barrel in Tony Champion's throat. "Y'all know anything about a killing down at Millard Station last night?"

At sundown, when Larrabee and Bob came riding into town sore-shouldered after long hours of chopping roots and hauling stumps, the town was full of talk about the capture of two members of the Murray gang—Tony Champion and Michael Kelly. Men who were usually even-tempered were talking of quick justice. Why go through the motions of a court trial they asked. Why wait for Murray's gang to escape again? Why not show Harmon Murray what we'll do to outlaws who terrorize our towns and farms? If they struck at Millard Station what's to stop them from doing the same thing here, to us and our wives and daughters? Why give these vermin another chance to ride out and terrorize and kill?

Larrabee and Bob brushed the horses down and fed them their can of oats, then washed off under the backyard pump. Larrabee had long since sold the chickens, so instead of their settling sounds in the hen house he heard nothing but voices through the trees. It was as if the woods themselves were buzzing with news of the Murray gang.

"Guess we're on our own for dinner tonight," Bob said.

Larrabee looked up at the blackened corner of the house. "Guess so."

"He was hell-bent to get himself killed, you know. Every now and then you run into somebody like that. I knew a feller on the lake that threw himself at a gator. Just like that. No reason for it."

Late that night Larrabee got up from his place by the fire and walked down to the jail. It looked particularly solid and inviolable. He knew that Fennell kept a dog in the yard to warn of anyone approaching, so he went to the heavy iron-studded door and, over the barking of the dog, told the deputy that the Irishman had stolen some money from him.

"Then you can kiss it good-bye," the deputy said through the slide-window in the door.

"If he tells me where it is, I'll give you half," Larrabee said. "I'm no robber. I'm just a citizen trying to get my money back."

The deputy squinted at him. "You're Anna Newhouse's husband, ain't you?"

"That's right."

"I was real sorry to hear about Anna. I knowed her at school. We used to attend at that place over there behind where May Dutton's is now. I hear that schoolhouse ain't even there no more." In an awkward gesture of friendship the deputy stuck his hand through the high window. "I'm Richard. Richard O'Dell. Whole passel of us went to that school for a time. I remember we put a coral snake in the schoolmaster's desk one time. Didn't that cause a ruckus! You want to come in? I'll hold the dog back. Your man ain't likely to tell you nothing though. Ain't neither one of 'em said nothing all day."

The two desperados were in the same upstairs cell. Nobody had bothered to bandage the gunshot wound in Tony Champion's arm and his shirt was caked with blood. One of the Irishman's eyes was purple and swollen shut. He sat on the floor with his back to the wall, going through the gestures of smoking his pipe even though he had no tobacco and no matches.

He looked up when he saw Larrabee but said nothing.

"Git what you can out of him," the deputy said. "I'll be downstairs."

"Tell me another story," Larrabee said to the Irishman. "This time tell me about a farmer at Millard Station."

Tony Champion jumped at the bars. "I killed him! I said I'd kill him when I went to jail and I kep' my promise. We didin't even take nothing off him. Just killed him. And glad to do it!"

The Irishman lifted his head and took his useless pipe out of his mouth. "Shut up, Tony. You do have a way of going on." He got up and walked to the bars. "Larrabee, did you by any chance come across my Bible when you were tidying up? Truth to tell, I could use it about now."

"I didn't see it, Mike. I'll look."

"I'd count it a favor."

"If you didn't kill anybody maybe it won't go so bad for you."

The Irishman shook his head. "Back to the old turpentine farm? Oh, I shouldn't think so. I have observed that the authorities tend to get riled up when one consorts with killers—unless, of course, one is in uniform."

Tony Champion's arm was starting to hurt. Wincing, he went to the back of the cell and pressed his head to the wall.

"Larrabee, there is one more thing you can do for me."

"Whatever I can do."

"Remember my name. It's not Kelly. It's Kierens. Hard to remember for an American perhaps, but a fine old Irish name. Can you remember that in case someone should come looking for me?"

Larrabee repeated the name, a strange name he thought, but it seemed fitting that a man so full of stories would make one of his own name.

"What do you think is going to happen, Mike? Are they treating you all right?"

"Yes, all right since I got here." He touched his bruised eye. "I got this on the way in. Things have been pretty quiet and gentle since. Well, and at least I have nothing to fear from Mr. Harmon Murray now that he's on the outside and I'm on the inside 'stead o' the other way 'round."

"If I find your Bible I'll bring it tomorrow night."

The next day was remarkable for what Bob and Larrabee were able to accomplish at the Preacher's Patch. It was as if they had finally achieved a well-oiled rhythm in the work of pulling pine stumps, because root after root gave in to them and the patient team of Tuscawilla and Maude. Bob straightened his back, put his hands on his hips and said, "You know, for the first time I can actually imagine this place as a farm. Mind you, I druther it was a lake, but we'll yet have time to put in the beginnings of a good vegetable crop. Hell, we can plant it all in corn and have us a crop out in May if it don't rain the whole time!"

"What do you figure," Larrabee asked. "Another week of pulling stumps before we can finally get down to business?"

"Brother, the way I feel right now, we'll have 'em all pulled by Friday, put the cabin up on Saturday, and take Sunday off!"

They were still in good spirits when they got back to the house. Larrabee had looked twice for the Irishman's Bible, had given up on that, and was looking for one Preacher Williams might have left behind. Finally he decided to see if Preacher Bonds didn't have one to spare. Absent-mindedly he walked toward the church instead of to the cottage inhabited by the young preacher and his wife. By the time he reached the square, he began to hear dogs barking and men shouting excitedly. He was crossing the street toward the darkened church when he was nearly knocked down by someone running toward the noise, jacket aflutter.

"They've got 'em!" the man yelled to an unseen companion. "They've got 'em out of the jail!"

Larrabee ran after him, not knowing what to expect, not knowing exactly what the man meant. Had Harmon Murray and the rest of his gang come back into town and sprung Tony Champion and the Irishman? As he ran, he realized that the voices were saying something else.

He found Richard O'Dell sprawled on the steps of the jail. Blood ran from his mouth but he was still breathing. He sputtered through broken teeth.

"A nigger and an Irishman. I never thought I'd take a pounding for the likes of them."

The mob was shadowy. Many of them were wearing handkerchiefs over their faces. They drew together as something rose above the fury of arms, hands and, sticks, and then pulled back as it fell into the thick of the men shoving their way down the street. As Larrabee caught up with them he saw, in the yellow flicker of a gaslight, the contorted face of Tony Champion. A few paces ahead, bucking amid fists and ax handles, was the battered Irishman, fighting with every breath.

Someone shouted in Larrabee's face. "One thing's sure—they ain't getting away this time!"

"Damn right!" said a man with a cut on his forehead. "They'll be lucky if they make it to the tree!"

"If he bites me again, they won't." said a third. "I'll pound the son-of-bitch right into the dirt!"

Larrabee ran to the front of the ungainly procession and grabbed at an arm to stop the men in the lead. An elbow caught him in the eye. He struck back, knocking the man beneath trampling feet. The crowd came on and he swung hard, connecting with a loud knock that doubled over one of the masked men. He saw a bottle coming at him and swung his arm to intercept it. Something cracked him on the forehead.

When he came to, he could still hear the mob but they were well down the street, no more than a dim roar in his ringing ears. He picked himself up, shaking his head to get his hearing back, and tried to run toward the noise, but his feet seemed caught in the mud, his legs heavy. He dragged himself to an iron trough and pushed his face into the cold water to regain his senses. He was moving faster now, but still unable to catch up with the mob as they crossed Liberty Street east of the square. He stopped and leaned against an orange tree to regain his breath. His lungs hurt and he was dizzy. He forced himself onward, but the mob was farther and farther ahead. He felt his way from tree to fence to light post until there were no more light posts and no more fences—only live oaks, half-lit by distant torches. He stopped for breath again, leaning heavily on the rough bark of an old oak. He sat down for a moment, only a moment he thought, then pulled himself up and moved on.

When he got up, the mob was far off and the dogs had stopped barking. He thought he must have lost his way somehow in that moment of rest beneath the oak. And then he saw them—the two long forms dangling from the outstretched arm of a giant tree. He thought at first that this was one of those spectacular oaks whose ancient branches hung almost to the ground, but as he came closer he saw the shapes better, saw the unnatural perpendicular attitude that made them stand out from the graceful curves of the moss-draped limbs.

The forms that had been so different from each other in life were remarkably similar in death. At first glance, the heavy-set black-skinned Tony Champion was almost indistinguishable from the slight, ruddy-faced Irishman, for both of their faces were now puffy and purple, their tongues black and hanging, their height and weight indeterminate. Their swollen hands were clumps behind their backs.

It was by their feet that Larrabee was first able to tell the two apart, for Tony Champion's fancy pointed boots swayed rhythmically at eye level, whereas the Irishman had lost a shoe and the big toe of one foot poked thorough a hole in a badly mended sock.

Chapter 49

John Howard turned sharply. The explosion had caught him off-guard.

"Really, John, you shouldn't be so jumpy! It's Independence Day—you should expect fireworks!"

Jane had spoken affectionately, but he didn't like being patronized. "In case you hadn't noticed, this is still a dangerous town. It's not always as harmless as fireworks."

She waved at a passer-by, a young man she had seen in the post office. He seemed to look at her in a special way. "Oh, now it's been fairly quiet for several months. Unless you make it a point of frequenting the square on Saturday nights."

"I'm glad that you feel so secure, but Harmon Murray, for one, is still out there. He killed a man in Fernandina the other day, you know."

She turned to him and shouldered her parasol. "No, I hadn't heard."

"Well, he did. Apparently it was a man who had testified against him, helped send him to the work farm. Now, I haven't testified against him, but I am in line to press charges for the break-in at the store last winter. Not to make you feel insecure, of course."

"You still think like a poker-player, don't you, John? Always ready to play the big card."

He pointed to some boys hunched at the edge of the Courthouse lawn. "They're about to set off another one. Let's see how brave we can be."

"At the rate he's going, they'll catch him, and I doubt that he'll live to see a day in court."

John Howard smiled and tipped his summer straw hat. Mr. and Mrs. Dutton were passing by in the finest landau he had ever seen. He thought they must have had it brought over from France.

"You're very bloodthirsty, my dear."

"What would be the harm, John? It would save all the expense of a trial."

"If you're talking about another lynching, don't. Lynchings are a blot on the community. They're primitive abominations. They do more harm than good."

"I swear, John, half the time I don't know what to expect from you."

Howard shook hands with a passing city council member. The square was so crowded that he was tempted to open the Emporium.

"You don't see a man like Dutton clapping his hands with glee at a lynching. That's because he knows how to work with the institutions. Henry Dutton *has* done pretty well, wouldn't you say?"

"We've been through that. I only said that I wanted a carriage that doesn't leak in the damned downpours."

"Such unladylike language! I'd say that by this time next year you'll have your carriage. If things keep going as they have been."

She gave him a brief, slightly improper hug. "I find this charming beyond words. You, a legitimate shopkeeper! Actually leading a stable existence."

"It so happens that the money in shopkeeping is getting to be passable. I don't mind selling hardware if there's money in it. Or corsets for that matter."

"Now, now. You'll make me blush."

"That'll be the day."

"To what do we owe these sudden profits in hardware?"

"To two things, my fair inquisitor. One little, one big. The little one is the rush of northerners into the county, a good steady increase now that we've put the plague behind us."

"The yellow fever."

"Of course. Let's not dwell on it, all right? And the other—the big thing— is phosphate. There are mines springing up all over the county. That's why Dutton opened his bank in the first place—to keep up with all that cash. But now the real stampede is on. People looking for it and people finding it. Between them they create a damned fine demand for hardware. I never would've thought such a fortune could be made on plain picks and shovels."

"But the real money is in phosphate, isn't it?"

"Don't goad me, my dear."

"I'm not. I'm testing you. If you were to gamble everything on phosphate or anything else, I think I might leave you."

"Then you're likely to be around for a long time. It takes money to make that kind of money. And we don't have it, not yet."

"It's hard to believe phosphate's worth anything. It looks like ordinary chalk."

"If so, it's chalk that turns the worn-out wheat fields of Europe fertile again. Henry has the Germans to thank for that landau of his."

Because the Fourth fell on a Saturday, the celebration combined the intensity of a holiday with the crowding of market day. All afternoon and into the night the air was filled with the sharp pops of firecrackers and the laughter of mischievous boys. The square was filled with picnickers and loungers, dogs and horses and stray chickens and hogs. All around, the bounty of the countryside was evident—early corn by the wagonload, bushel baskets of string beans and squash, and the biggest watermelons anyone could remember.

At night the Duttons threw another of their magnificent lawn parties. The house was stunning, gas-lit in every window of the new round tower, festooned with red, white, and blue bunting on the second-floor veranda, illuminated to the gables. On the front lawn a new bronze cupid sprayed water heavenward from a shepherd's pipe. Gracing the lawn further were a sundial and a fluted birdbath. Even though he lived next door, Howard hardly recognized the place.

Dutton looked positively regal, Howard thought, receiving guests in the gazebo formed at the junction of two shaded porches. He stood tall and straight, his thick white hair and dark brows prominent above the heads of the party-goers. He wore a fine linen suit, a pale blue silk cravat with a ruby stickpin, and a simple upturned collar that reminded Howard of a priest. When the conversation turned to Dutton's days with the Eighth Vermont Infantry and his sharpshooters at the Battle of the Cotton, Howard drifted away and fell into a conversation with an attractive brunette named Martha, Martha Newhouse, but it was broken off by a meddling drunk, B.F. Jordan, his former partner in the canal company, who spoke without being aware that his host was within earshot. "Feathered his nest right well, hasn't he? How come we didn't beat him to all that phosphate?"

That night, when he came upstairs to bed, Howard found Jane at the window, looking down at the Dutton's yard, where the Japanese lanterns were being lowered and extinguished. He put his hands on her shoulders and watched with her. "Dutton always has a theme, doesn't he? What was the theme of tonight's little get-together?"

Without taking her eyes from the lanterns she said, "I want you to marry me, John."

He removed his hands from her shoulders, took off his tie and pitched it on the bed. "I suppose tonight's theme was—let me see—Union. You know, by next Independence Day, we *will* be legally married."

She folded her arms. "John, a common-law marriage is more an accident than a choice. I want you to drive me to a church or a justice of the peace—I don't care which—and say the marriage vows with me."

He reached for a cigar but didn't have one handy. "I'm flattered, of course, that you want to yoke yourself to me in perpetuity, even though I don't own a crumb of phosphate."

At the same time, phosphate came into the conversation a few blocks away, at the Wards' house. Penny had asked Bob and Larrabee about their progress at their farm.

"Dismal," was Bob's reply. "Now that we've finally got all the stumps out, we can't get anything to grow. The potatoes we planted in June have hardly broken the surface and the sweet potatoes and cow-peas we put in last month might just as well not be there."

"What if you put some of Dutton's phosphate on there?" Penny wondered. "Might not have so much to lose tryin' it."

Larrabee pushed the window up the last inch. "That's for sure. I'll tell you, Bob still thinks I cheated him selling a half share for twenty-four dollars. And I'm beginning to think I *did*. Doesn't seem to be much but sand and clay out there once you get the trees and stumps off. And the mosquitoes are killers."

"You gittin' the cabin up all right?"

"We were getting eaten alive, so we up and bought a tent from the Guards. Now we don't seem to care so much if we get a cabin up. Just lazy I guess."

"I can see by your hands that you ain't lazy, Nathaniel. You just could use some luck."

"And maybe some phosphate."

"And maybe some phosphate."

Nelda and Martha and the preacher's wife had gotten into a conversation about letters. The preacher's wife wrote home to Alabama once a week and went up on the train every Thanksgiving. Because she had become homesick, Martha had resigned from her position in St. Julien and was helping Nelda to sell hats. But in her spare time, through a letter-writing campaign, she had been trying to find Caroline and Arthur in the wilds of Oklahoma. The last letter she had seen from Caroline was the one Larrabee had received just before Arthur had left New Orleans for the land rush. "I have a niece I've never even seen," she lamented. "Why haven't they written?"

Larrabee tried to put her at ease. "Maybe the same reason I haven't written. Too dog tired at the end of the day."

"We should go looking for them," Martha said.

Penny looked askance at that. "Now, Oklahoma may not be as big as China, but there's a parcel of country out there and you don't have any way of knowin' where they're at till they tell you. It'd be like ridin' from Pensacola to Tampa looking for some cow hunter. Sometimes there's nothing a body can do but wait."

Nelda offered more constructive wisdom. "Martha, you would be more settled if you found yourself some nice gentleman. I admit there don't seem to be many good ones around, but surely there's *one* in this town."

In the evening Larrabee walked with Martha to the house on Magnolia Street. "It hasn't gotten any better since the fire," he told her as they passed the Courthouse on their way toward the armory. "I'm afraid the rot's going to get it if we don't fix it proper. But that would take some real money."

"I don't want you to feel bad about the house," she said. "These things happen. Remember the Arlington?"

Indeed, they were looking at B.F. Jordan's store and the armory that had been built on the ashes of the great hotel.

"Anna would be sad to see the place like this," he said. "I haven't even had time to keep the garden up. She was so proud of that garden."

"Things change. We can't be living other peoples' lives. Does that sound cruel?"

"I don't know. I just wish I hadn't let the garden go."

The gate leaned heavily on its lower hinge and gave a rusty squeak as they passed through the scruffy yard on the uneven brick walk. Cracked as the shingles were, Larrabee had trouble believing that fifteen years had passed since he and Penny had laid them down on a couple of hot August afternoons. Back then the house had overflowed with the voices of children and the laughter of boarders. Now it was a sad, lonely place, reminiscent of the dead.

Larrabee had kept the privet under control by sheering the top off every few months, but it had gone wooden and ungainly. The gutter sagged over the porch. The gray paint was mostly gone from two of the repaired steps. Sandspurs sprouted along the walkway. Weeds poked up between the bricks. An empty whiskey bottle lay under an azalea. It seemed that the hot July sun had attempted to burn it all away. The whole ugly scene reminded Larrabee of the ruined Mississippi estate he had seen years ago. He tried to remember its name.

Martha changed her mind about going in. Maybe it was the swallows outlined against the watermelon red of the evening sky that made her suggest staying in the yard. The crickets put out their rapid pulsing song. From the woods came the steady *tunk-tunk* of a bullfrog. Tuscawilla and Maude shuffled to the fence, hoping for a carrot to top off their daily ration of oats.

"It's a beautiful evening," Martha said. "Calm and free. I read that in a poem somewhere. The setting sun always makes me ache to go west again."

Larrabee laughed softly. "You sound like a man."

"It's still a land of promise. Don't you wonder about Caroline and Arthur and Edgar—and your daughter?"

"I think about Flora all the time. And I wonder if she thinks about me. If I could get on a horse or a train tomorrow and go to her I would. But Penny's right. It's a big territory out there and there's no way of knowing where they are. So, sure, I have an ache too, and I guess it mostly comes at sunset. I guess disappearing runs in the family."

"You disappeared by coming here."

"That's right. Blame it on bad planning and a sorry sense of geography. I've spent a good deal of time looking at maps since then. I even know where China is. Anna set me onto that."

Martha smiled. The fireflies were out and blinked their mysterious yellow-green code. "Maybe you're right. Maybe I'm different for wanting to go back west. I was talking to Mr. Dutton at his Independence Day party, and he told me that when he was in the army, the South was the frontier for him. He said the more time he spent huddled over a campfire on winter nights, the more he longed to fight his way into warm old Dixie."

"You've been moving in some high circles, Martha. I believe you'll do well in this town."

She smiled. "Oh, they invited me just because I helped Mrs. Dutton try on some hats—as if she needed help. It was a day or two before the party, so she invited me on a whim. Of course, Mr. Dutton knew my father, but that was years ago. My attendance at the party was very improper. I was there without an escort."

"I'd call that a scandal all right."

"I met that elegant man that owns the store, Mr. Howard. He's charming after a fashion but—"

Larrabee turned and blocked her way. "Martha, you'd do well to steer clear of him. He's dangerous. He brings out the worst in people. Take my word for it as your—as your friend."

She tried to read his face for the meaning and motive behind his words, but he turned away from her to pick up a pine stick in the path.

They came to the summer kitchen. She brushed a cobweb with her hat. While he swept it away with the stick she removed the hat and began picking off the silky film.

He flipped the branch far out into the garden. "Most girls are afraid of spiders, aren't they?"

She put her hat back on and pinned it. "Most girls don't grow up with a rough older sister and a bunch of marauding boys."

He chuckled and looked from the charred roof to the woman in front of him. "I imagine both of us are tougher for having known Anna." When the barking of a distant dog died out, he added, "that's the first time in three years I've been able to laugh when I thought of her. I'm beholden to you."

Chapter 50

John Howard touched the carnation on his lapel and smoothed his cravat. He was not one for overdressing, but he wanted the exaggerated formality to make a statement. At least that had been his original intention when he and Jane had packed for the train. He had spent the better part of an evening drinking brandy and considering her ultimatum, and was convinced that she *would* leave him if he did not go through the legalities of marrying her. Now, with his standing in the community on the rise again, he could hardly afford the notoriety of being left by his wife—or the woman everyone believed to be his wife. And he felt that he had nothing to lose by making it a legal arrangement. If he died, she would inherit his estate, but he had no intention of dying and felt good, aside from the occasional pain in his stomach. He was thirty-eight years old and had a full life ahead of him as long as he didn't go walking downtown on Saturday night, and he felt less and less inclination to do that.

So he had decided to take the initiative and dictate the terms of the forced marriage, precisely when and where it was to happen, and he chose terms that appeared rather odd and arbitrary.

Actually, they weren't as strange as they seemed. He determined that he and Jane would be married in the town of Starke, about a third of the way to Jacksonville. In Starke they could avoid attention without having to travel too far. Years ago, when he owned the moss mill, he had sold furniture in Starke, but nobody would remember him from that, and Jane knew no one there. His only recent trip had been more than two years ago when he had bought the stock of a failed hardware store to set up the Sunrise Emporium. He and Jane could marry at the courthouse, spend the night in that hotel with the cupola, and be back in time to open shop on Monday, marriage certificate in hand. He offered to have it framed and hung in the front hall.

To his surprise, Jane had been delighted with the entire offer. She had purred and clung to his arm all the way to the depot, had talked almost incessantly about the groves and nurseries and farms along the way until he thought she must have suffered some kind of breakdown. But as the day wore on, he came to the conclusion that she was simply happy, as if some weight had been lifted from her mind, as if she were actually marrying some prince who had ridden into her dreams.

It was with a feeling of relief that he finally saw the vast strawberry fields and lumberyards of Starke.

They hired a hack and went at once to the hotel. The room was spacious and had a vast view of Main Street from one end of town to the other. Howard noticed with amusement that the chairs and ottoman and fainting couch were all products of the moss mill.

Jane was more than ever swept up in the spirit of being a bride and asked if she might have a bridal bouquet before they went to the courthouse.

"A bridal bouquet?" he repeated. "Where on earth do you expect me to find a bridal bouquet?"

She smiled and shrugged. "There's a whole town out there. I'll wait for you. I've waited six years. What's another half hour?"

Down in the lobby the heavy-set hotel clerk daubed gravy from his mustache and pointed down Main Street to a nursery that sold cut flowers.

"Even on Sundays," he wheezed. "They figgered out that they git some of their best business on the Sabbath."

Howard walked out into the bright sunshine of early afternoon and crossed the wide clay street, thinking to find a bearable restaurant for the night. He found the predictable procession of dry goods store and grocery, druggist, photographer, and livery stable. He was looking down at his walking stick when someone entering the livery stable brushed against him. He glanced up and looked into the eyes of a powerfully built black man who ignored the collision and moved on.

He had seen that man somewhere, but he was careful not to turn around. He walked on slowly, trying to place the broad forehead and shining onyx face, and most of all, the penetrating eyes.

Howard continued down the street to the nursery, where he bought a bouquet of evening primrose and poppy mallows, common enough in August, but vibrant and fresh with dew. By the time he got back to the hotel room he had all but forgotten the man at the livery stable. Jane kissed him and set about putting the flowers in a vase.

"They're as pretty as a picture," she said.

Then it came to him. He had not seen the man's *face* exactly. He had seen a sketch of it—in Sheriff Fennell's office.

He went to the window, parted the filmy curtain, and stared down at the livery stable.

Jane turned away from her bridal bouquet.

"What's the matter, John?"

"Harmon Murray's down there."

She put herself between him and the window. She kissed him. "I'm sure you're mistaken."

"He nearly knocked me over."

"All right. But if he is down there, they'll find him. Thank God we're safe up here."

Howard looked past her to the street. What if he were the one to tip off the law regarding the whereabouts of Harmon Murray? He'd be a hero. People would come into the Emporium and buy him out clean just for souvenirs. On top of that, the community would actually be rid of a double-murderer. All he had to do was say the word.

She cried. He did his best to reassure her. One by one, he pried her fingers from his lapels as if he were peeling off beggar weed after a walk in the woods. He left her sitting on the bed and hurried down to the lobby, where he made a discreet inquiry about lawmen.

A few blocks away on a side street he saw a black sign lettered in gold that read "S.J. Falon, U.S. Marshal." Behind the brick jail a heavyset man was washing a sloppy ox of a dog, holding him in an iron tub and scrubbing him with a short-bristled brush, a procedure neither of them was enjoying. The marshal had rolled up his sleeves, but the dog's splashing had wet him from his gun belt to his mustache and the lawman was threatening to shoot man's best friend.

As Howard came closer he understood why the washing was necessary. Apparently the dog had tangled with a skunk. Howard tapped his walking stick on the side of the jail.

"Marshal Falon I presume?"

"The same. Stand back unless you want a bath. Sit! You sit still, Goliath, or I'll tie you down."

"Sir, I have come to inform you that a fugitive is in town. Harmon Murray."

The marshal looked up. "You've seen him too, huh?"

"Then you know he's here?"

"I didn't say that. Every other Yankee, farmer's boy, and bootblack has seen Harmon Murray in the last two weeks. Or thinks he has. Where was he at when you saw him?"

"Across Main Street. Going into the livery stable."

Marshall Falon stood up. "When?"

"Not ten minutes ago."

"What makes you think it was Murray?"

"I saw a circular in the Alachua County jail. Murray broke into my store."

The marshal tossed his scrub brush into the tub. Goliath jumped out, shook himself off, and rolled in the dirt. The marshal paid no attention.

"How close a look did you get?"

"He damn near knocked me over."

"Was he alone or was somebody with him?"

"Alone."

"Mister, you go hide yourself. If you're talking through your hat about this, you won't want me to find you. And if you're telling the truth, you'll want to be out of the way. Was he armed?"

Howard thought hard. "I'm afraid I didn't notice, marshal."

"Well, was he carrying a rifle?"

"No, I'm sure he was not."

"Good. Go on, mister. You've done your civic duty. Just wish hard that this works out."

Howard took the back streets on his return to the hotel and went out of his way to go in the rear entrance. He found a service stairway smelling of lye soap and took it to the top floor. His neck tingled. He had the feeling that Harmon Murray was everywhere. He opened the door to the room with his key, not taking the time to knock.

Jane was arranging and rearranging her flowers.

"They'll get him," Howard said. "Half a dozen well-armed men are probably after Harmon right now. Half a dozen *angry* men."

As if at a signal, the street had become empty. Howard scanned it from one end to another until he saw the distant figure of a man carrying a rifle. The man moved in a shallow zigzag from building to building. A block behind him, across the street, walked another rifleman. Coming from the opposite direction were two, three other men.

"They're no amateurs," Howard said. "This could be it."

A stalk snapped in Jane's fingers. "Are you sure he's in the barn?"

"Not at all. But he was there a few minutes ago. He's probably not far." He moved against the glass for a better view. "That one there—the man in front coming this way—that's the marshal. He must've locked his dog in the jail."

Jane joined him at the window. "What's going to happen, John?"

"They'll surround the barn. They probably have two or three more men coming at it from behind. Probably not deputies. Old veterans maybe. Men who know something about shooting and being shot at. If he's in there, they'll flush him out. He's wanted for murder. He won't come out peaceably. They may have to smoke him out. There's eight or ten of them and he's probably alone. Who do you think will come out of it alive?"

"This is terrible. I don't care if he is a Negro."

"He's killed two men, Jane. He won't hesitate to do it again. You'd better hope it's the Negro who goes down."

Somebody came out of the livery stable with his hands up. A white man. The rifles of the marshal and his men came down. Two of the riflemen stepped cautiously toward the barn and went in. Howard heard a shot. The two men came back out and the posse split into two groups. One moved toward the courthouse, the other toward the depot.

"What was the shot?" Jane asked uneasily.

"Probably just nerves. Or trying to draw him out. They've given up on the barn."

"Don't sound so disappointed. We don't have to see Harmon Murray killed on our wedding day."

"If they don't find him it won't exactly make me look good. I'll be taken for just another excited farm boy or bootblack. To put it in Marshal Falon's words."

The marshal was just then taking a last glance into the livery stable. As he swung his rifle to his hip, another shot split the silence and he stopped a bullet with his forehead. His chin snapped back, his feet came out from under him, and he fell nose up, firing his rifle. The deputy with him ran around the corner of the livery stable and yelled for reinforcements under an outpouring of rifle fire. He blazed away until his revolver was empty and folded back against the side of the barn to reload as the wood all around him splintered and flew. Grabbing at bullets from his gun belt, the panicked deputy dropped his revolver, and as he stooped to snatch it up, he took a bullet in the shoulder. He spun into the open, where a second shot went through his liver and came out his spine. He stumbled into the middle of the street and died kicking.

In an instant Harmon Murray was gone, spurring a fast horse through a ripping crossfire.

When John turned back into the room Jane was sitting on the bed with her hands pressed to her eyes.

He pulled them away. "It's over," he said. "He's gone."

But it was not over. The marshal and his deputy lay in the street for half an hour before anyone dared to cart them away to the undertaker.

Chapter 51

Bob and Larrabee were in Duke's Saloon when Sheriff Fennell came in looking for men who could hunt.

Bobby La Rue was playing the piano and singing "Crossing the Grand Sierras." Some of the men were making fun of him for being at Duke's place instead of his own. Others were singing along with his high tenor voice.

All of it stopped when the sheriff came clomping in heavily armed, asking for volunteers. "Some of you remember Alexander Henderson, don't you? Harmon's man that tipped us off so we could get Tony Champion and the Irishman? Well, Harmon caught up with Henderson in High Springs the other night, and by the time he was through there wasn't much left. Now every nigger in the county's afraid to tell us a thing, so we're going to have to find him ourselves, and that means plenty of men. We're going to beat the brush until we've got him. And this time there won't be any lynching. We'll stretch him legal in the daylight so the whole town can see!"

The men in the saloon didn't jump at the chance. It was a dark night and there were thousands of places a man could hide.

"It might be sport for a day or two," Bob told Larrabee. "'At least it won't cost anything."

"Our horses aren't up to that kind of stump jumping," Larrabee said.

"We'll give you horses," Sheriff Fennell declared. "We'll give you guns. And full rations. The man's killed a federal officer. You'll have the full power of the United States government behind you."

"Well, I'd rather have it in *front* of me," Larrabee said.

The sheriff pulled out a chair and propped his foot on it. "If he's come down the line from Fernandina to Starke and over to High Springs, he's due to come through here any minute now. He hails from down by Archer so he may be on his way there. He likes to visit the ladies. We know that. If we keep watching those houses, we'll find him."

"Well, count me in," Bob said. "It beats farming for a day or two."

Larrabee cracked his knuckles. "All right. Tomorrow and Thursday. Period. I've got to pick up my patched-up boots and get our soil analysis on Friday."

"Soil analysis?" somebody hooted. "Ain't you fancy!"

"That's right," Bob snapped. "We want to know why the poorest soil in the county is putting up the poorest crop. Before we spend every last nickel putting phosphate on it."

"How many!" Sheriff Fennel boomed in the hollow room. "How many of you can I count on?"

Larrabee and Bob and five others rode out with him. At first light they met the posse at the jail, saddled up a pair of long-legged mares, holstered their cavalry surplus Winchester carbines, and loped down the Archer Road.

Bob smiled as they hurried along. "Damned if I don't feel like Johnny Reb!"

From the head of the column the sheriff was calling out procedures, most of which nobody behind him could hear.

"I'll bet he sure is sore about that appaloosa," Bob said. "Brung her all the way from out west somewhere—genuine Indian pony—and she gets shot by some nigger hiding in a shack. He wants to be the one to get Harmon whatever it takes. Matter of pride I suspect."

Larrabee was already looking through the trees, thinking Harmon might turn the tables and ambush the sheriff and his men. "Don't you suppose the marshal and deputy getting killed set Fennell off a little, too? Lawmen don't take to having their own kind mowed down."

Bob nodded. "Point well taken. Were you ever in a posse before, Larrabee?"

"Well, just once. Not so much of a posse as a search party. When Anna's sister Caroline ran off with Mr. Arthur Mayse. Preacher put up a hundred dollars to bring her back. I believe what he really had in mind though was preventing the union."

"Take more'n a hundred dollars to do that once the juices get to flowing."

Larrabee laughed. "You're right about that! A hundred dollars didn't do it."

"You suppose there'll be a reward for the skin of Mr. Harmon Murray?"

"The merchants have put up five hundred. What would you do if you had five hundred dollars?"

"I'll tell you what I'd do. I'd buy me the finest suit of clothes in the county, I'd polish my patched-up boots, and go courting Miss Laetitia Summerton. For just one day because that's all I could afford for five hundred. That's what I'd do. You?"

"Five hundred. I don't know. Guess I'd go to Oklahoma and look for Flora."

"Belle Starr is out there, ain't she? Queen of the outlaws. You'd have to watch out."

"You're mistaken. She was killed a year or two ago. Shot in the back. I read that somewhere."

They rode into one black hamlet after another, working southwest in their search for the outlaw's trail. The column fanned out in twos, interrogating men at hog pens and in cotton fields. They talked to women in front of one-room shacks in sandy yards hacked out of the woods. It was a long day of barking dogs and staring children, and heads that shook a little too long to be believable. The posse was most of the way to Archer by the time Sheriff Fennell gathered them together and called it quits for the day. They rode back into town tired, sunburned, and wet from a late afternoon dousing.

"Maybe farming ain't so bad after all," Bob said, scratching behind his damp collar. Then he added, "Yes it is."

They were at it again the next morning. They rode hard almost to Archer and picked up where they had left off, spreading out through the scrub. Larrabee hadn't been down that way for years, not since the terrible night of the search for the Confederate treasury, but he could read the tree breaks and brush as if he had never left. He and Bob picked out foot trails and cow paths and followed them to clusters of shanties and sheds where nobody admitted seeing Harmon Murray.

"Fennell said Harmon has three brothers living around here somewhere," Bob recalled. "You suppose anyone's talked to them?"

"Near Long Pond," Larrabee replied without interest. "Fennell himself has talked to 'em at least once even though he says they've never caused any trouble."

"All right. Don't get touchy. I was just thinking out loud."

Larrabee pointed through the woods. "Here's another clearing. May as well ask these folks."

Bob rode up to the wooden steps of the little clapboard house and tapped on the door with the muzzle of his Winchester. Two black men came out, scaring a chicken off the stoop.

"Afternoon," Bob said. "How you all boys doing today?"

"We sure doing all right," said the first man. "We just setting down to some lunch."

"Guess it is about that time. I'm Bob Harper and he's Nathaniel Larrabee. What're y'all's names?"

"I'm Elbert Hardy," the man said, "and this here's Perry Henderson."

"Henderson. You ain't no relation to Alex Henderson are you?"

"First cousin," Perry said proudly, as if it were a mark of distinction to have your relation blasted to tatters by a famous outlaw.

"Then you wouldn't mind telling us if you've seen Mr. Harmon Murray, would you?"

"I'd be proud to tell you, Mist' Harper, but I ain't seen him. No, sir. I sure ain't seen him."

"Nor has I," Elbert Hardy said quickly. "But if we does, we'll be the first to sing out. Yes sir. We surely will!"

"Y'all watch out for him now," Bob warned. His horse sidestepped nervously. "He's killed before, black and white, and he'll do it again if he gets the chance."

"We'll sure watch out for him. Yes sir," Elbert Hardy said. "We'll shoot his ugly ass if he comes poking around here."

Perry Henderson glanced at Hardy. "Sorry we cain't help you gen'men."

Bob and Larrabee rode to the edge of the clearing and watched the two black men go back into the house.

"You worried about those two?" Larrabee asked.

"I'm worried about most everything in these woods," Bob said. He watched a wisp of white smoke float up from the fieldstone chimney, then turned his horse back toward the road. "Well, let's finish it off and go home."

They got back to the jail, scratched and mosquito-bitten, and took their leave of Sheriff Fennell.

"He's out there, you know," the sheriff said, fingering the butt of his Winchester. "He's out there in those woods and we'll get him."

"So much for the five hundred I guess." Bob cut a chaw of tobacco as they walked back to the house. "I could sure use a drink tonight."

"Except now you can't afford it," Larrabee said.

"Tonight I'd swap old Maude for a cold beer. But then that's about all she's worth, the poor nag. It's going to be a comedown riding her after having those government horses."

"It'll be a comedown going back to that farm, too," Larrabee said. "If that's what to call it."

The house on Magnolia Street now smelled of mildew and burnt plaster. Bob started a fire in the kitchen stove while Larrabee pumped bath water into a bucket.

"Pleasant sunset tonight," Bob said as they waited for the bath water to heat on the stove.

"We'll have a change of season yet." Larrabee was thinking of Martha and her wish to look for Caroline and Flora. In another month or two Oklahoma would be cold traveling. She'd have to wait until spring.

Bob took a bullet out of his hip pocket and set it on the drain board. "I hope you've got some money. I seem to be plumb out."

As it turned out, they didn't need money that night. Duke served them drinks on the house in honor of their heroic efforts in the hunt for the desperado.

"Just don't let word get around," he said with a wink, "or I'll be run into the poorhouse treating everyone who rode with that posse—and some frauds to boot."

Bob and Larrabee accepted his offer with gusto. They were so tired that the drinks went right to their heads, and by midnight it was all they could do to find their way home. Bob never made it past the top step. Larrabee fumbled with the sticky front door for a while and then gave up and fell asleep on the porch swing. He woke up with an orange cat on his chest and a distant roaring in his ears. He got to his feet, swore never to drink again, and went looking for

Bob. He found him in the backyard, pumping water onto his head. He pushed him aside and got his own head under while the water was still gushing.

"What do you suppose we did last night?"

"I can tell you what we did, chief—and we did too much of it! I was broke. Now I'm broke and hung over. How's that for progress?"

"The drinks were free. I remember that. That Duke has a big heart!"

"And I've got a big head. I drink nothing but water for a week."

"That's all you can afford."

Bob swept his dark brown hair back from his forehead. "Do we have anything we can sell this morning?"

"Not that I can think of. Why?"

"We've got to pay for getting my boots mended. And that fool soil analysis. How do you like that? We can't even afford to get our own dirt back."

Larrabee took a drink of water and spat all the way across the chicken yard. "I think my hearing's gone bad."

"Do we have anything other than the horses?"

Larrabee had his fingers in his ears. He was opening and closing his mouth.

"What's the matter with you? You look like a bluegill in a fish bucket."

"I can't get that noise out of my ears. It's like a whole town full of people shouting."

Bob pulled Larrabee's hands down. "I hear it too. You may be dumb but you ain't deaf."

"How much for the soil test?"

"One and a quarter from that thief down at the land office."

Larrabee put his fingers to his eyelids and pressed. "There's twelve in the newel post. I was saving it for the taxes. You don't really need boots, do you?"

"We'll hitch up the wagon. That way if we need to buy phosphate we can pick it up on our way out of town."

"On credit."

"Is this a holiday?" Bob asked as they approached the square. "What is today anyhow? It's not the Fourth of July, is it?"

"No," Larrabee said. "More like the fourth of September."

"They're bringing him in!" somebody yelled, running across Liberty Street.

"Bringing who in?" Bob shouted after him, but the man disappeared into a crowd, hurrying toward the Courthouse.

"Bringing who in?" Bob repeated. "Is this another lynching?"

"No, they always do lynchings over toward the Sweetwater Branch," Larrabee said. "Whatever this is, it's at the Courthouse."

"There's a whole herd of folks charging in from the west," Bob said. "I've never seen so many people in my life."

In carriages and wagons, on horseback and on foot, hundreds of men, women and children were converging on the Courthouse as fast as they could go.

"I seen the box!" a boy yelled. "It ain't nothing but a big ol' crate! That's the way they're bringing him in!"

Larrabee caught one of the slower men by the arm. "Pardon me, neighbor, but what's all the fuss about?"

The man shook his arm loose. "Why, mister, you must be about the last one to find out! They got him last night! They got Harmon Murray and they're bringing him in!"

"In a crate?" Larrabee said dimly.

"He's dead," Bob suggested. "Otherwise he probably wouldn't have gotten in the crate."

They pushed their way toward the square. The streets were so packed with people of all kinds that it was impossible to see much of anything. Larrabee glimpsed Sheriff Fennell standing in the back of a wagon, gesturing to the driver. There was so much yelling that nobody could tell what was going on.

"I'm getting killed myself," Bob groaned. He was pinned between a large woman in a torn gingham dress and a field hand who was sneezing repeatedly. "Let's get out of here and go down to the land office!"

"You go ahead!" Larrabee shouted. "I'm going to see who got the five hundred dollars!"

Bob nodded as he was swept away by the big-boned woman and the sneezing field hand. Larrabee pushed toward the Courthouse fence. Just as he got to the gate it clanged shut, leaving the crowd pressing against the wrought iron bars. Somehow Sheriff Fennell and the wagon driver had managed to unload the crate and set it on the lawn. Then the sheriff set his attention to a whirlwind of people inside the gates. He finally separated them enough to free a slender young black man. Where had Larrabee seen him? In the clapboard cabin down near Archer. It was Elbert Hardy, one of the dozens of Negroes who had stonewalled Larrabee and Bob the day before. Sheriff Fennell was escorting him up the Courthouse steps.

An unfamiliar white man introduced Hardy to the cheering crowd. Grinning with triumph, Hardy jabbed his Winchester aloft with each cheer. Then he climbed up another step or two, and as the throng settled down, he spoke in a loud, wavering voice.

"Murray came to my house at nine o'clock last night and said he wanted to see me. I walked out to see him." He punched out certain words like a preacher making points about sin and damnation. "He said that he had heard that I was informing the *white* people that he was at Long Pond and that he had come there to kill me or I was to kill *him!*" The crowd took this as a cue and cheered until the sheriff waved his arms for silence. Hardy waited until the crowd settled down, then waited a little longer, milking the moment for all it was worth.

"He said he wanted *me* to go to Archer with him. He wanted me to go on a shooting spree with him. That way the *law* would be looking for me also."

A small scuffle broke out between two women next to Larrabee. One was standing on the other's hem and something had torn. Elbert Hardy's speech was lost for a moment.

"He looked at his *watch*. The same one he took from E. W. Paxton about six weeks ago. He said it was just past nine o'clock and he wanted to be in Archer by three."

Larrabee tried to remember where he had been at the fateful hour of nine o'clock. At Duke's Saloon with no chance of getting the five hundred.

"We walked out down the big road until we came to a little side path. He wanted me to go ahead but I slipped behind, just beyond the muzzle of my gun. He looked around about that time, and I let him have both barrels right in the head! He dropped to the ground without a *sound!*"

Confusion arose in the crowd as to whether the story was over. It had ended so abruptly, in such a matter-of-fact way.

Seeing the restlessness, Hardy licked his lips and added in a grand voice, "So that ended Mister *Harmon Murray!*"

This time the crowd got it. They let out three hearty cheers and again Hardy grinned and saluted with his Winchester. Sheriff Fennell turned him around and hurried him into the Courthouse, accompanied by a phalanx of newspaper reporters, deputies, and witnesses.

Now the crate on the lawn became the focus of attention. People were complaining that the sides were too high for them to see the body of the dead desperado. An attempt was made to prop the crate up on a board, but people on the other side complained that the new angle ruined their view and then the prop collapsed, slamming the head of the crate onto the ground. Finally a man came out of the Courthouse with a hand saw and began cutting down the sides of the crate while some of the people forced against the fence began to pass out.

Larrabee still had not seen the body and wasn't sure that he would anytime soon.

Now there was another commotion in the crowd behind him. Somebody was pushing people aside like Moses parting the Red Sea. Someone threw a punch and a fight broke out. The crowd continued to part.

"Make way! Make way! I'm looking for somebody!" It was Bob and he was so excited that nobody was going to stand in his way. He elbowed and butted his way up to the fence.

The man with the saw had two sides of the box cut down. Now people were complaining that he was blocking their view. He stepped back from time to time to trade insults with his critics.

Larrabee turned away from the fence. "Did you change your mind after all? It's quite a show."

Behind him the man threw down his saw and raised up one end of the crate as the nearest part of the crowd cheered.

Bob was bruised and breathless but wildly happy about something. Larrabee shrank back, afraid his friend's mind had snapped.

"The soil samples!" Bob panted. "I got the damn soil samples!" Across one cheek was a green line that looked like war paint.

Larrabee pushed away two boys who came between them, one stacked on the other's shoulders. "What'd they say? How much phosphate do we need, Bob?"

Bob laughed and shook his head. "Chief, we don't need phosphate! That's the last thing we need!" He held out his hands as if hefting a boulder before throwing it with superhuman strength. "We don't need phosphate at all because we're sitting right on top of a mother lode of it! Those crops weren't growing because they were sitting on solid phosphate. Three, four feet down— that's all there is out there! Nathaniel, we're *rich!*"

He threw his arms around his disbelieving friend and danced him all the way to the Courthouse fence as the crowd roared and Harmon Murray did a macabre jig of his own to each bounce of the packing crate.

Chapter 52

The coming of autumn now depressed John Howard. All summer long, wherever he went, he watched the oranges take shape and ripen on the trees. The trees that had replaced the live oaks on the square ten years ago had borne fine fruit for several seasons—the fruits of good government, according to a wag writing in the *Gainesville Daily Sun*. None of it cheered John Howard. He saw the oranges as a lost opportunity and calculated what sort of money he'd have if only he had invested his first poker winnings in citrus groves instead of diverting his resources—and energies—into one problematic enterprise after another.

The coming of fall made him think of the late Major Dennis now. Major Dennis had done so well, whereas—following in his footsteps—John Howard had done so badly. As fall came on, Howard smoked too much, drank too much, and fell into a bitter mood.

On a sunny afternoon when the sky was a pale cloudless blue against the galaxies of orange, Jane found Howard in such a mood. The leaves on some of the new imported ornamental trees had begun to turn crimson, but otherwise autumn had not yet made itself known except for the breaking of the feverish heat and the lifting of the heavy cloak of summer humidity. The gray squirrels chased each other from branch to branch without showing any interest in gathering. Collins had not yet lit a fire in the front room.

Jane came onto the side porch and sat down beside her common law husband. After the abominations in Starke, neither of them had spoken again of a wedding. He was at the wicker table in the pavilion, smoking a slender cigar and watching the smoke rise into the gray cedar rafters.

"So unhappy?" she inquired, gathering her skirts so as not to snag them on the wicker.

"I'm thinking," he said without looking up.

"John, maybe we should go away for a while. We could go to the exposition in Chicago. We could be up and back in a week."

"Chicago! Why the devil would I want to go up there?"

"It's supposed to be so grand! Don't you suppose the Duttons are going?"

"No doubt they are. They go everywhere else."

"It's opening next week. The vice president will give an address."

"Well, he won't be the vice president for long. The election's in three weeks. Cleveland's coming back in. So you can have your vice president."

"It's to have buildings from all over the world."

"You've been reading your *Ladies' Home Journal.* I can see that. Well, it so happens that I can't afford to get away for a week. I'm expecting two shipments, one from New York and one from Pittsburgh. I expect them to sell by the end of the year."

"John, we need to have *some* fun, you and I."

"You're having fun with the books, aren't you? That's a joke, my dear. Just what do you seriously have in mind—a bicycle ride?"

"I swear I'd do it if you would."

"You're safe there. Just because everyone else in town is peddling around on those fool things and running into trees doesn't mean I'm about to."

Jane sat back and folded her arms. "Well, why don't we at least go for a walk? It's such a beautiful afternoon."

At first the outing did little to improve his humor since it took them past one grove after another of orange trees hanging low with firm, ripening fruit. He found his thoughts shifting from Major Dennis to Henry Dutton, comparing them point by point. Dennis had run practically the entire county, Dutton had *owned* most of it at one time or another. Dennis had been an arch strategist and manipulator of men, Dutton had been able to produce money as effortlessly as an orange tree sprouted fruit. In fact, Dutton owned a fair-sized grove on what was now the east bank of Payne's Prairie. He owned oranges and a bank and phosphate mines. He even made big money from his old cotton gins. Without having any obvious interest in politics, he was involved in politics. He participated in the county government and influenced its workings without attempting to buy it. He was sociable—comfortable among men and women of all classes. And his success was unfailing.

Howard tapped his walking stick on the boards as he and Jane ambled down West Main Street, past the Land Office, past Miss Tebeau's School, toward open fields and groves.

"What's all that shouting?" Jane asked.

Only then did he become aware of it.

"We've had peace for a year," he said. "Ever since they brought Harmon Murray in. I thought we had become civilized."

"It's coming from over there." Jane pointed toward Ralph Pine's grove. "Let's go see what it is."

He reached toward her with his stick as if to catch her with it. "And who are you—Nellie Bly pursuing a story?"

"Come on," she urged, hurrying down a wagon track between rows of trees. "I think it's a baseball game in the park."

Howard grunted and quickened his step to catch up with her.

They came to an acre of pasture that had been given over to a ballpark. The game had drawn about a hundred spectators who lounged against wagons and sat on long benches improvised from barn boards and hay bales. Most of them were men and boys, but Howard noticed at once a familiar feminine face. He had seen her here and there in the streets over the months since Dutton's Independence Day party. He remembered her name from that interrupted encounter—Martha.

She was watching the game from the seat of a stylish new buggy. Standing beside her, dressed in a well-cut suit and Saratoga hat, was none other than Nathaniel Larrabee.

"I heard he was doing well," Howard said, half to himself.

"Who?" Jane asked. She was intent on the man at bat.

"Over yonder, my dear. Mr. Nathaniel Larrabee. Somehow he struck it rich I'm told."

"You're out of touch, dear John. He has one of the richest phosphate mines in the county. Haven't you ever heard of the Preacher's Patch Mine?"

That caught him by surprise. He had indeed heard of the Preacher's Patch Mine. Its foreman had been in the store more than once in the past few months. He was a man named Will Manning and he was the man wielding the baseball bat just now. Howard began to have an unpleasant sensation in the pit of his stomach, and this time he wasn't smoking.

"Whereabouts is this Preacher's Patch Mine and how did it come by its name? Do you know, Jane?"

She touched his arm lightly, as if tracing her initials on it. "Sorry. Haven't the faintest idea."

Will Manning connected with the ball, but it popped up high overhead, so that the catcher, a comparatively small man, threw back his head and angled his mitt for a straight drop. Will Manning winked in Jane's direction, shot his bare hand up, caught the ball, and handed it to the catcher, drawing a big laugh from the crowd.

"Oak Hall," Jane said, reading the team name on Manning's shirt. "I believe they'll do well. What do you suppose those men do for a living? Surely they can't support themselves playing baseball."

Howard tapped his walking stick in the sand. "You're quite right about that. The fellow you're admiring happens to be the foreman of the very same Preacher's Patch. He's a sort of tedious person named Will Manning. He has a tab running in the store. I wonder if Larrabee knows it."

"Why shouldn't he know it? We sell the best equipment money can buy. He'd be a fool to buy anywhere else."

"Yes. But you don't know Larrabee. He's quite capable of acting against his own best interests if his temper gets the better of him. You never know what he's capable of."

Jane glanced up at the scar on the side of his forehead, saw the firm set of his jaw, and began to regret that she had suggested this walk.

The game ended, and a small boy standing near Jane chased a dog onto the playing field. His mother asked Jane to hold her baby while she went after her older child. Before Jane knew what to say, she was cradling the infant in her arms as comfortably as if it were hers.

"She has the purest blue eyes," said an older woman, thinking in the confusion that the baby was Jane's.

It was true, Jane thought. The baby was looking up at her with clear, pretty eyes and a dimpled smile.

"Look at that face," Jane mused. "It must be a girl. Such a lovely smile."

The child shook her little fists as if in response to the compliment.

Then the girl's mother returned and took her back.

Howard felt someone nudging his elbow. "Say, mister, I heard you asking about the Preacher's Patch Mine."

He turned to see an unshaven man of about sixty chewing on a pine splinter. "It's up north and west of town. A old turpentine farm, lumbered off and all. Larrabee and his partner was trying to farm it when they found it was chock full of phosphate! Now they're plowing a damn sight deeper!" The grizzled old fellow laughed, making Howard wish that he would choke on his pine splinter. The man went on. "Pays a dollar a day a man out there. After a couple of weeks you can come into town and have a pretty good time. You ever in need of work, come on out! I'm the assistant foreman. I'll give you a fair shake."

The grinding, pinching sensation returned to the pit of Howard's stomach. He was irritated that the crusty old busybody had listened in on his conversation with Jane, but most of all horrified by the thought that he himself had once owned that very parcel of land and had sold it cheap—literally dirt cheap to that wretched preacher. All that time, he had owned one of the prime phosphate sites in the county without knowing it. All these years he had been risking his savings on one enterprise after another, losing and winning and losing again, when he had been sitting on a fortune—free of risk, free of worry, and perfectly legitimate. And the capper—the capper was that it had fallen into Larrabee's hands.

Late in December he was shaken again. Jane had a miscarriage. After seven years of sharing a bed, he had assumed that children were somehow not in the cards. Neither of them had brought up the subject. Neither of them seemed to care. Yet when Jane returned pale and shuddering from the house of the Doctors Robb, Howard could see that she was suffering not just physically but spiritually. She had not mentioned the pregnancy—after all it had been only two or three months—but she seemed devastated when it had failed.

He took pity on her. Saw to it that she had nurses on call around the clock, and when they couldn't please her, he dismissed them and brought in others. The fall was warm, but Jane seemed always to be cold, even beneath two feather comforters, with a pine fire blazing in the corner. He brought her hot tea and decked the armoire and bedside table with flowers from Tom Duforge's greenhouse. He read to her from *The Ladies' Home Journal* and brought her a stereopticon with which he showed her vivid street scenes from the capitals of Europe.

"Someday maybe we'll see them in person," he offered.

When the year turned, the weather turned. And on one magical morning icicles hung from the windowsills until almost noon, reminding him of his boyhood in New Hampshire—a boyhood that had been happy until the day his father had died, thrusting John overnight into the world of leather presses, sewing machines, and boot blacking.

Their visitors were few. Old Collins, of course, continued to rattle around downstairs, gossiping through the kitchen door and stealing naps whenever things got slow and quiet. But friends were scarce. Doctor Mrs. Robb—as they called her—came every few days, patted Jane's hand and spoke to her of time's curative powers. The occasional business associate paid a brief call, took coffee or tea, and made discreet inquiries about the well being of "the missus." These were men who sold farm and mining tools, men who rattled the china cupboard when they walked into the house, men who stole glances at their gold-lidded watches or allowed awkward gaps in the conversation to be filled by the ticking of the hall clock. The Duttons never came, although their colored man twice brought baskets of pecans and oranges.

So as the frost of January gave way to the drizzle and awakening buds of February, John Howard sat alone by his wife's bed and kept her spirits up as best he could, the way a man shivering in a cold, empty room keeps up the fire with what few little sticks of wood are available to him. He sat and wondered just what was wrong with his companion of seven years.

"It'll be better," he said as he left for the store one morning. "This year will be better. You'll see."

Chapter 53

Reverend Roland Bonds had lived in town for seven years yet still felt like a newcomer as he made the rounds of his congregation—and those he hoped to bring into the fold.

He tended to concentrate on the hard cases, those who had ceased attending church, those who came only rarely, those he knew to be ill or in a time of turmoil. Then there were the publicans and sinners.

It was unusual to find anyone home at the fine house rebuilt by Nathaniel Larrabee, the phosphate magnate. Mr. Larrabee was out at his mine by day, tended to come in rather late at night, and spent much of Sunday at the homes of others. He visited often the handsome cottage of Penny and Nelda Ward down toward Miss Tebeau's school and spent many a day at the farm of newlyweds Bob Harper and Laetitia Summerton down on the south edge of waterlogged Payne's Prairie. His absence was a shame because the house seemed to beg for laughter and small voices and a fatherly figure clasping his hands in grace at the head of the dinner table. Neighbors had said that the house had been that way not so many years ago, when it was in poor repair but rich with activity. Now it stood proper and quiet, like a bachelor at a cotillion, too timid to ask for a dance.

Next door, Iris Poinsett had finally found a husband. The minister took some satisfaction in that because he and his wife had chaperoned Iris and her young man during a picnic at Hidden Springs and for a long drive out to the Devil's Millhopper. At the latter place, Iris had leaned far over the rim of the giant sinkhole, had been overcome by dizziness, and was snatched back from almost certain death by the young man. There was good reason to believe that the near tragedy had brought the two young souls together for what would be their lifetime journey. The minister was happy about that.

He passed Curtis the iceman coming the opposite way on Liberty Street, smiled and waved and said something complimentary about Curtis' work as a deacon, and Curtis—who seemed to be turning a bit deaf—nodded and tipped his hat by way of a vague reply. Curtis had a new refrigerator wagon that kept the ice longer than ever and with less sawdust. Curtis had confided at one point that he had also been investing in railroad stock and had turned a pretty dime on the north-south lines. Reverend Bonds greeted the news with enthusiasm while wondering how much of the cold cash would find its way into the collection plate.

Ray Polk and his wife seemed to spend more and more time at Newnan's Lake. Ray had retired from the county government and somehow managed to spend most of his time—his Sundays certainly—fishing, while his wife continued to pump the wheezing church organ. For seven years Reverend Bonds had listened to her tattering one grand old hymn after another but had never been sure how much to blame the organist. He was afraid to buy a new melodeon and find out! He was concerned though that the church seemed to be losing the younger members of its congregation, and he once had a bad dream in which Mrs. Polk was huffing away at "Old Hundredth" while the deacons passed the collection basket. One by one, the deacons walked out the front door with the money baskets, except for poor half-deaf Curtis, the only person left in town who could experience Mrs. Polk's music without flinching.

Penny and Nelda Ward—now there was a couple! The old man came to church only for weddings and funerals and on rare occasions, baptisms. His wife came occasionally with her young friend, Martha Newhouse, a beautiful young woman who listened attentively to his sermons and occasionally questioned him afterward on weak points and omissions. He wondered if that wasn't why the breathtaking Martha was still unmarried. It seemed to him that perhaps she was too intelligent to marry. It was an idea that made him uneasy since it tended to make him evaluate his own wife's intellectual powers, a pursuit that seemed unhealthy.

No one had seen Dr. Willis in church for years, even during the service for the yellow fever victims. So far as Reverend Bonds could determine, the doctor had attended the wedding of Preacher Williams and Emma Newhouse in 1884 and no church service since. On Sunday mornings he saw patients. The minister had seen him admitting them through that side door on more than one occasion. Now that he was retired, though, what excuse did he have to stay away? Mrs. Willis attended often with friends, the Poinsetts and the O'Dells mostly, sitting near the melodeon as if to shield the rest of the congregation from what Mrs. Polk was doing there.

He was more concerned about the younger generation, the future of the church. There was J.J. Ward, son of Penny and Nelda. Rumor had it that he'd lost two or three fingers during some kind of rifle stunt with the Summerton boy. From what he could tell the two were almost inseparable. The Summerton boy, Jeremy, was said to be wild, impetuous, and cavalier. The Wards' son was more cautious and thoughtful, but when they got together they raced their horses through town, usually with barking dogs in pursuit. It would take a superhuman effort to get them just to sit still indoors, a miracle to get them to pay attention in church.

It seemed to Roland Bonds that the Negro churches had more fervent congregations, and he wondered if that verve was a trait of the race or a function of the poverty and disadvantages that made them a more tight-knit, heaven-looking people. To be sure, they had their bad seed. The late Harmon Murray and his men had proven that. But by and large, the denizens of the Porters Quarters and the outlying hamlets scratched into the hummocks filled their churches with soulful song on Sunday mornings. Preacher Bonds half wished that just once his congregation would sing like that—with the kind of heart that he had heard coming from some of those modest little Negro houses of worship.

Late in the afternoon he called on Mr. and Mrs. John Howard. Mrs. Howard had been ill, he knew, and had been convalescing slowly. On a warm day in March he had sighted her, white and drawn, sitting bundled in the sunlight in the porch pavilion. He had never seen either of them in church, but Mr. Howard had always been courteous and his wife pleasant, perhaps even interested one time when he had spoken of old Abraham and Sarah and the birth of Isaac.

He found John Howard at the Sunrise Emporium. The place had prospered enough that Howard no longer had to spend much time behind the counter facing everyone who drifted into the store. Howard had hirelings for that, slender young men who were more given to pleasing the customer. Howard spent most of his time dealing with salesmen and large-scale buyers and going over the balance sheets. When the minister found him he had just returned from the telegraph office. He was in the back room, looking at the previous day's quotations from the New York Stock Exchange.

Howard looked up at the minister and smiled.

"Well, God and mammon in the same room." He peeled off a pair of spectacles and motioned for Preacher Bonds to take a chair. "To what do I owe the pleasure? Nothing fatal I hope?"

The minister wondered if Howard thought he might be bringing some bad news about Jane.

"No, nothing fatal. I just thought I'd stop by. How have you been, John?"

"I'm well enough, but the stock market took a beating yesterday. I imagine our banking friends may be a little nervous today. Have you seen any of them—Dutton or the Pfifers? They might be able to use a little prayer."

Preacher Bonds smiled at the brazenness of the man. He thought that John Howard was trying to shock him by being irreverent. It was an attitude that all preachers seemed to run across from time to time. He also knew that John Howard was not exaggerating much. There would be little point in making small talk about how nice the store looked. Instead he asked about Jane.

"You may call on her if you like," Howard said pleasantly. "The longer days and warmer weather seem to be doing her good. She's a southern girl through and through. Wouldn't last a minute in the cold thin air and darkness of New

Hampshire."

Although the minister had scarcely sat down, he thought it best to take his leave on this positive note. He rose, shook the store owner's hand, and said that he would be pleased to stop by and visit with Jane from time to time. He wanted to go right over because his final call of the afternoon might go on for a while. He arrived at the house about five o'clock by his grandfather's rather unreliable gold watch. The old Negro, Collins, ushered him onto the porch where Jane was having tea in the pavilion. She had regained some of her color and sat straight in the ladder-back chair. She was wearing a stylish white cotton blouse with billowed sleeves and starched cuffs. Her collar was joined with a cameo brooch. Her gray wool skirt swept the painted gray of the porch floor.

The preacher began with his customary greeting, something about the weather. It was amazing how often that brought out what was on people's minds.

"Someday you must bring your wife by," she said.

He was so intent on her face that he wasn't sure whether she had said anything else before that. She looked older. Her face was thinner and there were the beginnings of lines at the corners of her eyes. And yet she looked more attractive now. Something in her eyes reminded him of a soft summer landscape after a devastating storm. For an instant he thought that perhaps he was to gain more from this visit than she was, that she had more to tell him than he could tell her of God's ways, God's mysterious ways.

She invited him to join her at the table, had Collins bring him tea. He asked about her health. It was the usual inquiry, hardly more than polite conversation.

"I'm quite well now," she assured him. She held the teacup in the palms of both hands instead of pinching it at the handle as a genteel lady of Mobile would do. He tried to picture his wife here with them and couldn't imagine what she would say to this woman who loomed like a thundercloud as if everything she said was so important that it might explode if handled wrong. "My husband has gone very far out of his way to restore my health."

"In sickness and in health." The minister smiled weakly. He mentioned Howard's qualms about the stock market.

"John doesn't have any cause for concern," she said. "He doesn't have any money invested in it. He's through with that kind of speculation. Everything we have is in the store."

She said this, he thought, with the tone of one denying an accusation.

"And a marvelous store it is, Mrs. Howard. The way this county is prospering you'll never be in want of customers."

"My husband has settled down a long ways," she continued. "I believe he's never been happier. Bad times can bring people together and make them see what's important, don't you think?"

Preacher Bonds nodded that he did indeed think so. He wanted to recite several cases in point, but for the life of him couldn't think of any.

He finished his tea rather hastily and rose to take his leave, looking forward to that last visit of the day.

Then she asked him a rather strange question. She asked him if he knew whether the local baseball teams had begun to play again.

He had no expectations at all from his stops at Duke's and he certainly didn't partake of the imbibing there. But he felt as surely as the Savior had associated with publicans and sinners that he should not shy from ministering to the saloon trade. Duke, of course, always kept things under control when he was there, and in turn the preacher was careful to absent himself before the rowdier element came charging in from the foundry, the fields and the trails. This particular Saturday evening proved a bonanza because the place was full but the crowd was well behaved. Bobby La Rue was spreading a new song on the piano and the men had stopped their dominoes and checkers to hear it. The preacher occasionally wished that Bobby would replace Mrs. Polk as the church organist but he wasn't sure he had the repertory for it. Bobby favored sentimental songs with no apparent moral and the occasional suggestive ballad, but at least he tended to get people stirred up no matter what he was playing.

"I hear this one's real big at the fair," Bobby was saying. "It's called 'After the Ball.' Here goes."

The preacher was a sucker for a waltz and he liked this one right away. Apparently the other men did too, because they sat back in their chairs with folded arms, smoking and chewing quietly right up to the very last flourish of notes. They clapped so loudly that Bobby had to play the song all over again. Duke spread his hands over the bar and gazed through the smoke with his big blue eyes, smiling as serenely as a babe asleep in its mother's arms.

It was then that the preacher noticed some of the other men in the room. Bob Harper was there and Nathaniel Larrabee, having beer and cornbread. And over by the stove was a scrappy little gamecock of a traveling tinker named Leo Bard who passed through town about once a year. He had foam in his beard and a smile on his face, suggesting to the preacher that he had been telling some of his tall tales before Bobby had started playing.

"Requests?" Bobby looked over his shoulder expectantly. "I have more than two hundred tunes in my repertoire."

Duke smiled at the men's reluctance. "Can't let you get away without doing everybody's favorite," he said.

Bobby laughed. "All right. But if I play it, I'll expect to see every one of you down at my cafe by this time tomorrow. We'll be running a special on spareribs." He launched into a flurry of introductory chords that evoked laughter from those in the know. It was a sentimental ballad overplayed for comic effect and over-sung to the point that an ancient basset hound out in the street was hauled in to sing along. The song was about a little girl looking for her father in a saloon. "Father, Dear Father, Come Home with Me Now" was an overwrought plea for temperance, and in a backward way, the theme song for Duke's saloon. Before it was over, most of the men were singing along on the choruses, and so was the dog.

The preacher noted with silent envy that in its way, this congregation, too, was more fervent than his own.

Chapter 54

Will Manning watched the ball sail over the back fence. He was so taken with the sight that he almost forgot to drop the bat and jog around the bases. It had been a tough scrap of a game for seven innings, and now the Oak Hall team had pounded the opposition with three runs. As he rounded second, he caught sight of the lady with the cameo broach and tipped his cap. She certainly deserved some recognition. So far as he knew she hadn't missed a game all summer.

After the game and the handshakes with the other team, he ambled over to Larrabee and Martha and their friends. Most of them had also made the games a habit, and it pleased him to think that his performance was part of what brought them to the field. It had been a good season. He had lost count of the runs he'd batted in, though he heard that some of the boys around town were keeping track of them. He was usually good for at least one home run per game. He rarely struck out and he played a good game in centerfield. He and the first baseman had three double plays to their credit. After a game he always enjoyed pressing the flesh and talking about the plays over fried chicken and biscuits.

He was careful to maintain a polite distance from Martha, not knowing what her relationship to Larrabee was. He made it his business to keep out of other people's business and so he didn't listen to the gossip about Larrabee and his late wife's sister. He just kept clear—polite and pleasant and at an arm's length. He was more intrigued by the woman in the centerfield crowd. She was a few years older and less pretty, but attractive all the same because she was so aloof and mysterious.

It was a fine summer night but Martha seemed not to be enjoying it. She didn't join into the conversation. It was hard to tell if she was even listening. Maybe she just found the topics uninteresting. The nation's economy. Silver and banking and the gold standard. Men talked a good deal about them and had strong opinions about them, but no one seemed to understand them. Now banks were failing, and formerly self-confident, successful men were starting to get nervous. You couldn't expect a pretty young woman to trouble her head about such things.

Larrabee noticed Martha's inattention too and mentioned it to her as they walked to Anna's garden.

She waited a long time before she answered. At first he thought she hadn't heard him.

They were in the side yard, passing the vacant paddock, when she told him that Barkley Duforge had proposed to her.

He stopped in his tracks. "Barkley? What's Barkley got to do with you?"

"He's been escorting me out. Some."

Larrabee tugged at his collar. He hated starch but it looked good, even in humid weather if you used enough.

"How come I never heard about it?"

She turned and looked at him. "Because you weren't here. He called on me while you were at the mine."

"Oh."

He started toward the garden but she blocked the way, took his hands in hers. "I'm twenty-two years old. I can't spend the rest of my life tending Anna's garden. I have gardens of my own—or want to." She released his hands and walked on. "Many's the time I wished we had gone to Oklahoma—you and I—to look for Carrie and Flora, brazen and improper as that sounds. If you had said the word, I think I would've gone the minute my bags were packed. But this place has a way of putting lead in your feet. So now—"

"Martha," he said, "Barkley isn't for you."

She flared up. "Who are you to say that?"

"Look, I can't say anything against Barkley. But he's a plain old boy from the county. And you—you're something else. You've seen the world way beyond this little place. He'll never want to look outside of it."

"Do you?"

"I don't know. I did once but I landed here by accident and just stayed. I didn't have the money to leave. And then there was Anna."

"And now that Anna's gone. And you have money. What's keeping you?"

"The mine, the business. There's a depression coming on and I'm going to have to work hard to stay free of it."

She smoothed the lapels of his linen suit, glancing up at him from time to time as she spoke. "And you see, Barkley won't have to fight the depression because he won't know the first thing about it. He'll plant his crops in the spring and harvest them in the summer and fall. He'll go out into the fields in the morning and come back to the house for lunch and supper. And I'll put up preserves and make watermelon pickles and, yes, have babies and help with the flower business. And care for the children when they catch cold. That's what I'll do out there in the county. I'll live my life and I'll know what to expect." She looked up at him. "Would you try to talk me out of that?"

The wedding of Martha Newhouse and Barkley Duforge took place on a crisp February morning when the sky was a cloudless blue and the dark green branches of the orange trees were laden with fruit. Some of the azaleas and red bud trees were already in bloom and the air was sweet with the promise of growing things. The ceremony was performed at the little frame Methodist church in Arredonda since that was where the young couple planned to worship. The minister there was a protégé of old Sam Carrington's, a mere boy by some accounts. He was more nervous than the groom, pacing and mumbling to himself when he thought no one was looking. But when the last guest had been seated he took his place at the altar, cleared his throat, and spoke out so boldly that even half-deaf Curtis could hear every word from the back pew.

Barkley was wearing some ancestor's old-fashioned black frock coat and heavy serge trousers. His boots looked like new because he had outgrown them quickly at the age of fourteen. He had squeezed back into them after thirteen years, figuring he could at least last through the ceremony, but he approached the front of the church with a pinched limp that set people to whispering. They could hear those boots creak with every step he took, and as he stood there forcing a smile he wanted nothing more than to rip those boots off and fling them out the arched window.

Martha looked a little pale, Larrabee thought, maybe because of the white dress and the harsh light of late morning. Despite the finery and trappings of the dress, which Nelda had helped design, Larrabee thought Martha had looked better in her old brown skirt and high-collared blouse, bending over a picnic basket with a strand of her dark brown hair falling across her forehead. He thought she had looked better tending Anna's garden, better on walks and at baseball games. Better when he had met her at the depot. He felt a stabbing in his heart when Barkley lifted the veil and kissed her.

After the wedding he rode his two-year-old sorrel mare down to the Summerton farm. He rode most of the way at a lope, partly because he wanted to give the horse a workout and partly because he liked the feel of the mud flying about him. It felt good to put the church behind him too. He wanted to put the church and the night behind him and he rode the mare hard, arriving at the farm windblown and spattered.

J.J. and Jeremy were already there, having left the wedding at the earliest possible moment and raced all the way.

"You boys shouldn't be so scared of weddings," Larrabee joked. "Someday you'll be wanting one of your own."

They had been playing catch on horseback with an orange, only J.J. had changed the rules and decided to bean Jeremy instead. Their Sunday clothes were streaked with pulp.

"When my time comes, me'n the missus'll just elope to the high hills!" J.J. laughed. He was trying to tell if Jeremy had an orange in his hand.

"The devil you will," Larrabee told him. "You'll have a bride in a fancy dress and a hat to beat the band and your boots spit and polished. It's the roughest ones that marry the fanciest brides. Today ought to've taught you that. Where were your folks, Jeremy?"

"Mother wasn't feeling so well this morning and asked if Bob wouldn't stay to home with her." He punctuated his statement by hurling an orange that caught J.J. square in the chest with a loud smack.

Larrabee prodded the sorrel toward the house. "You boys hit me with one of those and I'll pull you off those horses and spank you."

He was safe enough. The boys went galloping off to the grove to reload.

Bob was on the porch smoking a cigar. He was in his shirt and suspenders but he wore a fine powder blue derby.

"Ho, now! Who's the fine gentleman?" Larrabee came trotting up. "You look like a banker smoking that stogie."

Embarrassed, Bob flipped it onto the lawn. "You credit Laetitia for that, Nathaniel. She holds that a chaw ain't a fit form of pleasure for a cultivated man."

Larrabee let the sorrel graze on the greening grass. "I've been meaning to tell you that for years. Bob. Just didn't have the heart. Jeremy tells me the missus is under the weather."

Bob came down the steps smiling. "Not that so much, Larrabee. She's going to have a baby. What do you think of that?"

"I think *both* of us ought to be smoking cigars."

"She didn't want the word to get out till after the wedding. Didn't want to steal any of Martha's thunder."

"That's just like Laetitia," Larrabee said. "I believe that's the finest thing I've heard in a long while."

He looked out past Bob, down the long slope to the vast prairie that had replaced the lake. The tall grass was still flaxen, but patches of green shone all the way to the horizon. Along the rim that had been the shoreline the straight maples and sycamores and burgeoning sweet gums had already begun to leaf out. Here and there the eternal palms bent down to drink water long gone. As his eye followed the border between grass and trees, it occurred to him that his fortunes and misfortunes had come according to the caprices of this strange and wild land, and he wondered what Anna would have said about the events of the day.

Chapter 55

The laughter seemed out of place in the house, but Jane smiled to hear it. Everyone on the list had showed up and they were enjoying themselves immensely. Some of the men were talking about an eccentric old tinker they had seen in Duke's saloon a few months back.

"He's a sawed-off little feller named Leo Bard and he has the most outlandish tales you ever heard!" B.F. Jordan dipped his cup into the punch, and let it drip. "He told one about passing through Ohio one summer night when a storm came up. He knocked on the door of the nearest farmhouse and found himself face to face with the tallest woman in the world!"

"They wouldn't exactly be face to *face* if she was the tallest woman in the world," Jacob Ford said. He looked around to make sure that his sense of humor hadn't gotten him into trouble again.

"Anyhow," Jordan said, "this Bard fellow allows as how she lets him come in and sell her all kinds of bric-a-brac just for the companionship and then makes him dance a waltz with her!" He couldn't help laughing. "Can you imagine that wiry little bantam pressed up against P.T. Barnum's giantess, flying around the dance floor with a storm rattling the windows all the while?"

Jane burst out laughing. As the guests joined in, she glanced over at John and was glad to see that he was amused too. Finally, on his own terms, he was becoming accepted in the community.

Dr. Phillips flashed a knowing smile. "Tell what happened after that, Ben."

Jordan started to go on, but inhaled at the wrong moment and choked on his punch.

The doctor thumped him on the back and picked up where he had left off.

"With all this lightning—and the tallest woman in the world slinging him around the dance floor—"

"No, wait a minute. You forgot a part." Bobby La Rue had been invited to the gathering in the hopes that he would eventually play the substantial Hamlin & Mason piano that John had bought for Jane. Also, the Howards were frequent customers at his cafe and Jane had pressed him for advice about her party hors d'oeuvres. "You forgot the part about her being a widow and all."

"A widow, oh yes, well," the doctor continued, "the tinker—once he had recovered his wits from seeing this giant woman in the first place—had inquired as to the whereabouts of her husband and she had pointed to a dirt mound in the dooryard. So now the widow is slinging the tinker around like a rag doll and he's flying past the window when he sees this mound of earth open up and out comes the—"

"Tallest *man* in the world!" B.F. Jordan doubled over at the punch line.

"Now wait a minute." John Howard gestured with his punch cup. "I thought you said she was a widow."

"Well, that's what the tinker thought when she pointed at the dirt mound," Dr. Phillips said. "But she was actually pointing to the *root cellar* where she had shut away her man for being under the influence. He came bashing out of there and boy howdy was he mad! The tinker took off for dear life, leaving his merchandise behind, and that was the last that county ever saw of Mr. Leo Bard!"

A few nearby ladies had heard the last part of the story and joined in the laughter. One or two of them owned that the world should have more root cellars with good sturdy outside locks.

"You'd still need a man to dig 'em for you," Jacob Ford said.

A few minutes later he cornered John Howard in the study and asked if he might have a private conversation with him.

Howard put down the humidor he had been unloading and gave Ford a closer look. Back at the beginning of the year the man had secured a high position in the Dutton bank, a vice-manager's job. And recently he had added a second story to his house although he continued to dress in worn, almost shiny, suits and smoked cheap cigars that offended men and women alike. Howard thought of offering him one of his own Cuban Beauties but thought better of it and instead motioned for him to sit down and went over to close the double doors.

When he re-crossed the room he noticed that Jacob Ford was still standing.

Absent-mindedly Howard lit a cigar for himself. "How are things at the bank?"

"So far as I can tell, the bank is thriving," Ford said. "That don't quite go for me personally though."

Howard sat down and savored the taste of his cigar for a moment.

Ford was nervous. He smoothed the lapels of his shiny coat and touched the knot of his black silk tie.

"How about *you* then, Jacob? How are things going with you?"

Ford stood with bowed shoulders. The way he worked his fingers reminded Howard of one of the Negroes at the moss mill, hat in hand, asking for a raise.

"The facts of the matter are, I've made some mistakes," Ford confessed. "About two years ago I started putting a little money away. In railroad shares."

Howard leaned forward. "Railroad shares? Jacob, that's about the worst thing you could've done. Do you know how many railroads have failed in the past year alone?"

Ford nodded.

Howard sat back. "What do you expect *me* to do about it?"

"If you could just—just see your way clear to—You've been doing so good." Ford raised his gaze from the floor and looked Howard in the eyes. "If you could see your way clear to lend me a few hundred. I'd be—I'd be grateful."

"A loan?"

Ford looked back down at his feet. "Only until I can save something up on my salary. I'd pay interest, of course. Three percent? Or four maybe?"

Howard sat back again, watching Ford through a feather of cigar smoke. "You're working for a bank, man. Why not borrow from Dutton?"

Ford shook his head insistently. "That wouldn't do. Wouldn't do. I can't let the bank know I'm in this spot."

"I suppose not. Got any collateral?"

"Just the house. It's got a new room added on the back. We did that before the market started falling. I'm sure sorry about this."

Howard didn't know whether to pity Jacob Ford or laugh at him. Plenty of smart people had put their money into railroads. But the smartest of them hadn't risked more than they could afford to lose. The old poker-player's rule! Jacob Ford should've known it, should've lived by it. But then Howard remembered his own risk-taking and the Arlington. Only a well-timed fire had saved him from ruin.

He asked exactly how much Ford needed.

"A few hundred. Just to get through the year without losing the house."

"How much, Jacob? Two hundred? Three?"

Ford looked toward the window as if expecting to be prompted. Out on West Main Street the afternoon train came whistling in from Cedar Keys.

"Five?"

"Sorry, Jacob? I didn't hear you."

"Five hundred. Could you see your way clear to lend me five hundred? I could start paying you back by the first of the year, say a hundred a month?"

Howard tried to think of something Ford could give him back in return, other than the four percent. Absolutely nothing came to mind. He thought about what Major Dennis would do in this situation and quickly came to the conclusion that the major would send Mr. Jacob Ford packing.

He unlocked the top desk drawer, took out a book and wrote a check for five hundred dollars.

Ford snatched the check, folded it hastily, and tucked it in his breast pocket. "I won't forget this, John. I swear I won't."

Howard smiled. "See that you don't. There's that matter of repayment."

"Yes, yes—a hundred dollars by January first of '95. You've got my word on it."

"That's right. Your word as a fine old southern gentleman. I know you won't go back on that. Well, it's getting hot in here and Jane's going to be wondering where I've sneaked off to. Why don't we go back out and have a cup of punch, Jacob?" On the way into the front hall he gave his debtor a neighborly pat on the shoulder.

In the house on Magnolia Street, just after the turn of the year, Larrabee was talking money too.

"I'm glad that capital's not a concern, " said a stout man holding his derby with a firm grip. "But you're still talking about a big slab of country out there. Entire outlaw gangs go into it and disappear for months at a time. It's not like going to New York or Atlanta and looking somebody up in the city directory or talking to policemen. This is an entire territory you're talking about."

Larrabee threw another log on the fire and pulled his chair up to the round table. "I've probably spent more time looking at the map of that territory than you have, Mr. Blount, and I'm ready to pay you for your efforts, but I want regular reports, no matter how insignificant you think the information is. We know where they started out. That's where the trail begins."

"It's a trail six years old, Mr. Larrabee."

"Are you saying you can't do it?"

"Mr. Larrabee, would you know your little girl if you saw her?"

"I'd know her."

"Any distinguishing scars, birthmarks?"

"Not that I can remember."

"It'll make it hard to identify her—even if I do find her."

"You've got Carrie and Arthur." Larrabee had an old photograph of Carrie taken after her performance as Joan of Arc. "This is about ten years old. Her name is Caroline Newhouse. Her married name is Mayse. I don't have a picture of Arthur. He'd be about thirty-five now and probably on the heavy side." Larrabee put a finger to his chin. "He's got a little cleft right here. He's a couple inches shorter than I am and his skin peels when he gets sunburned. Carrie's a strawberry blonde. You can't tell from the picture."

Blount had listened with folded hands. "And what about the little girl? Flora. Can you give me anything to go on?"

Larrabee opened a battered cigar box. Slowly he took out a photograph the size of a playing card. It was a picture of Anna taken when she was about fifteen. Her face was turned away from the camera slightly, as if the photographer had taken it as a practice shot, but it had a spontaneity that appealed to the grieving husband. He had discovered it when he was boarding up the windows after the fire. He had set down his hammer and studied the photograph for a long time, speculating what Anna had been saying before it was taken, imagining that she was on the brink of smiling at the artificiality of the sitting. He showed it to Blount.

"This is her mother."

Blount attempted to take the photograph but Larrabee held on to it. "May I ask, sir, why you waited so long to look for your daughter?"

Larrabee looked at the photograph one more time, then turned it over, put it back into the box and closed the lid. He kept his hands on the box as if to keep the contents away from prying eyes.

"That would take a long time to explain, Mr. Blount. The reasons changed from one day to the next. But all in all, I thought I was keeping her safe."

Blount put a business card on the table. "There's my address at the home office in Memphis. It's going to take some traveling money. More than the usual case since we have such a cold trail. I'll start with the routine things—the registries of deeds, courthouse records—as soon as I figure out which courthouses to look in. Letters of inquiry. Sheriff's offices and, I'm sorry to say, cemetery records. You want to know about your little girl regardless if the news is good or bad?"

"That's right."

"I'll send you a progress report each month, by mail unless there's something meaty. Then I'll send a telegram with the headlines and a letter with the details. My fee is two hundred dollars a month."

"Yes, we agreed on that."

"I'll guarantee the expenses not to exceed an extra hundred dollars a month. Total three hundred at the outside. The money will be due in Memphis at the beginning of the month. The office will bill you. It's going to take five hundred to get things started. You can call the whole thing off anytime after the first month and we'll pro-rate the balance due."

"Whatever you need. Just be sure to send me a telegram as soon as you find her and see to it she stays where she is until I can get there."

They walked out to the gate. Blount let out a breath that spread like smoke before them. "Is it always this cold down here in February? I thought this was the tropics."

"It's been a cold winter," Larrabee said. "Back in December we had a freeze that nipped the orange trees. Killed the leaves and a good deal of the fruit. The paper said it got down to fourteen degrees. First time anybody could remember that happening. Most of that growth you're seeing came during a warm spell in January."

"Well, it feels like it's not much more than fourteen degrees right now." Blount pushed his Homburg down over his forehead, removed his glove, and shook Larrabee's hand. "Good luck to us, sir. I hope we can find your little girl."

With his hands stuffed deep in his coat pockets, Larrabee walked quickly down to the White Pine Stable. He had leased the aging Tuscawilla to Dobkin Murray and now had a sorrel máre that was too valuable to keep in the cramped paddock, so he boarded her at the stable and arranged to have her saddled by eight o'clock every morning but Sunday. The morning was unusually quiet. Not a door or a window was open. Not one child or dog ventured out. The pigs and chickens that customarily wandered the town were nowhere to be seen. This quiet morning was eerily reminiscent of the yellow fever epidemic, only with shivering cold instead of blistering heat.

Ralph Pine's boys huddled over the cast-iron stove in the stable office. Larrabee tapped on a fogged window and Ralph's older boy came out. He was going gray and his salt-and-pepper mustache looked as if it was frosting over. Near the door of the barn fresh manure steamed in the street. Larrabee turned up his collar and led the sorrel to a mounting step. He was slow getting into the saddle because the leg he had broken nine years before was stiff. He looked longingly at snug houses with smoking chimneys. Then he prodded the sorrel into a fast trot that soon took him up past the Courthouse, where he turned west on Liberty Street and began the long ride to the Preacher's Patch.

His hands were swollen with cold by the time he got there. He turned the sorrel loose in the sand patch behind the cabin and went inside. Bob was already there and so was Will Manning. Larrabee stood in front of the stove and watched his hands turn red.

"Half expected you to stay in today," Bob said.

Larrabee rubbed his hands together. "It'll warm up."

"Some of the old-timers are saying we're in for another freeze. This could be the big one."

"They've been saying that for years. Like the Second Coming."

"Today would be the day for it," Will Manning said.

"I'll bet this ain't but a spring day where you come from," Bob said.

"We didn't raise oranges in Elmira," Will Manning told him.

"How's the farm?" Larrabee asked Bob.

"Cold. We had frost most of the way to the prairie. Orange trees looking kinda sad. Two or three more days and we'll see if they pull through."

"Laetitia and the little one keeping close to the fire."

"Close as they can get. She's got two sets of wool on Ainsley. Can't hardly see nothing but those two blue eyes peeping out."

Will blew on the window and drew his initials in the fog. "Ainsley's going to grow up thinking she's a Yankee if this continues."

"Not hardly." Larrabee worked his fingers to see if the swelling had gone down. "Soon as she's weaned, Bob's going to fill her up on grits and collard greens and black-eyed peas and fatback. She'll be a Confederate through and through."

"Won't have to," Bob said. "With a name like Ainsley she'll be above eating collard greens. I don't care much for 'em myself. The Ainsleys were a fine old family of lowland Carolina. There was Ainsleys at the Battle of Yorktown. My mother was an Ainsley."

"Slave-holders I'll bet." Will squinted through the isinglass window of the stove to see if the fire needed more wood.

"I have no doubt some of 'em were," Bob said.

"Well, we could use some of those slaves this morning." Will warmed his hands in front of the flickering isinglass. "These men we've got aren't exactly taken with the cold."

Larrabee turned his back to the stove. "It'll warm up."

"Dollar a day ought to be enough to keep 'em going, even on a cold day," Bob said.

Will noted that some of Dutton's mines had gone from pick-and-shovel operations to large-scale works running railway carts.

Bob thought that would be a big investment.

"You'd get a damn sight more phosphate out of it," Will said, "and cut your labor costs. Before you know it, these men'll be wanting more money. A railway cart isn't ever going to do that. A railway cart's not going to join a union and pressure you for more."

"The unions aren't going to amount to anything down here," Bob said. "We can get convict labor from the state and pay 'em half what these boys are getting."

Larrabee didn't like either idea and told them so. "Before you know it, you two are going to be fingering gold watch fobs and busting your vest buttons. Aren't any of us out there scratching around in the cold. Let 'em have their dollar a day—and more. I'd say let 'em buy shares in the mine if they had the money."

"I wouldn't do that either if were you," Will Manning said. "This mine's not going to last forever."

"You ought to put some money aside," Bob told Larrabee. "That's what the Duttons of the world do. They diversify."

"So do plenty of men who go broke. The kind who buy railroad stock."

"I didn't say nothing about railroad stock, Nathaniel. What you need is a farm. Some cattle. Half a dozen orange trees and no more."

Larrabee tried to imagine a farm somewhere among the pines. His rows of corn and cowpeas bending under the generous sun quickly turned to a vast hole in the ground, a phosphate mine. And the farmhouse, empty of wife and children, became a lonely outpost at the edge of an abyss.

Chapter 56

In the heat of summer it was difficult to believe what had happened. Three days in February had destroyed groves all over the county and killed most of the winter vegetable crop. State production before the freeze had been six million barrels. Now some producers were saying that in the coming year they would be lucky if the number reached a hundred thousand. For miles around, farms folded. Property values for the frozen fields and groves dropped fifty percent. Fortunes evaporated overnight.

John Howard sorted through the developments in his mind as he fanned himself with his fashionable Panama hat. He studied every newspaper story, analyzed every overheard conversation as if it were the gospel. He read the advertisements for foreclosure sales and estate auctions and grew more and more restless in his respectable, secure store.

Jane heard him pacing at night and knew what he was thinking.

A week later a well-dressed man entered the store. Jane was at the counter talking to John while the new stock clerk put on a show of dusting and adjusting every little thing on the shelves. The man introduced himself as Bill Zeiss and asked if he might speak with John in private. Jane looked at Howard, trying to tell if he knew what this was about. His disinterested expression suggested that he did not. The two men retired to the office.

Mr. Zeiss explained that he was a real estate attorney representing a client who had an unusual opportunity for the right investor.

"You might be that investor, Mr. Howard." Zeiss spoke in a way that made Howard think of a collector carefully pinning a butterfly to pasteboard.

"I might," he shot back, "but my money is already invested." He glanced around the room as if the rows of ledgers on the oak shelves would explain what he meant.

The attorney went on. "You are perhaps not aware that some of the most valuable property in the county is available to the right buyer—for a very limited time. My client is most eager to sell and is ready to offer considerable incentives at this time—*considerable* incentives."

Howard eyed his visitor suspiciously. "By some chance do you mean orange groves?"

Mr. Zeiss looked at him as if he had just blurted out a state secret. "Some of the finest in the state."

"A moment ago it was some of the finest in the county."

"Some of the finest *anywhere*, Mr. Howard."

"Up until last winter I dare say. Why have you come to me?"

"Because you have a reputation, Mr. Howard. You've had extensive holdings in this area for many years. You've succeeded. You've been a responsible citizen interested in the welfare of the county."

It was strange to hear himself described that way. He wondered who Zeiss had been talking to.

"I haven't had any such holdings for seven years, Mr. Zeiss. I'm not interested in the sort of acreage you apparently have in mind."

"Hear me out, sir. Surely you know that the recent freeze was nothing but a setback. It was the first in sixty years. An extraordinary occurrence."

"There was that little cold snap in '86."

"Destroyed some of the fruit but not the trees. That sort of thing that can happen to any crop. In fact, it improves the stock."

Howard was impressed. This man had done his homework.

"All right, all right. Why don't we show our cards, Mr. Zeiss? Just what is it you're selling?"

Zeiss came to the edge of his chair. "Six hundred and thirty-three acres of groves. At half the assessed value."

"Six hundred and thirty-three acres! That's almost as big as the Walls plantation."

"Mr. Howard, that *is* the Walls plantation."

"*Walls* is ruined?"

"Mr. Walls will be pursuing an academic career in Tallahassee. At Florida Normal College."

The simple words spoke volumes. The freeze had ruined Walls. He had overextended his groves and three days of cold weather had finished him. He had lost it all. Twenty years of planning and building—gone in three days.

Howard showed Mr. Zeiss the door, but for days he was haunted by the thought of the plantation at the edge of the prairie. Most of what had made it great was still there. The cultivated land, the railroad spur, the grand brick house. In five, six years it might all be built up again at half the startup cost of a new place.

He went back to smoking too many cigars, spent more time with his hand on his stomach, his fingers slipped through the buttons of his vest as if he were posing for a photograph. He paced in his study and wondered how long the land of Mr. Josiah T. Walls would remain on the market.

On a Monday morning in mid-August he had a second offer, or rather appeal. He had just received his twelfth and final payment from Jacob Ford and he was feeling optimistic about money. The store was so hot that he had the windows thrown open wide, even though he was forced to arm himself with a fly swatter, and the clerk was kept busy cleaning up spots and specks. Before ten o'clock, Howard had removed his tie and was considering taking off his coat and collar when B.F. Jordan came in daubing his forehead with an oversized handkerchief.

"Like to die," he said, displacing his finely woven straw hat.

"Good day for a cruise on the lake," Howard said sarcastically. "How's business?"

Jordan gave a perfunctory nod to three women who were discussing a bolt of cambric. All three wore gray skirts, white blouses with puffed sleeves and broaches. All three had their brown hair pinned up in pompadours. They looked like triplets.

"I got a little offer for you," Jordan said.

Howard put down his fly swatter and invited Jordan into the office. He settled back into his leather chair and waited to hear that word again. *Oranges.*

Jordan tossed his hat onto the desk and wiped his forehead again. His hair was grayer and thinner than when Howard had last seen him.

"I won't tell you this is the deal of the century," Jordan said, "but it is a damn good deal, and I'm coming to you because I figure you're one of the few people in the county lucky enough to have some cash on hand."

Howard started to take issue with the word 'luck,' but Jordan plowed right over him.

"John, the canal company's going to fold. There isn't enough business on Santa Fe and the other lakes to support it. And on top of that my groves were taken out last winter. Mine and just about everybody else's. But the land's still good. Still good for oranges! It's just that I can't afford to put the money into to it and wait five or six years for the payoff. You can."

Howard started to take a cigar but changed his mind. "Ben, I also have this store. I don't know the first thing about oranges. It would have to be a remarkable deal to get me to invest in them."

"John, this is a remarkable deal. I'll sell you my hundred acres for what I paid for it fourteen years ago. Twenty percent down and the rest over five years, interest free. You can have a crop on it in five, six years."

"What about the freezes?"

"Hell, John. There may not be another one for twenty years. You know that. And something like that last one that killed the trees? When was the last time that happened? Not in my lifetime."

Howard looked through the half-open door into the emporium. Business was good, very good. The phosphate mines were continuing to prosper and he had the lion's share of their business, plus dealing with many of the farmers and builders for miles around. He had some money set aside, money he had planned on using to expand the store. But now that prospect seemed staid, predictable and unappealing. Politely, sympathetically, he turned Jordan down, wishing him luck with his financial predicament.

One thing became clear to him though: it was a buyer's market.

The first day of September brought the first bearable weather in weeks. Not that it was cool by any standard, but barefoot boys no longer hopped through the hot sand of the streets. Women no longer perspired through their corsets. It seemed as if fall might eventually arrive.

Someone from out of state bought the Walls property. B.F. Jordan's grove went for a fraction of its supposed value. The season was coming on again. People with oranges were going to make very good money from them.

On the fifth of September Ralph Pine was shot dead when the heat raised him past his usual level of irascibility, prompting him to insult a quick-tempered young cow hunter who had offered to buy one of his horses for a dollar and a half. Ralph's older son had shot the fleeing cow hunter out of the saddle and the boy had died writhing in the street while somebody ran for a doctor. The sons didn't have Ralph's compulsion to hoard. They went to John Howard and offered to sell him their father's fifty acres of groves for a very modest sum—and these were trees unscathed by the freeze.

Howard put them off. He dropped by Duke's saloon for the first time in several years, had two drinks of Colonel Jim's Kentucky Bourbon, and went home to wrestle with the idea.

It seemed to him now that *not* to buy would be irrational. The groves were healthy, productive, and practically under his nose. And fifty acres was more like a hobby than an investment. Collins came into the study and said that he was about to leave for the day, asked him if he needed anything else.

Deep in thought, Howard didn't hear him until the old butler repeated his inquiry twice more.

"Advice," he said when he had finally heard the question.

"I begs your pardon, Mist' Howard?"

"Nothing, Collins. But tell me. Do you fancy orange juice?"

"Orange juice? I shore does, Mist' Howard. I cain't hardly wait for the cold weather I craves it so!"

"Well, you just might be in luck. Good night, Collins."

That night he and Jane quarreled. Howard was most bothered by the fact that she seemed to be able to read his mind like a book. She knew what he was contemplating before he had said a word about it.

She knelt beside him as he sat in the big chair in the front room. She took his hand and pressed it as if she were preserving the last rose of summer.

"Haven't we been happy, John? Haven't you been happy these past seven years?"

"Now that's an interesting number," he said, glancing down at her.

"Seven years since you speculated. Seven years since we lost the land east of town. We've built back up. Solid. We've had steady money and no worries.

Why do we need to risk it? Don't we have everything we need?"

He withdrew his hand. "Oh, for pity's sake, Jane. This is hardly that big. This isn't speculation. I'm going to buy fifty acres. That's all. And we'll get a good price for the fruit too."

She stood up. "But it's the beginning, John, isn't it? Just the beginning."

He was beginning to find her distress annoying. "What if it is just the beginning? Fortunes have been made in oranges. And fortunes *will* be made. Look around you. Even some of the frozen groves are starting to come back."

"Just don't buy any more. Please, John."

He thought better of telling her that he hadn't bought *any* yet, but that he had made up his mind to do so first thing in the morning.

The winter of 1895-96 was much kinder than its predecessor had been. Just as John had predicted, fortunes were made. Those few who had producing groves were blessed with large, sweet oranges that fetched premium prices in the big northern cities of the eastern seaboard. The little grove that he bought from Ralph Pine's sons all but paid for itself before the season was over. If the younger Pines were at all envious or disgruntled, they didn't show it when Howard came into the stable to rent teams for his carriage. They seemed perfectly content to work with their animals at a plodding daily rate that must barely have kept them in hay.

By April he came to the point where he had more cash than he wanted to keep idle. He had the choice of enlarging the store again or putting the money into some other investment. Fifty, a hundred acres at a time, he bought old devastated orange groves and set about putting them back into production. He didn't tell Jane. Neither did he try to keep his purchases a secret from her. He knew that sooner or later she'd find out.

When she did, the argument was so loud that he went around shutting the windows so that the neighbors wouldn't hear.

"You promised!" she screamed.

"I did no such thing," he told her in a firm tone that he hoped she would find settling. He became aware that he was clenching his fists.

"Is it a sickness with you that you have to risk *everything?* Should you go to a doctor to find out what the matter is? Is there such a thing as a doctor for the mind?"

He wanted to throw her out of the house but thought it best to control himself—and her, too, if possible. "You've no doubt seen the books, Jane. You know how well those investments pay. I don't call it speculation. I call it agriculture. It's the backbone of this county."

A strand of hair had come loose and hung across her forehead, making her look like a madwoman in one of those terrible melodramas she had made him sit through at the opera house. She lowered her voice in a way that was more unnerving than her screams.

"What happens when the next freeze hits, John? Will you tell me that?

What happens then?"

He came toward her as if to pin her into the corner to make her listen. "Do you know when the last killing freeze was prior to last winter, Jane? I'll tell you. It was in 1835! Eighteen thirty-five, Jane. Sixty years ago! Now let's say the next freeze comes not in sixty years, not in fifty, or even twenty, but *ten* years. Will it ruin me? No! Because I intend to sell every last orange before then!" He raised his hand with outstretched fingers. "Five years, Jane. Five years from when I bought the first grove from the Pines. We'll be rid of it all by the year 1900. That I do promise."

She sat down on the bed, supporting herself against the footboard. "Just tell me you haven't mortgaged the store."

Chapter 57

Barkley Duforge laughed and took his joke one step further. "In fact, if our fields was as productive as Martha, we'd be proper rich farmers!"

His wife blushed and turned her head. It had been a mistake to come to the reunion. Women in a family way were supposed to stay out of sight. She was sure that her mother would have told her so. But she was in a family way *all the time.* Three babies in two-and-a-half years and another on the way. No one had told her that the Duforge women tended to give birth to twins. The one on the way could in fact be two. Barkley was happy and proud. Martha, on the other hand, was starting to wear out.

She studied the men lounging against the rail fence and envied them. The time came when their work was done. Hers never was—and never would be until the day she dropped down dead from exhaustion. She wondered how many childbearing years she had left.

"Got that mine dried out yet, Larrabee?" Duke Duforge gave him a friendly clap on the shoulder. Larrabee was a full-sized man but Duke made him feel delicate. The way his brother Tom put it, Duke had a way of "scaling you down."

"We've about got all the saltwater out, now we're working on the fresh." Larrabee was referring to the hurricane and tidal wave that had practically obliterated Cedar Keys. Grim jokes were going around about catching mackerel on Payne's Prairie.

"He's got his best man working on it," Will Manning said. He had been invited to the family gathering by dint of being an eligible bachelor who might take a shine to one of Tom's rapidly aging daughters, Tess or Mariana.

"Best man—who's that?" Barkley asked. He had just set his foot on a mound he had mistaken for a stump.

"Why, me, of course!" Will Manning's big smile and sunny boastfulness made him seem destined to become a member of the family.

"He was some kind of engineer in the navy," Larrabee explained. "Had to do with getting water out of unwanted places."

"In the navy, huh?" Tom took interest in the conversation. Something blooming in September was playing havoc with his sinuses, making him stuffy and irritable, but at least so far on this outing he had not had one of his famous sneezing attacks. "What kind of boat were you on?"

"All kinds," Will said proudly. "But mostly on a battleship. The *Iowa*."

Tom was impressed. "Them battleships have some guns on 'em, don't they? Now, that's *my* kind of law enforcement!"

"Well, and that's just what it is," Will replied. "The navy is the police force of the hemisphere and those battleships are the cops on the beat."

"I read in the papers the Congress is talking about sending some of those battleships out to help the rebels in Cuba." This was the longest conversation anyone had known Tom to have since he quit being sheriff. No one knew he'd been reading the newspapers, let alone thinking about what he had read.

"We won't do that," Will said wisely. "But we *will* use our firepower to protect American lives and property. And from what I hear, there's plenty of both in Cuba."

Tom snuffled. "You're sounding like you'd be ready to get right back on and get into the scrap."

"In a minute, if I could ship out on the good old *Iowa*. The Spanish ought not to be in Cuba. For four hundred years they've shown how badly they treat their colonies. They've made and broken countless promises. They throw men in prison on the flimsiest of pretences. Cuba can't remain Spanish in a hemisphere of free men."

Duke was impressed by the newcomer's rhetoric. "Now it sounds like you're running for Congress."

"No, but I'll vote for the men who are if they're in favor of a free Cuba."

He said the same thing a week later during a visit to Penny and Nelda.

Penny had been pulling weeds from the front walk. He stood up rubbing the small of his back. "Now don't you let our young fellers hear you make that speech. They'll be running off to Cuba 'stead of minding their business right here at home."

Nelda threw a stick to keep J.J.'s dog out from underfoot. "Oh, they're not going to hang around here pulling your weeds anyway. They know if you had any sense you'd hire a colored man to do it. One who's not fifty-eight years old."

Larrabee came to the conclusion that Will's restlessness stemmed from the slowdown at the mine. The hurricane, with its torrential rains, had set the digging back several weeks. They had to bring in pumps—Will's area of expertise—and still there were delays as heavy wagons bogged down in muddy roads, stretching to the limit the patience of man and mule. Some of the miners simply stopped coming to work, making the operation all the more difficult for those who stuck with it.

On top of that, the three of them—Will, Bob, and Larrabee—suspected that the mine was beginning to play out.

"Five years of digging," Bob said. "It's got to give out sooner or later, somewhere between here and China."

The drier weather of fall confirmed their suspicions. The plug samples had shown phosphate under most of the old Preacher's Patch, but they didn't indicate how shallow most of it was. The first digging site—near the road and beneath the sickly crop of corn and cowpeas Bob and Larrabee had planted—had been the mother lode. The rest of it was like tentacles that stretched out a good distance in all directions but it didn't amount to much. Their maps of the digging got more and more detailed and more and more indicative that the phosphate was coming to an end.

So was Larrabee's money. He had continued his search for Flora, spending greater and greater sums on investigators who disappeared for weeks at a time into the vast, rolling grasslands of the Oklahoma Territory. Mr. Blount—whose unpromising first name was Beverly—continued to telegraph occasional reports of his activities, but the language—the short words separated by *stop*— became increasingly routine. One communiqué failed to mention Flora at all and dealt entirely with clerk fees at some courthouse. Larrabee began to wonder if his daughter had ever existed.

On the tenth of January he stopped by Duke's place. A well-dressed stranger was twanging away on the piano and singing a Stephen Foster tune. Larrabee fell into a kind of dream, something about Flora picking tomatoes in the garden. Gradually he became aware of the lyrics.

> *Thou wilt come no more, gentle Annie,*
> *Like a flow'r thy spirit did depart.*
> *Thou art gone, alas, like the many*
> *That have bloomed in the summer of my heart.*

> *Shall we never more behold thee?*
> *Never hear thy winning voice again?*
> *When the springtime comes, gentle Annie,*
> *When the wildflow'rs are scattered o'er the plain?*

Larrabee got up and went outside. As he looked out at passing men and horses silhouetted in gaslight, a voice spoke to him from the darkness. It was Duke. He nodded toward the light that spilled from the swinging doors.

"You know, that's why I never got married. What you just went through in there. If I'd seen it coming I would've stopped him." He lit a cigarette that showed his kindly eyes. "That's about as deep as my relationships go—in there—a little bit of friendliness for every man who puts foot in the place without trying to throw something through the windows. That's as much as I was ever good for. I grew up seeing wives and children die from one thing and another. Never wanted to take the chance of losing my own. As long as there's liquor that saloon will be full of friendship. But that's just bits and pieces, Larrabee, nothing solid. That's why I envy you. Bad as it must've been to lose Anna."

The house on Magnolia Street seemed unusually large and empty. Larrabee lit the lamp by the front door and carried it into the front room. The fire had burned low, so low that he had to build it back up with pine sticks and twists of newspaper. The jumping dance of light and shadows brought back the people who had lived in the house during the twenty years he had known it.

The three girls flutter around the room then settle briefly at the piano where Caroline plays hymns and sentimental songs that occasionally derail into sharp jumbles of discordant notes. They are hardly more than outlines because you can't quite remember their faces as you first saw them, except for Anna, when she runs to the porch table red-faced and breathless after tricking the neighborhood boys into chasing her barefoot through a patch of sandspurs. The shade of Mrs. Newhouse comes in from the kitchen, not as you first knew her, but as you last glimpsed her ten years ago, getting onto the mail coach at Newnansville on the day you and Anna married. Preacher Williams descends the stairs, turns right at the wicker chair and comes into the front room, a worn Bible in his hand and a hymnal tucked under his arm, dressed in his winter black on his way to comfort some suffering member of his flock. He raises his hand for a moment of quiet in which to make some announcement, but the other boarders come filing past on their way into the dining room, where the empty chair of the late Mr. Newhouse presides at the head of the table. Duke is there, a little livelier and huskier than in recent years, and Bobby La Rue before the bald spot began to develop on the back of his head, and Nelda fresh as a spring hat. Penny takes a chair beside her. He has only a touch of gray in his beard. They sit down, the preacher says grace, the meal begins and then fades into the cold gray light of a winter night.

Two more figures enter the front room. You can see them clearly, images from not six years ago. Bob in his Saturday nightshirt with his thick brown hair slicked back, smiles at some forgotten joke. Trailing him is a red-hired Irishman casting his shining eyes about as if enemies lurk in the dark corners. He goes to the newel post, tries without success to lift the top, and glides through the front door.

Larrabee rubbed his eyes. He stared at the corner to the left of the piano. The little corral had been there, a patchwork of twine and ladder-back chairs that kept Flora out of harm's way for a few minutes at a time. Before she was even two years old she had figured out how to slip through it.

He wondered if she was still so good at escapes.

Chapter 58

John Howard thought it was a terrible idea and said so. "I'll not have you sharing a canoe with any colored man and that's that."

Jane tried to reason with him. "What can be the difference between poor old Collins paddling a canoe for me and any other Negro driving the carriage while I ride in the back seat? Will you tell me that, John?"

He glanced around to make sure that no one was overhearing the argument. It was the most beautiful spring day anyone could imagine and everyone in town apparently had decided to picnic at Bivens Arm. Howard had never thought much of the place. He found it cramped and mosquito-bitten, but since the draining of Alachua Lake, this surviving appendage of water had become very popular for boating and fishing, and its proximity to town made it easy to get to.

His collar itched and he was getting hot. He was eager to end the disagreement.

"All right. Since you insist on slithering though this excuse for a pond, *I'll* take you. But that'll be the end of it. One short trip."

He thought the canoe was dreadful. Cedar painted to look like birch bark. Jane probably had no idea how ridiculous they would look. He paid his quarter and nearly lost a shoe in the muck as he pushed off. He knew enough to stay low and balanced, but he had only a vague idea of how to make the thing go. While Jane sat smiling in the bow he thrashed around in the stern until they were somehow out on the dark brown lily-lined water.

Jane unfurled her parasol and watched the great white cranes and ospreys riding the updrafts above the hummock.

"You should look more cheerful, John. Winter's passed. Two winters without a freeze. The new trees have never looked better. Just three more years and we're clear."

The paddle stuck on something and he yanked it loose, spraying himself with that awful water. "Yes, of course. Glad to see you're keeping track for me. I suppose you've also noticed that business at the store has been leveling off."

She tilted her parasol to block the sunlight as the bow swung around. "As a matter of fact, I did notice. I fancy that the phosphate mines are starting to play out."

"Very astute. Not that it's going to put a dent in Dutton's fortune. But you see those groves will be just the thing to get us through a lean year or two. Then it's just a matter of time before commerce picks back up."

"That's the most balanced thing I've heard you say—ever. Picks and shovels will never rot or freeze or fall prey to worms. And there will always be a demand for them."

"Good God, Jane, I'll never know why you don't just wear suits and smoke cigars. You think more like a man every day."

"Not so much," she said with an enigmatic smile. The mild afternoon made her feel coquettish.

Howard's paddle hit something large that seemed to dive under the canoe. He drew back so abruptly that the canoe lurched to one side. Jane had been sitting on the cane seat, her back straight and her knees together. As the canoe pitched to the right, she threw her weight to the left, and the bogus birch bark marvel dumped its two flailing passengers into the grim water. As John worked at his backstroke—the only kind of swimming he knew—Jane's long skirt and shirtwaist began to pull her down. She panicked, screaming and splashing and sinking all the faster.

She was so distressed that she didn't see a large man onshore pull off his shoes, throw off his hat, and dive toward the overturned canoe. He swam toward her with long, powerful strokes so precise that they scarcely broke the water. As John fluttered and scissored his way toward shore, the large man surged toward Jane and put his arm around her waist as she was going under. It seemed a miracle to her that anyone could swim, let alone stay afloat without swimming, and his hold on her made her panic all the more. She tried to break free of his strong grasp and tore at his face with her nails. Then, without the least trace of malice in his face, he punched her on the jaw.

She came to with so many people fussing over her that she could scarcely breathe. They were all chattering like crows. She had no idea what they were saying. Somebody sat her up and she began coughing. Then she became aware that her shirtwaist was clinging to her breasts most indelicately. She became aware also of a sharp pain in her jaw. Her hair was matted. She pulled a weed from behind her ear and lay back down.

Her rescuer broke through the confusion. Dripping, he bent down and put a blanket over her. It smelled like deviled eggs. "You know," he said, "if you had just stayed with that canoe you could've floated in with it. Not that I minded going out to get you."

She wasn't sure what he was saying. She swept the water from her eyes, trying to remember where she had seen him. The sharp features, the thick dark hair and trim mustache, the blue-gray eyes touched with amusement. Then it came to her. He was the baseball player, the foreman at the Preacher's Patch Mine.

She struggled to get up but was seized by a wave of nausea. She lay back down. The last thing she needed was to humiliate herself further.

"Where's John?"

Someone made a comment about his swimming, how he looked like a water moccasin wriggling toward shore.

"The last thing I'd do with that water is swim in it," someone else said. "There's gators and snakes both in there. You're lucky you wasn't—" The voice broke off.

Someone had found a blanket for John too, a child's quilt in pink and light blue. His derby sat crookedly on his head, as if he was trying to wear it without getting it wet.

Collins drove them home.

A week later Jane had a visitor. The day had been hot and Jane sat in the shade of the pavilion, feeling sorry for the overdressed children who trudged to church, boys who sweated under black serge suits, girls awash in layers of petticoats and stockings. The church bells clanged on endlessly, leaving no room for doubt that this day belonged to unquestioned ritual.

John had gone to the store. Sundays were good for doing inventory, and he much preferred a weekly inventory to the insanity of an annual exercise. Collins came through the side door and interrupted her thoughts by informing her that a visitor had arrived.

Her first thought was of that odd little traveling salesman that clattered through town once or twice a year. He usually showed up in the spring. It was just a fancy though. The man who appeared on the porch was someone else entirely. It was the hero who had rescued her at Bivens Arm.

He looked quite different today. He wore a linen cutaway coat with fashionably high lapels and a matching vest, not one of those dreadful sack coats that were so popular. His trousers were creased as if he were in uniform. His tie was white satin. He carried a fedora.

Light-footed, he crossed the porch and stood before her, his face a little too somber she thought.

"Ma'am, my name's Will Manning and I've come to apologize."

"Apologize?" She looked up at him for an explanation. "Didn't you save my life?"

He looked at a loss for words. "I don't know. I'm just glad for the outcome. I'm sorry that I had to—that is, that I found it necessary to—to hit you. I'm afraid my navy training got the better of me."

"I'm afraid I don't know what you're talking about." It was true in that she had no recollection of the incident even though her face had been sore for most of the week. Somehow she had remained unbruised. Enjoying his discomfort, she turned her cheek toward him. "You see? Not a mark. Are you disappointed?"

Again he was tongue-tied. "Why, no, not at all. But I also want to apologize for what I said. It was unkind."

Now she was genuinely mystified but she thought this could be interesting.

"You're right about that. Just which part are you referring to though? And why don't you sit down? You look miserable standing there like that."

Eagerly he pulled up a chair. "Will Mr. Howard be joining us?"

"Mr. Howard's at the store doing inventory. He's over there every Sunday morning."

Will Manning remained standing. "Maybe I should come back at—"

"Mr. Manning, John is *always* at the store, except when I can talk him into going out for a little while. That's what we were doing last Sunday when you saved my life. So just what was it that you're here to apologize for?"

"I told you that you should've stayed with the canoe, that you could've drifted into shore with it even though it was upside down. You see, there's air trapped underneath an overturned canoe and you can float practically forever with one. In fact, with a little practice, you can even turn it back over."

"John has told me he was sure he hit an alligator with his paddle. That's what caused the accident in the first place."

"Well, there are ways to keep gators at bay, too, but I guess I'm not doing a very good job of what I came here to do."

"The navy didn't teach you how to apologize for saving someone's life."

"I guess not." He put his hand on the table. "But there it is. For whatever I said or did wrong, I'm sorry. I hope you'll accept my apology, Mrs. Howard."

He had slipped the loop, brought the fun to a sudden end.

She saw him again at a baseball game a month later. She walked down to the park on the pretense of checking on John's groves, the ones formerly owned by Ralph Pine. But in truth, at the end of April they were doing fine on their own. The fruit was gone and the white blossoms were out, even on the youngest trees. The grove was gloriously fragrant. She attended the games so regularly that she began to understand the rules and to see that Will Manning was a very capable player.

She doubted whether he had noticed her in the crowd. She was quiet among the noisy, milling multitudes. But after a particularly difficult victory over the Ocala Rush, as she walked back through the grove, there was Will Manning standing between two rows of trees. It was a windy afternoon, which took the curse off the heat and made the leaves cast a play of light and shadow across his tall figure. He stood with his weight on one foot as if he was about to burst into action, but he waited for her to come near.

"I saw you at the game," he said. He was hatless and his damp hair lay flat, parted just to the left of center. He looked at ease in his oat-colored uniform. The dark knee stockings showed the shapes of muscular calves. "You forgot your award."

He was talking in riddles again. "What award?"

"Why, the game attendance award, of course! Surely you know that the person who attends the most games in the season receives a game ball?"

She pursed her lips so as not to smile. "But I've hardly attended any games. I just stop by occasionally when I've been looking at the groves. Mr. Howard takes these groves very seriously."

"And so he should. They're fine groves." He held a ball out to her, offered it like some forbidden fruit balanced on his fingertips.

She took it and rolled it in the palms of her hands. "How can this be the game ball? It's never been used."

"It's for a game that hasn't been played yet," he said. She couldn't tell if he was simply saying the first thing that came into his head or if he had some deeper meaning in mind.

They were walking out toward the road.

"How are things at the mine?" she asked suddenly.

"Slow," he said without hesitation. "The poor devils. We've had to lay off half of them. I don't know what they'll do."

"Mr. Howard says that things are bound to get better in the next year or two. He blames it all on labor strikes and silver. Says we've been in a depression for four years."

"Your husband knows his business. But it's not just that. The mine's playing out."

"And what will you do?"

"What will I do?"

"If the mine closes down. Where will you go?"

"Well, ma'am, I think I may be going back into the navy, especially if I can get back on my old ship, the *Iowa*."

"And go back to pulling people out of the water."

"Not exactly. There's been trouble brewing down in Cuba and I'd like to help put a stop to it."

"Trouble? What kind of trouble?"

"Oh, the newspapers are full of the crisis. Every day there's a new story about Cubans being put in prison for no reason or the disappearance of men who speak out against the Spanish government. Something's going to give, and before it does we'll need to protect the lives of the Americans down there."

She had never heard anyone talk that way. She didn't know what to make of it. "That's very—very civic-minded of you."

"You've put your finger right on it," he said, his eyes full of fire and excitement. "It's like the whole hemisphere is our neighborhood and it's up to us to protect the weak from the bullies."

He seemed a little like a runaway locomotive to her. Once he got going on an idea, there was no stopping him. He talked politics the same way he played baseball, hitting hard, moving fast.

They came to the edge of the grove, where the bright light of day shone harshly on everything. As their paths separated she became aware again of the ball in her hands. With a long underhand sweep of her arm she threw it to him. He caught it without taking his eyes off her.

"Good catch," she said.

He came to her and pressed the ball into her hand. "Good throw." Then, suddenly, he was all manners again. He started toward the square, waved and called out with boyish cheer, "Thanks for coming to the game, Mrs. Howard! Please give my regards to your husband."

Chapter 59

The buds hardened and developed into dark green fruit that swelled into firm green balls hanging thick in the tall trees of the grove. The torrential rains of summer beat down the resilient young leaves without harm and sank into the sandy ground before the hot sun returned. The gray-green trunks broadened and rose and the lofty crowns of the tallest trees thickened and spread with new growths of glossy leaves. The hardy trees of the grove grew out, unbowed by winds, grasshoppers, or the weight of their own ripening fruit.

It was an easy place for meeting, the grove that graced the distance between West Main Street and the ballpark. A person might easily have a good reason for passing through its shady rows en route from the road to the park, and yet it was not often used as a shortcut because its owners were known as vindictive men. The first had been Ralph Pine, who had planted the groves more than twenty years ago—a man so mean-spirited that he had kept Dobkin Murray in debt for years just by renting a team to him, a man who had managed to get himself killed by passing a single harsh remark to a hot-headed cow hunter.

Then there was John Howard, who sent policemen after every boy who snatched a piece of penny candy from his counter. The ruse was always the same—that the boy had taken something of value also, or had acted as a diversion for one who had, though the merchandise in question was never found when the sticky-faced thieves were apprehended. Rumor had it that anyone caught crossing through John Howard's property would be prosecuted because the grove was posted with sternly-worded "no trespassing" signs that would make anyone think twice. The occasional violator did dare to go through, but Howard's grove was not a popular place.

Nonetheless, Will Manning cut through often, although it was not the most direct route to Larrabee's house, where he stayed most weekends. If he was seen passing through the trees after a baseball game, no one thought much of it. They assumed, perhaps, that he had some connection to the owner.

Jane Howard also was known to pass through from time to time to check on the groves on her way to indulging a surprising interest in the Oak Hall team.

The baseball season ended in October and the picking season began and the grove became a different place. Hoards of Negro field hands—men, women, and children—poured into it like ants on a sugar cookie. Men with large wicker baskets climbed tall ladders and picked their way from the bottom of the tree to the top and back down again and from one side to the other, while women and small boys toted the baskets to mule carts that conveyed the produce to Porter's brick warehouse a block east of the F.C. & P. depot.

Jane had taken it upon herself to drive to the depot to check the quality of the packing. She came back to the grove a good while later, although John wasn't there when she returned. He had gone to the telegraph office to make sure that the refrigerator cars were on their way. When people questioned the need for refrigerator cars in cold weather he had explained that the new cars would keep the oranges from freezing as they went north and would save them from rotting if they sat too long in the south. It was worth it to him to pay the extra freight.

The first payoffs were so good that early in December the Howards took a couple of days off to throw a Christmas party. The night was damp and gray but the south wind kept the temperature well above freezing. Only the older ladies complained about the cold as they stamped their feet and crossed the threshold. Jane had a cat now that would settle into the lap of any unsuspecting visitor and was valued as a sort of living muff that could keep hands warm even if the chair was away from the fire. Collins had long since stopped climbing the stairs, so Jane had hired a maid. Her name was Althea and she was said to be a cousin of the late, notorious Harmon Murray. She did a superb job of keeping the place in order although she was terrified of cockroaches.

By half past seven the house was filled with guests and the smell of perfume and pomade, shoe polish and cigars. Someone told Jane they had expected the McKinstrys to be there and wondered what could be keeping them.

"Well, let's just find out," Jane said with a bright smile.

Howard looked toward the ceiling. "Now you've set her off again. Any excuse will do."

Jane went to the back wall and lifted the receiver of the new telephone.

"An early Christmas present," John grunted. "Why I'll never know. A pickaninny with a note would be faster."

Still smiling, Jane cranked the telephone and hollered into the speaker. "Hello? Hello! Hello? Central?"

"Can we all say hello?" someone asked. "Will they hear us?"

"She's talking to the operator at the moment," Howard explained. "You'd think they'd be on intimate terms by now."

"Hello? Jenny? Would you ring fifty-two please? What? I said, would you please ring five-two?"

The guests quieted down to see what would happen next.

"Five-two! That's the McKinstrys. Yes! Will you ring them for me please?"

"She calls next door all the time," Howard said. "She could just as easily holler out the upstairs window."

Mrs. McKinstry bellowed back that they were on the way, and all of the guests shouted greetings at the slowpokes. They would've taken turns cranking and yelling themselves hoarse all night if Jane hadn't told them that Jenny went home at eight o'clock.

Jane drifted from one conversation to the next, finding that the women tended to talk about childbirth, canning, quilting, and schools—topics she knew very little about—except when someone said the Union Academy looked garish with a second story added. Jane thought it looked a little ungainly but said that the more students they could get in the better. Largely self-educated herself, she had determined that the sooner a person could read and had books at hand, the better off everyone would be.

The men's conversations roamed from the growing season to hunting—it was generally held to have deteriorated—to Cuba. A war of words had flared up between the Spanish and American governments.

"No," Dr. Phillips said, "not between the governments, between the *people.* Remember, Cleveland was as much against the Spanish as McKinley is."

It seemed strange to Jane that men could talk so fervently about people they had never met. It was as if Cleveland and McKinley were their billiard partners.

"There's plenty of fine sugar country down there," Ben Jordan reminded Dr. Philips with a genial poke in the vest. "We can manage it a darn sight better than Spain can. If I was you, I'd invest now. Prices are going to go sky high once we've taken the place over."

"Throw Spain to the mat and you'll get Cuba and Puerto Rico," said a third man. He was Ray Polk's nephew. He had made good money very quickly by managing foreclosure sales, but he wore a sack coat that was a size too small and his silver-plated watch fob was too big for the chain.

"What does Puerto Rico have?" Dr. Phillips asked with open hands.

"Rum!" roared the younger Polk and they all quaked with laughter.

Jane went back to the kitchen and dipped herself a cup of water. She felt strangely out of place at her own party. Later that night, after the guests had departed, she felt a headache coming on. After some complaining, John agreed to read to her from the book he had bought at the new tobacco shop across the square.

"I'm not sure it's suitable for a lady," he warned.

She lay back on the pillow and put her hand to her forehead. "Oh, John. It's the only thing we've got that I haven't read."

He settled in his chair by the fireplace and turned to the first page. "All right. We'll try it."

She smoothed the covers, waiting for him to begin. "John, what do you think of Cuba?"

He put the book down. "Cuba? What's Cuba got to do with anything?"

"I just wondered. That's all."

"Well, Cuba is a political matter and there's no reason for a woman to worry herself about political matters. It can only lead to—a headache."

"Do you think Cuba should be freed from Spain?"

"I have no idea whatsoever, except that the longer the revolt goes on the worse it'll be for business. You can't harvest sugar when you have a constant threat of insurgency. Better that they should all see to their business." He began to read.

She held up her hand.

"Now what?"

"You never told me what the name of the book is."

He turned back to the cover. "*The Red Badge of Courage* by Stephen Crane."

In late January John went to Savannah on a business trip. Part of the purpose, Jane was sure, was to take on the aura of substance and importance that businessmen got when they traveled. Anyone worth his salt referred casually to far-flung business trips, the farther the trip the more impressive, as long as people had heard of the place. Henry Dutton, of course, could toss off names like Paris and London without the least suggestion that he was trying to impress you because everyone knew that he made major cotton deals there. And now his phosphate holdings had taken him to Berlin and Munich too. For John Howard Savannah would have to do. Through a series of telegrams he had been negotiating with railroad managers there, trying to speed up the freight service, but the telegraph was such a limited medium of communication that he had decided to go up and wrangle face to face.

Jane thought it was also a way of showing his confidence in his business— the store and, in particular, the groves. He had a foreman now, who supervised the pickers as they moved from one grove to another like a conveyor belt. Jane thought that if anyone could turn orange trees into a sort of machine it would be John.

They were blessed with another cooperative winter.

Jane settled into a kind of contentment until one day in late January when she received a telephone call. Jenny informed her that a Mister Maine was ringing her. She had no idea who Mister Maine could be, and even when she spoke to him it was hard to tell at first because his voice seemed to be coming from a Mason jar. When she finally heard his voice clearly for a moment she nearly dropped the receiver.

"It's Will Manning."

She got a grip on the telephone. Collins was too deaf to hear her and Althea wasn't due until after noon.

"How are you?" She was reluctant to repeat his name.

"Fine! I just called to congratulate you on your groves. I see pickers in there just about every day! It's not the quiet place it used to be!"

"But it will be again!"

"Not as quiet as the little pond I'll bet!"

He had spoken of a lone oak that arched over a circular pool. It was about a quarter of a mile due north of the trading post. She got a better grip on the receiver. "No, not as quiet as that!"

"It's such a warm, sunny day. The pond must surely be a pleasant place by three o'clock!"

After lunch she had Collins bring a buggy from the White Pine Stable. She took the whip in one hand and the reins in the other and drove out to the warehouse and the depot and kept right on going. About two miles later, she turned north onto a sandy little hunting track. When she got to a small, dark pond, she stopped. A large live oak arched so low over the round sinkhole that it almost touched the water. Beside it stood Will Manning.

They met twice during that week, three times during the next. As a joke, Will started referring to himself as "Mr. Maine" when he called to make the arrangements, and they always spoke in a sort of code—a language of their own—that would be meaningless to anyone overhearing one end or the other of the conversation. Will spent less and less time at the mine, partly because there was less and less to do and partly because he didn't want to be a financial drain on Larrabee and Bob.

Will and Jane met for a discreet half hour at a time, sitting by the big oak tree at the brow of the pond. It was a mucky, scum-covered little puddle but it had a certain secluded charm, and to the two of them it was a glamorous place full of wonder and promise. They talked of their childhood homes, of their little pleasures and dislikes. Jane made a charade of reading Will's palm. At the end of her interpretation, he kissed her.

"I'm afraid I've been dishonorable," he said.

She continued to hold his hand. "Because I'm married?"

"Yes, of course. It's just that—"

She put a finger to his lips. "Well, I'm not. John and I were going to be married one time, but seeing two men gunned down in the street sort of broke the spell. So now you don't have to feel dishonorable. If you still want me."

He stopped telephoning after that. They worked out an even more private code. He would walk past her house and leave a heart-shaped piece of quartz on the fence rail by the front gate. If it was gone when he returned an hour later, he would know to meet her at the pond.

"I hate sneaking around like this," he told her. "As soon as I'm square with the navy, let's get married."

On February seventeenth, the day before John was due back, Will told her that he was going away.

"What have I done?" she asked.

He took her in his arms, kissing her hair. "Nothing, my precious, nothing!"

She drew back. "Then why? Because John's coming back?"

He kept hold of her hand and squeezed it. "One of our battleships was sunk in Havana harbor yesterday. Everyone is sure the Spanish did it. It's going to mean war. I have a duty to the navy and to the country to stop the Spanish."

She knew there was no point in arguing with him. "When will you go?"

"As soon as I hear from the navy." He lifted her chin with his fingertip. "I *will* be back when it's over. And we'll get our lives sorted out."

He kissed her again. When they got back to the road they went their separate ways.

Chapter 60

"Used to be, I thought I knew what patriotism was," Penny said, "but oncet you git outside of the country it seems a trifle fuzzy."

"At the rate we're going I'm not sure we'll ever *get* out of this country," J.J. said. He was looking for some sign that the train would speed up, but the scrubby cabbage palms and towering slash pines confirmed that they were still crawling along the edge of the prairie.

"These young bucks," Penny declared. "So full of piss and vinegar they can hardly stand up. If it's what you really want to do, J.J., I hope they don't care about them fingers of yours. But it's hard to believe a boy of mine'd be fighting in Union blue."

"General Wheeler's fighting in Union blue," Jeremy Summerton reminded him. "If he can do it, we can."

"You boys don't get your hopes up too high," Will Manning warned. "One thing you'll learn about the military—whether it's army or navy—they're big on paperwork. The war might be over by the time you get all the documents signed."

"I hope not!" J.J. accidentally kicked the seat in front of him. A private from New York, sweating in his new blue wool uniform, half turned to see what had hit him but thought better of starting a scrap. "There has to be enough Spanish for everybody to get at least one!"

"Them Spanish are probably saying the same thing about you boys. Now that's not something I was goin' to say when your mothers was around, but that's what war is—the other feller tryin' to git you as much as you're tryin' to git him. I just hope you end up with General Joe. He'll learn you how to take care of yourselves."

Larrabee had been looking at the uniforms worn by the men in the car. "All of these boys look like infantry. You two might have to settle for fighting on foot."

"That would be crazy!" Jeremy protested. "Making us foot soldiers. We can ride rings around the lot of 'em."

"Crazy is what the army's about," Penny said. "I don't care if it's Union or Confederate, American or Spanish. Crazy is what it's about. That you can count on."

Jeremy brought his elbow in from the window and brushed off a cinder. "Were you ever in the army, Mr. Larrabee?"

The window was stuck and Larrabee was pushing on the frame to loosen it. "No, I was too young for the last war and I'm way too old for this one. Unless they want to make me a general. In the cavalry."

"Cavalry's in the hands of a couple of colonels," Will said. "Colonel Leonard Wood and—can't remember the other one right now."

"All right then, I'll settle for colonel," Larrabee said. "Unless I'm too old for that too."

"We'll *all* be too old at this rate," J.J. complained. "I can still see the prairie back there. We should've ridden our horses down. We'd be half to Tampa by now."

They rattled down the Tampa & Jacksonville line, passing through one storm cloud after another. Despite the rain, most of the soldiers kept their windows open because of the heat and humidity that made the slow-moving train all but unbearable.

"This is a jog train all right," Penny said. "Almost as bad as what we had durin' the war. You know if Senator Yulee had let us move some of his tracks we could've held out another year."

Will Manning laughed. "You'd've run 'em right down to Tampa where most of that Confederate beef was going. Straight to Cuba. I've read some history."

"History!" Penny screwed up his face. "Well, I suppose it is at that."

They jerked and banged into the night. The windows streaked with rain. Cinders lit up the starless sky. Some of the soldiers played cards by lantern light, but the bumping of the train nearly knocked the lamp over and so they gave it up and settled for talking and smoking in the darkness. When the train stopped for water so did some of them, unbuttoning and pissing out the windows before the train took off again.

"I feel parched and roasted and hung out to dry," Penny said when the rising sun woke him. "What I'd like more'n anything right now is to be at Duke's havin' a cold beer, a good cold beer." He cleared his throat noisily, stuck his head out the window and spat. "Bob sure passed up an excitin' ride."

Jeremy took him seriously. "He wanted to see the front same as you and Nathaniel. He stayed home mostly for mother's sake."

"Anybody got any idea where we are?" J.J. looked around at the sand flats and scrub pines. "Must be down south somewhere."

Penny hauled out his silver-plated watch, an anniversary gift from Nelda. "According to my calculations we're about to pitch into the Gulf of Mexico at any moment. It's God-forsaken country, wherever we are."

Will Manning yawned and stretched and ran his hand over his hair. "We're about twenty miles from Tampa."

"Now how did you figure that out?" Penny asked.

Will smiled. "I asked the conductor while you were snoring your head off."

"Twenty miles! What's this train been doing all night?"

"Sitting. A passel of sitting," Larrabee said.

Penny settled back against the seat. "Well, that's what war is, boys. Settin' right where you are and then rushin' off like a decapitated chicken."

"Well, I'm ready for the rushing part," J.J. said.

But the closer they got to Tampa the slower the train went, inching its way in a series of fits and starts that made everybody hot, restless, and irritable. When it stopped again with screeching brakes, Penny hailed a conductor and asked what was wrong now.

"We're in Port Tampa!" the conductor shot back. "That's what's wrong."

Everybody jumped up and poked their heads out the windows. Nobody liked what he saw. The train had come to a halt in a field with countless others. Every one of the several tracks was clogged with boxcars. Soldiers were everywhere, dripping in their heavy blue shirts, which they wore with rolled up sleeves and open collars. Their white felt hats were stained about the bands. The men of the army sweated and swore and milled about the tracks.

"Look at the guidon!" Will said excitedly. "They're New Yorkers! The First New York Volunteers!"

They battled their way to the baggage cars and followed Will through the throng. Beyond the trains huge black smokestacks shot into the sky.

"Are those factories over there?" Penny wondered.

Will laughed when he realized what Penny meant. "Factories? Those are steamships, my friend! That's how we're getting to Cuba!"

"I was only funnin'," Penny said, sounding a little hurt.

Confusion ruled the day. Will couldn't find his commanding officer. J.J. and Jeremy couldn't find a recruiter. They all got hot and tired. Larrabee bought them each a lemonade from an enterprising Negro boy who carried a clump of change in his hip pocket. Nobody seemed to know when the troops were to ship out. A sergeant was stamping and cursing about some artillery pieces that had been dismantled and packed part in one boxcar, part in another, without any labeling whatsoever. Will Manning and the boys had been gone for an hour, off looking for somebody in charge.

"We've only got one hope," Penny said, dropping down onto a flour barrel. "That the Spanish are even more discombobulated than we are."

Just then the two boys came striding back. Jeremy was talking a blue streak, laughing and waving his hands. J.J. walked along with his eyes on the ground and his hands in his pockets.

"Yonder's a story of some kind," Penny told Larrabee.

Jeremy stuck out his hand. He was all smiles. "Say howdy to Private Jeremy Summerton, United States Army!"

Penny and Larrabee shook his hand. "One way or the other, you're in for an adventure," Penny promised. He put his arm around J.J. "What's your story, son?"

"Turned down flat, pa." The boy's disappointment was bitter.

"On account of them missing fingers? I'm sorry. But sometimes things turn out for the best. Your ma sure will be happy to see you when we git back home." He gave his son a consoling hug. "Yonder comes Will like a dog with his tail on fire."

"They're going out today," he reported breathlessly. "Today! It's no wonder everything's in such a jam. But by this time tomorrow I should be on the *Iowa*, God bless her!"

"Jeremy here has joined up," Penny said.

Will shook Jeremy's hand and gave J.J. a sympathetic look. "My friend, there's always an important job for the man who stays home." He patted the boy on the shoulder. Then he took Larrabee aside and thanked him for the good years at the mine.

"There'll be something for you when you come back," Larrabee said. "If you want it. It doesn't have to end here."

"I appreciate that," Will replied. "But whatever happens, I think I've come to a fork in the road." He took an envelope from the breast pocket of his coat. "When you get back to town will you leave this at the post office for me?"

Larrabee pocketed the envelope without looking at it. "You can count on it, Will."

"And have a drink at Duke's for me."

"Looking forward to it."

Jeremy was promising to write to J.J. "I'll see to it that you know as much about this war as I do. It's on account of me that you're not getting to go."

"If you mean the shooting accident, forget it," J.J. said. "That was a long time ago."

"I'll write," Jeremy repeated. "Every chance I get. And I'll whup a Spaniard for you."

With that the two warriors disappeared into the swarm.

After a few confused hours, Larrabee, Penny, and J.J. gave up on the train and bought horses for the ride home. Penny and Larrabee figured that J.J. could use a diversion from his disappointment, so they finished off the day drinking beer in a small saloon in Tampa. Then they looked around for a place to spend the night. The city was so swollen with civilians involved in the war that accommodations proved hard to come by. Long after sunset they tried a drafty old place far down the bay. The unpainted porch was decorated with strong-smelling conch shells, deep-sea sponges, and twisted fingers of driftwood.

"The bric-a-brac of the sea," Penny said. "Them sponges is right fragrant, ain't they?"

Larrabee didn't answer. He was staring at something on the wall of the dim lobby.

"Just look at all this stuff," Penny went on. "You'd think a ship come in here and busted up, wouldn't you?"

J.J. read the faded gilt letters Larrabee was looking at: "*La Belle Helene.* Is that foreign?"

"That ain't foreign," his father said, "that's the name board from a ship."

Hearing them come in, a clerk had approached the desk and turned the register toward them.

Larrabee asked him where the name board had come from.

"Hell if I know," the man said. "It's always been here."

When they rode out in the morning they were still tired, having spent much of the night batting at mosquitoes that came in through the high louvered windows. Penny complained of bedbugs and fleas. J.J. was somber. The day was hot and the horses slow. Larrabee wished he had brought his spurs.

"You suppose Jeremy's havin' as much fun as we are?" Penny waved his hat at the horseflies that seemed to be everywhere.

"I'm sure he's having plenty more," J.J. said with disgust.

"Maybe so," Larrabee said, "but I'll bet your folks are going to be a whole lot happier than his. You'll know how that is when you've got little ones of your own."

"Bob tells me you done give up on the detectives," Penny said. "I wish there was somethin' we could do, Nathaniel."

Larrabee turned in the saddle to see them better. "I figure even if I didn't do so much for my own, I went a long way to support the children of Mr. Beverly Blount. The last of the money went to plastering circulars all over the Oklahoma Territory. That was a year ago."

"You just never know," Penny said vaguely. "You just never know."

It took them three blistering days to get back home. At a crossroads called Garden Grove they learned from a stevedore that the ships were still in Tampa. Rumors that the Spanish fleet was waiting in ambush had made them steam back into port, and most of the frantic loading proved all for naught. Late the next afternoon, following the curve of a long lake, the three riders were caught in a downpour and took the opportunity to strip off their salty clothes and go swimming until thunder rolling over the water sent them packing.

The sun was coming down on the third day when they rode over a rise and saw the great prairie open up before them, blue on the north horizon. They spent the night at the farm with Bob and Laetitia and little Ainsley, who could never get enough of their stories.

"Let's just hope it's a real uneven scrap," Bob said after supper as the men sat on the porch steps eating watermelon. "This whole business has been more than tough on Laetitia. Seems like Colonel Summerton told her a thing or two about war."

Larrabee stayed on another day, Sunday, walking through the fields and orchards with Ainsley gripping his thumb and begging him to tell again about the train.

The growing season had been good to the farm. The vegetables had thrived in long rows that ran parallel to the old lakebed. Great broad leaves rose high, promising a steady crop of tomatoes and beans, potatoes, lettuce, beets, cucumbers, and squash. Bob had done well with May corn, had harvested and planted a second crop. Only the orange grove stood fallow and ruined, the grass tall between the fifteen-foot trees killed three winters back.

Bob's two hunting dogs came running up, tails wagging, and nearly knocked Ainsley over. She grabbed hold of her father's knee and righted herself.

"Honey, you're fixing to knock us both over!" Bob scooped her up and perched her on his arm. "Penny and J.J. was fairly eager to get home I guess. Did J.J. know his mother had already found out the army wouldn't take him without them fingers?"

"Not that I could tell. Penny wanted to play it all the way through. Wanted him to see some of it. It takes some doing to work the restlessness out of a boy."

"Don't I know it. I'll be glad when this is over and our boy comes riding down that road."

It rained steadily from evening until well into the next morning, and even in the afternoon the roads were still so muddy that the going was slow. Larrabee's horse lost her footing on the high side of a washout and began to limp. He dismounted and walked her for a mile, but she continued to be sore in her left hind leg. He spent the rest of the afternoon leading her into town.

He left her at the stable with Ralph Pine's older boy, stopped by the post office and dropped off Will's letter, then went home and set his saddle pack on the floor by the round table. He sat in the wicker chair for half an hour, staring out the window. Through the pines he could see pink and gray clouds wrestling for dominion of the evening sky. The grays were getting the upper hand. He felt a sudden need for companionship, washed his hands and face, and walked down to Duke's.

Some of the stores along the square were still lit and the Alachua Hotel was full of life. The tobacco store was selling books from a shelf set on the new cement sidewalk. In the few days that Larrabee had been gone, the gaslights on the corners of the square had been replaced with bright, outlandish electric fixtures on tall iron posts. In some ways this seemed like just another strange new town he had come to on his way back from Tampa.

Duke's was closed. The heavy black window shades were pulled low, even the one toward Roper's Hall, which had always refused to yield the last half-foot. It was a sight for Sunday morning, not for a weeknight. Even on Sunday afternoons Duke threw the shades back up and opened the door and windows while he swept up and aired the place out. Yet on this Monday night the saloon was shut up like a tomb.

Larrabee hailed a passerby. It turned out to be Bobby La Rue on his way out of the Alachua Hotel.

"Bobby, this isn't a holiday is it?"

"Not as I know of, Larrabee."

"Then why's Duke got his place closed?"

Bobby touched him on the elbow. "Say, you've been gone for a while, haven't you?"

"About a week, yeah."

"Larrabee, Duke's dead. They found him upstairs in his bed last Thursday. Doc McKinstry thinks his heart gave out."

Larrabee stared at the locked door and black shades. He had come back from a place where thousands of men were preparing to go into battle, where some of them would surely perish. That was a fact he could grasp. But, here in these familiar surroundings, it was beyond his comprehension that one man that he knew well had climbed the stairs to his room, gone to bed, blown out the lamp, and died.

Chapter 61

Jane hated the name on the envelope all the more because her own never appeared in the letter. But that had been the arrangement and, much as she hated it, she could see the wisdom in it. Althea had learned to come back from the post office without dallying. Jane pestered her to go early, get the precious letters as soon as the mail was sorted, and hurry back to the house. Each day she rose or fell according to what the maid brought back. The first letter arrived without a postmark just five days after Will had left for Tampa. She had no idea how it had come but she knew that he had written it on the train and that he went into danger determined to return to her.

The second letter came two days later. He was still in Port Tampa, sweltering with hundreds of soldiers and sailors. The ships were supposed to have gone out on June seventh and in fact had begun the trip to Cuba when suspicions arose that the Spanish fleet lay not far from Tampa Bay waiting to ambush them. So, Will wrote, the ships were called back into port, where everybody quickly learned that the ambush rumors were false. But then the ships were stuck in port until they could replenish their water supply and there weren't enough pilots to take them back out. As of June twelfth Will and his cohorts were still languishing at the docks, hot, dirty, and restless.

She waited a long, anguished month for the next letter. It was postmarked "Port Tampa, July 21" but it had been written at sea. Her heart skipped a beat as she saw the familiar handwriting.

It is now five weeks since I have seen your lovely face with its mysterious smiles and I miss you more than ever, like a man in the desert languishes for lack of water. There is plenty of water here, but little to drink. Don't take that metaphor too seriously, dearest! How I long to meet you again at our little body of water in the wild woods! To hear the jays and the mourning doves and feel the warm touch of your soft hands, to look into your deep eyes! I am feeling happy and melancholy all at the same time.

The war is won, except for the paper signing, and I was there to see it happen. On July 3rd we were on blockade as usual. It was a hot, still Sunday morning. The pale green water off Santiago Bay floated rather than chopped.

As you may have read in the newspapers, the North Atlantic fleet had been trying to beat Admiral Cervera the way Dewey beat the Spanish fleet at Manila. But he and his fleet slipped into the protection of the shore guns at Santiago Bay and we were forced to wait him out, sitting at the narrow entrance to the harbor.

On that hot, still morning of the third, suddenly he came out, Cervera with his four ships—the Maria Teresa, *the* Vizcaya, *the* Christopher Columbus, *and the* Admiral Oquendo. *I have to say, they looked more gallant than our lead-colored fleet, with their golden figureheads and red and yellow battle flags.*

We fired at once and our other ships joined in—the Indiana, *the* Texas, *the* Oregon *and the* Brooklyn. *We swung into an ungainly column and dogged the Spaniards as they tried to break free by running along the shoreline. Under our barrage* Teresa *burst into flames and turned for the beach. The* Oquendo *followed suit, set on fire by our broadsides. The* Vizcaya *made a good run for it but the* Brooklyn *and the* Oregon *nipped at her heels until she slowed. Then she went afire too and grounded on a reef. Our armed yacht, the* Gloucester, *closed in on two small but deadly torpedo-boat destroyers and sank them. The captain of the* Gloucester *had been the executive officer of the* Maine.

Lost in the smoke and close inshore was the Columbus, *but the* Brooklyn *cut off her escape. About fifty miles west she struck her colors and ran aground and the day was won after only an hour-and-a-half of shelling.*

How quickly men's affections turn! Once the foe was beaten our blue-jacket heroes ventured out to pull the wounded from shark-filled water and burning ships. We fed and clothed the rescued, tended their wounds, and prayed for their dead buried at sea.

Still it took two long weeks before the fall of Santiago, where we heard the gallant army was languishing in a standoff, under the threat of the tropical fevers.

It looks now as if the final t*'s and* i*'s will be written at last and this bitter-sweet adventure will come to an end. As soon as the Navy has had its fill of this seafarer (any day now, no doubt), I will be making my way back to a much smaller body of water and—if she has not thought better—to the "lady of the lake."*

He had signed with a single *W*. She kissed it and hid the letter with the other behind the wardrobe.

As the hot days of August unfolded one after the other, she began to think of herself as a kind of larval creature, ugly and unfeeling, bound in a soft wadding in which she had languished for months, years. She pictured herself at last developing into something beautiful inside her cocoon, something beautiful and mysterious—for she still had her mystique after all these years, some part of her being that men had been unable to penetrate. She pictured herself shedding her cocoon, spreading her beautiful yellow wings to dry, and then flying through the kitchen window, out beyond the well-trimmed privet and the moss-tangled oaks. She would beat her wings, take to the wind, and never look back.

Three weeks later, when Althea returned from the post office, John Howard was in the kitchen. He was drinking a glass of buttermilk, but the girl had the feeling that he was waiting for her. She held the letter behind her back and tried to act as if nothing was out of the ordinary but her nervousness gave her away. Howard held his hand out.

"What came in the mail today, Althea?"

She glanced out the back door to the rose bushes nestled against the wrought-iron fence, wishing she were on the far side of it all, walking barefoot toward the coolness of the Sweetwater Branch.

"You have a letter there. Just give it to me, Althea."

She clutched it all the closer. "No, sir, Mist' Howard. I dasn't."

"Come now, Althea. It's a letter for my wife, isn't it?"

"It's for me, Mist' Howard. It's addressed to me!"

Unwavering, he stretched his hand toward her. "So were the ones upstairs, Althea. But that was just a ruse, wasn't it? Just a little joke between you and Mrs. Howard. Tell the truth now."

She looked at the floor.

He reached behind her back and helped himself to the letter. She watched as he sliced open the envelope with his fingernail and began reading.

"It's a little vague, like the other ones. Vague but very complimentary. I don't suppose you know who *W* is."

"No, sir."

"I don't suppose you've seen any men in sailor suits loitering about the house while I've been gone? Maybe while I was in Savannah?"

"No, sir."

"Of course not." He refolded the letter and slipped it into his inside coat pocket. "This will be our secret, won't it, Althea?"

"I reckon so."

"I'll be able to tell if you inform Mrs. Howard."

"Yes, sir."

"Now to the cleaning. I'm starting to see mildew on some of the books in the study."

"Yes, sir." She started to go.

"And Althea?"

She turned at the dining room door.

"It's kind of fun to share secrets, isn't it?"

When Jane came home Howard was waiting for her in the front room. He stood so still, slouching slightly with his elbow propped on the cold marble mantle piece, that she didn't notice him until he spoke to her.

"There's a letter for you here."

Her blood froze. She got a tighter grip on the hatbox she was carrying and hurried upstairs.

He followed her into the bedroom.

"Would you like me to read it to you? You seem to like being read to."

She put the hatbox on the bed and opened it as if this were just another day in the long, hot summer.

"You had no right to read that."

"You had no right to receive it."

"I had *every* right to receive it!"

"Thirteen years in my house gives you license to do *this?*"

"That's right, John. Thirteen years in your house. Because that's all it is or ever was. Your house. A place to hang my hat."

"That doesn't justify this." He shook the letter at her.

"What is *that*, John? You've read it. What does it say?"

"It says—it says you are to meet him at some pond."

She laughed, embarrassed by his clumsy reference to something painfully close to her.

He looked up from the letter. "Don't you want to know when?"

She tossed her head, throwing a wisp of hair over one ear. "No, why should I?"

"Because he'll go away and never come back unless you're there." He held the letter out to her. "Go ahead. Read it for yourself. He's going to wait three times from seven o'clock in the evening until eight, and if you don't come he says—quoting here—I will banish myself from your life. Isn't that cavalier? I will banish myself from your life. I'm surprised he doesn't say forever. That's so much more romantic don't you think? So much more *passionate.*"

She snatched the letter from him and threw it in his face.

"All right. Just what do you think we've been doing, John? Nothing your impoverished mind can understand. I've done nothing to be ashamed of. Nothing! But what about you?"

"I don't know what you're talking about."

She came toward him with clenched fingers, as if she would swipe her claws across his face.

"I'm talking about Bill Zeiss, John."

"Bill Zeiss? The lawyer?"

"Yes, the *real estate* lawyer, John. While you were in Savannah he came by looking for you and told me all about the wonderful bargains you've been picking up. It seems that Mr. Zeiss sells orange groves. He said you're his best customer. That's the way he put it—customer."

"This isn't about oranges, Jane."

"No, not at the heart of it. It's about *trust*. I trusted you and you lied to me."

He put his hands in his hip pockets and took them out again. "I told you, I'll sell it all in just over one year now—at its peak—in January 1900. That plan has never changed."

"Neither have you. But I have."

"And I've got to say, it's not a flattering change. You used to be fun."

"That's because I didn't care. But now I do. I came here on a lark and got a good look at people who cared about who they were and what they were doing. They had—they had—I don't know— *honor*."

He laughed. "Honor? Isn't it a little late in life for you to hang your hat on *that*, Jane? Does your pond sailor know about you and honor?"

"He won't hold it against me."

"Maybe not. But then maybe you'll never know." He stooped and picked up the crumpled letter, smoothed it out, and slowly tore it to pieces that fluttered to the floor like snowflakes.

A month later, on the three designated evenings, a lone figure sat by a giant oak that arched over a small round pond in the woods. On the first day he brought a bouquet of camellias and roses. On the second day, a small leather-bound book of poetry. On the third day he sat smoking his pipe, watching the jays and mockingbirds flitter in the twilight sky, and listening to the mourning doves sing their long, sad notes.

Chapter 62

She had come despite the cold. She had walked to the White Pine stable, picked up a one-seat buggy and team, and driven the three miles to the pond. She had gone there from time to time just because it gave her some satisfaction to get away from John. It was only an hour or two, but it was an interval that belonged wholly to her. Bundled in a wool dress and shawl and blanket, she sat by the bending oak tree and watched the mallards paddling the dark water. Far to the north, rifle shots rang through the woods and she wondered what it had been like for him. Had the Spanish ships fired close to him? In his letters he had mentioned nothing of the danger to himself, only the quick end to the standoff at Santiago Bay and the gallantry of the sailors who went to rescue the vanquished Spaniards.

She ached to have those letters, even though he must have put her out of his thoughts by now. Nearly five months had passed since the three fateful days when he had waited in vain for her here. She imagined him walking briskly down the leaf-strewn path, whistling some jaunty sailor's tune as he came to the pond, certain that she would be waiting for him. Imagined his perplexity the first evening, his hesitant doubling back to the road, the return visit the next day and the one after that. What must he think of her? Then she wondered if he had come at all. Had there been some clue in the letters that would tell her what to think, what to do? John could have done her no greater harm than tearing them to pieces.

Her only salvation was in the little tasks that gave shape to the days and weeks. She walked to the groves although she no longer thought of them as her groves. She helped Hattie the fat cook plan the meals and went to the market herself to select the best produce and the most tender cuts of meat. She went to the occasional play or musical at Simonson's Opera House. She even walked to the post office and picked up the mail without any self-consciousness—and without any hope whatsoever that she would see another envelope graced by Will's precise slanting handwriting. Long ago, before she had even met John Howard, she had taught herself not to get her hopes too high, not to get them very high at all in fact. But with Will those cautions had been overturned and now she was paying the price.

Early in January John had begun complaining again about stomach pains. He had seen both Dr. McKinstry and Dr. Phillips without any improvement. On Dr. McKinstry's advice he had given up smoking cigars and had taken up instead the absurd habit of chewing sticks of penny candy. After a few weeks, though, he found that one of his back teeth was going bad, and he spent a miserable afternoon in Dr. Seigler's dentist chair. Jane instructed Hattie to overcook the roasts and vegetables and suggested that he might find milk soothing, but he rejected that idea as being even more humiliating than the penny candy. He did take the occasional glass of buttermilk.

"Good God," he barked, "at forty-six I'm not about to live on pabulum!" He flung his fork on the floor and stormed from the dining room.

As Jane sat alone picking at the mush of potatoes and peas on her plate it occurred to her that he was going through the same fits of temper he had attributed to Major Dennis just before the major's death at forty-five.

She was heartened, at least, that John had let up on his drinking ever since hearing that Nathaniel Larrabee had bought Duke's Saloon.

She thought, too, that the cold winter couldn't be doing his spirits much good. December had begun mildly enough. Some of the azaleas were already in bloom. But the end of the year had brought a light freeze that killed the azaleas and what was left of summer's beauty. January had been consistently cold but not unusually so, and recently some of the afternoons had been warm enough to make her throw her beaver coat over her arm as she walked about town. February had brought the promise of an early spring. Some of the red bud trees and dogwoods had begun to bloom and the oranges were fat and ripe in the groves.

It was one of those warm afternoons in February that lured her back out to the pond. She knew that most people would not think of it as a beautiful place, but to her it had taken on an attractiveness of its own. Will had told her that the pond was nothing but a sinkhole—a circular collapse of the porous limestone that supported most of the state. The surface either dropped down to the water table or the resulting depression filled up with rain and runoff. The origin of this particular pond, he had said, was less than romantic, and the pale green algae that spread over it gave it a particularly forsaken look. Once he had pried a piece of lime rock out of the sandy soil and thrown it into the pond, sending the scum cascading onto the muddy slope surrounding it. When the water had settled he had led her to its edge and shown her the image of a man and woman embracing, reflected in its dark, silvery surface.

"It's our wishing well," he had said, "and there's my wish."

Now, as the light began to fail, she lifted a rock and threw it into the pond.

As the noise died down she heard footsteps on the path behind her. She turned sharply.

"What did you wish for?" asked Will Manning.

As the team shook their harness, watching dusk settle over the woods, the butterfly emerged from her cocoon.

Later that night, as Larrabee warmed his feet by the fire, Will came in and sat down at the round table.

Larrabee looked up. "There's some supper on the stove if you want it. I didn't know if you'd be coming in or not."

Will ran his hand along the edge of the round table. It was hot where it faced the fire.

"There's something I ought to tell you."

"Not about supper, I imagine."

"You've sure given me a fair shake, you and Bob, and I can't take off without telling you why."

"Sure you can. Folks come and go all the time around here. There's not another war somewhere, is there?"

"I appreciate you and Bob giving me such a free hand at the mine. Not just anybody would've done that."

Larrabee stared into the fire. He was tired and discouraged. He wasn't sure that saloon keeping was his kind of work. He had put together just enough money to buy Duke's.

"We didn't know scratch about mining, Will. That's why we gave you your head."

Will smiled. "I know that's just you being you again. You'd give away everything you've got and say everybody else was doing you a favor. The fact of the matter is I'm going off with a woman."

"Don't think twice, Will. That's perfectly natural."

"No it isn't. She's married—or at least everyone thinks she is."

Larrabee's eyes flickered. "Ain't that kind of an obstacle?"

Will held his hand to the hot edge of the table. "It's a long story. But she wants to come with me. If there's one good thing about war it's that sometimes it helps you sort your thoughts out. Down in Cuba my thoughts kept coming back to her."

"And I guess she feels the same way about you. Where you headed for?"

"Washington. I have contacts in the navy. There's a place for me with the engineers if I want it. But I need to be up there within the week."

"Well, that's the way those decisions generally come up, isn't it? Now or never."

"We'll be leaving tonight. Taking a rig to Waldo and catching the morning train."

"I guess that's better than taking off in broad daylight. Her husband might see you standing there at the depot."

"Do you think the worse of me for this?"

Larrabee had been eating pecans, cracking them with pliers. He wadded the shells in a piece of the *Daily Sun* and tossed them on the fire. He watched the twist of paper catch on the ends.

"Will, if there's one lesson I've learned in the last twenty years or so it's not to pass judgment on other folks. You're a sound gent and you've got your reasons, whatever they are. I just hope it works out all for the best." He rubbed his hands together. "Seems like a cold night for running off, though. You'll be lucky if you don't freeze on the way to Waldo."

Will was silent for a long time, listening to the fat pine crackle and spit in the fire.

"You probably ought to know who it is I'm going with."

Larrabee thought for a moment. "My God! It's not Martha, is it? Because if it is, you'll have to buy tickets for all twenty-three of her pups or however many she's up to now."

Will chuckled softly. "No, it's not Martha. It's somebody else who used to watch me play baseball."

Larrabee sat up with a queer look on his face. "You don't uh—"

Will nodded slowly.

Larrabee whistled a long low note. "If that ain't a curious knot."

"Will you wish me well?"

"Sure. You got everything you need? Why don't you take one of those wool blankets from upstairs? As a keepsake."

"Thanks. I'll take you up on that. What'll you be doing, Larrabee?"

"Me? Just running that saloon I guess, now that the mine's played out. Duke made a living at it so I imagine I can. Especially now that it's got those fancy water spigots and electric lights."

Will leaned across the table. The fire brightened his face. "You oughtn't to live by yourself in this big old house. You ought to have yourself a wife and a family."

Larrabee was quiet for a moment, as if listening to the voices that seemed still to echo through the high-ceilinged rooms.

"You write now, Will, when you get the chance."

It was still dark when John Howard woke up. He thought he had heard some clattering under the window, but when he got up to look there was nothing to see. The pinewood floor was cold under his bare feet, and he was picking up another brick, warmed beside the fireplace to heat the foot of the bed, when he noticed that Jane was gone. She had been gone for a while. Her side of the bed was cold. One door of the wardrobe hung open slightly and he went to close it. As he did, the other door swung out, revealing that most of her clothes were gone. It was so late and he had slept so soundly that his thoughts were dead in the water. The empty wardrobe meant nothing to him. Going to the bedroom door, he could see no light in the upstairs. He fumbled around for a lamp, lit it, turned the wick back down, and went downstairs. The house was so terribly cold that he thought he must have come down with some sickness that brought on chills. The shadows of familiar objects lunged at him as he walked shivering from room to room. As the cold brought him to his senses his concern shifted from Jane to his oranges. He hurried to the study and held the lamp to the window, trying to get a look at the thermometer, but the glass was fogged, no—frosted—and he rubbed it with the sleeve of his nightshirt until he had a circle he could see through. Vainly he looked for the gray column of mercury. Holding his breath so as not to fog the window, he looked down from forty degrees to thirty, to twenty, to ten. He rubbed the glass again, held the lamp closer, squinted hard and then his eye saw the mark—at *six* degrees above zero.

He ran upstairs, nearly knocking the chimney off the lamp, threw off his nightshirt and stuffed himself into his clothes. At the front door he threw on his hat and an incongruously formal coat and ran from the house without bothering to close the elegantly carved door. He ran, sucking in the stinging air, all the way across the deserted square and down the vacant street to Ralph Pine's old grove—*his* grove now. He ran, coattails fluttering, down the path to the ballpark and soon found himself slipping on hard ground. He stopped and steadied himself against one of his trees. Its dark green leaves hung limp and withered. All but the thickest branches drooped. He pulled off the nearest piece of fruit and found it hard as a baseball. In the dim gray light of dawn he lifted his eyes to the treetops. Something cold drifted onto his cheek and melted. It was starting to snow. He dropped the orange.

It clattered on the frozen ground like a rock.

Part V
Harvest of Light
1899-1905

Chapter 63

THE MAN IN THE NEXT CHAIR was chattering away about the Courthouse Square. He had some theory that history moved in circles and he wanted to be sure that the barber didn't miss a word of it. Every time the barber turned his back to rinse the comb the man obligingly stopped and waited for him to turn around again.

"So you see, they cut down them oaks around the square and planted orange trees, and now that they're cutting down the orange trees, what you reckon they're going to put up there? Oak trees! You just wait'n see! Because one thing you can say about oak trees—they don't freeze! Ain't that right? I say, ain't that right?"

He was an older man and Larrabee found himself hoping that the talker would die right there in the chair and stop bothering everybody. They could take up a collection—about a dollar-and-a-half—and get old Sam Leary to do the burying—if he was still alive himself.

On Mondays Larrabee treated himself to the luxury of a shave at the place across from the Courthouse. It was a frivolous and wasteful self-indulgence, but he enjoyed the touch of the sharp razor through hot lather, and combined with his monthly haircut, that shave made him look the way a downtown businessman should. Larrabee figured he owed it to Duke's memory to look his best, and anyway, when you were unshaven, those electric lights down at the saloon were unforgiving.

The night had been muggy and the morning was warm, and Larrabee had flopped around fitfully on the sleeping porch so that he was still groggy, and more than once his barber had to ask him to lift his chin.

He had taken to watching the people walking past the wide arched windows. Each time he went through this exercise he was more surprised at the number of people he didn't know.

His barber was a heavy-handed man named Nick who had a suitably thick head of dark brown hair parted in the middle and slicked down with macassar you could smell from the Courthouse. He waxed the tips of his handlebar mustache and had fingernails trim enough to be the envy of the finest ladies in town. He lived just east of the Sweetwater Branch in a small house with a large yard in which he kept chickens, a sideline that Larrabee found hard to reconcile with the barber's starched and manicured person.

On this drowsy Monday morning, as the old man in the other chair droned on about history, Nick was telling Larrabee about his musical ventures. His voice was soft and polite as he drew the freshly sharpened blade across Larrabee's chin.

"Three of us fellows who like to sing have started up a barbershop trio," he was saying, "but there seems to be something missing."

Larrabee was watching a girl through the large backward letters on the window. She was overdressed for such a warm day, in a cut-down man's jacket that was still too big for her. She wore a pale blue gingham dress and black wool stockings. Most of the girls around town had long since taken to going barefoot and none of them were wearing coats. Larrabee deduced that this girl was wearing everything she owned.

Her clothes looked dirty but her brown hair was well combed and pinned. Her braids were tied with red ribbons. She was looking down, apparently at something on the sidewalk.

Nick was on to another subject, but Larrabee hadn't heard him. The girl had glanced up through the window. Her eyes were brown. She flipped one of her braids over her shoulder, looked back toward the sidewalk and smiled.

Larrabee bolted from the barber chair.

"Here now!" Nick raised the razor. "You've made me cut you!"

He all but knocked over someone passing the shop. The girl turned around to see what the commotion was.

She found herself eye to eye with a man who stared at her wild-eyed through a faceful of blood and shaving cream. He had a striped, hair-covered sheet pinned around his neck.

She was too surprised, too startled, to move.

The wild man looked at her hard with his blue-gray eyes.

"*Flora?*"

The cat she had been petting darted into the alley. She started after it. He seized her by the shoulder and the oversized coat started to come off. She screamed and tried to get away but he caught her elbow and turned her around.

"You're Flora, aren't you?"

She was frightened. She struggled to throw off his hand, but this time he held her fast.

"You're crazy! Leave me be or I'll scream!"

He eased his grip, afraid he was hurting her without knowing it.

"Go ahead. Go ahead and scream. You're my—daughter. That's enough to make anyone scream, Flora."

"I am not! I am not your daughter!"

"I'm afraid you are."

She looked at him, suspicious through welling tears.

"When's my birthday?"

He wiped some of the shaving cream from his face. He couldn't remember exactly. He knew it was near his own, sometime in January.

She pulled her arm away and started down the alley.

"Wait!" He cut her off and pulled his watch from his pocket. He opened the cover and showed it to her.

She took it from him, holding it as close as the gold chain would allow.

He let her look at the picture for a long time before telling her what she already knew.

"That's your mother. When she was about your age."

Flora closed the watch and clasped it in her hands.

"If you'd like to know about her, " Larrabee said, "I'd be proud to tell you."

He convinced her to come with him to Penny and Nelda's. She had no baggage, not even a change of clothes. She tagged along like a stray fawn, giving him the impression that at any moment she might bound away and disappear from his life forever. So he kept close to her, filling the silence with the explanation that Penny and Nelda had known her mother.

"When I first saw her she wasn't but about ten years old," he said. Then he added suddenly, "January tenth. Your birthday is January tenth, isn't it?"

Flora frowned and looked away.

"Well, that's it, isn't it? Why do you look like somebody just threw a rope around you?"

She stuffed her hands in her oversized pockets. "None of your beeswax."

They trooped along, listening to the sounds of the town. Plodding teams clattering through the sandy streets, boys calling to each other from windows, axes and saws taking down the dead trees in Ralph Pine's old groves, a rooster crowing. As they approached the Wards' house the dog let out a howl and then started barking. The girl drew back.

"Oh, that's just Mallet," Larrabee said. "He won't hurt you. Hell—heck, he don't even hurt rabbits" He repeated the statement as if to erase the inappropriate word.

"Well, it just so happens," Flora said, "that all dogs scare the hell out of me. Aunt Caroline had one that was supposed to protect us but snapped at us like a goddam wolf. "

J.J. came to the door and hauled Mallet back while Larrabee asked for Penny and Nelda.

"Daddy's on the terrace resting his back," he said, glancing at Flora. "Mama's due back from Matheson's any second. Y'all come on in."

"What happened to your fingers?" Flora asked.

"Bear got 'em," J.J. said without missing a beat. Larrabee had told him to use that story whenever he got tired of explaining.

The girl looked at him wide-eyed.

"'It isn't exactly polite to ask folks about missing parts," Larrabee told her. She followed him into the house with her hands behind her back.

J.J. dragged the dog toward the kitchen door and pushed him outside with his foot. "Go eat yourself a squirrel if you can catch one 'stead of stinking it up in here." On his way out, he closed the door behind him as he announced, "Uncle Nathaniel's here."

Flora was trying to get everything straight. "I thought you said he ain't kin."

Larrabee shook his head. "He ain't, isn't, but I've known him as long as kin. Known him since he was born. His folks lived in your mother's house before they were married. Seemed like we had half the town in there at one time or another."

Flora kept her hands to her sides as she looked toward the back door. "Is the dog gone?"

The door opened again and Nelda came through the kitchen talking to J.J. "You said there's someone with him?"

Larrabee straightened and touched the girl's shoulder. "Look who we have here, Nelda."

She took off her hat and peered at the new arrival, waiting for her eyes to adjust to the light. "Well, I—oh, land's sake, she looks just like Anna!" She rushed forward and put her arms around the girl. "Penny! Come see who's here!"

Her husband grunted and came in from the terrace muttering something about Nelda's habit of rousing him just when his back started to feel better. He was still partly bent over when he came into the front room.

"Why, hello. Who's this?"

"Look, for heaven's sake! Just have a look at her."

J.J. stood by with his hands in his pockets. He was only nine years old when Anna had died and had all but forgotten that Larrabee even had a daughter. He thought that Nelda's guess had been a matter of woman's intuition except that Larrabee looked so proud and happy.

"Why, how-de-do, young lady." Penny looked at Nelda. "You know who she kind of reminds me of?"

"Do tell," Nelda said.

He came forward and embraced the girl. "My, what a sight for sore eyes! But ain't you hot in that coat? J.J., git this child a lemonade! She makes me hot just lookin' at her."

Larrabee and Flora stayed at the Wards' for the rest of the day. Nelda drew the girl a bath and discreetly sent her maid out to get some clothes that Flora put on only after coming to the conclusion that her own were even dirtier than she realized.

"If it's all right, we'll get Camilla Mae to wash them for you," Nelda said.

Clutching her towel, Flora moved between Nelda and the soiled pile of wool and gingham.

"I'll wash it," she insisted.

Nelda stopped. "Of course. "She set down the clothes Camilla Mae had rounded up—a plaid cotton dress with a lace collar, a petticoat, cotton undershirt and drawers, dark stockings and a pair of rather formal tan calfskin shoes and a buttonhook. "You just come out when you're ready and if you need anything else, let us know."

"Larrabee was just tellin' me he come acrost her by chance outside the barbershop," Penny said when she came back into the front room. "Just like that."

"Where has she been all this time?" Nelda asked softly.

Larrabee let out a deep breath. "That's what I'm fixing to find out. But one thing at a time."

"Comin' all this way on her own," Penny said incredulously. "She'll have a story all right."

In the morning, Larrabee burned the breakfast bacon because he had been thinking about the girl upstairs. He trimmed it down as best he could and scraped the eggs to keep them from sticking to the skillet. He was still uneasy with the arrangement even though Nelda had set him straight.

"She's your *child*," Nelda had said. "Children are supposed to live with their parents. You've been looking for her all this time. Now that you have her, be her father."

"But I don't know anything about raising a twelve-year-old girl."

Nelda put her hand on his shoulder. "You'll learn. "

So after supper Flora had gone with him over to the house. He didn't want to pry but neither did he want to let slide the whole big question of how she had come to town—and why. They had tiptoed around it at the Wards.' Flora's answers had been consistently short and vague. She couldn't—or wouldn't—even tell them where exactly the Oklahoma homestead was. She described it in great detail but seemed to have no notion of what the nearest town was or even what part of the territory it was in.

She was a renegade. She reminded Larrabee of himself.

He put her up in the big southeast corner bedroom, the one that Anna and Caroline had shared. Looking a little small and out of place in the plaid dress, she trudged up the stairs clutching her old dirty clothes, found the room and closed the door behind her.

Now what, Larrabee wondered.

He stood outside the door for a moment, listening to the muffled sounds of her movements in the room. He heard a window open and hoped that she wasn't thinking of escaping through it. He listened for telltale footsteps on the sloping roof. Hearing none, he went downstairs and sat smoking his pipe in the wicker chair.

An hour later he slipped back upstairs and looked at the bar of light under the closed door.

He went downstairs again and smoked, ran out of tobacco, and paced in the front room. He ran his hand along the oak mantle piece. The dust kicked up a cloud in the lamplight. He carried the lamp through the room, finding dirt and clutter everywhere. He rolled up his sleeves and went about setting everything right, picking up and sweeping past midnight.

Then he returned to her room. Her light was still on. He longed to see her, wanted to embrace her, but didn't dare. He tapped on the door.

He heard the bed squeak and the floor creak and the soft sound of her sock-footed approach. A chair scraped and the door opened slightly.

"What is it?" she asked.

"I—I just wondered if you were all right."

"Sure I'm all right. Why wouldn't I be?"

"Well, I couldn't help noticing that your light was still on."

"I like the light on."

"Isn't it about time to go to sleep though? It's past midnight."

"I like the night."

That first night had not been a promising start. Now he had burned the bacon and the eggs weren't looking so good either. At last he made up his mind to be more direct and forceful with her. He put the bacon and eggs on a plate, went upstairs, and knocked on her door.

No answer. He knocked harder.

"What is it?" She sounded sleepy and more than a little annoyed.

"It's time for breakfast."

"Breakfast?"

"Yup, we generally eat it at the beginning of the day around here."

"Well, I don't want any. I want to go back to sleep."

"That's because you were up too late."

"What?"

"I said that's because you were up too late last night." He cleared his throat. "Tonight you'll go to sleep earlier."

She came stomping toward the door. "The hell I will!"

"The hell you—that's right, you will. Now will you open this door please?"

He heard the scraping of a chair again and then the door opened. She glared at him.

"Why did you have the door blocked?"

"That's none of your—"

"I know—beeswax."

She sat at the head of the dining room table, in the late Mr. Newhouse's place, glowering at her bacon and eggs.

"Don't they eat in Oklahoma?" Larrabee asked.

"Not like this," she said. "This is burned. Even Aunt Caroline could cook better than this."

"What else could she do?"

"What?"

"Never mind. Tell me about Caroline and your Uncle Arthur. And the boy. What's his name?"

"Edgar. Edgar went to work for the Morrows."

"The Morrows?"

"After Uncle Arthur defaulted on the loan. They live across the road."

Larrabee rocked in his chair. "Where is your Uncle Arthur now?"

"There's plenty of people would like to know that."

"Then what about Caroline?"

"She's at the home."

"The homestead?"

"Not the homestead, the *home*. The state home. It's in Oklahoma City."

Larrabee wasn't sure what she meant, but he didn't like the sound of it. "Where have you been living all this time?"

"With the Bassets. They live on the other side of the Morrows."

"Aren't you going to eat anything? You know, I don't cook for just anybody."

"It's a good thing."

He touched her hand. It was warm. His was cold.

"Tell me about the Baxters."

"The *Bassets*." She seemed to think he should know them.

"The Bassets."

"They had dogs. Two of 'em. They had three but Mr. Bassett shot one of 'em for killing sheep. And...."

"And what."

"Nothing."

"Why did you leave the Bassets?"

"Because there wasn't no place for me there."

"Do you think there is for you here?"

She looked up at him sharply.

He smiled and patted her hand. "Of course there is." He just wasn't sure what it was.

"Don't you think the Bassets are worried about you?"

"Not as much as they are about the money from the county."

"What money?"

"The money for taking me, of course. There was one boy who ran away and they kept taking the money as if he was still right there. They're probably doing the same with me."

Larrabee ached, realizing more than ever what a monumental mistake he had made in sending her away. "I want to show you some things and tell you some things," he said.

He wasn't sure where to begin. He led her into the front room. "There in the corner your mother and I made a little corral for you to keep you safe once you started to crawl. Sometimes she carried you like a papoose. You used to sleep with us in the corner room upstairs."

The girl took it all in without saying anything.

They went into the kitchen and he showed her the wood room. "She used to give you your baths in that tub because you carried on so much that she thought she'd stay drier that way. She didn't though. She had to change clothes after most of your baths."

In the corner of the room, stacked with newspapers, was a baby carriage. "I couldn't bring myself to give this away," he said. He took off the newspapers and pulled on the handle of the carriage while keeping his foot on the rear axle. The carriage turned into a highchair. "I guess you wouldn't remember this."

He showed her the hole he had burned in the arm of the wicker chair while waiting for her to be born.

He led her through the kitchen and out the back door to the profusion of weeds that had once been the chicken yard. He had long since paid one of Penny's carpenters to take down the henhouse. The grass in its place had grown tall and gone to seed. Behind its wire fence the garden was matted and yellow with spears of green poking up at random.

"Why are you showing me this?" Flora asked impatiently.

"It was your mother's garden. She used to have you out here while she worked in it. The two of you used to have long talks out here. She grew—"

"Beans."

"You remember?"

"No. I can see the stalks among the weeds. Why don't you take care of it?"

"I never had the time. Your Aunt Martha did for a while. Then we had a freeze last February. It killed just about everything that was left. But it looks like a few things are coming back."

"Back when she still made sense, Aunt Caroline told me you ran a boat or something."

"I did. The lake dried up."

"Is that some kind of joke?"

"It wasn't the least bit funny at the time, but now that you're here I'm glad it happened because I work nearby."

"Doing what?"

"I'm a businessman." That sounded silly so he told her outright. "I own a saloon. There's someone I'd like you to meet. He lives over this way."

He led her through the Poinsetts' back yard, past the brick building that housed B.F. Jordan's store and the armory. That side of the street, devoid

of its orange trees, was brilliant with sunshine and they crossed over to where
the great arching live oaks still spread their generous shade. They came to
a neighborhood of proud houses, tall and expansive, with turrets and porches
that fanned around corners, oval windows, and stories stacked like steamboats.
Picket fences and wrought iron went on as far as the eye could see. When they
were a block or two short of where Larrabee had shot John Howard, he turned
and led her up a narrow street.

Flora started to hang back. "Where are we going?"

Before he could answer, a large brown dog, a mongrel of hound and terrier,
jumped a fence and came at them. Flora screamed and ran.

Larrabee picked up a stick from an orange tree and stood his ground.

The dog stopped about six feet short of him and barked until it realized
that things had come to a standoff.

"You go on," Larrabee told the dog, "Go on, Tuck, while you still can. Go
on now. I don't have all day." He looked back and saw Flora huddled high in
a dead orange tree.

He turned and walked slowly back to her. The dog barked after him a
couple of times, snorted, and trotted back down the street.

Flora sat with one arm wrapped around the tree trunk and the other on
the branch above her.

"He won't hurt you," Larrabee said. "That was a half-wit mutt named
Tuck. He was just showing off. Will you come down now?"

She didn't answer.

He looked up at her. "You know, I was a pretty good tree-climber myself
when I was your age. We've got climbing trees around here like nothing you
ever saw in Oklahoma. And a sight better than the one you're in now."

She looked down the street to see where the dog had gone.

"I wish you'd come down, Flora."

"No."

He was at a loss. "Then do you mind if I come up?"

She didn't answer.

"Well," he said to himself, "I'm in it now." He spit on his hands and hauled
himself up to the first branch, about four feet off the ground. Something in his
shoulder popped. He grunted and climbed up to the next branch. A moment
later he was standing alongside her with the trunk between them.

"You know, this is higher than it looks," he said. "Now that I'm up here,
I'm not sure how I'm going to get back down."

He thought she looked awfully pretty despite the frown.

"When I was a kid back in Missouri we used to shake apples out of the trees
by getting up in the top and jumping up and down. Seems kind of crazy now."
He moved closer to the trunk and the limb he was standing on snapped. He
lost his grip on the trunk, dropped through a tangle of branches, and fell to
the ground on his back. The clouds spun around him as he tried to sit up. He

glimpsed Flora scrambling down from the tree hand over hand and lay back down to catch his breath.

She knelt beside him. "You still alive?"

He thought he heard concern in her voice, and he liked the sound of it. He looked up into her brown eyes. "I'm alive, but I believe I've taken root."

"Oh, this is terrible, terrible," she said quickly. "What if the dog comes back?"

Larrabee coughed. "The dog? If he comes back, I'll knock his head off. He wouldn't dare. Would you mind helping me up?"

Glancing around to make sure that no one else was nearby to do the job, she took him by the arm and propped him up against the tree. He dragged himself to his feet and leaned against the trunk.

"You know, I don't think that dog was as dangerous as the tree." He took a few steps and then had to support himself on the fence.

Flora looked at him, waiting to see if he would start blaming her for his fall.

"If you don't mind giving me a hand," he said, "I believe I'd like to go see Dr. Willis. That's where we were headed anyway. This just makes it a little more of a business call."

Reluctantly she went to the fence and stood beside him. He put his arm around her bony shoulder and they continued down the narrow street.

"What about the dog?" she asked again, looking toward the square frame house from which it had come.

"Forget the dog," Larrabee insisted. "Nothing's going to come between me and getting off my feet. Doc's house is just down there, past those palm trees."

The dog barked from the porch but broke off into a series of yelps that suggested his master's hard-handed disapproval.

When they came to the doctor's house Larrabee looked at the side door that had served as the patients' entrance. The black shingle with its gold lettering was still on the clapboard wall, but the door appeared to have been painted shut. They hobbled around to the front of the house. Larrabee sat on the gray steps and asked Flora to ring the bell.

When the doctor came out, leaning heavily on his cane, Larrabee tried to stand up but sank back down on the steps.

"No need to rise," the doctor said. "Pretty morning for a visit. How you doing, Nathaniel?"

"I'm doing rotten, doc. I took a fall."

Dr. Willis looked from Flora to Larrabee. "A fall? What kind of fall?"

"A fall from a tree, that's what kind."

"A tree. We'll they don't make 'em like they used to. Come in and let's have a look at you. Unless you'd like me to examine you here on the steps "

"I'm coming. I'm just slow." Larrabee pulled himself up by the rail and Flora helped him up the steps while the doctor held the door open.

They went into the cool dark foyer that smelled of bacon and fresh bread.

The doctor turned on his cane and looked down at Flora. "Young lady, either the floor's starting to give way or your stomach's growling. Didn't you have breakfast?"

"No, she didn't," Larrabee said. "The bacon was burned and the eggs were dry."

"Well, maybe they'll be better by lunchtime." Dr. Willis led them through a room of tidy, old-fashioned salmon-pink and green furniture and into his cluttered office.

Larrabee hadn't been in it for years. It smelled faintly like iodine and alcohol and must. Next to the big dusty roll-top desk stood the square table set with dusty chess pieces, a game interrupted long ago.

Flora helped Larrabee into the swivel chair. Dr. Willis propped himself against the desk and began to ask questions.

"Now tell me more about this fall."

Larrabee glanced at Flora. "I fell out of a tree. An orange tree."

"An orange tree. No wonder. Where was the tree?"

Larrabee thought he was being made fun of. "Down the street there."

"And how did you fall?"

"A branch broke."

"No, no. I mean, how did you land?"

"Well, I don't know exactly. I was kind of stunned."

"He fell on his shoulder," Flora explained. "Then he was flat on his back."

"As a matter of fact, we on our way to see you," Larrabee said. "Dr. Willis, this is Flora."

"I know," the doctor said.

"You could probably tell. She looks like Anna so much."

"Yes, but word gets around. Anyway, she looks as much like you as she does Anna."

Larrabee felt of flush of pride. It was the first time anyone had pointed out a similarity between him and his daughter. "Dr. Willis was with you the day you were born," he told Flora.

"Where exactly does it hurt?" the doctor asked. He set his cane against the desk.

"Well, it's sort of my back and my left leg." Larrabee wiggled in the chair.

Dr. Willis had him sit on a table and examined his leg for swelling, tapped lightly up and down his back, applied gentle pressure with his freckled hands.

"Are you being stoical or have I not found any tender spots?" he asked at last.

Flora watched from the corner, where she had been studying the chessboard.

"I just feel kind of sore and rattled," the patient reported with a little cough.

"I'm not surprised. I'd be surprised if you *weren't* kind of sore and rattled. Why don't you just sit here for a minute and see how you feel? You're not in a hurry are you? Young lady, how did you get all the way down here from Oklahoma by yourself?"

Larrabee had been postponing that question. He was afraid of what he might hear.

"By train," Flora said. "Who's playing chess?"

"I was. With the gentleman who was your grandmother's second husband. We used to play chess every Sunday afternoon. He was the trickiest chess player I ever ran across. Sneaky as the devil despite being a preacher. Generally whupped me, much as I hate to admit it. He moved to China and we played by mail for a while. Very slowly. You came all that way by train? All by yourself?"

"No."

"Somebody accompanied you then."

"No, I walked part of the way."

Larrabee lowered himself from the table. "Flora, don't you speak disrespectfully to Dr. Willis."

"Never mind," the doctor said, with a wave of his hand. "I'm sure Flora meant no disrespect. It was a very brave thing for you to take such a long trip all by yourself."

"It was just what I had to do," Flora said flatly. "It wasn't so brave."

The doctor straightened and picked up his cane. "Well, you help your daddy on home and make him lie down for at least an hour, will you?"

Flora nodded. "Were you white or black?"

It took the doctor a moment to realize that she was talking about the chess game.

"I was white."

"He was going to whup you again. In three moves."

Chapter 64

The more he thought about it, the madder he got. He figured his anger was good, the way a father was supposed to feel when he found out that his twelve-year-old daughter had gone bushwhacking halfway across the country alone on a train. His anger even brought him a strange happiness and contentment, but Larrabee was still uneasy about prying into Flora's past. Desperation had driven her to seek him out. Resentment at having been sent away in the first place had made her keep her distance from him. He was afraid that picking too deeply into her wounds would drive her away again. He decided to bide his time.

He scarcely let her out of his sight. He brought her with him when he went to the saloon in the midmorning. For a while she amused herself with punching the electric lights on and off and then settled down to playing with a box of dominoes that Duke had kept on hand.

The new tap had started to leak and Larrabee was trying to stop the drip. The saloon didn't open until noon and so, aside from the occasional neighborly visit and a man looking for a drugstore, they were alone. The eleven o'clock from Cedar Keys was pushing its way up West Main.

"Now tell me a little more about that train trip of yours," Larrabee said off-handedly.

"I just stayed on the train till I got where I was going," Flora said, not looking up from her dominoes. Apparently she was searching for one tile in particular.

"Well, where did you get on and where did you get off?"

"I got on in Grove Hill and I got off about half a mile down that way."

"How did you get on all by yourself like that?"

She looked at him for a moment, as if reluctant to give away a secret.

"I got on behind a lady with three children. Just like that."

"You didn't buy a ticket?"

"Nobody ever asked me for one."

"Isn't that lucky."

A sly look crossed her face.

"Well, you had to have some money. How did you eat?"

"The men on the train gave me money."

"The men on the train! What men?"

"The ones that bet against me."

"Flora, this is like pulling teeth. What do you mean, the ones that bet against you?"

"In checkers." She seemed to think that the answer was obvious. "Then checkers got boring so we played chess. They said it helped to pass the time. I whupped 'em all except for the one who had to get off in Atlanta."

"Where did you learn to play chess?"

"I don't remember. From Uncle Arthur I guess."

"Well, that's one thing he was good for anyway."

Someone came to the open door. He looked familiar but Larrabee couldn't quite place him. He was wearing a sweat-stained straw hat. His face was tanned and creased by the sun. His blue jeans were faded with wear and his green suspenders looked too tight on his bowed shoulders. His raveled gray shirt was buttoned to the chin and the sleeves were rolled up above his knobby elbows. He took off his hat and spat before coming into the saloon.

"I'd be looking for Miss Martha Newhouse," he said.

"Martha Newhouse? You're a little behind the times, pop. Martha Newhouse has been Martha Duforge for several years."

"I don't suppose a fella can get a drink." Licking his lips, the newcomer looked around hopefully.

"It's a little early," Larrabee said. "But you look thirsty. I imagine we can find something. What do you want with Martha?"

"Just stopped by to say howdy." The man sat at the bar and set his hat down. His thin white hair was streaked with black. He had a pennant mustache and a two-day growth of beard.

Larrabee remembered. He was the man from the barbershop, the one who had gone on and on about orange trees and history.

"Just stopped by, huh? Whereabouts are you from, mister? You're not from around here."

"I'm from all over!" The newcomer laughed, flashing a gold filling in an eyetooth. "And I kind of feel like I've been *spread*. First of all though I come from out Missouri way."

"I thought I heard some *show me* in your speech. Whereabouts in Missouri?"

"Northeast. Up close to the Iowa line."

"I'm from over in Liberty County myself." In his excitement Larrabee overpoured the man's beer.

"That's fine open country out there. Or at least it was when I was a young buck. It was all wild. And so was I, come to think on it."

"Then where'd you come to know Miss Martha?"

"In the Pacific! I helped fish her out of the drink when the *Marian* went down on the reef on her way into Honolulu. God, that was a sorry night! We couldn't tell if we was pulling out the living or the dead. We got Martha but her folks was lost."

"That was your grandmother and the other chess player," Larrabee told Flora. "They were on their way back from China."

The man soaked up half his beer with a single gulp and wiped his mustache on his sleeve. "Is Martha prospering then?"

Larrabee couldn't help smiling. "Yes, she's had what you'd call a fruitful life. You'll find her down toward Arredonda. About an hour's ride south, toward the prairie. You can pick up a horse at Pine's over there on the other side of the square."

"Say, I do appreciate it, mister. How much for the beer?"

"Not a thing. It's the least I can do for Martha's savior. I was married to her sister."

"So! Small world, ain't it? Thank you now."

He snatched up his hat and went back out into the daylight, spitting when he reached the street.

"Well, it has been an interesting week," Larrabee said. He gave up on fixing the tap and climbed onto a chair to dust the electric lights that stuck out conspicuously in the sconces that had held the gas globes.

"I didn't know you were from Missouri," Flora said.

"Sometimes I forget it myself," Larrabee said. "It's been a while."

"Your mother and father were in Missouri?"

"My mother and little sister. My father died just before I left."

"Why did you leave?"

He came down from the chair. "That's a long story."

"I've got time."

"You were telling me your story."

"There's nothing more to tell."

Larrabee shook his dust cloth at her. "Sure there is! How did you get all the way from Oklahoma to here by yourself? I could skin Caroline for letting it happen."

"I told you. I got on in Grove Hill."

"Well, you obviously had to change trains."

"So?"

"So how did you know exactly where to go?"

"I had a map."

He laughed.

"What's so funny?"

"Do you know where the Dakota Territory is?"

"You mean the states? North and South Dakota?"

"Yes, I forgot. The states, North and South Dakota."

"Sure I know. They're way up toward Canada. What's so funny?"

"You're one smart girl, Flora, smarter than a certain fella that came running out of Missouri. You get that from your mother. She had a love for maps. She was an unusual woman. I wish...."

"Wish what?"

"Never mind. Will you promise me something?"

She found the domino she was looking for and set it into the pattern she was working on. "I don't know. What?"

He tossed down his dust rag and came to the table. "Will you promise me you won't get on the train like that again? Alone."

She looked at him for a moment, weighing what he was asking.

"All right."

"Do you like it here?"

"I guess so. Do you?"

"Do *I*? It's home."

"Then why did you send me away?"

He pulled up a chair. Curtis was driving by in an ice wagon. He had three wagons now and three grown sons to run them, but he still drove on Wednesdays to keep in touch with his customers even though he now needed help hefting the ice blocks. The luncheon gong rang at the Alachua Hotel. The tap dripped steadily.

Larrabee reached across the table and touched her hand with his fingertip.

"I sent you away because I was afraid of losing you. That doesn't make much sense, does it?"

She waited for him to explain. She didn't look like Anna now. She was someone new.

"What it comes down to is this—when I lost your mother to the yellow fever I was afraid of losing you." A pullet came strutting through the open doorway. A small boy charged in, scooped it up and darted away. "I loved your mother. And I loved you and I thought you'd be safer in Oklahoma. I figured I'd get up the gumption to go out and be with you and we'd be safe. It didn't work that way. I hope you'll forgive me someday."

She gazed out the window, watching men unloading the ice wagon at the hotel. She ran her fingers down one braid then the other.

"I know it can't be too interesting to live here with me," he went on quickly. "But there are plenty of girls around here your age, plenty of things to see, folks who'll care about you. I can't do anything to fix my mistakes, but I'll sure do my best to do right by you now that you've come back to me."

She continued to finger her braids. "What about the yellow fever?"

"That's one lesson I've learned in these ten years. Bad things can happen anywhere. This place is no worse than most that way. It was just our bad luck that your mother died. The same could've happened in Oklahoma or China. That man who was in here a minute ago bears that out. Your grandmother and the preacher were about as far from the yellow fever as they could be and still they had bad luck. The water took them and spared others. Now that you're back I think the luck of our family must have turned for the better." He pushed back his chair. "Well, that's more of a speech than I intended to give. Explaining things isn't my strong suit."

She twisted her braids together at her chin, then let them go and gave him a tentative little smile. "I like the way you explain things. I just think you need more practice at it."

Chapter 65

For once in his life he welcomed the routine because it forged their lives together. As a boy on the farm he had rebelled against the monotony of plowing and planting, harvesting and putting up corn and hay. His short criminal career and flight from Missouri had broken the pattern and he had spent more than twenty years avoiding the predictable repetitions of days and seasons. His years on the *King Payne* had been as varied as the lake. Each day at the mine had a character of its own. Now he thought the time had come again to live by a pattern. Flora needed it. He needed it.

One part of their routine troubled him though. She still left her light on well into the night—all night so far as he could tell. She kept her old cut-down coat and gingham dress close at hand. She washed the dress, hung it out to dry and brought it in from the line as if it were made of spun gold and she kept the coat folded under her pillow. When she opened the door one morning he could see a gray coat sleeve poking out from under the pillowcase. She was not quite home yet.

At least she had stopped blocking the bedroom door with a chair.

On Sunday morning he took her to church although he hadn't attended since Anna's death. He had always felt ill-at-ease going through the rituals of hymns and prayers but thought that going through the motions might help bring them together. Flora didn't seem to care one way or the other about going. She wore a green-and-white checked gingham dress and a straw hat with a satin ribbon that Nelda had brought over. They came in late and sat in the back pew, following along in a shared hymnal without singing. Preacher Bonds' sermon was about the prodigal son and how he was welcomed with feasts and dancing by his father while his dutiful older brother received no such recognition. Larrabee found the preacher's logic a little hard to follow. He looked over to see if Flora was getting restless and found that she was paying close attention.

After the service, which—to Larrabee's relief—did not include the awkward communion of wafers and grape juice—Flora was duly introduced to the smiling, admiring churchgoers who clogged the aisle on their way out to shake hands and exchange greetings with the preacher.

Larrabee thought Flora must be smothering in the crush of gloved hands and sharp-smelling perfumes. She remained polite but aloof.

Like me, he thought. She takes after me in wanting to keep her distance.

They had Sunday lunch with Penny and Nelda—and J.J., who had started to buy and manage property west of town so that his father could spend more time at home.

"Isn't it just pine land out there?" Larrabee asked over pork chops and gravy.

"Pine lands and sinkholes and swamps—at good prices," J.J. added with a smile.

"Did a bear really bite your fingers off?" Flora asked, pointing with her fork.

Gently, Larrabee lowered the fork. "Flora, that's—none of your beeswax."

"They was shot off," J.J. volunteered cheerfully. "By my best friend. You like that story better?"

"They was?" Flora was fascinated.

J.J. assured her they were. "With a big ol' Confederate dueling pistol."

"That's marvelous!"

Larrabee did his best to change the subject. "What do you hear from Jeremy?"

"He's rocking along pretty good," J.J. said. "But his malaria's still flaring up."

"We're fixing to go down that way this afternoon to see the Harpers and the Duforges."

"Have you heard from Martha recently?" Nelda asked.

"She hasn't been up for a while," Larrabee said. "I figure she's a trifle tied down. That reminds me. There was a man came into Duke's looking for her the other day, said he had saved her out there in the ocean."

"Do tell. Flora seems to have a fondness for pork chops. How many days since you fed her?"

"I'm still working on my cooking," Larrabee admitted. "I guess I kind of lost my sense of taste what with fixing for myself all these years. So you say Caroline was a pretty fair cook."

Flora rubbed a spot of gravy from the tip of her nose. "No she wasn't. Most every day she made this rabbit stew that looked like puke."

"*Really?*" Nelda put her hand to her chest.

"How're things goin' down at Duke's?" Penny asked hastily. "You still callin' it Duke's?"

"Yep it's still Duke's. I couldn't see changing that. But business is slow."

"Well, you don't have all them cow hunters comin' into town anymore. The Spanish war pretty much put an end to them drives I hear. Ain't no market for them rangy cattle here and the Cubans can't afford to buy 'em."

"Makes it pretty quiet," Larrabee said.

They rented a horse and buggy at Pine's and set out for the Harper farm. Larrabee was still sore from falling out of the tree and he figured a long buggy ride might be just the thing to shake his bones back into place.

It promised to be a fine, mild afternoon. Once they got out of town they were no longer surrounded by the sorry spectacle of devastated orange groves. The lofty loblolly pines and profuse hardwoods crowded right up to the road. The bitterweed bloomed yellow along the roadside and snakeroot poked up its pale green maces where the witch-hazel and blackjack gave way to pastures and cropland.

Crows worked the newly planted fields of May corn, cawing harshly at the approach of the jostling buggy. Most of the month had been unusually dry and the road was hard enough to allow them good speed most of the way to the prairie. As the horse clopped along at a jogging trot in response to vague flicks of the whip, Larrabee told Flora the story of the *King Payne* and his thirteen years working on the lake with Bob Harper.

"What did you do before that?" she asked when she had taken it all in.

"Before that, why I just tried to keep body and soul together. Odd jobs."

"But I mean, why did you come here? You could do odd jobs in Missouri, couldn't you?"

He flicked the whip again, closer to the horse's rump this time. He needed a distraction. "No, I had to leave Missouri. I was very young. I'll tell you about it sometime."

"All right. Then how did you get here? From Missouri."

He laughed. "You should work for a newspaper. As a matter of fact, I took the train, part way."

"Did you tell your parents—your mother, I mean—that you were leaving?"

"No, I didn't. I had to go. Didn't have time to tell her."

"Kind of like me."

"Kind of," he admitted.

"Did you write to your mother?"

"I wanted to. But by the time I was able, she had moved."

"She never heard from you again?"

"No."

"That's very sad. Is she still alive do you think?"

"I don't know. I hope so."

"What if you were to go back to Missouri and look for her?"

"I'd like to. I'm just not sure it's the best thing."

"Why not?"

"It's a long story. I'll tell you about it sometime."

"Well, I think you should go back to Missouri and look for her. That's what I think."

"Maybe I will."

"Sometime."

"That's right. Sometime." He pointed down a narrow road, not much more than wagon ruts. "See down there? That's where Mr. Harper and I used to live. That's where the lake was once upon a time. Biggest lake you ever saw."

"Where did it go?"

"Into the ground. That's the way they do here. Some come out of the ground and some go back in. They call 'em sinkholes."

"I think you're trying to put one over on me."

"Am not. Cross my heart. That's the way it is down here."

"Then it's a real strange place."

"It sure is. You're going to like it."

When they got to the Harper farm the dogs came running at them and Larrabee had to hold Flora close while he drove the buggy onto the grass and up to the porch steps. Jeremy came out looking thin and tired. He was barefoot. He had his hands stuffed into his jeans pockets.

"Y'all dogs come off of there!" he commanded from the top of the steps. "Y'ought to know Nathaniel b'now. Come on now!" He clapped his hands three times and the dogs dropped their heads and scampered up the steps, wagging their tails in a plea for approval.

"I'll bet that's Flora," Jeremy said. "Hey, Flora, how you doin'?"

"She doesn't take to dogs," Larrabee explained. "Even scruffy old gum-flappers like those."

Jeremy poked one on the rear with his foot and ran them both of them off the far end of the porch. "Y'all come in. They'll stay back now. Bob and Mama are in the sewing room. Bob's trying on a dress."

Larrabee looked at Flora. "I'll come in to see that."

"It ain't no dress!" Bob hollered from the back of the house. "It's a gentleman's dressing gown!"

Larrabee and Flora followed Jeremy across the spacious front room. When they got to the sewing room Larrabee took off his hat and put his hands on his hips. "Now *there* is a picture! How's your dance card looking tonight, ma'am?"

Bob was standing on a chair while Laetitia pinned up the hem of the garment.

"This must be Flora," Laetitia said excitedly. She took the pins from her mouth and stuck them in a turtle-shaped pincushion atop a barrister's bookcase. She hurried to the girl, embraced her and kissed her on the cheek. "You must forgive my familiarity," she said, "but I've heard so much about you."

"What's that shiny stuff on your dress, Bob?" Larrabee pointed at the silk lapels.

"It *ain't* no dress," Bob insisted. "It is a dressing gown. You know, that's how that rumor about Jeff Davis got started. When the Yankees caught up with him in Georgia at the end of the war they said he was disguising himself as a woman when all it was—was a perfectly proper men's dressing gown he was wearing."

"Is that so? Well, I still think you're about the third prettiest thing in the room. Don't wear that gown just anyplace now, you hear?"

While Larrabee and Bob speculated about whether the mine might still have undiscovered phosphate deposits, Jeremy and Flora played caroms on a table in the corner.

Seeing that his shots lacked energy she asked him about his disease. "Just what is it you've got anyway?"

"Malaria," he said, missing his shot.

"That ain't like the yellow fever is it?"

"Not hardly. You can't catch malaria from a person. It's my own private disorder."

"My mother died of the yellow fever," she said. "My real mother."

"That was a long time ago," Jeremy said. "Doesn't hardly anybody get the yellow fever any more. Leastways not around here."

When they left the Harpers to see the Duforges and the now-friendly dogs were well behind them, Flora asked Larrabee about what Jeremy had said.

"That's right," he told her. "Your mother died a long time ago."

"Maybe there won't be no more yellow fever," she said.

He glanced back at a pair of Negroes digging a well. "You just make a wish on that and I'll wish too and maybe it'll be so."

Martha and her brood had also heard about Flora's homecoming. Half a dozen grubby-faced children pursued by barking dogs came rushing up to the buggy eager to see their new cousin.

"These all yours?" Larrabee asked above the fray of squeals and waving hands.

Flora sat still with her arms across her chest, turning pale as the dogs jumped and ran around the buggy.

"Only three plus this one here," Martha said wearily, jiggling a fat baby that had big dark eyes just like Barkley's. "There's one more in the house getting an earful from Asa."

Larrabee didn't bother to ask who Asa was, but he soon found out. It was the sinewy old codger from the barbershop, the one that had saved Martha from drowning. He came drifting out of the house with his thumbs hooked in his green suspenders. He was barefoot and spitting tobacco at a mother cat and her kittens.

"Well, it's you again!" Asa wiped his mustache. "You didn't tell me what a paradise these folks have down here. Never seen so many flowers since I left Hawaii."

"Atha's been telling me all 'bout whalin' thips," lisped a gap-toothed boy at his side.

Martha went through three names before she scolded him with right one. "Lewis! He's Mr. Moody to you. I've already told you that."

It seemed to Larrabee that Martha had come a long way back from China, and not just in miles. It was as if she had always lived on this shambles of a farm with its overflowing house, ramshackle barn, and slapped-together greenhouse.

When Larrabee explained about Flora's fear of dogs, one of the bigger boys—about six years old by the look of him—obligingly chased the hounds off toward the woods long enough for Flora and her father to make it into the house.

"Quite the spread you have here," Larrabee said, taking in the confusion of dilapidated horsehair sofas and cane chairs heaped with castoff clothes and playthings. He motioned toward the window. "Seems like you've tacked on to your flower house some."

"That's Barkley for you," Martha said. "He can't leave anything alone, you know. He's always cutting holes in the walls and hammering things together."

"Where is old Barkley anyway?"

"Up in the woods cutting out some dead blackjack for firewood, and he was going to cut some logs for the sawmill in Arredonda. Seems like we always need more lumber around here."

"How's Tom doing?"

"Doin' fine!" the former sheriff boomed from the kitchen. He came in carrying a terra cotta pot full of camellias.

He and Larrabee shook hands.

"How's the saloon business?" Tom Duforge sniffed and cleared his throat.

"Slow. I don't have Duke's touch I guess."

"I hear the cowhands are gone now. Since the war."

"That's part of it. How's the flower business? Pretty good looks like."

"These are some trash." The graying patriarch waved the pot casually in his large hand. "Not good enough to sell, but good enough to dress it up in here some."

"I sure miss Duke," Larrabee said.

"We all do," Tom said with a twitch of his nose. He looked like he was holding back a sneeze.

"I suppose you remember Flora." Larrabee put his hand on the girl's shoulder.

"Not looking like that!" Tom smiled down at her with his big broad face, reminding Larrabee of Duke. "She wasn't nothing but a pip last time I saw her! How are you, Flora?"

"What do you need all them dogs for?" she asked irritably. She held her hands bent back close to her hips as if expecting to be snapped at.

Tom laughed. "I'll be switched if I know! Just seems like we've got more every year! Dogs and kids! I don't know where they all come from!"

"You all will be staying for supper, won't you?" Martha seemed eager for the company.

"We'd like to, Martha. Sure appreciate the invite but we're figuring to get back to town before dark." Larrabee reached for his watch but it wasn't there. "Funny, I guess I forgot to take my timepiece this morning."

"Barkley's going to want to see you," Martha said with resignation.

"You can at least stay for a lemonade, can't you?" Tom set the camellias down on a water-stained table and rubbed his nose with the back of his hand.

While they sat drinking lemonade and chatted about Asa Moody and how he had come so far to see Martha, Flora glanced out the open window, afraid the dogs would come flying in baring their pointed teeth.

Larrabee stood up. "Will you be going up to see Barkley with us, Tom?"

The elder Duforge brushed the question off. "I see him all the time. And besides I do nothing but sneeze my head off in that field when it's dry like this."

Larrabee and Flora walked through the tall grass that sloped up to a thick stand of blackjack and maple. As they approached the woods they heard the echoes of Barkley's ax. Larrabee came on cautiously, expecting any minute to hear a tall tree crackle and fall. When he caught sight of a stout form bending over a tree, he waved his hat and whistled through his teeth.

"Nice to see you working!" he called out.

Barkley waved back. He was shirtless, which was awkward, but Larrabee figured it was too late to turn back now, so he went ahead and introduced Flora to her Aunt Martha's husband.

"Last I saw you, you wasn't nothing but a black-eye pea," Barkley said. "Your mama had you over to the Wards when I was there. I recall she used to wear you on her back." His freckled shoulders were shiny with sweat. He wiped his brows with a blue bandana.

"Fixing to make some lumber I hear." Larrabee looked up, measuring the height of the tree.

"Always am." Barkley rubbed his forehead with the bandana. "You probably heard *that* too."

"Pretty fair stand of blackjack."

"I thin it out every now and then." He offered Larrabee the ax. "It's just as much fun as it looks."

Larrabee put his hand up to decline the invitation. "I'm sure it is. My dad and I took down half an acre solid one summer. Including some walnut. Now that was some cutting! Looks like you've about got this one."

"It ain't as dead as it looks," Barkley said with annoyance. "But now I figure it's him or me. One of us is going to get carried out of here today."

He had cut into the light center of the tree with deep, well-aimed blows. It looked as if a good push would topple it, but when he tested it, Larrabee found it solid.

"I tell you what," Barkley said, catching his breath. "I'm sick of looking at this side. I'm going to take on the other for a while."

They stood back as he threw the ax blade into the untouched bark behind the cut. After three hard strokes they were surprised by a loud cracking sound. Larrabee grabbed Flora's hand and ran into the thick of the woods. Barkley dropped the ax and took off toward the field.

The tree came down with a splintering crash that seemed to crack the ground wide open. Larrabee picked himself up, wiped the dirt from his mouth, and looked for Flora. She was flat on her stomach with the hem of her Sunday dress twisted around her thighs. She got to her knees, shook her braids and coughed. Seeing that she was unhurt, Larrabee got up and ran toward the fallen oak.

He found Barkley beneath the trunk.

He was face up, his blue eyes blinking through the settling dust. Blood trickled from the corner of his mouth. His face was beginning to turn purple.

When he saw Larrabee he smiled. "I guess me and this damned tree *both* get carried out today."

"We'll get you out," Larrabee said quickly. He was pulling at snapped branches but the fallen trunk wouldn't move. It had caught Barkley about fifty feet from the base of the tree. The thing had split so that the fallen part was still propped on the upright, but there was no guarantee that it would stay there.

"Where are you hurt?" Larrabee continued to wrestle with the trunk.

"Hell, just about all over," Barkley sputtered. "And I can't hardly breathe."

"And I can hardly move this damn thing." Larrabee bent his knees, hooked his arms under the slanting trunk, and heaved.

Barkley wheezed. "That's some better."

"But I can't hold it." Larrabee eased the trunk back down.

"Well, that's ugly," Barkley said. His face was specked with blood from his efforts to get his wind.

Larrabee heaved again, becoming aware this time of Flora pulling beside him.

He dropped to his knees, his back throbbing. "It's no good, darlin'. I'll keep it off him as best as I can while you run down to the house and get help. Go on now. Get Tom, the old man, anybody you can, to come up here and help lift this thing."

She ran, losing her fine hat with the satin ribbon as she flew into the tall grass. She was within a hundred yards of the house when she heard the dogs. The hounds had been given their liberty again and now they were out chasing pheasants in the back field. When they flushed a quarry from the grass they jumped after it, yelping, tumbling back down and tearing off through the grass for the next one. When the first dog shot out of the grass, Flora stopped dead.

Back in the woods Larrabee had tried to dig Barkley out from under the trunk, but the ground was thick with roots. He tried to make a lever with a set of branches, but they were too small to be effective, and so he had gone back to lifting the trunk as much as he could to take the pressure from Barkley's chest.

"Looks like I just plain ran the wrong direction," Barkley wheezed.

"We'll get you out," Larrabee told him. "Just sit tight."

"Count on that!" Barkley's thin laugh turned into a cough. "Will you do me a favor, Nathaniel? If I don't get out of this will you see to Martha?"

Larrabee had moved to the other side of the trunk, hoping to find a better grip. "Don't talk foolish, Barkley. In half a minute the whole clan'll be up here and lift this thing off you." He looked toward the grassy field but saw no one.

Barkley blinked up at the overarching branches of blackjack and maple. "It's funny, but I always figgered you'd be the one to marry Martha. She favored you, you know."

"Shut up now, Barkley. Save your strength. You're going to need it to explain why you couldn't outrun a damn tree."

"You do me a favor now, Nathaniel. If this tree snuffs me out, you take it on down to the sawmill and have 'em plane it into coffin planks, will you, and bury it with me?"

Larrabee tried getting under the high end of the trunk and pushing it up with his back. The pain was almost unbearable.

"You dumb cracker. By the time they could plane this thing down and cure it, you'd stink to the stars. You forget about any damn coffin. You're just going to have to get out of this alive."

Barkley sniffed and blinked. As the trunk settled back down his face darkened.

Far out in the field the Duforge dogs were barking.

They had given up on pheasants. The girl was easier to get to. The hounds got up on their hind legs, pawing and licking her, but she was strangely unresponsive. She stood rigid with her arms crossed over her chest and her chin down, trembling, whimpering, terrified. They circled and leapt, nudging her with their cold wet noses, hoping for a pat on the head or some word of approval. But she stayed as she was, her fists locked over her chest, her eyes shut tight as she tried to maintain her balance while the big dogs collided with her.

She opened her eyes and looked back toward the woods.

Barkley gasped for air. "I feel like I'm drowning. Ain't that strange? Flat on my back high and dry and I feel like I'm at the bottom of a pond." The words rattled in his throat.

Larrabee looked at the ax. He wanted to chop the trunk away from Barkley, but he knew he couldn't, for even if he could hack through the hard wood fast enough, the pressure would surely kill Barkley before the trunk was severed.

He heard a strange reedy sound, shallow and staccato. Barkley was laughing.

"I always said I wasn't going to die sober. You ain't got a flask on you by any chance?"

Larrabee felt the blood drain from his face. "You shut up now, you hear me? You're going to be making a fool of yourself with liquor for years. And the next drink's on me. But you're going to have to get your sorry carcass up to Duke's to collect. You hear me?"

Barkley opened and closed his mouth but he was silent.

It was the dirty paw on her face that did it. That one insult shook loose a lifetime's memories of helplessness and anger. She struck out with her fist, caught the startled hound behind the ear and sent him tumbling into the grass. She sprang forward, gathered her skirt in one hand, and beat her way through the grass with the dogs in pursuit. She got to the house before they did.

Larrabee had gone back to scratching at roots when he heard the voices. He looked up and saw the entire Duforge family, toddlers and all, charging through the field with Flora in the lead. Men, women, and children all grabbed at the fallen trunk, dug in their heels, and raised it a precarious, wavering inch while Asa Moody took Barkley by the ankles and dragged him free.

Martha dropped to her knees crying beside her husband.

He lay rasping for a moment, then raised a dirty white hand and stroked her tousled brown hair.

"Well, now. I just had to get something off my chest."

"What do you think?" Tom asked. "You bust anything?"

Barkley looked up at him. "The tree."

Once Barkley had been put to bed and the household had settled down, Larrabee lit his pipe and told Martha that it was time for Flora and him to be on their way back to town.

"I wish you'd stay the night," she said. "It'll be dark before you get home."

He touched her tearstained cheek. "I'll see if Dr. McKinstry can come down and have a look at him first thing tomorrow. Best to get a start tonight for that." As she accompanied them to the buggy he asked how long Asa Moody was planning to be with them.

She shrugged. "Folks come down here and just seem to stay."

He made a stirrup with his hands and helped Flora into the buggy. "Why don't you tell him I've got a job for him at the saloon if he wants it. Tell him he can come up anytime. I'll be there."

He pressed her hand, climbed onto the seat, and headed the horse toward the road.

"It was brave, what you did," he told Flora as they drove the road that curved past the edge of the prairie.

She burst into tears.

He held her close, letting the horses set the pace. For a long time he tried to think of a way to tell her what was on his mind.

By the time he came up with the words and turned to tell her, she was fast asleep.

He drove straight to the house, tied the horse to the fence, and spoke to Flora, but she was still asleep, curled against the back of the seat. He lifted her, carried her into the front hall and upstairs. She lay limp in his arms. He brought her into her room and laid her gently on the bed. When he straightened the pillow, her bundled blue gingham dress fell to the floor and rolled open. Inside it were three things—a small whittled horse, a circular issued six years ago by detective Beverly Blount asking for information leading to the whereabouts of one Flora Larrabee, and the missing pocket watch, inside of which was the oval photograph of Anna.

Chapter 66

The clock he had bought to celebrate the first year of the Sunrise Emporium was broken, knocked from the mantel. Collins was nowhere to be found, although the heat and glaring sunshine suggested that he was well overdue. An empty flask lay in front of the fireplace. The front door hung half open.

John Howard's head hurt, but he didn't know why. He got up off the floor. Slowly his situation came back to him. The grove in town—the one he had bought from the Pine sons—hadn't been a total loss. Well, the trees had been. Frozen black like everyone else's. But the property was practically in the middle of town and he had been able to sell it to the hat woman and her husband, who had an interest in putting houses up on it. In his fuzziness he wondered why he hadn't thought of that—cutting the acreage into fifty-by-ninety-foot lots and tripling the price of the parcels once they had been built on. But then it didn't matter because he didn't have the money to put up houses, and certainly didn't have credit at the bank—any bank—to borrow. That was laughable.

The Walls property had damn near killed him. It didn't even have the lake to recommend it anymore. It had hundreds of absolutely dead young orange trees planted on the bones of the hundreds of other orange trees that had ruined Walls four years ago. Why not just sow salt into the ground and be done with it?

He had lost the store, but then he had never much liked being a storekeeper anyway. For desirability it was somewhere between digging up dead bodies and squandering on the Arlington. And speaking of the dead, wasn't it as if the late Major Dennis—the very late Major Dennis—had reached out from the grave and struck Howard down for disregarding his warnings about the folly of buying orange groves? The phantom of the major was surely enjoying the last laugh now.

As for the woman—Jane—that was embarrassing, humiliating, inconvenient, but not hurtful. After all, he had never gotten around to actually marrying her after that aborted effort in Starke because he simply didn't care that much. Women were not so hard to come by, were in fact much easier to come by than good investments. One good investment and the woman—or women—

would come as naturally as buds to a tree. But he *was* annoyed at having lost her to that letter-writing clod, that navy fellow. It was indecent and insulting after thirteen years of consorting to have someone with so little to offer come along and steal his woman away in the course of a few months. What do you suppose people were saying around town? Did it matter?

He hated this throbbing in his head and, worse, not knowing what had happened last night. Or was it the night before when the clock had been broken? Damn. It was a fine clock too. He had the grim thought that someone had thrown that bottle at it. Perhaps that was what people referred to as a drunken stupor, the last stop, he supposed, before delirium tremens and a twitching, frothing demise beneath passing feet.

Did he care? And if he cared, what did he care about? He thought back to 1888, the plague year, when he had braved the quarantine camp not out of courage but because of a self-destructive or perhaps fatalistic funk. Wasn't that worse than this? And hadn't he recovered—prospered in fact—until he had gotten—until he had reached beyond his grasp? Somewhere out there, beneath that beating sun, men were making money, quietly, steadily, and earning the respect of their fellow citizens while they did it.

The drinking had been an easy, foolish thing. It was no wonder preachers pounded their pulpits in condemnation of it. As long as he had a little money and no store to tend it was easy to spend a dollar here and five dollars there on liquor. Good stuff at first—the stuff Bobby La Rue sold in the bar at his cafe. But after a while it didn't matter because the taste blurred anyway. As long as he didn't take to buying the poison made by flint-faced men in the woods, he would be all right.

He had been drinking the morning he sold the frozen groves to J.J. Ward. The young man, barely twenty, had stood like a soldier while the notary put his seal to the contract at the land office. Howard felt the way General Lee must have felt at Appomattox, surrendering to his uncouth counterpart, General Grant. No animosity, just a hard suspicion that the other was completely unaware of all that was being surrendered. Howard wished that the scruffy old man had been the one to buy since he at least had a kind of stature in the community. But this young whip of a boy putting his mutilated hand to the documents seemed akin to General Grant arriving late for the surrender in the soiled uniform of a private.

The store and Walls' old groves had gone harder because they had not been a matter of choice. The Dutton Bank, holder of the loans, had simply gobbled them up. A junior clerk, brushed, bespectacled, and creased, had come by the house with the papers one Saturday morning. Weak and hung over, Howard had mistaken him for the Presbyterian minister, Mr. Bonds, until he remembered that Mr. Bonds must be forty-five years old by now, while the fellow coming up the porch steps couldn't be any more than thirty.

He introduced himself as Cecil Jordan. He came bearing a cover letter from the vice president of the bank, Mr. Eliot Polk, and the "instrument of surrender" as Howard referred to the collateral transfer document.

"Polk," Howard said, holding the paper at arm's length and still having trouble reading it. "I don't remember any Polk at the bank. I've always dealt with Mr. Dutton directly." An exaggeration, admittedly, but this confident young whelp needed to be thrown off balance.

"Mr. Polk is a lifelong resident of the city," the upstart replied, ignoring the remark about Dutton.

Howard looked up from the paper. "Polk. Good God, you don't mean Ray Polk? That old functionary."

"No," the young clerk said with complete composure. He was wearing a starched wing collar. His black bow tie was knotted precisely. He was not one to be flustered, had probably been through many of these surrenders since the freeze. "No," he repeated, "Mr. Polk is the *son* of Ray Polk."

"The son? Good God. He can't be more than twelve or fourteen."

"A good deal more than that, sir. Now if you would...." He gestured toward the papers.

Howard put his hand to his mustache. "Of course." He started toward the study. "You sure you don't need a witness for this, Mr....?"

"Jordan. No, sir. No witness is necessary."

"Jordan. I suppose you're going to tell me you're B.F. Jordan's great-grandson or something."

"No, sir. I'm his nephew."

"Well, thank God for that. I was beginning to feel like Rip van Winkle."

He made his way into the study, supported himself on the mahogany desk, and signed away the Sunrise Emporium and his title to the Walls property.

"There you are." He handed over the papers. "Thus are the proud laid low."

"I'm sorry, sir?"

"Never mind. May those properties bring the Dutton Bank all the joy they have brought me."

Two or three days later another young man came up the front walkway. Howard was on the porch, fanning himself with his copy of the instrument of surrender when he saw a young man approach. Before he reached the steps, Howard asked him what he wanted.

"I'm Winston Pine, Mr. Howard. I've come about an overdue bill."

Howard rose and picked up his walking stick as if it were a saber. "What are you talking about? I haven't rented anything from Ralph Pine for months."

The young man was short and thick-necked. He had powerful arms that looked as if they had wrestled horses and won. He came forward, up to the steps.

"Well, of course, not from Grampa. From my dad and Uncle Cleo. There was a horse and buggy taken clear to Waldo back in February and put on your tab."

Howard struck the porch rail with his walking stick. "What are you talking about? I haven't been to Waldo!"

"Sir, it was a lady and gentleman putting the fee on your tab."

"Well, God damn the both of them and you too if you don't get off my property!" He hurled his walking stick at the fleeing visitor.

"And God damn sons and grandsons!" he frothed before stamping his way back into the house.

Thinking back, Howard concluded that he had probably smashed the clock shortly afterward.

The rage and binge drinking and self-pity made his stomach hurt. One morning in August, glaring at a cardinal on the front gate, he decided that he could plunge on madly and drop dead in a welter of broken bottles or put his head under the spigot, shake off the past, and get on with his life. He gathered up all the bottles, carried them into the front room and smashed them in the fireplace, one by one, including a flask of Dr. Donner's Soothing Stomach Elixir that tasted suspiciously good.

He turned his back to the ruins and hit upon a simple principle. From now on he would dedicate himself to success with honor.

It was such an old-fashioned word, honor. His father had spoken of it the night before he had marched off to war, and Howard had never been sure what it meant. His father had died at Cold Harbor after having his big toe amputated. Where was the honor in that? Howard wasn't sure, but he had a dim sense that the future of the town lay in honor and that honor was somehow to be found in electric lights, running water, and paved streets. He thought he might be the only one in town with that insight, for no one he had talked to seemed to have his vision of a modern city. If someone did share his vision, he thought that great things could be accomplished by working with that person—profitable things.

Profit with honor. He liked that as a personal motto.

Now that he had rid himself of his dependency on liquor, he decided to make abstention a plank in his platform for community improvement. He would build on his old crusade against prostitution—which had succeeded so far as he could tell. He would champion the cause of a strong moral environment for the young—for the future prosperity of the town. Surely that crusade would produce valuable business contacts.

First he had to deal with the awkward matter of Jane. A man whose wife has left him would not be acceptable to upstanding citizens. He paced between the side door and the study, trying to think his way through that one. He longed for a cigar to help him concentrate, but smoking now seemed to pierce his stomach. He resorted to his fallback—sticks of penny candy that he nursed as if they were cigars. He avoided looking at himself as he passed the hall mirror.

As he walked and let his thoughts flow, he found himself building a plan. He liked it so much that he hurried into the study and wrote it out like a story.

Chapter 67

"Don't you see, it was all the worse for being on a Saturday," Mrs. Blalock said, twirling her spectacles on their silver chain. "And being the turn of the century, it brought out the very worst."

"Any excuse," Ruth Cramer echoed. Something in the chair cushion seemed to be causing her discomfort but she was doing a good job of maintaining her poise while shifting her shapely derriere.

"I do find it unfortunate that what should be an occasion for a rededication to rectitude is used by so many as a cause for degeneracy." Mrs. Blalock set her teacup down on the inlaid table at her side and smiled. "What would you say, Mr. Howard?"

Because he was looking at Ruth Cramer, John Howard didn't answer immediately. He thought of everything Mrs. Blalock said as water flowing from the kitchen tap, bubbling and transparent, harmless if you took in reasonable amounts, necessary to a point, but of no interest in itself. In any event, he was not inclined to take seriously women with Southern accents. Still he did recognize that Mrs. Blalock was not to be ignored even if answering her meant taking his subtle gaze away from those pear-like curves of Ruth's.

"Absolutely right," he said, knowing by Mrs. Blalock's smile that his bland reply had been well suited to her bland remark. Then he added, "and Duke's has become the worst of them all."

Mrs. Roland Bonds sat quietly, sipping her tea, cradling the cup in her hands rather than setting it down. Howard figured that she felt uneasy about being at a temperance meeting since the preacher shied away from political matters. Her blond hair had tarnished over the years and she had little lines at the corners of her eyes now. She had taken on weight that made her look matronly. Howard supposed that Mrs. Blalock had talked Mrs. Bonds into coming, perhaps to help evaluate his suitability for Ruth.

Although she was probably twenty years his junior, Howard could imagine making Ruth his wife. He knew hardly anything about her because she hardly ever spoke, but he knew that he was drawn to her, found it hard to keep his eyes off those voluptuous curves of hers, and occasionally he found himself imagining the underclothes that helped mold them.

He thought that the picture of Jane was a nice touch. It had been taken in 1891, on the morning of their abortive wedding trip to Starke. She was wearing a high-collared lace-trimmed dress. Her face was raised as if she were in the midst of some devout thought when in fact the photographer had asked her to look at a bobcat head mounted over the side door. Howard had tied a black satin ribbon around the corners of the picture frame. He rose for effect, stared out the window across the porch to where she used to sit, and touched the black armband on his jacket.

"My late wife used to say that the moral way was like growing a live oak tree, slower and more difficult, but resulting in something stronger and more enduring." He turned and looked at each of them. "How I wish she could be with us all today to share this cause we have devoted ourselves to." Then, lest Ruth be discouraged by his attachment to his deceased wife, he gently laid the photograph facedown on the table. He sighed, blinking, and clasped his hands behind his back. "Well, this is a new day, and it's up to us to lead the way to the community of the future—isn't it?"

Again, he looked earnestly at each of them. "If every man had the strength to resist temptation then, of course, we'd be in some other world, wouldn't we? But since we're in this world, it's up to us to remove the temptation, isn't it?"

Mrs. Blalock nodded. "Just so."

Mrs. Bonds smiled uncertainly.

Ruth looked up, her brown eyes luminous with admiration.

He sat down again and clasped his hands. "What do you think of this? We convince the commissioners to make this a *dry* county."

Mrs. Blalock was the only one who knew what he meant. She shook her spectacles enthusiastically. The other two were waiting for him to explain.

"A *dry* county. That's so bold, Mr. Howard." Her voice came from deep in her voluminous chest. "But how do we convince them? Most of the men on the commission have been known to take a drink I'm sure."

Howard put up his hands, acknowledging the point. "You are a keen judge of human nature, Mrs. Blalock. It *won't* be easy. It's the way of the oak— remember? Slow, but certain and enduring. Plus we have truth on our side! And the truth is that the future of this community depends on making it a moral community, as surely as it depends on electric lights and paved streets. Because what good are those things if the lights expose licentious behavior?" He thought the preacher's wife flinched here. "And of what value are paved streets that lead to saloons?"

Ruth Cramer started to speak but inhaled sharply instead. She was looking at something on the porch and the other two women saw it and stared round-eyed. Slowly Howard turned and saw a familiar face pressed to the window of the porch door. His hand went to his heart.

It was Jane.

She tapped on the pane with the handle of her parasol and let herself in. "Hello, John."

He looked from her to the three ladies, speechless.

Jane nodded and smiled quizzically at the ladies.

"John," said the phantom, "I wonder if we might speak alone for a moment." She motioned toward the study.

Slowly he took his hand from his chest.

"Ladies, will you excuse us? Just for a moment? I—" He forced a smile—a ludicrous, toothy smile—and edged toward the study. "This is urgent."

Mrs. Blalock and Mrs. Bonds stared at each other.

Ruth Cramer closed her mouth.

Howard didn't know whether to shut the study doors or not. He left them slightly ajar, hoping that the ladies wouldn't hear what he fervently hoped would be a short conversation. On his way into the room he caught sight of the thermometer on the porch. It brought back the bad memory of the killing frost and Jane's desertion.

He had just reached the mahogany desk and turned around when Jane said, "John, I want a divorce."

"A *divorce!*" Too late, he put his hand to his throat to stifle the word. He was sure the ladies had heard him.

She set her parasol on one of the leather chairs and took off her gloves. She was wearing an ivory-colored dress with a cameo broach at the lace collar. It was an expensive dress. Cold air seemed to swirl around her.

"Sounds odd, doesn't it, considering we never actually married. But it turns out that we ran afoul of common law after all."

He continued to stare. He wasn't sure what she was saying.

"Connecticut law requires a divorce—even from a common law marriage—before a marriage certificate can be issued."

Connecticut. The name sounded strange. She had taken on a whole new life and spoke of Connecticut as if he knew what she meant.

As if by magic, she produced a sheaf of papers from somewhere. She unfolded them and set them on the desk.

"This is a divorce decree. I've taken the liberty of having the witnesses sign it. All we need is your signature."

We. Who did she mean by *we*, he wondered.

She was looking for a pen. Seeing none on top of the desk, she helped herself to one from a drawer, and poked the point into an inkwell.

"This is preposterous," he said, looking at the pen she held out to him. "Sign it yourself. Why come all the way down here?"

"It's hard to explain. It's a matter of principle, John."

He laughed. "Principle?"

She continued to hold the pen toward him. "You'd have to know Will. Call it honor if you like."

"I *don't* like. If he was so honorable he never would've done what he did."

"Oh, John, that's all ancient history."

"It was not even a year ago. It may be ancient to you, but it's yesterday to me."

She glanced toward the front room. "Wouldn't it be easier for you just to sign, John?"

He took the pen and scrawled something that only vaguely resembled his signature. He flipped the pen into the corner and thrust the papers at her.

"You may go now."

She folded the papers and picked up her gloves and parasol.

"There is one other little matter."

"What other matter can there be?" He came toward her as if to back her through the doors.

"I believe I'm due something for the time I put in at the store."

"You *what*! God damn you, woman!" He was sure the windows had rattled, and wished he had not lost his temper. He took a breath and spoke quietly. "Get out of this house."

"You understand that Will doesn't know about this," she went on. "He would never approve. But we've had some tough times and this is my due. You couldn't've built that business without me."

"*You've* had tough times! You fool woman!" He pointed at the thermometer as if she would understand. "The *store* is ancient history! The *groves* have turned into houses for shopkeepers and clerks. All of that started the night you left! That's right. I lost everything but this shell of a house, so don't you go thinking you can squeeze a single nickel out of me because I don't have it. Now get out!"

When she balked, he picked up a brass paperweight and raised it as he came at her.

She backed through the study doors, blundered into the foyer, and disappeared through the front door.

When he went into the front room, tearing off the black armband, the only trace of the three ladies was three hastily abandoned teacups.

Chapter 68

They lifted their glasses and toasted the birthday girl. It was the finest day the house had seen in years.

"I remember *my* thirteenth birthday," Penny said. "I had a notion to get rich quick in the gold fields of California."

"I tell you," Asa Moody said, gulping his punch. "There was many more fellas went broke in those fields than ever turned a nickel. They were thinking hot instead of thinking cool. The cool thinkers made most of the money out there."

"Were you hot or cool?" Penny asked.

Asa laughed. "I was downright aflame! Had a real penchant for staying broke. That's one advantage of being a hundred and ten. You get a heap better at thinking cool."

"What do you suppose is keeping your father?" Nelda asked Flora. "He went out the back door to get your present a quarter of an hour ago."

"Oh, now, it hasn't been any more'n five minutes," Penny said. "You're just as itchy about this present as Flora is."

Dr. Willis sat with his back to the fire. "Now when I was thirteen, I—"

His wife looked at him. "Yes, Warren?"

He tapped his cane on the brick apron. "I forget."

Everybody laughed.

Larrabee came through the back door carrying a box tied in a pink ribbon. As he crossed through the kitchen they could see that the box was dented and dirty.

"I guess we can tell who wrapped it," Penny said.

Larrabee set the box down on the round table. "Better open it quick."

The box moved from side to side.

"What manner of magic is this?" Asa wondered with exaggerated curiosity.

Flora approached the box on the table as if afraid of soiling her white dress. She twisted one of the blue ribbons that Nelda had braided into her hair. Penny dug out his penknife and offered it to her, but she told him she preferred not to spoil the bow. She took her time untying it and then lifted the top off the box.

She shrank back, crossing her arms over her chest.

Dr. and Mrs. Willis stood up for a better look.

Nelda and Penny exchanged nervous glances.

Larrabee reached into the box. "Here, let me introduce you." He lifted out a brown puppy no bigger than his hand. "This here is—well, hmm. Come to think of it, he doesn't have a name yet."

Flora looked at the blunt nose and drooping ears of the thing in Larrabee's hands. She became aware of holding her hands across her chest and brought them to her sides.

"He looks like a lump of ginger root," she said at last.

Larrabee held the puppy a few inches from his face, letting its legs dangle.

"Well, then. Root, this is Flora. Flora—Root."

The puppy licked his nose and everybody laughed, even Flora.

"So here he is if you want him. Otherwise we can take him back."

"Take him back where?" Flora asked.

"Back to the alley by the saloon. That's where Asa and I found him a couple of days ago."

"Come *that* close to chucking a pot of hot water on him," Asa said. "Then I seen something moving down there and thought it was a 'possum or something till I got a closer look."

"That's how long you've had him?" Flora said. "Two days? Why didn't you say so?"

"I had to think about it," Larrabee said. "And then I remembered that your birthday was right around the corner so the two just seemed to fit together. We've had him back there in the summer kitchen, fattening him up."

"He weren't but a scrap o' hide," Asa added with a hint of pride. "Polished up pretty good. You can't even see his ribs anymore."

Flora reached out and touched the puppy on the top of the head. She liked the softness of it and stroked him gently. Her father started to drop him and in an instant she was holding the puppy in her arms.

"There must be some better name for him than Root," she said.

But nobody ever came up with one.

By April, when school let out, Root was big enough to follow Flora anywhere and they spent long afternoons in the garden, where Flora meticulously restored the rows of beans and carrots and radishes. She put in tomato stakes and planted seeds from B.F. Jordan's store and watched the plants break the ground and climb from day to day. In May and June the mosquitoes were so bad that even Root took refuge from them. He jumped and snapped and tried to hide under the grapevine that wreathed its way through the back fence.

Flora's best friend was a girl named Ida Derry. She had sat in front of Flora in school and was very good at language and social studies but had no patience for arithmetic and geography, which just happened to be Flora's best subjects. So the two had started doing their homework together and had become such enthusiastic collaborators that one time they fell into a lively consultation in class and paid for it by wearing dunce caps.

Ida was at the edge of becoming pretty and got along well with boys because she was accurate with a slingshot and never flaunted her good grades. She introduced Flora to her older brothers, Boone and Fondren, who weren't quite sure what to make of the new girl because she was so self-assured and her father ran a saloon. But they liked the way she could run and swear like a boy while still looking and dressing like a girl and they gallantly turned their backs when she climbed trees.

Fondren impressed Flora with his daredevil bareback riding. During the summer he often came by the house on Magnolia Street trying one trick after another. When he had gotten Flora's attention by whistling through his teeth he'd make a show of standing on the horse's back. One day after supper he took the stunt a step further. He pretended to lose his balance, shook and wobbled until Flora was convinced he was going to crash headfirst into the fence, then he stood up straight and tall, threw his arms out, and told the dapple-gray mare to start walking.

"There's not so much to it," Ida told Flora over Root's barking. "Bessie's so fat you could play shuffleboard on her back."

"If that's so, you come on up here and do it," Fondren told her.

Ida put her hands on her hips. "It so happens I don't like heights and you know it. If I got up there, I'd be *twice* as brave as you 'cause courage is nothing but overcoming your fears. Why don't you do something you're afraid to do?"

Mockingly, he put his hands on his hips. Then he leaned back slightly and put one foot in front of the other. "'Cause there ain't nothing I'm afraid to do," he said.

"That'll be the day," Ida told him. "Everybody's afraid of something."

"You think so?" He jumped down from the horse and nearly lost his balance, but righted himself. "If so, I ain't run into mine yet."

They all walked over to the Sweetwater Branch to look at one of the new houses that were going up. Despite his easygoing ways, Fondren had a kind of urgency about him that Flora liked. When he took a notion to do something there was nothing else in the world worth doing.

"I've a mind to see how those big houses are put together," he said. He boosted Flora sidesaddle onto Bessie's back and led the horse by the reins. Flora thought there was something elegant and exciting about their procession although Ida grumbled enough to take the shine off it.

"This had better not be more showing off," she said.

The house was bigger than most. It was still a skeleton in studs and joists and eaves although the wraparound porch and first story had been floored. Fondren vaulted up the steps and clattered from one airy room to the next, taking perfunctory looks at the way the joints came together and testing the soundness of the braces. Then he went upstairs, where the floor consisted of nothing but a grid of timbers set on edge. Boone came along and asked Fondren what he thought he was doing.

"Just having me a look around before they close it all up," he said. Arms extended, he started walking along one of the beams.

"If you was really brave you'd go a little faster," Boone said.

Ida shushed him. "It's bad enough as it is," she said.

Fondren was halfway across the beam now and starting to wave his arms. He had Root barking again. From her place atop the horse, Flora couldn't tell if he was showing off or in real trouble.

"It's a long drop," Boone taunted. "What was the name of that boy who fell through a floor and got maimed?"

"I'm not looking." Ida turned her back to the spectacle.

"Scared to do it and scared to watch," Fondren called back. A few more halting steps got him teetering to safety at the far wall.

"Now what?" Boone said. "You've still got to get back."

"I'm fixing to." Fondren smiled and started the return trip, this time with one hand behind him.

"Fondren, please stop." Flora came down from the mare and joined Ida and Boone on the unfinished porch.

"Can't stop till I get back, little friend."

He stopped in the middle of the beam, wavering as if the least breeze would hurl him to death or disfigurement.

"Something sure got him going," Boone said. "What if we all just walk off. Don't you suppose that'd put an end to it?"

Fondren glanced down to make sure they were all watching then fell from the beam.

Flora screamed. She thought Ida must have also and maybe Boone too for that matter. Fondren was hanging from the beam by his hands.

"Had you, didn't I? Didn't I have you?" He laughed and dropped six feet onto a pile of baseboard scraps.

Boone laughed too but the girls were angry. Against her better judgment, Ida had let herself be tricked again and Flora had humiliated herself by screaming.

Flora stalked off with Ida and Root at her heels.

"Well, now, come on, Flora!" Suddenly Fondren was falling all over himself to get back into her good graces. "It was all in fun. What if I promise never to do it again?"

She hadn't even heard him. She was still steaming. She wasn't sure why, but instead of marching home, she was heading toward a stand of live oaks, the dwindling remnant of woods that had been cut down to make way for a stucco cottage.

"Well, you know," Fondren said as the horse clomped along behind him, "I suppose there *is* something I'm afraid of."

Ida stopped in her tracks and turned around. "What?"

"You heard me. Flora, I'm afraid you won't ever speak to me again."

Again, he had caught everybody by surprise. Flora found the remark so outrageous that she was charmed despite the embarrassment of her scream.

"You *are* terrible," she said, not bothering to suppress her smile.

"So then, I've told you what I'm afraid of. What are *you* afraid of?"

She stopped smiling and answered without hesitation. "I'm afraid of being left."

None of her friends had expected such a serious answer. They didn't know what to say. Then Boone hastily brought them back to their world of cheerful innocence and foolishness. He blew a weird buzzing note on a blade of grass. He pointed to a gaunt figure in the distance. "Tell you what you *ought to* be afeared of—Mad Mary and her crazy daughter Joan, who everybody says was begat by John Howard. If they catch you coming down the street, either one of 'em, they'll latch onto your arm like this and talk your ear off in words you can't hardly understand. They're as scary as a pair of froth-toothed coons."

Fondren laughed. "That John Howard! He sure has trouble with his women. His first wife is a loony and the second one's a ghost."

Chapter 69

From time to time John Howard thought that he might be better off if he had simply murdered Jane. He had held the brass paperweight not six inches from the side of her insolent head. The action of a mere half-second could have made all the difference between his present embarrassing, wretched situation and a prosperous, respectable position among the town's businessmen. He imagined dragging her warm, limp body from the study and then his mind went blank. He thought there must be a well deep enough somewhere, but driving around the county looking for it could be very awkward, to say the least, with a dead woman in the back of the wagon. In his wildest fantasy he envisioned loading her into a catapult in the back yard and flinging her into the Gulf of Mexico, where she might be taken for flotsam from some passing boat or balloon.

With the first mild days of fall he felt the return of orange fever even though there was scarcely an orange to be found in the county since the killer freeze. It was a curse like malaria that came back despite his best efforts to be rid of it. True, there would be some sense in moving farther south, below the freeze line, and starting over with a new untarnished reputation. But that took money, imagination, and more energy than he seemed to have anymore.

At least he didn't have the constant reminder of orange trees everywhere he went. The streets and yards had been replanted with ornamental trees— red buds and dogwoods— that grew fast, lost their leaves in the winter and promised no fortune. Most of the land formerly given over to groves had sprouted an even more profitable crop for the patient investor—houses. Howard read in the newspaper that Penny and Nelda Ward had become the town's biggest sellers of commercial and residential land. Yet they continued to live in an unassuming cottage and the two of them continued to pound the streets in a battered buggy dragged by an unimpressive cross between a quarter horse and a big-hoofed Belgian.

Howard didn't have the money to buy vast tracts of land but he did scrape up enough for a down payment on a small, undistinguished brick building a block west of the square. Its occupants were a leatherworker and his son who, apparently, didn't have the sense to save up and buy the place themselves.

They had been paying rent for seven years and the landlord's widow was eager to sell, so Howard picked up the place at less than its assessed value, raised the rent ten percent—enough to cover the mortgage—and waited for the place to pay itself off. He liked that arrangement so much that he took out a mortgage on his house with the Pfifer Bank and used the money for the down payment on a second building—a warehouse—that he partitioned to accommodate four cramped tradesmen—a butcher, a dentist, a photographer, and a baker. That arrangement paid very handsomely, and within six months he had bought a third building, also brick. He liked brick buildings because they were so substantial and represented security and prosperity.

His quiet success helped him to put the scandal of the "ghost wife" behind him. He thought pleasurably of Ruth Cramer's pear-shaped curves until he read that she had become engaged to a lawyer recently arrived from Tennessee. For a few days he envied that lawyer the delicacies of his bed and considered taking the train to Jacksonville to resume his old habits of the flesh but soon found himself so busy renting buildings that he had no time to indulge himself so extravagantly.

He pressed on with his temperance maneuverings. He wrote letters to the editor of the *Daily Sun*, decrying the unwholesome and immoral goings-on at the town's notorious watering holes. He wrote vaguely of the future, the new century, and the opportunities awaiting the community that would embrace it. He attended—but did not host—temperance meetings. They took place after hours upstairs at the opera house. He mended his fences with Mrs. Blalock who, after more than a year, was easily convinced that the woman she had seen was the younger sister of his late wife, who had come to pick up the family Bible.

"It was sad for me to part with it," he sighed, "but, of course, it was more fitting for Jane's sister to have it."

A week later, Ruth Cramer turned up at the opera house. After some eavesdropping, Howard determined that the Tennessee lawyer had jumped from a second-story bedroom window with an enraged husband in pursuit and had left town with his leg and his reputation broken. Ruth had gained a little weight—the pear was now more like a rutabaga—but she was somehow even more voluptuous. Why the lawyer was in that other bedroom instead of Ruth's was beyond Howard's imagining.

In between votes on articles of a constitution for the Temperance League, as it was to be called, Howard arranged to accompany Ruth and Mrs. Blalock to a picnic. He was secretly hoping that Mrs. Blalock would somehow fall into a sinkhole, requiring him to console Ruth at great length.

He hired one of the better teams and buggies at the White Pine Stable, and on a splendid May morning the three of them set out for Boulware Springs. Mrs. Blalock blabbed on endlessly about the nobility of the temperance cause, to the extent that he wanted to knock her over the head with a whiskey bottle. But he concluded that in retaliation she would probably gore him with her outrageous hat, which was festooned with what appeared to be sharpened parsnips.

"God!" he sighed involuntarily as she reiterated her stance on the evils of absinthe—a drink unavailable anywhere in the state so far as he knew.

"I beg your pardon, Mr. Howard?" Her voice seemed to bubble up from some wellspring of commonplaces deep in her capacious bosom.

He came to himself at once. "It's the work of God—this grand countryside!" He drew a breath and patted his chest to show his invigoration.

"Well, there's no arguing that," Mrs. Blalock admitted, bewildered at what seemed an obvious observation. "Ruth, you've hardly said a word all morning. Whatever is the matter?"

"Where would she squeeze it in?" Howard muttered, cracking the whip to cover his words.

"I hope you're not ill," Mrs. Blalock said.

Ruth stretched her arms before her and wiggled her soft, smooth hands. "Oh, no, not at all! I was just enjoying the fresh air." Suddenly she pointed off toward the woods. "Look! Wasn't that a parakeet?"

"Not likely. I haven't seen one for years," Howard said. "They were all hunted out. For ladies' hats."

"Oh, how terribly cruel!" Ruth put her head out of the buggy and looked back toward the woods. "I'm sure *I've* never had one of those hats."

"They were too beautiful," Howard philosophized.

"They tell me the passenger pigeons are all gone," Ruth lamented. "And the buffalo."

"Oh, it's a big world," Howard said consolingly. "Don't you suppose there must still be a few banging around somewhere?"

The spacious, sloping lawns of Boulware Springs were well populated with picnickers and swimmers, but the well-trodden paths still led to the vastness of the old lakebed, Payne's Prairie, whose marshy acres were now all but impenetrable to humans. The trio took up a position beneath a live oak at the edge of a clearing that overlooked the springs and the white brick pump house.

Mrs. Blalock stuck to Ruth like a burr. She took her position as chaperone so seriously that Howard began to wonder why she didn't sit square in the middle of the picnic blanket and relay everything that was said between him and the object of his desires.

Something will have to call her away sooner or later, he told himself. But when it did, she called Ruth along too on some ruse, as if she required help with that most basic of functions.

When they came back, they had the ham sandwiches and deviled eggs that Ruth had prepared. Howard spoke of his fondness for deviled eggs but nearly choked when he bit the first one and found that she had made some mistake with the salt. He felt a desperate urge to spit—at Mrs. Blalock preferably—but forced himself to swallow the concoction and smile.

"Are you all right?" Mrs. Blalock asked innocently.

"Yes, yes," he reassured them. "Just a little clumsy."

"Oh, I'm *terribly* clumsy," Ruth sympathized.

Howard forced another smile. "I'm sure that can't be, Miss Cramer." He wasn't sure what to do with the rest of the deviled egg.

"Oh, but I *am*," she insisted.

She knew what she was talking about.

As they sat eating their sandwiches she thought she saw another parakeet. "There, look!" This time she poked her pointing finger in Howard's eye.

Startled and in pain, he lurched forward, planting his knee squarely in the potato salad.

"Oh, my, oh, *my!*" Ruth tried to make it better by getting a look at his eye, but he flung her prying fingers aside, struggled to his feet, slipped on a ham sandwich, and danced a grotesque little step to keep his balance.

"Dear, dear me!" Mrs. Blalock bellowed. "Are you all right, Mr. Howard?"

"God, yes! I mean, thank God, yes." He was trying to squeeze his eyeball back into shape.

"Are you sure? I could've sworn I heard something rip."

He had heard it too, but he wasn't sure what it was and didn't particularly want to know. He forced himself to smile at Ruth, but it must have come across more as a bloodthirsty baring of teeth because the girl burst into tears.

"Here, now," Mrs. Blalock chided. "There's no need for that."

Both Howard and Ruth thought she was speaking to them. They started to reply at the same time.

"Madame, it's only that I am half-blind and possibly crippled but—"

"Oh, I'm so sorry! I didn't mean to. It's just that—Oh, I'm so *clumsy!*"

"Please do *not* cry." Howard always felt ill-at-ease around weeping women. He never saw any point whatsoever in weeping and couldn't understand people who did.

Ruth took his request as an attempt to console her. "Oh, such a *kind* man!"

Howard didn't care what she thought as long as she didn't cause a scene. "Not at all. Just a harmless accident," he said almost sweetly as he hobbled off to wipe the potato salad from his britches.

When he returned Ruth was beaming again.

"She's just like our Florida weather," Mrs. Blalock said pleasantly. "One minute a storm and the next, sunshine!"

"How perfectly charming," Howard said. He had seen that awful phrase somewhere in one of the stories he had read to Jane. "How perfectly charming."

"I *know* it was a parakeet," Ruth said.

Howard looked at Mrs. Blalock. "Well, then let's say it was."

For the rest of the afternoon they got along famously. Howard ate heartily, except for the deviled eggs, perhaps thinking that by consuming the food he could avoid falling into it. The day remained mild. Great white clouds drifted across the sky without threat. A steady northwest breeze kept the picnickers' place in the shade pleasantly cool and mosquito-free. The infernal phantom parakeet stayed away.

As the conversation flowed, Howard determined that the voluptuous if rather dangerous Ruth Cramer had been a ward of the Blalocks and, upon reaching the age of maturity, as Mrs. Blalock called it, had remained in the household.

Howard's back began to hurt. He wondered whether the Tennessee lawyer hadn't fallen out of the bedroom window while attempting to save his eye from Ruth. He was sure now that the ripping sound had been some sinew.

On the way back to the buggy he had a terrible time walking. He felt his arms dangle before him and knew that he must surely be bent over, but he didn't dare straighten himself to find out because he was sure that he would be paralyzed.

"Is everything all right?" Mrs. Blalock looked at him with concern.

He managed to swing one of his dangling arms in the general direction of the spring. "Just hoping that the pump house there is adequate for our municipal waterworks. Town's growing so fast, you know."

He was aware of his voice sounding hoarse and gruff. And so it should. He was pinched with pain.

Mrs. Blalock shook her spectacles by the ribbon. "Now that's exactly the kind of thing a man would think about, isn't it? Pumps and engines and mechanical things. How *perfectly* charming!"

Chapter 70

It was a quiet evening, even for a Tuesday. A handful of men sat at the tables in Duke's Saloon, drinking beer and playing cards. Larrabee and Asa talked at the big corner table with the itinerant salesman and tinker, Leo Bard.

"I like this feller," Asa told Larrabee. "He's the only man around who's even more decrepit than I am."

"Why, thank you. I'll take that as a compliment." Leo Bard's new teeth clicked and whistled, so he sculpted every word, achieving the kind of credibility that all the great orators had—very useful in the selling trade. "Say, ain't this shaping up to be a nice little town! I've been coming here dang nigh every year since it weren't hardly more than a lonely crossroads and a trading post and now it's a bona fide city."

"She's tamed down some," Larrabee said. "It's been weeks since anybody's tried to ride a horse up to the bar."

"There was that feller with the trained monkey," Asa said. "Didn't that cause some havoc! Took us half the night to pry that little critter off a light fixture. Larrabee here won't admit it, but I say guns was drawn. Plugged in the knickers, that little booger would've come off of there right smartly too. Shame about all them bottles."

Leo Bard saw a chance to make a pitch. "Well, speaking of bottles, I've got something out in the wagon that may be just the ticket. Now don't you budge! I'll be back in a twinkle."

Asa watched him shuffle toward the door. "You seen John Howard lately?" he asked Larrabee. "He's walking just like that. Hanged if I don't think he's had a stroke."

"Won't anything stop John Howard," Larrabee said. "He may be getting slower but he'll keep right on plugging as long as there's a dollar in the county he can get his hands on."

"Did I see Flora and Ida take off a while ago?"

"They went over to Ida's to play *Logomachy*. Ida's folks don't approve of the girls spending time in a saloon, even if it is back in the kitchen on the slowest day of the year."

Asa clasped his hands behind his head. "Don't know how many places I've seen get civilized over the years. You know, pass through 'em one time and they've got kind of an edge to 'em. Pass through a few years later and all of a sudden the saloons has all gone to Sunday schools. Out west is like that now. Tough little Kansas towns going fat and sleepy. It's the way the country's going. Gives me a notion to strike out for the Pacific again. There's still some adventure to be had out there, I'll bet."

Through the swinging doors Larrabee could see Leo Bard's wagon. It seemed to be rocking from side to side as the salesman rooted around for something.

"You ought to take that old gamecock with you, Asa. You'd be quite a pair. The Pacific would meet its match."

"Did you ever get the yen to take off for places unknown, Larrabee?"

"A long time ago, even to *your* way of thinking. Seemed to me that adventure wasn't always such a treat."

The swinging doors opened and Leo Bard came shuffling back in with a small wooden crate in his arms. He set it down on the table and caught his breath. "Now this here is *something*. I picked it up in Georgia and ain't had but one of the twenty-four. I'll tell you, this here has a kick to it!"

"Have a sit, Mr. Bard." The chair was already out, but Asa pushed it farther with his foot. "You're all tuckered out. Looks to me like you could use another slug of that stuff."

Fanning himself with his hand, Leo Bard sat down and set his crooked fingers on the top of the crate. "Now this here—"

He noticed that Larrabee was watching three men at a table near the door. They had started to argue. One of them raised his voice and the man across the table threw cards in his face.

"That's starting to get ugly," Asa said under his breath. "You want me to go for the sheriff?"

"There won't be time." Larrabee got up and went to the bar. He was looking for the belaying pin that Duke had used to quell a thousand quarrels.

The argument got louder. Chairs came back and the table went over.

Asa made for the bar. "They've got guns, Larrabee. All three of 'em. They had 'em under their coats."

Just then Flora came through the doors. "Daddy, Ida says I—"

Guns sparked and banged. One of the three men went over backwards. Asa fell to the floor. One of the men bolted from the saloon, knocking into Flora on his way out. The third gunman picked himself up and drew his pistol. There was a loud cracking sound and he crumpled, his gun clattering as he went down. The only person standing was Larrabee, holding the belaying pin high.

Leo Bard stood up slowly and surveyed the damage. One gunman flopped and grunted in a puddle of blood. The other lay motionless at Larrabee's feet. Asa sat up against the bar with his hand pressed to his left shoulder. Flora stood gripping one of the swinging doors, staring wide-eyed into the smoke.

"Jesus Christ," Leo Bard drawled. "What happened?"

Asa was on his feet now. He was talking to Larrabee. "You sure put a stop to that. You stopped it good."

Larrabee lowered the belaying pin. "I hit him too hard."

Asa knelt down beside the crumpled man. "Is he dead?"

Flora ran over to her father and threw her arms around him. He dropped the belaying pin, kissed her on the top of the head, and gently took her hands away.

He knelt down beside Asa and put his fingers to the fallen man's throat. "He's still alive."

"That other one's making a real mess on the floor," Asa said. Blood had spattered the bar. The man was kicking and thrashing like a wounded deer.

"He'll make it," Larrabee said. "You're looking a little green yourself."

Blood was oozing up through the fingers Asa pressed to his shoulder.

"Well, it's the last day for this shirt," he said, "but yours truly ain't ready for the rag bin. It's just a graze. I heard the slug hit the wall behind me."

Seeing that Flora was still dazed, Larrabee kissed her again. "My darlin', will you go for a doctor? Doesn't matter which one. You know where McKinstry lives though, don't you?"

Still taking in the sight of blood and the men on the floor, she nodded, took two or three faltering steps backward, and ran out into the street.

By the time Flora came back with Dr. McKinstry the gunshot man had passed out. The man Larrabee had struck was still unconscious. Asa was sitting at the corner table with a wet towel pressed to his shoulder while, with unsteady hands, Leo Bard poured him a glass of the dark, mysterious new drink.

They had left the gunmen to lie where they had fallen. Larrabee had set the table and chairs back up. He was wiping the blood from the bar.

"It's quieted down considerable," Asa reported as Dr. McKinstry set his black valise on the table. "It's more like a Tuesday night again."

The doctor seemed not to have heard him. He lifted the towel on Asa's shoulder. "Rinse out that towel and put it back on. Looks like you were lucky."

Asa went behind the bar and did as he was told while the doctor looked at the man bleeding on the floor. He looked at the entry wound, which was in the fleshy part of the shoulder between the ribs and the collarbone. He rolled the man slightly and then laid him back down softly.

"He was lucky too, only not *as* lucky. The bullet went straight through." He asked Larrabee to press a towel to the man's shoulder while he had a look at the man lying by the table.

"What happened to this one?" He laid two fingers to the man's throat, raised his eyelids and had a close look at the side of his head.

Larrabee was leaning with his back against the bar. "I hit him. Hard."

"I'd say you did. Flora tells me there was a third one."

"He took off," Larrabee said. "Far as I know he wasn't hit. We'll tell the sheriff."

"Good idea. I don't want that other one coming back to finish these two, especially if they're going to be at my place. I can just about squeeze them in."

Larrabee left the saloon in the care of Leo Bard. When he and Flora had loaded the two men into a wagon and gotten them to bed in the medical annex at the back of Dr. McKinstry's house, they came back to find the salesman hawking bottles of his new drink from the corner table.

"It will be a night to remember," he promised his customers as they put down a nickel each to try the bubbling concoction. "That calls for a drink to remember."

Seeing Larrabee's disapproving look, he smiled and raised a foaming glass. "And for our host, a free sample!"

Larrabee studied the glass suspiciously and took a swallow. He choked and spat while Flora and the freshly patched Asa patted him on the back.

"What the h—devil is it?"

Leo Bard displayed a bottle proudly.

Frowning, Larrabee read the flowing script and snorted. "Coca-Cola."

The salesman stifled a belch. "Maybe we ought to try it cold."

For some reason, Larrabee was thinking about the gunfight in the saloon as he stopped by the back yard to watch Ida Derry cutting Flora's hair. He was glad that that the shootout had happened so fast because he thought he would surely have killed both men to put Flora out of danger. He knew that his reflexes were still that dangerous and he was of a mind to sell out and find some safer, more respectable livelihood.

The man with the shoulder wound had sneaked out of the McKinstry house a day or two after the shootout. The one Larrabee had hit was still complaining of headaches a month later. He had disappeared one night during a thunderstorm. The back fence gossip had it that the two had sworn vengeance against the third and had ridden off on one horse just as the sky opened up and the streets filled with water. That was the hearsay. It seemed to Larrabee that the longer he lived the harder facts were to come by.

"What's the matter with your braids?" he asked Flora, hoping to drive the gunfighters from his mind. "I like your braids."

Flora started to shake her head but Ida clapped a hand on her to keep her still.

"You want to lose an ear?" Ida said. "Just try shaking your head like that again."

Flora rolled her eyes and held as still as she could. "Daddy, braids are for little girls. I'm fourteen years old. Almost fifteen."

"You have the rest of your life not to have braids. Why not let 'em go a little longer?"

"Daddy, look at Ida's hair. Don't you like it?"

She had trimmed her braids and coiled them wreath-like around the crown of her head. Larrabee thought she looked like a young girl trying to look older than her years—older and more traveled. He didn't know what to make of it and didn't want to say the wrong thing.

"Sure I like it," he said. "That'll keep it out of the way for tree-climbing."

Through the comb and scissors Flora stared daggers at him.

Ida whispered something to Flora.

"I imagine the boys like the new look better," he ventured.

Ida squealed. It was as if he had heard some of what she had said.

He picked up a piece of stray kindling and chucked it toward the back steps. "Not that I don't trust you Ida, but I'm a little too squeamish to watch any longer. And I'm expecting a telegram from a bottler in Atlanta, so I'll go down and take care of that and see the new creation when I get back." He winked at Ida. "Don't you make her too beautiful or the boys'll give us no peace around this house. And save me a strand about that long for my watch fob."

Braving the scissors, Flora leaned forward. "Daddy, nobody wears locks of hair on their watch chains anymore. That's so old-fashioned."

As he walked the shady side of the street toward the square, his thoughts quickly returned to the saloon. Word of the shootout had spread through town overnight and the Temperance League had raised a shrill cry for closing down all of the "foul watering holes" as they called them.

"What those women need is jobs," Larrabee had declared after reading their letters to the editor in the *Daily Sun*. "Then they wouldn't have time to mix in other people's business."

"Ain't none of 'em you'd want working here," Asa had said. "Though a woman's touch might be just the thing for this place."

"We've been through that fifty times," Larrabee said, shaking the newspaper to turn the page. "The last thing we need is for the temperance harpies to start screaming about painted harlots consorting with the dregs from the planing mills and foundries."

Asa had made a big gesture with his hands. "We've got to have something to draw folks in here, short of another century party. It's not as if there aren't other saloons in town either."

"That could be a plus," Larrabee had told him. "If all of us saloon owners get together we can make a strong case instead of each trying to fight his own battle."

"A saloon league!" Asa had thought that was funny but not too likely.

It was a hot September day with the smell of rain in the air. Larrabee went down past the square to the Western Union office. He had already written out his message in the boxes on a telegram form and he had the piece of paper out to hand it to the clerk when the man plowed through the door and knocked him off the steps.

"Come back here!" shouted the telegrapher from behind the counter. He tore off his visor. "Where are you running off to?"

"To the paper!" shouted the clerk from the street.

"Keep your wits!" shouted back the telegrapher. "Use the telephone!"

The clerk stopped in his tracks and ran back up the steps into the building. Larrabee went inside and put his message on the counter, having decided to ignore whatever crisis the clerk was experiencing. The man, who looked like he might be one of the Poinsetts, was behind the counter cranking the telephone.

"Hello, Central. Give me 51! No, fifty-*one*! That's the newspaper! And make it snappy!" The telegrapher was sitting at his clicking key copying as fast as he could. After a few seconds of pressing the receiver to his ear and tapping the wall impatiently, the clerk shouted into the jutting speaker. "Get me an editor! I don't care which one. Someone in charge." He twitched and tapped for another half minute and then started shouting into the speaker again. "Jeff, this is Irv Poinsett. You're going to want a man down here. The president's just been shot. That's right. The President of the United States. I don't know. All it says is he was shot. In Buffalo, New York. I don't know. Just get a man down here. This wire is going crazy."

Larrabee picked up his message and walked back into the street. Big spatters of warm rain began to dot the boardwalk, but he took his time getting back to the house, listening to the pattering in the treetops. He heard doors and windows slam as people hurried inside, expecting a downpour. He was reminded of the way he had seen a Missouri town shut down when raiders came riding in.

By the time he got home, Ida and Flora had moved into the kitchen to finish the haircut. Flora looked out through Ida's fingers. "What's wrong, Daddy? You look like you swallowed a fly."

He thought for a moment about what to tell her and decided that she would find out soon enough.

"There's plenty of 'em out there to swallow," he said at last.

Eight days later when Irv Poinsett called the newspaper to say that the President had died, the town went into mourning. A black-bordered photograph of the martyred McKinley appeared on the barbershop wall next to the old lithograph of Robert E. Lee. Preacher Bonds himself climbed the narrow steeple steps of the Presbyterian Church and rang the bell. He stayed up late cobbling together a sermon likening the late president to the crucified Savior. "Go easy on him, boys," the dying president had said of his assassin, which the preacher called an echo of the Savior's "Forgive them, Father, for they know not what they do."

Fanning themselves all the while, many in the congregation wept.

Larrabee and Flora were at the Wards when Jeremy Summerton rode into town for a Sunday visit. Standing in the Wards' front room with his hat in his hand, Jeremy announced his engagement to a girl from Micanopy, sensing all the while a vague uneasiness in everyone he talked to. "You know," he said, "I saw the new President. down in Cuba. He was that colonel with the blue-and-white bandana on his hat, the one that led the charge up the ridge outside Santiago. What do you think of that? A boy from Payne's Prairie has seen the President of the United States."

He had to sit down after that because he was feeling fatigued and feverish from the ride. J.J. patted him on the shoulder with his partial right hand and told him to sit right there until he felt up to stirring.

"We're all feeling kinda winded today," he said.

Chapter 71

The courtship had gone on far longer than John Howard could have imagined. He had been pursuing Ruth Cramer for nearly three years, and in her way she had proven as elusive as the confounded parakeet she kept stalking. Her ornithological fancies seemed to have no end. She saw passenger pigeons where none had flown for years. She was capable of sitting for long, spine-numbing hours, peering up into the trees in the expectation of spotting some avian curiosity. They had at least shaken the imposing Mrs. Blalock from one of these birding sessions, but Howard felt that if Ruth had to choose between him and a Virginia rail, he would come in a remote second.

The Temperance League was progressing almost as slowly in its efforts to rid the community of that orphan-making, home-wrecking, demonizing agent of the devil, liquor. The county commissioners had not yet seen the light. Howard thought the ladies of the league were overdoing it. None of them had taken an ax to a whiskey keg yet, but their rhetoric was heating up. He thought that they were harping on the sheer wickedness of liquor when they should be emphasizing its negative economic impact.

"Morality is all well and good," he tried to tell Ruth. "But if you want a man to listen, hit him where it hurts most—in his pocketbook."

She had not heard. She was looking through an absurdly small pair of binoculars at what she thought was something exotic, whereas he could tell perfectly well without them that she was studying nothing but a common mockingbird. He felt ridiculous sitting on a tuft of Spanish moss while she gawked up at the sky. He considered putting an end to all the silliness by simply seducing her right there in the woods, pulling her hairpins one by one, undoing all twenty-two of the little buttons he had counted holding the front of her dress together, and burrowing through her cotton and muslin and lace fortifications underneath until the two of them were one, throbbing and writhing on a bed of oak leaves and pine needles.

When they were packing up the bird book and binoculars he inadvertently called her Jane. She didn't notice.

Sometime in the spring he was embarrassed by not being able to read the infernal bird book no matter how far away he held it. A new doctor—someone he had never heard of who was recommended by Dr. McKinstry—fitted him with spectacles. He carried them in his inside coat pocket but never took them out in public. He thought they made him look older than his forty-nine years.

Even after three years, Ruth still seemed in no hurry whatsoever to get married to him or to anyone else. She seemed to enjoy his company during the short intervals when they were alone. He sometimes wondered if she was feigning indifference to draw him out, but she seemed genuinely relaxed about what passed between them. He wasn't sure what to make of her. He did seem to spend more and more time thinking about her though.

On the first pleasant afternoon in March they went for a drive to Hogtown Prairie, a place that still attracted a wealth of bird life. Mrs. Blalock rode along in the back of the two-seater and, when they arrived at the greening marsh, she complained of fatigue and chose to stay in the carriage.

"Oh, we won't be out of sight," Ruth assured her.

"Not for a minute," Howard said with forced cheerfulness.

When they were down the path and out of earshot he did something that charmed Ruth. He took a peppermint stick from his breast pocket and offered it to her.

"I'm smoking these instead of cigars," he explained.

She played along and put it between her lips. "I don't believe I've ever smoked one. I suppose I look unfeminine."

"No—just the opposite. There's something very feminine about the way you look just now." He put one in his mouth and handled it just as he would a cigar as they walked along the grassy path.

"We've known each other for some time now," he said off-handedly.

"Yes, yes we have." She sounded a little absent-minded.

"We've had some pleasant moments together, you and I. And Mrs. Blalock."

"We sure have."

Before he knew it, he had a strange notion to propose to her. Partly he just wanted to see if he could get some response from her. Partly he thought it would be pleasurable to spend his days and nights with a woman who was so unflappable. He couldn't imagine that his investments would be of the least interest to her. He imagined that the house could fall down around her ears without causing her to raise her voice. And he was thinking this without being fogged by those pear curves of hers. She smelled of rose water and sun-warmed wool. He liked the smell, felt drawn to it, but at the moment was attracted to her visible charms, not the thought of entwining his legs with hers in a feather bed.

He glanced back at the carriage. Mrs. Blalock was gazing off in the opposite direction. Who could tell when this opportunity would come again? He pursued his notion.

"My investments have worked well for me. I have a house and a secure income. I have happy prospects for the future. The respect of the community."

She stopped and took the peppermint stick from her lips. Was she listening or had she seen her blasted parakeet again?

"I have everything a man could want. Except for one thing."

He bent to kiss her just as she was putting the peppermint stick back in her mouth. It poked him in the eye.

"Ouch!" At least he had avoided saying something far worse.

"Oh, dear! Oh, dear!" She dropped her peppermint stick and put a gloved hand to his eye.

He blinked. He had pulled back just in time. No harm done.

"Foolish of me. I—"

He felt her lips warm on his.

Her hat, that glorious amalgamation of silk roses and straw, shielded them from the prying eyes of Mrs. Blalock. Suddenly Ruth had become more mysterious than ever—and more irresistible.

She smiled, looked a little sleepy and cross-eyed. "You're so impetuous."

He was smiling too. "Impetuous? After knowing you for three years? After staring at about five hundred species of birds—real and imaginary—and spending countless hours with Mrs. Blalock wedged between us. Impetuous? I don't think so!"

"We do have a great deal in common, don't we?"

"Yes, yes, of course! And I suppose there has to come a time when Mrs. Blalock won't need to come along."

Ruth pursed her lips. "I suppose so."

"Ruth, what if we were to come to an understanding."

She stopped and looked up at him with her luminous brown eyes, shaded by her sloping rose-trimmed hat.

"An understanding?"

He really hadn't planned to go quite this far, but events seemed to be running away with him, with the two of them. Maybe he *was* being impetuous.

He put his hands on her shoulders, feeling her firm arms beneath the puffed sleeves of her dress. "An understanding that we will spend more time together, get to know each other better as friends or—or as—as husband and wife."

"I think I'd like that." She smiled as if ordering some tantalizing dessert at La Rue's Cafe.

So there it was, he thought. They were more or less engaged to be married. They had an *understanding*—one of the least appropriate words on earth to his way of thinking. He wasn't sure he understood anything at all where Ruth was concerned. Whatever it was, though, the understanding was between the two of them now. From what little he knew of Ruth, he doubted if she would even speak of it to her woman friends. It would be interesting to see if word got around.

In the meantime, there was the business of making money and furthering the temperance cause. He hit upon an idea that might combine the two and impress Ruth at the same time. The idea came to him in a strange way. He was looking at one of his buildings on the way home from the bank and he passed the fine new brick church the Baptists had put up two blocks east of the square on Liberty Street. He was reminded of his uncomfortable transaction with Preacher Williams—of feeling pressed into the pew as the preacher pressured him into selling the miserable turpentine still that later blossomed into the lucrative Preacher's Patch Mine. As he looked up at the Baptist Church's imposing arches and massive bell tower, it occurred to him that perhaps the time had come for another such transaction. Only this time he would be the one on the moral high road.

He hadn't been in Duke's Saloon for several years and was surprised that it had changed so little. The electric bulbs jutting out of the wall sconces where the old gas globes had been seemed out of place in this dingy relic of the town's unsettled days. The same drab pictures hung out from the walls as if they would come tumbling down at the stamping of a foot. The battered oak bar and dented brass rail had fared badly over the years. The bottles behind the bar seemed to be the same ones from a quarter of a century ago. One black window shade still refused to roll up all the way. There was still the same old smell of whiskey, sawdust, and felt. The horrible black upright piano still hunched against the far wall shamelessly exposing its chipped teeth. The unkind morning light glared through one of the swinging doors where a slat had gone bad.

Larrabee was standing on a chair, trying to reach one of the higher paintings with a feather duster tied to a broomstick. He didn't turn to see who had come through the doors.

"Your sixteen-thirty-two is on the bar," he said. "I'm doing you a favor."

Howard took off his hat. "Actually, I've come to do you one."

Larrabee swung around and tossed down the feather duster. The broom handle clattered on a tabletop.

"You really should not turn your back on the door," Howard said. "You never know what kind of desperado is likely to come in here. Is that a bullet hole in the bar?"

"You've seen bullet holes, John. You know what they look like." Larrabee came down from the chair. He stood with one hand on a table, as if holding himself in readiness, like a man with a gun.

"The place seems a little past its prime." Howard couldn't help smiling.

"It has its moments. It's eleven o'clock in the morning. You're a little early for a drink."

"And you're a little late. That's what I've come about. I want to make you an offer for the place. A good one."

"Not interested."

"You will be. The county's going dry. The commission's going to close down the saloons. You know that."

"I've heard plenty of talk. I've seen a few foolish letters to the editor in the paper."

Howard came closer. "Yes, well, the talk is going to come to fruition. It's for the good of the town. Clean streets, clean water—clean lives. You can be part of it or fall by the wayside. I'm offering to make it easy for you."

"By buying this place."

"That's right. Just the way the preacher took my turpentine still off my hands all those years ago—the one that turned into a gold mine for you. Only there's no gold in this place, no future."

"Then what do you want it for? A Sunday school?"

Howard smiled. "Sort of. Actually, it doesn't matter so much to me what's in it as what's *not* in it. I don't suppose you'd understand that. Are you looking at my scar? Wishing you'd shot an inch to the right?"

"I'm wondering about shooting wide of the mark, John. Who pulled the trigger at the Union Academy? They weren't trying to hit Major Dennis, were they?"

"Who knows, Nathaniel? That was twenty-five, twenty-six years ago."

"Same person behind running Caleb Green off his farm, don't you suppose? Or more likely, pressuring him to take a bargain price for it."

"You *do* have a long memory. You know, sometimes it's better to forget the past."

"And about burning out the soiled doves north of town? You hired Baldy for that, didn't you?"

"Now you're wide of the mark again. He wasn't there, Nate. Ask Penny Ward."

"Oh, even a busy bee like Baldy needed a hired hand from time to time. But he burned down the Arlington all by himself, didn't he, John?"

Howard ground his knuckle into a tabletop. "I came here to make you an offer, Larrabee. The best one you'll get in a month of Sundays."

"The answer's still no, John."

"Twenty percent over the assessed price. Cash today, Larrabee. Within the hour. That's twice what you'll get a year from now."

"Still no, John."

"Only a year from now you'll *have* to sell. And I'll be the first one in line. Sort of a matter of principle. I'm sure you understand what it's like to be driven by a principle."

"I understand spite, too. You want a saloon, go buy somebody else's."

Howard took a last look around the place. He wanted it more than ever but he knew that today would not be the day.

"All right then. We'll do it your way. " He put his hat on. "I'll be seeing you before long."

Larrabee followed him out the door. The morning light was harsh and hot.

"One thing, John. Don't send any of your boys down here. Even one broken window and I'll come after you."

Howard laughed. "You're behind the times, Larrabee. If anyone comes to see you it won't be boys." He leaned forward as if to share a joke. "It'll be *girls.*"

He smiled every time he imagined a hoard of ax-wielding temperance women descending on Larrabee's saloon. The thought helped him through an endless outing in which Mrs. Blalock was never more than an arm's length away. They were at Lake Alice, a dark, overgrown out-of-the-way pool popular with birds and alligators. Howard pictured Mrs. Blalock being swallowed whole by a particularly large lizard, leaving him and Ruth quite alone.

As it turned out, the three of them were thrown together. Howard's thoughts had passed on to raising the rent on the butcher, the photographer, and company when he felt the first big raindrop hit the brim of his hat. The storm came on so fast that even the horse was surprised. The nature-lovers ran from their lookout at the lake's edge and threw themselves into the buggy as the rain fell hard through the pines.

"There's no point in trying to get to town!" Mrs. Blalock bellowed as they attained the soggy main road. "The trading post is right over there!"

Howard felt his heart sink. "It's an awful place! We'd be better off going a little farther!"

"No! No!" the chaperone insisted. "How bad can it be? It's dry, isn't it?"

"Madam, I—" On the one hand, he was glad that she seemed not to know about Mary Leary's longstanding accusation that he was the father of her daughter. On the other, he had no desire whatsoever to find himself face to face with the madwoman or her repulsive offshoot. He pretended not to hear Mrs. Blalock's protestations. He flicked the reins and turned the horse toward town.

He felt her fat hand on his shoulder. "I say! We are getting quite wet back here! You *must* take us to that store!"

The road was rapidly dissolving. One wheel of the buggy sank down, throwing the two women together in the back seat. Howard cracked the reins. The horse pulled valiantly. The buggy rocked back and forth and settled down on its axle. The rain beat down like a waterfall. The canvas top offered little shelter. Mrs. Blalock bailed out of the buggy and landed ankle-deep in mud, letting out an unladylike sound. Despite her distress, Ruth followed and staggered through the mud into the tall grass on the other side of the road. Howard slapped at the horse's rump and the buggy hurled forth, nearly throwing him out. He drove up onto the grass and waited for Mrs. Blalock to waddle over. He got down long enough to help Ruth back in. He was so wet that he thought he might ruin his watch if he stayed out any longer. With his hat drooping down over his ears, he hoisted the wilted Mrs. Blalock into the back seat and drove to the miserable log and clapboard hovel.

He goaded the horse right up to the door and the three picnickers pushed their way into the dark, musty-smelling store where they stood dripping on the plank floor. Mrs. Blalock's voluminous dress appeared to have shrunk down several sizes. It now revealed her robin-like physique. Ruth kept a hand pressed to her throat. She had somehow lost one of the buttons between her breasts and she seemed to think the entire dress was in danger of coming apart. Her hair clung like moss about her ears, making her nose look oversized. A raindrop gave it a temporary hook. Howard's collar had come loose and his serge suit hung heavily, making him hot and itchy.

He turned and saw a lean, longhaired young woman looking at him from behind the counter.

"Don't just stand there!" he barked. "Get us some blankets." He extracted his wallet from an inside pocket. "Three blankets. How much do you want for them? Just make it fast!"

The young woman took off to the dim back of the store. The rain pounded on the ancient roof. A steady drip developed near the counter. The closed windows had started to fog.

"Hurry, woman!" Howard commanded. "It can't take you that long to find a few blankets!" He wrung water from his vest. "I'm sorry," he told Ruth, "but I warned you that it's a wretched place."

Still holding her throat, Ruth was taking in the room and its rows of neglected shelves laden with bolts of cloth that had lain undisturbed for years. "You've been here before then?"

He looked at his watch to make sure it was still running. "Me here? Not for ages! And only once. Once was enough. You can see why."

Mrs. Blalock was looking at the back of the store. A figure, tall, thin, and phantasmal seemed to float behind the girl.

"It's your father then, is it?" crackled Mary Leary.

Howard glanced at the windows, hoping that the rain had let up. It had not. The outside was nothing more than a gray blur. He whispered to Ruth. "She's completely mad. The entire family is blighted."

"What did she say?" Ruth asked.

Before he could answer, the girl approached Howard and smiled.

"This has got to stop once and for all," Howard said. "The joke has long since stopped being funny."

He thought Mary Leary looked frightful. She had become even thinner and her black matted hair was shot through with white.

"Get your father and his friends some blankets, Joan." Mary shoved the young woman toward the back of the store.

Howard became aware that Mrs. Blalock and Ruth were staring at him. They looked ludicrous in their wetness.

"This woman is mad," he repeated. "Ask anyone. Why she has chosen to vent her madness on me I'll never know."

"Ever since you came into the store to collect that money," Mary said. She seemed to have developed a slight lisp, making the situation even more bizarre. "Then we became one."

Mrs. Blalock let out a cry of disgust.

Ruth turned her head toward the door.

"Hear me out!" Howard demanded. "This is nothing but madness. The very idea is repulsive! Repulsive!" He called out to Joan as she straggled forth with the blankets. "Child, do you think for an instant that I am your father? Look at us! Do we have the least thing in common?"

"I take after my mother," Joan said.

Grudgingly, Howard accepted a blanket from her.

"It's true," Ruth said. "She and her mother are very much alike. Except for their hands."

Howard grabbed Joan's cold hand and held it up beside his own. "And is there anything alike here? You see? My fingers are straight." He thrust her hand away. "There is the evidence and here is my word. Never did I do more than try to collect a debt from this woman. A fifteen-dollar debt! And even that I never did." He pointed an accusing finger at Mary. "Old woman, I don't know who your consort was but it wasn't me! Do you dare to swear otherwise?"

"John, you've hurt her." Ruth came forward and lifted Mary by the elbow to keep her from sinking to the floor.

Mary doubled over, sobbing. "Just like before! Like a knife to the heart! To misuse me so!"

"Leave them to themselves," Howard said, pulling Ruth away. He pressed a silver dollar into Joan's hand and pushed his two companions toward the door. Before they were quite settled into the buggy, he slapped the reins and the faltering buggy jerked through the rain on the way back to town.

Chapter 72

Out in the street a wagon pulled up at the front gate. Nelda went to the door, thinking it might be one of Curtis' boys delivering ice, but this wagon was an odd old contraption, top-heavy and labeled in faded scroll letters.

"Oh, it's that traveling tinker," she said. "You never know when he's going to show up."

"Tends to be when it's cold up north," Penny observed. "This must mean an early winter."

Nelda always bought something just to be polite. She knew that some women would sit around for an hour or more looking at Mr. Bard's wares just because they had nothing better to do, but even in her advancing years, Nelda still had plenty to do. Although she had sold the hat business she still made the occasional piece on commission and was a corresponding member on the board of directors of the South Carolina company that had bought her out. On top of that, she spent more and more time working with Penny and J.J. on real estate transactions. While Flora and Ida looked on, she relieved Mr. Bard of two foxtail brushes and a paper of pins.

"He's starting to look older," she remarked on her way back into the house.

"Who isn't?" Penny said with a flip of the newspaper. "Except me."

"How long do you suppose he can keep poking along like that?" she wondered.

He poked along all day, stopping at homes and businesses all over town with modest success.

As afternoon faded into evening, he came to Duke's Saloon.

Asa was at the door, shaking out the rugs from the back room.

"Well, look who's here! If it isn't Mr. Tonic Water!"

Leo Bard climbed down from the wagon on unsteady legs. "How you doing there, sonny?"

"You ought to be sunning yourself somewhere," Asa told him.

"I aim to." The salesman dusted himself off. "Soon's I finish up here I'm going down to Tampa and flop on the beach."

"That so! And what're you hawking this trip?"

"Well, now. How'd you make out with that case of pop-and-fizz drinks I brought you last year?"

"Not so well. When we opened 'em they sprayed all over the place!"

"They did? You have to be careful with 'em, you know, or they'll come blasting out of there like a geyser."

"All we did was shake 'em a little to get the sludge off the bottom."

"Oh, Lord! We'll get back to that later. I wonder if I might trouble you for a glass of water."

"Sure! It's on the house." Asa waved him inside.

Larrabee and Flora had been discussing the merits of Ida's moneymaking scheme, selling tickets to a chess tournament. Larrabee wanted to know what she needed the money for.

"To help out."

"Oh, maybe we're not rich," he said. "But we're solvent."

"And to—"

"Hey, folks, look what the cat dragged in!" Asa tossed the rugs down in front of the bar.

"And to save up for the big fair in Saint—"

Larrabee squeezed Flora's hand. "Darlin', we'll talk about it later. How are you doing, Mr. Bard? It's been downright sleepy around here since your last visit."

"Howdy there, Mr. Larrabee. Howdy-do, ma'am. Sorry about your setback with those drinks. But I think we've got that sorted out for next time. I'll draw you up a list of safety rules."

Asa pulled out a chair for him. "You're looking a trifle peaked if I may say so. It was sort of hot today, wasn't it?"

"Sort of was. And I've had this here pain in my jaw for most of the afternoon."

"Toothache?"

Leo Bard winced. "Not very likely, sonny. These here are store-bought. Look at the bullet holes in that bar. How'd that rumpus end up anyway?"

"Couple of weeks later, two of 'em run off in a rainstorm chasing the other one," Asa said.

"It turned us into a temperance cause," Larrabee told him.

"Ax-wielding harpies beating down the doors? Begging your pardon, ma'am."

Flora gave him a puzzled look. She never knew what to make of the gruff yet cavalier Leo Bard.

"Nope, no axes yet," Larrabee said. "We've got Asa here guarding the place day and night. One look would stop 'em in their tracks. They've been putting the squeeze on the city council though."

"With the help of Mr. John Howard," Asa added. "He wants to buy this place and turn it into a library or something."

Flora perked up. "A library? That would be grand! But why does it have to be here?"

"He's making that up," her father said. "Howard just wants to put us out of business for the good of the community. And maybe to settle old scores."

"What scores, Daddy?"

"Never mind. Too many to go into."

"I hear he wants to give the place to some female for an engagement present. That's what I hear," Asa said.

Larrabee laughed. "Where'd you hear that?"

"Well, she's one of those temperance woman," Asa explained. "Place'd make quite a little trophy for the Temperance League."

Larrabee watched a familiar figure come scraping through the swinging doors.

"Looks like it's old home night! How are you, Dr. Willis?"

"I've been better but I'm not complaining. Or maybe I just did." He stopped and made a motion with his hands, his cane hanging on his arm. "Do you have any bottles of that port wine? We're suddenly out of it. Mrs. Willis took a shine to it."

"I've had one waiting for you in the back," Larrabee said. "I've been meaning to drop it by your house for at least a week."

"Now you don't have to. I suppose you've heard about J.J. Ward."

Larrabee stopped on his way to the back room. "What about him?"

"He's fixing to get married. Daughter of somebody he sold land to. Name of Smithson."

"Seems kind of sudden, doesn't it? He and Jeremy can make a double of it."

"We ought to toast 'em with a bottle of old Leo's witch's brew," Asa said smiling. "You bring any of that kick-pants drink with you?"

"Never without it," Leo Bard assured him. "It's all the rage. I can bring in a case if you like." He stood up and started for the door and then came to a halt. He stood slightly hunched over with his hands pressed to his sides.

"Get him," Dr. Willis said.

At first no one understood what he meant.

"Get him," Dr. Willis repeated. "He's going to fall."

Larrabee and Flora were there just in time to catch him by the elbows. "Put him down," Larrabee said. "Just set him down on the floor. Lay him down."

"What's the matter?" Flora asked.

Dr. Willis was beside them, leaning heavily on his cane. "Heart attack most likely." His voice was calm and quiet.

"Is he going to die?" Flora wondered aloud.

"He's breathing," Dr. Willis said. "That's progress." He timed Leo's pulse for half a minute. "He's pretty steady."

Leo Bard blinked up at the ceiling. "Where am I?"

"You passed out," the doctor told him. He loosened Leo's collar and shirt. "We're going to put you to bed and let you rest up."

Larrabee and Flora carried him upstairs to Duke's old room. Larrabee and Asa got him out of his clothes and into the sagging brass bed. Dr. Willis was searching the top of the chest of drawers.

"It's electric," Larrabee said. "Switch is on the wall."

The doctor found it and pushed the button, throwing the room into a pale, unwavering light. "His color's better. How're you feeling, Mr. Bard?"

"Like the time my wagon fell on me," the salesman rasped. The light showed the worst aspects of the room, the flaking ceiling paint and dingy rose pattern wallpaper.

"The best thing you can do for yourself is to lie right there all night," Dr. Willis said. "One of these kind gents will be right here looking after you."

"My horses...." Leo Bard began.

"We'll see to 'em," Asa assured him.

Leo dropped his head back onto the pillow. His white beard pointed at the ceiling. His Adam's apple rose and fell in his ropy throat.

"You just never know," he muttered.

Larrabee and Asa took turns watching at his bedside during the night. Flora slept at the Wards with Root curled up by her side. Early in the morning when she went back to the saloon Dr. Willis was already upstairs talking in low tones with Larrabee and Asa.

"You reckon he's out of his head?" Asa was asking. "It's such a peculiar request."

"Maybe peculiar," the doctor said. "But I don't see how it can do any harm and it might do a world of good."

"Then that's it," Larrabee said. "I'll go on out there right now."

"I don't suppose they have a telephone," Dr. Willis said.

Larrabee smiled at the thought. "They'd be the last ones in the county to get one."

Flora could contain her curiosity no longer. "What is it, Daddy?"

"Something you can help with, darlin'. Better to have a woman along for an escort. We'll get a rig and hit the road."

"Where are we going?"

"Out to the trading post. Mr. Bard has asked to see Mary Leary and her daughter."

By the time they returned, it was crowded and hot in the threadbare little room. Someone had pulled the black shade halfway down to block the midday sun, and white light showed through a dozen pinpricks that danced on the wall when a saving breeze caught the sash. On the telephone wires outside the window sparrows lined up. They fluttered off when a pair of cawing crows bore down on them.

Flora thought it was a combination of people to be found only in a dream. Leo Bard on the bed, looking as pale and creased as the sheets. Surrounding him, Dr. Willis, Dr. McKinstry, Asa, her father, and haggard old Mary Leary and her elongated daughter, Joan. Flora had thought her father would have to bring Mary and Joan in at gunpoint, but finally they had come along and clung to each other in the back of the carriage all the way from the trading post to the saloon.

Leo asked Mary and Joan to come closer. The daughter went at once and sat on the bed, but Mary had to be prompted by Larrabee. Once the room was quiet, the salesman licked his lips and began to speak in a thin, shrill voice.

"I've always thought of myself as a kind of comet, making my circuit, being seen by a passel of folks without ever really touching their lives. It's been a lonely life, watching towns grow up like kids from one visit to the next. Every now and then I was able to partake of what I saw. And one time back about twenty, twenty-five years ago I come into an old trading post on my way between here and the next town south." He looked up at Mary with dull eyes. "I come acrost a woman in distress, weeping on the floor and I comforted her. We comforted each other in a moment of weakness. Her distress and my loneliness." He held his hand out to Joan. "As the years passed and I saw this child around town I never had any doubt who she was." His crooked fingers wavered before her. Joan took them in her own.

Asa drew a breath. "If that ain't like two pieces of a puzzle fittin' together."

Leo's knuckles were white as he grasped Joan's slender hand. He swallowed. "When a man thinks of meeting his maker he gets the itch to set the accounts right."

Joan bent and kissed him on the cheek.

Mary sank onto the bed, weeping.

Asa nudged Larrabee and whispered. "I'm not so sure that bed will carry the three of 'em."

Leo patted Joan's hand. "When I die, what I have is yours. It won't be much. But it's yours." He sighed. "I've put off so many things."

He put off dying too. The next day Leo Bard took in some chicken soup that Flora had made and he felt much better. Dr. McKinstry came and pronounced his heart sound but advised very limited exertion for at least a month. The tinker followed his advice scrupulously.

"I kind of regret not being able to get down to that beach in Tampa," he told Asa. "But this here ain't so bad. That girl of Larrabee's makes a mean chicken soup."

"I'm kind of surprised that the wife and daughter haven't been by," Asa said.

"You just never know," Leo Bard replied. "It ain't like I'm so much to latch onto."

By Thanksgiving he was able to walk over to the stable to have a look at his team and feed them a handful of oats and a lump of sugar each. "They're like family," he explained. "We've been through so much."

"The Pine boys have been renting them out," Flora told him. "They're getting paid twice for keeping them."

"Like father, like sons," Larrabee said.

Leo was just about back in the pink by Christmas. He came close to setting the rug on fire with his pipe while Flora and Ida danced a two-step to Larrabee's harmonica playing. They had more visitors than usual, perhaps because people wanted to get a closer look at Joan's father. A very handsome new carriage stopped at the gate. J.J. Ward was driving it with his father at his side giving advice.

"Should've just bought an automobile," J.J. said.

"They ain't safe," Penny told him.

Nelda and a young blonde were talking in the back seat.

Flora ran out to greet them. Larrabee cast a cautious glance back at Leo Bard and his pipe and followed her down the front walk.

"That's quite the rig you've got there. That your Christmas present, J.J.?"

"No, it's a wedding present," Nelda said. "A little ahead of time." She introduced J.J.'s fiancée, Henrietta Smithson, a shy, soft-spoken girl given to blushing.

"Don't seem proper, does it?" Penny said.

Nelda leaned forward. "Whatever are you talking about now?"

"The boy's only ten or twelve years old."

"You just haven't taken a good look at him for ten or twelve years."

"They do grow up fast," Larrabee said. He had a strange feeling that he'd had this conversation before.

J.J.'s wedding was at the Presbyterian Church in January. Preacher Bonds officiated in a firm if uninspired voice. Flora had all the more trouble paying attention because she was wearing the cameo broach Larrabee had given her for her sixteenth birthday. The newlyweds moved into a fine new house with deep porches, bright white railings, four tile fireplaces and a square tower with two big oval windows in it.

"Damned if it don't look just like an old steamboat," Penny declared.

Early in February, Nelda was caught up in an uproar that arose when the state superintendent of education invited a former slave, the distinguished Booker T. Washington, to address a convention of county school superintendents. Nelda helped to sponsor the visit when she learned that the topic was to be Negro educational needs. Word got around that Mr. Washington would be speaking in the white high school, addressing an audience that would inevitably include white women.

The town was divided. The new mayor, William R. Thomas, supported the plan wholeheartedly. The issue became a topic of national discussion. The Jacksonville *Times-Union* saw nothing wrong with Mr. Washington's visit so long as he was discreet enough to remember his place in society. A New York paper ridiculed Mr. Washington's detractors. One in St. Louis suggested that Mr. Washington probably was too intelligent for the locals to understand anyway.

After calming the fears of his critics, the superintendent promised Mr. Washington a warm welcome, and on the night of February 5, 1903, two thousand people—black and white—crowded into the auditorium to hear an eloquent speech rich with appeals for improved education and cooperation between the races. The crowd applauded generously and enthusiastically. Men and women pressed the speaker's platform to congratulate Mr. Washington. Newspapers, north and south, praised the address.

The opposition quietly rethought their strategy.

Two weeks later, the speech was still the main topic of conversation when the wedding of Jeremy Summerton and Alyssa Burrows took place in Micanopy, just south of the Prairie. The wedding was conducted in the little white frame Methodist church. The stove sparked and spat as the minister spoke St. Paul's lines about it being better to marry than to burn. The reception at the farmhouse was so joyful and boisterous that, while dancing with the bride, Jeremy fell off the porch and tore his breeches, prompting somebody to predict in an undertone that the honeymoon would probably result in torn sheets and broken furniture.

In March a farmer coming in from Arredonda to buy oats reported that a man had died at the trading post. The deceased was Sam Leary, laid low by a fever caught in a cold rain.

"He ought to just bury hisself," said a man at the bar in Duke's. But Sam's more orthodox rivals, the Hutchinsons, did the honors since they were first to retrieve the body. Old Sam Carrington was selected to perform a traditional Methodist graveside service at Evergreen Cemetery. The oration, rich with hyperbole and imagination, dragged on in a drizzle that had most of the few attendees hacking and sneezing within a week. As for Reverend Carrington, who stood bareheaded as long as the rest of them, before the month was out, he too had gone to Abraham's bosom, singing hymns and clutching his tattered hymnal to the end.

By the middle of April it became clear that the Temperance League had won its battle to shut down the saloons. The city council had been convinced.

On a spring night Asa sat with his elbows on he bar while Larrabee boxed up the glasses. "Want me to shoot John Howard for you?"

"No thanks, Asa. I've spent too much time hating that man. Now I want to put it behind me and get on with my life. I'm just glad I could sell fast at a fair price before Howard could get his hands on the place. I imagine that's why he hasn't been by to gloat."

"What do you figure to do now?"

"Something else," Larrabee said. "Whatever the next thing is. Roper's Hall is being sold, too, you know. There's a man who wants to put a furniture store here."

"A furniture store!"

"Well, people have to have furniture, don't they? They've got to buy it somewhere. They may as well buy it here."

"A furniture store."

"That's right."

Leo Bard came creaking down the stairs. "Y'ought to have a big sale. That's what y'ought to do! Sell everything in the place in one big event!"

"I'm not much at selling stuff," Larrabee said. "And watch your step, old-timer. Bodies are bad for business. What business we have left."

Leo skipped the last step just to show he could do it. "You just let me take care of that! It's what I was born to do, and it's all you're going to get out of me for four months' board."

"Six." Larrabee looked around the room for something he thought somebody would actually want to buy. "What would you sell?"

Leo Bard shook a crooked finger. "Just you watch!"

Using his wagon as a platform while Bobby La Rue pounded away on the piano, he sold just about everything—the warped, shot-up pictures, the nicked-up tables and mismatched chairs, the strange old bottles and all, right down to the belaying pin. He chose a Saturday when the farmer's market was in full swing and auctioned the place empty in time for a late lunch.

The last thing to go was the piano. No one else bought it so Bobby did.

Climbing down the wagon wheel Leo Bard said, "Ain't nothing brightens up a sad day more'n hard money!"

"You done us proud," Larrabee said. "It was a smart move to get old Bobby to play the piano even if he was a little shaky."

Flora protested. "He was playing fine, Daddy. That was ragtime."

"It was nice of him to buy that piano for old times' sake," Larrabee said. "You're welcome to stay with us at the house, Leo."

"I appreciate that but I've got another scheme. I aim to go back home to Ohio."

"Back home to Ohio. To settle?"

"I'll know that better when I get there. But it'll take a while. I'm going by way of Hawaii."

"Hawaii!" As Flora spoke, Root yelped. Someone had stepped on his foot.

"Always had a hankering to see it. When I get back I'll shorten my route."

"That's a long way to go," Flora said.

Asa shrugged. "Well, he'll have a good guide. Me."

Early one morning a week later they drove to the vacant saloon and loaded the wagon with what was left of the liquor.

"Now don't you drink it all tonight," Larrabee advised.

"Only for medicinal purposes," Leo Bard said, patting his heart. He pulled the brake handle, freeing the wheels, and turned to Asa. "I ever tell you the story of when I spent the night with the giantess?"

Asa nodded. "*Both* endings."

"You'll have some new stories by the time you get to Ohio," Larrabee said. "You come back and tell us some of 'em."

Asa leaned down and gave Flora a hug.

"I know this is a world tour," Leo Bard said, "but I hope you don't mind stopping just down the road here on the way out of town."

"You're the one that's driving. But just where was it you had in mind? Oh."

Suddenly he had realized that Leo Bard was referring to the trading post.

Chapter 73

John Howard spent his last afternoon with Ruth Cramer without Mrs. Blalock. The rain had nearly ruined their relationship by forcing them into the confrontation with Mary Leary at the trading post. But now he was finally, joyfully, free of "the Leary curse" as he called it, and he welcomed the rain on this September day because it separated him and Ruth from their tenacious companion. The three of them had been window-shopping on the east side of the square and they were on their way back to Howard's house for coffee. Mrs. Blalock had fallen back to engage in an over-the-fence political discussion with an acquaintance, and suddenly the rain came down like lead shot. In the confusion Howard and Ruth ran one way and Mrs. Blalock the other. Before they knew it, Howard and Ruth were alone on his porch.

Her parasol—more for sun than for rain—had wilted but had kept them fairly dry so that they had the leisure of sitting back at the table in the pavilion and watching the deluge.

"Poor Mrs. Blalock!" Ruth said. "Where do you suppose she is?"

"I have no idea," Howard replied. Then they both laughed.

"This is rather improper." Ruth shook the rain from her parasol and adjusted her bodice.

"So it's true what they say. That everybody grumbles about the weather but nobody does anything about it."

She turned to hook her parasol on the porch rail and just missed Howard's eye with the point.

"Oh, my! I am so sorry!"

He smiled. "It's all right. I saw you coming." Just to be safer, he sat back. "Well, you and Mrs. Blalock and the league have certainly done a bang-up job. The last saloon in town closed day before yesterday! You must be looking forward to settling back down to more womanly pursuits."

Maybe it was just an effect of the rain, but he thought he saw a spark in her hitherto luminous brown eyes.

"Settling back down?"

"Why, yes. Now that the temperance battle is won."

"But don't you see? Temperance was just the beginning, just setting the stage."

He was puzzled. "For what?"

She stared at him. "Why, for social equality."

"Social equality? People bandy that catchphrase like a club. What the devil does it mean anyway? You mean having more Negroes give speeches in the high school?"

"Of course!"

"Whatever for? Isn't once enough?"

"John, don't you know that there's a plan to defeat the superintendent of education in the November election just because he helped sponsor Mr. Washington's speech? If he goes, the school principal will probably be fired. I hear there's also pressure being put on the Baptist minister, Mr. Holley, for offering his church as a place for the speech. We just can't have that kind of thing in the twentieth century."

He wanted to light a cigar but he didn't have one. "Whoever have you been talking to?"

"To myself!" She tapped a finger at the base of her lace collar. "And to plenty of other people who have their eyes open."

"You have your work cut out for you. I can see that."

She leaned forward, reaching across the table to him. "John, what about you?"

"Me? What about me?"

"John, this is your cause too."

"I beg to differ. My cause is to mind my business and let others mind theirs. The next thing you know, you'll be wanting to vote."

"Why shouldn't I want to vote?"

"Why should you? Surely you have enough to keep yourself busy without that."

Her brown eyes flared. "Why should we? Because half the population of the country is getting no say as to how it's run."

Suddenly she had gone from speaking of I to speaking of *we*. He had visions of women marching on the Courthouse with locked arms. Women and Negroes.

"As I recall, the Constitution talks about all men being created equal. *Men*. If you start throwing everybody into running the government the result will be anarchy. And God knows we have enough anarchists in the streets already. Look what happened to the President."

She shut her eyes and shook her head as if to erase everything he had been saying. "Nobody's talking about overthrowing the government, John! We're trying to make it stronger by giving it a broader base of representation, a greater source of ideas." She put a gloved hand on his sleeve and favored him with an earnest gaze. "Oh, John, you were so wonderful, so effective against the saloons! We need you for this fight."

He stood his ground." My dear, shutting down the saloons was a very specific task. Changing the U.S. Constitution to suit some vague notion about social equality is a big waste of time."

Her mouth came open. "A waste of time!"

"And besides," he went on, "you people are being naïve—or hypocritical—one or the other. Let's say you achieve your wildest ambitions regarding social equality. Can you honestly say that you'd be willing to live in the Porters Quarters—or have Negroes move into the houses on either side of you? Do you think the crusading Mrs. Blalock would abide with that?"

Ruth swept a strand of damp hair from her brow. "Nobody's talking about that, John. I mean, this is a town where a proper, respected Negro—an educator, a—a scientist—can't even talk to a group of teachers without outcry and scandal—and people losing their jobs. Isn't it worth fighting to change that?"

He eased up. "I have nothing against Negroes, Ruth, but there is such a thing as place."

"John, Mr. Washington was invited to luncheon on the White House lawn with the President."

"Yes! That's just my point. The President can afford to have a Negro take lunch with him. He doesn't live in the South. But once a whole class of people thinks it can push its way to the top of our institutions—our neighborhoods—there's going to be trouble. And that's the fire that Mr. Roosevelt is playing with." He found himself reaching for another cigar that wasn't there. "You know, even if I were completely sympathetic with your schemes, what about these people all around us? The people who pushed the poll tax through in '89. But not just them. The people who yammer about social equality, too. How many of them do you think will stand still for the kind of thing you're proposing? Go ahead. Take your crusade into the streets and courts and you'll see how quickly they turn on you. And if you tie your cause of getting the vote for women to your notion of social equality, you'll be a hundred years getting your vote. Care to bet on it?"

She sat back, watching the rain beat down onto the azaleas. The pines in the yard looked black. Toward the Dutton house the privet thrashed and flailed under the onslaught. Pools began to form where the ground had become saturated. The air had become cool, almost cold.

"What's going to become of you, John?"

His eyes narrowed. "What's going to become of me? I believe I'll do quite well, thank you. This town offers more opportunities than ever and I mean to take advantage of them. I'll do quite well."

"No, I mean—" She looked up into the thick gray rafters of the pavilion and at the broad clapboard walls with their windows vast enough for two men to walk through without bending over. "I mean, what will become of all this? Someday it will fall empty and be brushed away. And who will remember that once upon a time there was a man who rented buildings to a butcher and a photographer and a druggist? A worthwhile thing in its time, but who will remember you for what you have done to make the world a better place? When this house is gone and the butcher and the photographer are gone and—and you are gone. What will people have to remember you by? Only what you stood for and how you dealt with the men around you—and the women."

He tapped his finger on the tabletop. "I'm afraid you're a little ahead of me there. And anyway, it so happens that I'm not too concerned about being remembered. *And* it so happens that I concern myself with today, not the end of time. And—ordinary as it seems—the person—man or woman—who tends to the details happens to be the one who makes it possible for the grand thinkers to function. Who do you think paid taxes to put up the high school where your Mr. Washington gave his speech? Who put the lights up so that he could see his way across the square? And before that—if I may—who saw to it that this town was freed of unsavory women so that your knighted Mr. Washington didn't have to worry about stumbling over one of them on his way to give his lofty speech? Yes, well, you see, one of us has been busy around here for the past thirty years helping to put up this town so that certain other people would have a place to come and dream their big dreams and lord it over the rest of us."

She stood up abruptly, nearly knocking her chair over.

Slowly, he stood up too. "What's happened to you, Ruth? What happened to the girl who was content to look for the world's last parakeet? What happened to the *fun?*"

"People change, John. Some of them. I grew up."

"It's a rough world out there. You're welcome to stay here. With me."

She shook her head. "I can't imagine that anymore."

He handed her the parasol. "You'll need this. Good-bye, Jane." *The wrong name again.* It was a horrible, clumsy mistake and there was no way he could undo it.

She looked at him in disbelief. "Jane?"

"I'm sorry."

She swept together her skirts with one hand, put up the sagging parasol with the other, and ran down the steps into the rain.

Chapter 74

"But Daddy, *everybody's* going to be there! The whole world is going to St. Louis!"

Flora had run out of things to say so she was repeating herself with added fervor.

It struck Larrabee as a day too pretty for arguing. The sky was a clear blue more common to February than to April. Recent rains had turned the grass green and lush. He could smell the freshly turned earth in the garden. The sharp scent of backyard chives mixed with the odor of manure spread on distant fields. He had decided to devote the day to taking out the old paddock fence.

"You say Ida's going up to the fair with her folks?"

Flora nodded enthusiastically. "On the first of May. They say the Cascade Gardens have a thousand electric lights that show right through the water at night. They say there's even going to be Olympic games."

It was as if she were speaking a foreign language. He clipped the barbed wire, peeled it back to the next fence post and clipped again, stacking the pieces carefully so as not to snag his gloves.

"As long as you've saved up the money for it, I suppose you could go up with the Derrys. They'd probably be able to make room for you."

"Daddy, don't you see? I want to go up with *you*." She put her hand on the next fence post to get his attention.

He kissed her on the cheek. "I want you to see it, darlin', but I can't go."

"Daddy, why not? It's the perfect time! There's no saloon to worry about anymore."

"That's for sure." He'd had no idea that the buyer intended to knock it down. Then one day when he was on his way to buy tickets to the vaudeville at the opera house, there was the corner lot, open to daylight for the first time in forty years, strewn with chunks of brick and splintered wood.

Apparently John Howard had not bothered to buy the place. He didn't even come by to gloat when Roper's Hall was gone too. The place that had seen Caroline's early theatrical triumphs and the meeting to throw out poor Ronald

McMarris when the teacher was taken for a drunkard was now a shallow pit filled with scrap lumber. The furniture dealer was from Macon and probably had no idea what formative events those worn walls had housed.

"So then?" Flora had always been forceful. But now that she was fully seventeen years old and a high school graduate she was someone to be reckoned with.

He gave up and tossed down the wire cutters and gloves. Flora had come to look less like her mother, which made it even more difficult to argue with her. Larrabee had occasionally been able to charm Anna out of one wish or another, but those had been times when a man was more clearly the head of the household. Soon, all too soon Larrabee knew, Flora would be leaving to start a household of her own. He wanted desperately to hold onto her affection. He had no choice.

"Darlin,' I can't go to the fair because I can't go back to Missouri."

"Of course you can! You're from there."

"And that's just the problem. I've told you that one day I'd give you the story and I guess now's the time." He went back in his mind nearly thirty years and told her about the foreclosure on the farm, his father's death, and the failed bank robbery that netted him only ten dollars.

She took it all in as if it were a legend or a story about someone she had never met.

"It's true," he told her. "I still carry the gold piece from time to time, trying to think of the best thing to do with it. Seems like it should be put to some good use."

"But if all you took was ten dollars—"

He told her about the man at the river, about the exchange of gunfire and the empty saddle.

She held onto the fence post as if to keep from falling. "You did that, Daddy?"

"A long time ago. I wasn't much older than you are. And the times were different. Very different."

"That's why you never went back to see your mother and sister?"

"That's most of it. And once they were forced off the farm there was no way to know where they had gone. I wish I could undo it, and yet if it wasn't for that I never would've met your mother and that was about the finest thing that ever happened to me. It wasn't my choosing, but it was the grandest accident a person could wish for."

"That—the shooting though. It was so long ago. Whatever happened, it must've been forgotten by now."

"Maybe. But I've never been keen on re-crossing that river to find out. I can't do anything to fix it and people still get hanged."

"Did my mother know about this?"

"I told her."

"What did she say?"

"She said to get on with our lives and that's what I've been doing." He took her hand and pressed it in his. "Why don't you go ahead with the Derrys? You can see that fair for both of us."

She shook her head. "No, it wouldn't be the same. It's only a fair."

A week later they were playing badminton at the Wards house when Dr. Willis stopped by. "You know, what you need, Larrabee, is a profession that doesn't dry up. The lake went dry, the phosphate went dry, and then danged if the saloon business didn't go dry too! Get something that doesn't run out."

Larrabee looked at him and missed his shot. "Any suggestions?"

"No. Just the advice."

"I kind of had in mind to buy a little farm," Larrabee said. "I think I still remember how to open a furrow."

"A farm?" Penny said. "Now there's an idea."

"There's one not so far from the Duforges that's for sale," Larrabee said. "Looks like good rich mucky soil. Not too much sand."

He picked up the shuttlecock and lobbed it over the net.

Instead of hitting it, Flora caught it and asked him if he was serious about moving out into the county.

"It's a good piece of property," he said. He glanced over at Penny standing on the terrace beside Dr. Willis. Both of them were leaning on their canes. It reminded Larrabee of the vaudeville act he and Flora had seen at the opera house. "You've been down there, haven't you, Penny?"

"To the Duforges, sure," Penny nodded. "It all looks pretty good down there. You could grow most any kind of vegetable you want. Probably even apples and plums."

Without being aware of it, Flora was crushing the shuttlecock in her hand. "You mean we'd live there and everything?"

"That's the only kind of farming I know," her father said. "Anyway I never did much care for the idea of sharecropping. I suppose we'd rent out the house here in town and live on the farm."

"Daddy, we can't."

Larrabee shrugged. "I don't see as we have much choice. Got to do something."

Flora dropped her racquet and ran from the yard.

"Now, what do you suppose?" Larrabee scratched his head as she disappeared through the hedge in a flutter of skirts.

Dr. Willis walked from the terrace, steadying his cane with each step. "My boy, you have some very interesting moments ahead of you."

"She wants to go to the fair," Larrabee explained.

"I believe she wants more than that," Penny said. Slightly more nimble than the doctor, he joined them at the net.

"Well, I wish she'd just tell me." Larrabee laid his racquet on the grass.

The doctor put a hand on his shoulder. "My good man, five-to-one her problem is a boy. And if it's a boy, you may be the last person she tells."

"Well then, I'll ask her."

"At your own risk," the doctor said knowingly. "I may've raised a boy, but I've been around long enough to know something about the way the fair sex thinks. I'd give her a little breathing room if I were you. Sooner or later that boy's going to come around."

He came around a week later. The subject of the farm had not come up again. Flora had been helping Iris Poinsett—now Iris Collier—with the cooking and cleaning since Iris had gone through a difficult time with the birth of her third child. Sometimes Ida would come by and chat while Flora cleaned a chicken or beat a rug. Sometimes Fondren came with her. On a fine, mild April evening, Fondren came by the house on Magnolia Street and asked for Flora.

Before he and Larrabee had gotten through the pleasantries, there was a rustling on the stairs and Flora was at the door, prettier than ever for being slightly out of breath.

Fondren was nineteen years old. He had grown tall and hadn't filled out yet, so that he had a slightly caved-in, underfed look. He was not a bad horseman, but on his own two oversized feet he was slow and awkward. From next door you could hear him scuffing across the porch. His smile was good-natured but a little cocky. Flora had always had a soft spot for him because he and his big brother, Boone, had been kind to her when she had first come to town as a misfit.

"Evenin', Flora. I was just about to ask your dad if you could ride with me over to the house. We're pulling taffy."

"Last I heard," Larrabee said, "Flora didn't much care for being on horses." His hand was on the doorjamb.

She ducked under his arm. "Oh, Father, that was years ago! And anyway, Bessie is such a gentle horse that anybody would feel safe on her." Standing on the porch beside Fondren she asked, "May I go?"

Larrabee took out his watch and opened the cover. Captured in sepia, Anna looked out at him. "If you go straight to the Derrys. And you're back by nine o'clock."

"Of course!"

She hurried down the steps. Fondren made a stirrup of his hands and boosted her onto Bessie's broad bare back, where she perched sidesaddle as he hopped off the steps and onto the horse. The smoothness of the maneuver gave Larrabee the impression that they had done it many times before.

"Nine o'clock," he repeated.

Flora waved and then clasped Fondren's waist as Bessie clattered down the brick walk and out the gate.

All around, the crickets sang their rhythmic song, promising a long summer. Larrabee stood on the porch, smoking his pipe and wondering what had prompted her all of a sudden to call him "Father" instead of "Daddy."

In May Fondren began to send her post cards from St. Louis. One card had a painted photograph of the fountain-lined boulevard called "The Cascades." Another showed what looked like a grandstand called "The Olympic Pavilion." Ida wrote her a letter about food at the fair—a popular new sausage in bread called the "hot dog" and ice cream in a twisted waffle, an improvisation so popular overnight that everyone at the fair seemed to be carrying the so-called ice cream cones.

Larrabee spent many an evening hour pacing the porch, smoking his pipe and watching the moths bat at the electric lights. When the Derrys returned, Ida gushed about the fair. She and Flora sat in the porch swing looking at the stereoscope pictures Ida had brought back.

"They're not just of the fair," she said. "See, that one's Paris. Doesn't it seem as if you're really there?"

Indeed it did. Flora felt the image jump out at her. For an instant she imagined that she could walk down that tree-lined boulevard.

"Fondren wrote to you, didn't he?" Ida whispered.

Flora smiled and blushed and answered confidentially. "He sure did. Almost every day."

"Some days we couldn't get stamps," Ida said. "That's the only reason he missed. I'll bet he wouldn't tell you that."

Larrabee had overheard some of the conversation while he was adjusting the window sash in the sewing room. He wasn't sure what to make of it. Seventeen seemed awfully young for such a headlong relationship, especially if it involved his daughter. But he didn't know what to do about it. He was in over his head. He knew nothing about what was on the minds of seventeen-year-old girls. But he did know the thoughts of nineteen-year-old boys.

The Derrys pulled plenty of taffy during the summer, way too much in Larrabee's opinion. Every week Fondren came up the front walk on Bessie, whose fattening dapple-gray belly showed that she was eating the Derrys' entire yard down to stubble. Flora slipped onto the horse's broad rump and Fondren slid deftly into position behind the horse's high withers and they ambled along the front walk and down the street to the taffy pull. The anxious father paced on the porch, smoking and watching the fireflies dart and flash.

There were outings. To the cool shade of Hidden Springs, to the Wards' for an ice cream social, down to the Harpers for Fourth of July fireworks that arched over the prairie. They went to the Duforges, where Barkley showed off his new oak table.

"Am I right?" Larrabee asked, smiling as he ran his hand over the varnished wood. "Have I met this tree before?"

Barkley grinned and slammed his mug down as if to keep the table in its place. "The very same! Son of a bitch looks a heap better this way than it did laying across my chest. I been curing the lumber all this time with nothing but sweet revenge in mind!"

In August Fondren got a job at the foundry. On his third day at work he got into a fight with a supervisor, knocked the man onto the floor and kicked him in the head. Larrabee heard about it when he went down to pick up a new casing for the backyard pump.

"He's a nice kid," said the man who helped Larrabee set up the new pump. "Till you get his dander up. Ain't nobody going to cross that boy and keep his teeth to talk about it."

That night Larrabee and Flora quarreled.

"You haven't heard his side of it," she said. "The man must've been threatening him."

"Not once he was flat on his back," Larrabee said. "You don't kick a man in the head when he's down."

"You talk as if there's some kind of code to fighting for your life."

"What he did wasn't right. Take my word for it. I've been in some fights."

"So how can you judge Fondren when you have such a temper of your own?"

He put out his hands to embrace her but knew there was no point. "I had a temper. Sure I had a temper. And it got me into plenty of trouble. That's how I know what Fondren Derry is capable of. I'm not his judge and jury. But I *am* your father and as long as I am I won't let you—"

"And you won't stop me! I'm eighteen in January. I'll move out of this house if I have to."

They were at the woodpile. He picked up a full-sized piece of fat pine and threw it all the way over the garden fence. He caught a splinter in his finger doing it but he didn't let on.

"Look, look, this has gone way too far. Throwing over that boy isn't the end of the world. In fact, it's just the other way around. It can be the beginning of something good. Darlin', he's not for you."

"Daddy, did it ever occur to you that he's a lot like you?"

"Like me? That's crazy."

"What if my mother had turned you away because of *your* temper?"

They established an uneasy truce. She could continue to spend time with Fondren as long as she promised that the two of them would never be alone.

Chapter 75

"A great pleasure, Mr. Buckman!" John Howard pumped the hand of the man from Jacksonville. He had arrived late for the meeting at the Seminary, having been unable to find his glasses. Finally, in a fury, he had rushed off without them.

"Have we not met, sir? I could swear I've seen your face back in Jacksonville."

"I rarely get there anymore," Howard said quickly. "My business keeps me very close to town. Not like Hizzoner here, who seems to travel far and wide on behalf of our city."

Howard's new associates intrigued him. They were solid in every way, solid as oak and polished as brass. Henry Buckman was the first politician he had met who struck him that way. He was affable but businesslike, said to be a brilliant lawyer. Had an agenda for developing the state. Never spoke of personal gain. Never spoke of money at all except as it pertained to the state budget. He was a member of a new generation, building surely and steadily on the growth of the state.

Howard felt the same way about the mayor. Although he was not yet forty years old, William Reuben Thomas was one of the wealthiest men in the county. His family had built a fortune in an undertaking business and a hardware store on the west side of the square. He lived in a noticeable but not ostentatious frame home on West Main Street, a stone's throw from the Courthouse. The mayor reminded Howard of the late President McKinley, with his high forehead and tendency to turn his nose up when photographed.

"You know," Buckman was saying, "that the eight educational institutions in the state have been lobbying the legislature for money for years. But now that they've banded together, the legislature will actually have to begin listening to them. That's where my plan's going to come in."

Dr. McKinstry apparently had already talked with Buckman about the plan. He allowed himself a sly smile. "We're completely disinterested, of course."

"Of course." Buckman smiled pleasantly at the doctor's irony. "Just like

Fernandina and Lake City and—for that matter, Jacksonville—will be disinterested. Don't be deceived. It's going to be an uphill climb! Even if I get to introduce the bill, both the House and the Senate will have to pass it. Then there will be the detail of selecting the cities. You can be sure I'll remove myself from that part of the process. The governor will probably set up a selection committee and may God help them!"

Howard began to piece together what they were saying. He and other local businessmen had been invited to meet with Buckman to discuss a plan to put all of the state's higher educational institutions under one authority, a sort of state university system. Buckman had said in private conversations that along with the consolidation he would propose the creation of two new universities, one for men and one for women. The towns that picked up those two new universities could look forward to the biggest boom since the coming of the railroad. Tallahassee looked like a shoo-in for the women's institution. The site of the men's university would be hotly contested.

Buckman was on his way from Jacksonville to Tampa on business unrelated to the issue at hand. Having heard from a mutual friend about the transit, the mayor had arranged to meet with Representative Buckman in the parlor of the women's dormitory at the Seminary. He and a prosperous merchant, William Wilson, had teamed up with Dr. McKinstry to spearhead an effort to bring the men's university to town. Wilson had invited Howard and other businessmen with the idea of getting broad financial backing and unified support for the university. Wilson had been emphatic that the negotiations would be delicate, and since the concept was new to Howard he was content to confine himself to small talk and leave the substance to the men known as the Three Nabobs.

Howard was fascinated. This conversation was so different from what he was used to. It was as if each man were trying to distance himself from the prize. Buckman made it clear that he would propose the idea and push it hard but have nothing to do with who got the universities. The mayor made it clear that he and the others were merely supporting Buckman's idea without making any effort to influence him. Howard wondered how the mayor expected to accomplish anything. And yet, in a blind way, Howard had been clearing the path for the university almost from the start. By burning out the soiled doves, by paving and lighting the streets and shutting down the saloons, he had been working toward a grand design without knowing it. His motives may have been mixed, may have been for his own personal gain or vindictiveness, but who could know that? The appearance was of a man who had spent the past quarter century smoothing the way for the city's destiny. The crop of the twentieth century would not be cotton or oranges but *enlightenment*, and harvesting the light of learning would be an unfailing livelihood.

Two weeks later the mayor hosted another meeting upstairs at the opera house to determine what the town could offer the state to attract the university. The bulk of the land would come from the federal government but the town could offer land adjacent to the federal property. After filling the room with cigar smoke the businessmen came up with a package of five hundred acres west of the city, plus $40,000 or 320 acres west of town and fifteen to the east.

Everyone in the room agreed in principle to buy municipal bonds to get the offer off the ground. Then Wilson raised the matter of the Seminary.

"The state won't want to use it for the university but they can't afford to hang onto it either."

Howard was tempted to suggest insuring it and then blowing it up but he thought the joke might backfire. Too many of the men in the room still remembered the suspicious immolation of the Arlington.

The captains of industry smoked more cigars, paced and argued and stared out the window at the lights on the square, and then they came up with a plan to buy the old Seminary for $30,000.

Howard wondered what Major Dennis would have said. Surely he would have had a more direct approach. Surely he would have been able to work some sleight of hand that would cut the deal overnight. But the major was almost twenty years in his grave, and these were new times with a new way of doing business. Howard doubted that any other man in the room had quite his perspective on the matter.

In late October he felt the autumn blues getting a grip on him again. His business was moving along steadily. The buildings were bringing in good rent money, though nothing like what the mayor and his cronies must be making. William Wilson took over the brick block that housed B.F. Jordan's dry goods store and the now-disused armory. He was selling almost everything, with "departments" of merchandise almost vast as entire stores. It made Howard long a little for the days when he had owned the Sunrise Emporium, the days with Jane. It made him crave a cigar. He went across the square to the tobacco shop and bookstore and bought a box of Tampa Royals. He smoked three before his stomach began to hurt, and he counted that a good day.

He could afford a housekeeper, a cook, and a butler. He hired older people because they listened better and he thought they were less inclined to steal. Just before Thanksgiving he got sick while smoking a cigar, threw up in the azaleas, and gave the rest of the box to the butler. In the confines of his house and office he resumed his absurd habit of sucking on peppermint sticks. He declined all offers to smoke. Even the smell of cigars had begun to make him feel queasy.

His new dentist—no better than Dr. Seigler before him—said that he needed three teeth out. Howard put him off, figuring he was just trying to make a fast buck. A second dentist told him the same thing. Howard later realized that the man had been one of his tenants. He thought the man might be trying to get even with him for raising the rent. He swore off peppermint sticks and drank tap water and wondered when the devil Henry Buckman would put his proposal before the legislature.

His manner began to strike others as odd. He sucked on his teeth when they hurt, and it became such a habit that he wasn't aware of doing it. People in conversation with him lost track of what he was saying while watching his cheek move as if a mole were burrowing under it. Under this unfortunate affliction his mustache took on a life of its own, reminding the beholder of a tomato worm inching its way along the vine. So when Howard expounded on the excesses of the Temperance League—now the Women for Social Justice—the hearer was likely to look at him with a strange, pained smile.

When the talk turned to the university he was listened to less and less. The mayor was so articulate, so positive and optimistic in what he said that he was the center of attention. Clearly he, McKinstry, and Wilson were making plans of their own now, and everyone was riding along with them. Howard began to regret his commitment to buy bonds. He was glad that he hadn't signed anything.

In December he considered going to Jacksonville for a few days of carousing, but he was afraid of running into Representative Buckman. The legislator hardly seemed the kind to frequent such places, but he *had* referred to seeing Howard up there.

One morning Howard picked up the newspaper and saw an announcement that Miss Ruth Cramer was moving to New York to take a position as assistant director of the American Women for Social Justice.

"Well," he growled, "Within a week she'll probably poke the director's eye out."

The mayor had a Christmas party that was attended by the most successful people in town. Howard got himself organized well in advance and made it to the house at the beginning of the event so as to be there at the onset of any important conversation. His teeth had been giving him trouble again, which he blamed on the raw, wet weather.

"More like February," he said to the mayor's wife as he sucked at his teeth and toasted his backside at the fireplace.

She gave him a puzzled look and allowed herself to be drawn away by another arrival.

A rather stooped, ruddy, balding man was dipping himself some eggnog while his wife chided him gently. Aware of being watched, the man curtailed his dipping and raised his dripping cup. "Your health and a merry Christmas to you, sir! A happy 1905."

His wife was wearing silk and brocade. She was old and overweight but very tastefully dressed.

"It's John Howard, isn't it?"

He bowed slightly. "At your service. And I have the honor of talking to?"

"Mr. and Mrs. Pendleton Ward." The man downed his eggnog in a single gulp.

Nelda Ward came forward. "How have you been, John? We haven't seen you for a long time."

"Very well. Never better. Now that I think of it, it must be your son I've seen at some meetings lately."

"At the university powwows." Penny nodded. "Yes, it's practically all J.J. talks about."

Howard wondered if Penny had ever found out who was behind the beating he had taken at the cabins. He looked into the older man's watery eyes and saw no trace of malice there. "It's all *anyone* talks about," he said. "It'll be such a good thing. If it happens."

Nelda Ward gave him a reproachful look. "Oh, it'll happen. There's no better place for that university than right here."

Penny gestured with his frothy cup. "And free water too."

"Free water?" Howard wasn't sure he had heard right.

"Sure. We're going to offer that university free water now. You must've missed that meetin'."

Despite the fire, Howard felt a coldness come over him. So the plan was moving ahead without him. He wondered whose idea that had been. He looked around the room. Everyone was caught up in conversation, laughing, smiling, clapping each other on the back. It was as if he had begun to go deaf, hearing only muted sounds without being able to distinguish the words. He decided to play along with his cards close to his chest. If the people in this room were going to cut him out then he would look for an opportunity to do the same to them. With something as big as a state university at stake he could make major money *somewhere,* with or without the mayor and his merry men.

Chapter 76

Root barked and chased the girl on the bicycle, following her every move.

Ida laughed as if it were the funniest thing she had ever seen. Flora wobbled then righted herself, narrowly averting a collision with the Poinsetts' picket fence.

"Fly, my little fledging, fly!" Ida doubled over laughing in a most unladylike way.

Larrabee pushed his fedora back and folded his arms, enjoying the show. It was good to see the girls in high spirits again, and he was particularly pleased that his idea had brought it about.

"Have you ever ridden one of those things, Mr. Larrabee?" Ida was still giggling.

"Nope. I thought I'd leave it to Flora to show the way. They didn't have safety bicycles when I was a pup, just those killers with the gigantic front wheels. This is much more sensible. Who knows? I might even be able to make it go."

Flora came back at them careening drunkenly. Ida shrieked and pressed herself against the fence. Larrabee grabbed the handlebars and the bicycle skidded to a halt. Flora dismounted in a flurry of petticoats.

"Now *that's* a ride!" She fell into her father's arms and the bicycle rolled into the fence.

"I'm glad you like it," Larrabee said, "because I've got some news for you."

She regained her balance and straightened her hat. "Tell me!"

"It's more than just a birthday present. I'm going to start selling these things. At the stable."

Flora looked at Ida but saw at once that she wasn't in on the secret.

"I bought the White Pine Stable yesterday morning. We are now the happy owners of sixteen horses, four buggies, two rockaways, and one big rickety barn."

She threw her arms around his neck and hugged him so hard that his hat fell off.

"Come to think of it—two and a half rockaways. There's something back there that looks like a train hit it. I'm looking forward to putting 'em all together."

"So we're staying in town?"

"I couldn't see myself as a farmer after all these years. And at eighteen you're a little old to be starting as a farmer's daughter. I take you for a town girl."

She smiled at Ida.

"Our deal still goes though. You go with a chaperone when you're with her brother."

"How long, Daddy?"

"Till you're forty-two."

"Oh, you! I get to drink coffee though."

"That's right. But only if you can make it better than I can. Otherwise neither one of us ought to be drinking it."

That night after supper he told her the rest of his idea.

"I'm going to sell automobiles," he said.

She nearly dropped her coffee cup. *"Automobiles?"*

"Yup. It's about time I got a jump on developments."

"Daddy, why not just sell flying machines?"

"Too dangerous." He winked at her. "But you never know."

"Do you know anything about automobiles?"

"Not a cotton-picking thing. That's the next part of the plan. I'm going to go buy three or four of 'em. There's going to be a big show in July. In St. Louis."

She put her cup down.

"Sorry it wasn't in time for the fair. But then I just got the idea this morning when I woke up. I'd never given automobiles the first thought in my life and then all of a sudden there I was, getting out of bed and deciding to buy me some."

"What about the man at the river?"

"Well, that's the question." He got up and carried the dishes into the kitchen. "Seems to me it's about time to face the music. I've been thinking about it too much lately. I put it out of my mind for most of thirty years and now it's there every day. I kind of figure my life's going to be built on sand till I can fill in that part of it. And if I get through St. Louis all right I'll go back to the river to see what I can find out. And if nobody throws a rope around my neck, I'll go out to Liberty County to see if I can find my mother and sister. You want to come?"

"Yes, I want to come. But, Daddy, tell me one thing. Does it have anything to do with Fondren?"

"You'd better believe it does."

"You know, they say absence makes the heart grow fonder."

"Yup. But it also makes the heart forget. Whichever way you go with it, at least we'll know that you didn't rush into it."

"He hasn't been in any more trouble."

"I'm glad to hear that. I guess."

In February they had the gala opening of the White Pine Bicycle Club. Larrabee climbed onto one of his new purchases and after a shaky start led a column of eight grinning sportsmen wearing straw skimmers on an excursion all the way to the Devil's Millhopper. Flora and Ida brought up the rear, the ribbons on their broad-brimmed hats fluttering in the breeze. It was the best advertisement anyone could've concocted. Within a week Larrabee had sold every bicycle he had. He took the train to Jacksonville and bought ten more.

On a cool, sunny March afternoon the old board sidewalk in the heart of town gave way for cement, and when the sun rose the next day, it revealed a trail of embedded horseshoes that led all the way from the square to the former White Pine stable. For weeks people smiled at Larrabee and congratulated him on another spectacular advertising idea and laughed in disbelief when he said that he'd had nothing to do with it. Following the trail himself one day he had a closer look at one of the horseshoes and saw in the hardening mortar the faint outline of a feminine handprint.

The shoemaker on the other side of the square picked up on the idea and stenciled a line of red footprints going into his shop bare and coming out shod.

"Was that your idea too?" Larrabee asked Flora.

"No," she laughed. "And anyway, I wouldn't have used red paint, even if it does show up better. It looks like a crime scene."

A month later Larrabee had the house wired for electricity. "We came *that* close to burning the place down one time," he told Flora as they watched two of J.J. Ward's men drill holes in the walls. He thought back to the wild Irishman who had knocked the lamp over in his sleep. Fourteen years had passed since the bitter night of his lynching. It seemed like a century.

While the electricians were working, Flora talked Larrabee into having a telephone put in.

"You know, you can call all the way to Atlanta on this thing," she informed him.

"Just see to it you don't," he said. "Telegrams are expensive enough."

Their first call—two short rings and one long—was Nelda reporting that J.J.'s wife had just given birth to a son. "They're calling him Richard," she hollered.

"Richard," Larrabee bellowed back. "That's an awfully regular name for a Ward, isn't it?"

"I say—what?"

"I say that's an awfully *regular* name for a Ward, isn't it. Compared to his dad and his granddad?"

"I'll tell you what," she shouted. Somebody—it sounded like Penny—was laughing in the background. "We'll just come over and tell you about it!"

Larrabee hung up the telephone, put his hands in his pockets and snorted. "All the way to Atlanta, huh?"

A few weeks later the Harpers and Duforges came up for the weekend. The Wards joined them for Sunday dinner and a musicale. The house was full.

Larrabee, Bob, and Penny sat on the porch and smoked.

"That Martha sure has a pack of kids." Penny said, settling into a rocking chair.

Larrabee swayed gently on the porch swing. "I'd say so."

"Sounds like one of 'em's found your harmonica," Bob said. "You ought to ask him for lessons."

"Thanks. When I do, I'll come down and serenade you. Around midnight."

"Won't bother me. I'm immune. I heard it on the boat for what—fourteen years?"

Something crashed in the front room. Penny craned his neck and peered through the window. "We're in for it now. They've found the piano."

Bob took out a cigar and lit up. "Nelda tells me your Preacher Bonds is moving on."

"That's what I hear," Penny said.

"He's been here a while, hasn't he?"

"That's just it from what I hear. He figured twenty years was enough. That's what old Preacher Williams told him when he got here. Preacher was here just fifteen. Anyway, the Bondses are going back up to Alabama and take over a little church up there."

"Just decided to do it."

"Larrabee here's going back to Missouri."

Bob sat up. "Missouri! You mean for keeps?"

Larrabee shook his head. "No, not according to the plan anyway. I'm going up to buy some automobiles. We're going to sell 'em out of the stable if I get back."

"What do you mean, *if* you get back? Asa Moody and the tinker went all the way from here to Hawaii and back to Ohio. I'd think you could make it to Missouri and back. Wouldn't take more'n a couple of days each way."

Larrabee tapped his pipe and blew smoke. "Be quicker getting back than it was coming down I imagine."

Penny stopped rocking. "All these years, I never did hear just what it was brought you down here in the first place."

"Your guess is as good as mine, Penny. I was playing the cards the best I knew how, but I sure wasn't dealing 'em."

Penny thought he had changed the subject. "'Course from what I remember you never *was* much at cards."

"No sir." Larrabee started to sway again. "But all in all I can't complain about my winnings." He stood up. "I could use a little stretch. You want to come?"

"No, I'm too slow anymore. You young bucks go along. I'll try to keep them wildcats in there from levelin' the place."

"I can use it," Bob said. "I ate too much of Flora's blackberry pie. It sure was good."

Larrabee smiled. "I kind of took a liking to it myself."

He and Bob walked out the gate with Root trotting along at their heels.

"Automobiles," Bob said, fascinated. "You figure they're going to catch on? I always had the idea they were just toys for rich folks. What's this about you not coming back?"

"Just talk. I wouldn't have bought a stable if I wasn't planning to come back. I just hope that Barkley doesn't run it into the ground while I'm gone. Where is he anyway?"

"Last I saw of him he was snoring on the couch with three or four little Indians jumping up and down on him. One of the twins startled him and Barkley smacked him on the rear before he knew what had happened. Barkley asked to be forgiven and Ainsley piped up and said, 'Before you can be forgiven you've got to *forgive.*' Where do you suppose she came up with that?"

They walked in silence for most of a block and then Larrabee said. "I think she's onto something."

Bob asked, "Did she talk to you?"

"Ainsley? About what?"

Bob smiled and pulled a piece of lined paper out of his shirt pocket. He unfolded it. "She's been in there taking a census of the grand get-together. Look at this. She's got a list of everybody in the house and their age."

Larrabee looked at the painstakingly printed list.

> *Martha Duforge, aged 34*
>
> *Barkley Duforge, aged 39*
>
> *Lewis Duforge, aged 11*
>
> *Leon Duforge, aged 10*
>
> *Luke Duforge, aged 9*
>
> *Leah Duforge, aged 9*
>
> *Faith Duforge, aged 7*
>
> *Simon Duforge, aged 4*
>
> *Robert Harper, aged 50*
>
> *Laetitia Harper, aged 49*
>
> *Ainsley Harper, aged 10*
>
> *Pendleton Ward, aged 66*
>
> *Nelda Ward, aged 65*
>
> *Nathaniel Larrabee, aged 48*
>
> *Flora Larrabee, aged 18*
>
> *Emma Newhouse, spirit, aged 46*

Preacher Williams, spirit, aged 62
Anna Larrabee, spirit, aged 22

"That's quite a census, Bob. But what are those last three?"

"Search me. She just said she was counting everyone in the house, except for dogs."

"Well, she sure is thorough. I wouldn't be surprised if old Duke's rattling around in there someplace too. He spent many a happy hour at the table."

"Those aren't the kind of friends a feller's likely to walk away from, are they?"

Larrabee handed the list back. "Not likely. Given the choice, not likely."

Chapter 77

John Howard had to look closely to find the reports in the newspapers. After all, few people realized their importance. First there was the boxed paragraph stating that on May ninth Representative Buckman had introduced his bill in the House of Representatives. The bill was referred to the committee on State Institutions, which received it with a lukewarm recommendation for its revision. Representative Buckman helped to redraft the bill, and the substitute version was duly submitted. A little more clear and forceful than its predecessor, the new bill hammered away at Buckman's original idea. All of the existing state institutions of higher learning were to be consolidated into four institutions— a University of the State of Florida for men, the Florida Female College for women; the Florida Normal and Industrial College for Negroes; and the Blind, Deaf and Dumb Institute. Buckman's bill called for the Board of Control and the State Board of Education to assemble as soon as possible to determine where the two new schools—the men's and women's universities—were to be built.

Over the next ten days the newspapers reported that the debate in the legislature was heated. The bill provided that other existing institutions would be abolished. That set off a big scrap between those who stood to lose their old schools and those who might gain one of the two new ones. Somehow the bill still got through the House, by a respectable margin of thirty-four to twenty-two. It got through the Senate unscathed by a vote of sixteen to five. On June fifth Governor Napoleon Bonaparte Broward signed it into law and the fight was on.

The only real competition for the university was Lake City, a day's ride to the north. Howard compared what the mayor, Dr. McKinstry, and William Wilson had to offer with what Lake City had put on the table. The mayor and his men offered $40,000 cash. Lake City matched it. The mayor and his men offered acreage. Lake City also offered land—800 acres assessed at $20,000 to be sold for the benefit of the university. Dr. McKinstry offered free water. Lake City was surrounded by lakes, for God's sake, and so presumably also had plenty of water to give away. The mayor and his men offered to buy the tired buildings of the East Florida Seminary to take them off the hands of the state.

There Lake City had the trump card because it already had a university—a modern one at that, with several respectable buildings. As he sat in the pavilion drinking tap water, Howard let his mind work on the situation. He no longer had any use for the mayor and his men. They had cut him out of the deal, favoring the likes of the Wards, the colorless shopkeeper William Wilson, and the whole bland cabal. On the tenth of June he withdrew all of his cash from the Pfifer Bank, signed a promissory note for half again as much, stuffed the money into a valise, and took the train to Lake City, where he quickly bought a strategic parcel of three hundred acres at twice its market value.

The choice of cities was in the hands of ten men—the five-member Board of Control and the five-member State Board of Education. On June twenty-eighth the two groups met in joint session and invited any city to submit its qualifications as a site for one of the two new universities by July 5, 1905. During the intervening week the ten men, accompanied by Governor Broward, would tour each of the towns vying for the university.

Rumor had it that the members of the committees were split right down the middle—five for each city. Sipping his tap water, Howard hit on a simple scheme to swing the vote. In 1876 Major Dennis had thrown the U.S. presidential election almost single-handedly by stuffing a ballot box. Surely John Howard was up to the little matter of persuading *one* man to make the logical choice in locating a state university. His trump card was that he knew a member of the committee who was rumored to favor Mayor Thomas' proposition. He knew him from nights squandered on the seamier side of Jacksonville. Whether the man— a prominent attorney—continued in his profligate ways was anybody's guess, and in any case Howard risked tarnishing what was left of his own reputation by exposing the man, but he was confident that the attorney would prefer discretion. With very little effort the five-to-five would become six-to-four in favor of Lake City.

The decision was to be made at a meeting in Tallahassee on July fifth. In the meantime the gentlemen of the committees, accompanied by the governor, would be touring the two contending cities. When they arrived at the depot on June thirtieth, Howard was among the men of the town to greet them.

His old friend was there, pretending not to notice him. He was grayer, of course, heavier and careworn—from the responsibility of the decision no doubt. Engulfed by a boisterous entourage, the inspection party rode in open carriages to the Seminary, where a brightly uniformed honor guard startled them by discharging a howitzer. Then the procession hauled the inspectors to the proposed sites for the university. First to the east, the smaller and less impressive of the two, but close to town and within sight of some stately houses, the east being the side of town favored by the well-to-do. As for the land itself, Howard noted, not for the first time, that it was nothing outstanding. It was flat and covered with a mixture of hardwoods and pines. It reminded him of the blasted

Preacher's Patch, which had been mediocre as a turpentine still, but rich beyond anyone's dreams in phosphate. This land held no promise of phosphate,
little for turpentine, but plenty for building because of the neighborhood.

They went next to the western parcel, which was fully a mile from town,
also flat, and mostly given over to towering loblolly pines. Here and there he
noticed the telltale probings of the phosphate prospector. No one was taking
any chances. It was hard to imagine a school of any kind sprouting up on that
sandlot a mile of dirt road from the nearest boarding house or store. Howard
calculated that the men of the university would be about as close to Mad Mary's
trading post as they were to Wilson's huge store or the Dutton Bank. When
he thought of his cash fortune invested in Lake City cow pastures and scrub
pines, his palms sweated, but he convinced himself that he had right on his
side. Where would the university men be better off—on the well-kept campus
of trim buildings in Lake City or down here in these pine woods at the edge of
oblivion?

The day was hot despite an afternoon breeze. Men and horses were ready
to come in out of the sun. The entourage dragged back into town where the
inspectors were ushered into the parlors of the women's dormitory for lemonade
punch, petit fours and nonpareils. Howard bided his time. He kept his distance
from the man he knew until the time was right. When his acquaintance broke
from the rest and headed for the outhouses, Howard followed.

"Hello, Jake." Knowing the way better than the inspector, Howard was
waiting for him beside the privy by the time the man found it. "Or are you
not going by that name these days?" He smiled and came forward. "How have
you been?"

The man glanced over his shoulder to make sure no one else had heard.

"Oh, it's all right," Howard assured him. "Everyone else is still inside
lapping up the punch. Get over to the Peach House lately? Didn't we ever
have a good time over there! As I recall you liked very young—"

"That was a long time ago," the man blurted. "It's all in the past."

"That's the trouble with the past, isn't it, Jake? Just when we think it's
behind us it has a way of coming right back at us."

"I have other things to think about if you'll excuse me."

The breeze had picked up but the afternoon was hotter than ever. Crickets
clicked and droned. High in a pine tree, a blue jay looking faded in the hard
sunlight dove at an invading crow.

"Of course," Howard said. "You have the vote to think about. Whether
that university's to be here or in Lake City."

"That's right. Now if you'll—"

"Fortunes will rise or fall, depending upon what you and your friends decide."

The man looked around again. "What do you want, John? As if I didn't
know."

Howard couldn't help smiling. "Ah, but you don't know, Jake! You think I want you to vote to put the university here."

"Don't you?"

"You think that I'm going to threaten to tell the world about—what was her name, the one whose hair color kept changing—unless you vote to put the university here. Don't you?"

The man closed his eyes and put his hand to his forehead.

"I'm not going to twist your arm to put the university here. Why would I do that, Jake?"

The man's eyes remained shut, as if he hoped to open them and see Howard gone or to see that he had never been there.

"What then? I don't understand you at all."

"Everyone says that if the vote were held today it would be five-to-five."

"What of it?"

"Well, Jake, doesn't it make sense to vote for the place that already has a university? Isn't that the best thing for the state—and for all of us?"

The man took out a handkerchief and wiped his forehead, giving his derby an awkward tilt. "For God's sake, Howard, make sense. What do you want?"

"Isn't it clear, Jake? Will this help?" He held his fists toward the man. "In this hand, a letter to the editor about a man who savored the best—and worst—that Jacksonville had to offer. In *this* hand, a stipend to help us all forget the past."

The man couldn't believe what he was hearing. "You want me to vote for *Lake City*?"

Howard smiled.

"Why?"

"I told you. It's the better place. Believe me, I speak as one who knows *this* place very, very well."

He held out an envelope.

"You're crazy, John. Keep your money. I won't have anything to do with this."

Howard grabbed him by the vest and pushed the envelope at him.

"Take it, you fool! All you have to do is vote for the place that makes sense and the future is made for all of us. Take it!"

The man broke free and ran, tearing the envelope and spilling fifty-dollar bills on the ground. Howard stumbled backwards and dropped to his knees to snatch up the bills as they tumbled and fluttered toward the outhouse.

Chapter 78

Larrabee opened his watch and studied the face in the oval portrait. "I'm not sure you have time to pack anything else, darlin'. Besides, your trunk looks like it's going to blow up any minute now. We're only planning to be gone two weeks you know."

"Daddy, I'm hardly taking anything! Just be glad that fashions have changed and everything is so much simpler now. You want me to look good when we're in the automobiles, don't you?"

"You look fine. Just don't wear so much that you can't shut the door."

"Flora!"

They went to the window. Illuminated by the porch light, Ida looked up at them from the yard. She shifted her weight impatiently.

"It's half past eight! They're going to announce the vote any minute now and we won't be there!"

"Coming!"

Flora swept up her skirts and rushed downstairs.

Larrabee knew they were going to the telegraph office so he took his time catching up with them. He could hardly believe what he saw when he got there. It seemed as if everyone in the county had converged in the center of town. The streets around the square were thick with horses, buggies, bicycles, and people on foot. Small children rode on the backs of their fathers. It took considerable effort just to get near the Western Union office. It took him half an hour to find Flora and Ida. Fondren was with them and Boone, who had come to town in his Sunday suit.

"It's a day in history," he said. "I may as well look the part."

Fondren was scratching initials in a lamppost with his penknife. His own and Flora's, Larrabee figured.

By nine o'clock word filtered through the crowd that something was happening inside the telegraph station. Word circulated back. A false alarm. More and more buggies crowded into the streets. It was almost impossible to breathe. Larrabee looked up to see if it was going to rain but couldn't read the sky in the glare of the electric lights. Ida and Flora chatted excitedly about St. Louis.

"If we have time, we're even going to go to Oklahoma City and look for Aunt Carrie."

Larrabee looked at his watch. Ten o'clock.

"You suppose something's wrong?" Fondren wondered.

"Don't say that! I can't stand it," Ida told him.

"What could go wrong?" Flora asked.

"Well, if the word's bad, maybe the mayor will just skedaddle. Would *you* want to send a telegram saying that your town has lost the biggest break since the railroad?"

"Don't cause trouble," Boone said. "We'll get that telegram sure enough. Any minute now. You'll see."

Ten-thirty. Ida said she wanted to sit down, but there was no place to sit.

Eleven o'clock. Larrabee thought it would have been the best night ever for Duke's place—in the old days. He'd never seen so many people in one place, not even in New Orleans.

At eleven-thirty the crowd was thicker than ever.

Fondren yawned and remarked that it was like the Fourth of July, market day, and a lynching all rolled into one.

"How would you know?" his sister said.

"Daddy, is that who I think it is?" Flora pointed to a silhouette moving into the lamplight across the street.

It took Larrabee a minute to identify the man on the black horse as John Howard. "Rumor has it he's gambled every dime on Lake City. I've never seen him in the saddle before."

Suddenly the crowd pressed forward.

"They're coming out!" Fondren said. "See—he's waving the telegram!"

The crowd parted as the man pushed his way onto the sidewalk, waving the telegram like a flag.

"Quiet!" rippled through the masses. "Everybody be quiet!"

Continuing to wave the telegram, the operator shouted in a breaking voice.

"We win the university by a vote of six to four!"

Shrill hollering penetrated the roar of the crowd.

"Those are rebel yells sure enough!" Boone shouted to Fondren. Ida and Flora hugged. People slammed hammers against the iron light posts, making them ring from one side of town to the other. The bell in the Presbyterian Church clanged wildly. Men whistled, boys banged pilfered pots with serving spoons and ladles. The new fire siren growled like a thousand cornered cats. Somebody shot red streamers off the roof of the Alachua Hotel.

"I hear they're going to rename Liberty Street!" Fondren cried, red-faced. "They're going to start calling it University Avenue!"

Ida laughed. "They'd never do that!"

Larrabee saw lights moving down the street, burning through the throng like a branding iron. It was a torchlight procession, collecting scores of people as it passed.

"Have you ever seen the like?" Fondren asked Flora. "You'd think the whole world was here celebrating tonight!"

In the morning Larrabee woke to the sound of more ringing. At first he thought it was still night, that he had gotten knocked down in the street and was coming to in the middle of the crowd but, raising himself up on his elbow, he realized that the ringing was coming from the telephone. Two short, one long. He was on his feet ready to throw on a pair of pants when he heard Flora downstairs talking into the speaker. A moment later she was calling him from the foot of the stairs.

"Daddy, it's a Mr. Polk."

Larrabee finished dressing and went downstairs barefoot. "What's he want?"

She shrugged. She was holding her hand over the mouthpiece as if Mr. Polk could hear her even when she wasn't shouting.

Larrabee put the receiver to his ear and spoke in a firm voice. He refused to bleat into the telephone, as he called it.

"Yes? What is it?"

"Mr. Larrabee? You may not remember me. I'm Ray Polk's son." The voice was hollow and distant. "Eliot Polk is my name! I was wondering, sir...."

"What? Speak up!"

"I say, I was wondering, sir, whether you would be interested in becoming a member of the board of the Dutton Bank!"

Larrabee looked at the receiver. He wasn't sure he had heard right. "The bank board?"

"That's right, Mr. Larrabee. You've done such a darn fine job in the community all these years! We feel that you're just the sort of citizen we need on the bank board!"

Larrabee stared into the speaker for a moment.

"Well, I'll tell you what! I have a little out-of-state banking matter to attend to. And if I get back from that anytime soon, maybe we can talk about it! Mr. Polk?"

"Yes, Mr. Larrabee?"

"You don't by any chance own a bicycle, do you?"

"I'm sorry! A what? A bicycle? Why, no!"

"Well, when I get back maybe you'd like to buy one! You could ride it over here from the bank and we could sit and talk on the porch like civilized people instead of having to yell into this confounded contraption! Or we can just stand and scream out the windows at each other! It's only three blocks!"

Flora had been listening all the while. When her father hung up the telephone, she put her hand to her mouth, trying not to laugh.

"Go ahead," Larrabee told her. "Laugh all you want. He won't hear you. Especially if it's over the telephone."

"Daddy, he probably thought the telephone was safer than trying to get down the street. It's as crowded as ever out there."

"It is? What for?"

"The delegation. They're coming home this morning. Everyone's going to the station to meet them. They're putting together another parade, a fancy one this time, by the looks of it."

"You've been out there already this morning? When did you sleep?"

"Daddy, how can I sleep with all this excitement? Our train leaves in less than an hour! Mr. Poinsett will be here to pick us up in fifteen minutes."

Larrabee looked at his watch. The sixteen-year-old Anna looked back from her sepia oval.

"The time does get by, doesn't it? Good thing we packed yesterday. Do you suppose we'll ever get out of here in all the commotion?"

The scene at the depot was even wilder than the one at the telegraph office had been the night before. A line of at least fifty carriages hung with banners and bunting waited to greet the returning delegation, except for the mayor and William Wilson, who were staying in Tallahassee for another day. As she and her father made their way through the carriages, Flora stood up to get a better view.

"Look, Daddy! Look over there! Have you ever seen so many bicycles in your life?"

There they were. Every man, woman, and child Larrabee had ever sold a bicycle to, decked out in their skimmers and sun hats, a parade unto themselves.

"Never in my life," he said. "I've given up trying to guess what comes next."

Penny and J.J. were there in a rockaway, with Nelda and J.J.'s wife and baby in the backseat.

Larrabee called out to them. "You all part of the parade?"

Penny shook his cane. "No, we've got all day and tomorrow, too, for that! We're here to see you off!"

As Larrabee and J.J. wrestled their trunks onto the platform, the train came steaming up, saluted by a round of deafening cheers.

"This train yours?" J.J. asked.

"Soon as they turn it around," Larrabee said.

"We're all turning around today," echoed Flora.

Penny pumped Larrabee's hand as the cars banged back and forth on the tracks. "Y'all don't fergit to come back now. And don't wait too long or you won't even recognize this old place!"

The members of the delegation climbed into a couple of open carriages, drawing off most of the crowd as they headed toward the square. Porters finished loading the baggage cars and banged the doors shut as a conductor walked the platform calling, "Board! Board!"

Larrabee followed Flora up the steel steps onto the train. They turned, smiling and waving at the Wards, at the Willises, the Poinsetts and the Duforges, the Derrys, at the whole town.

A lone figure slowly crossed the platform, out to see if last night hadn't been merely a bad dream. Or perhaps merely out to shake off the memories that crowded him in the big empty house. Or perhaps only out for a cigar. Larrabee and Flora were just past the end of the platform when the train stopped and shuddered.

The man had followed the train past the platform as if he intended to escort it out of town. When the train stopped, he stopped and looked up at Larrabee.

"You won," Howard said. His face was pale and twisted in the sunlight that glinted off the train windows, but he was smiling as if he had overheard some off-color joke. "I suppose I did let myself become a bit vindictive, and yet I *was* holding very good cards—just not quite good enough! I'll be building back up again, of course, dime by dime if I have to."

The train let out a burst of steam and started to move. Howard looked away.

"John!"

He turned and saw Larrabee's hand fly up. Something bright made an arc, winking in sun-struck flight. John Howard swiped at it but missed. As the train pulled away, he stooped and retrieved the glittering thing from the gray sand and rubbed it with trembling fingers. It was old and worn, but as good as ever. A ten-dollar gold piece.

Epilogue
September 21, 1929

Dr. Billy Willis clapped shut his father's gold watch and slipped it into his vest pocket. He shook the rain from his umbrella, propped it against the porch swing, and then knocked on the screen door, trying to make himself heard above the jumpy jazz that filled the house. Finally he let himself in, went to the foot of the stairs and called out.

"Hello, Flora?"

A slender dark-haired girl, about fifteen years old, came in from the dining room. At first he thought she was Flora. He was thinking back thirty years.

"Why, hello *Rachel*." He was charmed by the girl's shyness. "At first glance you looked just like your mother. You all stay so healthy that I don't get to see that much of you. What's that you've got there on the Victrola? Not Paul Whiteman by any chance."

The girl's faint smile confirmed his guess. "It's called 'Whispering.' It's their signature tune."

"Well, it sounds more like shouting. But I kind of like it. It may be just the thing for our patient upstairs. A little racket can be good for stirring up a body."

The tune came to an abrupt end. Rachel hurried back into the dining room and put a stop to the rhythmic clicking that followed.

The doctor was starting up the stairs when Flora and Rex came in through the kitchen. Flora was saying something about a leak in the garage roof.

"It was cats and dogs for a minute there," the doctor said. "But it sure did cool things off. Sorry to be calling so late."

Flora laid her raincoat on the wicker chair and wiped a raindrop from her brow. "When you're married to a veterinarian and you have two teenage children, it's never late."

"How's the patient tonight?" They started up the stairs.

"He was sleeping very soundly after supper. I hope Rachel didn't wake him up with that so-called music of hers."

The doctor was quick to change the subject. "I've been itching all day to find out what happened when you and your daddy went to Missouri. What did he find out about the man at the river?"

Flora paused halfway up the stairs. "Nothing, I'm afraid. Nobody could tell us the first thing about what happened at the river. But since Daddy was never a very good shot with a pistol, he had reason to hope that he missed when he fired from a galloping horse. We couldn't even find anyone who remembered the robbery. The whole thing was forgotten, maybe even forgiven. The bank was being used to store grain."

Billy Willis steadied himself with the banister. "So using the ten dollars to forgive John Howard was probably the best thing he could've done with it, for both of them."

In the dining room, Rachel flipped the record over and the Whiteman Orchestra started playing "I'll Build a Stairway to Paradise."

The doctor listened for a moment. "I gather nobody rushed up to nab him at the automobile show."

"Oh, they rushed up all right—to sell him automobiles."

"So maybe he could've gone back home all along. "

"We did go back to Liberty County. Way out on a very bumpy road Daddy found his mother and sister not ten miles from the family farm. It was a bittersweet homecoming. We went up every summer for as long as his mother lived. Of course, that's where Charles and I met."

Dr. Willis chuckled and thumped his cane on the step. "I hear you married him because he beat you at chess."

Flora laughed. "You must've heard that from him. Well, he did beat me, after three games. It made quite an impression. I forgot Fondren pretty fast. Daddy was right about that."

"I sure miss your daddy. How long has it been?"

"A year. They called the search off a year ago today."

"Well, it's too quiet around here without him and Bob bringing in the big fish. The state ought to name Seahorse Reef after 'em."

Flora glanced downstairs, past the wicker chair to the front door.

"Sometimes I still expect to hear him coming in late, bragging about all the mackerel they caught on the reef. It's hard to have him just disappear that way."

The doctor touched her on the shoulder. "Another of those hard ambiguities."

"This is a strange thing to say," she added, "but I wish I'd gotten to know him better, wish I'd asked more questions."

They came to the top of the stairs and spoke in low tones outside the guest room door. Rex had followed them upstairs. He was unusually quiet.

"Did you go on to Oklahoma?" Billy asked. "You were going to look for your Aunt Carrie."

Flora laughed softly. "We missed her by just one week. She had run off with the director of the institution. As for Edgar, he saved up to buy a hundred and forty acres that turned out to be poor for farming but not so bad for oil."

The doctor smiled. "It was quite a family. I suppose by now it's all right to say that your mother was the first girl I ever kissed. That's one thing I wouldn't change for the world."

He nodded to Rex and with uncommon care the boy opened the bedroom door.

Flora bit her lip. "I'm afraid to look in here. Every time I do, I expect to find him—"

Rex slipped past her and stopped in the middle of the room.

Flora stared at the empty bed. "Good God. He's *gone!*"

The doctor glanced around the room, rubbing the back of his head. "Well, I *said* his heart was sound. Sound as a dollar. But where the dickens do you suppose he went?"

The little carved horse had fallen over. Flora stood it up beside the photograph of the two aged fishermen. "He talked about going home. We could check his house."

"His house? No, he lost that to the bank years ago. It's not even there anymore."

After they had finished searching upstairs and down, the doctor stood alone on the porch, smoking and gazing into the wet night, trying to imagine where the old man had gone. Then his thoughts drifted back to an earlier summer evening, an orange grove, and a girl named Anna.

Downtown, in the garish half-light at the edge of the Porter's Quarters, Richard Ward and his new girlfriend stumbled out of a speakeasy, bumped into a shifting shell of a man, parted briefly, and laughed.

"Hey, gramps, watch out!" Richard scolded in cheerful intoxication. "You don't know where you're going!"

As he veered into the darkness, John Howard concluded that truer words had never been spoken.

Afterword

Because my first aim in writing *Sand Mansions* was to recreate life in north central Florida as it was in the last quarter of the nineteenth century, I based the novel upon several histories of Gainesville and Alachua County, which yield a wealth of people and events more remarkable than any I could have made up. This book could not have existed without *History of Alachua County* by Jess G. Davis, *History of Gainesville* by Charles H. Hildreth and Merlin G. Cox, *History of Alachua County* by F.W. Buchholz, *Florida's Eden* by John. B. Pickard, and *Florida: A Short History* by Michael Gannon.

Among the characters in this book who really lived and behaved much as I have described them are: Major Leonard G. Dennis ("The Little Giant"), Josiah T. Walls, Harmon Murray, Tony Champion, the erstwhile priest Michael Kierens (alias Michael Kelly), Alexander Henderson, Elbert Hardy, Cary Dennis, General J.J. Finley, Richard Black, Thomas Vance, Henry Buckman, Henry F. Dutton, William Wilson, William R. Thomas, Carl Webber, Dr. James McKinstry, the doctors Robb, and Professor James Roper.

Nathaniel Larrabee, John Howard, and the others have dwelt in my imagination for so long that, to me, they are just as real.

The main historical events described took place in and around Gainesville, Florida between 1876 and 1905, including: the apparent—but possibly staged—attempt on the life of Major Dennis at the Union Academy in 1876; the stuffing of the ballot box affecting the presidential election of 1876; the burning hot air balloon colliding with the Courthouse in 1877; the burning, perhaps through arson, of the Arlington Hotel about 1886; the plan for New Gainesville and the devastating yellow fever epidemic of 1888; the disappearance of Alachua Lake in 1891; the depredations and violent deaths of Harmon Murray and his gang, the catastrophic freezes of 1895 and 1899; the temperance movement that made the county "dry" for sixty years, the controversial visit of Booker T. Washington in 1903; and the bitter competition between Lake City and Gainesville for the University of Florida after the passage of the Buckman Act of 1905.

Sand Mansions was so long in its development that it passed through many hands in many forms. Among those who gave me valuable advice were my mother, Marion S. Gilliland; Ants Oras; Terry Cassel; Karl Schmidt, who selected and read the first part of *Sand Mansions* for Wisconsin Public Radio's *Chapter A Day*; my brother Capt. Charles H. Gilliland, Jr.; David Poyer; Ken Potter; and my Americana professor at the University of Florida, John B. Pickard. My thanks to all of them for their candid and encouraging reactions to what was at times a trying experience.

Thanks also to the eloquent Ben Logan for his kind words about this book.

Thanks as well to Dennis Ryan for providing the military records of Josiah T. Walls and Henry F. Dutton and the military record and obituary of Major Leonard G. Dennis. Thanks to Sarah Brown for sending important historical source books my way; to Marion S. Gerber for her stories of old Gainesville; to my father, Dr. Charles H. Gilliland, for providing anecdotal links to the nineteenth century; to my son Jordan for the crucial technical support that turned a manuscript into a book; and to my son Ross for appearing on the cover. I'm grateful also to Sari Sanborn for making Stacie available for the cover of this book and for introducing me to cracker horses during pleasant rambles across Payne's Prairie.

At the end of this parade, heartfelt thanks to my other half, Amanda, who took the cover photograph, obligingly pored over every word of the story in its various forms, and put up with my many absences of spirit during a writer's odyssey.

Norman Gilliland
Madison, Wisconsin
June 26, 2004